# DIVISIONS

BOOKS BY KEN MACLEOD
FROM TOM DOHERTY ASSOCIATES

THE FALL REVOLUTION
*The Star Fraction*
*The Stone Canal*
*The Cassini Division*
*The Sky Road*

THE ENGINES OF LIGHT
*Cosmonaut Keep*
*Dark Light*
*Engine City*

*Newton's Wake*
*Learning the World*
*The Execution Channel*

# DIVISIONS

## KEN MACLEOD

ORB

A Tom Doherty Associates Book
New York

DIVISIONS

Copyright © 2009 by Ken MacLeod

*The Cassini Division* copyright © 1998 by Ken MacLeod
*The Sky Road* copyright © 1999 by Ken MacLeod

All rights reserved.

An Orb Book
Published by Tom Doherty Associates, LLC
175 Fifth Avenue
New York, NY 10010

www.tor-forge.com

Library of Congress Cataloging-in-Publication Data

MacLeod, Ken.
  [Cassini Division]
  Divisions / Ken MacLeod.—1st Orb ed.
    p. cm.
  "A Tom Doherty Associates book."
  ISBN-13: 978-0-7653-2119-0
  ISBN-10: 0-7653-2119-X
  I. MacLeod, Ken. Sky road. II. Title.

  PR6063.A2515C3  2009
  823'.914—dc22

                                                              2009002087

First Orb Edition: June 2009

Printed in the United States of America

0  9  8  7  6  5  4  3  2  1

# CONTENTS

# THE CASSINI DIVISION

*To Mairi Ann Cullen*

*Thanks to Carol, Sharon and Michael; to John Jarrold and Mic Cheetham; to Iain Banks and Svein Olav Nyberg; to Andy McKillop, Jo Tapsell, Paul Barnett and Kate Farquhar-Thompson.*

*Thanks also to Tim Holman for editorial work at Orbit; to David Angus for pointing me to the map of Callisto; and to the socialists, for the Earth.*

*Man is a living personality, whose welfare and purpose is embodied within himself, who has between himself and the world nothing but his needs as a mediator, who owes no allegiance to any law whatever from the moment that it contravenes his needs. The moral duty of an individual never exceeds his interests. The only thing which exceeds those interests is the* material power *of the generality over the individuality.*

—JOSEPH DIETZGEN, "The Nature of Human Brain Work"

# CONTENTS

# 1

## LOOKING BACKWARD

*There are, still, still photographs of the woman who gate-crashed the party on the observation deck of the Casa Azores, one evening in the early summer of 2303. They show her absurdly young—about twenty, less than a tenth of her real age—and tall; muscles built-up by induction isotonics and not dragged down by gravity; hair a black nebula; dark skin, epicanthic eyelids, a flattish nose, and thin lips whose grin is showing broad white teeth. She carries in her right hand a litre bottle of carbon-copy Lagrange 2046. Her left hand is at her shoulder, and on its crooked forefinger is slung a bolero jacket the colour of old gold, matching a gown whose almost circular skirt's hem is swinging about her ankles as she strides in. What looks like a small monkey is perched on her right, bare, shoulder.*

Something flashed. I blinked away annular afterimages, and glared at a young man clad in cobalt-blue pyjamas who lowered a boxy apparatus of lenses and reflectors with a brief apologetic smile as he ducked away into the crowd. Apart from him, my arrival had gone unnoticed. Although the deck was a good hundred metres square, it didn't have room for everybody who was invited, let alone everybody who'd turned up. The natural progress of the evening, with people hitting off and drifting away to more private surroundings, would ease the pressure, but not yet.

There was room enough, however, for a variety of activities: close dancing, huddled eating, sprawled drinking, intense talking; and for a surprising number of children to scamper among them all. Cunningly focused sound systems kept each cluster of revellers relatively content with, and compact in, their particular ambience. The local fashions seemed to fit the party, loose and fluid but close to the body: women in saris or shifts, men in pyjama-suits or serious-looking togas and tabards. The predominant colours were the basic sea-silk tones of blue, green, red, and white. My own outfit, though distinctive, didn't seem out of place.

The centre of the deck was taken up by the ten-metre-wide pillar of the building's air shaft. Somewhere in one of the groups around it, talking above the faint white noise of the falling air, would be the couple whose presence was the occasion for the party—the people I'd come to speak to, if only for a moment. There was no point in pushing through the crowd—like anyone here who really wanted to, I'd reach them eventually by always making sure I was headed in their direction.

I made my way to a drinks table, put down my bottle and picked up a glass of Mare Imbrium white. The first sip let me know that it was, aptly enough, very dry. My slight grimace met a knowing smile. It came from the man in blue, who'd somehow managed to appear in front of me.

'Aren't you used to it?'

So he knew, or had guessed, whence I came. I made a show of inspecting him, over a second sip. He was, unlike me, genuinely young. Not bad-looking, in the Angloslav way, with dirty-blonde tousled hair and pink, shaved face; broad cheekbones, blue eyes. Almost as tall as me—taller, if I took my shoes off. His curious device hung on a strap around his neck.

'Comet vodka's more to my taste,' I said. I handed the glass into the monkey-thing's small black paws and stuck out my hand. 'Ellen May Ngwethu. Pleased to meet you, neighbour.'

'Stephan Vrij,' he said, shaking hands. 'Likewise.'

He watched as the drink was returned.

'Smart monkey,' he said.

'That's right,' I replied, unhelpfully. Smart spacesuit, was the truth of it, but people down here tended to get edgy around that sort of stuff.

'Well,' he went on, 'I'm on the block committee, and tonight I'm supposed to welcome the uninvited and the unexpected.'

'Ah, thanks. And to flash bright lights at them?'

'It's a camera,' he said, hefting it. 'I made it myself.'

It was the first time I'd seen a camera visible to the naked eye. My interest in this wasn't *entirely* feigned in order to divert any questions about myself, but after a few minutes of his explaining about celluloid film and focal lengths he seemed unsurprised that my glazed-over gaze was wandering. He smiled and said:

'Well, enjoy yourself, Ellen. I see some other new arrivals.'

'See you around.' I watched him thread his way back towards the doors. So my picture would turn up in the building's newspaper, and a hundred thousand people would see it. Fame. But not such as to worry about. This was the middle of the Atlantic, and the middle of nowhere.

The Casa Azores was (is? unlikely—I'll stick to the past tense, though the pangs are sharp) on Graciosa, a small island in an archipelago in the North Atlantic, which is (probably, even now) an ocean on Earth. It was so far from anywhere that, even from its kilometre-high observation deck, you couldn't observe its neighbouring islands. The sea and sky views might be impressive, but right now all the huge windows showed was reflected light from within. The lift from which I'd made my entrance was at the edge, and I had to get to the central area within the next few hours, sometime after the crowd had thinned but before everyone was too exhausted to think.

I drained the glass, picked up a bottle of good Sungrazer Stolichnya, gave the monkey a clutch of stemmed goblets to hold in its little fingers, and set out to work the party.

'Nanotech's all right in *itself*,' a small and very intense artist was explaining. 'I mean, you can *see* atoms, right? Heck, with the bucky waldoes you can *feel* them, move them about and stick them together. It's mechanical linkages all the way up to your fingers. And to your screen, for that matter. But all that electronic quantum stuff is, like, *spooky* . . .'

She had other listeners. I moved on.

'You're from space? Oh, great. I work with the people in the orbitals. We do zaps. Say you've got a replicator outbreak somewhere, natural or nano, like it makes a difference . . . *anyway*, before the zap we all sorta wander around the evac zone, one, to check there's nobody there and, two, just to soak up and record anything that might get lost. You don't get much time, you're in an isolation suit that has to be flashed off you before you come out, for obvious reasons—takes most of your body hair with it, too—but even so, you can see and feel and hear a lot, and for hours or days, depending on how fast the outbreak's spreading, there's nobody else around for tens of kilometres. You know, just about every one I've done, I've picked up a species that wasn't in the bank. Genus, sometimes. Not known to science, as they say. Ran out of girlfriends to name them after, had to start on my actual *relatives*. And then you come out, and you sit around with the goggles and watch the zap. I mean, I like to see the flash, it's the next best thing to watching a nuke go off.'

The ecologist stopped and took another deep hit on the hookah. I waved away his offer of a toke. He sighed.

'The times when there's nobody around but you . . . You just gotta love that wilderness experience.'

I had reached halfway across to the centre of the room. I wanted to offer the stoned scientist a shot of vodka, but the monkey had, in a moment of abstraction, devoured my last spare glass. The man didn't mind. He assured me he'd remember my name, and that some beetle or bug or bacterium would, one day, be named in my honour. I realised that I couldn't remember his name. Or perhaps he hadn't told me, or perhaps . . . a certain amount of passive smoking was going on around here. I thanked him, and moved on.

'And don't *do* things like that,' I murmured. 'It's conspicuous.' A cold paw teased my ear, and a faint, buzzing voice said:

'We're low on silicates.'

I scratched the little pseudo-beast in response, and hoped no one had noticed my lips move. I felt a sudden pang of hunger and a need for a head-clearing dose of coffee, and stopped at the nearest buffet table. A woman wearing a plain, stained white apron over a gorgeous green sari ladled me a hot plate of limpets in tomato sauce. (All real, if it matters. I guess it must: my mouth waters at the memory, even now.) I decided on a glass of white wine. There were empty chairs around, so I sat. The woman sat, too, at the other side of the table, and chatted with me as I ate.

'I've just spoken to our special guests,' she said. She had an unusual accent. 'Such interesting people. An artificial woman, and a man from the stars! And back from the dead, in a sense.' She looked at me sharply. 'Perhaps you'll have met them before, being from space yourself?'

I smiled at her. 'How come everyone knows I'm from space?'

'Your dress, neighbour,' she said. 'Gold is a space thing, isn't it? It isn't one of our colours.'

'Of course,' I said. For a moment I'd thought she'd guessed it was a spacesuit. After she'd spoken, after I'd had a minute to observe how she moved, the subtle way her face cast its expressions, it was obvious that she was well into her second century. There would be no fooling her. She looked right back at me, her eyes shining like the pins in her piled-up black hair.

'Gold is such a useful metal,' she said. 'You know, Lenin thought we'd use it for urinals . . .'

I laughed. 'Not his only mistake!'

Her reply was a degree or two cooler that her first remarks. 'He didn't make many, and those he did were the opposite of . . . what's usually held against him. He thought too highly of people, as individuals and in the mass. Anyway,' she went on, complacently, 'some of us still think highly of *him*.'

I'd placed her accent now. 'In South Africa?' They were a notoriously conservative lot. Some of them were virtually Communists.

'Why, yes, neighbour!' She smiled. 'And you're from . . . now don't tell me . . . not near-Earth; not Lagrange . . . and you're no Loony or Martian, that's for sure.' She frowned, watching as I lifted my glass, looking past me at, perhaps, her memory of how I'd walked up to the table. Weighing and measuring my reflexes. 'Yes!' She clapped her hands. 'You're a Callistan girl, aren't you? And that means . . .'

Her eyes widened a fraction, her brows rose.

'Yes,' I said quietly. 'The Cassini Division. And yes, I've seen your guests before.' I winked, ever so slightly, and made a tiny downward movement with my fingers as I reached across the table for a piece of bread. Not one in a hundred would have as much as noticed the gesture. She understood it, and smiled, and talked about other things.


*The Cassini Division* . . . In astronomy, the Cassini Division is a dark band in the rings of Saturn. In the astronautics of the Heliocene Epoch, the Cassini Division was the proud name—originally given in jest—of a dark band indeed, a military force in the ring of Jupiter. You know about the ring of Jupiter—but to us it was more than a remarkable product of planetary engineering, it was a standing reminder of the power of our enemies. It was our Guantanamo, our Berlin Wall. (Look them up. Earth history. There are files.)

The Cassini Division was the Solar Union's front-line force, our collective fist in the enemy's face. In our classless society it was the closest thing to an élite; in our anarchy, the nearest we came to a state; in our commonwealth, it held the greatest share of riches. Its recruits chose themselves, and not many could meet a standard of that rigour. In terms of sheer fire power the Division could have flattened all the states Earth ever knew, and still had enough left over for a bit of target practice to occupy the afternoon. The resources it controlled could have bought everything on Earth, in the age when that world was owned—and it still stood ready for the exchange, to give as good as it got, to pit our human might against the puny wrath of gods.

In other words . . . the Division was there to kick post-human ass. And we did.

(And yes. I'm still proud of it.)


The South African woman might have had unsound views about Vladimir Ilyich, but she turned out to be one of the 'old comrades'. Although the International had long since dissolved into the Union, its former members maintained their contacts, their veterans' freemasonry. I'd never really approved of this, but it helped me here. She introduced me to one of her friends, who introduced me to another, and so on. By an unspoken agreement they passed me along their chain of acquaintance, moving me through the crowd a lot faster than I'd managed on my own. Only half-an-hour after I'd finished my coffee, I found myself among a small cluster of people, at the focus of which were the party's special guests: the artificial woman, and the man who had come back from the stars, and from the dead. Even five years after their arrival, they could still pull a crowd—all the more so because they seldom did, preferring to wander around and talk to people they happened to meet.

The artificial woman was called Meg. She didn't look artificial right now, and indeed her body—cloned from that of some long-dead Malaysian-American porn actress, I understand—was in some respects more natural than mine. Only her personality was artificial. It was a human personality in every way we'd ever been able to observe, but it was—she'd always insisted—running on top of a genuine artificial intelligence.

In which case the small, pretty woman standing a couple of yards away from me, elegantly smoking a tobacco cigarette, with her black hair hanging to her waist, and wearing a long black silk-satin shift and (unless my eyes deceived me) *absolutely nothing else*, was the only autonomous AI on Earth. A troubling thought, and it had troubled me ever since I'd met her.

The autonomous AI hadn't noticed me yet. She was looking at her companion, Jonathan Wilde, the man who had come back. Wilde, as usual, was holding forth; as usual, waving his hands; as usual, smoking tobacco, a vile habit that seemed hardwired into him and Meg both. He was a tall man, sharp-featured, hook-nosed, loud-voiced. His accent had changed, but still rang strangely in my ears.

'—never actually *met* him,' he was saying, 'but I did see him on television, and read some of what he put out during the Fall Revolution. I must say it's a surprise to find him still remembered.' He paused, flashing a quick, rueful smile. 'Especially since I'm forgotten!'

People around him laughed. It was one of Wilde's standing jokes that the ideas he—or rather, the human being of which he was a copy—had espoused back in the twenty-first century were now of interest only to antiquarians, and that his name was only a footnote in the history of the Space Movement. In some odd way, this very obscurity flattered his vanity.

As he stood there grinning he saw me. He stared at me, as if momentarily confused. Meg turned and saw me and gave me a welcoming smile. Wilde nodded slightly, and returned to his discourse. I didn't know whether to feel slighted or relieved. As the first person he'd seen on his emergence from the wormhole, I had some importance in Wilde's life . . . but I didn't want him introducing me as such, and thus letting everyone present know where I was from.

Meg stepped over and caught my hands.

'It's good to see you again, Ellen.'

'Yeah, you too,' I said, and meant it. Her personality might be synthetic, but its appeal was genuine. I'd sometimes wondered what she saw in Wilde, whose fabled charm had never worked on me.

'What brings you here?' Meg asked.

'You don't make yourselves easy to find,' I said lightly. 'So I thought I'd take the opportunity.'

Meg smiled. 'You're a busy woman, Ellen. You want something.'

'Oh, you know,' I said. 'Perhaps we can talk about it later?'

She was looking up at me, a small frown on her smooth brow.

'Of course,' she said. 'Things should quiet down, soon.'

I laughed. 'You mean, like when Wilde's spoken to everybody?'

'Something like that.' She drew me to a nearby seat, just outside the huddle, and I sat down with her. 'This is all a bit exhausting,' she said absently. She stroked one bare foot with the other, and stubbed out her cigarette. The monkey hopped from my shoulder and clutched the edge of the ashtray, its big eyes entreating me. I shook my head at it. It bared its teeth, then turned away from me and let Meg play with it.

Wilde's voice, carrying:

'—this whole thing: turning his sayings into a scripture, and him into a martyred prophet—it's almost the only irrationality you people have left! I think he would have *laughed*!' And with that Wilde's laugh boomed, and those around him joined in, hesitantly. The conversation broke up over the next few minutes, and Wilde ambled over and sat down beside me. The three of us were perched as if on a log in an eddied swirl. Around us people partied on; now and again someone would drift over, see no response signalled, and turn away. Some left, but most hung around, tactfully out of earshot.

We exchanged greetings and then Wilde leaned away from me and sat shoulder-to-shoulder with Meg.

'Well, Ellen,' he said. 'You got us where you want us.' He lit a cigarette and accepted a shot of vodka. He looked down at his glass. 'This has already had several other drinks in it,' he observed. 'Nice thing about vodka, of course, is it doesn't matter. Any taste is an improvement. I'm drunk already. So if there's anything you forgot to ask us, in the debriefing—'

'Interrogation.' I always hated the old statist euphemisms.

'—go right ahead. Now's your chance.' He swayed farther back and looked at me with a defiant grin.

'You know what I want, Wilde,' I said heavily. I was a bit drunk myself, and more than a little tired. Gravity gets you down (and space sucks, but that's life). 'Don't ask me to spell it out.'

He leaned forward. I could smell the smoke and spirits on his breath.

'Oh, I know better than that,' he said. 'The same old question. Well, it's the same old answer: no. There is no way, no fucking *way* I'm going to give *you people* what you are so carefully not asking for.'

'Why not?'

Always the same question, which always got the same answer:

'I won't let you lot get your hands on the place.'

I felt my fists clench at my sides, and slowly relaxed them.

'We don't *want* the wretched place!'

'Hah!' said Wilde, with open disbelief. 'Whatever. It won't be me who gives you the means to take it.'

It would have to be somebody else who did, then, I thought. I kept my voice steady, and quiet.

'Not even to fight the Outwarders?'

'You don't need it to fight the Outwarders.'

'Isn't that for us to judge?'

Wilde nodded. 'Sure. You make your judgements, and I'll make mine.'

I wanted to shake the answer out of him. I would have had no compunction about it. As far as I was concerned, he wasn't a human being, just a clever copy of one.

I also, paradoxically, wished I *could* regard him as a fellow human, as a neighbour. This just served to increase my frustration. If I could have taken Wilde into my confidence, and let him know just how how bad, how fast, things were going, he might very well have agreed to tell me all I needed to know. But the Division trusted him even less than he trusted us. Telling him the full truth might trigger things far, far worse. Wilde and Meg had both been in the hands of the enemy, were quite literally products of the enemy, and even now we weren't one hundred percent confident that they were— or were only—what they claimed, and seemed, to be. I thought for a moment of what it might be like if we ever had to treat them as an outbreak and hit them with an orbital zap. There would be no warning, no evacuation, no last-minute work for the ecologists.

The monkey-thing bounded from Meg's lap to mine. I let it scurry up my arm and nestle on my shoulder, and smoothed out the lap of my skirt. I looked up.

'That's fine,' I said. 'It's up to you.' I shrugged, the false animal's false fur brushing my cheek. 'You do what seems best.' I stood up and smiled at them both.

For a moment Wilde looked nonplussed. I hoped he'd be so thrown off balance by my lack of persistence that he would change his mind. But the ploy didn't work. I would have to go for the second option: more difficult, more perilous and, if anything, less likely to succeed.

'Goodbye,' I said. 'See you around.'

In hell, probably.


I leaned over the guardrail around the roof of the Casa Azores and looked down. The ground was a thousand metres below. I felt no vertigo. I've climbed taller trees. There were lights along the beach, bobbing boats in front of the beach, then a breakwater; and beyond that, blue-green fields of algae, fish-farms and kelp plantations and ocean thermal-energy converters, all the way to the horizon. Airships—whether on night-work or recreation I didn't know—drifted like silvery bubbles above them. The building itself, although in the middle of all this thermal power, drew its electricity from a different source. Technically the whole structure was a Carson Tower, powered by cooled air from the top falling down a central shaft and turning turbines on the way.

It was cold on the roof. I turned away from the downward view, wrapped the bolero jacket around my shoulders, and looked at the sky. Once my irises had adjusted, I could see Jupiter, among the clutter of orbital factories, mirrors, lightsails, satellites, and habitats. With binoculars, I could have seen Callisto, Io, Europa—and the ring. It was as good a symbol as any of the forces we were up against.

Our enemies, by some process which even after two centuries was, as we say, *not well understood*, had disintegrated Jupiter's largest moon, Ganymede, to leave that ring of hurrying debris and worrying machinery. And—originally within the ring, but now well outside it—was something even more impressive and threatening: a sixteen-hundred-metre-wide gap in space-time, a wormhole gate to the stars.

Two centuries ago, the Outwarders—people like ourselves, who scant years earlier had been arguing politics with us in the sweaty confines of primitive space habitats—had become very much not like us: post-human, and superhuman. Men Like Gods, like. The Ring was their work, as was the Gate.

After these triumphs, nemesis. Their fast minds hit some limit in processing-speed, or attained enlightenment, or perhaps simply wandered. Most of them distintegrated, others drifted into the Jovian atmosphere, where they re-established some kind of contact with reality.

Their only contact with us, a few years later, was a burst of radio-borne information viruses which failed to take over, but managed to crash, every computer in the Solar System. The dark twenty-second century settled down like drizzle.

Humanity struggled through the Fall, the Green Death, and the Crash, and came out of the dark century with a deep disapproval of the capitalist system (which brought the Fall), for the Greens (who brought the Death), and for the Outwarders (who brought the Crash, and whose viral programs still radiated, making electronic computation and communication hazardous at best).

The capitalist system was abolished, the Greens became extinct, and the Outwarders—

The Outwarders had still to be dealt with.


I checked that I was alone on the roof. The chill, fluted funnels of the Carson process sighed in their endless breath, their beaded condensation quivering into driblets. I moved around in their shadow, and sighted on, not low-looming Jupiter, but the Moon. I squatted, spreading the dress carelessly, and reached up and scratched the monkey's head and whispered in its ear.

The monkey began to melt into the jacket's shoulder, and then dress and jacket together flowed like mercury, and reshaped themselves into a ten-foot-wide dish aerial within which I crouched, my head covered by a fine net that spun itself up from where the collar had been. A needle-thin rod grew swiftly to the aerial's focus. Threads of wire spooled out across the deck, seeking power sources, finding one in seconds. The transformed smart-suit hummed around me.

'It's still no,' I said. 'Going for the second option.'

'Tight-beam message sent,' said the suit. 'Acknowledged by Lagrange relay.'

And that was that. The recipients of the message would know what I meant by 'the second option.' Nobody else would. My mission was confined to more than radio silence; the whole reason I'd come here myself was that we couldn't even trust word-of-mouth. The narrow-beamed radio message would be picked up and passed on by laser, which had the advantage that the Jovians could neither interfere with nor overhear it. It would be bounced to our ship, the *Terrible Beauty*, which was at this moment on the other side of the Earth, and sent on to the Division's base on Callisto. There would be a bare acknowledgement from Callisto, in a matter of hours. I was not going to wait around for it, not like this. I stood up and told the suit to resume its previous shape. When the dress was restored I gave it an unnecessary but celebratory twirl, and spun straight into somebody's arms. As I stumbled back a pace I saw that I'd bumped into Stephan Vrij, the photographer.

We stood looking at each other for a moment.

'The things you see when you don't have your camera,' I said.

'I didn't follow you,' he said awkwardly. 'I was just looking around. Last part of my job for the evening. It's amazing the crazy things people do up here, after a party.'

'Can you forget this?' I asked.

'OK,' he said. He looked away.

'Then I'll promise to forget you.' I reached out and caught his hand. 'Come on. I've had a lot of drinks, and you've had none, right?'

'Yes,' he said, looking a bit puzzled as I tugged at his hand and set off determinedly towards the elevator shaft. I grinned down at him.

'What better way to start the night?'

'You have a point there,' he said.

'Well, no,' I said, 'I rather hope *you* . . .'

Laughing, we went to his room.

When you are among another people, or another people is among you, and you lust after their strange flesh, go you and take your pleasure in them, and have sons and daughters by them, and your people shall live long upon the lands and your children shall fill the skies.

So it is written in the Books of Jordan, anyway. *Genetics*, chapter 3, verse 8.

I woke in a comfortable, if disorderly, bed. Stephan Vrij snored peacefully beside me. We were both naked, and I was under a quilt. I drew the quilt over him and he rolled over in his sleep.

From the angle of the light through the window, it was mid-morning on another fine day. The room was made of something that looked and smelled like pine, but it had never been cut into planks then hammered or glued together (which some people on Earth still do, as I later discovered, and not all of them because they have to but because they can afford the time to indulge such fads). Instead, it had been grown on-site, the walls and floor curving into each other, utility cables emerging like vines from the knotholes. Glossy monochrome pictures—of people, landscapes, seascapes—were stuck to the walls. They looked detailed and precise, just like photographs, apart from the lack of colour. Scattered about, on the low chairs and table or on the floor, was a rather embarrassing quantity and diversity of lingerie. Evidently I had been showing off, or the smart-suit had. My memories of the night were hazy, and warm.

I lay there a few minutes, smiling to myself and hoping I'd got pregnant. Doing so just before a war seemed perverse—it's traditionally done afterwards—but this war would be over before the pregnancy was noticeable. If we won, I might not be back on Earth for a long time, and we needed all the genes we could get. If we lost . . . but defeat wasn't worth thinking about.

I rolled out of bed and gathered the bits and pieces and set them to work reassembling themselves into hiking gear, apart from the one or two items

that would be serviceable as underwear. Not that I actually needed underwear in a smart-matter spacesuit, but they were very nice. So, in their own
way, were the shorts and socks, boots and rucksack that came together on
the floor. The suit always did have good taste.

The apartment was pretty basic and standard, and the functional logic of
it was familiar, so I had no difficulty in finding the makings of breakfast. I
brought the breakfast through to Stephan, and we ate it, and made love for
a final time. Stephan took some photographs of me, and I promised again
to forget him, and we said goodbye.

I suppose he has forgotten me, by now, but I like to think that someone
still has the photographs.


Down at ground level it was hot. The sun was high in the sky, enormous, so
bright I could see it with my eyes closed and so hot it hurt my skin. Even
the air was hot. It's one of the things they don't tell you about, like gravity.

Between the base of the tower and the beach were some low buildings.
Stores and warehouses of equipment for use by people working in the blue-
greens or playing on the beach, refreshment stalls, eating-houses, and so on. I
wandered along the shore road, looking for the tourist place.

Naked small children ran about, yelling, racing from the tower to the
beach and back. Somewhat older children lolled in shade and listened to
adults or adolescents as they talked earnestly in front of a flip-chart or above
a machine. Now and again a child would join one of these groups; now and
again a child would rise, nod politely to the teacher, and wander off to do
something else.

Two such children were minding the tourist place when I found it. The
store was easy enough to spot, a rough construction of seacrete and plastic
and what looked like driftwood, but was probably scrap synthetic wood. I
told myself it must be more solid than it looked, as I ducked under the sea-
silk awning and stood blinking in the cool, dim interior.

Inside, the walls were lined with sagging shelves, which were piled with
everything a tourist might need. Old tin boxes of gold and silver coins, new
plastic boxes of bullets, firearms oiled and racked, hats, scarves, boots. From
the ceiling hung a wide range of casual clothing: loose sundresses, seal-fur
suits, tee shirts and towelling robes. There seemed to be more possible desti-
nations than the number of possible tourists. I was alone in the store, apart
from a boy and a girl sitting on the counter with a chessboard between them.

The boy looked up. 'Hi,' he said. He waved his hand. 'Help yourself. If
you want something that isn't there, let us know.' He smiled absently then
returned to frowning over the chessboard.

I dug through clinking piles of dollars, roubles, marks, pounds, and yen to make up sixty grams of gold and a hundred of silver, in the smallest coins I could find. From the weapons rack I selected a .45 automatic and a dozen clips of ammunition. Food and other consumables I could get anywhere, and the suit had produced better boots, socks, etc. than anything here. But I couldn't pass up the chance of an amazing penknife with a red handle marked with an inlaid steel cross within a shield. It had two blades and a lot of ingenious tools. I was sure I'd find a use for most of them.

I said goodbye to the children, promised to pass on anything I didn't use (with a mental reservation about the knife), and stepped out again into the sunlight. After a few seconds I went back inside and picked up a pair of sunglasses. The girl's laughter followed me out.

Now that I didn't have to screw up my eyes to look up, it was easy to work out the location of the airport from the paths of the airships and microlights and helicopters. I followed the coast road for a couple of miles until I reached it. I got several offers of lifts on the way, but I declined them all. Despite the heat, and the gravity, and the moments of disorientation when some conservative part of my brain decided the horizon just *could not* be that far away, I had to get used to walking in the open on the surface of this planet; and soon, to my surprise, I found that I enjoyed it. The sea breeze carried the homely scent of blue-green fields, the distant converters shimmered and hummed, the nearby waters within the artificial reef sparkled, and on them swimmers and boating-parties filled the air with joyous cries.

The airport was on a spit of land that extended a few hundred yards, traversing the reef-barrier. Airships wallowed at mooring masts, 'copters and microlights buzzed between them. High overhead, the diamond-fibre flying-wings used for serious lifting strained at their cables like gigantic kites. I had arrived on one, from the Guiné spaceport, and it looked as if I'd have to leave on one. The thought of an airship passage was appealing, but it would take too long. I didn't know how much time I had to spare, but the final deadline, the Impact Event, was less than three weeks away. Whatever I did had to be done before that.

Just before the airport perimeter fence I turned and looked back at the Casa Azores. From here it was possible to see it, if not take it all in. A hundred and fifty metres square at the base, tapering in its kilometre height to a hundred at the top. The sides looked oddly natural, covered by climbing plants and hanging gardens, pocked by glider-ports, and by window-bays which shone like ice. Built and maintained by quadrillions of organically engineered nanomachines, it was almost as remarkable as a tree, and a good deal more efficient. The way of life that it and the surrounding aquaculture sustained was not mine, but it was one I was happy to protect. Plenty of interesting work, and plenty of interesting leisure; adventure if you wanted it, ease if you preferred that. Indefinitely extended youth and health. Anything that you couldn't get for the asking you could, with some feasible commitment of time and trouble, nanofacture for yourself.

The paucity of broadcast media, and the difficulties of real-time communication, were the only losses from the world before the Fall and the Crash. We had tried to make it an opportunity. All the entertainment and knowledge to be found among thirty billion people was (eventually) available on pipe, and live action provided by the steady, casual arrival and departure of entertainers and researchers and lecturers. The absence of artificial celebrity meant the endless presence of surprise.

Throughout the Inner System—Earth, near-Earth, Lagrange, Luna, Mars, and the Belt—variants of this same way of life went on. Cultures and languages were more diverse than ever, but the system that underpinned them was the same everywhere. In floating cities, in artificial mountains stepped like ziggurats, in towers like this or taller, in towns below the ground, in huge orbital habitats, in sunlit pressure domes, in caves of ice, most people had settled into this lifestyle: simple, self-sufficient, low-impact, and ecologically sound.

It was sustainable materially and psychologically, a climax community of the human species, the natural environment of a conscious animal, which that conscious animal, after so much time and trouble, had at last made for itself. We called it the Heliocene Epoch. It seemed like a moment in the sun, but there was no reason, in principle, why it couldn't outlast the sun, and spread to all the suns of the sky.

With our solar mirrors we controlled the polar caps. The glaciations and mass extinctions that had marked the Pleistocene were over; the next ice age, long overdue, would never come. With our space-based lasers and nukes, we could shield the earth from asteroid impacts. We could bring back lost species from the DNA in museum exhibits. Soon, any century now, we would control the Milankovitch cycle. We were secure.

No wonder they had so few tourists here: who would want to leave a place like this? I sighed, with a small shiver, and turned to the airport gate.

# 2

---

## AFTER LONDON

I got my airship journey, after all. The flying-wing route took me as far as Bristol, a city that was still a port for Atlantic traffic, though no longer for trade. The old city with its docks had been fairly well preserved, but the quays where sugar (exchanged for, and grown by, slaves) had once been landed now sustained only recreational craft. The new town was in the fashionable Aztec-pyramid style, with a projecting air-jetty about halfway up. We landed there at one p.m., having left Graciosa at eleven. I was lucky to catch the day's second flight to London. It left at around one-thirty in the afternoon, and would reach Alexandra Port about six. This is the sort of thing that happens when you travel inside an atmosphere.

Weather, of course, is another. I stepped out of the lift and on to the roof, to find large drops of water falling from the grey sky, on to me. I dug out of my rucksack a hooded cape—all part of the suit, naturally—and put it on. With the hood to keep water out of my eyes, it was easier to see where I was. The roof had the size and appearance of a small park—apart from the hills in the distance and the curious visual effects the rain made, it could have been under a municipal dome anywhere. I walked across the grass, past dripping trees and bushes, to where a small and gaily coloured dirigible was moored to a central pylon. Other people were also making their way over, a couple of dozen in all when we'd climbed the spiral staircase and crossed the gangway to the airship's gondola. My fellow passengers were dressed similarly to me, but most carried rather more equipment. From overheard conversations as we shook out our wet overclothes and took our seats, I gathered that most of them were—at least to themselves—serious eco-tourists, earnestly studying natural history or urban archaeology. But few had resisted the temptation to bring a rod or a rifle. The hunting and fishing in London was reputed to be excellent.

The seating was arranged in a manner more like a room than a vehicle, but I had no difficulty getting a seat by a window. The airship cast off on schedule, rising through the low cloud and then passing beyond it. After staring out the window for half-an-hour at deciduous woodland interrupted only by old roads and new buildings, I got up and wandered around asking people what refreshments they wanted, then went to the galley and prepared them.

While the coffee was brewing I was joined by a woman who introduced herself as Suze. She was small, brown-haired, hazel-eyed, dark-skinned. Very English. I figured her for being about her apparent age.

'Did you know,' she said as we poured coffee into mugs and tea into cups, 'that in the old system, there were people who did this as a full-time occupation?'

'Did what?'

'Serve refreshments on aircraft.'

I knew this perfectly well.

'Really?' I said. 'Why? Did they . . . enjoy it or something?'

'No,' she said earnestly, 'they did it because it was a way of getting what they needed to live on.'

I waved a hand at the rack of sandwiches. 'You mean this was all they had to eat?'

'No, no, it was because—'

She laughed suddenly. 'You're winding me up, aren't you?'

'Yes,' I admitted. I started pouring the coffee. 'Let's see if we can do the job better than the wage slaves, shall we?'

When we'd finished serving lunch to the other passengers we took our own trays. I saw that she, like myself, was making to sit alone, so I asked her to join me. We talked as we ate.

It wasn't polite to ask neighbours what they were doing, where they were going, and so on. You had to work around to it, and not pry if they didn't open up.

'Why did you tell me that thing about the old system?' I asked.

'At the moment,' Suze said, 'I'm a sociologist.'

I dragged up the unfamiliar word from old memories.

'Someone who studies society?'

She nodded. 'Yes, but there's not much to study any more!'

'How d'you mean?'

'Look around you.' She waved a hand. 'These days, you want to investigate society, and what do you find?'

It was a rhetorical question, but I really wanted to know her answer.

'Well,' she went on, 'it's all so *obvious*, so transparent. We all know how
things work from the age of about five or so. You go and try to find out, and
somebody will just *tell* you! And it'll be true, there are no secrets, nothing
going on behind the scenes. Because there are no *scenes*, know what I
mean?'

'Yes, of course,' I said, thinking *Ha! Little do you know, girl!* 'So what society do you study, if not our own?'

'I study the old system,' Suze said, 'and I do learn interesting things.
Sometimes I just can't help telling people about them. And anyway, it's a way
of getting people to talk.'

I snorted. 'Yeah, it's a great line,' I said. 'Almost anything you're doing,
you can say to someone, "Did—you—know—that under the wages system,
some people had to do this every day or *starve to death*?" '

She laughed at my mock-shocked tone and saucer eyes. For the next few
minutes we vied to suggest some activity to which the statement didn't apply, and found our resources of ribaldry and gruesomeness inadequate to
the task.

'All the same,' she said when we'd given up, 'it is fascinating in a way.' She
shot me a glance, as if unsure whether to go on. 'Capitalism had a sort of . . .
elegance about it. The trouble is, well, the old people, uh, no offence, aren't
very good at explaining it, because they hate it so much, and the old books . . .'
She sighed and shrugged. 'They just don't make *sense*. They have all these
equations in them, like real science, but you look at the assumptions and you
think, hey, wait a minute, that can't be right, so how *did* it work? *Anyway*,' she
went on, more firmly, 'it's the only interesting sociological question left.' She
looked out of the window, then leaned forward and spoke quietly. 'That's why
I go to London,' she confided. 'To talk to people outside the Union.'

Then she leaned back, and looked at me as if defying me to be shocked,
unsure that she hadn't misjudged my broad-mindedness. I didn't need to feign
my response—I was pleased, and interested. We had, of course, a network of
agents and contacts in the London area, and the old comrades could always be
counted on—but my mission was too secret even for them. Nobody knew I
was coming, or what I was looking for, although that information-leakage
couldn't be delayed much longer. I had expected to have to rely on hastily
learned, and possibly outdated, background.

Now I had the possibility of a guide. This could be a stroke of luck! Or
something else entirely, if I wanted to be paranoid about it. Her earlier
comments about there being no secrets were too transparent to be some
kind of double bluff; if she were involved in any secrets herself (other than

her—to some—distasteful interests) she would hardly have brought the subject up. And anyway, she was too young . . .

I studied her face, and tried to hide my second thoughts, my second-guessing of myself. You lose the knack for conspiracy, over the decades and centuries. The Division was not the Union, true enough, but even our politics had weathered and softened into non-lethality, like a rusty artillery piece in a mossy emplacement—all our destructive power was directed outwards.

I decided that, whether her presence was fortuitous, or the outcome of one of those hidden forces whose existence she'd so naively denied, I couldn't lose. If she was innocent, then I'd gain some valuable contacts and information—if not, the only way to find out was by playing along.

So I said: 'Hmm, that's interesting. Do you know many non-cooperators?' (That was the polite term; the others included 'parasites', 'scabs', 'scum', and—spoken with a sneer and a pretend spit—'bankers'.) It was considered all right to exchange coins with them for their odd handicrafts and eccentric nanofactures, and to employ them as guides—but most people shrank from any closer contact, as if the non-cos carried some invisible skin disease.

'A few,' she said, looking relieved. 'I'm studying, you know, trade patterns in the Thames Valley.'

'Trade patterns?'

'Most people think the non-cos live by scrounging stuff from the Union, but that's just a prejudice.' She grimaced; she was still talking in a low voice, as if not wanting the other passengers to overhear. 'Actually they're pretty self-sufficient. They make things and swap them among themselves, using little metal weights for indirect swaps. That's why whenever they offer to do things for tourists, they only do it for metal weights.' Suze laughed. 'There I go again. I'm sure you know all this.'

'Well, in theory,' I admitted, 'but it'll be interesting to see how it works in practice. The fact is, I'm going to London to find—a certain person.' I thought about risks. I'd be making inquiries after this guy as soon as we landed, among all kinds of people. No matter how discreet I was about it, word would get around. There seemed to be no harm in starting now. 'His name is Isambard Kingdom Malley.'

'He's *alive*?' Suze sounded incredulous. 'In London?' Comprehension dawned on her face.

'Yes,' I said. 'He's a non-co.'


Isambard Kingdom Malley was, or had been, a physicist. He worked out the Theory of Everything. The final equations. When I was as young as I

look, there was a fashion for tee shirts with the Malley equations on them.
TOE shirts, we called them. The equations, at least, were elegant.

Malley was born in 2039, so he was six years old at the time of the Fall Revolution. His theory was born in the early 2060s, in the brief surge of new
technologies and research advances that marked the period when the US/UN
empire had fallen, but the barbarians had not yet won. His last paper was
the modest classic *Space-time manipulation with non-exotic matter*, Malley, I K,
Phys. Rev. D 128 (10), 3182 (2080). It established the theoretical possibility
of the quantum-chaotic wormhole and the vacuum-fluctuation virtual-mass
drive. Its celebrated 'Appendix II: Engineering Considerations' pointed out
some practical problems with constructing the Gate and the Drive, notably
that it would require about a billion times as much computational power as
was currently available.

A week after the article's publication, the journal was shut down by the
gang in charge of its local fragment of the Former United States, for 'un-
Scriptural physical speculation', 'blasphemy', and (according to some sources)
'witchcraft'. There's a certain elegiac aptness in the thought that the paper
which pointed the road to the stars was published in what turned out to be the
journal's final issue: the West was still soaring when it fell.

Thirteen years later, the Outwarders built the wormhole gate and torched
off their interstellar probe, reaching for the end of space and time. That it
never did reach the expected end—that it was, in fact, still going strong, still
transmitting almost incomprehensible data from an unimaginable futurity—
refuted Malley's Theory of Everything, which had been based on the hitherto impregnable Standard Model finite-universe cosmology. But Malley's
was still the only theory we had. It fitted all the data, except the irrefragable
fact of the probe. Within the limits of our engineering, the theory still
worked. Nobody had come up with anything to replace it. (This was a sore
point with me. I sometimes thought it reflected badly on our society: perhaps, after all, it does take some fundamental social insecurity to sharpen the
wits of genius. Perhaps we had no more chance of developing further fundamental physics than the Pacific Islanders had of developing the steam engine.
Or—I hoped—it could just be that a Newton, an Einstein or a Malley doesn't
come along very often.)

I suspected that Malley would have been an Outwarder himself, but
he never made it to space. America's last launch sites were already being
stormed by mobs who thought rockets damaged the ozone layer, or made
holes in the crystal spheres of the firmament. He fled America for Japan,
and then quixotically returned to England at the time of the Green Death,
where he worked to the best of his growing ability and dwindling resources
as a medicine man, dealing out antibiotics and antigeriatrics to superstitious

settlers and nostalgic refugees, administering the telomere hack to frightened adolescents who understood it, if at all, as yet another rite-of-passage
ordeal. We knew he'd survived the century of barbarism, and that he'd registered to vote in the elections that formally abolished capitalism and established
the Solar Union. Evidently he'd voted against the social revolution, because
in the subsequent century of the world commonwealth he had retreated to the
wilds of London, a stubborn non-cooperator.

We badly needed his cooperation now.


Malley was apparently following the Epicurean injunction to 'live unknown'.
Suze had never heard so much as a rumour of him.

'Would you like me to come with you, at least part of the way?' she suggested. 'I could help you find your way around, and you could—well, to be
honest there are places I'd rather not go on my own.'

'Yes, I'd like that very much,' I said. 'That's real neighbourly of you,
Suze.'

She gave me a full-beam smile and asked, 'How do you expect to track
him down? Do you have any idea where he is? And why do you want to talk
to him, anyway? If you don't mind me asking.'

I scratched my ear and looked out of the window. We were again above
some low cloud, and through its dazzling white a town rose on our left.
'Swindon tower,' Suze remarked. Ahead of us the airship's shadow raced
like a rippling fluke across the contours of the clouds. I looked back at Suze.

'No, I don't mind you asking,' I said. 'I'll tell you the answers once we have
a bit more privacy. And then, it'll be up to you whether you want to come
along with me or not.'

'That's OK,' she said.

'Tell me what you've found out about London,' I said, and she did. By
the time she had finished, we were almost there. We looked out at woodlands and marshes, ruins and the traces of streets and arterial roads, at the
junctions of which smoke drifted up from the chimneys of huddled settlements. Suze began excitedly pointing out landmarks: Heathrow airport, its
hexagram of runways only visible from the air, like the sigil of some ancient
cult addressed to gods in the sky; the Thames Flood Barrier far to the east,
a lonely line of silver dots in the Thames flood plain; Hyde Park with its
historic Speaker's Corner, where the Memorial to the Unknown Socialist
rose a hundred metres above the trees, gazing in the disdain of victory at
the fallen or falling towers of the City; and, as the airship turned and began
to drift lower, our destination, the proud pylons of Alexandra Port.

The sight of Alexandra Port set the hairs of my nape prickling. It had
been one of the early centres of the space movement which was the com-

mon ancestor of the Outwarders and ourselves; there were people alive today whose journey into space had begun in its crowded concourses, waiting
for the airship connection to the launch sites of Guiné and Khazakhstan. Its
mooring masts were their Statue of Liberty, their Ellis Island.

Or their Botany Bay. My fingernails were digging into my palms. I turned
away and prepared to disembark.


The airship settled, its motors humming as they steadied its position, just
above the terminal's flat roof. A wheeled stairway rolled up to the exit and we
all trooped down. Two or three people working on maintenance boarded
the dirigible and began checking it over; although its automated systems were
more than adequate to the task, there's something about aviation which keeps
the habit of human supervision alive.

From the terminal's roof we could see an almost panoramic view of
London, its rolling hills hazy with woodsmoke. The trees were interrupted
here and there by towers whose steel and concrete had survived two centuries of neglect, and by broad corridors around ancient roadways. To the
east the Lee Water broadened out to the Hackney marshes and the distant
gleam of the Thames. On the nearby hills to the west the ruins of the old
brick buildings and streets were still, barely, visible as crumbling walls and
cracked slabs among the trees.

It was a common misconception—one which, to be honest, none of us
had ever found it politic to publicly correct, though the facts were there for
anyone who cared to look—that the Green Death was a single plague, the
result of a virus genetically engineered by some Green faction in a fit of
Malthusian overkill. More sober epidemiology has revealed that it was several diseases, probably natural, all of which hit at the same time and which
were spread by soldiers, refugees and settlers. The disorder, and the weakening of the social immune-systems of medicine and science, were indeed
partly the responsibility of the Green gangs and their many allies and precursors, going back through a century or more of irrationalism and anti-
humanism. Indeed, the panicky abandonment of the cities as plague-centres
was itself, in part, the outcome of that way of thinking, and it probably led
to more deaths than the diseases ever did. So, while the Greens weren't quite
as responsible as folk once thought for the billions of deaths, I find it hard to
reproach anyone for the so-called 'excesses' after the liberation. (The execution figures were inflated by over-enthusiastic local committees, anyway. It
wasn't more than a hundred thousand, worldwide. Tops. Honestly.)

The long-term effect of the Green Death wasn't on the size of the
population—which bounced back sharply after the social revolution, and
was now coming along very nicely, thank you—but on its distribution. Most

of the old metropoles remained empty, long after they became perfectly safe to live in. They were happily left, quite appropriately, to those who rejected the new society and preferred some version of the old.

The countryside, too, was reverting to the wild, as agriculture was replaced by aquaculture, hydroponics, and artificial photosynthesis. It was less frequently ceded to the non-cos than the old cities, however, because of its recreational value to people from the dense arcologies of the Union.

Alexandra Port itself had changed little, because it had never been abandoned to the ravages of nature or man. In the Green Death it had been a conduit for refugees going out and relief flowing in, and even in the West's century of collapse it had been maintained by the earthbound remnant of the Space Movement, its boundaries guarded, its personnel supplied from outside, a garrison in the midst of desolation.

It was all just like in the old pictures, I thought as we descended to the concourse: the People's Palace, retro-styled even when it was new, back in the twentieth century, and the newer, twenty-first-century terminal buildings and workshops sprawling across the crown of the hill under the high pylons. The only evidence of modern technology I could see was the escalator down which we rode and its continuation in the walkway which carried us to the exit. Their seamless flow of plastic—not nanotech, just clever—would have baffled the complex's early engineers.

We walked over to the People's Palace, now a guesthouse as well as a home for the people working in the port. I looked at the sun, and at my watch.

'Shall we stay here for the night?' I suggested. 'Go on our travels in the morning?'

Suze nodded. 'Yeah, it's too late to go travelling,' she said. 'I do know some places to sleep in London, but they're strictly something you do for the experience.' We checked at the board in the foyer and found there were plenty of vacancies; most of our fellow tourists apparently preferred the dubious glamour and adventure of finding accommodation in one of London's native inns or shooting lodges. We selected a double room in the west wing, and took our stuff up. There was a small stove, coffee, and other supplies in the room, and an invitation to the evening meal and/or later social activities. While Suze was showering, I asked the suit to make an unobtrusive sweep of the room. It found nothing, apart from the expected wildlife and the standard cleany-crawlies. There were definitely none of the other kind of bugs—not that I seriously expected any, but it was routine, like the airship inspection.

Suze stepped out of the shower just as the suit's agent was reporting back.

'Oh!' she said. 'A pet mouse. How sweet!'

'Grrr,' said the suit, but I'm sure all Suze heard was a squeak. I took a shower myself, and emerged to find that Suze had brewed some coffee and dressed for dinner.

'Thanks,' I said, taking the coffee. 'Nice dress.'

Suze looked down at it smugly. 'Fortuny pleats, they're called,' she said. 'You can just ball it up in a rucksack, and when you shake it out it still looks great.'

'Ah,' I said, 'I have something to show you.'

I climbed back into my clothes, which were still sweaty and crumpled from travelling. They all added up to only part of the suit—the rest being the mouse, and the rucksack with its contents—but there was still enough for it to do the Cinderella trick, and mimic net and lace from an archived memory of debutante froth. I twirled, and grinned at Suze's open mouth.

'Smart-matter spacesuit,' I explained, sitting down and patting its bouffant skirts. Suze was still goggle-eyed.

'You're from space?'

'Yes,' I said. 'The Cassini Division, in fact.'

'Wow!' Suze's amazed look turned to an awed, and slightly guilty, excitement which I'd encountered before. In a world of abundance, of peace and security, the Division was the biggest focus for the dangerous appeal of danger, the sexy thrill of violence. There were those who despised and feared it for that very reason, and those who—sometimes secretly, even from themselves—loved it. Suze, it seemed, was among the latter.

'That's why I want to talk to Malley,' I said.

'About the wormhole?' Sharp girl.

'Yes. We want him to show us how to get through it. To New Mars.'

'Start our *own* settlement?'

I shook my head firmly. 'We don't need another lot of deserts!'

Something—some sudden light in her eyes—told me her secret answer: we do, we do! Not everybody would feel that way, but I knew that enough did for Wilde to have seen that look all the many times he told his tales. No wonder he had the crazy notion that if we could go through, we'd colonize the place.

'So why do we need to go through?' Suze asked. 'Why now?'

'We need to go through,' I said carefully, 'because there's a chance that the people on the other side of the wormhole are tinkering about with the same entities that the Outwarders became—the Jovians—on this side. We're going to go through, and stop them, with whatever it takes.' (This was true, as far as it went, which was not very far.) Suze sat back in one of the armchairs and looked at me, shaking her head.

'Why don't people *know* about this? Why haven't we been told?'

'We're not keeping it exactly secret,' I said. 'It's just that we've released the information in scientific reports and so on, rather than making a big splash of it. So far, everybody who's managed to figure out what's going on must have agreed with us that there's no need to panic.'

'That may be right,' she said indignantly, 'but there is a need to discuss it! You can't just go and *do* something like that, without any, any—'

'Authorization? Actually, we *can*, in the sense that nobody could stop us. We wouldn't want to do that, because we—that is, the Division—would fall apart if we ever went against the Union, because we'd have a strong and well-armed minority who *didn't* want to go against the Union. But as a matter of fact, we do have authorization. We're mandated to protect the Inner System from outside threats, and if a possible post-human invasion coming out of the wormhole isn't one, I don't know what is.'

Suze still looked troubled. 'What about the New Martians?' she asked. 'I don't see them going along with it.'

I laughed. 'If they're still people . . . they're just a bunch of non-cos. And we know how to deal with *them*.'

Suze shot me an odd glance, and seemed about to speak, but whatever was on her mind, she thought better of it.

'Well,' she said brightly, 'enough of this. Let's go and grab ourselves some aircraftmen.'

Dinner was in the great hall, with one of the daily planning-meetings before it (we sat it out in the bar) and a dance afterwards. The hall, a former exhibition centre, was decorated with murals depicting episodes from London's history: the Plague, the Fire, the Blitz, the Death; the battles of Cable Street, Lewisham, Trafalgar Square, Norlonto; the horrors of life under the Greens (one particularly imaginative panel showed some persecuted rationalist tied to a tree and left to die of starvation and dehydration, gloating Green savages dancing around and a woman loyally lurking in nearby bushes, recording the words of the black gospel he croaked from his parched mouth); the joy and vengeance of liberation, cheering crowds welcoming the Sino-Soviet troops (the Sheenisov, as everybody still calls them) and stringing up Green chiefs and witchdoctors from their own sacred trees; the tense balloting of the social revolution. Uplifting stuff.

The other decoration in the hall, that of its occupants, was more attractive. Costume on Earth tends to follow local traditions and techniques; here, it was a native style, picked up (as we later noticed) from the non-cos: cotton, with lots of dyes and embroidery. Some of the clothes worn after work were far more beautiful than ours, but at least our party frocks marked us out as visitors. We had no lack of attention, and we did, indeed, pull an aircraftman each.

———

Early the next morning we made our separate ways back to the room in which neither of us had spent the night, gathered up our gear, and had breakfast in the main hall. In the daylight the murals looked lurid and naive rather than heroic. The sunlight through the roof panels was bright and warm. Suze spread out a map.

'Well,' she said, 'where are we going today?'

'Our friend currently lives in Ealing Forest,' I said. 'I have a kind of address for him. He hangs out in some non-co technical college, and he's known to scour the markets for old books and gear.'

'Easy,' said Suze. 'We drive down the main path to Camden Market, stash the car at the Union depot, then take a boat up the canal to the North Circular—' her finger jabbed at a trail marked on the map, then traced it to another thin line '—then down into Ealing.'

'You sure the canal's quickest?'

Suze nodded briskly. 'The roads are kept up by the non-cos, and they're just what you'd expect. The waterways are ours. Everything from the dredging to the lock-keeping is done by Union machines.'

'Why?'

She shrugged. 'It's the least obtrusive way of keeping a presence. And if we ever need to increase it, the canals have the great advantage of going round the back, especially with hovercraft.'

'Hmm,' I said. 'I wonder if we could get away with borrowing a hovercraft.'

'Too noisy. The tourists don't like it, and it makes the locals expect trouble.'

At the car-pool we selected a rugged, low-slung buggy with wheels that could, according to the spec, cope with any pothole or tree root in London. The controls were standard, but I didn't yet trust my reflexes in this gravity, so Suze took the wheel. We drove down the long, curving road to the southern exit, through a crowd of importunate people (for me, a new and alarming experience; for Suze: 'Just beggars and pedlars; you'll get used to it'), up and over a hill, and down into the wild woods.

The vehicle's compact electric engine was quiet. As we drove slowly along the muddy trackways, in the shade of tall oaks and elms dripping with the previous night's rain, we could hear constant birdsong, the occasional howl of a wolf or bark of a fox, and the far-off, uncanny whooping laugh of gibbons. Kestrels hovered high above the forest paths. Wood pigeons clattered among the trees, and now and again the vivid flash of a parakeet passed before our startled eyes. Every so often a small deer would bound on to the path, take one look at us and sprint away, its thudding hooves unexpectedly loud.

Most of the ruins on either side were covered with ivy, its green cables silently and slowly dragging the crumbled brickwork back into the earth. Some of the walls, however, bore the marks of recent repair, with clay and wattle or bricks cannibalized from other ruins making good the gaps, and the roofs—usually a floor or two lower than the originals—beamed and thatched. There were clearings where entire villages had been built from recycled materials, with not a trace of the original buildings left standing. We got used to treating rising smoke ahead as a signal to slow down and watch out for scuttling chickens, ambling pigs, barking dogs and racing, yelling children. The interest of the adults varied from covert and sullen to open and servile, the latter type frantically drawing our attention to wares that were depicted or described on garish signboards.

I put to Suze a question that had occurred to me from comparing old political maps with the current geographical ones: that the present communities might be remnants of the ancient, with Christian fundamentalists flourishing here, anarchic tribes around Alexandra Port, usurers still haunting the leaning towers down by the river, Muslims to the east and Hindus to the west . . . but she disabused me of this fanciful notion. The vast migrations of the Death and the dark century had literally walked over the great city, leaving of its former fractious cultures not a trace.

The human traffic on the path increased as, over the next hour, we approached Camden Market. There were few powered vehicles, and horse-drawn ones were only a little more frequent. Pedestrians generally walked in groups: gay parties of tourists with rucksacks and rifles, who waved and greeted us as we passed; and serious squads of non-cos, tramping with heavy loads on their backs, or on overburdened animals, or on similarly overloaded carts. The non-cos usually spared us no more than a calculating glance or a canny smile.

Camden Lock Market, a vast, trampled clearing at the intersection of several roads and a major canal, had the look of a place which the trees—and their worshippers—had never conquered. Like Alexandra Port, but for economic rather than strategic reasons, it had remained alive and functioning through all the disasters that had befallen the city. In physical extent it was actually larger than it had been in the twenty-first century, because some of London's other traditional markets, in the East, were now six feet under the Thames estuary at low tide.

Our first stop was the Union depot, a stockaded area on the edge of the market. Inside the casually guarded gate were a low garage, a warehouse, and a rest-and-recreation building. Suze gave the last a disparaging glance.

'For wimps,' she remarked. 'What's the point of coming here if you're not willing to mix?'

After we'd garaged the vehicle, hoisted our packs, holstered our pistols and wandered around for a few minutes, I began to see exactly what the point was. The place was guaranteed to give most Union people a severe culture shock. To me it looked like utter chaos, and sounded—to use words whose roots lie in ancient experiences of similar situations—like a barbarous babel.

The market consisted of: long fenced-off areas packed with sad-eyed beasts; marble tables running with the blood, piled with the flesh of beasts; fish swimming in glass tanks or flopping on slabs; canopied wooden tables stacked with pottery, weaponry, books, machinery, clothes, textiles, herbs, drugs, antiquities, foodstuffs; racks from which coats swayed and dresses fluttered in the warm breeze.

Each of the stalls and tables had behind it someone whose fulltime occupation was minding it, watching over it, talking to anybody on the other side of the table and passing wares over and taking money back. The sellers and the buyers filled the air with the sound of their dickering, bickering, joking, teasing, offering, refusing; and with the recorded music which every stall-holder, and most of their customers, discordantly inflicted on everybody else, played at an unsociable volume from portable devices which were aptly called loudspeakers.

Then there were the smells: of the animals and their dung and their slaughter, of the people and their sweat and the scents which failed to disguise it, of smoked herbal drugs which were, I began to suspect, not a recreation here but a necessity.

I stopped in front of a stall on which dried leaves of tobacco and hemp were laid out in labelled bundles, neatly sorted into open-topped boxes. The woman behind the stall was prettily dressed in an embroidered cotton blouse and a printed cotton long skirt, gathered at the waist with a drawstring. It was hard to work out her age—like many of the adult non-cos, she seemed to combine the detached watchfulness of age with the innocent selfishness of youth, and, on top of that, her cosmetics made a baffling mask: her cheeks reddened, the rest of her face whitened, eyes darkened and lips flushed, as if she'd been awake all night and was now in a state of sexual arousal. But she had an attractive smile.

'Suze,' I said, nudging, 'could we—?'

Suze grinned and nodded, then, when I reached into the pocket of my rucksack, frowned and shook her head.

'I'll do it,' she murmured.

She looked up at the woman behind the table, and fingered a leaf labelled 'Kent Ganja'.

'How much you got on this?'

'Best stuff, lady,' the woman said. 'Two grams gold, five grams silver an ounce.'

(That's what I later worked out she said. At the time her strange singsong went into my ears as: 'Besstuff laidy, two gramzgold five gramzsilveranahnce.')

Suze recoiled. 'Fackinell!' she said. 'Thassexpensiv init?' (I still haven't figured that one; I'll leave it as it sounded.)

'Nah,' said the woman. 'From cross the riveh, thatiz. Transport's fackin criminal. You won't get cheaper anywhere.'

She waved around at the rest of the market. 'Try 't an' see f' y'selves. You'll be back.'

'Not likely,' said Suze, taking me by the elbow and firmly steering me away. We'd gone only a few steps when the woman called out: 'Awright, I'll give you a special, just to try it aht. Frow in paypas, too.'

Back we went and the bargain, after a few more verbal exchanges, was concluded. To my surprise both the woman and Suze were smiling at each other, both apparently satisfied with an outcome which they had each insisted would, if repeated too often, reduce one or the other to complete wretchedness.

We sat down at a table a few yards away and ordered coffee and bread rolls stuffed with cooked meat which had almost certainly not been grown from blue-greens. I'm not sentimental about beasts, but I tried not to think about it too much—marine molluscs are one thing, vertebrates are something else. When we'd finished eating Suze built a small joint of tobacco and hemp, lit it and passed it to me after a few appreciative puffs.

'Good stuff,' she said.

I tested and confirmed this. 'Yes,' I said. 'Just like the woman said it was. But won't she . . . dislike you for the way you made her accept such a small amount of silver for it?'

Suze guffawed. 'She got a very good price—an acceptable amount of silver—for it. She's happy with the silver, and we're happy with the hemp. Oh, thanks.'

I looked at her as she drew on it again. 'So you were both lying?'

'No, of course not,' Suze chuckled. 'It's a convention. Like bluffing in a strategy game.'

'But why did you bother to go through it? Why didn't you just give her what she asked in the first place? I mean . . .' I shrugged, having enough nous to understand that saying out loud how much metal we had on us might not be a good idea.

'Ah,' said Suze. 'That's an interesting point. In theory, OK, all the Union tourists here could bring as much, uh, negotiables as they could carry, and buy anything they wanted. All that would happen is that the amount the locals expected for their goods would go up, and everybody would be worse off all round. That's one of the things that get explained to first-timers. It used to be called inflation when there were states.' She frowned. 'Sort of, except they used pretend money—'

I cut her off hastily, not wanting to get my head around yet another complication (*pretend* money? Say *what*?).

'OK, but if the woman had stuck with her first offer, what—oh! I see. You'd have gone to another stall.'

Suze grinned, passing back the joint. 'Make an economist of you yet.'

'Hah! Hard to believe, now, that the whole world was once run like this.'

Suze nodded soberly. 'This, and various combinations of this and pushing people around. Weird.'

We got up to leave, and were recalled by an indignant yell from the food-stall minder.

'Sorree!' Suze said to him, blushing as she passed him a silver coin. 'Keep the change.'

It took her even longer to explain to me about that: the custom of a price that wasn't a price, on top of the price; a sum that was never asked for, but whose omission was always resented. We wandered on towards the stalls of books and machines. The smoke, and the coffee and food, had shifted my brain chemistry in the way I'd hoped. They were helping me to adjust to what was going on around me, but I still let Suze do the talking.

She browsed the bookstalls and machine shops and nanotech tanks, making the occasional small purchase and apparently idle inquiries after Malley. Sometimes she used his full name, sometimes she just wondered aloud if anyone had heard of 'the scientist' or 'the old doc'. Most of the sellers seemed to know her by sight, and gave her less of a hard bargain than some other Union tourists were getting. At the last stall she picked up and leafed through an obsolete textbook of physics which she'd dug up from one of the plastic boxes at the foot of the stall.

'I wish I knew someone who could explain this to me,' she said, casually handing the book to the seller. He was plump, even for a non-co, pink-skinned, and wrapped in a curious multicoloured patchwork coat that made him look like some tubby wizard. He glanced at the book; his eyes narrowed and his grip suddenly tightened. He pulled the book back.

'Sorry, miss,' he said. 'Not for sale.'

Suze gave him her best innocent-tourist look.

'Oh? That's a shame. Why not?'

'I've been asked to save anything by this bloke Wheeler for the professor.'

'Sure,' said Suze. 'Professor Malley, isn't it?' She seemed to forget the matter, leaning forward and pouncing on a copy of the rare *Home Workshop Nanotech* (Loompanics, 2052). 'Hey, look at this!' She passed it to me and looked again at the stall-holder, eyebrows raised.

'Yeah, Malley,' he said. 'He comes by now and again. Ain't seen him for a few weeks, though.'

'He's still running a school down Ealing way, ain't he?'

'That's right,' said the stall-holder. His accent blended in with the local speech, but his diction was clearer, at least to me. Suze glanced at the price pencilled on the book's inside cover, and passed the man a gold coin, without her customary haggling. He seemed to take this as a payment for a little more than the book (I was beginning to grasp how these people's minds worked, I thought smugly) and went on:

'Funny you should be asking after him.' He scratched the stubble on his upper chin. 'Couple of your lot—' he coughed '—uh, Union members were through the other day, looking for him.'

I felt a jolt of surprise.

'Yes, he's quite famous really,' Suze responded lightly. 'I'm sure lots of people want to talk to him. I wonder if they're anyone I know?'

He shrugged. 'Hard to say, you people all—what I mean is, they were two blokes, right, about your age—real age—and about her height.' He indicated me. 'Tall, dark, but not—uh, more sort of Indian-looking than you ladies, if you know what I mean.'

'Did you notice,' I asked carefully, 'anything unusual in the way they moved?'

His face brightened. 'Yeah! That's it! Something about them bothered me. Couldn't put me finger on it. But one of them had a funny way of hanging on to the edge of the table, like what you're doing now—' I let go and straightened up, self-consciously '—and they both had a way of dropping things. Books they'd picked up.' He took a pencil from behind his ear and demonstrated, mimicking someone absently putting the pencil down a foot above the table, then turning back and looking for it where it wasn't. We all laughed.

'I think I know who they are,' I smiled. 'When exactly did you say they were here?'

'Must've been Sunday,' the man said. 'Weekend market. Today's mid-week.'

Today was—I had to think for a moment—Wednesday. I nodded and smiled. 'Thanks very much.'

'Be seeing you,' the stall-holder said.

'Cheers, Tommy,' Suze said, and we left, Suze intent on the old book she'd bought, pointing out to me its appallingly accurate instructions for building nanotech replicators using only a primitive computer, a scanning tunnelling electron microscope made out of television parts, and a few chemicals likely to be found under the kitchen sink in which the results could be 'safely isolated' according to the book's demonically irresponsible author, one Dr Frank N. Stein (probably a pseudonym, Suze told me solemnly).

' "Sold for informational purposes only",' she said, incredulously quoting the publisher's disclaimer. 'You know, the stuff in this book is *still* dangerous! You could start your very own outbreak with it!'

'Just as well you've got it out of the non-cos' hot little hands,' I said.

She glanced at me. 'Hmm,' she said. 'That's a point. Never thought of that.'

We had reached the end of one of the aisles of stalls. I walked on, until we'd reached the edge of the clearing. Suze followed me into the shade of one of the tall trees. We sat down on springy beech mast and gazed back at the ever-busier market.

'Well,' I said, letting out a long sigh, 'I had no idea they still made 'em like you, Suze. That was brilliant. You could be like one of those guys from the old days, a spy or a detective or whatever.'

'Ah, thanks.' Suze picked up a dried kernel and began picking at it with her fingernails. 'I suppose I am in a way. An investigator.' She shot me an awkward, almost embarrassed look, and I wondered, not for the first time, what social pressures—as undetectable to her, perhaps, as the pressure of the air she breathed—bore down on her from the society she wasn't investigating: her own. 'So there are other people looking for Malley.'

'Yes,' I said. 'And none that I know, I'll tell you that.'

'Perhaps they really are just students, keen on talking to a great physicist,' Suze said in a flat tone. 'What was that about the way they moved?'

'Spacers,' I said. 'Classic low-gee reflexes. Lagrangers or Loonies, if you ask me. Not from the Division, as far as I know.'

'But would you know?'

'I reckon so.'

Suze cocked an eyebrow at me. 'I know about need-to-know,' she said. She looked down again, then up. 'From books.'

I took this as a reproof, and had a momentary impulse to tell her everything. But I resisted it.

'That book dealer,' I said. 'You called him Tommy. You know him?'

'Chatted to him a couple of times,' she said. 'He's—he's ex-Union.'

'Really? Well, that explains the way he talks.'

Suze laughed. 'We're all so conscious of our superiority, aren't we?'

'I suppose so.' Well, we were superior. I'd never considered the matter. 'Why should anyone leave the Union?'

'I've asked him that,' Suze said. 'Couldn't get any answer out of him that made sense.' It sounded like an admission of personal failure. 'He didn't get on with neighbours, that's how he put it.'

'With thirty billion to choose from? I'm surprised he can get on with anybody.'

'I don't think he meant any particular neighbours.'

I grimaced. 'Weird. Anyway, it's his business.'

'That's *exactly* how he put it!'

I stared up at the sun-dappled leaves. A squirrel bounded along a low branch, looked at me and began scolding, just like my conscience.

'It's almost noon,' I said. 'I think I'd best be on my way.'

Suze's face fell. 'You don't want me to come along?'

I leaned over and squeezed her hand. 'You've helped me a lot, Suze. But . . . I really think it wouldn't be fair to get you further into this. It could be more dangerous than you expect.'

She expostulated further, to no avail; but with outward cheerfulness led me to the canal-boat dock, and said goodbye to me with an unexpected and more than neighbourly embrace.


I borrowed a small inflatable with an electric outboard. It could make five kilometres an hour, and even with the inevitable delays in locks, would only take a couple of hours to get me to the Union station at the intersection of the Grand Union Canal and the trail known as the North Circular.

The canal, under the oak and beech and overhanging willow that crowded its banks, was often dark. The towpath had not been maintained, so the only traffic was self-powered: the slowly chugging barges of non-co traders and travellers, the silently skimming launches, skiffs, and kayaks of Union trippers. Dredgers and other maintenance-robots went about their work, shiny metal crabs glimpsed crawling along the bottom or clambering on the banks. Shoals of minnows and sticklebacks lifted their noses to the surface, spotting the water like brief, local flurries of rain; herons and kingfishers took aim in response. Where the stone or brickwork bank was crumbled to the waterline, deer and wallabies looked up as I passed. The bridges were mostly recent, wooden; all but a few of the old stone bridges had long since collapsed, and their remains had been hauled from the water and dumped in unceremonious heaps at each side.

I settled back in the dinghy's air-cushioning, the tiller under one elbow, and relaxed my muscles while letting my mind freewheel, gradually overcoming the lingering effect of the joint. From the collar of my shirt I allowed a tendril of the suit to creep up my neck, over my jaw and cheek and around the back of my eyeball, where it patched into my optic nerve. It would be noticed by anyone closer than a few feet away, and probably recognized, but to anyone further away would look like a strange, hair-thin scar. For the moment I left it to maintain my position on a representation of the map, which with a deliberate wink I could view in front of my eyes like an after-image. Minute by minute the tiny bead of my real-time Global Position moved along the kinked and curved wire of the scaled-down canal.

I watched it all, and worried. Two men from space were after Malley, and they had three days' start on me. One of the more minor things I hadn't told Suze was that there was a faction—no, that was putting it too strongly—a school of thought in the Division (and, more widely, among the space settlers outside it, and even on Earth) which wanted to negotiate with the Outwarders, if such a thing were possible. As if! The very thought of attempting to negotiate with entities who could use any communication to corrupt your brain as easily as hacking a computer made me feel cold and sick. If the men looking for Malley were part of this group—appeasers, we called them—then we could be in the worst kind of trouble.

And there was no way I could call for help, without increasing whatever danger I was in.

The boat's engine had a bit more speed in it, for emergencies; I leaned forward, and pushed down hard on the stick. I reached the Union station a quarter of an hour earlier than I'd estimated. I deflated the boat, picked up another gas-cylinder for it, and packed it in another borrowed buggy. Then it was a matter of driving southward, picking my way carefully among up-heaved concrete slabs and fallen trees.

Traffic was slow on the North Circular.

# 3

## NEWS FROM NOWHERE

Gunnery's going ballistic. The alarms set bulkheads drumming, periodontal ligaments resonating: my whole jaw aches as I slam into my seat. I bounce back, then it grabs me and hugs me in. Suit goes rigid for a second (*I can't move!*), everything goes black for a second (*we'll get that bug out of the next release or somebody DIES!*), then the optical fibres cut in and the joints articulate and my fingers are tapping the armrest pads and I'm in charge.

'Shut that noise!'

My teeth and ears sing with relief. I'm looking straight ahead. The Gate is sixty-odd miles away, right in the sights, as always, and the number of invading ships or projectile comets or Lovecraftian unspeakables heading straight at us is, count 'em, *none*.

'If this is another bodging drill I'll—'

'THIS IS NOT A DRILL,' says the ship. Its voice drops as the magnification racks up; lenses zoom, cameras click. 'Look.'

It's tiny. The graticule reading shows, what? 24 *inches* across. In starboard Fire Control, somebody laughs. My first thought is *welcome back, Pioneer 10!* It is, indeed, like some early space probe: body like a spider's, brain like a gnat's; but (second thought) *not one of ours*. It matches none of the space-craft designs humans have ever built (I know them all, like the faces of old friends) and the apparently solid instrumentation of the thing is (*click, click*) suddenly, blatantly, nanotech stuff. Fractal depths of smart-matter come into focus as the zoom increases and the probe continues to drift towards us: surfaces flowing, crawling—

I hit the cut-out and the view dwindles to a speck. There wasn't enough definition to implement a Langford visual hack (*but you would think that, wouldn't you?*) and I set the micro-scale babbages skittering across print-out and they report back in seconds that it's clear. No nasty viruses have impacted our retinae, raced up our optic nerves and taken over our minds (*but they would say that, wouldn't they?*) and paranoia beckons—

Enough. Ignore your feelings. Trust the computers.

(And yes, I *know* the Langford hack is just a viral meme in its own right, replicating down the centuries like an old joke, wasting resources every time we act on the insignificant off chance that if someone could think of it, somehow it could be done. What kind of twisted mind *starts* these things?)

There are two dozen ships in the wing this watch, and since just before the alert (all of ninety seconds ago) every ship-to-ship radio has been shut down and physically unplugged: total radio silence is the ships' first reflex, even before they warn their crews. Decades of nothing coming through but the odd rock, decades of drills for every imaginable (and then some) contingency. Everybody in the Division has to do it, the stints come round regular as orbits, and every time it's drilled into you that if something does happen, you're on your own.

We're all right behind you. But when you're up against the superhuman, the orders run in reverse: the first is *sauve qui peut*, the second is 'havoc', the third is 'no quarter' . . . you get the picture. Our swords are permanently notched.

Thinking for myself is what I'm here for. At this moment the glorious possibility of First Contact is clamouring with the alarming thought that this thing originates with our long-departed—or ever-present—enemies. The little probe has closed its distance by ten miles, and seems to be decelerating: its puffs of reaction-mass volatiles another piece of evidence that it isn't some long-lost voyager.

'Hailing it,' I say, and key out a standard all-bands interrogative and a single radar sweep. To my surprise there's an immediate response. The babbages chatter for a second and then my suit's interpreters spell out the message:

'Cometary mining vessel NK slash eight-seven-one out of Ship City to unidentified, please respond, over.'

I don't take it in; my mind's still full of clutter about this craft's being (since it's obviously not the enemy coming back and telling us resistance is useless, etc.) a genuine alien space probe. To my lasting embarrassment, the only thing I can think of (but did I think?) is to hit the video transmission and say, my voice squeaky with astonishment:

'Speak *Angloslav*, robot?'

More computer chatter, then a human voice:

'English?'

'Yes, English,' I babble happily, still speaking falsetto, still hearing space opera, 'you pick it up from old transmissions, yes? Language has changed—'

At that point the video input starts up, the image grainy through anti-virus snow. It's the face of an old, old man. He's had the telomere hack, and some fairly primitive rejuvenation, but that's it. The significance of all the machine has said dawns on me. This is no alien emissary, but something almost as strange: the digital ghost of an escaped prisoner, one of the Outwarders' bondsmen who, two centuries ago, had fled their orbital work camp for whatever lay beyond the Gate.

'Much has changed,' I tell it.


Remembering my first encounter with what turned out to be the replicated minds of Wilde and Meg could still make my ears burn, as I found when the recollection came to me while I drove down a relatively clear stretch of the trail, just north of Ealing Forest.

I knew roughly who or what he was straight away. He had no idea who we were, and was surprised when we told him. I don't think he believed us. Partially overcoming our mutual suspicions took hours of talk, followed by almost direct physical contact before Wilde and Meg would accept that we were human. Even after we had taken the stored cells they'd brought with them (kept like a lucky charm through all their robotic adventures) and re-grown bodies for the pair of them, and transferred their minds to the new brains, I could never bring myself to think of them as human. Their tale of what had happened to them did nothing to reduce my unease.

Wilde told us that the human and ex-human labourers had hacked a path through a spun-off 'daughter wormhole' to a just-about-habitable world they called New Mars. The uploaded ones had turned themselves back into humans, and were 'now' (thousands of light years away, and thousands of years in the future) turning New Mars into a new Earth, in a rather cavalier terraforming process which exploited the local system's large complement of comets.

Society on New Mars was what Wilde called a free market anarchy. To us, it sounded more like a multiple mutual tyranny. The most powerful person in it was our oldest surviving enemy—a man called David Reid, the original owner of the forced-labour company. He had in his possession copies of the stored mind-states of the Outwarders, and was open to the argument that it would be safe to reboot them Real Soon Now.

Imagine our delight.

I brought the buggy to a halt beside a six-foot-high hawthorn hedge, a sort of natural barbed-wire entanglement, just a few paces before the gap in that hedge containing the gate of Ealing Technical College. I turned off the engine, and sat back for a moment, stretching and relaxing muscles that had tensed in the long and alert drive here, and looked around. The College was a mid-twenty-first-century building whose steel, concrete and glass had been built for blast. Its squat, three-storey bulk had survived the machinery of a more insidious destruction a lot better than the score or so of older buildings in the clearing that surrounded it. These had long since been reprocessed into low dwellings with all the usual accompaniments of non-co post-urban life, children and dogs and pigs and shit.

It was about four in the afternoon. The shadows of the forest's hundred-foot oaks and elms covered a good quarter of the clearing. A hundred yards away, on the edge of the forest, smoke rose from behind a small shed from which the ringing of repeatedly struck metal could be heard; a low-tech version of a forge, I guessed, wondering idly what it was called. The few adults about treated me with more than usual non-cooperation, pointedly ignoring my presence and sharply tugging away any children who didn't. I left the rucksack in the back—like a fierce dog, it could look after itself— but made sure my holstered pistol was obvious as I walked to the gate.

The gate, of stout creosoted wood, was on a latch, evidently designed to keep out any animal less intelligent than a dog. I closed it behind me and strolled up ten yards of flagstoned path to the main entrance. To left and right of the path were vegetable gardens, with plots marked out in stretched string and lettered labels. A young man, kneeling on an old sack and poking at the soil, looked up at me incuriously.

On the concrete slab above the double doors some original name had been chiselled off, and the new one carved in, with much embellishment of leaves, hammers, sickles, and glassware to mask this necessary vandalism. The windows on the ground floor were little more than slots; on the other floors they were a more normal size. Glancing up, I saw that several of them had been cracked, in a time so distant that some green algae or moss had settled there and spread along the zigzag flaws. Tough glass. The walls themselves, of course, were covered with ivy.

I pushed at the door, which swung open to admit me to a broad foyer with stone stairs ascending to left and right, and a wide U-shaped wooden barrier in the middle, behind which a young man sat, smoking a pipe and reading a book. No one else was about, though a murmur of voices and the sounds of machinery carried from other parts of the building. There was a strong smell of non-mineral oil, presumably used for lubrication rather than cookery. Lighting was provided by the doorway, the stairwells, and a very bright tube above where the man sat. ('I've never met a non-co yet,' Suze had told me, 'who was too proud to generate electricity, or too poor to steal it.')

As the door swung back behind me, the man glanced up, laid down his pipe casually and kept his hand where it was, behind the sill of the desk. He eyed me warily as I walked up. He had a thin face and narrow beard, and was wearing a homespun cotton shirt.

'Good afternoon, lady,' he said.

'Good afternoon, man,' I replied with equal formality. 'I wonder if I could speak to Dr Malley?'

He bristled. 'I'm afraid not,' he said. The muscles of his right arm tensed.

'If he's busy, I'll wait,' I said, glancing around as though looking for a seat.

'It ain't that,' he said. 'Waiting wouldn't do no good. Dr Malley says he don't want to see no more of you people.'

'Any more of what people?'

He looked away, looked back defiantly.

'Space people.'

Ah.

'Listen, young man,' I said. 'I've come a long way to see Dr Malley. Even longer than you think. And I'm not going to be stopped by you, or even by whatever laughable weapon you have your hand on. Using these things fast takes practice, and I have a couple hundred years' head start.'

Sheepishly, he withdrew his hand.

'And now,' I said politely, 'I'd thank you to take me to see him.'

I sauntered behind his sullen walk, all the way up two flights of stairs and along a dim-lit corridor to a room on whose brass nameplate showed (among more curlicued foliage, within which the roman capitals lurked like ruins) the name of Dr I. K. Malley.

'Knock and enter,' I said quietly, and he did. I followed him into a small of-fice with a wide window whose evidently thick and old plate glass distorted the outside view. Wooden shelving along the walls bowed under the weight of books and papers, which also partly covered the floor. The room smelled of old paper, worn carpet, pipe-smoke, whisky, and sweat. It had two chairs, one of them behind the desk, which was edge-on to the window. Hunched in it, looking up at us, was a man whose apparent age must have stabilized about thirty, but who had not touched an antigeriatric for at least a hundred years. His hair and stubbly beard were white, his skin dark and lined, his eyes grey, cold as a Martian winter.

'I thought I *told*—' he began. Then he looked at me and waved a hand with weary resignation. 'It's all right,' he said in a dull voice. 'It wouldn't do any good, anyway. They'll just keep coming.' There was a half-empty bot-tle of whisky on the desk, and a full glass.

The young man went reluctantly out, scowling in response to my farewell smile. Malley turned to me and motioned to the room's other seat, a worn leather armchair by the window. I told him my name and held out my hand. He looked slightly surprised, and stood up and shook it. His grip felt like an old leather glove fitted closely over a metal hand. He was tall, but stooped, and he wore an open-necked check cotton shirt and twill trousers. All his clothes seemed too wide for his girth and too short for his limbs. He folded himself back into his seat and leaned his elbows on the desk.

'So what do you bastards want now?' he said without preamble or apology. He took a sip of his drink, and hooded his eyes.

I shrugged and spread my hands. 'Dr Malley,' I said, 'I must tell you I have very little idea what you're talking about. I'm here on behalf of the Cassini Division of the Solar Defence Group, and I assure you that no one else has been sent to see you.'

Malley fiddled with the bowl of his pipe. His fingers were stubby, their tips ingrained with grey ash and yellow tar.

'Day before yesterday,' he said, 'a couple of chaps turned up out of the blue, and told me they were from space defence. Said they were checking out rumours that I was dabbling in AI work. Total bollocks, of course. I just teach the local farm boys basic electronics. Any bright sparks that turn up, I throw a bit of Feynman and Hawking at them.' His eyes flashed conspiratorially. 'And a bit of Malley. The few who make any sense of it invariably fuck off and join the Union, no matter what I say.' He unzipped a leather pouch and began filling the bowl, hands working automatically as he gazed sadly out of the window. 'You could say I've been lowering the average intelligence in these parts—a crime in my book, but not, I guess, in yours.'

He snorted a laugh. I smiled encouragingly; not that I quite understood what he was saying word for word, but I got his drift.

'So,' he went on, lighting up his mixture with an antique Zippo, 'it was a bit of a surprise to be leaned on by two of your heavies, leaving me with subtle warnings about dire consequences. The words "outbreak" and, I think, "red-hot smoking crater" happened to crop up in the conversation. Just like the good old days under the Yanks. No black suits with bulges at the shoulder, but otherwise, *plus ça change*.'

This, I have to say, gave me pause. There was no *law* against dabbling with artificial intelligence (or against anything else, for that matter). There was not even a Union rule against it. For anything not covered by Union rules (just about everything) we'd settled on the iron rule: 'Do What You Can Get Away With.' But touching off an outbreak—of artificial intelligence, disease, nano-assemblers, or any other kind of replicator—was something you couldn't get away with. Your neighbours would ostracize you, or boycott you, and if one of the essential amenities they chose not to supply turned out to be, e.g., your next breath, why then that was something that—when the matter reached the agenda of a neighbourhood moot—*they* would get away with.

And at worst, if an outbreak actually began to spread, the Inner System's own space defence forces would apply the orbital zap. I had never heard of them coming down and threatening people before the fact. It seemed rather illiberal.

'Excess of zeal,' I said, partly thinking aloud, partly bluffing. 'I'll have it looked into. But I assure you the Division has nothing to do with it. We have a rather different proposition to put to you.'

'Yes,' he sighed, 'I'm sure you do. Hard-cop, soft-cop, and all that.'

Could it be? The thought that someone else in the Division, or in the wider Solar Defence apparatus, might be playing games with my mission was so enraging that for a moment, fortunately, I was speechless. After a second or two I gathered my thoughts, and calmed down: I might be out of practice at conspiracy, but not at self-control. I shrugged.

'I know nothing of that,' I said.

'So what do you want me to do?'

'Dr Malley,' I said, smiling, 'do you know what the people on the other side of the wormhole, the people Wilde told us about, call it? They call it the Malley Mile.'

'I've seen the tapes,' Malley said dryly. 'Flattering, isn't it?'

I had hoped so. Time to lay on some more.

'We find ourselves,' I said carefully, 'in a position where we urgently need to understand the wormhole. And on our own, we can't. There's only one person who can help us, and that is you. Would you like to come with me to Jupiter, and do some real physics?'

Malley was taking a sip of whisky as I said this, and he snorted so hard it went up the back of his nose. He spluttered, coughed, then leaned back and laughed.

'So it's come to this! Thirty billion people in your utopia, and you have to come to me! You people really disappoint!'

I smiled. 'I know what you mean, Dr Malley. And I think what we want to do may change all that, in the long run. The Division is not the Union. That's all I want to say, for now.'

He rested his chin on a cat's-cradle of fingers and looked at me.

'Hmm,' he said. 'Interesting. That used to be called the Wolff gambit.'

I raised my eyebrows; he shrugged. 'Look it up.' (I never did.) 'Anyway,' he went on, 'you're too late.' He refilled his tumbler, and raised it to me in an ironic toast:

'Here's to the scientific genius of Isambard Kingdom Malley.' He knocked it back and slammed the tumbler down. 'And here's what has long since pissed it away. This, advancing age, and corrupting youth.'

'No!' I stood up. 'You're wrong! Those are symptoms. Your real problem is this: you worked out the most beautiful and successful physical theory a human being ever developed, and then superhuman beings went right ahead, used it, applied it, took it to the limits and *disproved it*! And you have never gotten over the suspicion that, to go beyond your theory, you'd have to go beyond your human limitations. And now, you can't even do that!'

'Precisely,' he said. He refilled the tumbler, again. 'Thanks to you people!'

'Us?' I said, stung by the injustice of this accusation.

'Yes, you—with your armlock on space development and on computer work, your endless cold war with the Jovians. The Cassini Division has a very cushy number out there, while the rest of the human population gets fobbed off with a sort of static comfort. Restricted without their noticing, rationed without knowing what they're missing. The rations are generous, I'll give you that, but basically what you so grandly call the Solar Union is the civilian hinterland of a war economy.'

This was beyond arguing about.

'Think what you like,' I said. 'But why not come and see for yourself?'

Malley took out a penknife, unfolded a yellowed steel spike and began poking about in the bowl of his pipe. I looked away. There was a scrape of flint and the now-familiar smell of burning dried weed refreshed itself in the room.

'It's tempting,' Malley acknowledged. 'To be honest, I'd love to see the gate—the Malley Mile, ha-ha!—up close. I'd be delighted to find a way through it to the world Wilde described, which sounds so much more interesting than this one.' (I almost jumped—I hadn't even raised the matter of navigating the wormhole, which was what we really wanted him to do.) 'But like I said, it's a waste of time. I can't handle the math any more. It's a young man's game, and the young man who was Malley is no more.'

He really was sounding dangerously close to maudlin. I sat down again, and leaned across the desk and looked earnestly into his somewhat bloodshot eyes.

'Age and alcoholism,' I said, 'are curable. As you well know. A couple of treatments and you'll feel better than you can remember, better than you can now even *imagine*. You'll have access to the biggest computers the Division has, the best instruments, decades of observations. All we want you to do is show us the way to New Mars. If you do that, you can do whatever else you can get away with, just like the rest of us.'

Malley leaned back, sucking on his pipe. I'd never noticed before the horrible bubbling sound the tar and spittle make in the things.

'It's a deal,' he said.

It took me a moment to work out that this meant he agreed.

'You mean, we have a plan?'

'Yes!' Malley chuckled. 'Indeed we do. We have a plan.'

My plan, at this point, was to retrace my route to Alexandra Port, and get the next airship connection to a flying-wing flight to Guiné, and the next laser-launcher to rendezvous with the *Terrible Beauty*, the fusion clipper on which I'd arrived, which was currently parked in low Earth orbit. On the way—a recent update—I intended to show or describe to Malley some of the features of Union society, from which he'd so carefully exiled himself these past one hundred years: the gigantic Babbage engines churning through their Leontiev material-balance matrices, the sea-farms, the miles-high skyscrapers, the miles-deep caves, the (almost deserted) great hall of the Central Planning Board with its golden statue of Mises . . .

Alas for plans.

'Isn't there anyone you want to say goodbye to?'

Malley was stuffing books, instruments and stashes of tobacco into an overnight bag with every indication of being ready to leave there and then. He gave me a wintry smile.

'What do you think?'

'You're not in a close relationship?'

'No doubt the village whore will miss me.'

I blushed and looked out the window; changed the subject.

'Why's this place built like a fortress, anyway?'

Malley coughed at dust stirred up by his rummaging.

'Police station. The windows do open, by the way. I understand this was so that prisoners could dive out of them.'

Not entirely sure what he meant (or, perhaps, not wanting to believe I understood) I fiddled with a lock and latch. The window swung open, and I leaned out to inhale a breath of uncontaminated air. After my first long sigh of relief I looked across at the nodding treetops, the lowering sun, and down—

In front of the college was a crowd of about fifty people, mostly adult, and all clutching some kind of weapon: rifles, shotguns, even—like peasants out of an old horror movie—pitchforks. Some were crowded around the gate, others formed a wide semicircle around the buggy, above which the ruck-sack part of my suit had transformed itself into a hornet-cloud of buzzing defence-motes.

I must have said something to draw Malley's attention. He stuck his head out the window beside me.

'Oh, shit!' he said.

'Is this the doing of that nice young man in reception?'

'Probably,' said Malley.

'Why?'

He turned to me and frowned. 'You really don't get it, do you? People live here because they *don't like* you guys! And they don't want you taking me away.'

'You can tell them you're going because you want to!'

He retracted his head. 'I can try.'

The people around the vehicle were backing off from the futile and painful task of attempting anything against the defence swarm. They moved through the crowd at the gate and, being apparently more adventurous spirits, began to lead them to the main door. Someone looked up and saw me. Yells rose and the move towards the door became a surge.

They'd be up the stairs in about a minute.

'Suit!' I screamed, tapping instructions on to my cuff. The swarm above the buggy circled once then made a beeline for me, and as I ducked back inside they crowded over me and reformed. The whole of my outfit flowed and reshaped into its basic spacesuit form. The suit went rigid, everything went black (two releases on, and that one-second bug was *still* not fixed) and then became clear and mobile again.

Malley stared open-mouthed as my clothes changed into seamless matt black close-fitting armour, with a faceless black ball for a helmet and massively over-muscled shoulders.

'Nanotech spacesuit,' I explained impatiently. 'Out on the window-sill, now!'

He hesitated, then heard the sound of running feet in the corridor. He grabbed his bag and clambered out, half-sitting under the swung-up window. I followed him on to the ledge and wrapped my arms around him. 'Hang on,' I told him unnecessarily.

'Rope,' I requested, and jumped. From the shoulders of the suit a couple of cables extended, one end grabbing the window-ledge by pure adhesion, the other lowering us rapidly to the ground. We landed gently. I looked around. The crowd's vanguard were looking down at us from the window as the cables snaked back into the suit, the crowd's stragglers were standing around between the gate and the doorway, looking at us with expressions that I still remember with somewhat malicious satisfaction.

Malley was tottering on his feet beside me, wheyfaced. He'd vomited over the suit; already it was thirstily absorbing the organics. I picked Malley up, like an actor in a Killer Robot outfit carrying off an actress in a Torn

And Revealing outfit, and bounded to the buggy. The crowd scattered around me. I set Malley down in the passenger seat and hopped into the driver's seat.

I had underestimated the crowd. They were not some panicked mob, but a peasant village, watching what they saw as the suborning or abduction of a well-liked and much-needed teacher. Those who'd gone up the stairs were streaming back down, and those who hadn't were closing around the buggy. Students, young men mostly, added to the numbers pouring out of the college doorway. They made no threatening approaches, giving it a good few yards' clearance, but they formed an increasingly solid mass around us. I looked out at a wall of people dressed in their colourful wools and cottons, their broad leather belts; at their competently held, though crude, weapons, their smooth and hostile faces.

Well, at least they should see my face. 'Scroll helmet,' I murmured, and the globe around my head opened at the top, the aperture widening, then narrowing, as the smart-matter flowed back into the temporary ring-seal resting on my collarbones. I turned to Malley before anyone could react and said:

'Could you please explain things to them?'

Malley shrugged. His hands were quivering. He wiped the back of one hand across his mouth and stood up, gripping the rim of the buggy's windshield.

'Hey, friends!' he called out. 'Listen to me! Thanks for your concern, but everything's all right. I'm going away for a short while with this woman from the . . . outside. I'm going of my own free will. So please don't worry! Let us through, please.'

The tallest and toughest-looking man in sight shouldered his way to the front and stood right in our way.

'I'm sorry, Dr Malley,' he said. 'But we ain't sure you *are* going of your own free will. Those space-folks, those *socialists*, they can do things to your brain so's you *think* you're doing what you want, but you're doing what *they* want, see?'

'Not *that* old lie,' I muttered under my breath. I should have guessed that the non-co dominant ideology could only be a full-blown paranoid delusional system.

'I'm sure they can,' Malley said. He'd recovered some of his poise. 'But I very much doubt that they can do it in half an hour.'

The tall guy looked nonplussed for all of two seconds.

'Well then,' he said with implacable logic, 'she must've threatened you. That they'd zap the village, or some'ing. It's all right, Dr Malley, you tell us! We ain't scared of them!'

'I assure you—' Malley began, but I knew it was of no use. Argument would get us nowhere. I couldn't credibly threaten Malley, and if it came to threatening the crowd my pistol (now inside my suit, and pressing painfully against my hip) was no match for their guns. Whether the suit could recreate the helmet in time to protect me from a shot was an experiment I didn't care to try.

'Scroll helmet up,' I whispered, and turned on the engine. In the moment of blackness I reached up and caught Malley's shoulder.

'Get right down!' I yelled, pulling hard. With the other hand I caught the wheel. I groped with my foot for the control pedal and pushed it down. The buggy leapt forward and as the view cleared I saw the man in front of us hurl himself out of the way at the last possible second. The others did likewise, scattering like skittles. And then we were through, careering down the village street in a flurry of chickens and a shower of stones. One or two shots were fired, but they whizzed overhead—I doubted that they were seriously aimed to hit. The only people between us and the end of the village were more interested in getting out of our way than in stopping us. But one of them, glimpsed as we hurtled past, was holding a rectangular chunk of plastic with a yard-long thin rod poking up from it. He held it with one end at his mouth and the other at his ear, and was speaking rapidly into it.

I had a nasty suspicion that this was a radio.


'I told you I taught them electronics,' Malley said a few minutes later, as we bounced along yet another forest track, heading in completely the wrong direction for any return to Alexandra Port.

'How irresponsible can you get!' I yelled. 'Radios can pick up viruses, you know that.'

'Yeah, and melt in your hand—so what!'

'What about *mind* viruses? Have you thought about that?'

'Of course I have,' Malley said, struggling to get the seatbelt on. 'They're just a fancy term for ideas you don't like.'

'Ideas *who* don't like?'

'You lot,' Malley said, waving his hand around his head. 'The Union. The Division. It's just censorship.'

I laughed so hard that the buggy swung dangerously as I steered around a log. 'Sure, like taking what you want is rationing!'

'Exactly my point,' Malley said, with unaccountable triumph.

I sighed. 'Dr Malley, I have great admiration for you and all you've accomplished, and I can even see you've been doing good to these people, but I respectfully suggest that you're a bit out of touch, or maybe misinformed—'

'Hah!'

'—and you'll see things differently once you get out to the Division.'

'No doubt,' Malley chuckled, wheezing. 'No doubt I will.'

The map—still patched to my eye—showed that we were nearing Gunnersmere, one of the first fens of the Thames Estuary. The village of Under Flyover was marked as a straggle of houses along the shore. Ahead, I could already see the trees thinning, oak and beech being replaced by alder and birch.

'What do you think they were using the radio for?' I asked.

Malley gave me an evil grin. 'Oh, warning ahead, probably.'

'Skies above, man!' I applied the brake gently and we slithered to a halt in a spray of leaf mould and beechnuts. Suddenly our surroundings seemed very quiet, apart from sinister cracklings under the trees, and deserted, apart from flitting shapes in the long shadows. 'You mean we're heading straight into an *ambush*?'

'*You* are,' Malley said calmly. 'I would have stopped you any minute now, but I was waiting to see how long it'd take before you realized you needed my local knowledge to get you out of this.'

I took a deep breath. 'OK, Dr Malley. I need your local knowledge. That, or a rescue chopper.'

'Maybe both. First things first. Let's get this buggy off the road, preferably somewhere not too obvious. There's a bit of exposed roadway a couple of hundred metres ahead, and some ruins alongside. Tracks shouldn't be too conspicuous, especially in poor light.'

I restarted the engine and let the vehicle roll forward quietly to the area Malley had indicated, where the chances of wind and weather had laid bare the cracked tarmac. I sought out a ruin whose approach wasn't itself covered with plants or plant remains, and found one with a battered concrete ramp leading to the gap where its doors had been. Within a minute or two we had the buggy stashed inside a rectangle of crumbled wall, within which nettles, willow-herb and hemp grew to a height of over six feet. I looked down at the former contents of the rucksack, scattered forlornly in the rear well of the buggy. I changed the suit into a rucksack and a dappled black-and-green jumpsuit, then repacked, with the weighty addition of the deflated boat, its electric outboard engine and fuel cell, and the spare gas cylinder.

'That's one possible way out,' Malley acknowledged.

'Now what?' I asked.

'Do you have any way of contacting the nearest Union outpost?'

Outpost, indeed. 'Not directly,' I said. 'I could contact them via my ship. It'll be above the horizon in about—' I blinked up the watch floating in my left eye, and checked '—fifteen minutes. But I'd really rather not do that, or send out some general distress—'

At that moment I heard a rhythmic thudding along the trail in the direction from which we'd come.

'What's that?'

'Galloping horse,' Malley said. 'Get down!'

We ducked behind the wall. I drew my pistol, wishing as I did so that I'd known of the properties of nettles before changing my suit: my hands were coming up in a nasty rash. The thudding sound got closer, then slowed and changed to a clatter as the horse encountered the stretch of paving. As it drew level I peered out through the stems of weeds.

A young woman was sitting on the back of the strange, huge beast, holding on and controlling it by an arrangement of leather straps and metal footrests. She was riding quite slowly now, looking from side to side. Her clothes were filthy, as were the sides of the horse, and a trickle of blood was drying below a bruise on her temple. As she turned to the right, almost facing me, I recognized her.

'Suze!' I called, standing up.

She jumped and the horse shied and whinnied, then she tugged on the straps she held and said something, and the beast settled. Malley, with a grunt and a glower, straightened up and followed more slowly as I skipped over the tumbled brickwork and down to the path.

'Are you all right, Ellen?' She looked past me at Malley, and her eyes widened. 'Is that—?'

'The great man himself, yes,' I said. 'But Suze, what about you? What happened?' Not that it was hard to guess.

'I followed you,' she said. 'I know you didn't want me to come, but—'

'It was a kind thought,' I said.

'Well.' She smiled down at us, uncertainly. 'I took a barge up the canal and borrowed Bonnie here.' She patted the horse's neck. 'I've ridden her before, and she's much better on the forest paths than a buggy, you know. When I rode into the village back there the locals saw I was Union, and some sort of riot started, all yelling and running. They pelted me with stones and, uh, shit. I didn't know what was going on, so I just put my head down and dug in my heels. And here I am.'

Here you are. Another innocent to look after.

'Anybody follow you?'

She shook her head. 'What about you?' she asked.

I introduced her to Malley and outlined our plight.

'Oh!' she said, peering anxiously around. 'You mean there might be people out looking for us right now?'

'Yes,' I said. 'Over to you, Dr Malley.'

'Call me Sam,' he said, possibly irritated by Suze's star-struck glances at him. 'Everybody does. Short for Isambard. Right. Suze, can you put a call through to Alexandra Port, arrange a chopper pick-up?'

'Yes, of course, Doc—Sam.'

'OK.' He closed his eyes and pinched his forehead with thumb and fore-finger, looking as tired as I felt. 'You do that, ask them to be ready for take off in about an hour. We make our way through the trees to the east of the path, around the back of the village, hide out by the shore, and then no doubt Ellen here will be able to give them our exact coordinates from her magic suit's gee-pals link, right?'

I nodded.

'Okay,' said Malley. 'Suze, you're going to have to say goodbye to the horse, I'm afraid, but I assure you the locals won't maltreat her.'

Suze removed the horse's harness and sent her cantering away southward with an affectionate slap on the rump. Then she unclipped a narrow-band transmitter from her belt, tuned it to the nearest communications satellite relay, and called up Alexandra Port. She frowned and shook her head.

'Message got through, but there's no acknowledgement.'

Malley shrugged. 'Try again when we get there.'

He turned, and Suze and I followed him under the trees to the east of the path. The way through the trees, bearing generally rightward, was much harder than one might expect. They were old woods, so the canopy was high and thick enough to choke off most undergrowth. However, the ruins un-derneath the deceptive layers of leaf mould more than made up for this lack. We banged our shins on hidden blocks, plunged knee-deep into hidden pits. What appeared to be a dead branch could turn out to be a disconcertingly solid and sharp prong of rusted metal. Malley persisted in staying in the denser part of the wood, and walked its treacherous footing with confi-dence, carrying his overnight bag like somebody heading for a transport terminal. We concentrated on avoiding injury and struggled silently—or at least inarticulately—along behind him.

After about half an hour of this Malley began to bear a little further right and we shortly emerged in a more open area of long grass dotted with bushes and low trees. The water was about a hundred yards away and at this point was almost two miles across. A mile to our left was Under Flyover with its surrounding fields and gardens. Only a few pillars remained of the structure which had given it its name.

Spread out across the fields was a line of people with dogs, working their way systematically towards where we were and communicating with other people, no doubt out of sight in the forest, with their hand-held radios. We crouched down and Suze tried again to raise Alexandra Port.

'Nothing,' she said. 'I don't understand this. It's like they're deliberately ignoring us!'

'Could this be policy?' I asked her. 'Is it something to do with the ruckus we—I—caused back in that village? Like, if you stir up the non-cos, you're on your own?'

She shook her head fiercely. 'No way. You'd have some explaining to do, but we always pull our own people out. Hey, we even help non-cos if they ask for it.'

Malley grunted. 'Huh, usually those who least deserve it—village hooligans or thieves.'

Suze was agreeing with him and the searchers were getting closer.

'Enough,' I said. 'Here's what we're going to do.'


What we did was run hell-for-leather down to the shore. I tore through the long grass, not bothering to hide or dodge, slid down banks, felt my feet grit on gravel, and pulled the inflation cord of the boat. Putting the gas cylinder and the motor in place was the only preparation we'd made.

The dinghy *whoomphed* into shape in about five seconds, even as I was throwing it forward onto the water. Suze came panting, Malley puffing, behind me and we all splashed through the shallows and pushed the boat out until the water was knee-deep, then clambered in. It all took less than a minute, which was more than enough time for yells and yaps to break out. By the time the first of our pursuers had reached the water's edge I had the engine started and we were about ten yards out. A couple of men waded in after us and a dog plunged in and bravely paddled in our wake.

I looked back. They were gaining on us, but as the water got deeper the advantage changed. By the time the water became too deep to wade, we were beyond their reach. Somebody whistled, and the dog too turned back. By now six people had gathered on the bank, and as we turned and headed downriver I noticed that one of them was speaking into a radio.

'What do you think he's up to?' I asked Malley. For answer, Malley pointed back along the shore, to Under Flyover's long wooden jetty. Four men were just visible, running along the quay. They scrambled down a ladder and into a boat. With the four of them working two pairs of oars, it pulled away from the quay and gave us chase.

'They haven't a chance,' Malley said, just before two of the men shipped their oars and raised a mast, then a sail.

'Looks like they do,' said Suze.

With the sail up their rate of closing on us increased visibly, though I figured it would take them at least half an hour. I steered a course away from the shore, hoping to pick up the main current and gain some much-needed speed.

'What *is* this?' I demanded of Malley. 'This is crazy. They must know you want to come along with us, you could have got away easily back there if you didn't. They can't all believe that story about me brainwashing you, or whatever. So why are they still chasing us?'

He shrugged. 'I don't know. I'm more surprised that your lot haven't responded to our call.'

Not quite my lot, but he was right. It was most disconcerting. I looked around. The sunlight was by now at a quite acute angle, and the scene—the sheet of water over which we moved, the wooded banks curving to the left ahead of us—would in other circumstances have been idyllic. Waterfowl swam or skimmed the widened river, and its surface was otherwise marred by only a few small craft . . .

'What about those other boats?' I asked Suze. 'Surely some of them are Union visitors?'

'Yes, but it's hard to say which—ah!'

She pointed downriver to a tiny vee of white spray. 'We're saved! That's a Union patrol boat!' Carried away by excitement, she began waving her arms and shouting, although the boat—a hydrofoil, I now saw—was still a couple of miles off. She desisted after a moment and stripped off her shirt and began waving that.

'What does a patrol boat have to do?' I asked.

'River rescue, mostly,' said Malley.

'And maintaining a presence, as they say,' Suze remarked, flapping her shirt and all but standing up.

'Do they ever interfere with non-cos?'

Malley scowled and shook his head. 'Maybe they should—the Thames boatmen are inclined to take what the traffic will bear. Daylight robbery.'

I didn't understand this, but Suze gave it an appreciative laugh.

The hydrofoil's course shifted a fraction. 'They've seen us,' I said. I looked over my shoulder. The men in the boat were working the sail again, tacking off in a different direction. Within a few minutes the hydrofoil—a thirty-foot launch, painted white, its ensign the Union's starry plough—had cut back its engine and dropped into the water, and circled behind us and hove to alongside. The woman at the wheel waved to us and called out: 'Hi! You having trouble with those people?'

'Yes!' I yelled. 'Thanks for coming to help.'

'That's fine,' she said. 'Where are you going?'

I thought for a moment. 'Alexandra Port—but the mouth of the Lee would be fine, if you want to give us a lift.'

'Sure. No problem. Come aboard.' She threw us a rope, and we pulled the wallowing dinghy in to a small ladder at the side of her boat. First Malley, then Suze, then I climbed in, and I used a boathook to haul the dinghy up after me. The woman, who introduced herself as Carla, had long blonde hair and a suntanned face and a smile that showed crooked teeth. Her yellow jumpsuit had a small patch with her name and 'River Patrol' stitched on it.

'Did you pick up a call?' Suze asked. 'We tried to hail Alexandra Port.'

Carla shook her head. She motioned us into, the cabin in front of the cockpit, and re-started the engine. 'Make yourselves comfortable,' she yelled. 'Tell me about what happened when I've got this thing on course.'

The boat picked up speed, the foils dug into the water and we lifted off. Malley lit his pipe, Suze settled to gazing out of the window, and I stood beside Carla and told her a conveniently edited version of what had gone on. She was as baffled by the non-response as we were. We crossed Gunnersmere, Hammersea, Southwater and had just reached the City Basin when Carla remarked: 'There's a lot of non-co boats on the river this evening . . .'

I had noticed the boats, but not having any basis for comparison hadn't known it was unusual. Rowing boats, sailboats, skiffs, steam-launches, smoke-trailing woodburners, and barges were visible all across the pool, their courses at first uncoordinated, and then—as I looked again and again—obviously converging. On us.

Carla noticed it a few seconds after I did. She frowned and tried her communications equipment. The microwave laser pinged off whatever satellite it was tuned to, but no response came back. The boats were still at a distance—a few hundred yards all around—but were slowly surrounding us. Suze and Malley came out of the cabin and we watched in silent puzzlement and growing dismay.

'This is too much,' I said. 'No more miss nice girl. Carla, please take *fast* evasive action before they block us off completely.'

She grinned and gave me the thumbs-up and pulled out the throttle. The boat shot forward, then began a curving course towards the City towers, which gleamed gold and bronze in the low sun, like drunken, armoured Goliaths wading out to meet some aquatic David. Between them and us were a couple of non-co craft: a four-man rowing boat, perhaps similar to the one that had first followed us, which skittered across the water like a surface-tension bug; and a much slower, heavier wood-fired puffer that chugged with shocking determination across our bows. Carla touched the wheel, once to left, once to right. The rowing boat was swamped, and I glimpsed white faces from the steam boat's decks as we hurtled past its stern with yards to spare. Then we were in among the leaning, looming towers, our reflection speeding and flashing in their glassy flanks.

I stepped carefully to the rear deck and squatted down and flowed the suit into its dish aerial form, and sent an urgent call to the *Terrible Beauty*.

The others were clinging to any available handhold, and looking at me in bemusement as I stood up with the reconstituted clothes climbing back over my skin.

'Twenty minutes,' I said. Our wake set waves crossing and recrossing the geometric spaces of the boxed canyons. The non-cos' vessels prowled about the flooded buildings but kept well back.

'Until what happens?' Carla asked.

I grinned, suddenly cocksure again, already back in my own world, already far above this one, with its conspiracies of non-cooperators, its unresponsive rescue services, its general principle of leaving far too much to a natural world and a prehistoric humanity that pounced on any moment of weakness.

'Watch the sky,' I told them. '*Terrible Beauty*'s coming down.'

It was Malley who spotted it first, a new and brighter evening star low in the glare of the sunset. Although it was coming down, it seemed to climb, as it moved away from the horizon and towards us. Twice it seemed to flare, and broader secondary flashes drifted away. Then, closer, it really did flare, with a thunder that tumbled down to us through miles of air, and that was as suddenly replaced by the screaming whistle of the aerobraking flues. Plumes of superheated air founted from its surface, then the third and final parachute was deployed, a half-mile-wide canopy of monolayer carbon filament on which the huge ship floated like the seed beneath a thistledown.

'Head for mid-channel,' I told Carla. She complied, barely able to take her gaze away from the descending ship. The harrassing boats fled from its encroaching shadow in a widening circle of accelerating haste. We nosed out from among the towers and set a course to meet it, as if in perverse defiance of the surrounding panic.

'Oh, oh!' cried Suze. 'It's beautiful—terrible beauty all right!'

Its surfaces glowing like a lantern, curved like a shell, intricate like a vase; its shape like the paradoxical egg of an alien, avian species that lived in higher dimensions; its sound like a choir of angry angels or a host of adoring devils, the *Terrible Beauty* released its drogue, which flitted out of sight above the towers and trees, and no doubt made more than one fortune for whoever found it; fired its attitude jets and its final retro-flare, sending roiling clouds of steam across the water towards us, and settled at last on the riverbed of the pool of London.

'That,' said Malley, 'is the most *shocking* waste of delta-vee I have *ever* seen.'

Carla looked at me sidelong. I nodded: 'Full ahead.' The hydrofoil surged across the few hundred yards that separated us from the improbable object on the river. As we drew closer the water hissed and bubbled, and the foils failed to support our craft. Carla moved a control lever and the hull sank back; skilfully she adjusted our speed until we came almost to a halt beneath the spaceship's curving overhang. Around us, the silvery bellies of killed or stunned fishes flashed in the churning water. Some of them had undoubtedly been cooked alive; I found myself hoping that the intake valves—already open and gulping in water, thirsty to replace the squandered reaction-mass—would filter some of them off to the commissary. It was probable: like many of the Division's mechanisms, the ship had a sensitive nose—and a ravenous appetite—for usable organics.

About fifty feet above us, at the *Terrible Beauty*'s widest diameter, a hatch unlidded and a face peered down at us: Tony Girard, currently the security officer on the ship.

'Hi, Ellen!' he shouted. 'Sending a ladder down.'

I caught the plastic ladder as it reached the boat, and turned to Malley. 'After you.'

Malley grinned at me, all cynicism gone from his face. He looked like a small boy about to go on a carnival ride. He picked up his bag, looped its longest strap across the back of his neck and under his armpits, and set off up the ladder.

'Carla,' I said, 'we'll obviously wait till you're well clear before we lift, but will you be all right?'

She made a performance of shading her eyes and looking around the now almost deserted stretch of river. 'I'll be fine,' she said. 'There's a Union station at the mouth of the Lee. I'll find out there why nobody answered your call—or mine, and why there weren't any other patrol boats around to help.' Her expression darkened. '*Somebody's* gonna have some hard questions to answer.'

'Contact us when they do,' I said, scribbling a note of our call sign and passing it to her, along with the money I'd taken from Graciosa. 'And thanks for everything. Anybody gives you trouble, you just give us a call.' I jerked my thumb at the ship, and she smiled—grateful for the moral support, but probably not taking my promise seriously. This is a mistake people make about the Division, but each person only makes it once. I smiled, half to myself, and grasped Suze's shoulder.

'You were great,' I said. 'You helped me a lot, and it was real neighbourly of you to come after us.'

'Even if it wasn't necessary!' Suze laughed. 'Forget goodbyes, Ellen. I'm coming with you.' She put her hand on one of the steps of the ladder.

'What? You can't—'

'I can,' she said confidently. 'Anybody in the Union can join the Division if there's a ship available to take them, and—' she patted the hull '—here it is.'

She was right. It was a rule, but in practice it was only applied by experienced spacers from the Inner System defences joining the Division as a natural progression, and by members of various administrative committees coming out to exercise what they supposed was democratic oversight. We had long experience in dissuading starry-eyed youngsters from Earth, but ultimately we could only dissuade, and—if the new volunteer turned out to be useless—gently disillusion them with some really boring tasks.

'But Suze!' I expostulated. 'You've got a job to do here. Something's up among the non-cos—all this radio communication, nobody knew *that* was going on. You'd do better to use what you know to help the Union find out—'

She held up her free hand. 'No,' she said. 'I'm useless for that now. The non-cos saw me with you, and we've seen how fast word can spread. They won't trust me any more, and they'd be right! And if you're really going to— where you said—I wouldn't miss that chance for anything. I'm coming.'

And with that she turned away and climbed swiftly up the ladder. I watched her almost halfway, then looked at Carla. She had an ironic smirk, as if to say, *you'll have trouble with that one*. The only response I could think of was to shrug and spread my hands.

'That's life,' I said, shaking my head, and then followed my new comrade up the ladder and into the ship.

# 4

## THE STATE OF THE ART

The sound of that hatch sealing behind me was the most welcome I'd heard for some time. Tony Girard caught me by the forearms, and then let himself be swept into a hug.

'It's great to be back!' I said when I'd let go of him and he'd stood aside, red-faced, as we stepped out of the airlock. The inner hatch closed behind us and we heard a brief, muffled surge as the airlock filled with water. The deck thrummed under my feet, the curving walls of the narrow corridor enclosed me, the familiar shipboard smells of metal and plastic and blue-green, of endlessly recycled air and water and organics, filled my grateful nostrils. 'That was a brilliant landing, I must say.'

'Great to have you back,' Tony said. 'Especially with such success.'

I turned the sides of my mouth downward. 'Wilde would've been better. He *knows* the way—'

'And who's to say it still works? We'll get more out of Malley in the long run. You did fine.'

'Hope you're right. Have to dry him out and give his brain a reboot first.'

Tony laughed. 'Two tabs from the medical bay. I've pulled worse cases out of brawls in Aldringrad.' He motioned me to precede him along the radial corridor. 'Who's the little sweetie?'

'Calls herself Suze,' I told him. 'Don't know her other names. She's just volunteered. I met her by chance, and she's been helpful. She's a sociologist—'

'A what?' I glanced back at him. He rolled his eyes up, then down. 'Oh, right, I see.' He blinked hard, shutting off his suit's encyclopaedia.

'Check her out,' I advised. 'She's nice, but—' I spread my fingers and waggled my hand where he could see it over my shoulder.

'Gotcha,' he said. 'You had some trouble with the locals?'

'Minor trouble,' I said. 'No tissue damage to anyone—but something serious is going on. Malley was leaned on by a couple of guys who claimed to be from the Inner System's space defence, and the descriptions of them check out, low-gee reflexes and all that. Hinted that he was a potential source of an outbreak. He denies it, but what he's actually been doing is teaching electronics to the non-cos—no harm in that, but the grubby sods are using radios.'

'Mind viruses could have been the worry.'

'Possible,' I said. 'Or maybe the appeasers have picked up some hint of what we're up to. The local Union rep is looking into it, she'll be in touch.'

'I'll keep an ear out,' Tony said. We'd reached the internal doorway to the mid deck. 'Oh, and Ellen . . .'

'Yes?' I paused, my hand on the plate, and looked back at him. He eyed me up and down and mimed disapproval. 'You can't face the rest of the crew dressed like *that*.'

'Oh.' I looked down at my torn jumpsuit, stained webbing, scratched boots; thumbed the straps of my backpack. 'I suppose not.'

I put down the bits of hardware I'd accumulated and hesitated before transforming the suit. In the natural human environment of free fall or low-gee most of us went for some permutation of closely fitting and lightly floating; but we weren't going to enjoy that comfortable condition for some time, and I'd need some padding. I selected the appropriate parameters, and let the suit come up with something to match them. I found myself in a bulky, quilted one-piece with the arms and legs sealed at the wide cuffs to skintight gloves and socks. It had a thrown-back anorak hood which could quickly convert to a helmet in an emergency. Deep pockets were on the front of each thigh. The whole thing was presumably modelled on its race memory of a Project Apollo spacesuit, except that it was rendered in pale pink satin quilting, and embellished with a deep pink satin sash and lot of lace, ribbons and bows, all pink.

The suit has its little moods, sometimes.

'Oh, very dignified,' Tony said. 'You look like somebody's great, great grandmother in a bed jacket.'

So that was what was on its mind. There were several layers of clothing underneath; from the feel of them, the suit had elaborated further on the maternal-boudoir theme. Perhaps it had registered that I was pregnant, even though I hadn't asked it to check. It was quite touching, in a way.

'I *am* somebody's great, great grandmother,' I reminded Tony, as I gath-

ered up the pistol, ammo, and clasp knife. He looked at the last with cov-
etous interest.

'A Swiss Army knife!' he said. 'Can I have that?'

'No,' I said, pocketing it. 'You can have the gun, though. I think our new
recruits will expect it of the security officer.'

'Yeah,' he said as I pushed the plate and the door slid open. 'I just don't
think they'll expect that suit of the skipper.'

The mid deck is the control area on a fusion clipper. Circular, fifty feet
across and fifteen feet high, it's shielded from the engine by the main water
tanks, and from external radiation by shells of water between the outer and
inner hull. It looks and feels like a greenhouse, warm and slightly humid,
with illumination provided by water-filtered sunlight and electric lamps;
the instrumentation and cabling intertwined with the hydroponics and the
inevitable coiled tubes of transparent plastic through which the algae circu-
late. In a sunstorm the whole company—usually up to sixty, counting crew
and passengers—can crowd into it, but most of the time it's occupied only by
the active crew. On this trip there were no passengers, so we were all there.

My wonderful team, my gang. Tony Girard beside me, my security expert,
whose conspiratorial skills went back to the old faction fights in Lagrange.
Jaime Andrades, the navigator, who joked that his talents came from his
Portuguese ancestry, but who was a pure-black survivor of the famously
disastrous Angolan moon colony. Boris Grobovski, the gunner, who'd spent
his first century of adulthood with the Sino-Soviet mobile artillery, in their
slow but inexorable advance from Vladivostok to Lisbon, spreading democracy from sea to shining sea. Andrea Gromova, the pilot, who had started out,
before the Fall, boosting antique Energias crammed with bonded labourers
from the privatized gulags to the asteroid mining camps, then gone over to
the revolution in the battle of New South Yorkshire. Lu Yeng, the computer
specialist; at seventy, she was the youngest, born on Callisto. Her parents had
come there in the initial negotiations between the Union and the Division.
The intensity of her experience with neutralizing Outwarder viruses more
than made up for her relative youth, although in political terms she was a bit
naive, retaining an odd reverence for Kim Nok-Yung, Shin Se-Ha and other
finders of the true knowledge.

None of the crew so much as raised an eyebrow at my suit when Tony
and I strode out on to the mid deck. Eccentricity is policy. Suze and Malley
were sitting together on the edge of an acceleration couch, and they had
some difficulty not laughing out loud. I gave them a withering glance, and
grinned and waved at the other crew members, who were spread out around
the circle of a dozen or so acceleration couches.

'Thanks, everybody,' I said. 'That was an excellent landing. Congratulations to Jaime and Andrea.' The navigator and pilot waved back. I walked straight over to the nearest acceleration couch and lay down. Tony settled in another couch, hauled down a boom-borne instrument resembling a television screen with handlebars, and began scanning.

'Tony,' I asked after a minute, 'are there any people within a mile of us?'

He kept twisting the bars for a few seconds.

'Nah,' he said. 'None on the water, for sure, and any who're too deep in the trees for me to pick up should be safe enough.'

'Sound the alarm anyway,' I said.

The internal alarms on a fighter-bomber are cacophonous. The external alarms on a fusion-clipper about to lift from a planet are calculated to wake the dead and send them running anywhere out of its range. We only heard it faintly ourselves, but it still set our teeth on edge. I let it sound for ten minutes while we went through the final checklist: everybody strapped in, water-intake valves closed, fusion lasers powered up, flight path clear . . .

'OK, comrades,' I said, 'let's lift.'

Andrea eased out the fusion regulator, and the ship rose, slowly at first, shuddering from nose to tail.

'Fifty feet,' Andrea intoned. 'One hundred, hundred and fifty, two hundred . . .'

'At two thousand feet, go for the burn,' I said.

'Eat proton death, Canary Wharf!' said Suze.

'Hey, come on,' I said. 'A few broken windows.'

Ten seconds later Andrea pulled out the regulator all the way, and a succession of invisible people started an unkind experiment to find out how many could lie on top of me. By the time we reached orbit, they'd piled up seven deep.

The drive shut off, and they all went away. I unbuckled and let myself drift for a moment, enjoying the sensation while it lasted. 'Everybody all right?' I called out. Everybody was.

'Okay,' I said, 'don't get too happy in free fall. We're going to pick up some ice, and then we're boosting all the way at one gee.'

'Thank god for that,' said Malley, who was clinging to his couch as if he were afraid of falling off. Suze had the silent, pale look of someone who is determined not to think about being sick. Several crew members made mutinous moaning noises.

'Shut up, you lot,' I said. 'I've been in one gee for three days, while you've all been loafing about in orbit. You can live with it for another ten days.'

'But we've *already* lived with it for ten days,' grumbled Andrea. 'On the way in.'

Malley rolled on his couch and looked over at me. 'So you'll have been in one gee for all of twenty-three days? I wonder how the human frame can stand it.'

'It can't,' I said, launching myself over to float above him. 'Hence many of the ills that flesh is heir to. Which reminds me.'

I grabbed a boom and pushed myself over to the medical bay and clicked out three surgeries.

'Just swallow these,' I told him on my return. He clutched the colour-coded capsules and looked at them suspiciously.

'What'll they do?'

'One's to stop your addictions—you'll still enjoy a drink or a smoke, but you won't need them—one to rejuvenate you—circulation, muscle tone, skin and so on—and one to burnish up your synapses.' I grinned at his suspicious look. 'Just the hardware—the software's still down to you. No commie brain-washing involved, honest.'

'I guess I have to trust you sometimes,' he said wryly, and placed the sur-geries in his mouth and swallowed hard. 'All I feel right now is I could do with a drink.'

'Better wait until we're under acceleration,' I said. 'Squirting from bulbs ain't much fun.'

Suze observed this with dull interest.

'I don't suppose,' she asked plaintively, 'you have anything for space sick-ness?'

'I'm afraid not,' I said. 'You just have to get used to it.' I refrained from adding the bit about the first six months being the worst.

Suze fixed her gaze on something above her and nodded, her lips set in a thin line. I felt sorry for her, but at the same time a little amused that she'd come up with the same request as every other newbie we'd ever lifted. A cure for motion sickness, indeed! What did they expect from medical nanotechnology—miracles?


'What's with the imperial units?' Malley asked, as we watched and listened to Andrea guiding us in to dock with the ice tanker.

'You'll hear arguments about human scale and intuition and convenience and so forth,' I explained, 'but the older and coarser characters in space will sum it up in two words: fucking NASA. Most of the space settlements were built with ex-NASA stock or to NASA spec way back in the early days, and ever since then it's been too much trouble to change. We're locked into it.'

'Yeah,' said Andrea. 'Which is why we are now two point five seven miles from a hundred thousand metric tons of ice. You've just gotta love the con-sistency of it all.'

'Mind you,' Malley chuckled, his teeth clenched on an unlit pipe, 'I suppose I should be grateful. The Malley One Point Five Eight Kilometres just
wouldn't have the same ring to it.'

Even Suze managed a laugh, though she was still looking a bit green.
The thought of the mess she could at any moment make impelled me to
seek out a couple of suits. I hauled them over and thrust one each to Malley
and Suze.

'What do I do with this?' Suze asked, drifting away with her arms wrapped
around a twenty-pound, eighteen-inch ball of rubbery glop.

'Just let it get to know you,' I told her. It was already flowing around her
waist and across her midriff. 'It'll take the form of a set of basic fatigues and
backpack in the first instance, and it'll show you how to vary that if you
want. It can mimic almost any texture and external appearance you specify.'
I waved a satin-gloved hand, pink lace flurrying around my forearm. 'If you
don't specify the details, expect surprises! But no matter how frivolous it
may look, it reacts to vacuum before you can blink. If you go outside, or if
we have, uh, a *sudden loss of cabin pressure*, it snaps into a spacesuit. Grab an
oxy bottle if you can, but if necessary it can work on a closed-loop basis indefinitely.'

'What about the clothes we've got on?' Malley asked.

'They will be assimilated,' I assured him. 'The suit can reprocess just
about anything.'

Suze looked around, rather wildly, as the smart-matter crawled up her
arms.

'What about going to the toilet?' she said.

'There's a place called the head, over there—oh, you mean if you're outside in the suit?'

'Yes.'

'Like I said,' I reiterated patiently, 'the suit can reprocess just about anything.'

At this point she gave the suit an opportunity to demonstrate this ability
and several others, including that of catching projectile droplets. I left them
to it.


An hour later we had replaced the reaction-mass and fuel used up in the
*Terrible Beauty*'s unscheduled planetary surface excursion, and were accelerating at a steady one gravity in a more-or-less straight line across the plane
of the ecliptic to Jupiter—or rather, to where Jupiter would be in ten days'
time. After five days, we'd turn off the engine, swing the ship around, and
decelerate at one gravity the rest of the way. This, as anyone will tell you, is
not the most fuel-efficient way to get around. Most of the transport in the

Solar System hardly used any fuel at all, and was pretty fast even so; with a big enough light sail you can get from Earth orbit to Mars orbit in weeks, Jupiter in months. We had no compunction about using fusion-clippers, on the minority of journeys for which we didn't have weeks or months to play with.

(As it happens, fuel efficiency, or even reaction-mass, wasn't the limiting factor. With the laser-fusion drive and the practically inexhaustible amounts of ice available, we could have used clippers for everything. The limiting factor was the availability of ships.)

The return to weight made Malley and Suze a lot more cheerful, and the rest of us a little less. We made our way down the stairwell from the command deck to the commissary. It was a slightly smaller room, also circular, with several small tables and one big round table, more than adequate for all of us. In the centre of that table was the serving lift, and at each setting was a menu mat. I sat down with Malley on one side and Suze on the other.

'You can dial up quite a wide range of foods and drinks,' I explained, 'but for obvious reasons anything made with boiling water is a speciality of the house.' I scrolled the menu. 'May I recommend the Thames salmon, freshly caught?'

Most of us made the same choice, tapping the appropriate lines on the menu, and the steaming, almond-flaked dishes rose from the centre of the table and were passed eagerly around. Now that it had the template, the kitchen could carbon-copy 'freshly caught' Thames salmon till the drive went out, but the real thing did have a thrill. It's subjective, but as Malley (slightly drunk on Tranquilitatis 2296, and high on the first buzz from the swallowed surgeries) tried to tell us, value was all subjective anyway. He seemed to think he was making a point, and we politely deferred to this misconception.

We finished eating and shoved the plates back into the middle. The lift silently sank away with them. Malley fished in his pocket (his suit had based its initial form on what he'd been wearing, and had a quaint tweedy appearance) and pulled out his pipe and tobacco.

'Is it OK to smoke on the ship?' he asked.

'Sure,' I said. 'We're sitting sixty feet above a fusion torch, man. Fire is the least of our worries.' I hoped he'd give it a rest when the addiction passed, though. Various comrades unthinkingly wrinkled their noses, until someone tapped a command on their mat to increase the ventilation.

By the time we reached the coffee I had introduced everybody: Andrea, Jaime, Boris, Tony and Yeng. Suze looked at me when I'd finished and said: 'But Ellen—who are you?'

We all laughed. 'Ellen May Ngwethu,' I said. 'I was born in 2041, in a Lagrange space settlement, so I'm almost as old as Malley—I mean, Sam! Fought in the initial split between the Earth Tendency and the Outwarders, and on Earth during the dark century. I worked on Earth Defence for a long time, then moved out to Jupiter. I've been in the Cassini Division for the past, let me see, seventy-odd years, and right now I'm on the Division's Command Committee, and I'm the liaison on the Jovian Anomaly Research Committee. That's a non-military, scientific body which is responsible to the Solar Council and has the next-to-final say in what the Division gets up to. The Solar Council has the final say.' I smiled around the table. 'In theory. In practice, the Division does what it pleases.'

Suze looked slightly shocked, Malley smug.

'I know the theory,' Malley said. 'In theory, everyone does what they damn well please. "The free development of each is the condition of the war of all against all", or some such nonsense.'

Yeng frowned at this comment; Malley turned up his hands. 'Screw the politics—I gather from what you've just said, Ellen May Ngwethu, that you are what in a more openly hierarchical arrangement would be called a member of the General Staff. A top military officer and politician. So—what the fuck are you doing getting your hands dirty, rolling about in the mud on the kulak reservation, all just to lift an old physicist?'

'Good question,' I said. Malley looked me in the eye and began fiddling with his pipe; I wished I had something equally distracting with which to occupy my hands. 'One part of the answer is that we don't work the way you think—our committees may look like a hierarchy if you draw them out on a schematic, but that's all. It genuinely isn't some kind of concealed top-down structure. So if the Command Committee wants certain kinds of job done, it doesn't have some poor minion down below to send off and do it. We're elected to do a job, and I was the best for this one.

'The other part of the answer is that we need to keep what we're doing secret. Apart from the Division's Command Committee, the only people who know that we're planning an assault through the wormhole are those of us on this ship.' I looked around. 'We're it, we're the team, and you're in! If you don't like what we're doing, you're both free to pull out, but not to leave the Division's space until it's all over.'

Malley and Suze both looked troubled and about to speak. Suze said it first: 'But who are you keeping all this a secret *from*?'

'From the Jovians,' Tony said.

'But—but—' Malley was almost stuttering, as his synapses misfired with excited articulation. 'The Jovians, the Outwarders, they're, they're just mad, they're trapped in their own virtual realities!'

I glanced around the team, and caught minute nods and shrugs.

'Not any more,' I said. 'But it's a long story, and we've all had a long day. Tomorrow for that. Let me show you around the ship.'

One thing that distinguishes a fusion-clipper from most spacecraft is that its internal layout has a definite 'up' and 'down'; and because this one was only carrying the crew there was plenty of room in which to show Malley and Suze around. After dinner I used my remaining energy to climb up and down stairways all over the ship and explain all that could be explained.

The fusion-clipper's hull is like a somewhat pear-shaped egg, two hundred feet long and seventy across at its widest diameter, which is occupied by the commissary and the command deck. The narrow end tapers to the jet, and contains the fusion torch, the main water tanks, and the life-support systems. Above, or forward, from the command deck are the sleeping-quarters—cramped, but festooned with climbing plants and recycling tubes (hard to distinguish, in practice) which give it a more open feel. Above that, clustered around the big glass eye of the heat shield, are the active-defence laser cannon, for dealing with any wandering space junk which (at the sort of velocities a fusion-clipper can reach) *all* has to be dealt with.

Our tour ended in the sleeping gallery which, typically for this class of ship, was deliberately designed to resemble a cliff-face of caves overlooking the central air well, whose bottom was the transparent mid deck roof and whose top was the transparent forward heat shield, through which a a distorted but distinct pattern of stars could be seen. The erratic, silent flaring of incoming dust and meteoroids, vaporized by the reflex lasers of the ship's active-defence system, provided a soothing analogue of the shooting stars in a natural sky.

Malley leaned over a guardrail and looked up and down.

'Why the recyling plant?' he asked. 'The journey times are days or weeks. Why not just carry supplies?'

'Not all the journeys are so short, and they don't all end at ports,' I said.

'Hmm,' he said. 'Colonizing.'

'Well,' I shrugged, 'there's the Kuiper Belt, and the Oort.'

'And New Mars?' Suze asked mischievously.

'We plan ahead,' I agreed. They both laughed.

Malley stretched and yawned. 'You were right,' he said. 'Time for bed. Now where did I leave my bag?'

I retrieved their luggage, such as it was, then showed them their cabins and crawled into mine. With just enough room to stand up and to lie down in, its rounded walls veined with translucent tubes ferrying swirling swarms of engineered noctilucent protozoa, it was like an undersea cave, with the sand-coloured foam rectangle of the bed its only furnishing. I let the outer garment of the spacesuit change into a thick quilt and pillow; and discovered that for the inner layers the suit had extended its range of textures to fluffy knitted wool and brushed silk tricot, and its range of colours to ecru, beige, and several shades of peach. It was all very cosy. I unfastened a few bows, pulled the quilt over my head, and went to sleep.


'You want to live in a dream world!' I accuse.

I'm clinging by my left big toe to a hole in an angled aluminium bracket, floating at right angles to the kid I'm arguing with, and squirting jets of hash beer into my mouth from a nozzled plastic bottle that once contained something quite different (whose taste lingers) in the crowded recreation-deck (or, inevitably: 'wreck-deck') of an Earth Defence battlesat abandoned to squatters and orbital decay and it's 2062 and I just know it can't be, and I'm dreaming. So the accusation doesn't carry much conviction.

The kid is about nineteen and must be a recent arrival: he's fat, and no-body gets—or stays—fat in free fall (it's that great weight-loss diet we have). His face, dotted with more eruptions than Io, calls to mind all the pizzas he must've stuffed in it. His eyes tend to bulge: the modern equivalent of peb-ble lenses, due to several corrective cornea ops for reading-induced myopia. Disdaining the hops and hemp as unhealthy, he's sucking some vile cocktail of smart drugs, spiked with euphorics. He knows everything.

'You're the dreamer,' he says. He waves a hand at the window, thirty feet away on the other side of the wreck-deck. Through the mass of drifting drinkers, through clouds of smoke and stray droplets, the image of a brick-red surface crawls past. Madagascar, I'd know it anywhere. 'You're still stuck in commie altruism. You want to help people who're beyond help. They're doomed. "Earth—the Third World", ha-ha. Time to grow up and get with the programme, Ellen. Time to move it out. There's a big universe out there.'

'My point exactly.' I gesture, too, at what's now the Indian Ocean. 'And Earth is part of it. You want to live in a virtual reality.'

'Not entirely.' He smiles, showing bad teeth. 'We'll pay a lot of attention to the outside—we'll have to, if we're gonna turn all that dumb mass into smart-matter. Matter that thinks, and dreams. A world of wonders, where you can be anything you like, not what chance and your genes have made you.'

'I don't want to turn the universe into a big computer running virtual re-alities,' I tell him. 'And don't call me a "commie altruist", by the way. It's just ordinary human concern. I just don't like to see people suffer, so it would be very *unselfish* of me to ignore ten billion people blundering into the dark.'

'You won't have to see them suffer,' he tells me, with insufferable assur-ance. 'You can just *edit them out*. Anyway, their problems are *their* problem. Why make them yours?'

'Because I care about them, and if that sounds altruistic, just think of it this way: I'm selfish enough to want to be, oh, the princess of the Galaxy!

OK—at a pinch, I'd be happy just to live forever in a Galactic Empire. I *personally want* to see a universe crowded with people having a good time.'

I wave expansively at the wreck-deck, to illustrate.

'People!' He snorts. 'Where's your ambition? We can do better than that.'

'You want to be machines.' I knock back a shot of the drink. 'I don't.'

He shrugs. 'If you want to live in space, you're better off as a machine than as a bag of sea water. The human body's design spec is: a spacesuit for a fish. Machines are at home in the universe.'

I give him a grin so wide and delighted that he thinks I like him, and I come back with a quote from a dated dystopia that had a huge resonance for me when I was a kid: *This Perfect Day* by Ira Levin. (Not that we were in any danger of that perfect day, or any other, but the book spoke to me.)

' "Machines are at home in the universe. People are aliens." '

He's still smiling back, still thinks I'm agreeing. The hash beer drives me to stoned and pissed elaboration: 'Strangers in a strange land. Marx was wrong—we aren't alienated *from* our humanity, alienation *is* humanity. We're always capable of stepping back and looking at what we're doing, from the outside as it were—we have an outside, *inside*, and it's as infinite as space. No Turing test can come close, no matter how good it is at faking an organism. Machines calculate; people count. Machines have programs; people have purposes.' I stop and stare at him and take another shot of beer. 'So there.'

'People are machines too,' he says. 'And machines will have all we have, once we've transferred our minds to them.'

'That's what you call it. Stripping your brain away layer by layer and modelling it on a computer is what I call *dying*.'

'It's transcending,' he says. He slaps his chest, almost setting himself spinning. '*This* is dying. "The meat is murder." '

'Yeah,' I say cruelly. 'If I had *your* body, I'd want to be something else.'

He doesn't take this as the crushing put-down it's intended to be. 'Yes,' he says, still smiling. 'When I upload, I might model my virtual body on yours.'

My attention is distracted by the television screen at the end of the bar, where my parents' faces have appeared, talking to me in a language I don't understand, smiling, reassuring. Their twitching, dead-but-galvanized bodies are drifting in front of the screen, attached by pipes that are sucking up their brains. 'Goodbye, Ellen,' they're saying, 'goodbye. See you in ten thousand years.'

Furious, I turn back to the kid, but he's already changed, from slob to blob, a paramecium shape buzzing with fractal cilia, a patch of which snows to pixels and freezes to a face—my face.

'I like your body,' he says.

'In your dreams!' I yell at him. 'In your dreams!'

And I wake.

The quilt cuddles me, the pillow drinks my tears.

'Hush,' it soothes. 'Everything will be all right.'

The following morning I got up at about 1100 hours, ship time (which, conveniently for those of us who'd boarded yesterday, was the same as GMT), and made my way to the mid deck. Rather to my embarrassment, I was the last to arrive, and the rest of the team had honoured the occasion by setting their suits to various approximations of nattily masculine militarism. Andrea and Boris were entertaining Suze and Malley with a demonstration of the active-defence system, which although automated, could be overridden to provide a spectacular shoot-'em-up game with (mostly tiny, but fast) meteoroids as targets. The others were amusing themselves in less productive ways.

I grunted a good-morning to all of them and had a solitary and thoughtful breakfast in the commissary, chasing the wisps of disturbed dream away with strong coffee. I took my third mug with me back up the stairs and sat down on a couch.

'OK comrades,' I said. 'We're in session. Yeng, would you like to chair?'

She nodded, pushing away her goggles and nanotech tank, and clapped her hands. 'Come *on*, guys. Turn the aiming-computers back on and come over here.'

Andrea, Boris, Malley and Suze dragged themselves away from the manual fire controls and settled down on the ends of couches. I got a shy smile from Suze, a cocky grin from Malley. The surgeries' work, though by no means complete, had transformed his appearance overnight: straightening his stance, smoothing the skin on his face, wiping the wrinkles from around his eyes.

'Your little pills have certainly done something for my reflexes,' he said. Boris spread his hand and made a rocking motion: 'Considering what you started with . . .' The two men laughed; I hoped it indicated, at however tentative a level, the beginning of friendship.

'Suze, Sam,' I began, 'the rest of us all know what I'm going to tell you, but each of us may be able to answer different questions, so . . .'

I worked the long, low seat's controls, raising the central overhead cluster of instrumentation and lowering a boom on which was suspended a holographic projection apparatus. Tendrils snaked out from my gloves into the system's interface. The electric lamps turned off, and I keyed up a football-sized image of Jupiter, softly glowing. I set it spinning with exaggerated speed in the light from the outside, under the refracted, multiply-distorted images of the real stars above us.

'A brief history of the Jovian system,' I said. 'Let's start with how it was before the Outwarders got underway with Project Jove.' The four Galilean moons shuttled around it, the Great Red Spot turned with the planet's coloured bands. 'Here's the first indication that something big was going on, which we noticed in 2090. Real archive tape from the Farside Observatory.'

Ganymede disintegrated—not exploding, not flying apart, just separating into millions of bits which, on this time-lapsed view, immediately spread out to form a ring.

We'd all seen it before—it's the Zapruder film of astronautics: the most widely known image, and the most thoroughly studied and argued-over sequence of photographs, in the history of space exploration. The technician who recorded it had a sense of humour as well as a sense of history, and I played the audio tape of his (alleged) first reaction: 'Oh my stars, it's full of gods!'

Small polite laughs all round. 'OK,' I said, 'we've all heard it. But he was right. And we *still* don't know how they did it, even in principle. Sam Malley proved the concept of the Gate and the Drive, and nanotech and uploading were all understood well in advance—essentially as far back as the nineteen-eighties. But shattering the biggest moon in the solar system came as, um, a bit of a shock.'

The most frightening moment of my life, to be exact. I nodded to Tony, who took up that side of the story.

'We all,' he said, 'couldn't help remembering that the Outwarders had announced their intention of turning everything except the stars into smart-matter, starting with the smaller asteroids and working their way up, all the way to what they called "Jupiter-sized brains". They had a saying: "If it isn't running programs and it isn't fusing atoms, it's just bending space." So we were all rather concerned when we saw that.' He gave us a thin smile. 'Especially those of us who lived on the Moon.'

Malley looked up from doodling something on a pad he'd conjured from the knee of his suit. 'There may be ways of deriving the, uh, *planet-wrecker* from the same schema as the Gate,' he said. 'I've given it some thought over the years, but I've never taken it far. I'll work on it.'

'Good,' I said, smiling as warmly as I could. 'Well, on to the Gate.' I ran the tape forward again, focusing in on the ring and magnifying the view to what had been the limits of our telescopic resolution back in the twenty-nineties. A complex cat's-cradle of girders rapidly took shape, a three-dimensional web of black threads just inside the ring. At the same time the face of Jupiter was transformed, its bands fractured by crosscurrents. I cut to close-ups of the structure.

'These shots are from files retrieved from a construction robot by the so-called artificial woman, Meg, who was Jonathan Wilde's companion in

that robot body,' I explained. 'The black struts are—prosaically enough—
polycarbon I-beams, though they have complex internal machinery. The
small robots you see rocketing about and apparently working on the structure are the bonded labour force, each of them with a copied human mind
running on its onboard computer.' I paused, compressed my lips for a moment and took a deep breath, then continued. 'Now *that*—' I froze the
frame, then let it run on—'is a very different kind of upload. It's what we
called a "super-organism" and what the ex-human workers on the project
called a "macro." It's a smart-matter object, a constellation of trillions of
nanomachines, and one of many. Each of them contains literally millions
of minds, mostly replicated—and enhanced—descendants of the original
Outwarders. Wilde refers to them as "the fast folk," and the term has caught
on, because it's apt: their minds are thinking and experiencing at least a
thousand times faster than ours.'

We all sat and stared at the macro, a nightmarishly gigantic and multicoloured amoeboid shape, its fractal surfaces seething, its pseudopodia
bulging and retracting as it oozed around the girders. Its size dwarfed the
tiny, tinny-looking robots of its pressed servants.

'You've never shown these close-ups to people on Earth,' Suze accused.
I nodded briskly.

'That's right,' I said. 'We've kept them to ourselves, for now. All anybody
in the Inner System has seen is the fuzzy blobs that showed up in some pictures we got at the time from a spy probe before it was detected and destroyed.'

'Very democratic of you,' said Malley. 'Didn't want to cause panic, is that
it?'

'Not exactly,' said Tony, leaning forward. 'If you're like me, Dr Malley,
I'm sure you're feeling a reaction of unease or even dread, which is objectively rather hard to justify. We ourselves find it difficult to explain, and
suspect it may be deliberately induced by some subtle effect of the surface
patterns. If that's the case it was presumably intended to overawe the labour
force. Tests on our own personnel have shown that this response might
readily translate into a desire for precipitate action against the present-day
descendants of these entities. That's a pressure we'd prefer to avoid.'

*For the moment*, I thought. I went on quickly, showing the subsequent
stages of the construction project in fast-forward. The structure suddenly divided, a smaller, circular section detaching itself. The Jovian surface swirled,
its equator dotted with what looked like waterspouts which soared in curving
trajectories to the ring. A hairline circle around the ring glowed white-hot.
The newly separated structure seemed to fold in on itself, and there, hanging
like a film of soap in a ring, was the Gate itself: a mile-wide circle of stretched
space, its edge shimmering with all the colours of the spectrum.

'The Malley Mile,' I said. Malley gave us all an ironic bow. 'If you watch closely you'll see the moment where it divides into two just-overlapping circles, the two sides of the wormhole. There. The small dark object at the centre is the Outwarders' ship, or probe, which . . .'

A line of light stabbed at a tangent from the glowing line around the great ring, straight for the centre of the Gate.

'. . . goes away.' Everybody blinked; everybody drew breath, even those who'd watched this scene a hundred times. 'Taking one side of the wormhole with it. Observe how the plasma jet apparently just *stops* when it reaches the Gate. There can be not the slightest doubt that the jet is passing from the local region of space-time into—somewhere else. But in case anybody's wondering, we did manage to track the probe for the first few minutes.' The grainy images flashed up, showing a streak of light and a blurry dot. 'As you can see, there's the plasma jet, coming apparently out of nowhere and crossing a few hundred yards of space to the probe, where it's transformed into kinetic energy via what we presume is, ah, a Malley virtual-mass drive. We calculate that the probe reached almost the speed of light in a month. After that, things get complicated, because both sides of the wormhole are in the same reference frame.'

Suze was looking puzzled. I smiled at Malley. 'Sam, over to you.'

Malley shrugged. 'To simplify drastically . . . it's not really correct to refer to "both sides" of the wormhole. The ship is travelling at some arbitrarily close approximation to the speed of light, and therefore experiences relativistic time dilation—time runs slower on the ship than it does back home. The truly paradoxical feature of the wormhole is that both ends are in the same place. So anything passing through one end of the wormhole arrives at the other end in ship time, which after, say, a year, could be hundreds of light years away, and hundreds of years in the future. With continued acceleration, the probe reaches the edge of the observable universe in thirty shipboard years. So, thirty years from launch, anybody passing through the wormhole arrives instantly at the same location. It is, if you like, a time machine to the future.'

Suze grinned around at us. 'If you say so.'

I laughed. 'Meanwhile, if that's the word, quite a lot had been going on around Jupiter.'

The planet's surface was mottled, the sites of the still-soaring tornadoes expanding into new variants of the Great Red Spot. I pulled up time-lapsed shots from the records recovered from Meg's AI mind. The macros changed as we watched, their original feverish internal activity speeding up, then slowing to a stop. A few of them seemed to crystallize, and drifted off towards the Jovian atmosphere. The rest visibly shrivelled, rotting to skeletal shapes like the veins of dead leaves.

A new shape burst on the scene, crashing through the dead macros and their vast construction site like a stone through cobwebs. The viewpoint zoomed towards it, revealing a long, jury-rigged assembly of spacecraft and habitats, spinning crazily on its axis and following a precarious course along the line of the plasma jet. And then the viewpoint was evidently *on* the cobbled-together ship, the hot white line strobing past. The shot ended in a burst of blue light.

'Cherenkov radiation,' I said. 'They went through the wormhole—well, through a side-branch of it, a daughter wormhole—and, as we know, found a new home. Now we'll leave them for the moment, and pull back to see what happened on this side.' I switched to the telescope view: the fountains of gas, and the jet that they had fed, ceased.

'We're not sure,' I said, 'whether that was planned, the probe having reached some point where it could continue to accelerate without further input from base; or whether it was a result of the disaster that you saw unfolding there, or whether indeed it was a response to the escape of the labour force on that remarkable excuse for a starship.'

Suze was grinning from ear to ear.

'It was quite a feat, that escape,' she said.

'It sure was,' said Andrea. 'I still shudder every time I look at it.'

'Why didn't they just head for home, for the Inner System?' Malley asked.

I shrugged, hiding a moment of pain. 'Partly because, ironically enough, they didn't have the supplies for such a long journey in, uh, *real space*—it would have taken them years to get back to the nearest human settlement in *that* thing, and partly because their leaders—it wasn't exactly a democratic setup, being an orbital labour camp—had decided they wanted to go to the stars.'

'Also,' Tony added, 'I suspect the post-humans systematically misled them about what was going on in the Inner System. Wilde certainly thought we jammed their communications, which is more or less the opposite of the truth.'

'OK,' Malley said.

'Right,' I went on. 'The next thing that happened, about a year later, was the beginning of a flood of disruptive radio-borne computer viruses from somewhere inside the Jovian atmosphere. It took us a long time to recover, and even longer to get out there ourselves. Within five years, however, our telescopes were picking up something with which most of you are by now so familiar that it's hard to imagine how awesome it seemed at the time.' I laughed briefly. 'There must be kids today who think this appearance of Jupiter is *natural*.'

The planet's image blurred, the orange banding known since Cassini himself dissolving briefly into chaos, then settling into the new configuration it had shown for the past couple of centuries: vast hexagonal upwellings, like Bernoulli convection cells in boiling water.

'As you can see, they were able to affect their environment—deliberately or not, we can't say. Bear in mind the speed the original post-humans worked at—if it was maintained, the entities we now call the Jovians must have done that over five or six thousand subjective years, so it could have been just a by-product of their activity. Every five years or so, these cells collapse and reform, and the radio output changes. We think this represents the repeated rise and fall of post-human cultures in virtual realities, though for all we know they could just as well have degenerated to pre-human levels of intelligence, and all this might have no more significance than the work of coral polyps or bees. The viral messages themselves could be simply a defensive reflex, the equivalent of a squid's cloud of ink or a plant's insecticides.'

Yeng raised her hand, exercising her chairperson's right to interrupt. 'That wouldn't make it any less dangerous,' she pointed out. 'Biological diseases aren't intelligent either, but they can still threaten us, and the computer viruses which something out there is generating are definitely a threat.'

I nodded emphatically. 'Yes . . . which is why our communications are such a bind, and why our most important computers are such lumbering monsters, and *all* our computers, right down to the nano scale, are mechanical. But that's only part of it. Now and again there's some kind of attempt at launching things out of the atmosphere. These attempts have increased over time. Which is where we come in.'

What followed was basically a propaganda video for the Cassini Division, showing the constant vigilance of the orbital fleets patrolling just outside the Jovian atmosphere, zapping anything larger than a grain of sand that looked like heading the wrong way; and the long watch on the Gate. A voice-over carefully explained that the latter wasn't the complete waste of time that it might seem, because we also spooled in the data sent back from the probe, which constantly deepened our knowledge of the far future of the universe. Malley shared with me a sceptical smile.

I paused the video. 'All this is now, sadly, out of date,' I said. 'Because something new has happened.' I bookmarked the place for later use and brought on some new footage.

'This is recent,' I said. 'The last couple of months. We haven't, uh, put it on general release yet.'

The huge upwellings died away, as they had two-score times in the past. When they were renewed, clusters of bubbles appeared within them, bobbing into visibility and then sinking back. Each time they returned to the surface, the clusters had expanded and proliferated, linked up by long and (on this scale) thin black lines. I maxed the res, showing dark shapes shuttling within these black lines, moving in both directions.

'Oh, shit,' said Malley.

'Quite,' I said, running overflight scans. 'It does definitely look like some kind of stable, organized form of life, with habitats, technology, transport. So far, that's the best detail we've got. Perhaps most significant of all, there are narrow-cast beam messages passed between these clusters. We haven't yet interpreted them, but they sure look like intelligent communication. There's every possibility that what we're seeing is evidence that the Jovians have finally got out of the recurrent traps of their inherited virtual realities, and have emerged as a new species. They are developing and changing fast—we're getting traces of flight paths through the atmosphere, and the speed and frequency of these flights are increasing by the week.'

'Wow,' said Suze. 'Aliens!'

'No,' I said. 'Post-humans—a superhuman, post-Singularity form of life, that may be as far above us as we are above the ants. Or will be, Real Soon Now.'

I looked around the circle. Malley and Suze seemed puzzled, but not worried; my crew were united in grim resolution.

'Is this why you're so keen to get through the wormhole?' Suze asked. 'So we can—you can—escape, if necessary?'

'That's part of it,' I admitted. 'And part of it is as I said to you—we don't know what's going on on the *other* side: If it's anything like this, we want to know.'

'There is something else,' Boris said. 'Something you should know.' He nodded to me; I ran the standard spiel at the place where I'd stopped. It showed off our distant expeditions in the Kuiper Belt using lasers and tactical nukes to topple cometary orbits in towards the Inner System, sending them swinging around Jupiter and on to Mars or the Belt.

I stopped it and brought up the lights. We all sat back and looked at Malley and Suze. All of us, I suppose, felt as tense as I did; we had decided, in long debates on our journey to Earth, that Malley (or Wilde, if we'd got him on board) would have to know the full story, because it would be impossible to conceal it from him once he started work on the wormhole problem, and he was unlikely to take kindly to being duped.

Malley's mouth opened, then closed. He swallowed hard and spoke.

'You're not serious,' he said. 'You can't be—are you telling us you're going to actually set up a cometary bombardment and destroy the new Jovians?'

'Yes,' I said. 'That's exactly what we're going to do. As soon as we saw this new development, we set things in motion—literally—out in the Kuiper

Belt. It took a lot of work, but it's ready now. We've set up a train of massive comets, and they're due to arrive in less than three weeks. We'll give them a nudge at the last moment, and there'll be a succession of impacts all around the planet. It should work—the new Jovians seem more vulnerable than whatever is making the upwellings. Those bubbles you see are just that, bubbles in the atmosphere. Most of their technology seems to be based on manipulation of electromagnetic fields, gas flows, and large-scale chemical reactions. We are going to direct a stream of fast, heavy comet nuclei into the Jovian atmosphere, hit them with a force greater than a million nuclear wars, and wipe them out for good.'

'But we don't even know if they're hostile!' Suze protested. 'Have you tried to contact them?'

'Of course not,' Yeng said. 'They're still churning out the same old viruses. If we deliberately opened communication with them, who knows but they'd send even more destructive viruses back?'

'You must be able to build in safeguards,' Malley said. He rattled his unlit pipe between his teeth. 'I don't see the justification.'

'They're capable of supplanting us,' Tony said. 'At least, there's a strong chance that they are. They present a threat to us just by existing. Isn't that justification enough?'

Suze and Malley both shook their heads. 'It's a bad thing to do,' Suze said. 'We could learn from them. We could persuade them to stop the virus broadcasts. They might not be able to harm us. They might not even be aware we exist!'

'Here's hoping,' said Andrea. 'That way, they have no chance to fight back.'

We all laughed, except Suze and Malley.

'What about the morality of it?' Malley asked.

Most of us shrugged or smiled. Yeng frowned. 'Morality?' she said uncertainly. 'What's that?'

Some of us smiled; Malley barked a laugh.

'It's an ideology,' Suze said. 'People used to think that there was a very powerful intelligence that controlled the universe, and that it told them what to do. Later they found out there was no intelligence controlling the universe, but for about a century or so after that they thought the *universe* told them what to do. Some of them had doubts about that, but they thought that if people didn't believe it they would start raping and killing and hurting each other.' She grimaced. 'I've never understood why they thought that, because some people were raping and killing and hurting other people all the time anyway. The reason most people weren't doing that is because they didn't want to in the first place, or because they knew they couldn't get away with it. We know now that if we want other people to stop doing bad things we have to *make* them stop and *not* let them get away with it. Which is why we have the Union!' she concluded triumphantly, a little out of breath, but evidently pleased that her arcane studies had made some contribution.

'OK,' said Yeng, 'I understand. It was something people believed before they had the true knowledge?'

'That's right!' I said. 'Exactly. So, Sam, you were saying?'

Malley glowered at me. Then his expression relaxed and he shrugged. 'All right,' he said. 'If that's the way you see it, fine. I think all this "Do What Thou Wilt Shall Be The Whole Of The Law" crap is as satanic as the man who first said it, but let that pass.'

I nodded. It was easy enough to let that pass, because it made no kind of sense to me.

'So to put it in your terms,' Malley went on, 'I don't think it would be to our advantage to destroy the Jovians. They are a form of intelligent life, presumably they're sentient, and disrespect for sentience is a danger-ous thing. A bad precedent. And secondly, as Suze pointed out, we could benefit from some kind of peaceful interaction with them, if that's at all possible.'

I stared at him, somewhat shaken. I had known he was old, and had been a non-cooperator most of his life, but for a genius he seemed remarkably obtuse.

'First of all,' I said, 'you're right about sentience. We do have to respect it, each and every one of us, if only for our own peace of mind. But only humans are sentient. Those things out there are just jumped-up computer programs! They may give the appearance of sentience, but if they do, it'll be a protective coloration. You can have a deep, meaningful conversation with your suit—hey, you can have a sexual relationship with it, if that's your thing—but nobody thinks *suits* are sentient. It's just something that suits have evolved, by a kind of natural selection, in order to get along with hu-mans. The Jovians, if we communicate with them, will no doubt seem sen-sitive, but they can no more feel than the eye-spots on a butterfly's wing can see.'

Malley tilted his head back and roared with laughter.

'And you people sneer at ideology!' he spluttered, when he'd calmed down a bit. 'That's the most airtight piece of dogmatic, closed-loop think-ing I've ever heard! You really mean to say that no robots, no uploads, no artificial intelligences are truly sentient and worthy of our concern?'

'Absolutely,' I said. 'It's self-evident.'

'And even if you were right, what's the *advantage* to you, or us, or any-body, in crushing those "butterflies' wings", blind though they may be? Eh?'

'Let me explain,' I said patiently. 'There are no signs of intelligent life anywhere else in the universe. The Outwarder probe has gone a long way, and none of the data coming back from it has shown a smidgin of a trace of a signal. We're alone, apart from the Jovians. If they are superior to us, no matter how friendly they seem to be, we'll always be at their mercy. I will not live at the mercy of anyone or anything. This our best, last, and only chance to have the universe to ourselves, and we're going to take it.'

Malley stood up and looked around at all of us, not angry, not impatient; a bit sad, as though some of the aging damage he was beginning to slough off had settled back on him.

'Not with my help, you're not,' he said.

# 5

---

## THE COMING RACE

Malley stalked over to the stairwell and went down to the commissary. Suze rose, looked at me anxiously, shrugged and followed him.

'Meeting's over,' Yeng said. She glanced around, unsure how to take what had happened, then decided to look on the bright side. 'Time we all had some lunch.'

Lunch was usually a relaxed occasion. This one wasn't. We hung around the smaller tables in the commissary in ones and twos. Suze was with Malley on one side of the room, I with Tony on the other. All the talking was in low voices.

'Think we've blown it?' Tony asked.

I shrugged. 'Callisto's buzzing with talk about the bombardment. We couldn't have kept it from him, not without isolation that would've made him suspicious and—non-cooperative!'

Tony stroked his beard, and looked searchingly at me. 'Suppose we're wrong,' he said softly. 'When I think about what we're proposing to do— well, between you and me, Ellen, I sometimes have qualms about it myself. Suppose the Jovians *aren't* flatlines, suppose they really are conscious, just like you and me but far better, with a deeper and richer inner life. After all, they may have naturally evolved away from the earlier Jovians, and they're no longer some kind of new releases of the old mad uploads, but a new species, a new flesh. Wouldn't that make the impact event like, say, some troop of chimps using rocks to beat out the brains of the first humans?'

I fought down my dismayed surprise at this incipient flinch, this *line wobble* as the old comrades would say, coming from—of all people—my security officer and oldest ally. I fought down my indignation. If Tony had qualms, then certainly others would, too, and he was doing me a favour by expressing them.

'All the more reason to do it,' I said, clapping his shoulder fraternally. 'Look where not doing it got the chimps.'

We understood each other perfectly. In our two hundred years of acquaintance, we had never had a sexual relationship (not counting quick drunk fucks, of course). He just wasn't my type, nor I his. But in every other way we knew each other quite intimately. Not that we agreed on everything, at least not at once, but we knew how to get agreement or agree to differ. We knew how each other's minds worked.

I knew what was going on in Tony's, right now. Although he intellectually accepted the true knowledge, he had never been *taken* by it—unlike me, to whom it had struck home with the force of a revelation.


The true knowledge . . . the phrase is an English translation of a Korean expression meaning 'modern enlightenment'. Its originators, a group of Japanese and Korean 'contract employees' (inaccurate Korean translation, this time, of the English term 'bonded labourers') had acquired their modern enlightenment from battered, ancient editions of the works of Stirner, Nietzsche, Marx, Engels, Dietzgen, Darwin, and Spencer, which made up the entire philosophical content of their labour-camp library. (Twentieth-century philosophy and science had been excluded by their employers as decadent or subversive—I forget which.) With staggering diligence, they had taken these works—which they ironically treated as the last word in modern thought—and synthesized from them, and from their own bitter experiences, the first socialist philosophy based on totally pessimistic and cynical conclusions about human nature.

Life is a process of breaking down and using other matter, and if need be, other life. Therefore, life is aggression, and successful life is successful aggression. Life is the scum of matter, and people are the scum of life. There is nothing but matter, forces, space and time, which together make power. Nothing matters, except what matters to you. Might makes right, and power makes freedom. You are free to do whatever is in your power, and if you want to survive and thrive you had better do whatever is in your interests. If your interests conflict with those of others, let the others pit their power against yours, everyone for theirselves. If your interests coincide with those of others, let them work together with you, and against the rest. We are what we we eat, and *we eat everything*.

All that you really value, and the goodness and truth and beauty of life, have their roots in this apparently barren soil.

This is the true knowledge.

On this rock we had built our church. We had founded our idealism on the most nihilistic implications of science, our socialism on crass self-interest, our peace on our capacity for mutual destruction, and our liberty on determinism. We had replaced morality with convention, bravery with safety, frugality with plenty, philosophy with science, stoicism with anaesthetics and piety with immortality. The universal acid of the true knowledge had burned away a world of words, and exposed a universe of things.

Things we could use.


'It's the Rapture for nerds!'

Now that's a breath of fresh air, I think, and turn to see who's come up with this well aimed sneer at the Singularity. It's a guy bumping alongside me, a slender man with straight black hair gelled to a quiff, a sharp beard modelled on Lenin's, a slim gentle face and darting dark eyes. He's enjoying the laughter he's spread on our side, the discomfited smiles on the other.

It's 2065 and we're back in the wreck-deck, but the recreation area is now much expanded, as is the space station, which has just been boosted to a higher orbit. We are here to celebrate that work's completion. There must be hundreds of people here. To begin with we were one big crowd, but as the arguments have gone on we have, almost literally, drifted apart. We have polarized to opposite sides of the deck.

The arguments have been going on for years, but we've always worked together. The two sides, of which those here are a small sample, are loosely based on two waves of space settlement. The first lot had peaked in the twenty-forties, and consisted of pioneer settlers and the forces in Earth Defence who'd gone over to the Fall Revolution. The second lot had come up in the late twenty-fifties, and early twenty-sixties, and were the product of a quite different process: a deliberate abandonment of Earth by technicians, engineers and scientists—and the desperate rich—who had developed an increasingly advanced technology and launch capability in increasingly isolated and beleaguered enclaves. They'd shot their bolt in the catastrophically botched and counter-productive 'Space Movement coup' of 2059.

They still have stuff coming up, though, and all along they've been using bonded labourers—criminals making restitution, mostly, and political and military prisoners from the losing side in the Fall Revolution and subsequent conflicts—to build and defend their infrastructure, in space and on the ground. To us, this seems little better than slavery, not to mention a sneaky undercutting of the Space Movement's traditional private-enterprise

or voluntary-labour ethos. To them, it's payback for the long years of re-
pression before the Revolution, and for their continuing harassment by the
fragmented governments and frantic peoples of Earth.

Understandably, they have no interest in using the now-enormous and
self-sufficient space presence to aid those from whose ignorant wrath they've
barely escaped. We, from the first wave of idealistic or avaricious colonists,
are convinced that aiding Earth is exactly the way to overcome that ignorant
wrath.

We call ourselves: the first settlers, the Earth tendency, the beautiful
people, the star warriors.

We call the others: the others, the outsiders, the nerds, the new lot.

The others call us: the Earth-Tenders, the greenies, the commies, the
mundanes, the dirt-farmers, the Space Family Robinson.

The others call themselves: the Outwarders, the Singularity Gang, the
Futurists, the post-humans.

Their dream is the Singularity. Ours is the Galactic Empire, or the Federation, or whatever. It makes them laugh.

And right now we're laughing at them, or at least the dozens of people
within earshot of this man's gibe are laughing at a roughly equal and opposite group of Outwarders.

'That stuff is just *stupid*,' he goes on. 'I can't understand how anybody
ever fell for the idea that a computer model of the brain is the same as the
brain. Talk about mechanical materialism! It's about becoming a machine,
it's death, and wanting it is *sick*.'

'You wouldn't say that if you knew you were about to die,' says the nearest Outwarder, a young man (but we all look young, now) who doesn't
match our favourite nerd stereotype because he's eschewed the coke-and-
pizza diet for a different Outwarder vice: body building. He floats, tanned
and oiled and naked, in a slow-spinning lotus posture, doing something dy-
namic and clever with the squirted stream of his drink. 'We already have
back-ups of people who got killed guarding Canaveral, you know that?'

He catches a wobbling sphere of liquid in his lips, and swallows it, his
next rotation bringing up a questioning smile.

'And you're going to run them?' I ask.

'Sure,' he tells us. 'As soon as we have a few bugs out of the virtual-
environment software.'

The man beside me laughs. 'So your slave soldiers get promised paradise
when they die! Stay with that idea, guys, it worked for Mohammed.'

This second religious allusion leads the oiled man to ask, challengingly,
'Have you ever read anything on the strong-AI resurrectionist position?
Even something classic, like *The Physics of Immortality*?'

'Nah,' says the bearded man. 'Life's too short!'

The Outwarder stops his rotation with a perfectly-timed toss of his empty drink-bulb, and looks coldly at my sniggering face.

'Here's a thought from it,' he says. 'Brief enough for you: refusing to accept intelligent robots as *people* is equivalent to racism.'

'So?' says the man at my side. 'So I'm a racist. A *human* racist.'

'Fine by me,' I chip in, knowing that the Outwarder is playing the racism card with my dark skin in mind. He scowls at me.

'Here's another—claiming that human selves can't be implemented on computers is tantamount to accepting death, for everybody, forever. Is that so fine by you?'

'I can live with it,' I say. The man beside me gives an appreciative chuckle, and adds:

'If you allow us to live.'

The Outwarder smiles, looks around at the jostle of his fellows, then back at us.

'Of course we'll allow you to live,' he says. 'On wildlife reserves, like the other interesting animals. Some of us may prefer to think of you as pets. Sentimental post-humans will no doubt campaign for "human rights"—it'll be one of those fluffy causes, like old-growth forests and spotted owls. Wouldn't it be much better to join us, and be as gods?'

Something twists inside me. Everything is suddenly clear. I have what I later understand as the beginning of the true knowledge.

'We *are* as gods!' I snarl. '*We* are the top predator here. *You* can become machines if you like, but then you'll be dead, and we'll be alive, and we'll *treat* you as machines. If we can't use you, we'll smash you up!'

'If you can,' he says.

I look straight back at him. 'If we can.'

He makes a dismissive gesture, and turns away.

The man beside me performs a mid-air somersault, and floats before me, grinning, arms spread. He seems to think he's just given me a fly-past salute.

'That was good,' he says.

'Hey, I liked what you said,' I tell him. ' "The Rapture for nerds." '

We laugh like it's an old, shared joke, and introduce ourselves. His name is Tony Girard, and he's on the space station's management board, responsible for keeping an eye on the Outwarder component of its inhabitants. The liaison is important—the just-completed boosting of the station has been done with the new rocket engines, which look like they've been injection-moulded from diamond, and are nanofactured by the Outwarders. But he can't help getting into arguments with them.

'They say we're evil,' he says. 'I tell them we are.'

'But we're not!' I protest.

'Not from our point of view. We are from theirs. Reactionaries, counter-*evo*lutionaries, pulling back from the next stage in human development.'

'Yeah—extinction!'

I think about being evil. To them, I realize, we are indeed bad and harmful, but—and the thought catches my breath—we are not bad and harmful to *ourselves*, and that is all that matters, *to us*. So as long as we are actually achieving our own good, it doesn't matter how evil we are to our enemies. Our Federation will be, to them, the evil empire, the domain of dark lords; and I will be a dark lady in it. Humanity is indeed evil, from any non-human point of view. I hug my human wickedness in a shiver of delight.

I tell Tony some of this, and he nods.

'It's very liberating,' he says. 'Wearing the black hats.' He draws, spins and cocks an imaginary six-gun. (Like all of us, he has a real one on his hip.) 'Saves you a lot of soul-searching. As long as you avoid hitting your own side, you're doing the right thing.'

'Perhaps we're the Indians. The natives.'

Tony likes this. 'That's right,' he says. 'Doomed but brave. A drag on the wheels of progress. Shooting arrows at the iron horses of Manifest Destiny.'

'They are such mechanists,' I say.

'Yeah,' he says. 'That's why I like to wind them up.'

I laugh so much I find myself clinging to him, and later that day-cycle we have the first ever of our quick drunk fucks.


I smiled at Tony, perhaps more warmly than usual, and stood up and caught Yeng's eye, then flicked a glance to the table where Malley and Suze were sitting head-to-head. Yeng nodded. We each picked up our trays and wandered over.

'Mind if we sit down?'

Malley looked up, looked at Suze. 'Not at all,' he said.

I sat down beside Malley, and Yeng slipped on to the bench beside Suze and flashed her a quick smile. Suze looked down at her plate, then up.

'Sam and I have a question for you,' said Suze. 'I'm Union, he's non-co, and it turns out we both have the same question. Independently.'

'OK,' I said.

'Would you be willing to at least *try* to contact the Jovians, before destroying them? Would you at least try to come to some arrangement?'

The idea of contact with the Jovians made my skin crawl; but I also felt its attractions. The danger appealed to my recklessness, my hatred of the Jovians fuelled my curiosity about what they were really like, and, above all,

we needed Malley's cooperation to get through the Malley Mile. That was
the bottom line.

Yeng looked about to speak. My look signalled her to be quiet.

'We'd consider it,' I said. 'I can't speak for the Division, of course, but I
wouldn't say it's ruled out. Why?'

'I'd feel a lot happier about working with you,' Malley said, 'if I knew for
sure the Jovians really were a threat to us. A clear and present danger. And
opening communication with them is the only way to find out.'

Suze nodded agreement. 'When the folks back home find out what
you're doing, which they will—and you *are* going to let them know before
the event, aren't you?—I think *they'd* like to know for sure, as well. It would
be a rotten shame to wipe out things—even if they *are* just things—that
could help us, and that could turn out to be the only friends we have in the
whole universe. Like, what if they are gods, but gods on *our* side?'

So Suze was an appeaser, I thought sadly. I wondered again if she'd
somehow been sent to spy on me, and dismissed the thought, again.

'All right,' I said. 'We'll do it.'

'How?' asked Malley.

'Shortly after we get back,' I said, 'a fleet of remote probes is due to begin descent into the Jovian atmosphere—essentially to spy, to get a clearer
and closer view of what the comets are going to hit. Their telemetry—
radio, radar, laser—could easily be adapted for a first stab at communication. I'll put as strong a case as I can for doing it, and you and Suze can
argue for it too, if you think that'll help.'

Yeng's eyes flashed surprise; disagreement scored her brow.

'It's dangerous!' she said.

'Sure it is,' I said. 'But if anyone can build the firewalls, it's you. There
must be contingency plans somewhere, hardware and software designs,
right?'

She nodded reluctantly. 'Good guess.'

It was more than a guess, but Yeng didn't need to know that I knew more
than I needed to know.

'So go to it,' I said. 'Let's make some good use of our nine days.' I turned
to Malley. 'And you'll help us with the wormhole?'

'If you do as you say, yes.' He picked up his pipe and ran its stem across
his upper lip, inhaling gently through his nose, then put it down. 'I'll start
work on it now—I mean, I can hardly help thinking about it. When we arrive I'll use all the research facilities you've promised me, and *if* you lot
show some indication of having made a sincere attempt to avoid . . . war,
because that's what it is, then I'll share my results with you.'

'It's a deal,' I told him. Malley nodded; Suze smiled back at me; Yeng
looked vaguely puzzled. 'We have a plan,' I added, for her benefit.

'I have a lot of plans,' Yeng said. 'This is great! Such a challenge!' She grinned at me, her sweet, small face lighting up. 'Don't you worry, Ellen May, you'll have the best protection possible.'

She jumped up and almost ran up the spiral stair, so eager was she to start work on her anti-virus software design.

'What did she mean?' Malley asked. 'Why should it be you who opens communication?'

I knocked back my now-cold coffee. 'Same reason. I went to get you,' I said. 'If somebody proposes and pushes some daft, dangerous idea, it's only fair that they should have the fun of trying it out.'

Malley gave me an odd look. 'You must get through a lot of leading cadre that way.'

'We don't have "leading cadre",' said Suze.

'In the Division, we do,' I said. 'Only we don't lead from behind.' Suze looked so concerned that I had to relent.

'We do take back-ups,' I assured her.

Back-ups were controversial. After I'd left Malley talking to Andrea about the available recorded observations of the wormhole gate, and left Suze talking to Tony about *her* interests and observations, I sat and drank more coffee and worried about back-ups.

There were several methods, in principle, of taking back-ups: non-invasive scanning techniques for the living, smart-matter infusions for the dying or newly dead. The end result of all of them was a stored snapshot of the brain's state, down to the last neuron and synapse. This state could be replicated in a 'blank' brain, usually but not necessarily that of a forced-grown clone of the original. The Outwarders had perfected this process long ago, back in the twenty-fifties, and we'd learned it from them. They'd subsequently perfected the far trickier task of 'running' the copied mind, advancing the recorded brain-state from its final instant to the next instant, and the next . . . whether in control of a robot body, or in a virtual environ-ment, or in some combination of both. This they called uploading, and this we did not do. It required the cooperation of autonomous artificial intelli-gence, and it had a logic of its own which led—unless interrupted by main force—to the Singularity, the Rapture of the nerds as Tony had called it.

Because: once the mind was out of the meat, once it was running in sili-con rather than carbon, and surrounded with artificial intelligences that could give it every assistance, there was nothing to stop its running a thou-sand times faster, and expanding its capabilities—its available knowledge, its sensorium, its memory storage and access—just by *plugging more stuff in*. The uploaded mind could be upgraded, and every upgrade made the next more feasible, and quicker to implement. That way led to runaway artificial intelligence excursion: Singularity.

The Outwarders had regarded this as no bad thing, and the supplanting of humanity as long overdue. We, the ones who'd intended, for whatever reason, to remain human, might even have been convinced. The haunting thought that uploads had no thoughts, no souls; that they were flatlines, mindless emulations of the mind, that subjectivity was (as the finder Shin Se-Ha had wryly said) 'an emergent property of carbon', might have come to seem absurd even to us; were it not for the fact that the supposed super-humans had almost all, to all appearances, gone mad; and the exceptions, the survivors of Project Jove who became the Jovians, had gone bad.

Bad for us, anyway.

The experience, and the long, low-level conflict that followed, had hard-ened our first quibbles and quarrels with the Outwarders (way back when they'd been of the same flesh as ourselves) into a theory which—as Malley had pointed out—was embarrassingly like an ideology: machines don't think, they calculate; only people count; uploads are flatlines, and copies are not originals.

Which, for anyone contemplating taking a back-up, was a disturbing thought. For anyone who woke up to find that they *were* a copy taken from a back-up, it was even more disturbing.

So I had been told; and soon enough, if my proposed encounter with the new Jovian entities went badly, I would know for myself.

Or rather . . . somebody else would, somebody just like me, with my name, my face, my memories, including my memory of thinking this very thought. I wished her well.


Up on the command deck Malley was sitting in an acceleration couch with its back tilted up to make a seat. Yeng sat in a similarly adjusted couch sev-eral yards away. In front of each of them was a computer interface screen of a type standard throughout the Union and the Division. It was made of two sheets of thin, tough glass, about three feet by two, with a quarter-inch thick layer of multicoloured liquid between them. The multicoloured liquid was nothing but clear water swarming with nanomachines, which scurried about and held up fine particles in various colours, according to in-structions transmitted by chemical and electrical impulses, thus forming the graphics, the moving pictures, and the text.

Malley's screen was blank except for a scrolling block of text. His fingers moved along the pad angled at the base of the screen. I couldn't distinguish whether he was writing or reading, or whether the symbols on the screen were our data or his calculations. His pipe jutted from the corner of his mouth, and small puffs of smoke rose from it every few seconds, each puff drifting gently upwards until the current from the ventilation whipped it away. I knew better than to talk to him, and I doubt he would have talked back.

Yeng, however, looked up at me and seemed eager to discuss what she was doing. She shifted on her seat and motioned to me to sit down. There was plenty of room, though I took up more of it than Yeng did.

One of the advantages that this kind of computer had over the old-fashioned, and dangerously vulnerable, electronic computer was that it doubled as an engineering workshop and biochemical laboratory. You could physically isolate a little box—a fixel, it was called—on the screen, and set up an entire nanofacturing complex. It might be too small to see, but it was a small matter to get the rest of the screen to display what was going on.

The screen I was looking at displayed a line along the top, and a dozen or so columns. Yeng pointed. 'Latest variant of their radio transmission,' she said. 'Signal lasts ten seconds. I'm testing it against an array of input devices—radio, television, radar receiver, mechanical computers of various sizes that might pick it up accidentally—even human visual pigments. Running.'

The message was played, in a silent and invisible pulse represented by a wavefront advancing from the line at the top of the screen to the top of the array of columns. All the devices handled it—or completely failed to react to it—except one, whose column started flashing. Yeng cleared the rest and enlarged that view. Trapped in the circuits of a miniaturized version of our standard radar input, the signal had set up a standing-wave pattern which, as soon as Yeng connected the radar with a clutch of nanocomputers, duly propagated into them and burnt them out.

'Nasty,' I said. 'They're hacking babbages now. That's new.'

Yeng smiled. 'Indeed, but I think I can see a way to neutralize it.' She tagged the message, and moved on to a fixel containing a complex organic molecule, large numbers of which had recently been detected escaping from the Jovian atmosphere. That molecule turned out to have the interesting property of jamming the gears of one of our hull-maintenance nanobots.

'Hmm,' said Yeng, sucking the end of a strand of her long blue-black hair. 'Must have picked on something of ours that drifted the other way. Unless the meshing is accidental, which seems unlikely.' She called up a 3-D model of the gearing mechanism. 'Hmm,' she said again. I decided it was time to leave her alone.

'Messages for you,' Yeng said.

It was the morning of the fourth day out. We had settled into a routine. There wasn't much for the crew to do, apart from reading, watching moving

pictures, looking out at the stars, playing games or music and trying to seduce Suze into the constant slow dance of our convoluted relationships.
Malley was now engrossed in studying recorded observations of the wormhole Gate, gazing for hours at the strange images, then departing to stare at
a sheet of paper which was, very gradually, filling up with pencilled equations. Yeng was working her way through decades of predesigned anti-viral
software, updating the programs, throwing them into battle with trapped
Outwarder viruses (some of them computer viruses, some of them almost
literally biological viruses, molecular engines of destruction) and breeding
from the survivors. (And *that* Darwinian process had to be watched, too—
for what better way to infiltrate a system than to subtly direct, through manipulating the virus attacks, the evolution of its anti-infiltration software?)

She'd just taken a break to check our mailbox. The few unavoidable real-
time communications, mostly on arrival and departure, were handled more
directly, through the comms rig—though even there the defensive barriers
had to be active. The mailbox was for less-urgent or personal messages, and
each of them went through a cryptographic quarantine whose processing
kept billions of nanotech babbages busy for seconds on end. She passed me
a small vial containing a culture of nanomachines on which the incoming
laser communications had been recorded and decrypted.

My suit ate it, and played the messages over my eyes.

'You are in deep trouble, Ellen May Ngwethu,' the first message began,
without preliminary. The face of Sylvester Tatsuro, current chairman of
the Command Committee, frowned upon me. 'The Research Committee
has just passed a vote of no confidence in you, so you're no longer our liaison with the social admin. They've asked us to divert a clipper to Lagrange
to pick up a representative of the Solar Council, no less, who will be heading out here to investigate personally what's been going on. There's a lot of
concern about our possible intentions.' He allowed himself a brief smile.
'Which no one outside the Division knows yet. Our self-discipline has held
the line, *so far*. But the Earth Defence bodies are indulging their usual jealous pique towards us, and arousing all kinds of suspicions. Fortunately they
have the wrong end of the stick entirely, in that they're hinting that we've
become appeasers! Apparently your clumsy extraction of Malley has caused
something of a sensation, and various people who saw you talking to Wilde
have been speculating in public. Naturally, the genuine appeasers are making a big thing of this, suggesting that we've seen sense at last and are about
to open contact with the Jovians. I've put out a communiqué saying that's
the last thing we'll consider, and that our vigilance remains as high as ever.'
Another quick smile. 'I didn't see my way clear yet to point out that we're
on a *higher* alert than ever. And just to wrap up, Ellen, all this talk has
aroused interest in Jupiter, and one or two astronomers on Farside have

been jolted out of their routine rut and are looking closely at the planet for the first time in decades. They've already noticed some . . . oddities.

'You have, in short, stirred up a hornets' nest. We're all giving you covering fire, of course, but when you arrive you'll have some explaining to do. I don't expect any reply to this message, by the way. Be seeing you, comrade.'

There was a pause of perhaps a second before the image closed down. In that moment, Tatsuro's head inclined in what could have been a nod, his eyelid flickered in what could have been a wink.

Weeks ago, we had come to a private agreement on what to do, if the worst came to the worst: Plan B. It was something we dared not talk about; even thinking about it made me uneasy. But whatever my mistakes, Tatsuro needed me to carry it out. He would defend me against accusations—give, as he'd said, covering fire.

That I still had his confidence was the only comfort I could draw. The rest of the message left me uncomfortable and indignant. I held off from allowing myself any further reaction and let the suit play the next message.

It was from Carla, of the Thames river patrol. The view was of her sitting in a small room, with screens and papers lying around.

'Message to Ellen May Ngwethu on the *Terrible Beauty*,' she began, awkwardly. 'Uh, Ellen, I shouldn't really be telling you this, but hey, you seemed pretty sound. I've found out why you didn't get a response to your calls for assistance from Alexandra Port. There were a couple of neighbours from Earth Defence around there just about the same time, warning about some radio communications going on among the non-cos, and the possibility of Jovian viruses leaking through. Well, we all saw that the non-cos were using radios, and it turns out that Alexandra Port and the river patrol and so on had all had an emergency shut-down when all that radio babble started, just in case.

'The Earth Defence chaps have been talking to our committee, and it seems they were investigating that man you picked up, Dr Malley. They were waiting to see what he would do, and I have to say they were not best pleased when *Terrible Beauty* suddenly swooped down and carried him off. They're kicking up a bit of a stink about it, and it's all over the discussion tubes back here.'

She stopped and sighed. 'To tell you the truth, Ellen, they're saying Malley and the Division have been in cahoots for some time, and that all those radios the non-cos were using so carelessly were encouraged by Malley—and yourselves—as part of some scheme to try out the effects of people picking up Jovian communications—*testing* them on the poor non-cos, rather than on our own people. You can imagine what a fuss that's causing.'

I could, all right.

'Well,' Carla concluded, 'I'll have to leave it at that. I'm sure it's all some big misunderstanding, so it's over to you now. All the best.' She gave a rather forced smile and I saw her hand reaching forward to switch the recorder off.

Yeng's concerned face came into view as the virtual image faded out. 'Are you all right?'

'I'm fine,' I said, standing up.

'It's not any . . . personal bad news, is it?'

I smiled and put my arm around her shoulders. 'No, Yeng, it's nothing like that. Just a little political problem, is all.'

After a watchful moment she turned back to her screen. I stood looking at her back, and at the equally oblivious Malley, for a few seconds, then I sought out Tony. He was lounging on one of the side benches in the commissary, reading a book—I could see his eyes saccade, scanning the invisible page. He blinked it away as he heard my approaching steps, and raised his eyebrows. By way of reply I inclined my head slightly towards the corner table, where Boris was talking to Suze, over a rapidly emptying bottle of ice-clouded vodka and a couple of glasses. He was matching her sips with gulps.

Tony gave me a small nod, flashed five fingers and returned to his book. I picked up a coffee and climbed up the stairwell, past the command deck to the sleeping gallery, and into my room. Five minutes later, as signalled, Tony followed. He tapped on the hatch and ducked in, and sat down in front of me on the spread quilt of my outer suit.

'Still going for the mumsy look, I see,' he remarked. 'Mmm, I don't know if I can contain my lust.'

'You'd better,' I said. 'There's something under all this that seems to be containing *me*—'

'Oh, stop it . . . anyway, Ellen, I don't suppose you asked me here to tear it off you, so . . .'

He listened to my summary of the two messages. Then he lay back and stared up at the ceiling, his hands clasped behind his head.

'I think we've been set up,' he said. 'The Earth Defence . . . comrades . . . are probably trying to muscle in on our patch. *They* don't think we're going for appeasement, no way, nor that we're doing *human experiments* on the non-cos. They think we have some kind of plan to win the war while nobody's looking, take all the credit, declare the Solar System up for grabs, and grab a big chunk of it ourselves.'

I stared at him. 'Earth Defence think *we* are tooling up for a . . . what, a counter-revolution? Dissolving the Solar Union? That's crazy.'

'It's part of their job to worry about that sort of thing,' Tony said.

'All right, I'll take your judgement on that one. But what I most want to ask you—'

'Yes?'

'—is what you've found out about our little sweetie.'

'Ah, modesty forbids,' Tony said gallantly. 'But apart from that: she's basically just a nice girl. She's grown up in the Union, and she can't really imagine anything different. Because all the conflicts she's ever actually been in *have* been settled by discussion, literally around a table.'

He sighed. 'Passionate global debates about what species to bring back this year. It's a bit . . . disorienting, talking to someone so young. It's been a long time since I gave anyone the third degree, and I wasn't giving her anything like that—'

He smiled, looking somewhere else.

'Notwithstanding any screams you may have heard.'

'Do lay off. You think she's clear?'

'Yes. I'd say she's just a nice, normal girl who doesn't know how tough life can be. The youth of today, eh?'

'There is one thing she's . . . hard about,' I said. 'She wants the virus blanketing to stop. She wants expansion.'

'She told you that?'

'No,' I said. 'I guessed.'

'Well, you guessed right. She told me she's really excited about New Mars.'

'So is Sam Malley,' I said. 'And he did tell me that. Maybe if what Suze really wants, deep down, is an end to the standoff, then—'

'She might be winnable on our way of ending it, if it comes to that?'

'Yes. And she might have an influence on how Malley sees it, especially if—well, they do have a lot in common.'

Tony stared at me, the bioluminescence sending bands of light down his face. 'You are incorrigible, Ellen.'

I shrugged. 'I must admit he's looking and smelling better every day—'

'You really do owe me one if I lose Suze's sweet young body to that old reactionary.'

'If you insist.'

'Anyway,' he added a minute later, 'we can't have the gang thinking we're having a secretive discussion, or something.'

'No,' I agreed, trying to find the release-spot for the most impenetrable of the suit's inner layers. 'People might talk.'

That evening I sought out Suze after dinner, and settled down with her in a corner.

'Interesting conversation with Boris?'

Her glance shone. 'He's amazing! An actual Sheenisov veteran! I've never met one of them before. It's like . . . history talking to you.'

'Well,' I said, 'it isn't always reliable history. Boris's memories may have got a bit screwed up along the way.'

(This was the charitable interpretation.)

'What! No tribes of folks with two heads? No yetis? No lost legions of reanimated US/UN casualties?' She smiled.

'I'm afraid not. Not as he describes them, anyway. There *were* weird things on the steppe and in the European forests, and hallucinogen weapons were among them. That, we know for sure, so we can't be too sure about the rest.'

'Yeah, I know,' Suze said, sounding regretful. 'Anyway.' She peered at me from under her brow. 'You didn't come to talk about the battle of democracy. You came to talk about the battle that's coming up.'

'That's true,' I admitted. 'I'm sorry to be so—'

'It's all right,' Suze said. 'I've had these conversations in the past. You say something *way* out of line, and nothing will happen except folks will argue, maybe, but sure as nature you'll find one of the old comrades dropping by for a friendly chat to put you straight.'

'I'm not one of the old comrades!'

'Oh, but you are,' Suze said. 'I'd know that look anywhere. Tolerance that comes from total confidence that you're right.'

I had to smile and nod and shrug to this, because I knew that look myself; even if I'd never recognized it in the mirror.

'OK, Suze, the fact is—we *have* to win. They've been plaguing us, we've been zapping them, for centuries. Nobody has ever said we shouldn't be doing it. This is just . . . finishing the job.'

Suze looked troubled. 'Yes, but it's so final! Everything will change.'

I nodded briskly. 'That's right. But if we don't, everything will change, but for the worse. This way, things will change for the better. We'll be able to expand properly at last. And we have to. Have you *seen* how many kids people are having?'

Suze smiled wryly. 'Yeah. But what you're proposing reminds me of . . . things I've read about, from the old time. *Lebensraum*. Manifest Destiny. All that.'

I almost regretted coming (almost) clean with her and Malley. But this kind of argument would have to be had, and soon, with everybody. When the Solar Council representative arrived, he or she would not be fooled, and would tell everybody. Then the water would hit the fuel-rods in a big way.

'It isn't like that, Suze,' I said. 'Honestly. The Outwarders—the Jovians aren't people. They're nothing like people. They're just smart computer viruses, and this is our chance to wipe the disk for good. And if we don't take that chance—' I hesitated here, because this was the core of the Division's morale, our Central Dogma, and it didn't go over well with folk who'd led more sheltered lives '—they'll destroy us, or use us, as soon as *they* get the chance. It's them or us.'

Suze looked thoughtful. 'OK, I can see that,' she said. 'I try to imagine my mind being taken over, like happened to the old computers back in the Crash, and—' She shuddered. 'I'd do anything to prevent that. I'd rather die.'

'Good on you,' I said. 'But it won't come to that, because we'd rather *kill*.'

'But you'll try to talk first? As you promised?'

And as our own chairman had almost promised we wouldn't.

'Of course,' I said.

Our conversation moved on to less weighty subjects, and when we parted after a few drinks I was fairly sure that the tried and tested technique of the friendly chat from one of the old comrades still had a lot to be said for it.

# 6

## VALHALLA

'It's funny,' Suze said. 'I always imagined Jupiter from Callisto would fill half the sky, and that everything else would be dark.'

'You're getting blasé, girl,' I told her. 'Jupiter's more than a million miles away, and it still looks big enough to me.'

It was 08.48 GMT on the tenth day. We were in a low orbit around Callisto, its surface of cratered ice with its characteristic appearance of pellet-struck glass. Valhalla's bull's-eye shock-rings slid by below us, giant Jove rose above the horizon in front of us. On both bodies the works of mind were evident: the honeycomb upwellings of the Jovian hive, still monstrous to my eyes after two centuries; on Callisto the bright green-and-gold bubbles of the equatorial crater villages, the dark towers of the defence-lasers, the long white lines of the mass-driver tracks along which blocks of ice were hurtled into space. Callisto has four times more water in its icy crust than Earth has in all its oceans; slingshot around Jupiter, those blocks of ice were sent on slow transfer orbits to the Inner System—the water we'd picked up in Earth orbit had come all the way from here, and it was *still* worth doing; far more efficient than hauling water up Earth's deep gravity-well or scraping frost from Luna's polar shadows.

Between this outermost of Jupiter's major moons and the planet itself was the ring: the near edge showing at this angle and distance as unbelievably sparse lights, which, as the eye took in the longer view, combined to form what seemed a solid crescent band of white. The sun was still recognizably the sun, but its light was just bright enough to look like broad daylight, not so bright it dazzled and burned; much more natural than it looks from Earth.

'Everybody strap in!' yelled Andrea. 'Braking in two minutes!'

We launched ourselves away from the wide CCTV screen and towards the couches. I strapped in and reached out for the still-floundering Suze, and pushed her gently to her place. She wallowed, grabbed, and turned. Malley had stayed strapped in throughout our minutes in free fall. His eyelids were closed tight, their compression forming the only wrinkles in his rejuvenated face. He and Suze were now on a par, physiologically, but his reflexes, the habits and expectations of his nervous system, remained those of a man who'd lived two hundred and sixty years in the same one gravity. Suze, with less to unlearn, was adapting quicker.

'Braking burn in ten, nine, eight . . .'

There was no real need for a countdown, but Andrea too had old habits. The deceleration this time was shorter and less severe than the acceleration from Earth. *Terrible Beauty* came down and settled into its landing cradle like a well-caught egg. The silence left by the sudden absence of the unheard note of the drive was filled with ominous creaking noises.

'Water melts under the torch,' I told Suze and Malley. 'That's it refreezing. The cradle we're resting on has legs that go deep into the ice, so we're quite safe.'

We all stood up and grinned at each other and bounced around a bit in the low gravity, shouting and caromming off each other and generally acting as if a weight had just been taken off us, which it had. Suze and Malley stared at us and made cautious, experimental little hops.

'It's good to be home,' I said, passing out air-tanks like bottles of champagne. I clapped mine to the front of my suit and the suit's surface flowed around it.

'That's all there is to it?' Malley asked.

I nodded, guiding them through the equally rapid and simple processes of making the suits vacuum-ready. My own suit absorbed some of its more exuberant embellishments as it shrank to fit. I could feel the inner layers flowing away from their nightwear images to a more functional chin-to-toe insulating one-piece. I pulled the hood over my head and murmured, 'Helmet up.'

'You look very funny,' Suze said. She looked around. 'I guess we all do.'

'It's practical,' I said. 'The colours make you more visible out on the surface. In accidents and emergencies, that can save your life.'

'Yeah,' said Malley, gesturing at his magenta carapace. 'You wouldn't want to be seen dead in it.'

We made our way to the airlock and went through in pairs to a lift-platform cranked up by the landing cradle. I took Suze through with me and as we waited for the others she gazed around at the landing-field. We were a hundred feet above the surface, and had a good view of miles of flat and dirty ice, dozens of gantries and landing cradles, scores of crawling vehicles, and hundreds of people in their bright suits, looking from this height like an anomalous species of idiosyncratic, multicoloured ants. One of Valhalla's ring-walls marked the horizon. Ice-blocks from a distant mass-driver soared overhead like meteors going the wrong way at a rate of about one a minute.

I felt, as always on returning here, a sense of homecoming, literally light-headed at being safely back and only minutes away from the warm human tumult of the ice-caverns, and an absurd gratitude to the godless, mindless forces that had placed this precious oasis of water so conveniently within the reach of man. The first wave of space-settlers had a saying, something between a litany and a running joke, which went: 'If God had meant us to go into space, he'd have given us the Moon; if he'd meant us to terraform, he'd have given us Mars; if he'd meant us to mine asteroids, he'd have given us the Belt; if he'd meant us to colonize, he'd have given us Callisto.' And so on. The details, and the name and gender of the deity allegedly responsible varied, but the message was the same. There were even attempts to reformulate it in more philosophically correct terms, as a special case of the anthropic principle, but they always struck me as rather forced.

If there was, as almost everybody now thought, no God, then all one could honestly say was that the human race was just unbelievably lucky. There had to be some winner of the cosmic lottery, some species which every chance event, from the passing of the dinosaurs to the coming of the ice, had worked to bring about, and then to light the fire of reason; and on whose birth as a space-going people the configuration of the planets had been favourable, and the stars themselves had smiled: the true horoscope of our real destiny, infinitely greater than anything imagined in the petty prognostications of astrology.

Other life was certain: the Solar System was dusty with organics, and on extra-solar planets our best telescopes could see the biospheres; Wilde's reported New Mars had multicellular organisms, fossil beds and coal. Other minds there might be; but the great silence of the sky spoke with an unanswerable unanimity. Whatever triumphs these other minds had attained, radio communication and space travel were not among them. The stars were ours alone.

I looked out over the busy, cluttered, cheerful scene of the landing field, watching as a covered walkway to the nearest tunnel mouth rolled itself out towards us. Two by two the others joined me, leaning on the platform's guardrail, silent in their own thoughts. My helmet's newly built laser-link buzzed.

'This is a bleak place,' said Suze.


We travelled from the landing field by descending elevator and rapid tunnel-train to the Division HQ at Valhalla base, six miles from the field and a mile under the ice. The elevator's descent was for much of the way a free fall, with only a gradual deceleration at the lower end. The tunnel-train, likewise, was able to coast for most of its journey on blades like skates, running in channels of perpetually melted and refrozen ice. On the way, Malley asked about ice-quakes; I told him Callisto was the most stable of the major moons. He didn't look reassured. All those recent-looking craters can give the wrong impression.

The Division HQ was a warren of tunnels and chambers lined with a spray-on insulation which smelled faintly of tar and which was coloured according to a scheme so complex that it had been abandoned as soon as it was implemented. We stood outside the inner door of the main airlock while our helmets scrolled down. The air was cool, carrying more of the smell of humans and machines, and less of plants and recyclers, than that of the ship. The distant vibration of air-pumps could be heard, and felt through the floor.

Ahead of us a hundred yards of bright-lit yellow corridor extended to a junction with a blue corridor. Along that corridor people passed every few seconds, in the familiar low-gee stride known as the 'lunar lope.' To allow for the upper part of the lope's trajectory, the corridor roofs were never lower than about nine feet high.

'No guards?' Malley asked. 'No reception?'

'We don't—' began Suze; was stopped by Malley's gesture and smile. 'OK, OK.'

The crew members were all changing their suits into low-gee styles. Suze let her suit revert to the default fatigues and pack. I went for blue fake-leather trousers and top, a crinkly transparent blouson, and a shoulder-bag. Malley surprised me, and possibly himself, with a Medieval-scholar ensemble of leggings, breeches, tunic and cloak with a lot of black fur.

I led the way along the corridor, turned left, then along until the blue changed to a red-and-white tiling, looked at the hand-lettered sign tacked to the wall, turned right at the next junction and stopped at the door of the newly hacked emergency meeting-room. Here, at least, there was a guard, a man in heavy armour, armed with a couple of pistols and a light machine gun. He recognized me and nodded.

'We're expected,' I said.

I knocked and went in. Expected we might be, but those present were busy at their tasks, and it took a few minutes before a meeting could be convened around the table that occupied the first section of the big room. It was a long table, eighteen feet by six, and it had about twenty chairs around it. The part of the room it occupied was tacky with fresh insulation. Behind it was a display screen and a cluster of terminals, and behind that a bank of medium-scale babbages whose gentle clicking and whirring filled any silences. About a dozen people were working among them, looking somewhat harassed: as members of the Command Committee, principles notwithstanding, they didn't have much recent experience of such low-level tasks. The far end of the room abutted on raw ice, and dozens of robots were working at extending the room, melting the ice face, draining off the water, filtering out the organics, uncoiling cables and power lines into freshly melted ducts and applying insulation behind the advancing front of their activity. Beneath the insulation, the new stuff in the walls would eventually freeze into place.

Sylvester Tatsuro was the first to look up from the babbage which he was laboriously programming and come over to greet us. He was a small and stocky man, with receding black hair which he'd never bothered to replace, and narrow dark eyes. He was wearing a sort of belted robe in green fur. His sleeves were studded with display-units, and he had a small control bank hung from a strap around his neck.

He shook hands with Malley, nodded at Suze, and turned to me.

'Why is she here?'

'I want her here,' I said. 'Voice but not vote, obviously. I met her by chance, but she's been helpful, and I think she has a point of view which may be useful for us to hear.'

Tatsuro shrugged. 'She's your responsibility,' he said. 'If you wish to retain her as an adviser, that's fine.'

'I've joined the Division,' Suze said.

'Welcome, comrade,' said Tatsuro. 'But on this committee, you're strictly an adviser. You may leave whenever you wish, but no unauthorized communication outside the Division is permitted. Any such will be noticed at once, and action taken.' He smiled briefly. 'I sound like a cop from the old time reading your rights—but I'm sure you understand why this rule is necessary.'

'Of course, neighbour,' Suze said. 'I understand. I feel very proud to be here.'

'Good,' said Tatsuro, smiling with every appearance of sincerity. 'As to the rest of your gang—' he added, speaking to me.

'My crew stays,' I said.

After a moment of eye-lock, he nodded.

'What's going on here?' Malley asked, indicating the far end of the room.

Tatsuro glanced around. 'We're setting up the information filters for the

return data from the probes that are due to enter the Jovian atmosphere in
a few hours,' he said. 'Naturally most of the detailed processing will be
done by our scientific teams, but we get the first look. The first chance to
make sure there are no mind-viruses present.' He smiled thinly. 'One of the
privileges of our position.'

'Spoken like a good socialist,' said Malley.

Tatsuro responded with a half-smile and a shrug, as if he didn't want to
argue, and rapped loudly on the table.

'Gather round, comrades,' he called out gruffly. 'That stuff can wait.'

One by one the other committee members left off what they were doing
and made their way to the table. I indicated to the other crew members that
they should spread out among the committee rather than sit in a group, and
I myself sat down between Malley and Suze, with Tatsuro at right angles to
me, not across. I was not going to give him even the slight advantage of sitting opposite me, if he wanted to make this a confrontation over my actions
back on Earth.

It seemed he didn't. The first item on the agenda was, of course, us; but
the committee—all familiar faces, some old friends—listened to my summary account with only a few questions. It was when I mentioned my agreement with Malley that the frowning and muttering began.

'Contact hasn't been in any way considered,' said Tatsuro. 'It implicitly
changes the basis on which we're acting. It re-opens questions which were
settled long ago.'

'Circumstances have changed,' I said. 'I have little confidence in getting
anywhere with the Jovians, but if it's what Dr Malley here needs to convince him to share his work with us, I'm more than willing to try.'

Tatsuro shook his head. 'It's far too dangerous. We can't afford to lose
you, Ellen, and we can't let some *negotiation* lose us time.'

'We can continue preparations for the impact event,' I said. 'Contact, if
it should happen, need not get in the way. If there are negotiations, I imagine they can be complete before the impact event, and in time to avert it if
they're successful. If there are post-human minds down there, one thing we
know is they'd think fast. And as for the danger, well—is it any worse than
making direct observations?'

'If I may?' Yeng said. Nods around the table. 'It is worse, Ellen—with
communication you necessarily open yourself more than with observation,
and give more away. But I've strengthened the firewalls, and this—' she
waved at the back of the room '—has obviously been set up to filter incoming observations, and to isolate them.'

'Correct,' growled Tatsuro.

'So between them,' Yeng went on, 'it should be more than enough. But
I recommend a back-up, just in case.'

We argued for about an hour, but finally it was agreed. And once we'd come to agreement—a consensus, in fact; there wasn't even the need for a vote—those of us directly involved went straight to work, while the meeting went on.

Yeng applied the back-up process—the equipment was to hand, because whoever had drawn the short straw, or volunteered, to handle the close-up observations would have needed one anyway. It took forty minutes, every second of which were, for me, deeply unpleasant: it starts with a tendril up a nostril, and ends with a painkiller for the worst headache you can imagine, a real migraine and *petit mal* combined, with thunder in your ears and a dirty yellow lightning in your eyes, as the pain flips over into synaesthesia.

And then it fades, to a dull relief. I stood looking at the cubic inch of smart-matter in my hand, within which my soul was stored, until the tiny block was absorbed seamlessly into the suit, vanishing like a cheap trick: nothing up my sleeve.

'Takes it out of you,' Yeng observed sympathetically; then we both saw the ambiguity, and laughed. I felt better, and stood up. The Command Committee had moved on to discussing the forthcoming visit from the Solar Council delegate. As usual in the Division, they were quite capable of focusing on one thing at a time, and leaving those who were implementing a previous decision to get on with it.

During my backing-up ordeal the television screen had been moved to one side, and Malley was using it to observe the Gate up close and in real-time. The Gate's outline was clearer now than on the old recordings, because over several decades we'd cautiously attached an array of instruments and rockets around its circumference. The instruments we used for observation, the rockets to shift its location, gradually boosting it from low Jupiter orbit to its present position among the outer moons. The current image on the screen came from a fighter among the usual swarm that stood watch.

Where the television screen had been was now a smaller screen showing incoming Mission Control data about, rather than from, the shower of probes currently converging on the planet; and a control deck and wraparound helmet, for the privileged individual who was about to follow them down.

'I've reprogrammed some of these remotely,' said Yeng. 'They're standard gas-giant divers. There's a prerecorded message—just a hailing and query—for you to fire off on the wavelengths the Jovians use for what we think are their communications, and an isolated core for any reply.'

'How will I know which ones to fix on?'

'They're the only ones you'll get through to. Don't worry, they're a big enough fraction of the total for you to have a good chance of getting close.'

'OK,' I said. I looked at the Mission Control display. 'Five minutes to entry. Here goes nothing.'

Malley turned from his own screen and gave me a thumbs up as I sat down and put on the VR helmet.

Jupiter loomed, and in I fell.

It was the clarity of the light that struck me first. I knew intellectually what to expect, but I'd got used to seeing Jupiter from above, and from far away, as a roiling mass of clouds and upwellings. Close up, the scale of the spaces between those clouds was a visceral shock. There were chasms between the pillars of cloud in which Earth could fall in sunlight all the way to the metallic-hydrogen core.

The hundreds of probes, elaborate but expendable, stamped out like bottle-caps in the nanofactories, were passively aerodynamic: gliders with the shape and approximate size of stone arrowheads, their faceted surfaces glittering like chipped chert, their shafts the thin rods in which the drogues were stacked. The filaments of their aerials trailed behind them, parallel to the shafts. The probe heads had ailerons and rudders, so their flight could be controlled, but with a minimum two-way delay of twelve seconds such control could only be gross.

As they hit atmosphere at a hundred thousand miles per hour I was flicking from probe to probe, seeking out ones that seemed to be heading in interesting directions. The first one on which I settled was spiralling down in a clear updraft in which one of the bubble-clusters (I was not prepared, yet, to call them 'cities') was drifting upwards. I tagged another, which headed straight for one of the 'walls' of the convection cells, and stayed with the first as it descended. The pink and orange clouds streaked past.

Behind me—as I couldn't help thinking—the drogues deployed one by one, and one by one were whipped away. By the time the last had gone, the probe had slowed to a mere fifty thousand miles per hour and was two hundred miles deep in the atmosphere, hurtling in a tightening circle down the well of clear hydrogen towards the bubble-cluster. I nudged the probe's control surfaces and brought its descent almost to a halt, circling the cluster like a stacked airliner. The bubble-cluster was a thousand miles in diameter, made up of hundreds of translucent bubbles. This much our telescopes had already shown; and the hint of movement within.

Closer . . . now I could see the black threads, each at least a quarter of a mile wide, which radiated from the cluster and vanished into the cloud walls. That the threads connected with other such clusters seemed incredible, given the distances involved—but the only other explanation, that they were some kind of intake and/or outlet pipes, was so far without evidence, tempting as the thought that they were mere sewers and ventilators might be.

Closer still . . . the apparent translucence of the bubbles sharpened to transparency: multiple hexagonal panes set in a lattice of sturdy-looking white struts. Behind them was movement, unmistakable, definite. I hit the 'send' key and swooped around again. On a reckless impulse I slewed the probe into a close pass across the top of the bubble-cluster. All I saw, of course, was a minute-long blur, followed by darkness as the probe plunged into the clouds.

I disconnected from the probe and flicked to the data, running the recording in slow motion, stepping it down and down until I seemed to be drifting along; increasing the magnification until each panel was as clear and close as a cockpit window.

And saw behind those windows—looking out, crowding, visibly following the tiny object's flashing flight—deep violet eyes in gigantic faces, faces sweet and calm as those of any imagined angels. Their bodies too were like angels': with long, trailing cascades of gold or silver or copper hair, and sweeping diaphanous robes of rainbow light, each breastplated with a sunburst of jewelled filigree. Their features weren't sexless, or androgynous— they were differentiated into the variant ideals of masculine and feminine beauty. The interior of the bubble glowed and flickered with the radiance of their beating wings. Not like the wings of insects, or birds, or bats, but perfect parabolas, curved like magnetic fields, shimmering like polar lights; wings made from aurorae.

As I watched, they changed, flowing into the shapes of fantastic fish, of floating multicoloured scarves, of showers of flowers, of flaring fireworks. The vision ended as the probe passed beyond the cluster.

I replayed it, this time accompanying the images with the message I'd sent, and found that a response had been received. I hesitated, then went ahead and ran it through the firewall filters. What came out was not any kind of virus, but a quite straightforward message composed and sent repeatedly as a second-long sequence of English. The machines stretched out the burst, sampled it to a sound that sang in my ears, letters that shone before my eyes:

'Responding to probe: we welcome your message. Standing by for further communication. Informally—hi guys and gals! It's been a long time! Let's talk! See you soon!'

The beauty of the Jovians, the warmth—and indeed the colloquial informality—of their message, should have been enough to melt all hostility, all suspicion. The gaiety of their display, the tones of welcome and love in their voice, made me yearn to see them and speak to them again. I ducked out of the VR helmet and put it down and looked up at Yeng. I could feel my cheeks strained with smiles, damp with tears. Yeng smiled at me and glanced above my head. I swivelled the gimballed seat and found the rest of the crew and of the Command Committee crowded behind me.

'Well?' said Tatsuro. 'You made contact?'

'Yes,' I said. My voice quivered.

'No hacking? No viruses?'

Yeng shook her head. 'It's all clean,' she said. 'No viruses.'

'None at all,' I said. 'See for yourselves. Look and tell me if those aren't the most beautiful creatures you've ever seen. They're . . . ravishing. Seductive.' I sighed, remembering. 'And obviously capable of communicating with us. Whatever they've gone through, they've kept some continuity with humanity.'

The images I'd seen were replayed again, this time on the screen. Suze and Malley watched them, rapt. The crew and the Committee studied them more warily.

'What do you think?' asked Tatsuro. The others were, for a moment, too absorbed in what they'd seen to speak, so I got in first.

'Why don't we have a look at some of the other Jovians?' I said. 'The ones I *wasn't* in contact with. Let's see how typical this is, before jumping to conclusions.'

Reluctantly the others pulled themselves out of their contemplative admiration, and set to work. A few probes had passed as close, or closer, to other bubble-clusters as had the one I'd been tracking, and images of the clusters' inhabitants could be extracted. Their appearances varied widely, and changed rapidly as we watched. The 'angel' form I'd first encountered was among them, but there were many others no less beautiful. The most common basic shape resembled a butterfly, with the parabolic, colourful wings, like those of the 'angels', extending from a central column or core. The sunburst shape, which on the 'angels' had appeared as a breastplate or pendant, was a feature of all the Jovian entities, though sometimes masked by their current form.

'That jewelled object seems to be your basic Jovian,' I said. 'The CPU, perhaps? It sits in the glowing shape around it like a magnet in its fields—'

'Which it may well be,' said Yeng. 'The wider form is like a controlled aurora, almost a television picture, which the Jovian can vary at will.' She smiled. 'They seem . . . playful, whimsical . . .'

'Jovial!' someone said.

'It suggests,' Tatsuro said seriously, 'a degree of commonality with ourselves that the old Outwarder macros with their amoeboid shapes did not. Their reaction times show that they are still "fast folk" but their appearance is more . . . appealing, and they each seem to be distinct individuals. I have to say that one's automatic reaction to these entities is quite the opposite of

the horror and hatred that the macros seem to incite.' He waved a hand
through some virtual display of his own, creating a sequential display of the
beautiful, flickering images. 'When people see them, I don't think they'll be
as eager to destroy them as we are—or *were*.'

The members of the Command Committee were nodding gravely,
stroking their bearded or beardless chins like peasant elders listening to an
intellectual. I glared at them all, amazed that they could be so swayed.

'Isn't it obvious what's going on here?' I said. '*This* is the mind virus, the
killer meme. The fast folk have simply adapted to an environment that contains humans with more power than they have—for now. Their beauty is a
lure, precisely calculated to trigger our aesthetic reactions. That message,
that display, was their first line of defence. We have to smash through it, or
we're doomed.'

# 7

---

## THE IRON HEEL

That was the start of the argument. The other CC members knew as well as I did that life is a fight in which beauty is a weapon: an instrument of survival, like a baby's cry or a child's smile. They knew that the message I'd recorded—and any other communication—could be the output of a flatline. They knew . . . but why go on? They had the true knowledge.

So I still find it difficult to forgive, or indeed to understand, the next decisions of the Command Committee. Each decision went to a vote, and each vote was carried by twelve to two (me and Joe Lutterloh, our comms specialist). The committee decided: to release all the Jovian images and other probe data to the rest of the Division; to prepare for a direct contact, using a (heavily firewalled) radio link; and to cooperate fully with the Solar Council delegate, due to arrive in three days. There was still plenty of time to deflect the incoming train of Kuiper-Belt comets—all of them had guidance rockets attached, and right up to the last few minutes all it would take to divert them from the usual harmless slingshot swing around Jupiter would be a brief burn.

Tatsuro seemed to win over most of the committee with the argument that there was nothing to lose, and possibly a lot to gain, by doing things this way. The Division had originally intended to present the rest of the Union with a *fait accompli*, to give the Jovians no warning—but we'd known that there might be some problems later. This way, we'd pull the rest of the

Union into the decision. If coexistence with the Jovians turned out to be impossible—or was voted down—then the Jovians would still have no time to react if we went ahead with the bombardment. From the Jovians' point of view, the incoming comets would appear no more threatening than our normal import traffic, until the final, fatal, fine adjustment to their course.

I thought, and argued, that this was assuming rather a lot about their capacities. Unfortunately, by opening the question of negotiation in order to get Malley to cooperate, I'd let the other committee members rediscover any doubts and hesitations they may have had—as well as exposing them to the insidious sight of just how attractive and appealing the Jovian entities could appear. I consoled myself with the thought that Malley's cooperation was, in the long run, the most important thing from my point of view.

The Command Committee's deliberations had been held *in camera* only because of the possible virus threat. With that apparently out of the way, the meeting was as open as all our meetings usually were, and all its decisions were open to appeal to the Division as a whole. The emergency meeting-room would be kept up, however, as an operations room to handle the direct communication. During that contact, it would again be isolated.

Malley, of course, was delighted at how the debate had turned out, and was eager to get on with his study of the wormhole. Suze too seemed pleased by it, and a little relieved when I showed no sign of hostility to her—or to anyone else who disagreed with me. I took my defeats in the votes with every sign of good grace. Inwardly I was seething, but it doesn't take two hundred years to get a grip on that sort of thing. I've been good at it since my teens. (My *late* teens, admittedly.)

As are others. Tatsuro didn't get to be the chairman for nothing. At the end of the meeting he said mildly:

'Ellen, you are obviously not keen to participate in the negotiations, and you have little to contribute to the scientific analysis of the survey data. May I suggest that, until further notice, you continue to work with Doctor Malley, giving him all practical assistance on the wormhole navigation problem?'

I agreed, of course, and the rest of the committee were more than happy to have me occupied in something I agreed with, rather than reluctantly participating in something I didn't.

'We have much to do,' Tatsuro said. 'But I suggest further that the crew of the *Terrible Beauty* take some time to get some sleep. You in particular, Ellen, must be quite exhausted. You can begin work with Doctor Malley in the morning.'

I smiled and nodded. As we rose to leave, Tatsuro turned so that his face was, for a moment, visible only to me. I saw his almost undetectable wink, and knew our concord held.


Suze stayed behind with Malley, who was given a work station at the far end of the room to continue with the wormhole observations. The rest of us headed for the suite which we shared as a crew, though several of us would undoubtedly be going elsewhere tonight. (Night and day in the Callisto caverns had nothing to do with that satellite's inconvenient rotational period— they were arbitrarily based on GMT, like our ship time. For many they had little to do with their sleep patterns, either, which were often based on staggered shifts and distorted by anti-sleep drugs. The latter had a limited usefulness: the circadian rhythm was buried deeper in our cells than our genetic tinkering or pharmaceutical intervention could reach, and the brain's requirement for regular sleep is—though more recent in evolutionary time—even less amendable.)

I stood aside to let the others in, then let the door click into place behind me and leaned back against it. The suite was as we'd left it when we'd been scrambled three weeks earlier. All the items of clothing or crockery left lying around had no doubt been patiently and mindlessly cleaned in our absence, which was just as well. The plants had been dusted and watered. The low ceiling glowed with its familiar dim evening light, the kitchen was humming quietly to itself, and the bedrooms off the lounge were sighing with invitation. The mailbox was politely silent; though probably bursting with messages from our colleagues and friends and forebears and offspring, it knew better than to remind us of this when we'd just come home. I looked around at Boris, Yeng, Tony, Andrea and Jaime.

'I don't know about you, comrades,' I announced, 'but I am not for any discussion. It's been a long day, and a long trip, and we all need some R&R. I'm up for a high-alcohol drink, a low-gee Jacuzzi, and some low-gee sex. In any sequence, all at once, and more than once.'

' "If", "Else", and "Repeat",' Yeng grinned. 'Still the basic program logic.' She caught Tony's hand. 'We'll have a drink, but we're going out.'

'I guess that's decided,' said Tony. He squeezed Yeng's hand, kissed the top of her head, let go her hand and bounded over to the drinks cabinet, where he started dialling up responses to shouted orders. Andrea and Jaime wanted to do their own thing too.

'That leaves us,' I said to Boris. 'So, big gunner, you wanna make it with me, or just leave me with my suit's imagination?'

He put his arm around my shoulders and boosted me towards a couch.

'Ah, Ellen, of course I stay with you. All the girls in all the bars in Callisto . . .'
He paused, looking dreamy and regretful, until I gave him a friendly kick,
'. . . couldn't drag me away from my good lady to whom I'm eternally grateful.'

I first met Boris in 2110, on a military mission to the Sheenisov. We met
on the frozen Lena outside Yatkutsk. He was a giant in furs, I a sexy space-
woman in my new smart-matter spacesuit, with its bubble helmet and black
sheen. An angel more of death than of mercy, I was delivering home-brew
kits for turning Siberian ore and Russian rust into shiny, perfectly ma-
chined small arms. His voice was like black molasses: American accent,
deep, rich; it reminded me of Paul Robeson, and it still does. I could never
forget it, or him.

Over the next nine decades I saw Boris, or he saw me, in many odd circumstances, but I could never stay, and he could never go. Eventually we
found each other in the last battle, against the last believers, the last crazy
altruists to risk their mortal bodies and potentially immortal minds for god
or country or duty or other people's property. I pulled him from a wrecked
and burning tank in the suburbs of Lisbon, and took him with me to orbit
and grew him all back, and I never let go of him again.

'I don't want your gratitude,' I said, reaching up with one hand to grab a tall
vodka-and-ice from Tony, and reaching down with the other. 'That wasn't
why I pulled you out of the tank. It was pure selfish lust, comrade, and that's
what I want from you.'

And that was what I got. We did the If, we did the Else, we did the Repeat, we did the Do Until exhaustion. There are those who swear by free
fall, but give me low-gee any day, or night. There's more *purchase*. As for
one-gee and above . . . it's OK for a bit, but it does you in. How Earth ever
got to its present population, I'll never know. Cloning, possibly.

But eventually, we slept. I dreamt of angels, and sometimes woke with a
start and with memories of other things, and clung to Boris until I rejoined
him in sleep.


It's 2089 and things are falling apart: as below, so above. Every day, every
hour brings a new disaster to our screens, picked up from the dwindling
number of functioning news services and the vastly larger, but also diminishing, numbers of communications amateurs and hackers and pirates. The
net that brought the world together is dying in its arms. It's been years since
any rocket that didn't carry a warhead has lifted from the surface. We're on
our own now: hundreds of thousands of people, millions of bugs and beasts,
more millions of humans and other animals *in potentia* as frozen sperm and
eggs, *in vitro* as cell samples and recorded brain-states; countless digital

ghosts; together they make up the space-based fraction of the biosphere. They add up to millions of eggs in hundreds of baskets; no longer, thankfully, in one. Spread out across near-Earth, Lagrange, Luna, Mars and the Belt, humanity and its animal allies are safe against anything short of a nearby supernova. The sky won't fall, now; but Earth will.

The Green Death is in its early stages. Already, the biomedical laboratories where the only hope of a cure could be found are being put to the torch. The Greens are leading the mobs, happy to divert the unfounded suspicion from themselves. I, at this time, am absolutely convinced that the Greens have deliberately engineered the Death in a genocidal sacrifice to their evil goddess, Gaia.

So, with this awful warning of the consequences of the kind of thinking all of us have always opposed being shown in lurid and distressing detail before our very eyes, the two factions of the space movement, Earth-Tenders and Outwarders, unite in adversity to face the challenges of the future . . . No. We're arguing over resources, we're on the verge of *fighting* over resources—water, primarily. We're bleeding all the solar power we can spare into the capacitors of high-energy lasers. We're checking our nukes.

The Outwarders have—appropriately enough—long since moved out, or been pushed out, from the old near-Earth battlesat in which I still live. They've moved out to Lagrange 4—most of the traditional Space-Movement types, for reasons buried deep in Space-Movement tradition, settled at the other Lagrange point, L5—where they're building the fleet for their Jovian expedition; and they're mining the Moon.

That's one source of conflict. They want Lunar polar water ice for their expedition. We want it for our survival—there's ice out in the Belt, but its transfer-orbit delivery is a slow trickle. The allocation of rights to exploit particular patches of Lunar ice would have been tricky to work out, even with the best of intentions and a decent legal system in place. (Discovery? First use? Present possession? Does the first satellite identification count? The first landing? The first staking-out? The first successful mining-plant?) In these benighted days we're all experts on libertarian property acquisition theory—trouble is, every claim has at least one respectable theory behind it, and a squad of underemployed legal experts in front of it, with guns.

I'm worried about the Lunar polar mines, because my parents—with whom I keep in touch, though we haven't breathed the same air for decades—are managing one of them, on behalf of one of the old Space Movement's front corporations.

Meanwhile, we—the Earth-Tenders—are using up resources in quixotic efforts like orbital medicine-drops (not as useless as it sounds, by the way—we drop medical *nanofactories*) and orbital zaps of whatever military force look like this week's bad guys (big mistake) and servicing communications satellites that would otherwise just *die* (good move, except that the military bad guys [q.v.] use them too). And the Outwarders claim, using whatever theory of property is to their immediate purpose, that at least some of the resources we're allegedly wasting on aid for the stricken populations of Earth belong to *them*. For example, they helped to boost this station to its present orbit; we paid them, but they now claim rent for the *orbit*, back-dated, with interest.

'Fucking property rights,' I say to Tony as I keep an eye on the deep-space radar. 'It's enough to make you turn communist.'

We're seated criss-cross, each looking at a screen behind the other's shoulder, in one of the station's modules that barely has room for both of us, let alone for the tangle of cables and tubes and floating obsolescent equipment. Outside the open hatch of the module, other people are work-ing, moving slowly in the sluggish stale air.

'Hah!' Tony doesn't look away from the computer on which he's collat-ing loyalty checks on the station's eight hundred and fifty-six personnel. 'You're a communist already, Ellen, you just don't know it. When did you ever pay for your supplies, or get paid for your work?'

'Ah, that's, that's different,' I say, waving my hands. I have genuinely never thought of it that way, never given a moment's thought to the way of life in the settlement in which I've been raised—a crowded can at Lagrange called New View—or in the battlesat. 'I mean, that's all just among our-selves. We all know what has to be done, and what we can afford to use, so there's no problem. What I meant—and only as a *joke*, for fuck sake—was that all this crap about who owns what was making me feel a bit . . . *bolshie*, isn't that the word?'

'I see,' says Tony. 'Like the Sheenisov.'

The Sino-Soviet Union, a rabble of collective farmers and Former Union and ex-PLA veterans whose ragged red armies are currently besieging—or, if you listen to their broadcasts, relieving—Sinkiang.

'I thought they were more into restoring democracy.'

'Yeah, for now, though I don't know how democratic it all feels when their partisans roll into town and call a meeting. But for the long run, when the Sheenisov have conquered the world—' we share a laugh '—their theorists advocate the weirdest kind of communism I've ever heard of: everybody owns nothing, or everything.'

'Sounds like every dingbat communist since Munzer—'

'No, no—every *individual* owns *everything*. The whole goddamn universe.'

'Including every *other* individual?'

'Only to the extent that you can.'

'Nice if you can get it. I just want to be princess of the galaxy.'

'Modest of you, my sweet. But that's the catch—the universe is yours to take, *if you can*.'

'So what's to stop me?'

'Only the other contenders, and your possibly reluctant subjects. And the size of the universe. If you can get around all that—go for it, gal!'

'Oh. I see. And there was me thinking that eating people is wrong.'

Tony does glance sideways at me, now. 'Eating people is *wasteful* . . . but seriously, if you think it's wrong, fine. I entirely agree. So do something about it. Arm the prey! Set up taboos. Give them teeth! Just don't think that announcing your moral convictions affects any part of the universe further than your voice can reach.'

'And they want to base *communism* on this . . . this unlimited selfishness? What's to stop it all degenerating into a war of all against all?'

Tony shrugs. 'No doubt they expect we'd come to some kind of arrangement.'

I'm telling him all the reasons why this'll never work and he's dividing his attention between talking to me and grumbling to himself about a Minskyite clique in cee-cubed (you're asking *me*?) when the alarm goes off and I realise it's me that's done it, set it off by reflex, even before my conscious mind has registered that there's a blip on the scope and it's closing *fast*.

'Shit shit shit SHIIIT!!!' I announce, helpfully. Fingers tapping, keying the message to Command-Control-Comms (and hoping the Minskyite clique, whatever they are, knows which side of the bulkhead their air is on) and the blip is suddenly blurred by a burst of debris from the side just as the station lights dim under a power drain and the object is filling the screen then clearing it to the top right and it's gone, as I duck and feel there should have been a *whoosh* as it passed overhead.

'Hundred-ton rock on collision course deflected by laser burn,' says a calm voice in my ear. Needless to say the whole process from detection to deflection has been automatic—both I on the watch, and the gunnery crew, are just there to make sure we know what's going on. Here in a purely advisory capacity, as the US/UN grunts used to say.

The alarm cuts out and the lights come back.

'What the fuck was *that*?' says Tony.


I'm swinging the screen's viewpoint, as the computer labours to patch in data from drogue cameras and other settlements. The cluster of habitats and ships at Lagrange 4 comes into sudden focus. Where each one had been was a point of actinic, atomic light—for a moment, I think they've been hit; that *we've* hit them. Nuked them.

And then I see them move. The flares are fusion torches, not fusion war-heads. The Outwarder fleet is making its orbital transfer burn, heading out to Jupiter. Our comms net is buzzing. Other pictures begin to flash up:

Teletroopers bounding across the lunar surface, smashing into the mining-camps, seizing control of the mass-driver. They've used it to punch a few warning shots at us, and it's still sending load after load of precious water to rendezvous with the Outwarder fleet.

Our people in the camps dying—shot or gasping vacuum. I see security-camera footage of teletroopers stooping over the dead, applying clawed de-vices to their skulls. My fist is at my mouth, my teeth are biting on my knuckles.

Later my parents' names appear on the list of the missing.

The face of David Reid, the owner of the bonded-labour supply com-pany, looms on our screens in a final message from the Outwarder fleet. It's like a hostage video—face haggard, stubbled; voice stumbling, eyes glanc-ing now and then to the side.

Some apology, some expression of regret.

Then the smooth, confident face of one of the Outwarders cuts in. They were still human, then. If you call that human. He tells us what they've done.

My knuckles begin to bleed.


The Outwarder spokesman told us what had happened to our people in the mining-camps. The lucky ones had been killed outright. The rest had been brain-scanned before their bodies were left to gasp vacuum. The Outwarders left us the details of their claim to the mines: they had records of having bought up the front-company years ago, something we could no longer check, and which they'd hitherto neglected to tell us. Our use of the mines had been theft, according to them, a crime aggravated by our resistance to their teletroopers. They claimed compensation, which they were going to recover as labour from the people whom they'd 'uploaded.' They'd use their recorded and rerun brain-states to operate their robots: much cheaper and quicker than AI.

They never did tell us which of the dead had been scanned, and the des-iccated corpses we recovered later didn't show up traces that could answer the question. For years after, I had nightmares about its being done to my parents. They'd appear anachronistically in dreams of other times, speaking to me on television screens. After the conflict, I didn't just have an ideological dislike, and aesthetic distaste, for the Outwarders. Hatred was flash-burned into my brain.

Which is one reason why I wasn't too worried about the Command Com-

mittee's decision to negotiate with the new Jovians. The night after the decision I now and again found myself lying awake in the dark, cuddled up beside
Boris's obliviously sleeping bulk, thinking about it all. No matter how beautiful the Jovians appeared, no matter how specious their messages might turn
out to be, there were still enough people alive who remembered, and who
would never forgive. That was not, of course, the rational reason for destroying the Jovians—but it was related to it. The brief experience of what can
happen to those at the mercy of superior power had left me, and many others,
with the implacable resolve never to allow the existence of any power superior
to the power which we shared. There can only be one dominant species, and
humanity was not about to relinquish that position. (Or, if it was, I was not
about to let it.) But the emotional memory of what the Outwarders had done
to us, and what their Jovian descendants had done to Earth during the computer crash, should help to harden hearts when it came to the crunch.

When it came to the crunch . . . I smiled to myself, and went back to
sleep.


I got up before Boris, in the slowly increasing daylight-spectrum light of an
artificial morning, and checked my e-mail. (Electronic bandwidth was far
too precious, and too laden with multiply-redundant safety measures, to be
squandered on anything less than urgent news or real-time links. Hence,
chemical mail.) Some of it was practical, some personal or sentimental: these
days, I didn't exactly have a family, beyond the intertwined relationships of
the crew, but I had descendants. I replied to those letters that needed a reply,
sending the little coded molecular message-bearers swirling off down the
capillaries, into the circulation of the base; and beyond it, to the crater towns:
Skuld, Trindr, Igaluk, Valfodr, Loni . . . There was nothing in the mailbox as
urgent as my current work, so I left a coffee percolating for Boris and headed
for the operations room.

It was a slow progress for me. The corridors were crowded, and everybody I met seemed to want to talk to me. The committee's discussion and decision, and the images from the probes, had all been flashed around Callisto's
fibre-optic network. Every forum for argument, from screens to streets, was
overloaded with nothing else.

'—you're right Ellen, we should hit them and not waste any more
time—'

'—waited long enough—'

'—wait and see—'

'—sorry to say this, Ellen, but I think your position is way off beam—'

'—forget the comets, we can rig some nukes that'll disrupt them, they
look pretty delicate—'

'—give them a chance, it's not as if *they* did it—'

'—magnetic fields, right? Well, a polar hit with one good EMP burst—'

All the time my senses were bombarded by the colourful clothes, the beautiful faces (how right we had been, back at the start, to call ourselves the beautiful people); their insistent, vigorous voices, the absolute confidence of all the conflicting opinions; the eager, earnest children literally jumping up to have their say. I had my say too, but I avoided argument. I was happy with it all, not annoyed. Even those who disagreed with me strengthened my conviction that I was right: that this self-chosen people, this fractional distillation of humanity was worth more than anything or anybody else in the universe. There has to be some source of value, some measure, some criterion, someone for whom 'good' means 'good for us'—and we were it. There was more vitality in our one million than in all Earth's billions together, more beauty in us than in any pretty pictures the Jovians could project.

Still, entering the relative quiet of the operations room was a relief. Since yesterday it had lost its newly hacked look. With the instinctive biophilia of all space settlers, people had brought fast-growing plants whose leaves and tendrils were already spreading across the nutrient-rich insulation. A coffee machine had been set up, and cleany-crawlies—those cockroaches of cleanliness—were burrowing into the inevitable drifts of discarded plastic cups. The robots at the ice-face had extended the room by at least ten yards overnight, and the racks and rows of machinery had kept pace. Cameras for the news-threads were present and active, according to the suit.

A few members of the Command Committee were present. Some had just arrived, one or two had been there all night. Clarity Hardingham, the youngest CC member, younger even than Yeng, looked up at me. She was interfacing with one of the computer banks, evidently through a virtual-image display: I could see the focus of her eyes, and the apertures of her green irises, changing moment by moment. Judging by the dark areas around her eyes, she had been up all night. She flicked her auburn curls back from her temples and blinked away the display.

'Good morning, Ellen,' she said. 'Grab me a coffee, will you?'

I passed one over to her. 'You look like you should be drinking cocoa,' I told her.

'Ah, sod it,' she said, knocking back a drug tablet, followed by a sip of coffee. 'This is too exciting for sleep. For me, anyway. I've been more or less holding the fort since about four.'

'Doing what? Comms protocols?'

'Aagh! I wish! Well, I was working at that earlier, so I can't complain. No, what I've been doing for the past four hours is sampling opinion—we'll run a proper poll nearer the time, when we have to make a decision. This is just preliminary, sounding out what the comrades think our negotiating position should be.' She grinned quirkily, scratching her ear. 'That's if we have one. There's a lot more than two in twelve agree with you out there, Ellen.'

'I'm not surprised.'

'Well, me neither. But of those who do want to negotiate, I reckon the biggest issue is putting an end to the viral assaults. Next, coming to some agreement on . . . spheres of influence, if you like.'

'Literal spheres,' I smiled.

Clarity nodded. 'Yes! Most comrades seem keen on the idea that the Jovians should have Jupiter, and we'll have the rest.'

I stared at her gloomily. 'That is so stupid. All right, let's just say *premature*. We know the Jovians have gone from nothing to some kind of culture in a matter of weeks, their powered flights are increasing all the time—'

'No, Ellen, we've been tracking that further while you've been away. The flights haven't increased, nor the number of clusters. They may have reached some plateau in their progress. After all, remember they may have inherited all their technological information from their precursor entities, and are now simply implementing it, so their earlier rapid ascent needn't indicate that they're, oh, recapitulating human development from the stone age up on a faster platform.'

'That could make it worse, from our point of view,' I said. 'What if during their precursors' time in virtual reality they were all along doing design-ahead work? We've only *assumed* that the old Outwarder macros went crazy, and that all their descendants up to now have been crazy too. We could be wrong. The ones that have now emerged into the real world could have countless generations of R&D simulation behind them, which they could implement at will.'

Clarity shrugged. 'You're right, it is premature to argue over how we negotiate before we know what they're capable of, which is why the *next* highest item on most people's agenda is finding out more about exactly that, and getting some kind of reliable access to confirm any story they give us about what they're up to.'

'Inspection rights? At least that strikes a note of healthy suspicion.'

'You could put it like that.' Clarity drained her cup and tossed it towards the big table. '*You* would.'

We both laughed, but I could hear the slight tension in her throat, and in mine.

The other CC members hadn't looked up from their work when I came in, and were still absorbed in it. I didn't interrupt. I spent the next hour or so in front of an unused interface, pulling up summaries of the night's work, an increasing number of which were modified and updated as more people came in. The science teams, safely distant in other warrens, were evaluating the physics and chemistry of the Jovian entities: the most solid results so far were that the bubbles were made of laminated sheets of monomolecular diamond; that the 'wings' were, as we'd thought, made up of a flow of ionized molecules in electromagnetic fields; that the 'bodies' were a combination of these with hologram projections; and that the whole display was not just decorative or expressive but a means of communication, a language of light. The core of the Jovian individual, the brain and engine of the thing, was the elaborate structure that had appeared as a jewelled breastplate on the angels. This object was itself aerodynamic, and drew its energy directly from the fast winds and vast electrical pulses of Jupiter's atmosphere, which even at its calmest was (from a human point of view) a ceaseless violent storm.

It struck me that the Jovian body was a tough structure. Disrupting the displays, even cracking the diamond bubbles, might be as easy as the nuclear enthusiasts I'd encountered thought. Destroying their source would take exactly what we had planned.


Malley and Suze came in at 0900 GMT, with the smug, sleepy look of people who had spent a first unexpected night together. I disengaged from the interface and stood up.

'Good morning,' I said.

Suze smiled shyly; Malley grinned. 'Hi,' he said. He passed a hand over his reddened eyes. 'God, is there coffee in this place?'

I brought over three cups and we made our way to Malley's workstation. Suze dragged a couple of extra chairs over and we sat down. Spindly chairs; on Earth they'd have crumpled under us.

'How have you been getting on?' I asked.

'Oh,' said Suze, 'we've been getting on very—'

She stopped and giggled.

'Well, yes,' Malley said. He smiled at her again. 'Suze has a really charming notion that getting off with a non-co is some kind of decadent perversion—'

'I do *not!*'

'I must say it adds something to the, ah, energy of the reaction. Not that it needs much adding to—you were right about those rejuvenation treatments. I had forgotten it was possible to feel this good.' He sighed and stretched. 'On the other hand—I feel very strange. Part of it's the gravity, the conditions, and part of it is . . . you people. Your people. They're not what I expected, even after spending days with all of you in the ship. The crowd out in the corridors are so . . .' He shook his head. 'You in the Division aren't like the people in the Union, at least from what I've seen. The Union people seem happy enough, and free too in their way, but you out here have more *edge*, more discontent with themselves. You, Ellen, and your crew, well . . . it's hard to say, but you are different again, you seem to carry more of the past.'

'We do,' I said. 'Several of us are almost your age.'

He looked at me curiously. 'No, even Yeng has it—a sort of hardness in the eyes.'

'Yeah,' said Suze. 'It's the "old comrades" look I told you about.'

'Hmm,' I said. 'I don't know. You strike me as pretty tough yourself, Sam.' I flicked my hand sideways. 'Another time . . . What I wanted to ask you was, how are you getting on with the math? Are our miracles of neural nanotech reviving your genius?'

Malley laughed. 'That's one of the things about you that I was talking about, Ellen. You can say something like that without cracking a smile, and yet treat other matters with the most appalling levity. Anyway, as you say. Later for psychology. The answer to your question is, yes, I am making progress, but it's slow—and I don't think it's because of my brain's age. The "engineering considerations" I once blithely summed up as beyond the wit of man are beginning to look a bit more tractable, and as for the theory of the quantum-chaotic manifold, even my own old papers are beginning to make sense to me again.'

I wasn't sure whether he meant this ironically or not.

'OK,' I said. 'You heard what the man said, last night. I'm supposed to give you all necessary practical assistance, starting this morning. That obviously includes giving you access to all the observations, all the calculating machinery you might need, and so on. But it's more than that. If you want to observe the wormhole Gate up close, or send a probe through it, or for that matter go through it yourself—we can make it possible.'

'I suppose it would be best to do things in that order,' Malley observed. 'Observation, test probes, expedition. Rather than the reverse.' He smiled, as at a thin joke, and for a moment, despite the glowing success of his rejuvenation, looked like an elderly academic from one of those twentieth-century lecture tapes whose science has remained valid, however bizarre the diction or the clothes appear to their modern students. 'However . . . it's the practical calculation which has to be solved first, so yes, I would appreciate as much computing power as you can spare, and a walk through your available mathematical software. Oh, and a lit search, don't want to reinvent the wheel, eh?'

I set him up with all of these and a connection to our wormhole physics team; they had decades of experience of sending probes into the wormhole, and none whatsoever of any coming back. When he was comfortably enmeshed in the virtual-reality workspace I turned to Suze.

'There's something very important you can do,' I said. 'If Sam finds a way of getting us through, we may need you to help us find our way about on the other side.'

'New Mars?'

'Yes,' I said. 'Imagine an entire planet of non-cooperators, if you can.' I frowned. 'Now I come to think about it, there are only half a million or so, which is probably less than you've got on Earth . . . but this lot have a world to themselves. I'd like you to take a look at the files we've built up of Wilde's accounts of New Mars, and some of the images his little spacecraft had in its storage.'

'I'd love to,' Suze said. 'It's a dream, it really is.'

'Each to their own,' I said.

Suze laughed. 'You don't like it?'

'I don't like what I've seen of New Mars, or what Wilde told us about it,' I said, as I guided her to the most recently built workspace, at the far end of the room. Closest to the ice-face and the busy, tiny robots, it was the one least likely to be coveted by CC members. 'For me it just confirms something I've thought for a long time: people in an owned world are owned.'

Suze sat down and began adjusting the workspace to her own preferences. All I could see of this process was off-centre hologram images, dim in the full-spectrum light, and subtle twitches of Suze's facial muscles as she settled into the scene. She turned to me and smiled, as though from a distance.

'That isn't how they see it,' she told me, and before I could reply she had slipped the sound system over her ears, and was away.


By about ten o'clock all the CC members had turned up. None of them looked as if they'd had much sleep, and not for the same reasons as Suze and Malley (and, for that matter, myself). They had probably collapsed into a few hours' deep sleep after staying at work most of the night. Several of them resorted now to stimulant drugs, as well as making full use of the coffee machine.

I'd used the time until their arrival in checking out the current flightworthiness of the *Terrible Beauty*; according to the maintenance team, it was entirely sound, so all I had to do was reserve it for my own crew. There were two reasons for doing this; one was that it would be quite inconvenient, but all too predictable, to find that all the fusion-clippers were already assigned or in use just when we needed one; and the other was that, like myself, the rest of my crew were far more familiar with the handling and operation of fighter-bombers than of fusion-clippers, and our experience with the *Terrible Beauty*'s individual quirks would make our next flight in it easier.

Tatsuro took a seat at the head of the long table.

'Why are you here, Ellen?' he asked.

'Doctor Malley is fully occupied,' I said. 'If he requires further help from me, he has only to ask. In the meantime, I would like to remain here.'

'Very well,' said Tatsuro. Other members began to wander back from the other end of the room, and sat down. Clarity smiled at me, and took a seat beside me; others looked somewhat reserved. Tatsuro called the meeting to order.

'For the benefit of any who were not present last night,' Tatsuro began, with a flash of his eye at me, 'we've finalized our equipment for opening a secure communications channel. Our surface teams have arranged a narrow-beam transmitter-receiver, connected by a completely independent and isolated cable to a screen and speakers in this room. The wavelength and location with which comrade Ellen established contact yesterday will be used as the basis for our first attempt. During the contact, this room will be isolated, and anyone who doesn't wish to participate is free to leave.'

We all looked at each other. Nobody made a move.

'All right, comrades,' said Tatsuro. 'Ellen, will you please ask Doctor Malley and comrade Suze to leave.'

Malley and Suze, when I'd interrupted their respective attention-trances, flatly refused to do any such thing.

'Wouldn't miss this for anything,' Malley told us. Suze just looked stubborn.

Tatsuro gave a small shrug. 'It's your life,' he said. The two of them sat down together at the table, Suze beside me, Malley beside her. I squeezed Suze's shoulder.

Joe Lutterloh, the committee's electronics specialist, went around the room checking each news-thread camera location and disconnecting it. We could hear a murmur through the walls as the people outside, like everybody else in the Division who was watching, found their screens going blank.

The big screen was moved into position at the end of the table, and a camera was mounted on it. The isolated cable was connected up to both, via a likewise isolated computer through which the message, if any, would be filtered. A small cable was unwound and trailed across the table to a control pad in front of Tatsuro.

'Ready,' said Joe.

He rejoined the rest of us at the table. We all shuffled our seats around until the arrangement resembled a broad U-shape, with Tatsuro at one end and the screen we all faced at the other. Each of us could see all the others. Tatsuro gave a final glance around, as though to check that everybody was still willing to be present, and pressed a switch. The tiny light on the mounted camera glowed red. The prerecorded hailing message went out, several times, along with an image of the room and our silent, waiting selves.

Time passed, perhaps a minute; it seemed longer. Then the screen lit up with a picture. There was no fuzziness, no moment of tuning. It came into focus at once. It wasn't any of the shapes I'd seen. Instead, it showed the head and shoulders of a young man, wearing a plain white tee shirt and apparently standing casually in the interior of one of the bubbles. I could see the hexagonal patterns of the panes, as from a great distance. The more familiar—since yesterday—forms of the Jovian entities drifted and shifted in the great spaces between the man and the domed roof, like strange birds in an aviary. The man looked like a typical North American, mainly Caucasian with a good mixture of the usual other races. His face was unexceptional: healthy, good-looking, alert and friendly. The image could have come from an old NASA commercial, and possibly did.

He smiled and waved. 'Hi,' he said. 'Thank you for getting in touch again. To us, it's been the equivalent of two years since your first contact, so we've had time to prepare our response. I'm operating at your speed, by the way—we can interact directly.' He smiled. 'Apart from the light-speed lag, of course. I see Doctor I. K. Malley is among you. We're honoured, sir.'

Malley grunted something. There was a pause of a few seconds. The Jovian smiled.

'As you know, what you're seeing now isn't how we usually present ourselves to each other. But it isn't just a mask—we're of human descent, and we have much in common with you, perhaps far more than you think.'

No doubt we could say the same to gorillas—or to goldfish.

'But,' the friendly face continued, 'we are of course post-human. We don't wish to hide that, or play it down. We know of the long history of discord between those who took our path, and those who chose to remain within the human frame.'

His gaze, uncannily, fixed on me. 'Ellen May Ngwethu,' he said, in a wondering tone. 'It's amazing to see you here. Your old opponents from the wreck-deck send their regards.'

He raised an open hand, then clenched it to a fist in what, from his quizzical expression, I judged to be an ironical salute.

'How do you know me?' I asked, keeping my voice steady. The delay in the response gave me plenty of time to quail.

'We are individuals,' the Jovian said, moving the clenched fist, turned inwards, to his chest. 'Not a hive, not—' and here he paused to smile '—a "Jupiter-sized brain". But memories are shared, and nothing is lost. Some who were with you are with us, and some of their memories are with me. I hope you'll come to see us as alive, as a different flesh, and not as a simulation or a soulless mimicry. We have thoughts and feelings that may be wider and deeper than we remember from our human phase, but are otherwise like your own. We're people too, Ellen, as we hope you'll come to see.'

I made no reply, and after the inevitable delay the Jovian's attention shifted.

'Tatsuro, isn't it?' he said. 'No doubt you have questions for us.'

'Indeed I have,' Tatsuro said urbanely. 'But first, let me say how much I, and most of us here, welcome this opportunity to talk things over. I will be frank with you. As you may know, we represent a defence force which has spent most of the last couple of centuries—which to you must be almost geological ages—in conflict with your kind. Your continued broadcasting of viral programs, and generation of destructive molecular machinery, remain an inconvenience to us. Their first occurrence, shortly after your arrival in the Jovian atmosphere, resulted in many millions of deaths, and gave the final push to an already tottering civilization.

'Your emergence from virtual reality into, as you put it, a different flesh, changes the situation, but in a way which—as I'm sure you'll understand—many of us can't help regarding as a threat. Your predecessors, the human beings with whom you affirm your continuity, left us with no cheerful prospect for the future of humanity, in a Solar System dominated by post-human entities. We're interested in what you have to say on these points.'

Perhaps because of the length of Tatsuro's statement, the Jovian's reply began immediately. It gave a superficially reassuring impression of a conversation, but on second thoughts it only confirmed the alien superiority of the being confronting us; he must have been able to deduce, from subtle clues in Tatsuro's voice, expression and posture, the exact moment when he'd subconsciously intended to stop speaking, and precisely timed his response to arrive a moment after that. Doubtless he was processing Tatsuro's last few sentences while apparently speaking the first of his own. I felt hairs prickle on my forearms.

'This has come as a shock to us,' the Jovian was saying. 'We assure you that we weren't aware of this viral sabotage. We are grieved to learn that it did you so much damage, in the past. Please bear in mind, we have only just emerged from what you refer to as virtual reality, and which we remember as a kind of nightmarish dreamtime. The last two months, to you, have been about a century and a half to us. We've spent most of it in our own struggles for survival—in developing, as you see, the rudiments of a material culture in what remains an exceptionally harsh environment. When we realized how much time had elapsed between the wormhole starship project and the present, we were astonished and, I must admit, appalled. The viral sabotage is—at the very least—not under our conscious control, and may not be—even indirectly—our doing. There are physical, mechanical processes—the post-biological equivalent of vegetation—underpinning our existence, and the viruses may be a reflexive, defensive product of that, like the natural insecticides of plants.' He gave a self-deprecating smile. 'Or maybe it's just our natural smell. Sorry about that, folks. It may give you offence, but it isn't, on our part, an offensive action. We'll do our best to find out what's causing it and, if possible, put a stop to it.'

He registered, with another smile, the nodding that had been going on around the table from everyone but me, and continued.

'We obviously have a lot of problems to overcome about our common past. One of the things we hope to gain from our contact with you is a better understanding of what happened during our . . . dreamtime, how it came about and how any harm that was done in that time can be repaired, or at least some restitution made. And that brings me to your very understandable concerns about the future.

'The first thing I'd like to say, on behalf of all of us, is this: please, we urge and implore you, don't hold against us the wild statements made by the alienated adolescents some of us once were, long ago. Would you judge an adult by every spiteful or foolish word spoken in childhood? We are much further advanced from our origins than that! And as for things said by some who should have, perhaps, known better—the philosophers and predictors of the post-human, most of whose speculations were committed to text before even one AI existed in the world—please don't turn these guesses, fearful or inspired, against us now. Please judge us for what we are, not for what some roboticists and science-fiction writers hoped or feared we might become.

'Ellen, and others present, used to joke about our emergence as "the Rapture for nerds". Well, we weren't all nerds, you know! And for us, it hasn't exactly been a Rapture. There were great and exhilarating times, ages to us, in the early years. Since then, since our catastrophe, it's been a long and agonizing process of evolution, in every sense of the word, during which we learned to turn away from the dreams and nightmares that our new capacities made possible, and turn again to the real and only universe, the one we share with you, and with all life. We have laid no plans against you. All we ask of you is to live in peace with us. To let us enjoy the part of this system that belongs to us, and yourselves to enjoy what is your own. We hope that you will go further, and explore with us the possibilities of what we can accomplish—together. The choice is yours.'

It was indeed, but I wondered how many of who heard this message would understand what the choice it presented was.

The Jovian spread open his hands. 'This contact is putting quite a strain on our resources, friends. We'd like to leave you now, to consider it, and we look forward to your reply.'

The screen went blank. Tatsuro fingered his control panel, and the camera's light went off. A moment of silence was followed by shiftings and sighings as people relaxed.

'Well,' Tatsuro said, 'that was a remarkable message. Something to think about. The Command Committee meeting is adjourned while we do some thinking about it. Don't all speak at once.'

Everybody did, but Tatsuro resolutely ignored them while he rose and strolled to the coffee machine and helped himself. Others followed suit, and within a minute we were all standing around. It was quite a smart move on Tatsuro's part, because it gave us a breathing spell, a chance to unwind after the tension of the contact. In the huddle around the coffee machine, I found Malley in front of me.

'I happened to glance at you during the last part of that message,' he said. 'I hope we kept a tape of how our side looked from the camera. Your expression was a classic.'

'Oh?' I reached the machine and keyed up some espresso. 'How so?'

Malley grinned, over the rim of his cup. 'Hmm,' he said. 'I once saw a late-twentieth-century newspaper photo of a mad Moscow bag lady clutching pictures of Stalin and the last Tsar and looking into a shop window full of televisions showing the new politicians making promises after the counter-revolution. You had *exactly* the same look on your face.'

'Sometimes, Sam,' I said, 'I have only the vaguest idea of what you're talking about. But if you mean I looked somewhat sceptical, and perhaps a little hostile, then—'

'Yeah, that's about it,' he chuckled. Then his face became more serious. 'It's almost frightening, Ellen, to think that if I hadn't insisted on your making contact, you'd never have had the chance to hear what the Jovians had to say.'

'Yes,' I said. We were moving sideways, letting the pressure of bodies shift us out of the crush. I found a clear part of the edge of the table and sat down. 'Without that message, we might never have known just how hostile they are.'

Malley nearly spilled his coffee. '*Hostile?* That was as generous an offer of peaceful cooperation as you could hope to hear.'

I shook my head. 'Sometimes I might sound prejudiced, but contrary to what you might think, I *can* imagine what a generous offer of peace from the Jovians would be like. I'm not saying I'd believe it, or even if I believed it that I'd accept it, but I can imagine it. And what we've just heard was not that.'

'Frankly, I'm amazed,' Malley said. 'What problems do you have with it?'

'I'm still adding them up,' I said. 'The devil is in the details.'

Malley grimaced. 'All right. I'm a scientist, not a politician.'

'How's the science going?' I asked lightly.

'Ah.' Malley looked down, then looked me in the eye. 'As you said: the devil is in the details. It's all a matter of getting the angle of entry to the wormhole right—that's how you end up coming out of the daughter wormhole, and not up the arse of the probe. Once you've got that, it's straightforward. But I'm a long way from getting that. Even the physical measurement of the angle depends on how you define the location of the quasi-surface, and that's technically a bit tricky. Still . . . that's what we're here for, eh?'

While everyone was milling around Joe and Clarity were running diagnostic software on the message records. As far as they could tell, the message was clean. As soon as this was announced Tatsuro banged on the table and reconvened the meeting.

'OK, everybody,' he said. 'We know the message contains no Trojan-horse viruses or semiotic-trigger traps, so I propose we release it to the Division without delay. Anyone disagree?'

Nobody did.

'Fine,' he said. 'Carried *nem con.*'

Joe reconnected the cameras. Again we heard sounds from outside. Tatsuro hit some keys and the conversation between the Jovian and ourselves began to replay on the outside screens, while our continuing discussion was being shown on other threads.

'Next item: anyone totally opposed to continuing the contact?'

Again, no objections.

'Then I suggest we move quickly to a response,' said Tatsuro. 'From what the Jovian said, the fast folk are as fast as ever—a thousand times faster than us. Let's not give them two subjective years between messages, this time. You've had time to sort out your first impressions; here are mine.

'The account we've received of how the present . . . implementation of the Jovian post-human intelligences came into existence fits perfectly with what we've figured out ourselves. They have some continuity of memory with their human progenitors, which is not a surprise, although their recognition of individuals among us is, I may say, disquieting to experience. They are obviously making an effort—an effort which they at least want us to believe is at some cost—to show us, literally, a human face. They've made a statement which we should weigh carefully, but which on the face of it is an appeal for cooperation and an offer to live in peace. To me, this suggests that they do not, as yet, have enough power to defeat us in all-out conflict—and that we, for now, have the power to destroy them. At their present or possible rates of progress, this balance could rapidly tilt the other way. So far, they've shown no signs of any ability to project their power beyond the Jovian atmosphere—other than by radio messages, of course, and the odd molecule boiling off into space, which they claim is not their doing.

'The expressed dismay at the damage the radio-borne viruses have caused, and the disavowal of responsibility for them, are again among the possibilities we've considered ourselves. We can't confirm it, but I think we should give them the benefit of the doubt.

'Now . . . as to the appeal for cooperation. The points made about not judging them by their progenitors, or by the speculations of pre-Singularity thinkers, are well taken. But they have a further implication. If the Jovians continue to develop, and manage to avoid the virtual-reality trap, then they or their descendants could soon be as far beyond their present selves as they are now beyond their past. They now look back at their past selves, and in effect disown them. The shadow of the future, which to them, now, may loom genuinely long, would be to us a painfully short period before their defection. In a matter of days or weeks, they could look back on their present selves and dismiss their concerns and promises as those of infants—or less than that.

'How can we bind them to their promises, without superior force? And how can we keep our force superior? We can't—we either *trust* them, or destroy them.'

Tatsuro placed his hands, palms upward, on the table, and his gaze slowly tracked around us all. He raised his eyebrows, and then sat back.

I was surprised and relieved that he'd said all he had. He, at least, had not been carried away by the Jovian's rhetoric. Others didn't welcome the cold water he'd poured on their hopes. I could see that from their faces, but nobody seemed willing to speak.

So I did.

'There is one more point,' I said, 'which could bear clarification in the next exchange. The Jovian said that they wanted to enjoy their own part of the system, and leave us to enjoy ours. It would be very interesting to know just what parts they mean—what they consider theirs, and what ours. I seem to remember that this kind of property right was one of the issues we originally fell out about. He, or it, also mentioned repairing or recompensing harm done during the period of their so-called dreamtime. He said nothing of who was to compensate whom, for what.'

'But surely he meant—' someone began.

'No!' I insisted. 'We can't assume they mean the harm *they* did to us! They might mean the harm we did to them. Some very rich people became Outwarders, and they could still claim that we—that is, the Union—stole their property in the social revolution. In terms of their legal system, the bloodsucking usurers owned half the Earth, and they might want it back, and the rest as interest! The way I take what the Jovian said, our choice remains the same: we hammer them with the comets, or we live under their iron heel, submitting to whatever enslavement it would take to pay them off for their so-called property.'

'Oh, Ellen!' said Clarity. She looked at Tatsuro. 'Sorry. Uh, comrade chairman. Ellen's comment I'm afraid sums up what's precisely the wrong approach we should take to this situation. The idea that these post-human beings would be *interested* in Earth, or in interest—whatever that is—when they have the whole universe in front of them and the whole future before them, is just dragging up old fights. I don't think we should even *mention* it. I'm not saying take them at their word, but let's show them the sort of basic goodwill we show to any stranger, and not get bogged down in ancient history.'

A ripple of amusement went around the committee at this fifty-year-old's allocation of the youth of most of us to ancient history. Suze raised her hand. Tatsuro nodded.

'Comrade Tatsuro,' Suze said, 'my sympathies are with Clarity, but I would like to say that Ellen has a point. If the Jovians do think in the way she described, then they could feel themselves justified in almost anything. On the other hand, if they have some version of the true knowledge, then anything they wanted to do to us would be its own justification, once they have the power. It would be very helpful if we could get them to demarcate now what's to count as theirs, and what as ours, and to agree to build in that distinction to any future versions of themselves—something they can't go back on without severe internal conflict. So that whether they're moralists or egoists, they'll go on respecting us.'

Tatsuro gave her an encouraging smile, and said: 'Comrade Suze, you may be right, but that still comes down to trusting them. Without power, respect is dead. But our power needn't be the capacity to destroy them— our own infants, and many lower animals, have power over us because our interests are bound up with theirs. Because *we* value *them*, and because natural selection has built that valuing into our nervous systems, to the point where we cannot even wish to change it, though no doubt if we wanted to we could. This is elementary: the second iteration of the true knowledge. The question we really have to answer, then, is whether the Jovians have come to value our independent existence.'

'That,' said Joe Lutterloh, speaking up suddenly, 'comes back to surviving as wildlife or pets.'

The discussion then heated up, and went on for an hour or so until Tatsuro stopped it with nothing more than an impatient drumming of his fingernails on the table.

'Comrades,' he said firmly, 'I think we've discussed this to the point where we have more than enough to bring to our next contact. *However* that turns out, I am more strongly persuaded than ever that Doctor Malley's work on the wormhole must continue in parallel.' He looked over at Malley, and at me. 'I accept your reasons for wanting to witness the first contact, and to confirm *our* sincerity in making it—but can I take it that you're satisfied?'

Malley nodded.

'Very well. I'm sure you're keen to return to the wormhole problem. Ellen, I think you've said all you need to say. I don't see your contributing further to the discussion, or the negotiation. Am I right?'

'I guess so,' I said.

'All right. See to it that a part of the far end of this room is sound-screened off, so that Doctor Malley can continue his work without distraction, and give him any further help he needs. If any developments require your attention, we'll let you know.'

I stood up, gave the rest of the committee a comradely smile, and accompanied Malley back to his workstation. After a moment of hesitation, Suze followed.

'Well,' she said, 'that's us put in our place!'

I clapped her shoulder. 'Not to worry. Tatsuro is actually paying us quite a compliment, however it looks to the others. He's saying our work is as important as anything that's likely to come out of the contact.'

Malley sat down at his workstation and gazed at the screen. He grasped his temples in his fingertips and rubbed. 'You know, Ellen, he's right. Because what we're trying to do is get to the stars!'

'That's the spirit,' I said. I looked back at the group around the table. Joe was once more disconnecting the external cameras. Another contact session was about to start. I wondered how far the Jovians would have changed in the time since our first contact, and how far we had.

'Come on,' I said. 'Suze, help me round up some robots to spin us a sound-screen.'


Over the next three hours I helped Malley with locating and collating thousands of recordings of the Gate, and with running through the navigational data from Wilde's spacecraft, which had come through the wormhole the other way. Frustratingly, the paths were not commutative: it was not possible to take the path from the New Mars system and run it in reverse. Outside, through a plastic partition that let through light but not sound, I could see the committee going again and again into contact with the Jovian emissary. Suze was immersed in her study of New-Martian society, occasionally muttering to herself.

About 1500 GMT Clarity strolled in carrying three mugs of coffee. We all stopped work and leaned back and smiled at her gratefully.

'Clarity, you should be charity,' Malley said.

'How's it going?' I asked.

Clarity wrinkled her small, perfect nose. 'All right, I suppose,' she said. 'The Jovians are being very friendly, and they're not just showing that man-image now. There are other forms crowded around him, and sometimes they seem to be relaying replies through him. It's like they've understood we're getting used to them.'

'Any progress on the virus front?'

'No, they still say they haven't pinned down the source of it themselves.'

'Hah. What about the issue of who gets what?'

'Oh, that! The Jovian was very taken aback that it should even come up. Insisted that they had no plans for any use of the system beyond Jupiter, which as he pointed out was quite big enough.'

I favoured her with an evil grin. ' "No plans" still doesn't mean anything, beyond what it literally says, which isn't much. And *nothing* is big enough for exponential growth, which is what the old Outwarders were really keen on.'

She shrugged. 'As you keep reminding us. Enjoy your coffee.'

'Thanks.'

Malley watched her walk away, and Suze watched Malley. I caught Suze's eye and smiled.

'It's the rejuve,' I murmured.

'What?' asked Malley.

'Nothing.'

'You know what you are?' Malley said to me. 'You're a hawk.'

'Hey, I like that,' I said. 'I thought we all were out here, I just didn't expect everyone to go all dovish as soon as their faceless enemies put on a face to talk to.'

Malley took his pipe out of a pouch on his belt, and clenched it between his teeth. He put it down again and took a sip of coffee. 'You know,' he said, with some regret, 'I'm not sure I even like the *taste* of tobacco any more.' He dropped the pipe and caught it again, several times, as though fascinated by its slow fall. He tilted his seat back and stared at the screen and poked around in his virtual workspace.

'Back to work,' he said.

He continued for another hour, and then he suddenly stopped. I was talking quietly with Suze at the time, as she refreshed my memories of the intricacies of anarcho-capitalist legal theory—something some of the Outwarders had bored me with back on the wreck-deck, and of which New Mars was an insanely logical outcome. It was like Ptolemaic epicycles, an endless addition of reinvented wheels. Why, I kept wondering, couldn't these people *see* the answer?

Malley's inarticulate sound of frustration interrupted us.

'Is there a problem?' I asked.

'Is there a fucking problem.' Malley took out his pipe again and this time stuffed it with tobacco and lit it, puffing furiously. Small machines stopped what they were doing and sniffed the air. Some of them hastily extemporized firefighting equipment, and began to gather round.

'I can't do it,' Malley said. 'The whole thing depends on the angle you make to the wormhole when you pass into it. I can't get it from the angle the mutineers' colony ship made back in 2093—the wormhole goes through a cycle whose period I don't know, and so far, calculating it is beyond any of the resources we've got. There's a key to it somewhere, but it's mathematically intractable. You'd have to have built the wormhole to know what it is.'

'You can't even make a best guess?'

'Oh, sure,' said Malley. 'I can make a best guess. Wouldn't bet my life on it, though.'

'You don't have to!' I said. 'We'll test it with a probe. See if it comes back . . .'

Malley jabbed at his screen with the stem of his pipe. 'Sure,' he said. 'Trouble is, we could be testing probes from now until doomsday. I mean, my best guess is no better than the best your chaps have come up with, and *they* haven't had anything back.'

I fought to hide my dismay. There was no way we'd have time to mess around with test probes. We'd all been counting on Malley, confident that with his deep theoretical knowledge and our masses of data, he'd find us a path through.

Malley looked up at me, frowning.

'Something's puzzling me,' he said.

'Yes?'

'This space-time path back here from New Mars . . . how come we have that, and not the one the other way?'

'Well,' I said, 'it's kind of funny. Wilde had the return path in his onboard computer, and we've been able to access it. The outward path—which may not even be a valid solution any more—he had in his head, so to speak. I mean, there was a time when both "his head" and the return path were stored programs in the same computer, but even if we'd known, we still can't hack human minds, even minds in computers. No access path, no memory addresses . . .'

Malley smiled, thin-lipped. 'I know that. What I was wondering is how Wilde was able to work out the return path from New Mars. Do the New Martians have super-advanced computers, or lots of brain-boosted physicists, or what?'

'Not exactly,' I said. 'Over on New Mars, they have the stored original mind-states of the Outwarders, and the stored minds of some of the subsequent "macros" before their catastrophe. What they did—and it still gives me

the shivers to think about—was make copies of them, then restart the copies
in a controlled environment—a standard nanotech tank, as it happens—then
ask them to work out the return path, and when they'd got the answer to that
question and a few others, like how to resurrect a lot of human minds and
bodies they also had in storage . . . they, well, they basically tipped in the
bleach! Something called Blue Goo, actually, a nanotech specific for wiping
out nanoware.'

'Jesus!' said Malley. 'You mean they generated an entire post-human culture in a virtual reality, asked it a few deep questions, and then *destroyed* it?'

'Yes,' I said. I chuckled at the appalled look on his face. Even Suze was
astonished by this part of the story, which the Division hadn't chosen to release. 'OK, it was a bit risky—I wouldn't trust a post-human culture, even if
I did have it in a bucket. But, you know, full marks for initiative.'

'And zero for morality,' Malley said. 'That's like a small-scale version of
what you had in mind for the Jovians and with less excuse.'

I nodded briskly. 'Wilde does have his own take on the true knowledge,'
I said. 'Even if he is a non-co.'

Malley sighed. 'Let's not get into that. So how did they get the original
path, the path through the daughter wormhole to New Mars?'

'Oh,' I said, 'they got it from the Outwarder macros.'

Malley stared. 'The Outwarders *gave* it to them?'

I spread my hands. 'One, or several, of them did. We don't know if it
was a deal they had arranged all along as a payment for the operator of the
bonded-labour company—a man called Dave Reid, a very nasty piece of
work who's probably still top dog on New Mars—or if the daughter-
wormhole was set up by the Outwarders for other purposes, and Reid and
company just managed to extract the information as the Outwarder macros
were degenerating.'

'Ah,' said Malley. 'It has occurred to me that we could do the same ourselves. We could just ask.'

I really had not thought of that.


Tatsuro was sitting at the head of the long table, doodling on a pad and
combing his receding hair with his fingers. Committee members stood or sat
around, talking and drinking coffee. Another contact session had just been
completed, virus-scanned, and relayed to the rest of the Division. Clarity
was elbow-deep in a display of the state of current opinion about the talks so
far: shifting, by the look of it.

Malley and I walked up to Tatsuro.

'We have a problem,' I told him. 'And a possible solution.'

As he listened, I watched his expressions; almost undetectable, under the smooth surface of his skin. Alarm, disappointment, anger, doubt, and a faint glimmer of hope.

'I suppose it's worth a try,' he said at last. 'But it does let them know we're going through.'

'They'd find out as soon as we did go through,' I said. 'At least, we have to assume that they could.'

Tatsuro nodded slowly. 'Perhaps. Although I must say, observational astronomy from inside the Jovian atmosphere is probably a bit tricky, even for them. Anyway, if we ask them for the path, we need to do so without getting them worried about our intentions.'

I shrugged. 'Surely we have an understandable interest in another human society—'

'Aha!' said Malley. 'How about this? The Jovians may still have some, ah, bones to pick with the mutineers, yes? And so do you, I would imagine. Didn't the labour-force operator conscript some of your people into his labour gangs?'

'That's one way of putting it,' I said sourly. It was something I'd thought over before—that the responsibility for those long-ago raids and deaths might rest more with Reid's company than with his clients, the Outwarders. Not that it mattered.

'So tell them that,' Malley said. 'Tell them you want to extract some retribution for what was done. The Jovians might well consider that a *very* understandable motivation.'

'Especially if they think it gets them off the hook,' said Tatsuro. 'OK, we'll do it on the next contact.'

'By the way,' I said, 'just who are we in contact with? Do we know that they're in any way representative?'

'Like us, you mean?' Tatsuro asked dryly. 'Rather more so, I would say. We've had evidence that the contact is being monitored throughout the Jovian population. The "man" we see is a construct, presenting a consensus or majority view.'

'Sum over histories,' said Malley.

The preparations for contact were gone through once more. It was becoming a routine, as was the contact itself. Again the face appeared. The first few exchanges concerned matters arising from earlier sessions, which I hadn't seen. Then Tatsuro broached the subject of the wormhole and the path to New Mars.

For the first time, the Jovian speaker hesitated. 'One moment, please,' he said. His face suddenly became abstracted, the resolution fading until it looked like a hollow mask. The flitting shapes of the individual Jovians in the sky around him went through agitated transformations, spinning into girandoles, stretching into long columns, building themselves into dark edifices . . .

'This might not have been such a good idea,' someone whispered.

Shut up, I didn't say. My lips were dry.

The Jovian speaker's colour and texture returned like a flush.

'Sorry about that, folks,' he said. 'The information you asked for was buried quite deep in our archived memories. Also, some of us weren't too keen on giving you it.' He smiled. 'But the rest of us won them over, so here it is.'

Tatsuro's fingers scrabbled on the control panel as a line of pulsing light along the bottom of the screen indicated a raw-data transmission. It was over in less than five seconds.

'That's all you need,' said the Jovian. 'Give our regards to our former employees, and please assure them that we bear them no ill-will for having baled out when they did. Goodbye for now.'

The image blinked off.

'Wow, fuck,' said Malley. 'These things are sharp.'

I tried to laugh. People were looking at the empty screen, looking at us.

'You stirred up something there,' said Clarity.

'That's the first indication we've had of dissension among them,' said Tatsuro. 'I suggest you give the data we just received a *very* thorough virus-scan.'

I called up Yeng and asked her to come along. Together with Joe and Clarity, she combed through the data with everything she'd got. It checked out clean. Malley loaded it into his workspace, and found that it meshed with his own incomplete calculations.

By this time it was well into the evening. Yeng, Suze and I were seated around Malley. Behind us, other work was going on. When Malley leaned back and nodded silently, we all let out a whoop that caused some distraction.

'We test it first,' I said.

I dialled up a drone and downloaded the data into its navigational computer. I patched in a view on Malley's screen, and we watched the whole mission, from the tiny rocket's launch to its carefully angled insertion in the wormhole. That took about an hour. We'd warned the patrol fighters, hanging in orbit in front of the Gate. Even so, the probe's re-emergence put them on full alert. I could imagine the jangled nerves.

The probe had nothing on board but a telescopic camera—photographic film, not television. One of the fighter-bombers scooped up the probe and ran the film for us, past one of their own telemetry cameras.

We looked at the grainy images of an unfamiliar starfield, and the spec-

trum of an unknown yellow sun, and at the distant red globe with its tracery of canals.

'Fucking amazing,' said Malley. 'Just seeing this. I wonder if I ever really
believed it before.'

I slung my arms around the shoulders of Malley, Yeng and Suze. 'Believe
it,' I said. 'We're going there. Tomorrow.'

# 8

## CITY OF THE LIVING DEAD

Tilted, Jupiter's ring cut a white segment into the forward view. Ten miles ahead, also at an angle, hung the vastly smaller ellipse of the Malley Mile. At this distance the boosters and attitude jets clamped to its circular rim showed as tiny black beads spaced out around its rainbow ring. A fighter-bomber, the *Turing Tester*, stood by beside us, ready to move into our exact present position shortly after we'd vacated it.

The *Terrible Beauty*, with the currently uncrewed fighter-bomber *Carbon Conscience* clinging to its side like a black fly squatting on a white egg, was about to make its final thrust towards the wormhole Gate. The whole crew was on board, along with Malley and Suze. Malley, despite protests from Tatsuro and others, had insisted that he was certainly not going to stay behind. Whose goddam theory was it, anyway, he wanted to know? Whose name was on the thing, eh? Suze's equivalent insistence had more logic behind it: we actually needed her, because she was the only one who seemed to have a feel for how New-Martian society worked.

'Angle of approach 1.274066 radians,' said Jaime.

'Course confirmed,' said Andrea. 'Distance nine point seven five miles, relative speed one hundred and twenty miles per hour.'

'Check.'

It was all down to them now; them and the onboard computer, which was really flying the ship. But, moved by an impulse that goes all the way back to Vostok and Mercury, when people are in a ship they like to have the final say. Maybe it's an illusion, maybe it would be better to let the machines handle it all, but when you start thinking like that, where do you stop? You don't, is what, and you end up with all machines and no people. Come to think of it (I thought, floating in my straps, an inch above my acceleration couch and trying not to think too much) you end up with exactly what we were fighting against.

'Eight miles.'

Right now, as I watched the Malley Mile expand in the screen overhead, I didn't have much sense of control. We were falling into a hole in the sky, and there was nothing I could do about it any more.

'Six miles.'

'Ready for the burn,' Andrea sang out. 'Three minutes.'

We had to go through under acceleration, Malley had told us. He had tried to tell us why, but lost most of us by the fourth equation, and that was keeping it simple. I glanced over at him. He was lying on a couch next to me. As far as I could see, he had his eyes tight shut. His lips were moving. He turned over, and opened his eyes.

'Ah,' he whispered, 'you caught me at it.'

'At what?'

He closed his eyes again for a second, then opened them and smiled. 'Praying.'

'I didn't know you were a believer.'

'Not as such,' Malley said. He stared fixedly at our looming goal on the screen above us. 'But I understand God listens whether you're a believer or not.'

This was no time for philosophical debate. 'Yes,' I whispered back. 'That's what Andrea says about her St Christopher medal.'

'I heard that,' said Andrea. 'Don't you believe it. I may be sentimental, but I'm not superstitious.'

Malley smiled and seemed to relax somewhat.

'I've seen God,' Boris contributed, from the couch to my left. 'In the sky outside Brno.'

'You mean you got caught in smart rain from an obsolete Hanseatic psychochemical munition,' I said. 'Don't confuse things.'

'I know what done it to me,' Boris said placidly. 'And I know what I seen.'

'Pipe down, you back there,' said Andrea. 'Boosting in ten seconds, nine, eight . . .'

This time the acceleration was gentle, building up slowly to a half gee; but the wormhole gate came at us in a rush. Before I could think, before I could wonder, before Malley could pray again, the screens flared briefly blue, and then went black.

'Cutting the drive,' said Andrea. The small weight went away.

Jaime's voice rose above the sudden silence.

'Is that *it*?'

Andrea flicked though screen images, stabilizing on the red crescent of the planet we'd seen the day before, sixty-two thousand miles away and dead ahead.

'Yes,' she said. 'That's it. We're through.'

Jaime was checking the starfield against an astonomical atlas in the navigational computer. The babbages ran for a few seconds, the fixels flickered and laboured; the catalogued 3D picture incremented the proper motions of the stars, and after several iterations meshed with the outside scene. Jaime examined the tank's readout.

'Ten thousand light years from home, and just over ten thousand years in the future, at a rough guess,' he said. 'Welcome to the Sagittarius Arm.'

'Wow,' said Suze.

'I think you spoke for all of us,' I said. 'Stay strapped in, everybody. Yeng, would you please run us a scan?'

Yeng complied quickly, hauling her interface down from the clustered banks of computers and checking that it was isolated from the rest, then cautiously sweeping the radio portion of the electromagnetic spectrum and sample-scanning apparent messages into her anti-virus software.

'It's busy,' she said.

'Take your time,' I said.

'It's *really* busy. I've never seen anything like it. There are signals at *every possible* wavelength! Scanning them all for viruses would take forever.' She waved a hand helplessly at the screen, down which a string of samples was propagating. 'Nothing there, but that's just the beginning, just a tiny fraction.'

'Try a random sample right across the spectrum,' I suggested.

That took about an hour, during which time we drifted further from the daughter-wormhole Gate and closer to the planet. We put this time to good use. First, we rotated the ship and decelerated, so that we could flee straight back through the wormhole if Yeng's investigations turned up anything nasty. Next, we placed a small communications satellite in a fixed position relative to the wormhole, a position it was programmed to hold. It was also programmed to point a communications laser at the correct angle for the beam to get through to the *Turing Tester* on the other side. (Light, having no mass, could get through without acceleration, which would of course have been impossible in any case; Malley's further explanation of how only coherent light could do it was, I'm afraid, lost on me.)

I tested the link, nervously, with Malley at my shoulder.

'*Terrible Beauty* to *Turing Tester*, are you receiving me?'

Seconds passed.

'*Turing Tester* to *Terrible Beauty*, receiving you loud and clear. Are you in the right place?'

'Yes, we are,' I said. 'Ten thousand light years from home, according to Jaime.'

Another short delay.

'Just passed on your message to the Command Committee. Tatsuro's coming through now.'

The voice changed. 'Congratulations, comrades, you just made history. Small step, giant leap and all that.'

One small step for the Jovians, one giant leap for us.

'Thank you,' I said. After a few more exchanges, mainly technical, we signed off.

Next we spun out a mirror and set it up in front of the ship and a little to one side, so that we could make visual observations through *Terrible Beauty*'s forward telescope. By sheer good luck we'd arrived just at the time when the planet's major settlement, Ship City, was coming around the middle of the crescent limb and turning to the night. The lights of smaller settlements were sprinkled across the dark side, and shortly the five-armed shape of the city joined them, a bright neon star. There were more settlements than Wilde had told us about, and the city seemed bigger and brighter than he'd described.

'Looks human enough to me,' said Tony.

'Well, it ain't,' I said. 'According to Wilde, four of those arms are inhabited, if that's the word, by robots running wild.'

'The lights are on, but nobody's home?' Malley said mischievously.

'Exactly,' I said. 'So let's not make assumptions, OK?'

'Looks like somebody's making assumptions about us,' remarked Boris.

'What?'

'No challenges,' he said mildly. 'They must assume we're friendly.'

'Thank you for sharing that,' said Tony. 'I've always thought the null hypothesis didn't get its fair share of publicity.'

'Stop bitching, comrades,' I said.

'Who's bitching?'

They continued in this vein for some time.

'*When* you've all *quite* finished,' said Yeng. She pushed the apparatus away from her, and the spring-loaded boom lifted it back to the cluster. 'You might like to hear my preliminary report on a random sample of radio signals.'

'We're listening,' I said.

'They're clean,' she said. 'A lot of encrypted stuff, but nothing that does nasty things to anything I've thrown it at. Definitely just dead data, not live programs. So, would you all like to hear a little of what goes on in a system

where humans have the spectrum to themselves and don't have to worry
about—' deep doomy voice '—"parasite programs from monster minds"
shorting their circuits and eating their brains?'

'Yes, go ahead,' I said.

We all sat up a little on our couches—or rather, pushed ourselves away
with our elbows—to listen to what people without Jovian jamming to worry
about had to say. Yeng, with an impish smile, reached up for a switch and
fiddled with a dial. The command-deck speakers filled the level with the
most doleful music I'd ever heard. A sad, throaty voice was singing along,
with lyrics I had to search my most distant memories to make sense of: the
themes included unemployment, alcohol abuse, desertion, betrayal, sexual
frustration, jealousy, religion . . .

'That's *terrible*,' said Tony, after a couple of minutes of open-mouthed
listening. 'It must be hell down there.'

Suze laughed. 'Not hell—capitalism.'

'Yes, yes, yes,' I said. 'But what sort of music *is* that?'

'Country,' said Malley. 'Or maybe western.'

'Give us something else,' Boris pleaded. 'Anything.'

'Sure thing,' Yeng drawled. (The infection was already getting to her.)
She turned the dial through a couple of banshee howls, and settled on a
wavelength just as a voice announced: '—and I'd like to welcome you all
to the Black Wave, Ship City's first and best blues and soul station, here to
help you make it through the night . . .'


To be fair, not all the music beamed out by the local radio stations was an
incitement to suicide: some of it was definitely a provocation to murder.
This fitted right in with what we saw on broadcast television, which at first
sight indicated a society where murder was commonplace; but Suze and
Malley assured us that Wilde had been right in his descriptions of this in
his original interrogation—it was just faked, staged, pretended violence for
entertainment. Most of it was, anyway. Lethal combat was a legal spectator
sport, as Wilde had told us and as we now soon confirmed. We floated
about, watching the screen with an appalled fascination.

'This is *sick*, man,' said Boris. 'Hey, I've seen more killings in the last
half-hour than I ever saw in the Hundred Years' War.'

'You did most of your killing at long range, as I recall,' I said. 'What you
saw is one thing, what you did is another. Anyway,' I added, pointing at a
losing player being dragged out of a stadium, to cheers, 'he'll be back on his
feet—well, when they find them—in a few days.'

'Nasty head wound,' said Yeng.

'They all take back-ups just before they go on, so all he'll lose is the memory of the fight. That's how they see it.'

'But not you?' Malley asked.

I shook my head, emphatically. 'Death is death, and I don't see the comfort in knowing that a clone with your memories is going to exist in the future.'

Malley pushed himself away from the wall he was about to collide with, and immediately drifted off in a direction other than the one he'd intended.

'I think,' he said over his shoulder, 'that we've just encountered yet another of your incorrigible ideas, Ellen. It's right up there with this "machines aren't conscious" bug in your mental program.' He grabbed at a plant through whose fronds he was moving, and succeeded only in breaking off a leaf.

' "Consciousness is an emergent property of carbon",' Yeng quoted gleefully. 'So stop hurting our plants.'


We'd needed this interlude of slacking-off, to recover somewhat from the tension we'd all felt about going through the wormhole—greater, to me anyway, than that of any other manoeuvre I'd experienced; at least since dropping in on the battle of Lisbon, which was a long time ago. To cross that space-time gulf was scarier than landing a shuttle through flak, and in retrospect it was no less troubling. I turned my mind resolutely from reflecting on it. It would be some time before the awe at what we'd done struck home to us, and I wanted to be safely home before it did. The radio and television broadcasts, misleading though they possibly were about the texture of daily life, had also been useful in mentally preparing us for arriving in a very alien society.

But it had gone on long enough.

'OK, comrades,' I yelled. 'Stop laughing at the sex channels and get back to your posts. We got work to do.'

When everyone had drifted—or, in Malley's case, been hauled—back to their couches, I attached myself loosely to my own and positioned myself to see and be seen.

'Right,' I said. 'We've established, at least provisionally, that New Mars hasn't yet had a runaway Singularity. If it has, somebody's making sure it looks and sounds like it hasn't—but we can't rule that out. The obvious way to check is to send down a few small, unobtrusive probes and see what it's like close up. But first, we want to let them know we're here. As far as we know, we haven't been spotted yet, but we certainly will be as soon as we start our approach burn and go into orbit.

'We've been through all this before, but let me go through it one more time. They don't have space defence in a military sense, but they do have laser-launchers, and spacecraft with missile and laser capability. They use them whenever one of their incoming comet fragments looks like it might fall in the wrong place, or fall too hard—terraforming by cometary bombardment is a bit of a risky business. Their lasers aren't powerful enough to burn us out of the sky—they only use the laser-launchers for little robot craft like the Wilde simulacrum came back in—but they could do us a lot of damage, and even the fighter-bomber might find their missiles too hot to handle. They have a charmingly casual way with nukes, by the way.

'So let's do this by the book. The first thing I suggest we do is for Suze and Yeng to compose and send a nice, reassuring hailing message, and for Jaime and Andrea to put us on a course which plainly is aiming for a high orbit around the planet. Geostationary, or to be precise—' I paused, smiling at my own pedantry '—*neo-areostationary* above Ship City would be ideal.'

'Not right above it,' said Tony. 'Too intimidating.'

'OK, just so long as we stay above the horizon. Before we start hailing, I'd like Boris to power up a dozen probes—little ones, mind, whose final stage will just float through the air like a leaf—and have them ready to fire them off shortly after orbital insertion. Meanwhile, I want you in Fire Control from the moment before we start signalling to well after we're sure we're welcome; and you and Jaime be ready to scramble the fighter-bomber. Yeng, you could scan for any response to our message on the aerospace-traffic control channels, or whatever they have, and Suze can do the same for the news broadcasts. It shouldn't be too long before we're the number one item.

'Finally . . . last we heard, they don't have a state here. All to the good, no doubt, but what they have instead is a lot of competing defence companies. It ain't like the Division, or even the Union—we don't worry about tooled-up people, because we aren't violent. These people may not be as violent as you'd think from their television, but they're a bit, ah, touchy and unpredictable.' I looked enquiringly at Malley.

'I think that's safe to say,' he acknowledged.

'Right,' I said. 'Let's do it. By the book.'


We got our first reply very quickly. This historic first contact between the Solar Union and humanity's first and only extrasolar colony went as follows:

'This is Solar Union passenger spaceship *Terrible Beauty*, out of Callisto via the Malley Mile, calling Ship City traffic control. Requesting permission to enter geostationary orbit and—'

'GET THE FUCK OFF this channel, kid. I'm warning you, you're endangering traffic, and we're triangulating your source *right now*. You are in deep shit, you little scumbag. OK, we've got you, we—'

Long pause. 'Uh oh. Jonesy, we got a bogey. I say again, we got a bogey. Condition Yellow. Going over to encryption Zero-Prime, I say again, Zero-Prime as from now, *kcchchchgh* . . .'

'Try another channel,' Suze advised. 'See if their competitors are more open-minded.'

Yeng worked her way through a succession of rebuffs from Ship City ATC Inc, Reid Industrial Airways, Lowell Field Control Tower, Barsoom Buddies, Xaviera's Friendly Flight-Control . . .

'When you said to go by the book, Ellen, you might have told us you meant the Yellow Pages,' Malley said.

I had to laugh (and yes, we did have Yellow Pages, even in the moneyless commonwealth); but we could all imagine the calls that were undoubtedly going on, to yet another list of companies: the ones that sold protection from incoming space-junk. We also knew that the people on New Mars had what seemed to them good reason to worry about things coming at them out of the wormhole. Five years earlier, Jonathan Wilde's robot copy had disappeared through the Malley Mile, desperately worried that the Jovian fast folk were about to take control of its other end. This concern had been misplaced, but he'd never reported back . . .

And our own intentions weren't entirely friendly. If the New Martians had known just what they *were*, they'd have scrambled every interceptor they had, and blown us out of the sky.

Suze called out: 'We're on the news!'

Yeng leaned over and swung a display screen around so that we could all see it. It showed an excited small boy, talking very quickly in front of a picture of a blurry but recognizably ovoid blob.

'—the UFO is still moving slowly towards us from the wormhole Gate. According to a well placed source, it claims to be a human expedition from the Solar System! Sources remain tight-lipped, however, about whether this claim is true—or whether the fast folk back home are pulling a fast one on us! Are we about to face a real invasion—or a virtual one? Software Seduction Services urges everyone to update their anti-virus systems. Don't take chances—call this number now!' A long number appeared at the bottom of the screen. 'And now . . . we bring you, live and exclusive, an outside broadcast of Mutual Protection's crack comet-busters scrambling from Lowell Field! No job's too big for Mutual Protection—and no job's too small! Is *your* home or business as safe as it could be? Call Mutual Protection, and you too can enjoy the security that only the most experienced protectors can provide, in a proud tradition that stretches all the way back to Old Earth, and is still out in front on New Mars!'

'And off it,' the kid ad-libbed admiringly, as the screen filled with a startling floodlit view of scores of needle-shaped rockets leaping into the night sky like the arrows at Agincourt, the snarl of engine after engine rising and merging into one baying yell.

At the bottom of the screen was another number to call.

'Boris, Jaime, get in the fighter-bomber,' I said. 'Don't separate until I tell you, unless you see incoming. Jaime, give us an estimate on how long these rockets will take to arrive—'

'They won't,' Boris said flatly. 'That picture is *bullshit*, Ellen. Archive footage or outright fake. These are last-ditch anti-missile missiles. Type we used to call Citizens. No use for comet-busting unless the comet's almost on top of you. It's a diversion—'

The alarm went off and the forward view lit up with laser fire meeting its targets. Heavy thuds resounded through the ship—not hits, as my first shocked notion was, but decoys being launched from the hull's tubes in a crazy, confusing non-pattern to distract any radiation-seeking incoming missiles with a bewildering variety of radio, radar, and infrared emission profiles.

'Strap down!' yelled Andrea. Our suits, responding to the alarm with the equivalent of conditioned reflex, were already hardening around us, tightening our straps. Andrea fired the attitude jets and, while the ship was still rolling over, engaged the fusion drive. The acceleration pressed down on me like a smothering, giant hand. Despite all the support of the suit, my ribs were almost cracking under the strain of breathing. I began to black out, then felt my skin prickle all over as the suit started slipping oxygen directly into my blood through micrometre-wide tubules. The forward view—what I could see of it through the flaring patches that the weight on my eyeballs was generating on my retinae—was a storm of expanding spherical flashes.

And then we were in free fall again. I lay gasping painfully. The suit's multitude of tiny needles withdrew, their infinitesimal pains indistinguishable from the pins-and-needles of returning circulation.

'Stay where you are!' Andrea's warning was again redundant—none of us could have as much as raised our heads. 'We did it,' she went on. 'We outran them.'

Boris was scanning engagement and damage reports.

'Not too bad,' he said. 'Hull damage is within tolerance. *Carbon Conscience* is intact and seems to have fought pretty well on its own account.'

'What *happened* there?' Suze asked plaintively. 'Were we attacked?'

'Sure were,' said Boris. 'Nothing too sophisticated, though. Looks like they had a small swarm of comet-breakers parked around the wormhole. They weren't much use against active-defence. Wasted the decoys on them, really. Pity about that.'

'Why,' I asked, staring in disbelief at the swelling dark circle in the forward view, 'are we heading straight for New Mars?'

'Ah,' said Andrea. 'Sorry, comrades. Reflex, I'm afraid. I can make a course correction if you—'

'No, no, leave it for now.' I was beginning to reconsider our approach, literally as well as figuratively. The television news was still coming through.

'—the UFO has punched through our first line of defence and is now *heading straight towards us*! Stay tuned for—'

'"UFO", indeed!' said Malley. 'Bloody cheek.'

'What's a UFO?' asked Yeng.

'Something people believed in before they had the true knowledge,' Malley flipped back.

'Yeng,' I said, before her moment of puzzlement could turn to hurt, 'I wonder if you can access the New Martian communications network, and *call that number?*'

'Call up Mutual Protection?'

'Yes, why not? Suze, do you think you could talk to them? Do a deal?'

Suze laughed. 'I don't know about that, but I could make them very confused.'

'It's worth a try, anyway,' I said. 'OK everybody, stay strapped in. Enough of trying to persuade them not to be paranoid. We're going to give them something to *really* worry about. Andrea, give us a three-gee course towards them, then spin us round and bring us down anywhere that looks uninhabited and not too far from Ship City. Suze, Yeng, keep trying the numbers. Boris, Jaime, get in the *Carbon Conscience* and ride along as long as you can; disengage before we hit atmosphere, make an aerodynamic landing, and use up all the firepower you need to get us through.'

'That's what I like,' said Boris. 'Covering fire for a contested landing. Takes me back.' He disengaged from his couch and followed Jaime in a straight dive for the transfer airlock.

I decided that reminding him that he'd never done any such thing, and that I had, would be bad for his morale. A minute or so later he called us up from the fighter-bomber and announced that he and Jaime were ready for the burn.

'Good,' I said. 'Now let's show those non-cos what we're made off.'

'Here's hoping they don't have to work it out from our scorched DNA,' said Andrea, just before the drive kicked in. This time the gee-force was less than in our evasive manoeuvre, but it was considerably more prolonged. The moment of free fall during the roll-around provided no respite—parts of me that were enduring a dull ache took the opportunity of the weight coming off to report in as acute pain, and didn't shut down when the deceleration began and the weight came on again.

'Disengaging,' said Boris. 'See you on the ground, if you make it.'

'I love you too,' I said. 'Take care.'

In the lateral view the complex insectile shape of the fighter-bomber shifted away on a parallel course by a brief burst of its jets, and fell rapidly behind us. Then its main drive lit up and it shot past us again, on its own different, perilous, and necessarily one-way descent.

Suze and Yeng simultaneously said something, hard to make out as their voices strained against the weight on their chests.

'Say again please,' I said heavily.

'We're through,' groaned Suze, her voice making it sound as if she meant that we were finished. 'We're in contact with Mutual Protection. They seem to be taking us seriously. Got them on hold right now.'

'Put them on the main screen,' I said. 'Patch me through.'

A serious-looking young man's face appeared above me. 'Hi,' I said feebly. 'We're about to make a powered landing outside your town, and we want to assure you we're friendly and ask you to keep your missiles off our backs. We can fight them off anyway.' This was a bluff, but my face was probably so distorted that my expression was unreadable. 'But we'd rather land peacefully.'

'You the starship that calls itself *Terrible Beauty*?'

'Yes,' I said. Starship, I thought. That's better than calling us a UFO!

'Can you offer collateral?'

'Call what?'

'Excuse me,' said Suze, cutting in. 'We can offer at least one ton of gold as collateral against any damage.'

'Ah.' The young man frowned, trying too obviously not to look impressed. 'Is that imperial, or metric?'

Before this negotiation could go further we hit the upper layers of the atmosphere, and the picture went hazy and then black. The air of New Mars is thinner than Earth's—not that we were relying much on aerobraking. The outside view went red, and comms and active-defence could do very little. Nor could we. We just had to lie there and hope that the shrieking and buffeting were caused by our passage through the air and not nearby airbursts, each of which could be the last thing we knew. Malley seemed to be praying again, and I almost wished I could do the same, even with his agnostic reservations. But I'd been a good materialist in too many foxholes to relent now. All I would ask of a god is unconditional love and close air support, and I could rely on Boris for both.

The drogues jolted us three times, four, five—the thinner air meant more were needed than on Earth, even with the lesser gravity. There was a final flare of the jet which piled on the gees and helped deploy the struts, and then we were down. I could hear nothing but the creak of my chest and the pneumatic sigh of the settling struts.

'We're down in one piece,' said Andrea. 'No incoming missiles, and *Car-*

*bon Conscience* just checked in. They're spiralling down and report no ground fire.'

People attempted a cheer. Andrea lined up a comms laser on the relay at the wormhole and passed on the news of our safe landing.

Painfully, making full use of the suit's power-assistance, I moved to a sitting position and stood up.

'Everybody OK?'

They all struggled upright.

'Feel as if I've been in a fight,' said Tony. 'Where are we?'

'Forty miles outside Ship City,' said Andrea. 'In a field covered with some kind of monoculture.'

'It's something people do when they don't have hydroponics,' Malley said.

'A non-co thing, is it?' asked Yeng.

I was pleased to see her beginning to be sarcastic back.

A short while later we discovered that it was indeed a non-co thing, as I peered out of the airlock hatch to see a man standing in semi-darkness, just outside our circle of lights and the wider circle of ruination our landing had caused. He was holding what looked like a shotgun. The land around him was level in all directions, with low, lit mounds here and there which I guessed were dwellings of some kind. The stars seemed closer than they do in space, and, strangely, brighter.

'I don't know who or what you ay-are,' he shouted. 'But you pay-ay for this day-mage, or you git the hail off mah lay-and.'

'What payment do you want?' I yelled back, giddy with relief and quite prepared to offer the man a ton of gold, imperial or metric.

'Hey,' said Suze, from behind my shoulder. 'Let me handle this.'


The farmer, who introduced himself as Andrew Calvin Powell, turned out to be quite different from the non-cos I'd encountered in London. After a few minutes of narrow-eyed dickering ('What's that in grey-ams?') he seemed delighted by what Suze offered by way of compensation, and invited us all to 'Come on in and way-at fer the helicopters.'

'Military helicopters?' I asked, glancing anxiously back up the ladder.

The man laughed, white teeth flashing in his friendly, sunburned face. 'Good Lord no, may'am. Last I heard, Mutual Protection had taken you all under their wing. No, you're getting a visit from the city big shots, them as have been dragged out of urgent business meetings—and beds and bars! They won't be here for a good hour at least, while they get their act together. And your pals in the stealth bomber have lay-anded safely at the airport, where they're talking to reporters.'

I signalled for the rest to come down the ladder. There was little point in

staying with the ship—it was more than capable of looking after itself, and
so were we. Our suits could maintain encrypted radio contact with it—or
with the fighter-bomber, when that was closer. In fact, we could do better
than that, I thought, and tapped my cuff as though I had an itch under it.
The tiny beaded eyes of nanocameras formed, barely noticeable, in the
suit's fabric.

'How do you know all this?' I asked, as we gathered around Powell and
set off across eight hundred yards of ploughed ground towards the glowing
windows of his house, which was in the shape of a long, low mound. 'Was it
on television before you came out?'

'Don't you hay-ave cortical downlinks?'

'Well, in a way,' I said carefully. 'We just don't use them for *news*.'

He gave me a sideways look. 'Same old Reds, eh? Controlled news and
lousy consumer electronics. Way-ell, at least you're fray-endly, like the old
New Viet Cong back home.'

'Hey,' said Tony, tramping along beside me through the muddy field, 'I
remember them.'

'Wait a minute,' I said, before Tony could launch into political reminiscence, 'it isn't like that. We have problems with electronics, sure, but that's
because of the fast folk. We have all the fancy tech we want, but we've just
developed it in a different direction.'

'My old grandpaw told me the goddamn Russkies useta say that,' Powell
said, with maddening slowness and imperturbability. 'And the only things it
was true of was the Energia booster, the Mig fighter and the AK-47. The
rest of their kit was cray-ap.'

Behind me I could hear Malley laughing.

'Oh, come on,' I said, 'how do you think we can see in the dark?' I waved
a hand in the dimness.

'Not with gene-spliced visual intensifiers, I'll bet,' said Powell.

I blinked my contacts to a higher acuity and said nothing until we arrived at Powell's back door. He stood back on the doorstep and gestured for
us to go inside. Just before I did so, I got the suit to repel all the mud from
my boots, and to go through a spectacular transformation as I stepped dramatically over the threshold into the brightly lit room beyond.

I turned around with a twirl of skirt, noticing with a downward glance
that at least some of the suit's cameras had cleverly turned themselves into
visible beads. 'Do people here have clothes that can do that?'

Powell grinned. 'That's a very fine dress, may-am,' was all he said. He
waited for us to step inside—the other women followed my example, each
in her own fashion—and came in and racked his shotgun at the door, then
led us through his house.

The first room we passed through was just a store: bare walls of concrete—much the same as sea-crete, except that the limestone component is fossil—with racks and shelves of tools and seeds and parked robots. Then Powell led us along a corridor, past closed wooden doors, into the main part of his house. Somewhere along the way the flooring changed to a deep carpet, which Powell stepped on to without even shaking the mud from his shoes. A few steps later his shoes were clean. I couldn't quite catch how it was happening. The carpet's pile shimmered slightly as he walked on it; that was all.

From outside, the house had looked quite large, an artificial grass-covered knoll, about thirty yards long by four high. Inside, it looked even bigger, because it turned out to be thirty yards square and partly underground. We came out of the corridor on to a balcony that ran all around a sunken atrium, whose roof was a layer of glass, behind which we could see torpid fish and the ripple-distorted, starry sky. The lighting was brighter in the lower level, which was furnished with what looked like leather-covered sofas and chairs and a few tables. A woman was sitting at one of the tables, and as we entered she stood up and smiled at us. We trooped after Powell down a stair that followed the curving wall to the floor, past a pool with tall plants growing up from it and fish swimming around.

All around the walls were screens, apparently blank; a few large, still pictures of people, and Earth landscapes; and a great number of unfamiliar objects, most of them vaguely organic in appearance but probably artificial. They clung to the walls or squatted on shelves or hung from the ceiling. You never quite saw them move, but at a second glance they gave the disconcerting impression that they just had.

'Folks, meet my wife,' said Powell, turning around and looking at us all.

The woman who'd been sitting at the table stepped towards us, smiling. She was about five foot six tall with a sturdy, curvy build which her rather tight, gem-beaded red dress did little to conceal and much to enhance. Her blonde hair cascaded around her shoulders in elaborate curls and waves. Her face was covered with cosmetic make-up, quite unnecessarily: it was young and pretty underneath all the powder and colouring. She held out her hands and grasped mine between them.

'Well hi there,' she said. 'I'm real pleased and honoured to meet you. My name's Abigail, and you must be Miss Ellen May.'

'Just Ellen, neighbour Abigail,' I said. 'I'm pleased and honoured to meet you too.'

'Oh, how kind of you,' she said. Her accent was less noticeable than Andrew's, and in fact from that point on I stopped noticing his. The main thing I noticed about her voice was the warmth. As I introduced the rest of the crew she greeted all of them like long-lost friends. She had heard of

Malley, and seemed awe-struck to meet him. By the time the introductions
were over Andrew—or someone, or something—had covered the table with
an inviting array of bottles and glasses. The couple insisted on sitting us all
down on the biggest sofas and serving us drinks, than sat down facing us by
the table and served themselves.

Andrew Powell raised his glass. 'Peace and freedom!'

We drank to that. I felt a bit bad about what we all might think of it, any
day now; but we could always hope. There was a moment of awkward pause,
not surprisingly: the etiquette of first contact between people from two long-
separated human societies was in its early days.

'It was brave of you,' I said to Andrew, 'to go out to us with nothing but
a shotgun. You didn't know who we might be, or how we might react.'

He waved his hand. 'Not real brave,' he said. He and his wife shared a
smile. 'Abigail here had you covered from the house, with enough firepower to stop a regiment.'

'Ah,' I said, thoughtfully. 'But you'd have been in the line of fire, yes?'

He shrugged. 'Backed up just the other week. Some memories I'd be sorry
to lose.' Another shared smile, a nudge and a giggle from Abigail. 'But anyway, I weren't that worried. Had you lot figured for a human expedition ever
since the first reports this evening. Just gosh darn lucky you landed on my
patch. I'll be showin' off that site for years, and prob'ly charging admission!'

Abigail must have misinterpreted our puzzled expressions. 'Oh, you see,
we don't have no problem with resurrection. We both fell asleep way back
in the twenty-first, and we were raised again only five years ago. Which
is why—' she waved around, with a look of slight embarrassment '—we're
still only moderately well-off, as you can see. I mean, we can't really afford
to have children yet. But we have each other, and our little farm, and God
has been kind to us.'

Her thick eyelashes emphasized a few quick blinks.

'Didn't have no truck with religion until I died,' said Andrew awkwardly.
'But that experience kind of concentrates one's mind on spiritual things,
and when I found myself buck naked and dripping wet and looking up at a
Red Cross chopper, I tell you I just got down on my knees and praised the
Lord.'

'What you might call a born-again Christian,' said Malley. The rest of us
didn't quite get why Andrew and Abigail laughed so much they had to clutch
each other for support.

'You could say that,' Andrew gasped, knuckling his eyes. He took a deep
breath and spoke more seriously. 'But apart from the, uh, relief and thank-
fulness and so on, when I had time to think about it I figured, well, if mere
man can do that then you'd be a *damned* fool to think the Almighty couldn't

raise all the dead in His own good time, and I knew that only Jesus could stand between me and His righteous indignation on that day.'

He grinned at our politely frozen faces. 'OK, that's me done my witnessing to you godless communists, and you'll hear no more gospel from me unless'n you ask for more, and I'll gladly give it. But the good book says not to cast your pearls before—'

'It sure does,' Abigail interrupted, with apparently unnecessary haste. 'Now let me get you all another drink.'


Our forty minutes or so of enjoying the hospitality of Andrew and Abigail did us all a great deal of good, though at the time it seemed only to give us a little relaxation and a sense of unreality arising from the sudden change from our dangerous descent to this scene of sumptuous comfort. As soon as they'd got past the 'witnessing', which they apparently regarded as something they had to do, however briefly, to any stranger, they chatted to us easily. Mainly about themselves, but even this was a courtesy, as though they didn't want us to feel we were being interrogated. We all knew that the time for that would shortly come.

They proudly called themselves 'dirt farmers'; vegetables grown in real soil were a luxury here, supplied to exclusive restaurants for sophisticates who claimed to be able to tell the difference from the carbon-copy, and who could afford the—considerably more evident—difference in price. (I had to give Yeng an unobtrusive nudge at this point.) Variety was their speciality— Andrew explained how much searching of the gene-banks he had to do to keep ahead of changing fads. Most of the work on the farm was done by what they called 'dumb machines', and not by what they called 'hired help'. (Another nudge to keep Yeng quiet.)

Their questions about the Solar System were carefully general. We answered with similar care. They expressed relief that Earth was well populated, respect at our assurance that it was prosperous, and only wry regret that it had all 'gone communist' (as they put it) since their demise.

'I don't think you'd find it anything like what you think of as communist,' Malley said. 'And I'm not part of their society, so maybe you can take my word for it.'

'I'm sure you folks like it just fine,' said Abigail soothingly. 'But for ourselves, we like it here.'

'Every man under his own vine and under his own fig tree, and no one to make him afraid,' added Andrew.

'Things must have changed a bit since Jonathan Wilde left,' I suggested.

'Since he *left*? Oh—I see what you mean.' Abigail shook her head. 'Now that I do call unnatural, having another copy running. Anyway, you're right, things sure have changed. You know, in the old days, before the Abolition, they didn't even give civil rights to robots who were as smart as any human being, if not a darn sight smarter!'

'They had androids and gynoids walkin' about, lookin' just like people,' said Andrew. 'God only knows if they have souls, but they sure do have minds of their own, and anybody could just own one like it was a brute beast!'

Before we could respond—our looks of surprise, perhaps even, in my case, of shock having been interpreted by Andrew as sharing his dim view of this unenlightened past state of affairs—there was a distant chime.

'That'll be the big shots' delegation now,' said Andrew. He looked down at a panel on the table, which hadn't been grey and glowing last time I looked. 'Landing in a couple of minutes. Best get up to the patio.'

As we rose to our feet Abigail said: 'Just one thing . . . it was courteous of you ladies to turn on those pretty dresses for visiting us, but I think when you're going to be on television and all, you'd best *look* like you'd just stepped out of a spaceship, and not out of a cab on the way to a dance, if you don't mind my saying so.'

Oh, well, I thought, there'd be other chances to show off. But I felt a slight pang as my layered chiffon, Yeng's brocade cheongsam, Andrea's tiered lace and Suze's silver velvet sheath melted and flowed back into variants of high-gravity, on-duty gear.

Andrew grinned as the transformation was completed. 'There's already a group on the nets that says the whole thing's a fake got up by the defence companies to drum up business. Don't know if you looking like spacers will make them any less suspicious.'

Abigail approved of my blue denims and high boots. 'But you want to put some darker colour in that jacket, and maybe a mission patch or two . . .' So when we all marched up the stairs, around the balcony and out on to the patio, we each had a round blue patch with Earth's starry plough and a picture of the *Terrible Beauty* over our hearts.

The wide patio was also sunken, about six feet below ground level, open, and brightly lit. Over to the left, above the banking around it, was another flat illuminated space, on which a small helicopter was parked. Above it a much larger helicopter hovered, silent apart from the *whap* of the rotor-blades. It slowly descended close by the smaller one, beside which it looked like the adult of a strange species standing over its infant. I think it was something clever in the ground plan, and not any more advanced technology, that kept the downdraught blowing above our heads and not into our faces.

The helicopter's side door folded away, and a set of steps folded out. In the moment before anyone appeared, it occurred to me that I felt as if we, and not they, were waiting to meet the aliens.

A man stepped down the ladder, with a slow dignity which was only partly due to the care which he had to take with the high heels of his tall boots. His medium height and slim build were further extended by a stovepipe hat and an open frock coat, both black, and a colourful waistcoat over a white shirt with a black bootlace tie. A holstered pistol completed the look: the law west of Pecos, to the life. He walked over to the rim of the patio, looked to left and right, found the steps and made his way down.

Close behind him followed another man and two women, with a whole crowd of other people behind them. I just had time to recognise the second man—it was David Reid, who'd supplied the Outwarders with bonded labour, including some of ours. Our old enemy—

And then the man in the tall hat was shaking my hand.

'Hello,' he said. 'My name's Eon Talgarth. I'm pleased to welcome you to Ship City, of which'—his smile twisted a little—'I'm the somewhat reluctant Chief Justice. And you must be Ellen May Ngwethu, acting captain of this expedition?'

'That's right,' I said. 'Pleased to meet you, neighbour.' His voice and accent reminded me, oddly, of the London non-cos; he'd stabilized his age at about forty, but he was much older than that, possibly older than I was—an eerie thought, which impressed me more than his ridiculous judicial fig.

'Yeah, I reckon we're all neighbours now,' he said. He turned as if to introduce these new neighbours, but any opportunity for formal introductions had been lost: everybody on one side was indiscriminately shaking hands with everybody they could find on the other and introducing themselves or introducing somebody else. Talgarth looked momentarily at a loss, even taken aback, before he shrugged and relaxed. Reid, I noticed, was working the little crowd expertly—probably avoiding me, for the moment, and trying to make a friendly impression on my comrades. Abigail and Andrew, on a sudden inspiration, began handing out drinks, and shortly we were all behaving as if we'd just arrived at a slightly formal party.

'Comrade?' someone said in a friendly, but slightly diffident, voice. I turned, smiling at this unexpected greeting.

The girl in front of me had long fair hair that sprouted straight up from her scalp and then fell back in a mane between her shoulder blades. She wore a belted jump suit which showed off her muscular but definitely female frame. Almost as tall as me; big blue eyes, wide grin, thin, sharp nose; striking rather than beautiful, but I was inured to beauty.

'Ellen? Hi.' She stuck out her hand and I shook it. 'My name's Tamara Hunter,' she went on. 'Very pleased to meet you.'

'Likewise,' I said politely. 'What's your—'

'—part in all this?' She scratched her head. 'I put up a bit of a fight to get on this delegation. Just so the business folk and the judges didn't have it all to themselves. I'm a union official, actually, in the inter-syndical.'

'You negotiate terms for the wage slaves?'

'Exactly!' she said, looking pleased. 'A dirty job, but someone's got to do it.'

'We have these too,' I said, wryly.

Tamara looked around, as if concerned that she might be overheard.

'Is it really true,' she asked, leaning closer, 'that in the Solar System you have anarcho-communism?'

I thought over this unfamiliar word. 'We don't have to sell ourselves, and nobody tells us what to do, so I suppose you could call it that.'

'Wow!' she said, her eyes shining. 'Just knowing that is *possible*, that it can *work*, will make a huge difference here.'

'I don't know about that,' I said, mentally comparing what Abigail and Andrew considered modest prosperity with the conditions that had brought about Earth's social revolution. 'It's not just a question of ideas in people's heads—'

'Stop plotting there, Hunter!' a man's loud voice said. 'Time enough for that later.'

The man who spoke came up and firmly grasped my hand. He had black hair down to the collar of his sharply cut cotton jacket; dark brown eyes, thick black eyebrows, smoothly tanned skin; and the look of ease and unshakeable self-confidence which in our society marked out the 'old comrades', and in this one, I guessed (correctly, as it turned out), the rich.

But there was more than that. He was terrifyingly old, among the oldest people alive, and unlike even his contemporary Wilde, he'd lived as the same body, the same man, for over three hundred and fifty years. Again unlike Wilde, he had both the desire and the capacity for power, and had grown strong and proficient in its use.

'Hi, Ellen May,' he said. 'My name's Dave Reid. I'm happy to meet you, at last. You know, I heard about you back in the old days, from, well—' he laughed '—the Outwarders, I have to say!'

'Your former clients send their regards,' I said, rather more coldly than I had intended, 'and their assurance of no hard feelings about your . . . departure.'

'Do they, indeed?' He seemed surprised and pleased. 'Well, as I say, later for that. This is a great occasion.'

I sipped my drink. 'So everyone keeps telling me.'

He grinned, unperturbed. 'It is a bit of a mêlée, isn't it? I don't think anyone ever worked out the protocols for contact between socialist and capitalist anarchies. Your comrades in the *Carbon Conscience* have been telling reporters all about your society. Fascinating stuff.'

'I'm sure it is,' I said, wishing I'd briefed Boris and Jaime on what and what not to say.

'Used to be a socialist myself, you know,' Reid went on. 'Gave it up as a bad job.' He grinned at Tamara. 'Maybe I should have stuck with it.'

Then he looked at me, and through me, his face momentarily bleak. With a shake of his head he smiled again.

'"Battles long ago",' he said. 'Speaking of which, Ellen, Dee has something to tell you—'

A woman was stepping delicately towards us on stiletto heels. She wore a short dress of black lace over a longer one of white crepe, all wow and flutter. She had black hair, pale skin, green eyes, broad cheekbones and a warm smile.

'Hi, Ellen,' she said. 'I'm Dee. Pleased to meet you.'

'Hello,' I said, trying to keep the ice from my voice.

'I'm Dave's partner,' she went on. 'I used to be his, ah—'

His mechanical squeeze. A clone with a computer in its skull. Just a fucking machine.

'I know,' I said. 'Wilde told us about you.'

The gynoid woman shook my hand; I felt, or perhaps imagined, an electric tingle in her touch. She smiled up at me with disconcertingly wide, bright eyes and parted lips.

'So he made it back,' she said quietly. 'And Meg too?'

Meg—Wilde's companion, the artificial woman. Another walking doll, another fucking machine.

'Yes,' I said. 'They both made it.'

'Ellen,' Dee said. She caught my hands. 'My mind works . . . differently from yours. I have access to all the old company records, and to the city's nets. I have something to tell you. Many of the people here, as you know, were revived from the fast folk's robotized workforce. Your parents were . . . not among them.'

'They were never among them?' I asked. 'It's not just that they didn't make it in the ship?'

'We all made it in the ship,' Reid said. 'I made damn' sure of that. I didn't leave behind anyone, human or ex-human, alive or dead, who'd been conscripted or volunteered to my company.'

I looked down at him and unclenched my teeth and nails. 'I'm relieved to hear that,' I said. 'I truly am. I am happy to know that my two hundred years of nightmares about them being enslaved in robot bodies were only bad dreams, even if it does mean I'll never see even their copies again.' I stopped and took a deep breath through my nostrils. 'I can live with that, Reid, but I can't forget who killed them.'

Reid shook his head firmly. 'It wasn't me, or my company, who carried out those raids,' he said. 'It was all the doing of the Outwarders. I just saved what could be saved, and gave people a chance of a new life. For which I've received no complaints.'

'Very well,' I said. I grasped his shoulder and smiled at him, in a way that made a very satisfying shadow of fear show briefly on his face. 'Now I know who I'm looking for, and I'll take your word that it isn't you.'

Reid took a step backwards as I let go of his shoulder. His jacket was creased there, and damp. I automatically wiped my hand on my thigh. The two women looked at me with expressions of indistinguishable compassion. Eon Talgarth, the judge, perhaps drawn to the edge of our little group by the intensity of our conversation, broke an uneasy silence.

'If it's justice you want, Ellen, if that's among your reasons for coming all this way, you can find it here.'

I shook my head. 'I'm sorry,' I said. I lowered my voice. 'This is a great occasion, a happy occasion, and I don't want to spoil it.' I indicated the more cheerful fraternization going on around us, hoping that the comrades didn't take it too far. 'But you should know something about us, about me. I don't seek justice. We don't believe in justice. We have the true knowledge. There is no justice. But there is defence, and deterrence, and revenge. That's what I want. And I will have them all.'

Reid, to my surprise, smiled and stepped forward again. Though shorter than I, he held my gaze as though it was he who was looking down.

'I know what you mean,' he said. 'I've been there. If you want to take your revenge on the fast folk, be my guest!' He waved his arm expansively. 'I can fly you at a moment's notice to the place where we store their templates. You can revive them, tell them exactly what you're going to do to them and why, and make them die a thousand deaths before we flood the tanks with Blue Goo. And then, if you want, you can do it again. And again. And—'

'Stop.' I caught his arm. 'Enough.'

The vast futility of my deepest and darkest, though not my most secret, motives for coming here made me feel cold and sick and dizzy. My hope against hope of meeting copies of my dead parents had been one, and I was racked by its simultaneous disappointment and relief. My desire for revenge on the entities who were incontestably the closest to the original Outwarders had just been exposed by Reid as equally, achingly empty. There would be no point in tormenting, no satisfaction in punishing, entities with which I didn't even have enough empathy to take pleasure in their pain, if pain it was. It would be as futile as stamping on a recalcitrant machine.

There could only be one deterrence, one defence, one vengeance for me, and that was to send them to the same oblivion as they'd sent my parents and so many others: an eternal death without hope of resurrection. Nothing I said or did now could be allowed to imperil that.

I smiled at Reid. 'You're right, of course,' I said. 'It's just one of those fantasies, isn't it? When you spell it out, when you have the chance to act it out, you see how tawdry and childish it really is.'

'Well, it's understandable,' he said. 'I know how you must feel.' He clasped my forearm. 'Come on. We'll have reporters buzzing about in a few minutes, and you'll have to talk to them. When you've got that out of the way, you can all come and see the city.'

'Yes,' I said. 'I'm looking forward to that.' My knees were shaking. Reid noticed, and guided me to a seat beside a patio table. He twitched his eyebrows at Talgarth and the two women, and they slipped back amongst everybody else, standing and talking. Reid sat down beside me and uncapped a silver hip flask and passed it to me. I sipped something fiery, and passed it back.

'It's not the same,' Reid admitted regretfully. 'I really hope you still know how to make single malt.'

I had to smile. The man had, despite his reputation for ruthlessness, a disarming ability to put one at one's ease.

'You'll have to ask the people in Japan about that,' I told him.

'Oh, God,' he said. He took another sip. 'And you really do have a world without money? What do you use instead—computers?'

'Yes,' I said proudly. 'We don't do much planning, but for what we do, we use computers. The biggest in the world.'

Reid's head rocked back, his laugh bayed at the sky, and he didn't see my bleak moment of remembering just why our most important computers were built of brass and steel and looked like the very locomotives of history, incorruptible analytical engines that nothing could divert or deflect.


The year is 2098. Below me a city drifts past, its old towers of concrete and glass overshadowed by recent nano-built spires and surrounded by the shantytown sprawl that predates, and will outlast, the buildings which have grown above it like fungi on a damp, dark soil. Beyond even the shanties, the vivid green of the forest with its grey-brown scars of road; higher even than the towers, and rising still, and multiplying, the columns of oily smoke.

The smoke is rising from crashes. Here a tower is burning, upward from the twentieth floor where a helicopter is spattered on the side of the building like an insect on a windshield; there traffic is gridlocked by numberless collisions; elsewhere an airliner has fallen out of the sky, and set ablaze acres of wooden shacks.

I float in the station's telemetry deck, and the unmanned cargo airship floats above Lagos, its scanning cameras showing me scenes I can do nothing whatsoever about. This was a successful city, until half a day ago. The West Africans, decimated again and again by the plagues of the twentieth century, are almost immune to the last great plague of the twenty-first. They have survived the Death, and have even accommodated the floods of European refugees which fill the shantytowns and swirl about the towers. They still have oil, they still have computer networks. Here civilization is still rising, not falling.

Until now.

The computers are crashing, and with them everything that depends on them: traffic control, air traffic control, *aircraft* controls, industrial processes, stock control, telecommunications, and electricity supply. With predictable prisoner's-dilemma rationality, people are looting food from the suddenly dark and warming refrigerators before it spoils, raiding the shops before they're stripped, arming themselves before they're robbed, taking to the roads and heading for the villages before anybody else gets the same idea, and each discovering that everyone else is doing the same.

We're in a bad way ourselves, running everything on manual or back-up or emergency. Our computer programs have been reduced to gibberish, the viruses have shorted systems, wiped memory cores, crippled machinery . . . but our basic systems are robust, they've been jerry-built and jury-rigged and worked around so often that nothing short of physical force can disable them. We still have air and food.

The people down below are in a worse circumstance. They're paradoxically far more reliant on a network of artificial organization than we are. Lagos's biggest export is financial services, pulling in even more than its dwindling oil. All that is gone now.

The people I helplessly watch struggling in the streets are worse off even than they know. There's no help coming from anywhere, because everywhere is in the same plight. With an eerie, awful certainty, I know that a very high percentage of those people are already dead, as dead as if they were walking around—as, elsewhere, in other cities, not a few at this moment are—in the elliptical downwind teardrop zones of fallout from burning reactors.

The airship crumples into the side of a nano tower, and the picture dies.

The door of the helicopter opened again and reporters swarmed out and began hovering and buzzing about, just as Reid had said. I'd thought he'd spoken figuratively, but he hadn't. The 'reporters' were tiny helicopters, carrying microphones and cameras and loudspeakers; some of them had the ability to project a hologram of a human figure which lip-synched along with the questions from the speaker.

'They'll look quite solid when you've tuned your contacts,' Reid assured me.

'I'm not sure I want them to,' I said.

I gathered the team again into a group and we all faced the cameras and mikes together. Boris and Jaime, I guessed, must have satiated the requests for basic information about us: most of the questions I was asked (and it was I who was asked, the local media having appointed me the spokesman of the expedition) felt like the reporters here were just mopping up.

'You seemed surprised at the sight of us, Miss Ngwethu,' said a spectral youth a few feet away. 'Don't you have fetches and 'motes back in the Solar System?'

'Of course we do,' I said. 'But as I'm sure you've heard, we have problems with our electronic communications, thanks to our local versions of the fast folk. In any case, even if we didn't, I doubt if we'd use them for . . . what do you call it, news gathering? We do make limited use of them, for exploring or monitoring dangerous environments and so on.'

'So what do you use for news gathering? Do reporters have to go around in person?'

'We don't actually *have* reporters, as such,' I said. 'I mean, some people run newsletters and pump newsfeed pipes, but nobody has to pay them much attention.'

'So how—' The reporter paused, baffled. 'How does anyone know what's going on?'

'Oh! That. Well, everybody in the Union can report anything to anybody, and attend or listen in to any meeting of the social administration and say anything they like about it. Or at it, come to that, unless they start wasting everybody's time and get thrown out.'

'So your Central Committee, this Solar Council, could have hundreds of thousands of people turning up at its meetings, and all shouting at once?'

'Of course not,' I said indignantly. 'I suppose in theory, yes, but who would want to? Apart from the Solar Council delegates, that is, and some of them practically have to be pushed. It's all very practical, and frankly a bit *dull*. Local meetings are far more interesting because they have more to do.'

'Does that apply to your organization, the Cassini Division?' asked the hologram.

I thought about this. 'No,' I said.

'Why not?'

'Fighting is different. Sometimes we need to keep secrets, but not for long.'

The reporter hesitated for a second, and another seized the opportunity.

She had straight blonde hair and looked about twelve years old. 'Why have you come here?' she asked.

I gave her my best smile. 'We're very interested in finding out what has happened to the only other human community, and in establishing friendly relations with you. And of course we have a scientific interest in the wormhole—the Malley Mile.'

She gave me her best 'I wasn't born yesterday' look; rather funny, considering her age and mine. 'Apart from that.'

'Isn't that enough? Why else would we want to come here?'

'To impose your system on us, perhaps?'

This idea had genuinely not occurred to me. Our intention of wiping out the local fast folk, or destroying what Reid had called the templates, was secret and sinister enough for me to worry about anyone's guessing it. But not this. I just laughed.

'You seem to be doing fine as you are,' I said diplomatically. 'And you can't have socialism unless most people understand it and want it and are willing to do something to get it. From what I know of New Mars, this is not the case—yet.'

This raised an appreciative laugh all round, and Talgarth stepped forward with his hand raised. 'Ladies and gentlemen,' he said to the phantom figures and their rotary haloes, 'I'm sure our visitors will have a great deal to tell you all very soon. Meanwhile, I'd like to give them some hospitality and privacy.'

We'd been having plenty of both until Talgarth and the other leading citizens and their accompanying swarm of inquisitive remotes turned up, but I was not complaining. We said goodbye to Abigail and Andrew, and were escorted to the big helicopter. I found myself in a window seat beside Tamara. As the machine lifted off I waved to Powell and his wife, who waved back. The last thing I saw of them before we turned out of sight was Andrew Powell setting off across his field with a swarm of remotes beside him, heading for the ship. I knew he would have the sense not to go too close to it, but I rather suspected that this was not true of the remotes.

I leaned back with a smile, already enjoying the flight.


Tamara and I got chatting about life on New Mars and on Earth, laughing at each other's misconceptions, and about our pasts. I was gratified and embarrassed by Tamara's awe about mine, and encouraged her to talk about her own.

She said she'd been an Abolitionist.

'What's that?'

Abigail and Dee had mentioned the Abolition, but I hadn't yet followed up what this meant.

'We used to be a small group of anarchists—some social, some more into the lifestyle thing—who believed that using conscious machines as tools was wrong, you know, like slavery. But five years ago, all that changed.'

'You don't believe it any more?'

Tamara looked at me, visibly decided I was joking, and laughed more at the oddity of my supposed humour than at its content. 'No, we changed people's minds! It all came out of a complicated string of court cases involving Wilde, the copy of Wilde in the machine, Dave Reid's ownership of Dee, and of course the fast folk. After that a lot of owned sapients took to claiming self-ownership, and some people sided with them, and the new people from the dead couldn't see how anybody could treat robots like that—they didn't have the prejudices that the first humans here had.'

'Yes,' I said, 'Wilde told us about that. He said things were getting pretty hot just as he left.'

'They sure were! Closest we've ever come to a revolution, everybody outside in the streets arguing.'

'What happened about the fast folk?' I asked lightly.

Tamara's expression darkened. 'Well, after Reid and Wilde used them to start the resurrection—it's still going on, we're bringing back dead people from the smart-matter storage all the time, about a million over the past five years, which is why the city's grown so much and all the new settlements are springing up—they wiped out the copies of the fast folk they'd revived, and Reid's still sitting on the stored originals. Still scared of another bad Singularity.' She paused thoughtfully. 'But now that your Jovians have started acting reasonable and aren't going mad or anything, maybe that'll change too.'

'I'm sure it will,' I said, 'Reid won't be worrying about a bad Singularity for much longer, not if I have anything to do with it.'

Tamara's pleased look in response to this true but ambiguous statement shamed me a little. I turned to the window and looked down at the city below and before us, three of its five arms foreshortened, their long streets with their radial canals joined by the ring canal, a glowing starfish in the night.

# 9

## A MODERN UTOPIA

Airports are quiet places, where people make their leisurely way along covered walkways to the waiting craft. Around the sides of the concourse are tables with drinks and snacks, open-sided rooms with stores of the kind of supplies you might need and are likely to forget, racks and shelves where you can browse and, if you like, take away a book or journal or disk. There's a knack, a *politesse*, of picking just enough entertainment for you to have finished at the end of your journey, or at the end of one of its stages, so that you can casually place it on another airport's shelves. At some airports there'll be a group of musicians or a troupe of acrobats or whatever. You can stay within sight and sound of them, or move away. The only barriers you'll encounter are to keep you from wandering into danger. Sometimes you'll help other people with their luggage, sometimes you'll ask for a hand. If you have a long wait for your flight, you might feel like joining in some of the support activities, making sure that more hurried passengers get their refreshments or books or help with heavy luggage or small children. That's what airports are like.

Not in capitalism, they're not. When I emerged at the end of a long corridor from the busy landing field into the main concourse of Ship City's aerospace port, with my comrades beside me and the leading citizens behind them, I was greeted by hundreds of enthusiastic people behind a barrier, a swooping flock of reporters, a dazzle of clashing colours and a blare of sound. Every square yard that wasn't absolutely required for passengers or people waiting for them was occupied by a stall or shop or kiosk, each of which had its own fluorescent rectangle above it advertising flights or drugs or socks or cosmetics or lingerie or insurance or back-ups or cabs or hotels. The public-address system thumped out urgent-sounding music made all the more unsettling by frequent, and equally urgent-sounding, interruptions.

Meanwhile, other activity, apparently unrelated to our arrival, was going on. The wide passage between us and the welcoming crowd was being traversed from right to left by a succession of small automatic vehicles slowly hauling laden trailers, and of briskly striding men and women and—this was my first such encounter—what looked like ape-men of various species. Among them robots, few of which were remotely humanoid, stalked or skittered. Outside the terminal building, at the far end of the landing field, the distant sounds and flares of heavy lifting shook the air and lit the night. None of the humans or hominids or robots hurrying past in front of us spared us more than a curious, if friendly, glance.

I hesitated, unsure about how to get across this stream of light but persistent and swift traffic. Talgarth walked past me and strode out into the midst of it and, facing the oncoming flow, held up his hand. This imperious gesture enabled us to get across to just in front of the barriers. Yells and smiles greeted us, hands reached out to touch us; recorders and babies were held above heads. Talgarth led us past them all, along the barriers and around a corner into a quieter area, from which even the tiny news-copters were turned back. There were padded benches along the walls. Jaime and Boris were sitting there, looking somewhat drained, but talking earnestly to two young women in identical sky-blue jackets and matching skirts. When they saw us approaching they said their goodbyes to the women (who immediately stood up and assumed strange fixed smiles) and rejoined us.

Andrea hugged Jaime and I hugged Boris and everybody milled about for a few minutes, until Talgarth herded us all together again like a supervisor on a children's outing and led us between a pair of big glass sliding doors to the edge of a flat expanse of tarmac, where a lot of vehicles were parked, one of which awaited us.

It was about twenty-five feet long and eight feet high, with large windows at the side and a low-slung chassis. A man in a grey uniform, wearing a grey peaked cap, stood outside its open door and gave us another example of that oddly impersonal smile. Talgarth stepped aside and motioned to us to enter the vehicle. Inside there were rows of seats covered with something like leather, a fitted carpet on the floor, and a smell of fresh plastic in the air. I made my way to the rear seat and sat down beside Boris. Talgarth sat in the seat in front of us, and the rest of the crew filled up the adjacent seats. Reid, Dee and Tamara all got on too. The others who'd been with them stayed behind, waving at us from the kerb, looking simultaneously self-important and left out.

As the driver closed the door and got behind the steering wheel I said to Talgarth, 'It's neighbourly of you to lay this on for us.'

'The mini-coach?' He smiled. 'They're standard airport-to-city transport.'

'Well, thanks anyway,' I said. 'Where are we going?'

'Reid's booked a hotel floor for you, in the same building as his offices,' Talgarth explained. 'We'll go to his offices first, if that's agreeable, because we'd like a chat with you all privately before we arrange any other social functions.'

'Fine,' I said. 'We have a lot to discuss.'


The airport was between the proximal ends of two of the city's arms. Behind it lay miles of open flat ground, some of it apparently water-covered: as I glanced back through the big curved and rounded rear window, pools flashed back reflections of the jet of a rising rocket. As it faded, another flared. There was a *lot* of heavy lifting going on. Ahead, along a couple of miles of wide, open road, rose the centre of the city. The buildings in the two converging arms on either side of us became higher the closer they were to the centre, which was dominated by a cluster of tall, slender towers. They were not as tall as the towers of Earth, or the trees of the Lunar crater-domes, but they were more graceful than either, lifting the gaze and catching the breath. Their lower reaches were linked by spiral or otherwise curving ramps, giving the whole complex an appearance like the fine metalwork of a decorative headdress. Among them were other buildings, rounded, polyhedral; and tall glass rectangles like those I'd—only a fortnight ago—watched *Terrible Beauty* land beside.

All the buildings blazed with lights, from windows and flood-lamps and displays. We stared ahead, entranced.

'It's beautiful,' Suze said. Reid, sitting in front of her, turned around and said over his shoulder:

'It is, and it's also a little joke on us. The more delicate towers and the elegant geodesic domes were designed by the fast folk, based on old illustrations of futuristic cities—just to say to us, "look, we can do this better."'

'They did, too,' said Malley. His chuckle resounded above the electric hum of the bus. 'I remember those old skiffy covers myself. Bloody spiral ramps—nobody ever got them looking right, but whoever built this did.'

The driver, I noticed, wasn't doing very much, and most of the other vehicles on the road seemed to be driverless. The driver was a formality, a gesture towards the notion of some people serving others, being at their beck and call; another of those capitalist things, like the air stewardesses that Boris had been talking to, and was now telling me about . . . I listened sceptically: he seemed unduly impressed by their wage-slavish solicitude.

'But are they any more friendly and helpful than neighbours helping out with refreshments on a transport?' I asked, my mind going back to how I and Suze had met.

Boris shrugged. 'Maybe not,' he said grudgingly. 'But they do it all the time, and they do it to get what they need to live on, and that makes it all more . . . intense.'

'Ha!' I caught his arm and snuggled up beside him. 'That's *kinky*, that is,' I murmured in his ear. 'You're just an old Sheenisov state-capitalist at heart. Bet you've been secretly into employer-and-employee sex-games for years.'

'I have *not*,' he growled indignantly, then turned and touched the side of my nose with the tip of his and grinned. 'Couldn't never get anyone to play, anyway, but if that's what *you* want—'

'Go employ yourself,' I told him, very quietly. No one even in the adjacent seats could have overheard my crudity. But Dee must have had—perhaps not surprisingly—superhuman hearing, because she turned around and looked back at us from the front of the bus with a friendly and wicked smile, as though she knew exactly what we were talking about. I felt my cheeks burn a little, and I looked away.

The mini-coach was now gliding along a street, between tall buildings. At the bases of the tall buildings the pavements were quite wide, and quite crowded, even at this late hour in the evening. The traffic was denser here, and slower-moving, and as we passed, people (and the startling, ubiquitous quasi-people, the enhanced apes and re-engineered hominids and the au-tonomous machines) on the street would turn and stare for a moment, and look around them and smile.

'How do they know we're in this bus?' I asked.

Dave Reid, up at the front, snorted. He gestured at a flat grey screen be-hind the driver's seat. 'It's because we're—ah, sorry—' It seemed that all he did was to snap his fingers, irritably, and the screen suddenly showed a pic-ture of our coach, from above and behind. I looked back through the rear window, and spotted the pursuing remotes. The others on the bus laughed. 'Don't encourage them,' Talgarth said, as I faced the screen again and saw the back of my head in a zoomed-in shot which then zoomed disappoint-edly out.

The news-copters were still hovering above us when we stopped at the foot of a tower like a great concrete treetrunk, with tall windows distrib-uted apparently at random, close to the centre of the city. Talgarth and Reid preceded us out of the coach, gesturing at the remotes as if waving away flies. As I got off I thanked the driver and said goodbye to him, making eye

contact for the first time. He smiled with a slightly startled look, and smiled
a bit more when Dee paused on her way out and slipped him a tip.

Inside, the building was furnished in fake leather and real wood and the
inevitable potted plants and indoor ivy, with some of the walls left as bare
concrete. The vast, deep-carpeted reception area had the polite hush of
posh. The lift, which had a grey-uniformed attendant to push the buttons,
was big enough to take us all, comfortably. It was also fast, its acceleration
almost enough to make my knees buckle.

Reid escorted us to a room along the corridor from the lift. It was a large
anteroom to a small office, whose heavy wooden desk and deep-set window
were visible through its open doorway. An oblong arrangement of deep fake-
leather armchairs and sofas, around a long, low wooden table with glass ash-
trays; subdued ambient light; black-cylindered spotlights picking out wall
pictures, plants, and the drinks cabinet.

'Sit yourselves down,' Reid said. He took off his jacket and slung it over
the back of a seat at the top of the table, marking his own territory, then
busied himself at the drinks cabinet. Talgarth hung up his hat and coat,
pushed back his shirtsleeves and sat down, unbuttoning his waistcoat. Dee
and Tamara waited for us to take our seats, and then sat down together.

The chair I found myself in, with Boris on my right and Malley on my
left, faced one of the large, well-lit framed photographs on the wall. Most
of them showed Reid posing with new weapons systems or talking to what
I guessed were capitalists and their hired men. The one opposite me showed
Reid and Dee standing together on a wide step outside a vast arched doorway with a crowd of people around them.

The man standing beside Reid looked just like Jonathan Wilde, and the
woman standing beside Dee looked just like Dee: same height, same build,
same face. I realised with a start that I was looking at Dee's original, and
Wilde's copy, the one who had stayed here. The two men wore black coats
and trousers and colourful ties, and the woman standing beside Dee was
wearing a long, narrow green dress of understated elegance.

Dee was wearing a smug smile and a very fancy white satin dress with fitted
bodice, gigot sleeves and a full floor-length skirt, all decorated with beadwork,
cutwork, panelling, stitching, lace trimming and organza fluting: not one expensive cheap trick of exuberant, eye-filling excess had been missed. On her
head she wore a silver tiara from which a waterfall of embroidered tulle cascaded down her back and across the wide, ruffled pool of the skirt's train. The
whole saccharine confection seemed to be the costume for some carnival
where considerations of visual impact overrode those of taste; I nudged the
suit to record it, for the next time I wanted to make a big entrance at one of
our wilder parties.

Reid placed some trays of glasses on the table, then bottles of spirits, beer, tonic water, plain water, and cola. 'Help yourselves,' he said, and while we were doing so he sat down in the seat at the top of the table with a bottle of beer in front of him. When we were all sorted for drinks he leaned back in his chair and ran his fingers through his long, thick black hair several times, in a rather distracted way, then lit a cigarette. He let out a long, smoky sigh.

'Well,' he said. 'Nothing like a bit of peace and quiet. This room is about as secure as you can get, and it's also inside a Faraday cage. Chicken wire in the concrete, I understand; quite effective.' He glanced at what looked like a wristwatch, and then at me. 'So, Ellen, I'm afraid your encrypted television signal won't get beyond the walls.' He grinned. 'Just letting you know; it's not a problem. Feel free to record anything and report back to your committee or whatever—I'll give you comms facilities and complete privacy, afterwards, if you want.'

I nodded. 'Fine.'

'Good,' Reid said. He looked around at us all. 'So let's get down to business. If you want to do deals with people here, it would pay you to deal with us first. Talgarth owns a court, which at the moment is accepted by the other courts as . . . a final court, particularly for human-machine interface problems. Dee and I run the biggest protection agency, which funnily enough is the one which has taken your contract. Tamara has the ear of a significant part of the city's population, not to mention a capacity to call a general strike at a moment's notice.'

Tamara smiled and spread her hands. 'Not really.'

'You're too modest,' said Reid. 'We're not in charge here, we certainly don't see eye to eye, and I'm much less of a city boss than I was before all the formerly dead people started arriving.' He smiled wryly. 'But any of us could make or break your chances of getting on well with the people and machines of this city—I'm not saying that as a threat, just a fact. I presume you have some similar status back where you come from, and aren't'—his eyes crinkled—'just a bunch of rank-and-file cosmonauts.'

'We are, in a way,' I said. 'We have no special status, but we do have a mandate to negotiate and take whatever action we think is necessary.'

'On behalf of thirty billion people?' asked Reid, looking at me through narrowed eyelids and a haze of smoke. Somewhere an extraction fan started up.

I shrugged. 'More or less, in that we'll have to answer to them, and they voted for the broad outlines of what we're here to do.'

'And what's that?' Reid asked, with deliberate casualness.

I took a sip of whisky and water. The taste for it could be acquired, I decided. Malley was fiddling with his pipe, Suze examining her fingernails.

'We're here,' I said carefully, 'to make certain that the fast folk on your side of the wormhole are no threat to us, just as we can ensure that those at our end are no threat to you.'

Reid and Talgarth leaned forward at the same time, with the same alert, cautious expression.

'What do you mean by that?' asked Talgarth.

'Wilde—' I shook my head. 'The other one, the one you call Jay-Dub. He told us that the whole question of "robot rights" was bound up with that of reviving the fast folk, and that when he left, the robot rights side of the argument seemed to be winning. Naturally, we were concerned. I have to say I was relieved to hear from Tamara that you are still resisting any suggestion of reviving them. Can you guarantee that the question will remain closed?'

'What guarantees would you accept?' Reid asked.

*Nothing short of their destruction*, I thought. 'What can you offer?' I asked. Reid knew well that I hadn't answered his question, but he didn't press me on it. He leaned forward, elbow on knee, fingers with cigarette at his lips. 'How about my—our—continuing conviction that it would be unsafe to tamper with them again?'

'You've tampered with them once,' I said. 'And the results, as far as you're concerned, have been entirely beneficial—you've been reunited with people you'd lost, you've gained a population that seems to have materially increased your city's prosperity, you got . . . Jay-Dub through the wormhole, and so on. Now, I don't remember much about capitalism, but some of us do, and I think it's safe to say that at some point the temptation to let the genie out of the bottle again, get a few more useful answers to intractable problems, and thus give your company some competitive edge, could be hard to resist.'

Reid leaned back and looked straight at me. 'That's an entirely valid point,' he surprised me by saying, then didn't surprise me at all by going on, '*however* . . . I think you can rely on my not doing it until it's safe.' He looked over at Talgarth. 'What was it I offered—to let anyone do it who could provide an isolated space platform ringed with fire-walled lasers and dead-fall nuclear back-ups?'

Talgarth smiled and nodded.

'Hey—' said Boris, with that look shown in cartoons by a light bulb going on and blocky capitals spelling *IDEA*.

'*Nevertheless*,' I interrupted firmly, 'you then did it, with, what? *Blue Goo* instead of heavy weaponry, and you got away with it. What's to stop you doing that again?'

'The rights of the fast folk,' Reid said, quite seriously.

'*What* "rights"?' I asked. If we'd been discussing a bacterial culture, I couldn't have been more surprised.

'Oh, you know.' Reid waved his hands about. 'The usual. Life, liberty, and the happiness of pursuit.'

I sat back and laughed. 'But seriously,' I said. 'What's to stop you?'

Reid crushed out his cigarette and glared at me.

'I *am* serious. It would be wrong to do again what we did five years ago. It was wrong at the time, but'—he grimaced—'we didn't know any better. It would be all right to revive the fast folk and be ready to defend ourselves against them—that's the lasers-and-nukes scenario—but not to revive them and then wipe them out as soon as we'd got from them what we wanted. So you needn't worry about us doing that.'

Talgarth nodded agreement. I frowned, trying to figure this out. Dee and Tamara were watching me even more narrowly than the men were.

'You offered to do it for me,' I said. 'For my revenge.'

Reid gave me a cold smile. 'An offer I knew you would refuse. You're an intelligent woman.'

I wondered how he'd have reacted if I'd accepted, but thought it best to drop that uncomfortable question and return to the main point.

'You're telling us we can't trust you not to revive them, but we can trust you not to wipe them out if you do?'

'That's about it,' Reid agreed cheerfully. 'But, as I say, we wouldn't revive them without adequate defence, and there's not much chance of that in the foreseeable future.'

I could foresee quite a few futures in which Reid's idea of 'adequate defence' might differ from mine, and where in any case he'd have a strong motivation to deceive himself about how much defence he'd need. But I let that pass, for now, and tried to work around it.

'According to Wilde,' I said slowly, 'you used to think very differently. You used to think that the fast folk, in fact all AIs and uploads, were flatlines—not really conscious. And now, you're saying our whole safety depends on your continuing to believe the opposite. What changed your mind?'

Reid gave us all a big, stupid, happy smile. 'Dee,' he said.

I shook my head and glanced around at the comrades, then at Dee, who was fixing a steady gaze on me. I had the uncomfortable feeling that she knew what I was thinking.

'I don't quite understand,' I said, lying diplomatically.

'That's quite understandable,' said Reid dryly. 'It's a matter of experience. I found that I couldn't go on thinking of Dee as I used to before she became autonomous.' He smiled at Dee. 'Before she walked out on me. Looking back, I have to say that my, uh, relationship with her before then was a bit sad and sick, but you have to allow for local custom. Gynoid or android mates were a success-symbol for rich people. Very capitalist.' He smiled, with a flicker of embarrassment. 'Anyway, after all the trials and challenges she put me through, after the resurrection, after I got to know her again . . . I found it impossible to regard her as anything less than a person. Not a cunning imitation, not a flatline, but a real woman, whom I loved and who *loved me*. And because I had frequently, notoriously, and publicly denied that she or any other artificial people were real people, I had no choice but to acknowledge the error of my ways in a very public and decisive manner.'

He glanced up at the big photograph opposite me, and then smiled at Dee again. 'I married her.'

So *that* was the occasion! Marriage meant a public declaration of a sort of mutual possession: an odd, ancient custom, rare in the Union but apparently widespread here. And Reid had made that commitment, to this machine in a pretty body and a pretty dress, after owning her and using her for years. I hoped my face showed no trace of my revulsion.

'Ellen,' said Dee, 'it really doesn't matter what you think about us—about me.' She stood up and walked around the table and sat herself down on the edge of it, just in front of me. I couldn't avoid her green-eyed gaze. 'I know you think I'm a machine. "Just a fucking machine", yes? But *I* know I'm human, and if you were to know me for any length of time, you'd find you couldn't treat me in any other way. You can't own me, you can't use me, you can't switch me on and off. You can try! And if you had the power to force me, you could get some use out of me. But you wouldn't get much, and you wouldn't get *me*. If you want to get all that can be got out of this machine, with all its capacities, you have to let *me* decide to use those capacities. If I'm a machine, Ellen, I'm one that doesn't—*can't*—function properly unless it's free.'

She reached forward and touched my face. I didn't flinch. 'And so are you. So let's just try to be nice to each other, shall we?'

She stood again and walked back to her chair and sat down beside Tamara. I looked sideways at Suze, who was looking at Dee; at Yeng, who was looking at the floor.

'I reckon,' said Malley, 'that somebody just passed the Turing test.'

There was a moment of laughter, tension released. Reid reached over and caught Dee's hand. 'She passed it long ago,' he said.

Dee smiled at him, and then at me. The warmth of her smile chilled me as much as the passion and cogency of her reasoning had, and the gentle touch of her soft fingertips. It was like one of those uncanny moments when you're looking at what you think is a twig or a leaf, and suddenly it spreads wings and flies away.

'All right,' I said to Reid. 'I accept that your views about machine consciousness aren't likely to change.'

Yeng was still examining the floor. Suddenly her head jerked up. 'So *what*?' she said fiercely. 'You can all believe that if you like. The denial of machine sentience is not part of the true knowledge, it's just an opinion the finders had, a—' Her hand mimed her search for a word just out of reach.

'*Obiter dictum*,' suggested Talgarth gravely.

I doubted that Yeng had heard the phrase before, but she nodded briskly. 'Yes! Something like that. All the things Dee said, they're part of the true knowledge. It's just the same with people. If we want to make the most of our lives we have to get the most out of each other, and that means not treating people as less than what they are.' She paused and frowned, as though puzzling something out. I felt for her: the cognitive dissonance of being taken in by Dee's startling mimicry must have been painful. 'Unless we get more by doing that, of course, which doesn't happen very often. If we meet machines that the same applies to, we can live with it.' She laughed, without humour. 'We might have to! None of this changes the other problem, of how we deal with machines far more powerful than us, which—or who, for all I care—could be *more* than people. We can't live with beings to whom we are like ants.'

' "And we were in their sight as grasshoppers",' Reid said, apparently quoting some obscure text. '*Why* do you think we can't coexist?'

'Because they'd have power over us,' Yeng said, explaining the obvious.

'Having more power than us,' Reid said with equally heavy patience, 'doesn't mean the same as having *power over* us.'

'All right,' said Yeng, 'but they'd have it, and they could always use it, just like you did to the fast folk you revived.'

'Ah,' said Reid. ' "They". That's interesting. I understand you're negotiating with these Jovians. How are you doing it?'

I glanced around the team. No one flashed any warning looks, so I explained how the contact had been made and how the communications were being carried on.

'So,' said Reid when I'd finished, 'how many of them are there?'

I shrugged. 'Millions, possibly. Thousands at least.'

'And they're some kind of hive mind, right? Some gigantic collective entity?'

'No,' I told him, not sure what he was getting at. 'They say they're individuals, and all the evidence we have indicates that's what they are.'

'Some kind of totalitarianism, then? Each subordinate to a single will, as Lenin put it? Or some angelic anarchy where they all agree on the obvious common good?'

'Of course not,' I said impatiently. 'We've noticed signs of disagreement among them, and they take time out for discussion and then come back to us.'

Reid shared a grin with Talgarth. He smacked his palm with his fist. 'Hah!' he exulted. 'Knew it!'

'Knew what?' I asked.

'That you people would be negotiating with the Jovians as if they *were* a hive entity. And as if you were, come to that!' He chuckled darkly. 'And you've made the same mistake with us,' he added. 'When I said we weren't in charge here, I meant it. While we've been talking, quite a few enterprising people have been acting. People who have been thinking ahead, designing ahead, planning ahead, during the five years it's taken for a confirmation to come back through the Gate that it was safe to go through. And now it has—now *you're* here—they've been scrambling to get ships in orbit, ready to go through themselves. Bit of a jostle to be first, but I'm sure the protection agencies are keeping order in the queue of ships that must be building up right now outside the wormhole.'

He took a swig of his beer and lit a cigarette, blatantly enjoying our startled looks and Tamara's smouldering outrage—this was apparently news to her, too.

'To do what?' I asked, shouting above the rest.

Reid leaned back and clasped his hands and made cracking noises with his knuckles. 'To trade,' he said. 'What else?'

I laughed. 'They won't get much profit out of trading with us,' I said. 'And anyway, they don't know the way through.'

'Indeed they don't,' Reid said. 'But I do. I got it from the fast folk, remember, just as I got the path for going the other way. And I'm going to sell it.' He affected a glance at a wristwatch. 'Any time now, the bids should be coming through.'

Tony leaned forward. 'Very clever,' he said. 'But quite frankly, they'll be wasting their money. The businesses you're about to sell this secret to aren't going to be too happy when they find we don't need anything you've got to offer, and nothing on our side is for sale at any price. Either because we'll share it for free, or we won't give it to you for anything. Like Ellen said—not much profit in that.' He took this as his turn to sit back and look smug.

'I wouldn't be too sure of that,' Reid said. He waved his hand airily. 'Not that it matters. Most of the companies I'm talking about aren't that interested in trading with people in the Solar Union, anyway.'

'So who—?' I stopped, unwilling to accept the obvious answer. 'Oh no. You're not.'

'We are,' Reid said calmly. 'We're going to trade with the Jovians.'

For a moment we were all stunned into silence. It was Yeng who spoke first, her normally high voice raw with anger and concern.

'This is insane,' she said. 'Just *look* at yourselves! I've seen how comms work here—you have radio for everything, electronic computers everywhere, including your bodies, and lots of you have cortical downlinks! Direct electronic interfaces with your brains, right? You're just *ridiculously* vulnerable—

absolutely naked to viral assault and takeover. You're a *culture medium* for the things! The Jovians could *eat* your minds alive, and you'd never know.'

'We've considered that,' Reid said calmly. 'We're confident that our countermeasures will hold them off, should the Jovians behave as treacherously as you people seem to expect.'

'*Countermeasures!*' Yeng's voice spat contempt. 'We've had two centuries of front-line struggle against their virus plagues to develop countermeasures, and we still wouldn't contemplate what you suggest.'

Reid shrugged and smiled. 'We're pretty sure we've done better, because—' He stopped. 'We have better computers,' he finished, rather lamely I thought; but he might have had more to say, and not said it.

'I don't—' I began, then Boris raised his hand and shot me a quick glance.

'All irrelevant,' Boris said. 'Because if your ships go through the Malley Mile, you can rest assured the Cassini Division—our defence agency, our ships—will destroy them. The Division will assume anything coming through is hostile, unless they hear different from us.'

'Then,' said Reid, 'I most strongly suggest you do just that. Contact your Central Committee—or whatever—and tell them to let us through. Because if you don't, and your ships attack ours, the Mutual Protection fighters covering the traders will take whatever action is needed to defend them.'

Boris and Andrea guffawed at the same moment. The rest of the team looked at least amused. Even Malley had a faint, sceptical smile at Reid's apparent bluster. Malley had seen our ships, and Reid had not.

'They can try,' Boris said. He laughed again. 'They can try!'

Reid stood, and wandered over to the wall and leaned on his hand against it, beside a picture of himself alongside a sleek machine, something like a World War Three jet fighter aircraft. He drew on his cigarette and gave us a cool, appraising look. I knew what was coming next, so I spoke first.

'I presume you've already checked over the *Carbon Conscience*,' I said. 'Scanned it, maybe tried sending a little fly-camera in. Do tell us what you've found.'

'Indeed we have,' Reid said, with a slight involuntary backwards sway that cheered me a little. Boris bristled; my quick black look made him back down. 'We got a lot closer to it than we did to the *Terrible Beauty*.' This time it was his turn for a brief inward gloat, as I betrayed my surprise. 'Oh, yes, Mr Powell had our remotes on the job as soon as you'd left,' Reid went on. 'Very helpful and friendly bloke, absolute soul of kindness, as I'm sure you'll agree. Now, about the *Carbon Conscience*.' He gazed over our heads, his eyes flicking back and forth in the way of someone looking at a virtual image. 'It's a good fighter, I'll give you that. But so was the MiG-29, and we all know how that performed against the Polish EFAs.' He paused, frowning. 'Maybe we don't all know. Not very well, is how. And let me tell you, if your fighter-bombers come up against *these*'—he jerked his thumb at the spaceplane in the photo—'they'll never know what hit them.'

'So you didn't get inside it?' I asked, in as casual a tone as I could manage.

Reid shrugged. 'Didn't need to,' he said, equally lightly. 'Outside inspection was enough.'

Boris almost made another forward lurch; at my sharp gesture, he sat back again, glowering. I hoped Reid had seen that—I was only just able to restrain myself from punching the air and shouting, 'YES! Just you try it, you banker!'

Because if they hadn't been able to penetrate the fighter-bomber's passive defences, they would certainly not be able to defeat it in combat. It was an ugly, insectile thing, that fighter; it looked more like an ornithopter than a spacecraft, let alone a spaceplane; but it was built for the most difficult combat imaginable, close-quarter fast manoeuvering in space, and it had evolved out of two centuries of zapping anything bigger than a molecule that dared to lift from Jupiter, and from even longer experience of split-second work within disintegrating comet nuclei.

The only problem I could foresee with pitting our fighters against Reid's was one he almost certainly wouldn't have thought of: so few of our pilots had ever killed a human, and those few so long ago, that they might fatally hesitate at the death. It wasn't a weakness that those on his side were likely to share.

'Our fighters are fully automated,' Reid said, 'no humans in the loop at all. That puts your side at a further disadvantage, don't you think?'

*Oh no it doesn't*, I thought with a surge of joy. We'd cream them without a fleck of carbon on our consciences.

'I see you disagree,' he went on. 'Perhaps you should see how they're made.' He made a slapping motion with his hand. The lights dimmed further, and above the table a hologram flashed into view. Six feet high, it showed a dark, pitted nodule, slowly tumbling end over end. On its surface, smudges of light seethed; and small bright things, like iron-filings, drifted off.

'Carbonaceous chondrite, with nanofactories,' Reid said. 'Now let's look a little closer.' The hologram shrank to a patch of the body's surface, which then expanded. The seething smudges became vast constructions of pipework and drillheads and vats: the small bright things, tens and hundreds of spaceplanes like the one in the picture.

'This is speeded up, of course,' Reid allowed. 'Each fighter takes a day to be put together by the assemblers. But as you can see'—the view zoomed back again—'we have a *lot* of assemblers.'

The hologram vanished and the lights came back up. While we were still blinking, Reid strode over and sat down again.

'Even if you think your fighters can beat ours one-to-one—which I don't—you have the attrition to consider. It won't be one-to-one. More like hundreds to one, and they'll keep on coming.'

The room fell silent. We could still beat them, I thought. We had more than the fighter-bombers to count on. We had the far more powerful lasers on Callisto; the nuclear-armed orbital forts; the entrenchments on the other moons. We had the Inner System defence-forces. If it came to the last ditch, we had the population of Earth itself.

But the New Martians would have more than fighter-bombers, too, and they might have gods on their side—and not just the Jovians, even if they did find allies there. They had their own fast folk, in their smart-matter storage tanks up in the mountains; assuming they weren't already up and running, a deception of which I reckoned Reid was wholly capable.

The attrition would indeed be terrible, on both sides; and we still had the Jovians to deal with. We couldn't afford the diversion.

I smiled and rose to my feet. 'Isn't it great how talking things over can prevent fighting?' I said. 'How did we get into all this talk about fighting, anyway? Of course you can come through. If you want to deal directly with the Jovians, you're welcome to try. It's at your own risk, as the capitalist small print always puts it. You may even be doing us a favour, by running that risk on our behalf. We can look after ourselves, whatever happens.'

My crew were looking at me with barely concealed dismay. Even Malley and Suze looked troubled. I turned completely away from Reid and his partners, and gave the comrades a tremor of a wink.

'So, Dave,' I went on, turning back to him, 'about that offer of a secure communications room? I think it's time to take you up on it.'


'Hard suits, radio comms, deep crypto,' I said. Our clothes gelled, then set to armour around us. The small room at the top of Reid's tower had a shelf all around it of communications-control panels, with more help menus than we could use. All idiot-proof, Reid had cheerfully assured us, closing the door behind him.

In their reconfigured suits the comrades resembled faceless humanoid robots with anodized aluminium finishes in a variety of bright colours. No one could so much as read our lips, and the deeper masking of cryptography would keep our communications safe, unless New-Martian computation was so far ahead of ours that we might as well give up now. The comrades' voices contended in the dead spaces of the crypto channel.

I hit my override control. 'Try to talk one at a time,' I said wearily. I was hungry, and irritable, and among the first people in history to suffer starship-lag. 'Boris, the chair recognizes you.'

'Ha, ha, Ellen. What are you playing at? We can't let them through, definitely not now.'

'We can't fight them *now*,' I said. 'None of us, I hope, has mentioned the impact event. Eight days away now. We need our forces intact for that, just in case . . . We could stop a determined breakout from this side, *or* we could make sure the comets don't get diverted the wrong way. We can't count on doing both.'

'These aren't the only options,' Tony said. 'And we still have to do—'

'I know, I know,' I said.

'Do what?' asked Malley.

'Make sure Reid doesn't touch off another runaway Singularity,' I said. 'If he hasn't already. Don't worry, we'll deal with that. Right now, the decisions aren't up to us. What we have to do is contact the Division, and let them decide. Yeng, please go to it.'

Yeng complied, and while she was setting up a laser-link to the communications relay satellite (by now, presumably, somewhere among a growing fleet of ships that shared its orbit, and the wormhole's) I called up a display inside my helmet and did some rough editing of the suit's record of recent events. I made sure that Reid's most informative statements were there in full, so there'd be no doubt as to what he was saying.

'Ready,' Yeng's voice said. 'Encrypted conference link—you'll all see the committee as a virtual view in you helmets, and they'll see our faces.'

Worried faces, on both sides.

'Are you all right?' Tatsuro asked. 'We haven't had any contact for over an hour, since you went into that tower.'

'We've been in a Faraday cage,' I said. 'We're all right. There's been an . . . unexpected development. Tell you about it in a minute. How are things at your end?'

Tatsuro massaged his eyebrows, leaving tiny, paired dishevellments. 'Fine, fine,' he said. 'The Jovians have finally managed to shut off the viral transmissions. That's at least a token of goodwill, but we aren't opening any radio channels just yet. Their own atmospheric traffic has started to increase again. Also, they've detected the incoming comet-train. They can see it's heading for a slingshot orbit, but they raised the matter with every appearance of concern.'

'Can't say I blame them.'

'We've told them it's routine—for Martian terraforming—showed them records of our previous cometary flybys, which they've checked against what they call dreamtime archives. They seem reassured. Now, about your position. The relay has detected and reported a build-up of ships on your side. What's going on?'

It took me about ten minutes to tell them, with clips of our discussion projected straight through from my suit to their screens. The consternation thus sown was almost amusing to watch; the angry, murmured discussions echoed and amplified our own. I concluded with my assessment of the odds.

'Well,' said Tatsuro when I'd finished, 'this is certainly a complication. I would prefer that you had not said to Reid that his side's ships could come through. Is that not rather a matter for the Solar Council, or at least for its delegate?'

'Oh,' I said. I'd almost forgotten that little matter. The Solar Council delegate had—or represented, rather—the ultimate power over us. For all the Division's immense, concentrated power, it could not prevail against the will of Earth and the Inner System Earth Defence forces—not in the long run, not with attrition to consider.

'Her fusion-clipper has just gone into orbit around Callisto,' Tatsuro continued. 'With a few Inner System fighters attached. Can we wait for the hour or so it will take for the delegate to arrive?'

'The decision can't wait,' I said. 'Reid is selling the coordinates to the merchant fleet at this moment.'

Tatsuro shook his head reprovingly, but with a glint of wry amusement in his eye as he said: 'You might have tried to argue for a delay of . . . a little over a week!'

'We could still do that,' I said.

Suze raised her hand and spoke up. 'If I may, neighbours . . . comrades. I don't think that would work. We're dealing with capitalists here. They'll *expect* us to stall, and suspect us of stitching them up—that is, of doing our own deal with the Jovians and cutting their side out of it.'

'Which might not be a bad idea,' said Clarity, frowning at us across light years and millennia.

'Oh, it would!' Suze said. 'If I know anything about these people, they'd just batter on through. Race each other to be first to cut a deal. Their whole way of life is based on taking high risks for high returns.'

'And not much risk, at that,' I said sourly. 'They've probably all taken back-ups, and they'll all try different approaches and keep on trying until one succeeds.'

'Or until the Jovians infect them all and turn them into puppets,' said Yeng. 'Puppets who can fight us in space.'

Tatsuro made a chopping gesture with his hand. 'Whatever. I move that we let them through. I agree with Ellen's analysis. If what Yeng fears does happen, we are still in a better position to fight if our own forces are intact. However, I think we should insist that some of our own fighters go through the wormhole and take up positions on the New-Martian side.'

'Opposed,' said Joe Lutterloh. 'We shouldn't open the Solar Union to the bankers, and we shouldn't let them trade with the Jovians, who are still a danger to us.'

After a few more minutes of discussion the vote was taken on letting the traders through. Eight in favour, four against.

Tatsuro didn't pause for a second. 'Carried,' he said, as the hands went down. 'So, comrades, go and tell Reid his traders and fighters can come through, on the condition that our fighters can do the same. Let us know if he agrees or not. Obviously you should make every effort to return to your ships. I appreciate why you had to leave them, but don't leave them for too long. Get your ships back into space, if you can, and stand by for a bombing run—by yourselves, or the other fighters—on the place where the fast-folk templates are stored. And meanwhile'—he looked around at the Command Committee, a slow, sly smile forming on his face—'we'll work out how we're going to explain all this to the Solar Council delegate. Goodbye for now.'

I waved to the Committee, more bravely than I felt. Yeng switched out the link. Malley and Suze's voices were yelling in my ears. Tatsuro's passing comment was the first they'd heard about our real plans for the fast-folk templates. I waved my arms frantically for silence.

'It's only a contingency plan!' I shouted on the override. 'Only if Reid does something crazy with them! Don't look at me like that! We still can't trust them.'

'Don't worry,' Malley said grimly. 'I don't much care what happens to the templates, they're not conscious anyway. You can trust me not to tell.'

'And me,' said Suze. 'I just wish you had sooner.'

Her voice was thick with disillusion. I looked around at Malley, Suze, and the comrades, and as my glance slid helplessly from one blank bubble to the next, I realized that I couldn't tell which was which.

'All right,' I said. 'I'm sorry. Now let's go and talk Reid into letting us do it.'

Before the world commonwealth was established, one objection to it that always came up was *But who will do the dirty work?*

I always used to answer *me*, and I was right.

# 10

## IN THE DAYS OF THE COMET

One after another, the ugly, bristling, articulated fighter-bombers came out of the wormhole; a whole squadron of them, their names heroic, ironic, or plain daft: *Gai Phong, Debug Mode, Virus Alert, Luddite Tendencies, X Calibre, Acquisitor, General Arnaldo Ochoa, Codebreaker*, and *Necessary Evil But Still Cool*. And one after another, the slow, laden freighters of the merchants and the fast, sharp fighters of their mercenaries went in. Even on the screen in the aerospace port, with the news-child's prattling commentary jamming the silence, the sight remained awesome and uncanny: ship after ship vanishing in a flash of blue light, as if annihilated.

The same thought must have struck Andrea. 'What happened to the law of mass-energy conservation?' she asked. 'Did it just go away, with those ships?'

Malley leaned over from the bench beside me. 'Good point,' he said, jabbing his pipe-stem, like a lecturer's pointer, at the screen. 'The answer is that the mass of the wormhole at this end increases, and at the other end decreases, by the same amount as has gone through.'

We were sitting, with Reid and Dee, in the same quiet area of the port where Boris and Jaime had waited. I watched the screen with silent satisfaction as our fighters took up positions around the wormhole and deployed a scatter of attitude-control booster drones which clamped themselves around its perimeter. Reid had conceded this degree of control over the gate to us. I wasn't sure whether I'd convinced him it was the only way to get the people on our side to agree to his side's ships coming through, or whether his confidence in the superiority of capitalist technology made the entire concession irrelevant to whatever *his* longer-term plans might be.

I was listening intently to the conversation, and trying hard not to show it; Andrea was still puzzling over Malley's answer.

'So,' she asked, 'does that mean one side of the wormhole would just fade away to nothing if enough mass came through from the other?'

'In lay terms,' said Malley cautiously, 'yes. But bear in mind that the mass can go *negative*.'

I leaned back, hands behind my head, gazing up through the roof, and tuned my tone to idle curiosity.

'What does that mean, in physical terms?'

Malley laughed. 'I don't know, to be honest. The rest of the wormhole—the main wormhole—can balance a negative mass, and thus keep the original gate open, up to a certain point.'

'How much, though?' Andrea sounded worried.

Malley shrugged. 'Depends on its total virtual mass, which I don't know. A lot more than those ships, anyway.'

'The gate on the other side masses oh point nine five seven million tonnes,' Dee said, unexpectedly. 'On this side, a lot less: only about a hundred thousand. If we keep up the traffic, we'll have to ensure that it balances. Unless we want to find out what negative mass means, in physical terms.'

'We're safe enough for now,' said Reid. 'The ships that went through probably don't mass more than a thousand tonnes each.'

'I don't see our side sending twenty-odd thousand tonnes the other way,' I said, with now-easy flippancy.

'Ours are coming back.' Reid glanced over at me and grinned, as though challenging me to deny it. 'Aren't they?'

I returned him an equally unfriendly grin. 'Of course.'

The entire port was much quieter than it had been when we'd first arrived. The welcoming crowds had gone, and the heavy lifting had all been done. Only a few passengers, for the outlying settlements I guessed, wandered or hastened through. Even the news remotes, with an appropriately gnatlike attention span, had drifted off. For the New Martians it was the middle of the night; for us, early afternoon. Discarded disposable plates and the remains of likewise disposable food littered our surroundings. Now we were waiting for the auto-piloted arrival of the *Terrible Beauty*, and for the refuelling of the *Carbon Conscience* to be completed. There was a certain amount of tension in the air, and a lot of smoke. Malley was puffing his pipe, Dee and Reid chain-smoking cigarettes. The habit seemed common in capitalist societies; if we had to wait much longer, I'd be tempted to take it up myself.

'What do you intend to sell, and to buy?' Suze asked.

'If I knew that,' Reid said, 'I'd probably be doing it myself. The folks who're going through have given it a lot more thought than I have.' He spread his hands. 'Information, I guess.'

'They may get more information than they bargained for,' Yeng told him, darkly. 'And you'll get it, too.' She stood up and paced forward and pointed at the screen. One of the defence-agency fighters had hung back from going through, and was deploying a relay drogue, much larger than ours, on the same alignment. 'I can't *believe* your complacency. I hope we get off this place before the Jovian viruses come down the line, straight into your heads!'

Dee laughed.

'You don't get it, do you?' she said. 'We do have open systems, yes, and we are personally vulnerable—I more than most, I should say—to mind-hacking. That's exactly why we're not worried about it. We've *had* to develop countermeasures, very good ones, so we can protect ourselves from business competitors, criminals—or bloody kids!'

Yeng shrugged. 'Maybe so,' she said doubtfully. 'But if you're up against conscious—well, supposedly conscious—entities with processing-power vastly greater than yours, I can't see it doing much good.'

'But we—' Dee began. She looked at Reid. He shrugged.

'Oh, tell them,' he said. 'They'll figure it out for themselves eventually.'

'All right,' Dee said. She stood up and faced us all, as Yeng returned to her seat. 'I'll tell you.' Her tone, and her expression, altered slightly, as though some different personality were in control. 'Consciousness—or the emulation of consciousness, if you insist'—she smiled, her usual self flashing momentarily back—'*costs*. Selfhood has a very high cost in processing-power, and that cost increases with the amount of information it has to integrate. It's not something that just *drops out* of increased complexity, as some people used to think. It has to be actively *designed in*, either consciously by us or unconsciously by natural selection. So it's quite possible to build hardware more powerful, and software more complex, than any brain or mind in existence: computing machines that don't even act *as if* they're conscious, that don't have *interests*, and that don't object when they're used as tools.'

Her possession passed, her self-possession returned. She stepped over to one of the long seats, and expertly flicked the fluttery hem of her skirt under the crook of her knees as she sat down. I smiled at her. She, and Reid, had been right: no matter what I thought, in the innermost depths of my mind, about the innermost depths of *her* mind, it was impossible to be with her, to converse with her, and not give her the benefit of the doubt, not act *as if* her mind *had* innermost depths, and not to quite simply *like* her.

She smiled back.

'And these tools,' Reid added, 'we have. That's why we're confident we can deal on equal terms with beings greater than ourselves. We have ways of amplifying our power to more than equal theirs. Golems to stand up for us against the gods.' He crushed his cigarette and stood up. 'Products of good old capitalist competition. You should try it, sometime.'

I found myself thinking of the great analytical engines of our socialist planning, whose spare capacities had increased over decades of stability in which more and more decisions had come to be made locally, and only the most general, those concerning the most widely used resources, had to be made globally or even regionally. I thought of our smart-matter suits, and our domestic cybernetics. Perhaps we'd all along had gods—or golems—on our side, whose aid it had never crossed our minds to invoke.

About to say something of this, I looked at Reid, and then tracked his gaze to a falling spark visible through the concourse's transparent roof.

'Your ship's coming in,' he said. 'Time to go.'


Free at last; free fall at last! It had taken hours—hours of shifting the ships and coupling them together, an awkward job in one gravity; half an hour of negotiation between Suze and one of Reid's employees over our debt to Mutual Protection, and another half hour with the port company, over services they'd allegedly rendered and definitely wanted paying for—and finally a painful five minutes of boost, to get ourselves quickly into this orbit. Reid's last words to me had been: 'I hope I see you again.'

'Me too,' I'd said, sincere only in my hope that I never did.

I unclipped my webbing, pushed myself away from the couch and executed a joyous somersault, ending up just in front of the forward view.

I hauled the gross-focus bars of the display screen, rotated the fine-focus handles. Although the wormhole was still a long way off on our slowly closing trajectory, the forward telescope's field—transmitted through lenses, mirrors and fibre-optic cables—showed our destination clear and sharp: the rainbow ring of the daughter wormhole—like its parent, a mile across—and the glittering clutter of the surrounding ships. Our ten fighters and Reid's one; our relay drogue small, theirs large.

I fiddled with the controls and swung in another view, an enhanced night-time image of Ship City and its environs.

'OK comrades!' I called out, rolling around again. They'd all unstrapped and were flying around the command deck, enjoying not only the free fall but the respite between getting out from under capitalism and having to face a bit of democratic accountability from our distant socialism. I grinned at them all and gave them a big thumbs-up.

'Mission accomplished—so far!' I announced.

'Yeah?' said Malley. 'And what did we accomplish?'

'A lot,' I said. 'We've confirmed that the New Martians are just what they seem to be: real people, even if they do have funny ideas about what counts as people. We know for sure they're at risk of losing that, if Reid or someone else gets too cocky about reviving his fast folk again. And from what that nice anarchist comrade Tamara told me, we have good reason to think the fast-folk templates are still where Reid originally stashed them— up in the range of hills called the Madreporite Mountains.'

I pointed it out, and paused as a much more vivid marker made the point: a long bolide-trail in the atmosphere, and the flash of its impact. Another followed, and another.

'That's it,' I said above the sound of indrawn breaths. 'There, near where they direct their comet fragments, at the source of that long channel leading into the city. We got the exact coordinates years ago, out of the artificial woman's—Meg's—data-files. So if we or any of the other fighters gets the go-call, we can lob a nuke into the cave-mouth and blast them and the whole mountain to blazes.'

'You've got *nukes* on this thing?' Malley asked indignantly.

'On *Carbon Conscience*,' Boris said. 'That bird's got a fifty-megaton egg, man. Nice clean laser-fusion job, in case you're worried.'

'Consider me reassured,' said Malley. 'No doubt a few fifty-megaton city-busters will come in real handy if the New Martians should have the bad luck to fall short of your definitions of what counts as people.'

'There is that,' Boris said thoughtfully.

'No!' I said, shocked. 'We're not going to do that!'

'Why ever not?' Malley floated up, his voice heavy with sarcasm. 'According to you, you wouldn't be killing *people*.'

'Too dangerous,' I explained. 'Wouldn't be like Jupiter, with vulnerable entities at the bottom of a gravity well. It'd be a massive breakout, with millions of ex-human puppets and a space-going capability. If there's another Singularity here, we cut and run.'

'Run where?' asked Andrea.

'Through the wormhole, if possible,' I said.

'And if not?' Malley hung in front of me, hanging on my words. I waved a hand airily in his face.

'We keep boosting until we use half the reaction-mass, back ourselves up if we absolutely have to, and at the first likely looking clump of matter the ship finds, we download and spend the rest of the reaction-mass decelerating. And then, well . . .' I smiled at his frown. 'We have the makings of a nice little galactic empire of our own right here. With your beauty and my brains, neighbour . . .'

Malley's anxiety dissolved in a guffaw.

'And I shall call you . . . Eve!'

'Mitochondrial Eve,' Suze said firmly, catching Malley's hand.

'Plenty of good genes in the cold-stores,' said Boris.

I turned away before Malley could suspect there was even a sliver of a chance we were serious. (But it was part of the standard kit of a fusion-clipper, even so: the haunting fear of a runaway torch, or of everything going wrong in our cold war with the Jovians, was the real reason the ships relied on recycling rather than supplies, and stored the frozen seeds of a viable population and the smart-matter blueprints for its infrastructure and technology in their vaults.)

'Enough,' I said. 'We got work to do. Jaime, Andrea, could you please haul yourselves over to the nav gear and the long-range viewing-kit. We need to track all the moving matter around us, all the ships and missiles and especially all the cometary junk. We don't want to wander into the path of one of *their* comet-trains.'

(*Indeed we don't*, I thought to myself.)

'Don't worry about our deep-space radar being pinged,' I added. 'They know we're here, and they know we're not hostile.'

'We've paid for our protection,' Suze reminded me.

'Handy stuff, gold,' I agreed. 'And Yeng, I'd like you to help Andrea and Jaime with mapping comet-streams—their courses and timing *must* be public knowledge somewhere. As well as that, I need two channels—one to see if there's any readable information coming from their comms drogue . . .'

'Newscasts, probably,' Suze said. 'Subscriber only, if I know them.'

'So try subscribing,' I said.

Yeng grinned. 'And the other channel?'

'Same as before,' I said. 'Patch us in to the Command Committee.' I caught Malley's *you're for it now* smile, and smiled defiantly back. 'Time to find out what the democratically elected delegate of socialist humanity thinks of what the heroic defenders of socialist humanity have been getting up to.'


I recognized the Solar Council delegate at once, which surprised me. As the Solar Council—like all the other councils, from local to global—was directly elected, and I was theoretically one of its constituents, I shouldn't have been surprised. Local councils tended to be made up of people with local reputations, and so on up. The Solar Council's delegates should have been known to everyone in the Solar System, usually for their decades if not centuries of good, competent work in relevant fields; the re-gerontocracy, as some of our younger and more cynical neighbours put it. But by and large I trusted the people in the rest of the Union to choose people whose previous experience and reputation they trusted (and now and again to throw in some absolute beginner who had made enough of a fuss about something to get their name bruited about) so, apart from my recently lost position on the Jovian Anomaly Research Committee, I generally stuck to my little intrigues in the Division and left wider affairs alone. However, even I had heard of Mary-Lou Radiation Nation Smith.

She was, I think, Navaho, if it matters; in any case, a member of one of the all-too-many tribes—Aleutian, Kazakh, Aboriginal, Uighur, etc.—who'd been unwilling or unwitting participants in the old society's nuclear tests, and who now formed a loose but active lobby calling itself the Radiation Nation. They were united, not by ethnicity—which the Union only encouraged as a basis for cultural, and definitely not for administrative, association—but by a quite understandable though, I sometimes thought, exaggerated concern that we were a little too careless with our civil-engineering and outbreak-zapping and forest-clearing nukes. *Yes*, they'd say, *we can stop cancer and fix chromosomes and regenerate ecosystems, but there could be unknown losses, uncalculated risks* . . . it was a legitimate point of view, despite all the mutterings about Greens under the machines, and as a respected biologist and statistician, Mary-Lou Radiation Nation Smith had the qualifications to back it up.

Black bangs framed her face, dark eyes shone out of it. She was sitting beside Tatsuro, whose uncharacteristically frayed appearance—the hairs of his head, eyebrows, and moustache sticking out as if static-charged—contrasted with her well-groomed composure.

'Ellen May Ngwethu,' she said, as if it were the name of some particularly loathsome disease. 'Comrades and friends.' She swept us all with a glance, making a similarly distasteful diagnosis. 'And the distinguished non-cooperator Dr Malley. I'm pleased to meet you all at last, even at such a distance. *Especially* at such a distance, I should say. Your energy and enterprise are quite astonishing. We on the Council had *no idea* you were planning such bold initiatives. Not only have you set up a scheme to destroy the Jovians, you've simultaneously entered into negotiations with them! No doubt you have already worked out what to do if these superhuman minds see through your *highly plausible* cover-story, and respond. I look forward eagerly to our surprise when you demonstrate your surefire, foolproof stratagem to prevent their entirely predictable fury from wiping us out. Don't spoil my suspense by telling me in advance—not that telling us *anything* in advance is one of your habitual faults.'

She paused, placed the palms of her hands together and the fingertips under her chin.

'Well?' she said. 'I've heard the CC comrades' . . . explanations. What do *you* have to say for yourself?'

'Comrade, ah, neighbour Radiation Nation Smith—'

'Just call me Mary-Lou,' she said sweetly. 'Or neighbour Smith, if you prefer formality. My middle names are a soubriquet—like your last.'

From her point of view it may have been an inappropriate reminder of just *why* I'd chosen that old slogan for my name. *Ngwethu!* Freedom! I had it, and at the relevant point of application, perhaps more than she. The sting of her whiplash sarcasms faded, and (embarrassing to relate, but there it is) a few half-forgotten bars of that haunting anthem *Nkosi Sikelele Afrika* hummed through the back of my mind.

'OK, Mary-Lou,' I replied. 'We in the Division have a mandate to contain and destroy the Outwarder threat, and that's exactly what we're doing. I've assumed all along that our actions would be accountable to the Union, and that if necessary a global poll would be taken before the final decision—the issues are well known, and have long been discussed, so there should be no problem.'

'*No problem*,' she said, in a dead level tone. 'Of course, keeping our decision a secret from the Jovians is simply a matter of radio silence and complete self-discipline by billions of people, many of whom would be appalled at the suggestion of what you plan to do, not to mention what you've already done. You know, I can *almost* imagine that being possible, were it not for your other impressive feat. Opening contact *and* hostilities with the Jovians wasn't enough for you.'

She shook her head. 'Oh, no. As a final flourish, you manage—a mere hour before my arrival—to open the Solar System to a vigorously expanding capitalist society, and an anarcho-capitalist one at that. I'm sure if you'd had the choice between New Mars and some tedious statist tyranny with whose tedious statist tyrants we could at least have made some kind of deal that *might actually stick*, you'd still have picked New Mars, out of pure scientific curiosity as to which anarchy would subvert the other first. Let me tell you that your curiosity may be well justified . . . Dr Malley!'

Malley jumped (in as much as one can, in free fall) like a student caught dozing in a lecture.

'Yes?'

'I'm in no position to remonstrate with you—as a non-cooperator, you can't be expected to live by our rules. However, you do have to live with the consequences of your actions. Here are some consequences of yours: after decades of virtual radio silence from Earth, your brave experiment in encouraging your students to make and use radios has led to something of a happy babble of electronic communication. Our non-co friends heard that I was on my way out here, and decided to spread the news to the handful of non-cos in *space*. You'd be surprised to learn how much ill-informed comment on my well known concerns has flashed around the Solar System in the last few days. Evidently the New-Martian traders have monitored it closely—not difficult, because in absolute terms there isn't much radio traffic, *yet*. A couple of hours ago, I received a *personal message* from one of these ships, offering me "an unrepeatable, ground-floor offer"—whatever that is—for an "import concession"—I know what that is, thank you—for "alpha-emitter-assimilating biomechanisms"—whatever *they* may be.'

'How did you respond?' asked Malley, with what I thought commendable nerve.

'I told them to shop off,' was the somewhat coarse reply. 'However, we shortly afterwards picked up another version of the same offer, beamed towards Earth for anyone who cares to take it up. It's one of *thousands* of similar propositions directed at Earth, which in turn are the merest *fraction* of the communications going on between the traffickers' fleet and Jupiter. Most of the latter are heavily encrypted, so we don't even know what the offers they're making *are*.'

None of this came as a surprise, but it was all happening faster than I'd expected. I hadn't foreseen that the inevitable contact between the dominant non-cos of New Mars and the marginal non-cos of Earth would result in so much information leakage that keeping our plans from the Jovians would be well nigh impossible.

'All right,' I said. 'I see your point. That just means we'll have to act first and take the vote later—that's if most people aren't so relieved to be rid of the Jovian threat that it'll be obvious to anyone what the majority view is.'

Mary-Lou Smith lost her expression of detached, ironic appraisal. She shot me a look of hot fury.

'Act first, vote later?' she said. 'On an issue like this? What a disgusting attitude to your fellow human beings!'

'It isn't my attitude,' I protested. 'It's what's required by the realities of the situation.'

'Yes! Realities which you've brought about!' For a moment she looked as if she were about to start banging her head on the table. Then she drew her shoulders back and took a deep breath.

'Enough,' she said. 'We must deal with the situation as it is, and uncover the reasons for this mess when we have time. The whole relationship between the Union and the Division has to—'

She stopped herself, stood up and took a few steps backwards, so she could see all of the Committee as well as all of us. 'As I say, enough. Here's what I propose to transmit to the Solar Council, and what—on my mandate from the Solar Council—I *instruct* you to implement immediately, pending the Council's decision. One, you absolutely must not provoke the Jovians by giving them any reason whatever to fear a cometary bombardment. That means you must divert the comet-train into a wider and irreversibly safe orbit *now*. Second, you must step up fighter-bomber patrols on this side of the wormhole, and make no compromises with the New Martians on that. We have to make clear to them that they're here on our sufferance. Third, you must prepare to jam all radio transmissions within the Jovian sub-system, and between it and the Inner System, whether from the Jovians, the New Martians, or the non-cos.'

She strode forward and sat down again. 'That is all,' she said. 'Any questions?'

Nobody said anything. Quickly scanning the faces of the others on the Committee, I registered that most of them showed nothing but relief; in the case of Clarity and one or two others, more than relief. I took in their tentative smiles, keeping my own face carefully neutral. Only Joe Lutterloh showed anger, which he was equally visibly restraining. Tatsuro looked at me gravely. The tiny downtilt of his head could have been a cryptic nod, or an unconscious bowing to the inevitable. Mary-Lou might not have much immediate power to bring to bear on us, but a greater constraint applied. The Division couldn't go against the explicit will of the Union, or even of its authorized delegate; without being irretrievably split. And if we tore ourselves apart, we risked being easy prey for the enemy.

Well, if the others were too intimidated to talk, I was not.

'You propose a risky course,' I said. 'We've taken some risks too, I admit, but we always had the final fail-safe of the comet-strike to fall back on. Anything conceded to the Jovians—or the New Martians—could still be negated with that. Now you want to strike this weapon from our hands, and leave us defenceless.'

Smith jumped to her feet and leaned forward, fists on the table.

'Ellen May Ngwethu!' she shouted. 'I have had *enough* of your inflexible attitudes! I've heard *more* than enough of your devious speeches! I've had it up to—'

She stopped, leaned back, drew breath. She bowed her head for a moment and massaged her temples, then looked up at me and smiled.

'Excuse my outburst, neighbour. I understand your situation better than you do. You've endured two centuries of apparently endless conflict, two centuries for your personal dislikes to rankle into hatred. You've had even longer for the harshest aspects of the true knowledge—its dark side, if you will—to overwhelm its truth. Because the truth is the *whole*, and in raising the aspect of struggle way out of proportion to that of cooperation, you've turned it into a *lie*. If you could see yourself—as I have, I've had time to sample the records of this Committee, and those which you and your comrades have been sending back—in all your implacable belligerence, your *imperviousness* to the reasonable appeals of rational beings, whether the

Jovian speaker or the New-Martian gynoid, to be recognized as such . . . if you could see all that, I hope there is still something in you that would be ashamed.'

I stared at her, shaken despite myself. 'I've done nothing out of personal malice, *nothing* I'm ashamed of, and nothing that goes against the true knowledge.'

Mary-Lou shook her head slowly. 'There are two sides to the true knowledge, and you have forgotten one of them, despite your name. There is not only *amandla*—power. There is also *ngwethu*—freedom.'

'I know that,' I said calmly. 'And we'll lose both if we throw away our last chance to destroy the Jovians while we still can!'

For a split second, Mary-Lou literally staggered, as though I'd hit her. Then she said:

'All right. Let me speak to you in a language you understand. We are not throwing away our last chance to destroy the Jovians. *There never was a chance.* As soon as a stable, reality-oriented Jovian culture emerged, there was *no chance* that it could be destroyed by anything we could throw at it. These are beings whose *evolutionary ancestors* disintegrated Ganymede and punched a hole through space! How many *hours* do you think it would take for them to develop some response that could swat aside your comets like flies? And as soon as you brought back the first pictures, and the first messages, there was *not a chance* that the people of the Union would react to the Jovians' emergence with anything but hope, and to their destruction with anything but horror. You've seen how a typical Union member, Suze, a typical tough-minded non-co, Dr Malley, and even your own Command Committee have reacted. They've all drawn back from the brink, to varying degrees, and they're right! Our only *chance* of survival is to survive *with them*, and the only effect of attempting to destroy them would be to *make* them the deadly enemies you seem to take for granted they are.'

She turned to Tatsuro. 'Which reminds me,' she said. 'I heard no dissent from my instruction, except from Ellen. Do you wish to take a vote?'

Tatsuro nodded wearily. 'Those for accepting the delegate's instructions.'

All the hands on the other side went up, except Joe's.

'Those against.'

Me, and Joe. I smiled at him. He shook his head, lips compressed in a thin line, and drew a finger across his throat. I don't think anyone else saw the gesture. Behind me, I distinctly heard Yeng say: 'Shit.' No one else spoke.

'Carried,' said Tatsuro. He took his control panel from its strap around his neck, and jabbed in a long series of firing-codes.

'It's done,' he told Mary-Lou. 'The jets are firing, the nukes are flaring. The cometary masses have been shifted to the orbit you requested.'

'Let me confirm that,' she said. 'No offence, neighbour.'

She spoke briefly and quietly into a personal phone, waited a few seconds, then nodded.

'OK,' she said. 'The local observatories have confirmed it.'

Her shoulders moved as though a weight had been lifted from them. 'And now,' she said, 'Ellen. Let me try to reassure you about the Jovians.'

My heart was thudding, my mouth dry.

She sat down on the edge of the table, leaning on one hand, twisting her body a little to face me, in a pose of casual conversation. 'They're not *monsters*, you know. Why should you expect beings more powerful and intelligent than ourselves to be worse than ourselves? Wouldn't it be more reasonable to expect them to be *better*? Why should more power mean less good?'

I could hardly believe I was hearing this. Glancing quickly over my shoulder, I saw Andrea, Jaime and Yeng working at their screens but listening intently, and the rest giving Mary-Lou all their attention. I searched for my most basic understanding, and dragged it out:

'Because good means good for us!'

Mary-Lou smiled encouragingly and spoke gently, as though talking someone down from a high ledge. 'Yes, Ellen. But who is *us*? We're all— human, post-human, non-human—machines with minds in a mindless universe, and it behoves those of us with minds to work together *if we can* in the face of that mindless universe. It's the possibility of working together that forges an *us*, and only its impossibility that forces a *them*. That is the true knowledge as a whole—the union, and the division.' She laughed. 'So to speak! In fact, exactly so—the Union, and the Division!'

Images of the Jovians, in all their multifarious forms, processed through my mind. My skin felt as if small, chill, unpleasant things were crawling over it. I remembered the cold, lively metal of the robots, the warm flesh of Dee's fingertips; and I knew that my response to those machines, however edgy, however suspicious, however prejudiced it might be, was not the same as my cold intellectual loathing of the Jovians, beautiful though they were. The robots and the gynoid and all their kind, conscious or not, had become part of *us*, whereas the Jovians—

'You mean you would contemplate a union—with *them*?'

Mary-Lou nodded briskly. 'Of course. With those who wanted to. You may not know this, but the Jovians have the true knowledge, in their own terms. Some of their practices are even socialist!'

God help us all, I thought, heretically. 'That,' I said, 'only makes them more dangerous. More powerful, because more united, like we're dangerous to them, or *were* until *you people*—'

I stopped my words, too late. Mary-Lou chopped her hand downwards.

She pushed herself off the table, a slow, graceful motion in Callisto's low gravity, and brushed her hands together as if to remove some light dust.

'That's it,' she announced. 'End of discussion. If we are now *you people*, then we aren't in any kind of union *with you*. I have nothing more to say to you, Ellen. *Go away*. Just keep out of trouble, don't make any more trouble for us, and let someone else sort out your head, because I won't. Goodbye.'

She raised her hand above her shoulder, glanced at Tatsuro, and snapped her fingers impatiently. Tatsuro gave me a last, helpless look, reached for something out of sight, and the screen went dead.

It was all down to me now, I thought. Time for Plan B.


I rolled in the air and grabbed a stanchion. The comrades, and Malley, were all staring at me, or at the blank screen. The command deck had never sounded so quiet.

'So that's it, I guess,' I said.

'And very glad I am,' said Malley. Suze looked at him, looked at me, and nodded.

'It's over,' she said. 'Come on, Ellen. The decision's made. The die is cast. The comets won't crash, and Mary-Lou's won the Committee to her way. All right, there are risks, but she's right—there'd be more risks in yours. We'll just have to accept it, and hope they made the right choice.'

'Hope,' I said.

Hope was there, lighting up the eyes of Suze and Malley. The faces of the five other comrades didn't show hope, nor share the dread I felt. They were lost in their own thoughts, the worst of which may have been that they might have to choose between me—between us, the team—and the Union, or even the Division. For all our fierce individualism, we'd all—consciously or not—drawn strength from the Union, not only in the obvious objective sense but also in our selves. Mary-Lou had been right about that, at least: 'good for us' had two sides.

Now I'd have to work with this feeling, get it on my side—and so on everybody's, whether they knew it yet or not.

'Nothing's over,' I said. 'We have *not* been expelled from the Union, or even from the Division, and whatever Mary-Lou may think, I'm *still* on the Command Committee until I hear otherwise.' I waved behind me at the blank screen. 'If the comrades choose to throw me out, fine—the first thing they'll do is tell us. They haven't. Until they do, I'll carry on as a member.'

Malley scowled, Suze shrugged, the others brightened slightly.

'OK,' I went on. 'There's something I have to tell you. For a long time now, Tatsuro and I have had . . . an understanding. We both knew things

might come to this, and we knew we'd need a fall-back position if even the
comet-strike were . . . struck out!' I smiled, and coaxed some flickers of response. 'Whether by the Jovians, or by our own decision. We knew we might
come to that decision. We knew we might even agree with it ourselves. We
weren't—I wasn't—as dogmatic about the Jovians as Mary-Lou made out. *I*
was the first to argue for attempting contact, remember, against a fair bit of
opposition.'

'Come off it,' snapped Malley. 'That was just to get my cooperation.'

'Of course,' I said. 'But it was hardly an act of blind hatred, was it? *I*
risked my own mind making the first contact. You know how I feel about
back-ups, and whatever you may think of that view, it's sincerely held. The
risk was real, to me. I trusted them enough to take their path through the
wormhole—a risk we all shared, yes, but I sure wouldn't have taken it if
I thought the Jovians were *monsters*.'

'You've made your point,' said Malley. 'So why didn't you make it to
Mary-Lou?'

'I know a hopeless fight when I see one,' I said. I shrugged. 'She has her
point of view, fair enough, but I think she's biased towards a non-violent
resolution, and blinded to the other possibilities. Don't get me wrong—
nothing would please me more than to find that she's right, that we and the
Jovians can coexist and cooperate and so on. That they won't turn out as bad
or mad as their predecessors. But until I'm convinced of that, until we all
know we're safe, I am going to do my best to ensure that we do have a last
resort. *Only* as a last resort, and *only* if it's them or us, and everyone for
themselves. And it's one that *won't* threaten, won't even worry, the Jovians,
until or unless they threaten us.'

Jaime and Andrea glanced at the screens at which they'd been working,
then smiled at me with dawning comprehension.

'This is what Tatsuro and I agreed,' I went on. 'The real reason we came
here. Because here we have comet-trains all set up for us—ones the Jovians
need never see, and which can strike at them without warning. We can send
comets through the wormhole.'

'But the comets aren't—' Tony began.

Malley shot him a dry smile, and to me, one of grudging respect.

'Very elegant,' he said. 'Relative motion.'

'Yes,' I said. 'We're going to move the *wormhole*.'


It wasn't as simple as that, but the process of setting it up convinced the
comrades that at some level I still had authorization for what I was doing.
And I had; in as much as Tatsuro and I had indeed privately agreed on
this contingency plan before I'd even set out to find Wilde or Malley.

The fact that the Division's fighter-bombers, around both ends of the wormhole, responded to my requests was evidence enough (not least to myself) that I hadn't been thrown off the Command Committee. Not yet, anyway.

I sat beside Yeng while she sent the encrypted instructions, to the squadron on our side and to the *Turing Tester* on the other. The action of the latter was crucial, but it passed almost unnoticed in the general rede-ployment of fighter-bombers around the Malley Mile, on which—ironically enough—it was Mary-Lou who had insisted. The *Turing Tester* pulsed its own instructions to the wormhole Gate's attitude-control rockets, which fired off in a sequence of brief puffs. Slowly, over several hours, almost im-perceptibly, the great rainbow ring swivelled on its axis to face the surface of Jupiter.

Meanwhile, we drifted closer and closer to the daughter wormhole Gate. Neither our fighters nor the lone, auto-piloted sentry—which, I was amused to note, actually did belong to Reid's Mutual Protection company—challenged us. Jaime and Andrea steadily mapped the incoming stream of cometary fragments, which fell almost hourly on uninhabited parts of New Mars, after perhaps decades of slow, directed infall from this system's equivalents of the Kuiper Belt or Oort Cloud. We calculated that we could reach a sufficiently high speed to make an effective bombardment within anything from thirty minutes to two hours, with the ship dragging the worm-hole at up to thirty gee if we had to pick the shorter approach: the maxi-mum tolerable acceleration for that length of time, even with full use of the support capacity of our smart-matter suits.

'How do we grab the wormhole?' Malley asked.

'It's been done before,' I said. 'It's set up. The little attitude-control drones were designed for the original orbital shift we gave the Malley Mile back home. They've clamped around it, and they have secondary clamps that can grab on to the ship's lifting-gear cables. We can do it—the gate will be tilted at an acute angle behind us, we'll be at its centre of gravity, and our jet will be firing into it, going—'

I raised my eyebrows. Malley shrugged: 'Who knows?'

Just before the encounter, we'd have to cut the drive, disengage from the wormhole's perimeter and fire the drones' attitude jets to fine-tune the an-gle of the wormhole, so that the comets would follow the same course as had the departing ships, and explode out of the other side on a straight course for the surface of Jupiter. The combined velocities of the daughter worm-hole Gate and the comet fragments would deliver enough kinetic energy to spread devastation for tens of thousands of miles around their points of impact. It would be best if we could simultaneously get the ships on the other side to move the far mouth of the wormhole, sweeping it like a gun muzzle across Jupiter, and preferably on a course that would take it all the way round, but we couldn't count on that best-case scenario. Nor could we count on the configuration lasting for a Jovian nine-hour day, carrying the exit gate around the planet. What we could count on was hitting the Jovians hard.

Yeng had found several commercial channels, and several internal company reporting channels, which were either not encrypted or easily hacked. We kept our forward lasers trained on the New Martians' comms drogue. We stayed near our acceleration couches, watched the screens, and waited.

Hours passed.


I was keeping an eye on a narrow-band monitoring channel, relayed from a camera and a mike in an upper corner of a room in a ship. Not encrypted, nothing special. Full colour, sleety image, mono sound, trickle feed. Probably just one of those capitalist things: management spying. Maybe something more benign, a sort of online black box. It was certainly not that ship's main comms channel, which was sending back an unbreakable flood of coded data. It showed a constant, unwavering view from inside one of the trading vessels—its command deck, by the look of it. Much less cluttered than ours, no recycling equipment, none of the trailing tubes and climbing tendrils. Five acceleration couches, moulded and resilient and glistening, like black jellies. Four men and a woman in identical blue fatigues, drifting around, checking instruments, watching their outside screens; joking and chatting. They didn't seem to have much to do. They were excited about being in the Solar System. One man had been there before, which gave me an eerie feeling when it became clear from his conversation that he'd been one of the uploaded slave-minds in the Outwarders' construction robots.

The real work of their mission was being carried on by their ship's computer, which they referred to as the Bitch, apparently in honour of the ship's name, which was *Running Dog*. I was not as bored as they were, partly because of my still-simmering tension, and partly because—as generations of producers of visual wallpaper have shown—there's something hypnotically watchable about people in space, just as there is about watching planetary surfaces from space.

Snatches of conversation, picked up by that unobtrusive mike, narrowcast to a nearby drogue, lasered at a critical angle into the wormhole, cutting through millennia of space and time, bounced to another relay, beamed by radio to—no doubt—some bored watcher on New Mars, picked up by Yeng's eavesdropping aerials, to finally be heard by me:

'Bitch is hot!'

'Yeah man, she's got her tail up now. Musta met another Jovian.'

'Meeting a minds.'

'Sniff, sniff.'

Laughter.

'Reds still around the Mile?'

'Like flies on a shit. Don't like it, man, don't like it at all.'

'Home says not to worry.'

'Don't trust them, but. Fuck. It's their territory—'

'Says who?'

'Home, that's who. We don't know what they can do yet, anyway.'

(No, I thought, you don't.)

'Not a whole helluva lot, not if they're like the commies we useta know and love.'

'Ha-ha. Didn't know you were that old.'

'Looked good on the tel, though. See the tall black one?'

'Yuh-uh!'

Ribald noises. About me, I realized, and felt flattered. The men rolled and somersaulted, trading ineffectual pokes and punches. Then a voice cut across their laughter; the woman's voice, like a dash of cold water.

'*Something's wrong.*'

'Wha—'

'Look at the board! What the fuck!'

'Bitch, are you all right? Bitch?'

They were diving backwards to their couches, which caught and embraced them in swiftly emerging pseudopods of glassy black jelly. As soon as they'd smacked into place the five astronauts were working very hard, very fast. I could see their heads move, tracking virtual head-ups; their fingers flex over invisible keys. My own movements were almost a reflex of theirs—I was yelling, patching the view from this channel into the other screens and tiling in theirs.

On a news channel, one of the merchant ships—which a sidebar swiftly tagged as the *Running Dog*—had begun to move strangely, yawing under irregular thrusts from its attitude jets.

'They seem to be having some—' A child's puzzled voice.

'Boris!' I shouted. 'For'ard laser now! Get ready to hit the comms drogue! Yeng! Screen out all encrypted input now! Andrea, warm the torch!'

The voices of the *Running Dog*'s crew were still coming through.

'Can't raise the Bitch! Can't raise the Bitch!'

'Shaddap shaddap, we're trying. Shit shit shit shit, drive's not responding.'

'*Running Dog* to home, *Running Dog* to home. We got a bad situation here. Engine out, Bitch haywire. We're getting sorta rolling motion, irregular. Say again please, say again please . . . shit. Comms are out.'

'Lights are on.'

'Nobody's home.'

'Ha ha.'

'Running audit now . . . OK guys, we're in deep shit here, deep shit. Bitch seems to have taken a massive data hit, she's down . . . No! She's running!'

'The hell she is, she's not—oh fuck. Gotta report this, gotta—Shit! Comms are still out.'

'Hey, the monitor!'

Faces turned, looking straight at me.

'If anyone's getting this,' the woman's voice said, quite calmly, 'please act fast. We think our onboard computer has been hacked into and taken over—'

'A fucking Jovie's uploaded on us!' another voice yelled, and meanwhile in the background a third voice was intoning: 'Holy Mary Mother a God pray for us now and at the hour of our *hey, wait a minute, guys, everything's back to normal, it's cool, look*!'

As I watched, their expressions changed from frantic concern to calm relief. The woman was making waving motions at the monitor.

'Cancel that,' she said urgently, smiling. 'False alarm. Sorry, folks, false alarm! Electrical glitch, Jovian atmosphere storm, that's all, panic over.'

The men behind her were moving in a completely different way than they had before, heads and arms working away in a new virtual space; there was nothing wrong with their movements, except that they were all making the *same* movements, in unison. Four heads turned as one, smiling at the monitor as their hands reached and fingers flexed in their synchronized puppet ballet.

'Boris,' I said.

On the forward view the twirling parasol of the New Martians' comms drogue flared at the focus of our lasers, and flash-burned instantly to a million fragments of twinkling foil.

Andrea hit the drive as all the other screens went out.


It wasn't a long burn, just enough to kick us into a closing orbit with the Gate. We had only a few minutes in which to act. Lots of things seemed to happen at once.

'Enemy fighter spinning around,' Boris announced calmly. 'Firing. Missile launched and closing. Active-defence—'

The forward view lit up, with a big flash then lots of small ones as the active-defence lasers mopped up the missile's fragments.

'Fighter taking evasive action. I'm realigning the laser. Over to automatic fire. Target destroyed.' He thought about it for a second, and added: 'Yee-hah!'

'What'd they attack us for?' Suze demanded.

'For burning the drogue,' I said.

'Should be grateful.'

Jaime was running a plot on the nearest comet-train, and Andrea was aligning the ship to match his calculation. Our attitude jets fired, again and again, sending us on a giddying roll. Yeng passed the data to the fighter-bombers, and the *Necessary Evil But Still Cool* sent its own message to the Gate's little attitude-control jets. By the time we were ready to dock with the Gate it was lying at an odd angle, apparently 'below' us, like a tilted plate, and we were sliding backwards 'above' its mile-wide face. On some screen I noticed, out of the corner of my eye, that our own small comms drogue was darting about like a flea on a griddle, squandering its fuel in a mindless attempt to hold the correct position, relative to the disc of the Gate, for picking up the Division's messages. Zap it too? No—I was confident, even now, that the Division's computers and comms weren't going to fall for the Jovian outbreak.

The ship was now lined up for a straight blast into a course to intercept the comet-train, and to continue along 'up' that infall orbital path. The hull shuddered repeatedly as the grappling lines were fired. They snaked out, and were snared by the perimeter clamps. Andrea played another subtle but sickeningly violent crescendo on our own attitude jets, adjusting our alignment as the lines took the strain of the Gate's mass.

One hundred thousand tonnes, Dee had said. Plus another twenty thousand for the score of ships that had sailed through it on their bright bold enterprise . . . and had encountered at least one entity which had found the temptation, or competitive necessity, of *getting in first* as powerful as theirs. I thought of Dee, and wondered how her vaunted competitive countermeasures were holding out against whatever had come down the line from the poor, possessed *Running Dog*. Doing better than I expected, I hoped, for my sake—and hers, I realized, in a sudden pang of anguished solidarity with a self that, human or not, was at least as singular as mine.

'Holding position,' Andrea said.

'*General Arnaldo Ochoa* to *Terrible Beauty*.' Yeng was patching the message through to my phones. The voice was almost languid. 'Situation back home severely compromised. Situation here totally confusing. Please advise.'

Whoever that was had the right stuff, all right! I cut in the override on the Division's all-ships channel:

'Hi guys and gals, *Terrible Beauty* here. Situation as follows. At least one New Martian merchant ship, with crew, has been taken over by a Jovian upload or personality copy. That is confirmed, repeat confirmed. Comms drogue destroyed by us to stop viral spread. We don't repeat do not know if we did this in time. Observe extreme caution with all incoming comms of New-Martian origin. We are about to blast off with wormhole Gate in tow. Intend to try punching local comet-train through to hit Jupiter. You have two minutes to get clear or attempt to return home.'

The languid voice returned. 'Thanks for the clarification, *Terrible Beauty*. Good luck. We see heavy fighting back home. All ships have been recalled. We're leaving. Do you wish continued updates from our own comms drogue?'

'*Yes!*' shouted Yeng, the sheer volume of her voice carrying it to my over-ride.

'Patching you through.'

The scene, relayed from the home system by the—for now—stable and on-position drogue, flashed up on the virtual screens of the suits, which were still tensing and hardening around us. It came from an external camera on the *Turing Tester*, loyally on station in front of the Gate.

Jupiter was bang in the middle of the view, as I'd hoped. The rest of the view sparkled with the flashes of distant laser hits and was scored by the scorch of particle-beams, and snowed by the chaff thrown out in efforts to deflect or diffuse both. Missile trails and kinetic-energy tracers added to the battle's blaze. Two or three of the trading vessels were in sight, each surrounded by a swarm of fighters. One was heading away on what looked like an entirely orthodox evasion course. The others were wallowing in the same bizarre way as the *Running Dog* had when its systems were first suborned. I could almost feel the strivings of the new minds in their unfamiliar frames, new impulses racing through controls, and the struggles of whatever parts of the ships' programming resisted its new master. The ships' yaw and pitch were resultant of these conflicting forces. Through the whole confused scene flitted the dark shapes of our own fighter-bombers, their violent manoeuvres dodging at least the kinetic-energy and missile weapons, but even in the first seconds of our observation, two were successfully targeted by particle-beams, and burst in silent agony.

One by one, the fighter-bombers on our side darted past, seeming to pass over our heads from the camera's viewpoint, our whole ship rocking as each fighter's mass passed through the Gate. I counted nine, then heard a now-familiar voice.

'*General Arnaldo Ochoa* says goodbye and good luck.'

'Goodbye,' I said.

For a tenth and final time, the great drumhead of stretched space to which we were attached resonated as the fighter-bomber went through. I saw its black, bat-like shadow-shape flit sideways a moment after its exit. We were on our own now.

Then I saw, heading straight towards us, filling the view, the bulk of a merchant ship. Something burned into its side, but it ploughed on. The last thing that the *Turing Tester*'s camera showed was an out-of-focus image of its looming forward shield. The last—and, while we were watching, only— sound to come through that channel via the comms drogue was a voice breaking in, by some frantic feat of hacking, to yell the warning:

'*Running Dog!*'

Our ship shook as the thousand-tonne mass passed through, simultaneously subtracting the same amount from the virtual mass of the Gate. A cable broke, lashing across the forward view. For an entire second, as I cut from the now-blank internal screen to an outside camera which Yeng had instantly and reflexively patched in, I watched in frozen shock as the huge ship rose from the wormhole Gate like a missile from a silo, with the wreck of the *Turing Tester* crumpled across its prow.

As soon as it cleared the Gate, its attitude jets fired with far greater precision than its earlier efforts had shown. Its new mind had mastered its controls, and it was turning its main drive away from us, and its blunt forward shield towards us.

'Andrea!' I tried to shout, but she'd already engaged the drive. The most violent acceleration I'd ever felt slammed down, crushing my shout to a grunt. The *Running Dog* vanished instantly from view, then reappeared as the camera swung to track.

'Boris,' I groaned. 'The nuke.'

'Can't,' his stronger voice came back. 'No time to program its course.'

'OK,' I breathed. 'Just send *Carbon Conscience* with it, kamikaze run.'

'Hope you mean kamikaze *autopilot*.'

'Don't—waste—breath . . .'

He wasted neither breath nor time, but it was a long minute before he'd punched the instructions through, and our very own fighter-bomber sprang from our side and flashed away, instantly outrun by our acceleration.

Yeng switched to its nose-camera, and—in less than a minute, its fuel burned off in one final sprint—we saw what it saw as it closed for the kill. We saw *Running Dog*'s bulk loom again. We saw the silent, shocking sphere of the fifty-megaton nuclear explosion . . . but not in that camera.

I swear we saw it through our hull.


The white afterimages of everything faded slowly, to be replaced by the red pulse of pain. I wasn't breathing—the suit was doing that for me—and the pinprick tubules of the suit's oxygen-supply were forged to hot blades stabbing through my almost-collapsed lungs.

*Going for the short fast run*, Andrea's message spelled out, in green letters on the wavering scarlet screen of my visual field. *Free fall in 20 mins, first encounter in a further 20.*

*Can't you run it longer more speed?* Boris asked.

*Outa gas*, replied Andrea.

Out of reaction-mass, to be precise. Nobody had any more questions. I hoped Andrea had allowed some reserve to get us home, wherever home was now, but I hadn't the heart or the strength to ask.

Jaime flashed up data about our target comet-stream: a long, rich train of fragments, nicely lined-up long ago by the New Martians'—or ultimately, ironically, the Outwarders'—automated machinery, far out in the system's vast cloud of unconsolidated ice and organics: still gigantic and irregular flying icebergs hundreds of yards across, each mined with chemical explosives synthesized *in situ* by the smart-matter that infiltrated it. These explosives were primed to detonate before its final fall on New Mars, breaking the masses into manageable morsels for the planet's atmosphere to ablate and its surface to absorb.

Something was troubling me, something I'd forgotten. I struggled for the elusive thought, crushed as I was in that press of acceleration, and suddenly it seemed I had it—what if they broke up before hitting *Jupiter*? I dismissed it as unlikely—the nanomachines on the comet-chunks wouldn't mistake a gas-giant for a small and rocky world.

And anyway, there was nothing we could do about it, nothing at all. This was, in every sense, our last throw.


The crushing pressure ended. We all drew a first breath, and let it out in a common howl of pain just before the suits mainlined opiate derivatives into our blood, metered out precisely to cancel the agony and not to overshoot us into euphoria. Not that there was much risk of that.

'OK,' said Andrea, her voice shaking. 'We have twenty minutes to get clear and get this thing lined up. Stay in your seats.'

A quite redundant instruction, I thought, as I strove to twitch my fingers and call up screens. After about a minute, I succeeded. The suit's infiltration of my body was not withdrawing, this time; it still had work to do, as had everyone else's—the first screens I pulled in showed their physiological readouts. They were all alive, and conscious, and undergoing massive assistance and repair.

And I was not.

I stared at the screens, hardly believing what I saw, hardly believing that I was not seeing with my own eyes, or nerves, or brain. My brain had not shut down completely: it was keeping my body going, all right; but what Dee had called the cost of sustaining consciousness, of maintaining self-hood, had been passed elsewhere. The suit had shunted my mind straight into itself, running me as an update of the model it had taken, days earlier, for my back-up before the first Jovian probe.

So now I knew. I knew how a simulated mind experienced the world. There was no difference whatsoever.

At least, none that I, as a simulated mind, could tell.

Why had the suit done that? Why to me?

At that point I found a difference in my experience. I had an acute awareness of the suit's presence, its own awareness, as a loyal, living thing; and of its answer.

*There is not only you*, it said. *Potentially, there is another here. You are carrying a foetus. I optimize, based on your implied preference. The choice remains yours. You can override mine if you wish.*

I did not so wish.

As from a great distance, I watched Yeng disengage the grappling lines, Andrea boost us to a stable position a couple of miles from the wormhole Gate, and Jaime play the Gate's clamped-on attitude jets to bring it all to precisely the right angle for the oncoming comet-stream.

'That's it,' Jaime said. 'Just made it, the drones are almost out out of gas themselves.'

'Three minutes to go,' said Andrea.

The comets were closing so fast that, even at this late moment, they were still invisible to the forward telescope. Even if their reflected light could have been picked up, they'd show no proper motion against the background of stars, until the last few seconds before interception. Only the deep-space radar clocked their approach. I lay still, my fingertips keying in codes to flip through outside views: the system's sun—small compared to how ours had looked from Earth, big and burning in my Callistan eyes; the distant ochre disc of New Mars; and the paradoxical ellipse of the gate.

'Two minutes.'

She counted down the last minute. As she said 'Two!' I saw, in one of my screens, something moving against the stars: the first comet, seen with—not quite—the naked eye.

'One!'

'Ze—'

Cherenkov backwash flooded all our sight.

The other fragments followed with less than a second between them.

Blue light strobed. Ten cometary masses, each of them weighing in at hundreds of thousands of tonnes. Four passed through the Gate, adding their mass to our side of it—and subtracting it from the other.

'We must be into negative mass, now,' Malley said. 'I wish I could see what it's like.'

We were in free fall, but we all stayed in our couches, too exhausted to move, and perhaps afraid to. We had nothing to do but wait, and watch the process by which we hoped to accomplish the destruction of a world. I knew, now—now that I too was a copied mind running in smart-matter—that the Jovians were not flatlines; that they were, indeed, a superior species not just in the reach of their power, but in the depth of their minds. They, like us, had infinite space within, subjective worlds; they were not just entities, but beings.

And at this moment—no, at another moment, ten thousand years in the past—our first shots at them were crashing down, smashing those subjective worlds; our crude rocks were bashing in thinner skulls and deeper minds than ours. If, that is, we had succeeded in our aim.

It came to me, then, that what we *were doing* now had *already been done*, that the interactions of the Gate and the comet fragments in our immediate future had consequences in the far past—that, in some sense, the battle was already over. The universe within ten thousand light years of the Sun was already being colonized by our descendants, or theirs. There was no way of telling, of course—they, or we, might 'already' have near-lightspeed Malley Drive ships, dragging new wormhole gates, but if they 'had' penetrated further than New Mars, they wouldn't arrive until so many years in our future. The thought gave me an odd, fatalistic reassurance, when it wasn't twisting my mind in knots that only Malley, perhaps, could have unravelled.

I lay there and waited. What would be would be.

The Gate was still open; still hurtling along the orbital path of the other incoming comets, ready to intersect the next stream—as it did, half an hour later. These were larger, less shaped, but still small enough to go through. As was the next stream, and the next, until finally, ten hours and countless cometary fragments later, we reached the limit of the wormhole structure's capacity to sustain a negative mass.

Malley grunted, as if some calculation had been confirmed.

'Now we know,' he said.

The remaining fragments we encountered passed through where the Gate had been.


No longer held together by the tension of the Gate, its rim broke up into sections: dull arcs that drifted apart and then, very slowly, together, under the attraction of the enormous, invisible mass of some exotic matter which was all that remained of the warped space they had contained. It continued to move outwards, against the infalling stream of comets, out towards their source.

# 11

## LOOKING FORWARD

Move or copy?

The suit's query could, for me, have only one answer. I had no wish to leave a second self hanging around in the suit's circuitry. Nevertheless, my second self had second thoughts. Was I—the real me, existing now, at this moment, about to die? About to commit suicide, for the sake of another person, who would wake with my memories, back in the presently unconscious meat? Or was I—the copy—about to murder *my real self*, who would otherwise awaken, with no memory of what had transpired between the loss of her consciousness and its recovery?

Once you start thinking like that, I realized, there is no end to it.

'Move,' I said.

Something happened then, in that brief, eternal moment when I sparked across the gap between the suit and the skull. I saw a hundred billion stars, as they might be after a hundred thousand years. It was, of course, a vision, a hallucination; or an intention, a programme, a plan; but what I do not know to this day is whether it was mine: whence it came, and to whom it was vouchsafed.

I saw a galaxy of green and gold, its starlight filtered through endless, countless habitats; the federation of our dreams. And behind it all, in the walls of all our worlds, an immense but finite benevolence, a great engine of protection and survival; a god on *our* side, a terror to our enemies and a friend to us, worlds without end.

A god who smiled, its work to see; and who now smiled on mine.

Someone was shaking me. I struggled, in too-solid flesh.

'Ellen!' Boris was asking. 'Are you all right?'

I opened my eyes and cracked an awful smile (I know, because I've seen the recording that Boris's eye made).

'I'm fine,' I said. 'I just . . . passed out for a moment.'


'Situation report,' said Andrea, briskly. 'We're almost out of reaction-mass, although of course we can still get all the power we need from the drive. We're in an orbital couple with the dark matter, or whatever, where the Gate was, and heading rapidly outwards towards the local comet-cloud. We don't know if New Mars has fallen to any final transmissions from the *Running Dog*, and we don't know if our bombardment did in the Jovians. It was a lot weaker, after all, than the massive comet-strike we had set up in the Solar System.' She paused, gazing at the star-speckled forward view. 'And now the Gate is gone, we'll never find out.'

'Until the first Malley Drive ships turn up,' I said, grimly. 'Ours or theirs.'

'Why ships?' Malley asked. He seemed amused.

I stared at him. 'Well,' I began, 'assuming somebody can reinvent the virtual-mass drive you postulated, and which the first fast folk built for their probe, it can travel at close to lightspeed, and we're ten thousand light years away but ten thousand years in the future, so—'

I stopped, suddenly feeling stupid, as everybody got the point at the same time, and laughed.

That ten thousand years was time enough for any radio signals from the Solar System to reach us; signals that originated immediately after we left.

'It won't be easy to pick up,' said Yeng. 'I'll have to build a radio *telescope*.'

'How long will that take?' I asked.

Yeng frowned. 'Some time,' she said. 'I'd have to dig out our last parachute, which is of course not much use to us now, and rejig some hull-maintenance robots to paint it with a monomolecular foil mesh. It's half a mile across, so it should be sensitive enough, especially as we know where to point it.' She mentally calculated. 'It'll take several hours, at least.'

'*That* long?' snorted Malley. 'Good grief, woman, I thought you were talking about *years*.'

I'd been reckoning on months, but I didn't say it. I smiled at Yeng and said:

'OK, that's great. But I think the *first* thing we have to find out is if New Mars is all right. Because if it isn't, we could be in real trouble, real soon.'

Despite protests—somehow, the thought of waiting was even more intolerable, now that we knew we could find out—we went ahead and re-ran the procedure to check the New-Martian radio traffic. Yeng worked her way through her entire armoury of defences, and found them all clear, relaying the same insistent and wholly human commerce as she had found before. The incidents of the past hours were being analysed by many loud and conflicting voices. Nobody knew we were still in the system, and we had no intention, just yet, of telling them.

New Mars, at least, was safe. We left the radio on, in celebration. The New Martians' old music, with its perverse celebration of strange sad yearnings and desperate desires, began again to infiltrate our own minds like a viral meme. It formed the soundtrack as we all pitched in to help Yeng deploy and adapt the bubble-thin parachute, a process we called our STI project—the search for terrestrial intelligence.

It was a nervous joke. We didn't know what we'd find. We didn't speak of our fear that what we'd find would be the incomprehensible—or all too comprehensible—voices that told us that our exile, and our great proud crime, had been for naught.

When the telescope was completed, we all hung in the air around Yeng, on the command deck. Every sound was loud: the air conditioning, the murmur of the ship to itself, the ping of the radar, our breathing. Yeng ignored them all, working through the first faint signals her great dish aerial had picked up. She ran them through every check, through her hardware and software, the analyser fixels flickering in their game of life. For long minutes, she studied them, then without a word, without looking around, she flicked the speakers on and rotated a dial.

The command deck filled with the sounds of human beings from the far past: talking, singing, arguing, squabbling, claiming and disputing—a sound immediately redoubled by ourselves, doing much the same, but louder. Then we stopped yelling, and listened again. Most of the broadcasting was still being done by non-cos, and there was—just as on New Mars—a lot of ill-informed speculation, but it was obvious that our strike had been a success. The Division's internal messages were, as we could have expected, narrow-beamed, and nothing so far had leaked in our direction.

We drank a lot of alcohol that shift.

Some time later I found I'd eaten a pizza topped with synthesized anchovies, olives, banana and pineapple. I had never eaten such a revolting combination before, and I vaguely wondered about it as I licked a final ice cream before falling asleep. I slept for hours, longer than anyone else. I woke up among them all, still on the command deck, and was promptly and quite publicly sick.

Suze looked at me with a funny, speculative grin.

'Comrades,' I said, 'I have something to tell you.'

It was a month or so later that Yeng's telescope picked up the first signal directed at us: a television signal, open and unencrypted. The call sign had us all leaving whatever we were doing, literally in midair, and rushing to the nearest screen. Tatsuro's face appeared. He was sitting in a virtual conference-space, with some of the Command Committee members, a group of people in New-Martian commercial uniforms, and, to my surprise, Jonathan Wilde. (The copy of . . . but I'd stopped thinking that way. I had reformed.)

'I feel very strange saying this,' Tatsuro began. 'This message is to be sent by the most powerful transmitter we currently have, and will be repeated, on more powerful transmitters as they become available, for at least some years to come. It will not, of course, reach its intended recipients for ten thousand years. If you're receiving this, you know how strange the circumstances are. But I have to assume that you're there, in the future, and that to you this message seems almost immediate. So—

'To the crew of *Terrible Beauty*, we all send our thanks. Your comet-strike was just sufficient to disrupt the Jovian post-humans. To the best of our knowledge, they are extinct, not only from your actions, and ours, but also from fighting amongst themselves. You need not worry that you destroyed entities which might have been friendly to us—any that were, I'm afraid, were destroyed by other Jovians, who were in the process of a frantic race to upload copies of themselves into anything they could reach. Strangely enough, the target of their outbreak was the New-Martian trading ships rather than ourselves. Our computers were almost impervious to the Jovian viruses, whereas theirs were, ah, rather more vulnerable, as it turned out. Our latest investigations and reconstructions show that the Jovians were aiming for the Malley Mile, from which they could have mastered the entire span of the wormhole, and with it a large part of the universe. You saved more than you knew.

'Whether you saved the humans and post-humans of New Mars, we don't know. If you have not, or if this message is being received by our enemies, I hope the destruction of the Jovians is a sufficient warning of the terrible acts of which our species is capable. For we are going to build new virtual-mass quantum-fluctuation drive ships, and new wormhole gates, as soon as we have the capacity. We will re-establish contact with New Mars. And now, I'll wish you well, and pass the transmission to the survivors of the New-Martian trading expedition, who have messages of their own.'

One by one, the New-Martian men and women came up, each speaking a heartfelt, and heart-rending, personal message—some, in a way that struck me as strange, addressed to their own copies as well as to friends and relations. One of them finished by saying:

'This is just a general message to all of you out there. We'll do our best to maintain one-way communication—we'll keep in touch, until they build the ships. Of course, unless they build another gate as well, the ships will be one-way, too, as far as getting back to this place and time is concerned—but we're coming home. And you don't need to worry about how the Solar Union people will treat us—Wilde here has lived off their hospitality for years, according to his needs, as they say. But what most of us want is to do some business, with the non-cooperators if no one else—but I think we'll find more trading partners than that. There are a lot of energetic people on Earth, and now they can use electronics as they please, they are going to *boil off*. Things are going to change around here. We *will* see you again.'

Wilde had learned from the traders about the survival of his other self and his resurrected wife. He had messages for them, and for me.

'Ellen May,' he said, 'I thought you could defeat the Outwarders without finding the way to New Mars. Well, I was mistaken, and you've done both. You know what I feared—that your people would invade New Mars, a place for which I have . . . a certain affection. Now, looking around me, I wonder just who has invaded whom. Life may surprise us.'

He shrugged. 'That's all. Good luck.'


I'm looking out of what we still, from habit, call the forward view. The sun of New Mars is a tiny, distant disc, barely noticeable against the other stars. We are in the thick of the comet-cloud, but this thickness is only visible in simulations, not in reality. All around us is what looks like empty space, apart from our very own comet, surrounded by the frail-seeming, diamond-strong structures we've built from its material; and the strange ruin of the Gate.

Exotic matter is useful stuff to have around. It pulled us into a close orbit with an even bigger chunk of normal matter: cometary matter, hundreds of millions of tonnes of it, rock and ice and organics. It took us five years, give or take, to get out to the cometary cloud, so by that time we were ready to appreciate our gain. These days, the remnant of the Gate has begun to acquire its own accretion disc. It is, as Malley once put it, an attractive feature.

Every home should have one.

Home . . . is here, in one sense. In another, it's ten thousand light years away—and ten thousand years in the past. (Although I still find myself thinking that *we* are ten thousand years in the future.)

The solar sources grew and multiplied—at the time we first heard them, they increased by the day and the hour. Within months they were detectable by much less sensitive receivers than ours, including those on and around New Mars.

The transmissions tell the ongoing tale of the struggle which that New-Martian trader foresaw, and whose conclusion no one can foresee: between the Union's common ownership and the unstoppable appropriation of the Solar System's resources by individuals and groups; a story intently followed by ourselves and by the New Martians. It has the immediacy of daily news, and the poignancy of ancient history, which nothing we can do will alter and whose ultimate outcome, if any, was settled millennia ago. It's already the subject of numerous documentaries, frequent debates, and several completely fictitious and laughably imaginative New-Martian drama serials.


The comet-cloud is vast, and we are used to communicating by narrow, cryptic channels, by winks of laser in the void. Around us the broader, more open signals of the New Martians and their robot comet-miners fill the spectrum. We know all that they do, and they know we're here, but little more. We keep contact to a minimum. We're happy with that, for now: we want to build a world of our own out here, out of rock and ice and carbon-compounds and weak sunlight, before we venture back to a world owned by others.

One day the Solar Union, or whatever replaces it, will have built its own near-lightspeed Malley Drive ships. And ten thousand years later, which could be any day now, they'll turn up here, perhaps dragging a new worm-hole. I don't much mind if the people who arrive don't share our views. They certainly won't share our property. We may, by then, have the beginnings of our own little galactic empire quietly accreted around us, out here in the depths of the comet-cloud. When we have enough mass processed, we'll start growing people and animals and machines from the seeds in our stores, and we can grow a long way before anyone even thinks to stop us.

I'm scanning the analyser readings of a new lode, frowning over the sparse traces of metal, when a small body cannons into me and a voice says, 'Ellen, they're talking about you!'

Stef is four years old, lanky and bright. He looks a bit like his father, the photographer I met on Graciosa, but he'll grow taller than his father: my genes, and his microgravity environment, will see to that. It's a struggle getting him to keep up his induction isotonics, in addition to all the usual fights about brushing teeth and washing hair. He claims his suit takes care of all that, and it does, but that's not good enough.

'Back home?' I ask eagerly.

Stef shakes his head, impatiently. To him, the Solar Union is almost unreal, a mythical past, a tale we tell him of our Heliocene days. New Mars is, in every sense, more immediate and vivid.

'In the *world*,' he tells me.

'OK,' I say. 'Patch it through.'

Stef sticks his hand inside the open front of his suit, and tugs and twists the smart-matter fabric in exactly the careless, undocumented way I've always tried to argue him out of. To no avail, so far. He regards the suit as something between an imaginary friend and an intelligent stuffed toy, and treats any attempt to impose a system on their private language as just that, an imposition.

The image on my screen dissolves and is replaced by one of those late-night discussion programmes that New-Martian television stations put out for the slenderest of minority audiences, the sort of people who probably work in or around the media themselves and affect to despise the rubbish they put out for everybody else.

The format is utterly conventional, with a young presenter—a teenager, and thus more mature than most local newscasters—and a few older heads discoursing earnestly around a table. I recognize the bishop, who is probably, whether she realizes it or not, by now the Pope; the rabbi; a Reformed Humanist spokesperson; a couple of Post-Resurrectionist clerics—and David Reid.

'—calling it *justifiable genocide* is, shall we say, uncalled for,' one of the clerics is saying. 'I understand your need to be provocative, of course.' A quick, we're-all-in-this-together smile to the presenter. 'But I think we need to consider it in more, ah, morally neutral terms. We are, after all, talking about *machinery*.'

Reid leans forward, as usual establishing his priority to speak with a wavy trail of smoke. The presenter, knowing her limitations, wearily nods.

'Rubbish,' Reid says. 'If you want to talk about morality, you can't leave out machinery. We *are* machinery. The point is, I doubt if anyone could have done what *had* to be done to the Jovians without having a pretty hard attitude to the sufferings of machines. Mind you, the Outwarders had a pretty low empathy with the sufferings of humans, and the Jovians inherited that flaw, so—'

'Original sin?' interrupts the bishop. 'I'm surprised at you!'

The two Calvinist clergmen smirk politely. Reid shakes his head.

'They showed it by their actions,' he says. 'By what they did to our ships.'

'Ah, but was that enough to condemn an entire . . . species?' the Reformed Humanist asks. 'I suspect Ellen May Ngwethu and her crew acted precipitately, but with a degree of premeditation, a refusal to consider alternatives, which in itself—'

'We live in a tough world,' says the rabbi. 'As my people have tradition-ally put it, life is short and shit happens.'

A few minutes of free-for-all follows.

'What everybody here seems to be forgetting,' says the presenter, trying to get a word in edgeways, 'is the evidence from the Solar System, which at least suggests that the Jovian outbreak was *no threat whatsoever* to the people in the Solar Union. So, in effect, whatever we think of what the crew of the *Terrible Beauty* did, it was to our benefit.'

'And to that of the new societies emerging in the Solar System,' one of the clerics adds. 'They wouldn't exist without the ending of the Jovian threat, which, whether we approve of it or not, the Cassini Division accomplished.'

The Reformed Humanist nods gravely. 'At some cost, moral and material, to themselves.'

The next comment, if any, is drowned out by Reid's cynical guffaw, and then he says: 'What *else* are communists *for*?'

The complacent laughter of all the good liberals around the table light-ens the tone of the rest of the discussion, to which I pay not the slightest at-tention. I'm hugging the kid to my side and looking at the cheerful, chatting faces, and thinking, *Just you wait, you bankers! Just you wait!*


Our day will come, again.

# THE SKY ROAD

*For Mic*

# CONTENTS

# 1

---

## THE LIGHT AND THE FAIR

*So it came that Merrial found him
in the square at Carron Town*

She walked through the fair in the light of a northern summer evening, looking for me. Of the hundreds of people around her, the thousands in the town and the thousands on the project, only I would serve her purpose. My voice and visage, mind and body were her target acquisition parameters.

I sat on the plinth of the statue of the Deliverer, drained a bottle of beer and put it carefully down and looked around, screwing up my eyes against the westering sun. The music faded for a moment, then another band struck up, something rollicking and loud that echoed off the tall buildings around three sides of the square and boomed out from the open side across the shore and over the water. The still sea-loch was miles of gold, the distant hills and islands stacks of black. The air was warm and shaking with the music and heavy with scent and sweat, alcohol-breath and weed-smoke. People were already dancing, swinging and swirling among the remaining stalls of the day's market. I caught glimpses and greetings from various of my workmates, Jondo and Druin and Machard and the rest, as they whirled past in the throng with somebody who might be their partner for the hour, or for the night, or for longer.

For a moment, I felt intensely alone, and was about to jump up and plunge in and seek out someone, anyone, who would take me even for one dance. It was not normally this way; usually at such occasions through the summer I had got lucky. Like most of my fellow-workers, I was young and—of necessity—strong, and my vanity needed no flattery, and we were most of us open-handed strangers, and therefore welcome. But I was in a serious and abstracted mood, the coming autumn's study already casting its long shadow back, and in all that evening's gaiety I had not once made a woman laugh, and my luck had fled.

She walked through that dense crowd as if it wasn't there. I saw her before she saw me. Her long black hair was caught around the temples by two narrow braids; the tumbling waves of the rest showed traces of auburn in the late sun. That golden light and ruddy shadow defined her tanned and flushed face: the large bright eyes, the high cheekbones, the curve of her cheek and jaw, the red lips. She wore a gown of plain green velvet that seemed, and probably was, made to show off her strong and well-endowed figure. Her gaze met mine, and locked. Her eyes were large and a little slanted, and they caught my glance like a trap.

There is, no doubt, some bodily basis for the crude cartoon of such moments—the arrow through the heart. A sudden demand on the sugar reserves of the cells, perhaps. It's more like a thorn than an arrow, and passes in less than a second, but it's there, that sharp, sweet stab.

A moment later she stood in front of me, looking down at me quizzically, curiously, then she came to some decision and sat down beside me on the cold black marble. The hooves of the Deliverer's horse reared above us. We stared at each other for a moment. My heart was hammering. She appeared younger, more hesitant, than she'd seemed with her first bold gaze. Her irises were golden-brown, ringed with green-blue. I could see a faint spatter of freckles beneath her tan. A fine gold chain around her neck suspended a rough mesh of gold wire containing a seer-stone the size of a pigeon's egg. It hung between her breasts, its small world flickering randomly in that gentle friction. An even thinner silver chain implied some other ornament, but it hung below where I could see. The dagger and derringer and purse on her narrow waist-belt were each so elegant and delicate as to be almost nominal. There was some powerful undertone to her scent, whether natural or artificial I didn't know.

'Well, here you are,' she said, as though we'd arranged to meet at this very place. For a couple of heartbeats I entertained the thought that this might be true, that she was someone I really did know and had unaccountably, unforgivably forgotten—but no, I had no memory of ever having met her before. At the same time I couldn't get rid of a conviction that I already knew her, and always had.

'Hello,' I said, for want of anything less banal. 'What's your name?'

'Merrial,' she said. 'And you are . . . ?'

'Clovis,' I said. 'Clovis colha Gree.'

She nodded to herself, as though some datum had been confirmed, and smiled at me.

'So, colha Gree, are you going to ask me for a dance?'

I jumped to my feet, amazed. 'Yes, of course. Would you do me the honour?'

'Thank you,' she said. She took my hand in a warm, dry grasp and rose gracefully, merging that movement with her first step. It was a fast dance to a traditional air, 'The Tactical Boys'. Talking was impossible, but we communicated a great deal none the less. Another measure followed, and then a slower dance.

We finished it a long way from where we'd started—fetched up close to the outside tables of the biggest pub on the square, The Carronade. Some of the lads from work were already at one of the tables, with their local girls. My mates gave me odd looks, compounded of envy and secret amusement; their female partners were looking lasers at Merrial, for no reason I could fathom. She was attractive all right, and looking more beautiful to my eyes with every passing second, but the other girls were not obviously less blessed; and she wasn't a harlot, unless she was foolish (harlotry being a respected but regulated trade in that town, its plying not permitted in the square).

Introductions were awkwardly made.

'What will you be having, Merrial?' I asked.

She smiled up at me. She was, in truth, almost as tall as I, but my boots had high heels.

'A beer, please.'

'Fine. Will you wait here?'

I gestured to a vacant place on the nearest bench, beside Jondo and his current lass.

'I will that,' Merrial said.

Jondo shot me another odd look, a smile with one corner of his mouth turned down, and his eyebrows raised. I shrugged and went through to the bar, returning a few minutes later with a three-litre jug and a couple of tall glasses. Merrial was sitting where she'd been, ignoring the fact that she was being ignored. I put this unaccustomed rudeness down to some petty local quarrel, of which Carron Town—and the yard and, indeed, the project—had plenty. If one of Merrial's ancestors had offended one of Jondo's (or whoever's) that was no business of mine, as yet.

The table was too wide for any intimate conversation to be carried on across it, so I sat down beside her, setting off a Newtonian collision of hips all the way along the bench as my friends and their girlfriends shuffled their bums away from us. I filled our glasses and raised mine.

'*Slàinte*,' I said.

'*Slàinte, mo chridhe*,' she said, quietly but firmly, her gaze level across the tilted rim.

And cheers, my dear, to you, I thought. Again her whole manner was neither shy nor brazen, but as though we had been together for months or years. I didn't know what to say, so I said that.

'I feel we know each other already,' I said. 'But we don't.' I laughed. 'Unless when we were both children?'

Merrial shook her head. 'I was not here as a child,' she said, in a vague tone. 'Maybe you've seen me at the project.'

'I think I would remember,' I said. She smiled, acknowledging the compliment, as I added, 'You work at the *project*?' I sounded more surprised than I should have been—there were plenty of women working on it, after all, in catering and administration.

'Aye,' she said, 'I do.' She fondled the pendant, warming a fire within it, and not only there. 'On the guidance system.'

'Oh,' I said, suddenly understanding. 'You're a—an *engineer*.'

'I am a tinker,' she said in a level tone, using the word I'd so clumsily avoided. She spoke it with a pride as obvious, and loud enough to be heard. A snigger and a giggle passed around the table. I glared past Merrial's shoulder at Jondo and Machard. They shook their heads slightly, doubtfully, then returned to their conversations.

Justice judge them. As a city man I felt myself above such rural idiocies—though realising her occupation had given even me something of a jolt. Whatever passed between us, it would be less or more serious than any fling with a local lass. I leaned inward, so that Merrial's shoulders and mine defined a social circle of our own.

'Sounds like interesting work,' I said.

She nodded. 'A lot of mathematics, a lot of'—and this time she did lower her voice—'programming.'

'Ah,' I said, trying to think of some response that wouldn't reveal me to be as prejudiced as my workmates. 'Isn't it very dangerous?' I resisted the impulse to look over my shoulder, but I was suddenly, acutely aware of the massive presence of the hills around the town, their forested slopes like the bristling backs of great beasts in the greater Wood of Caledon.

'*White* logic,' Merrial explained. 'The right-hand path, you know? The path of light.' She did not sound as though the distinction mattered a lot to her.

'Reason guide you,' I responded, with reflex piety. 'But—it must be tempting. The short cuts, yeah?'

'The path of power is always a temptation,' she said, with casual familiarity. 'Especially when you're working on a guidance system!' She laughed; I confess I shuddered. She fingered her talisman. 'Enough about that. I know what I'm doing, so it isn't dangerous. At least, not as dangerous as it looks from outside.'

'Well.' Despite the electric frisson her words aroused, I was as keen as she was to change the subject. 'You could say the same about what I do.'

'And what do you do?' She asked it out of politeness; she already knew. I was sure of that, without quite knowing why.

'I work in the yard,' I said.

'On the ship?'

'Oh, not on the ship!' A self-deprecating laugh, not very sincere. 'On the platform. For the summer, I'm a welder.'

She slugged back some beer. 'And the rest of the time?'

'I'm a scholar,' I said. 'Of history. At Glaschu.'

This was a slight exaggeration. I had just attained the degree of Master of Arts, and my summer job was a frantic, frugal effort to earn enough to support myself for an attempt at a doctorate. Scholarship was my ambition, not my occupation. But I refused to call myself a student. Merrial looked at me with the sort of effortful empathy with which I'd favoured her self-disclosure. 'That sounds . . . interesting,' she said. 'What *part* of history?'

I gestured across the square, to the statue's black silhouette. Behind it, from the east, the first visible stars of the evening pricked the sky.

'The life of the Deliverer,' I said.

'And what have you learned?' She leaned closer, transparently more interested; her black brows raised a fraction, her bright dark eyes widening. Without thinking, I lit a cigarette; remembered my manners, and offered her one. She took it, grinning, and helped herself to the jug of beer, then filled my glass too. 'You wouldn't think there'd be much new to learn,' she added, looking up through her eyelashes.

I rose to the bait. 'Ah, but there is!' I told her. 'The Deliverer lived in Glasgow, you know. For a while.'

'A lot of places will tell you she lived there—for a while!' Merrial laughed.

'Aye, but we have evidence,' I said. 'I've seen papers written with her own hand, and signed. There is no controversy that it was her who wrote them. What they mean, now, that's another matter. And a great deal of other writing, printed articles that is, and material that is still in the—you know.'

'Dark storage?'

'Yeah,' I said. 'Dark storage. I wish—' Even here, even now, it was impossible to say just what I wished. But Merrial understood.

'There you go, colha Gree,' she said. 'The path of power is always a temptation!'

'Aye, it is that,' I admitted gloomily. 'You can look at them, labelled in her own hand, and you wonder what's in them, and—well.'

'Probably corrupt,' she said briskly. 'Not worth bothering with.'

'Of course corrupt—'

She shook her head, with a brief, small frown. 'In the technical sense,' she explained. 'Garbage data, unreadable.'

Garbage data? What did that mean?

'I see,' I said, seeing only that she'd just tried to explicate part of the argot of her profession; another unseasonable intimacy.

'All the same,' she went on, 'it must be strange work, history. I don't know how you can bear it, digging about in the dead past.'

I had heard variations of this sentiment from so many people, starting with my mother, that exasperation welled within me and I'm sure showed on my face. She smiled as though to assure me that she didn't hold it against me personally, and added, 'The Possessors don't work only through the black logic, you know. They can get to your mind through their words on paper, too.'

'You speak very freely,' I said. For a woman, I didn't add.

She took it as a compliment, and thus paid me one by not recognising the stiff-kneed priggishness that my remark represented.

'It's the tinker way,' she said, giving me another small shock. 'We talk as we please.'

I couldn't come back on that, so I ploughed on.

'We have to understand the Possession,' I explained self-righteously, 'to understand the Deliverance.'

'But do we understand the Deliverance?' she asked, teasing me relentlessly. 'Do you, Clovis colha Gree?'

'I can't say,' I said—which was true enough, though ecological with the truth.

'Good,' Merrial said. 'We would not claim to understand it, and we knew the Deliverer better than most.' A sly smile. 'As you know.'

I nodded, slowly. I knew all right. Despised and feared though they sometimes are, it is not for nothing that the tinkers are known as the Deliverer's children. They worked her will long ago, in the troubled times, and the benison of that work has protected them down the generations; that and—on a more cynical view—their obscure and irreplaceable knowledge.

I had heard rumours—always disparaged by the University historians— of a firmer continuity, a darker arcana, that linked today's tinkers and the

Deliverer, and that reached back to times yet more remote, when even the Possession was but a sapling, its shadow not yet covering the Earth.

Her hand covered mine, briefly.

'Don't talk about it,' she said.

So we talked about other things: her work, my work, her childhood and mine. The glasses were twice refilled. She stood up, hefting the now empty jug. 'Same again?'

I rose too, saying, 'I'll get them—'

'I insist,' she said, and was gone. I watched the sway of her hips, the way it carried over to swing her heavy skirt and ripple the torrent of hair down her back, as she passed through the crowd and disappeared through the wide door of The Carronade. My friends observed this attention with sardonic smiles.

'You're in for an interesting time, Clovis,' Jondo remarked. He stroked his long red pony-tail suggestively, making his girlfriend laugh again. 'Looks like the glamour's got you.'

Machard smirked. 'Seriously, man,' he told me, 'take care. You don't know tinks like we do. They're faithless, godless, clannish and they don't settle down. At best she'll break your heart, at worst—'

'What is the matter with you?' I hissed, leaning sideways to keep the girls out of the path of my wrath. 'Come on, guys, give the lady a chance.'

My two friends' expressions took on looks of insolent innocence.

'Ease off, Clovis,' said Machard. 'Just advice. Ignore it if you like, it's your business.'

'Too damn right it is,' I said. 'So mind your own.' I spoke the harsh words lightly—not fighting words, but firm. The two lads shrugged and went back to chatting up their lassies. I was ignored, as Merrial had been.

The late train from Inverness glided down the glen, sparks from the overhead wire flaring in the twilight, and vanished behind the first houses. A minute later I could hear the brief commotion as it stopped at the station, a few streets away. The clouds and the tops of the hills glowed pink, the same light reflecting off a solitary airship, heading west. Few lights were on in the town—half past ten in the evening was far too early for that—but the houses that spread up the side of the glen and along the shore were beginning to seem as dark as the pine forest that began where the dwellings ended.

Farther up the great glen the side-lights and tail-lights of vehicles traced out the road's meander, and the dark green of the wooded hillsides met the bright green of the lower slopes, field joined to field, pasture to pasture all the way to where the haunches of the hills hid the view, and the land was dark. Somewhere far away, but sounding uncannily close, a wolf howled, its protracted, sinister note clearly audible above the sounds of the town and the revelry of the fair.

The square was becoming more packed and noisy by the minute. The drinking and dancing would go on for hours. Jugglers and tumblers, fire-eaters and musicians competed for attention and spare cash, with each other and with the hawkers. The markets on summer Thursdays were locally called 'the fair', but only once a month did they amount to much, with a more impressive contingent of performers than were here now, as well as travelling players, whirling mechanical rides and, of course, tinkers; the last pursuing their legitimate trade of engineering and their less reputable, but often more lucrative, craft of fortune-telling.

The train pulled away, trailing its sparks along the Carron's estuarial plain and around the Carron sea-loch's southern shore.

Merrial returned with a full jug, a bottle of whisky and a tray of small glasses. Without a word she placed the tray and the bottle in the middle of the table and sat down, this time opposite me. She filled our tall glasses, put down the jug and gestured to the whisky bottle. 'Help yourselves,' she said.

My friends became more friendly towards her after that. We all found ourselves talking together, talking shop, the inevitable gossip and grumbles of the project, about this scandal and that foreman and the other balls-up; ironically, the girls seemed to feel excluded, and fell to talking between themselves. Merrial, showing tact enough for both of us, noticed this and gradually, now that the ice was broken, returned her conversation to me. Jondo and Machard took up again their neglected tasks of seduction or flirtation. When, a couple of hours later, she asked me to see her home, their ribaldry was relatively restrained.

The square was noisier than ever; the only people heading for home, or for bed, were like ourselves workers on the project who, unlike the locals, had to work on the following day, a Friday. We walked through the dark street to the north of the square and across the bridge over the Carron River towards the suburb of New Kelso. Merrial stopped in the middle of the bridge. One arm was tight around my waist. With the other, she waved around.

'Look,' she said. 'What do you see?'

On our right the town's atomic power-station's automation hummed blackly in the dark; to our left the fish-farms, warmed by the reactor's run-off, spread down to the shore. I looked to left and right, and then behind to the main town, ahead to New Kelso, across the loch to the other small towns.

She smiled at my baffled silence.

'Look up.'

Overhead the Milky Way blazed, the aurora borealis flickered, a communications aerostat glowed pink in a sun long since set for us. The Plough hung above the hills to the north. A meteor flared briefly, my indrawn breath a sound effect for its silent passage. To the west the sky still had light in it; the sun would be up in four hours.

'I can see the stars,' I said.

'That's it,' she said, sounding pleased at my perceptiveness. 'You can. We're in the very middle of a town of ten thousand people, and you can see the Milky Way. Not as well as you could see it from the top of Glas Bhein, sure enough, but you can see it. Why?'

I shrugged, looking again back and forth. I'd never given the matter thought.

'No clouds?' I suggested brightly.

She laughed and caught my hand and tugged me forward. 'And you a scholar of history!'

'What's that got to do with it?'

She pointed to the street-lamp at the end of the bridge's parapet. Its post was about three metres high; its conical cowl's reflective inner surface sharply cut off all but the smallest upward illumination. 'Did you ever see lamps like that in pictures of the olden times?' she asked.

'Now that I come to think of it,' I said, 'no.'

'A town this size would have had lamps everywhere, blazing light into the sky. From street-lamps and windows and shop-fronts. The very air itself would glow with it. You could see just a handful of stars on the clearest night.'

I thought about the ancient pictures I'd peered at under glass. 'You know, you're right,' I said. 'That's what it looked like.'

'Some people,' Merrial went on, in a sudden gust of anger, 'lived their whole lives without once seeing the Milky Way!'

'Very sad,' I said. In fact the thought gave me a tight feeling in my chest, as if I were struggling to breathe. 'How did they stand it?'

'Aye, well, that's a question you could well ask.' She glanced up at me. 'I thought you might know.'

'I never noticed, to be honest.'

'And why don't we do it?' She gestured again at the electric twilight of the surrounding town.

'Because it would be wasteful,' I said. As soon as the words were out I realised I'd said them without thinking, and that it wasn't the answer.

Merrial laughed. 'We have power to spare!'

It was my turn to stop suddenly. We'd taken a right and were going down a path past the power-station. I knew for a fact that it could, when called upon in a rare emergency—such as when extra heating was required to clear snow from a blizzard—produce enough electricity to light up Carron Town several times over.

'You're right,' I said. 'So why don't we do it? I've seen pictures of the great cities of antiquity, and you're right, they shone. They looked . . . magnificent. Perhaps it was so bright they didn't need to see the stars—they had the city lights instead! They made their own stars!'

Merrial was slowly shaking her head.

'Maybe that was fine for them,' she said. 'But it wouldn't be for us. We all get—uneasy when we can't see the night sky. Don't you, just thinking about it?'

I took a deep breath, and let it out with a sigh. 'Aye, you're right at that!'

We walked on, her strides pacing my slower steps.

'You're a strange woman,' I said.

She smiled and held my waist more firmly and leaned her head against my shoulder. I found myself looking down at her hair, and down at the scoop neckline of her dress and the glowing stone between her breasts.

'Sure I am,' she said. 'But so are we all, that's what I'm saying. We're different from the people who came before us, or before the Deliverer's time, and nobody wonders how or why. The feeling we have about the sky is just part of it. We live longer and we breed less, we sicken little, sometimes I think even our eyes are sharper; all these changes are hard-wired into our radiation-hardened genes—'

'Our what?'

I felt the shrug of her shoulder.

'Just tinker cant, colha Gree. Don't worry. You'll pick it up.'

'Oh, I will, will I?'

'Aye. If you stay with me.'

There was only one answer to that. I turned her around and kissed her. She clasped her lips to mine and slid her hands under my open waistcoat and sent them roving around my sides and back. I could feel them through my silk shirt like hot little animals. The kiss went on for some time and ended with our tongues flickering together like fish at the bottom of a deep pool; then she leaned away and gripped my shoulders and looked at me and said, 'I reckon that means you're staying, colha Gree.'

Suddenly we were both laughing. She caught my hand and swung it and we started walking again, talking about I don't know what. Out on the edge of town we turned a corner into a little estate of dozens of single-storey wooden houses with chimneys. Some of the houses were separate, each with its own patch of garden; others, smaller, were lined up in not quite orderly rows. Even in the summer, even with electricity cables strung everywhere, a smell of woodsmoke hung in the air. Yellow light glowed from behind straw-mat blinds. A dog barked and was silenced by an irritable yell.

'Hey, come on,' Merrial said with an impish smile.

I hadn't realised how my feet had hesitated as the path had changed from cobbles to trampled gravel.

'Never been in a tinker camp before,' I apologised.

'We don't bite.' Another cheeky grin. 'Well, that is to say . . .'

'You really are a terrible woman.'

'Oh, I am that, indeed. Ferocious—so I'm told.'

'I'll hold you to that.'

'I'll hold you to more.'

She held me as she stopped in front of one of the small houses in the middle of the row, and fingered out a tiny key five centimetres long on a thong attached to her belt but hidden in a slit in the side of her skirt. The lock too seemed absurdly small, a brass circular patch on the white-painted door at eye level.

'So are you coming in, or what?'

Lust and reason warred with fear and superstition, and won. I followed her over the polished wooden threshold as she switched on the electric light. I stood for a moment, blinking in the sudden 40-watt flood. The main room was about four metres by six. Against the far wall was a wood-burning stove, banked low; above it was a broad mantelpiece on which a large clock ticked loudly. The time was half past midnight. On either side of the stove were rows of shelves with hundreds of books. In the left-hand corner a workbench jutted from the wall, with a microscope and an unholy clutter of soldering gear and bits of wire and tools. Rough, unpolished seer-stones of various sizes lay among them. The main table of the house was a huge oaken piece about a metre and a half square, with carved and castered legs. A crocheted cotton throw covered it, weighted at the centre by a seer-stone hemisphere at least thirty centimetres in diameter, so finely finished that it looked like a dome of glass. Within it, hills and clouds drifted by.

Merrial stood by the table for a moment, reached up behind her head and removed a clasp from her hair, so that the two narrow braids fell forward and framed her face. Then she lifted the chain with the talisman, and the other, finer silver chain, from around her neck and deposited them on the table.

The place smelt of woodsmoke and pot-pourri and the bunches of flowering plants stuffed into carelessly chosen containers in every available corner. The wooden walls were varnished, and hung with an incongruous variety of old prints and paintings—landscapes, ladies, foxes, cats, that sort of thing—and tacked-up picture-posters related to the project. An open door led to a tiny scullery; a curtained alcove beside it took up the rest of that end of the room. I presumed it contained the bed.

But it was to a big old leather couch in front of the stove that she drew me first. She half-leaned, half-sat on the back of it, and began unbuttoning my shirt, then explored my chest with her lips and tongue—and teeth—as I applied myself to undoing the fastenings down the back of her dress, and working my boots off. As I kicked away the right boot the *sgean dhu* clattered to the floor. By this time she had unbuckled my belt, and with a shrug and a step we both shed our outer clothes, which fell to the floor in a promiscuous coupling of their own. Merrial stood for a moment in nothing but her long silk underskirt. I clasped her in my arms, her nipples hard, her breasts warm and soft against my chest; and we kissed again.

We moved, we danced, Merrial leading, towards the curtained alcove. She pulled away the curtain to reveal a large and reassuringly solid-looking bed. I knelt in front of her and pulled down her slip and knickers, and kissed her between the legs until she pulled me gently to my feet. I managed to leave my own briefs on the floor.

We faced each other naked, like the Man and the Woman in the Garden in the story. Merrial half-turned, threw back the bedcovers and picked up from the bed a long white cotton nightgown, which she shook out and held at arm's length for a moment.

'I won't be needing *that* tonight,' she grinned, and cast it to the floor, and me to the bed.

I woke in daylight, and lay for a minute or so basking in the warm afterglow, and hot after-images, of love and sex. Rolling over and reaching out my arm, I found that I was alone in the bed. It was still warm where Merrial had slept. The air was filled with the aroma of coffee and the steady ticking of the clock—

The time! I sat up in a hurry and leaned forward to see the big timepiece, and discovered with relief that it was only five o'clock. Thank Providence, we'd only slept an hour and a half. With the same movement I discovered a host of minor pains: bites on my shoulder and neck, scratches on my back and buttocks, aching muscles, raw skin . . .

The animal whose attacks had caused all this damage padded out of the scullery.

'Good morning,' she said.

I made some sort of croaking noise. Merrial smiled and handed me one of the two steaming mugs she'd carried in. She sat down on the foot of the bed, drawing her knees up to her chin to huddle inside her sark, its high neck and long sleeves and intricate whitework giving her an incongruous appearance of modesty.

I sipped the coffee gratefully, unable to take my eyes off her. She looked calmly back at me, with the smile of a contented cat.

'Good morning,' I said, finding my voice at last. 'And thank you.'

'Not just for the coffee, I hope,' said Merrial.

I was grinning so much that my cheeks, too, were aching.

'No, not just for the coffee. God, Merrial, I've never . . .'
I didn't know how to put it.

'Done it before?' she inquired innocently.

Coffee went up the back of my nose as I spluttered a laugh.

'Compared with last night, I might as well not have,' I ruefully admitted.
'You are—you're amazing!'

Her level gaze held me. She showed not the slightest embarrassment. 'Oh,
you're not so bad yourself, colha Gree,' she said in a judicious tone. 'But you
have a lot to learn.'

'I hope you'll teach me.'

'I'm sure I will,' she said. 'If you want to stay with me, that is.' She waved
a hand, as if this were a matter yet to be decided.

'Stay with you? Oh, Merrial!' I couldn't speak.

'What?'

'Nothing could make me leave you. Ever.'

I was almost appalled at what I was saying. I had not expected to hear
myself speak such words, not for a long time to come.

'How sweet of you to say that,' she said, very seriously, but smiling. 'But—'

'But nothing!' I reached sideways and put the mug on the floor and
shifted myself down the bed towards her. Without looking away from me,
she put her mug down too, on a trunk at the end of the bed, and rocked
forward to her knees to meet me. We knelt with our arms around each
other.

'I love you,' I said. I must have said it before, said it a lot of times through
the night, but now there was all the weight in the world behind the words.

'I love you too,' she said. She clung to me with a sudden fierceness, and laid
her face on my shoulder. A wet, salt tear stung a love-bite there. She sniffed
and raised her head, blinking her now even brighter eyes.

'What's wrong?' I asked.

'I'm happy,' she said.

'So am I.'

She regarded me solemnly. 'I have to say this,' she said, with another un-
ladylike sniffle. 'Loving me will not always make you happy.'

I could not imagine what she meant, and I didn't want to. 'Why are you
saying this?'

'Because I must,' she said. Her voice was strained. 'Because I have to be
fair with you.'

'Aye, sure,' I said. 'Well, now you've warned me, can I get on with loving
you?'

She brightened instantly, as though some arduous responsibility had been lifted from her shoulders.

'Oh yes!' she said, hugging me closer again. 'Love me as much as you like, love me for ever!' She pulled back a little, looked down, then raised her gaze again to mine.

'But not right now,' she added regretfully. 'You have to go.'

'Now?!' We had fallen out of our mutual dream into the workaday world, where we were two people who didn't, really, know each other all that well.

'Yes,' she insisted. 'You have to get back across town, get . . . washed, and ready for work and catch the bus at half past six.'

'I can catch it from here.'

'The hell you can. People will talk.'

'They'll talk anyway.'

'People around here, I mean.'

I climbed reluctantly off the bed. Merrial slipped lithely under the covers and pulled them up to her chin.

'What about you?' I asked, as I searched out and sorted my clothes.

'I'm an intellectual worker,' she said smugly as she snuggled down. 'We start at nine.'

She watched me dress with a sort of affectionate curiosity. 'What have you got on your belt?'

I patted the hard leather pouches and fastened the buckle. 'The tools of a tradesman,' I told her, 'and the weapons of a gentleman.'

'I see,' she said approvingly.

'So when will I see you again?' I asked, as I recovered the *sgean dhu* and stuck it back down the side of my boot.

'Tonight, eight o'clock, at the statue? Go for something to eat?'

I pretended to give this idea thoughtful consideration, then we both laughed, and she sat up again and reached out to me. We hugged and kissed goodbye. As I backed away to the door, grudging even a moment without her in my sight, a flickering from the big seer-stone caught my eye. I stopped beside the table and stooped to examine it. As I did so I noticed Merrial's two pendants: the talisman—the small seer-stone—now showing a vaguely organic tracery of green, and on the silver chain a silver piece about a centimetre in diameter which appeared to be a monogram made up of the letters 'G' and 'T' and the numeral '4'.

The table's centre-piece was all black within, except for an arrangement of points of light which might have been torches, or cities, or stars. They flashed on and off, on and off, and the bright dots spelled out one word: HELP.

I glanced over at Merrial. 'It's reached the end of its run,' I remarked.

'Reset it then,' she said sleepily from the pillow.

I brushed the stone's chill surface with my sleeve, restoring it to chaos, and with a final smile at Merrial opened the door and stepped out into the cock-crowing sunlight.

*and she threw her arms around him*
*that same night she drew him down.*

# 2

## ANCIENT TIME

*Death follows me*, she thought, as she rode into the labour-camp. There was something implacable about it, like logic: it follows, it follows . . . The thought's occurrence had nothing to do with logic; it appeared like a screensaver on the surface of her mind, whenever her mind went blank. It troubled her a little, as did another thought that drifted by in such moments: *where are the swift cavalry?*

The gate rolled shut behind her, squealing in its rusty grooves. The wind from the steppe hummed in the barbed-wire fence and whipped away the dust kicked up as she reined in the black horse. A guard hurried over; he somehow managed to make his brisk soldierly step look obsequious, even as his bearing made his dark-blue microfibre fatigues look military. He doffed a baseball cap with the Mutual Protection lettering and logo.

'Good morning, Citizen.'

That title was already an honorific. Myra Godwin-Davidova smiled and handed him the reins.

'Good morning,' she said, swinging down from the horse. She could hear her knee-joints creak. She lifted the saddlebags and slung them over her shoulder. The weight almost made her stagger, and the guard's arm twitched towards her; but she wasn't going to accept any help from that quarter. 'That will be all, thank you.'

'As you wish, Citizen.' The guard saluted and replaced his cap. She was still looking down at him, her riding-boots adding three inches to her five-foot-eleven height.

She patted the big mare's rump and watched as the guard led the beast away, then set off towards the accommodation huts. As she walked she pulled off her leather gauntlets and stuffed them awkwardly into the deep pockets of her long fur coat, and tucked a stray strand of silver hair under her sable hat. Hands mottled, veins showing, nails ridged: tough claws of an old bird, still flexible, but a better indication of her true age than her harshly lined but firm face, straight back and limber stride. Her knees hurt, but she tried not to let it show, or slow her down.

The camp perimeter was about one kilometre by two. Beyond the far fence she could see straight to the horizon, above which rose the many gantries and the few remaining tall ships of the old port. It had been a proud fleet once. How long before she would have to say, *all my ships are gone and all my men are dead?*

As if to mock her thought, a small ship screamed overhead; she caught a glimpse of it: angular, faceted, translucent, a spectral stealth-bomber shrieking skyward from Baikonur on a jet of laser-heated steam. The trail's after-image floated irritatingly in front of her as she turned her gaze resolutely back to earth.

One of the camp's factories was a couple of hundred metres away, a complex of aluminium pipework and fibre-optic cabling in a queasily organic-looking mass about fifty metres wide and twenty high, through which the control cabins and walkways of the human element were beaded and threaded like the eggs and exudate of some gargantuan insect. The name of the company that owned it, Space Merchants, was spelled out on the roof in twisty neon.

As she approached the nearest workers' housing area it struck Myra, not for the first time, that the huts were more modern and comfortable than the concrete apartment block she lived in herself. Each hut was semi-cylindrical, its rounded ends streamlined to the prevailing wind; soot-black polycarbon skin with rows of laminated-diamond windows.

This particular cluster of accommodation huts was in two rows of ten, with the rutted remains of a twenty-metre-wide paved road between them. A gang of a dozen men was engaged in repairing the road; the breeze carried a waft of sweat and tar. The men were using shovels, a gas burner under a tipping-and-spreading contraption, and a coughing diesel-engined road-roller: primitive, heavy equipment. On the sidewalk a blue-suited Mutual Protection guard lounged, picking his teeth and apparently watching a show in his eyes and hearing music or commentary in his ears.

The loom of Myra's shadow made him jump, blink and shake his head with a small shudder. He started to his feet.

'No need to get up,' Myra said unkindly. 'I just want to speak to some of the men.'

'They're on a break, Citizen,' he said, squinting up at her. 'So it's up to them, right?'

'Right,' said Myra. Physical work counted as recreation. It was the intellectual labour of design and monitoring that taxed the convicts' nerves.

She turned to the men, who waved to her and shouted greetings and explanations: she'd have to wait the few minutes it would take for them to finish spreading and rolling some freshly poured tarmac. Not offering one to the guard, she lit a Marley and let the men take their time finishing their break. She'd always insisted that her arrivals and inspections counted as worktime for the labourers.

Her spirits lifted as the Virginia and the Morocco kicked in. The labourers had their yellow suits rolled down to the waist, and were sweating even though the temperature had just climbed above freezing. Most of them were younger—let's face it, *far* younger—than herself; dark-tanned Koreans and Japanese, muscular as martial arts adepts—which, indeed, some of them were. She enjoyed watching them, the effect of smoke amplifying the underlying undertone of lust, the happy, hippy hormonal hum . . .

But that reminded her of Georgi, and her mood crashed again. Georgi was dead. Sometimes it seemed every man she'd ever fucked was dead; it was like she carried a disease: Niall MacCallum had died in a car crash, Jaime Gonzalez had died—what?—*seventy* years ago in the contra war, Jon Wilde had died in her arms on the side of the Karaganda road (on snow that turned red as his face turned white), and now Georgi Davidov had died in the consulate at Almaty, of a heart attack. (They expected *her* to believe *that?*)

There had been others, she reminded herself. Quite recent others. It wasn't every man she'd ever fucked who was doomed, it was every man she'd ever *loved*. There was only one exception she knew of. All her men were dead, except one, and he was a killer.

Even, perhaps, Georgi's killer. *Fucking heart attack, my ass!* It was one of their moves, it had to be—a move in the endgame.

A door banged open somewhere and the street suddenly swarmed with children pelting along and yelling, their languages and accents as varied as the colours of their skins. Few of the camp's bonded labour-force were women, but many of the men had women with them; there was every inducement for the prisoners to bring their families along. It was humane, but politic as well: a man with a woman and children was unlikely to risk escape or revolt.

Surrounded by children calling to their fathers, poking fingers in the hot asphalt, crowding around the machines and loudly investigating, the gang knocked off at last, leaving the guard to mind the newly tarred road. Myra savoured his disgruntled look as she crushed the filter roach under her heel and stepped out into the centre of the untarred part of the street.

'Hi, guys.'

They all knew who she was, but the only ones among them she recognised were two members of the camp committee, Kim Nok-Yung and Shin Se-Ha. The former was a young Korean shipyard worker, stocky and tough; the latter a Japanese mathematician of slender build and watchful mien. Kim seized her hand, grinning broadly.

'Hello, Myra.'

'Good to see you, Nok-Yung. And you, Se-Ha.'

The Japanese man inclined his head. 'Hi.' He insisted on taking her saddlebags. The whole gang surrounded her, flashing eyes and teeth, talking to each other and to her without much regard for mutual comprehension. They shooed away the children and led her into the nearest hut. Its doorway film brushed over her, burst in a shower of droplets with an odour of antiseptic, and reformed behind her. She blinked rapidly and shrugged out of her heavy coat, throwing it on to one of a row of hooks that grew from the curving wall.

Her first deep breath was evidence enough of how effective the filter film was at keeping out the dust. At the same time, it brought a flush to her skin as her immune system rushed to investigate whatever she'd just inhaled of the nanoware endemic to the building's interior. She followed Kim into the dining-area, an airy space of flat-surfaced furnishings—some a warning red to indicate that they were for heating, others white for eating off. The chairs were padded black polycarbon plastic. Around the walls, racked on shelves or stacked on floors, were thousands of books: centuries' worth of classics and bestsellers and blockbusters and textbooks, as if blown from the four winds and fetched up against these barriers. It would have been the same in any of the huts. The next most common items of clutter were musical instruments and craft equipment and products: plastic scrimshank, spaceships in bottles, elaborately carved wooden toys.

As they sat down around a table Myra felt prickly and on edge. She tugged her eyeband, a half-centimetre-wide crescent of translucent plastic, from her hair and placed it across her temples, in front of her eyes. A message drifted across her retina. 'Nanoprotect56 has detected the following known surveillance molecules in the room: Dataphage, Hackendice, Reportback, Mercury, Moldavian. Do you wish to clean up?'

She blinked when the cursor stopped on the Proceed option, took a deep breath, held it until her lungs were burning, then exhaled. The faces around the table were incurious and amused.

'Cleanup in progress,' the retinal display reported. Myra took a deep breath. It felt cool this time, as well as smooth.

'So we have privacy,' one of the Koreans said, with heavy irony.

'Ah, fuck it,' Myra said. 'Happens every time. You gotta assume they're listening.' There was bound to be something else her current release of 'ware wasn't up to catching: she imagined some tiny Turing machine ticking away, stitching sound-vibrations into a long-chain molecule in the dirt. She took a recorder—larger and less advanced than the one in her mental picture—from her pocket and laid it on the table. 'And I'm listening. So, what have you got for me?'

A quick exchange of glances around the table ended as usual with Kim Nok-Yung accepted as the spokesman. He rustled a paper from an inner pocket and ran a finger down the minutes; Matters Arising started with the routine first question.

'Any progress on POW recognition?'

Myra was touched by the note of hope with which he asked the question, the hundredth time no different from the first. She compressed her lips and shook her head. 'Sorry, guys. Red Cross and Crescent are working on it, and Amnesty. Still no dice.'

Nok-Yung shrugged. 'Oh, well. Please make the standard protest.'

'Of course.'

As they ticked their way down the list of complaints and conditions and assignments and payments, Myra noticed that the whole pattern of production in the camp had changed. The intensity of the work, and the volume of output, had gone up drastically. Twenty engines and a hundred habitat modules completed for Space Merchants in the past month! Nok-Yung and Se-Ha were subtly underlining the changes with guarded glances and shifts in tone, but they weren't commenting explicitly.

Myra looked around the table when they reached the end of the agenda. No one had complained about the speed-up. They didn't seem troubled; they had an air of suppressed excitement, almost glee, as they waited for her to speak. She checked over again the figures in her head, and realised with a jolt that at this rate most of the men here would work off their fines—or 'debts'—in months rather than years.

Another endgame move. Myra nodded slightly and smiled. 'Well, that's it,' she said. 'Don't overwork yourselves, guys. I mean it. Make sure you get in plenty of road-mending, OK?'

The prisoners just grinned at their shared secret. She reached for the saddlebags, as though just remembering something. 'I've brought some books for you.'

The men leaned inward eagerly as she unpacked. They weren't allowed any kind of interface with the net, and nothing that could be used to build one: no televisions or computers or readers or VR rigs, not even music decks.

Nothing could stop Myra carrying in whatever she liked—the saddlebags
were legally a diplomatic bag—but any electronic or molecular contraband
would have been confiscated the moment she left. So hardbooks it had to
be. The prisoners and their families had an unquenchable thirst for them.
Myra's every visit brought more additions to the drift.

This time she had dozens of paperbacks with tasteful Modern Art covers
and grey spines, 20th Century Classics—Harold Robbins, Stephen King,
Dean Koontz and so on—which she shoved across the table to the men
whose names she didn't know. For her friends Nok-Yung and Se-Ha she'd
saved the best for last: hardbooks so ancient that only advanced preserva-
tion treatments kept them from crumbling to dust—

Rather like herself, she thought, as the books passed one by one from her
gnarled hands: an incredibly rare, possibly unique, copy of Tucker's edition
of Stirner; the Viking *Portable Nietzsche*; and a battered Thinker's Library edition of Spencer's *First Principles*.

Kim Nok-Yung looked down at them reverently, then up at her. Shin
Se-Ha was in some kind of trance. Nok-Yung shook his head.

'This is too much,' he said, almost angrily. 'Myra, you can't—'

'Oh yes, I can.'

'Where did you get them?' asked Se-Ha.

Myra shrugged. 'From Reid, funnily enough.'

All the men were looking at her now, with sour smiles.

'From *David* Reid? The owner?' Kim waved his hand, indicating everything in sight.

'Yeah,' said Myra. 'The very same.'

There was a moment of sober silence.

'Well,' Nok-Yung said at last, 'I hope we make better use of them than
he did, the bastard.'

Everybody laughed, even Myra.

'So do I,' she said.

She settled back in her chair and passed around the Marley pack and accepted the offer of coffee.

'OK, guys,' she said. 'The news. Everything's still going to hell.' She grimaced. 'Same as last week. A few shifts in the fronts, that's all. Take it from
me, you ain't missing much.'

'A few shifts in *which* fronts?' asked Se-Ha suspiciously.

'Ah,' said Myra. 'If you must know—the north-eastern front is . . . active.'

Another silent exchange of glances and smiles. Myra didn't share in their
pleasure, but couldn't blame them for it. The two encroaching events that
filled her most with dread were, for them, each in different ways an earnest
of their early liberation.

She said her goodbyes, wondering if it was for the last time, and took her now empty bags and stalked away through the restitution-camp streets, and mounted her horse and rode out of the gate, towards the city.

Thinking about Reid, trying to think calmly and destructively about Reid, she found her mind drifting back. He had not always been such a bastard. He'd been the first person to tell her she need never die. That had been eighty-three years ago, when she was twenty-two years old. She hadn't believed him . . .

*Death follows me.*


'You don't have to die,' he told her.

Black hair framed his face, black eyebrows his intent, brown-eyed gaze. Dave Reid was dark and handsome but not, alas, tall. He wore a denim jacket with a tin button—a badge, as the Brits called them—pinned to its lapel. The badge was red with the black hammer-and-sickle-and-4 of the International.

'What!' Myra laughed. 'I know it feels that way now, everybody our age feels like that, yeah? But it'll come to us all, man, don't kid yourself.'

She rolled back on her elbows on the grass and looked up at the blue spring sky. It was too bloody cold for this, but the sun was out and the ground was dry, and that was good enough for sunbathing in Scotland. The grassy slope behind the Boyd Orr Building was covered with groups and couples of students, drinking and smoking and talking. Probably missing lectures—it was already two in the afternoon.

'Seriously,' Dave said, in that Highland accent that carried the sound of wind on grass, of waves on shore, 'if you can live into the twenty-first century, you have a damn good chance of living for ever.'

'Says who? L. Ron Hubbard?'

Dave snorted. 'Arthur C. Clarke, actually.'

'Who?'

He frowned at her. 'You know—scientist, futurist. The man who invented the communications satellite.'

'Oh, *him*,' Myra said scornfully. 'Sci-fi. *2001* and all that.' She saw the slight flinch of hurt in David's face, and went on, 'Oh, don't get me wrong, I'm not saying it's impossible. Maybe hundreds of years from now, maybe in communism. Not in our lifetimes, though. Tough shit.'

Dave shrugged and rolled another cigarette.

'We'll see.'

'I guess. And the rate you smoke those things, you'll be lucky to be alive in the twenty-first century. You won't even get to first base.'

'Och, I'll last another twenty-four years.' He sighed, blowing smoke on to the slightly warm breeze, then smiled at her mischievously. 'Unless I become a martyr of the revolution, of course.'

'"I have a rendezvous with death, on some disputed barricade",' Myra quoted. 'Don't worry. That's another thing won't happen in our lifetimes.'

The shadow of the tall building crept over Dave's face. He shifted deftly, back into the sunlight.

'That's what you think, is it?'

'Yeah, that's what I think.' She smiled, and added, with ironic reassurance, 'Our *natural* lifetimes, that is.'

Dave hefted a satchel stuffed with copies of revolutionary newspapers and magazines. 'Then what's the point of all this? Why don't we just eat, drink and be merry?'

Myra swigged from a can of MacEwan's, lowered it and looked at him over its rim. 'That's what I *am* doing right now, lover.'

He took her point, and reached out and stroked the curve of her cheekbone. 'But still,' he persisted. 'Why bother with politics if you don't think we're going to win?'

'Dave,' she said, 'I'm not a socialist because I expect to end up running some kinda workers' state of my own some day. I do what I do because I think it's right. OK?'

'OK,' said Reid, smiling; but his smile was amused as well as affectionate, as though she were being naïve. Irritated without quite knowing why, she turned away.


The city was called Kapitsa, and it was the capital of the International Scientific and Technical Workers' Republic, which had no other city; indeed, apart from the camps, no other human habitation. The ISTWR was an independent enclave on the fringe of the Polygon—the badlands between Karaganda and Semipalatinsk, a waste-product of Kazakhstan's nuclear-testing legacy. A long time ago, Kapitsa would have looked modern, with its centre of high-rise office blocks, its inner ring of automatic factories, its periphery of dusty but tree-lined streets and estates of low-rise apartment blocks, the bustling airport just outside and the busy spaceport on the horizon, from which the great ships had loudly climbed, day after day. Now it was a rustbelt, as quaintly obsolete as the Japanese car factories or the Clyde shipyards or the wheat plains of Ukraine.

Myra, however, felt somewhat cheered as the mare took her through the light traffic of the noonday streets. The apple trees were in bloom, and every wall had its fresh-looking, colourful mural of flowers or stars or ships or crowds or children or heroes or heroines. Real ancient space-age stuff, an effect enhanced by the younger—genuinely young—people enjoying the chilly sunshine in the fashionable scanty garb, which recalled the late 1960s in its jaunty futurism. She looked at girls in skinny tights and shiny, garish minidresses and found herself wondering if they were cold . . . probably not, the clothes were only an imitation of their nylon or PVC originals, the nanofactured fabrics veined with heat-exchangers, laced with molecular machines.

The bright clothing gave the people on the street an appearance of prosperity, but Myra was all too aware that it was superficial. The clothes were cheaper than paper, easily affordable even on Social Security. Over the past few years, with the coming of the diamond ships, the heavy-booster market had gone into free fall, and unemployment had rocketed. The dole was paid by her department out of the rent from Mutual Protection, and it couldn't last. Nostalgia tourism—the old spaceport was now a World Heritage Site, for what that was worth—looked like the only promising source of employment.

Before she knew it, the horse had stopped, from habit, outside the modest ten-storey concrete office-block of the republic's government on Revolution Square. Myra sat still for a moment, gazing wryly at this week's morale-boosting poster on the official billboard: a big black-and-white blow-up of the classic Tass photo of Gagarin, grinning out from his cosmonaut helmet. She remembered the time, in her grade-school classroom on the Lower East Side, when she'd first seen this human face and had formed some synaptic connection between Gagarin's grin and Guevara's glare.

Space and socialism. What a swindle it had all been. She shook the reins, took the mare at a slow pace around to the back, stabled it, wiped the muck from her boots and ascended the stairs. The corridors to her office—at the front of the building, as befitted a People's Commissar for Social Policy and Prime Minister Pro Tem and (now that she came to think about it) Acting President—were filled with a susurrus of hurrying feet and fast-fading whispers. Myra glanced sharply at the groups she passed, but few seemed willing to return her look.

She closed the door of her office with a futile but soul-satisfying slam. Let the apparatchiks worry about her mood, if she had to worry about theirs. The last time she'd sniffed this evasive air in the corridors had been just before the first—and only—time she'd fallen out of power, back in 2046. Then, she'd suspected an imminent move from the Mutual Protection company and its protégés within the state apparatus: a *coup d'état*. Now, she suspected that Mutual Protection and its allies were into the final moves of a much wider game-plan, as wide as it could be: a *coup du monde*. Or *coup d'étoile*!

She stalked to the window, shedding her coat and hat and gloves in quick,

violent movements, leaned on her knuckles on the sill and scanned her surroundings in a spasm of fang-baring territoriality. No tanks or tramping
feet sounded in her city's streets, no black helicopters clattered in her country's sky. What did she expect? There were days at least to go before anything happened—and, when it did, the opening blows would be overt in larger
capitals than hers; she'd be nipped by CNN sound-bites in the new order's
first seconds.

She sighed and turned away, picked up her dropped clothes and hung
them carefully on the appropriate branches of a chrome-plated rack. The
office was as self-consciously retro-modernist as the styles on the street, if a
little more sophisticated—pine walls and floor, lobate leather layers at random on both; ornaments in steel and silver, ebony and plastic, of planetary
globes and interplanetary craft.

She dropped into the office chair and leaned back, letting it massage her
shoulders and neck. She slid the band across her eyes, summoned a head-up
display and rolled her eyes to study it. The anti-viral 'ware playing across her
retinae flickered, but there was nothing untoward for it to report; here, as in
all the offices, the walls had teeth. Her own software was wrapped around
her, its loyalty as intimate, and as hard to subvert, as the enhanced immune-
systems in her blood. It was personal, it was *a* personal, a unique configuration of software agents that scanned the world and Myra's responses to the
world, and built up from that interaction a shrewd assessment of her needs
and interests. It looked out information for her, and it looked after her investments. It did to the world nets what her Sterling search engine did for
her Library—it selected and extracted what was relevant from the vast and
choppy sea of data in which most people swam or, more often, drowned.

Having a good suite of personal 'ware was slightly more important for a
modern politician than the traditional personal networks of influence and
intelligence. In the decade since she'd recovered power, Myra had made sure
that her networks—both kinds, virtual and actual—were strong and intertwined, strong enough to carry her if the structure of the state ever again
let her down. Though even that was unlikely—her purges, though blood-
less, had been as ruthless as Tito's. No official of the ISTWR would ever
again have the slightest misapprehension of where their best interests lay,
and no employee or agent of Mutual Protection would fancy their chances
of changing that.

She'd have to consult with the rest of Sovnarkom soon enough—a meeting
was scheduled for 3 p.m.—and round up some of the scurrying underlings
from the corridors to prepare for it, but she wanted to get her own snapshot
of the situation first.

Myra's personal didn't have a personality, as far as she knew, but it had
a persona: a revolutionary, a stock-market speculator, an arms dealer, a spy;

a free-wheeling, high-rolling, all-swindling communist-capitalist conspira-
tor out of some Nazi nightmare. It had a name.

'Parvus,' she whispered. The retinal projectors on her eyeband summoned
an image of a big man in a baggy suit and a shirt stretched across his belly
like a filled sail, scudding along on gales of information. He strolled towards her, smiling, his pockets stuffed with papers, his cigarette hand waving as he prepared to tell her something. She'd never come across a recording
of the original Parvus in action, but she'd given this one the appearance of
one historic Trotskyist leader, and the mad-scientist mannerisms of another,
whose standard speech she'd once sat through, long ago in the Student Union
in Glasgow.

'Give me the big picture.'

Parvus nodded. He ran his fingers through his mop of white hair, fur-
rowed his brow, grinned maniacally.

'*Jane's*, I think.' He flicked an inch of ash, conjured a screen. Her gaze
fixed on an option; she blinked, and the room vanished from her sight;
again, and Earth fell away.


Her first virtual view, spun in orbit, was from *Jane's Market Forces*—a publicly
available, but prohibitively expensive, real-time survey of military deployments around the world. She was running the next-but-one release, currently
in beta test. It had cost the republic's frugal defence budget nothing more
than the stipend to place a patriotic Kazakh postgrad in the Stockholm International Peace Research Institute's equally cash-starved IT department.
(That, and an untraceable credit line to his comms account.) Myra, long
familiar with the conventional symbols and ideographs, took it all in at an ab-
stract level: colour-coded, vectored graphs in a 3-D space, with other dimensions implied by subtle shadings and the timing of pulsations. That photic
filigree hung like a complicated cloud-system over the relatively static his-
tograms depicting the hardware and the warm bodies. The physical locations
and quantities of personnel and *matériel* could provide only a basement-level
understanding of the world military balance, just as the location of physical
plant was only a rough cut of the state of the world market. Second by second, market and military forces shifted unpredictably, their mutual inter-
penetration more complex than any ideology had ever foreseen. With most
of the world's official armies revolutionary or mercenary or both, and most of
the conflicts settled in unarguable simulation before they started, everyone
from the bankers down through the generals to the grunts on the ground
would shrug and accept the virtual verdict, and change sides, reinforce or
retreat in step with their software shadows—all except the Greens, and the
Reds. *They* fought for real, and played for keeps.

It was like the old Civilization game, Myra sometimes thought, with a new twist: Barbarism II. Nobody was going to wipe the board, nobody was going to Alpha Centauri. They were all going down together, into the dark . . . Just as soon as enough major players decided to contest the incontestable, and put the simulations to the audit of war.

But, for the moment, the dark was full of twisting light. And in the real world, blinked up as backdrop, one front was more than virtual, and closer than she'd like. Beyond the northern border of Kazakhstan, itself hundreds of kilometres north of the ISTWR, the Sino-Soviet Union's ragged frontline advanced in flickers of real fire: guerilla skirmishes and sabotage on one side, half-hearted long-range shelling and futile carpet-bombing on the other.

The Sheenisov—the name was subtly derogatory, like Vietcong for NLF and Yank for United Nations—were the century's first authentic communist threat, who really believed in their updated version of the ideology which communistans like the ISTWR parodied in post-futurist pastiche. Based in the godforsaken back-country of recusant collective farms and worker-occupied factories, stubbornly surviving decades of counter-revolution and war, armed by partisan detachments of deserters (self-styled, inevitably, 'loyalists') from the ex-Soviet Eastern and ex-PRC Northern armies, they'd held most of Mongolia and Siberia and even parts of north-west China since the Fall Revolution back in 2045, and in the years since then they'd spread across the steppe like lichen. Myra detested and admired them in equal measure.

Of more immediate, and frustrating, concern: the Sheenisov were outside the virtual world, a torn black hole in the net. Their computers were permanently offline; their cadres didn't trade combat futures; they refused all simulated confrontation or negotiation; like the Green marginals in the West and the Khmer Vertes in the South, the Reds in the East put all to the test of practice, the critique of arms. Even *Jane's* could only guess at their current disposition.

But their serrated south-western edge was clear enough, and as usual it was cutting closer to her domain than it had been the last time she'd checked. Like, this time yesterday . . .

She sighed and turned her attention from the communists to tracing the darker deeds of a real international conspiracy: the space movement. Somewhere in that scored darkness, reading between those lines of light, she had to find the footprints of a larger and more ragged army, impatient to assume the world.

Her first step—acknowledged by the system with startled gratitude—was to update the information on Mutual Protection's labour-camp output. When this was integrated and plausibly projected to the company's whole global archipelago, a first-cut re-evaluation of relative military-industrial weightings sent ripples through the entire web. Just as well she was working with a personal copy, Myra thought wryly. This was information to kill for (although already, presumably, discounted by Mutual Protection itself, which must surely know she knew).

She zapped the speculative update with a flashing 'urgent' tag to the People's Commissar for Finance, and a less urgent summary to the comrade over at Defence. Then she invoked her ongoing dossier of space-movement activity, meshed in the new output figures, and sent it to all the commissars, with her own interpretation.

The 'space-movement coup' had been talked about, openly, for so long that it had become unreal—as unreal as the Revolution had been, until it had finally come to pass. Myra herself had cried wolf on the coup, once before. But now she felt herself vindicated. And, again, David Reid was involved.

Her former lover had built up Mutual Protection from a security-service subsidiary of an insurance company into a global business that dealt in restitution: criminals working to compensate the damage they'd done. Originally touted as a humane, market-driven reform and replacement of the old barbaric prison systems, its extension from common criminals to political and military prisoners after the Fall Revolution had given it an appalling, unstoppable logic of runaway expansion, in much the same way as the use of prison labour in the First Five-Year Plan had done for the original GULag.

For more than a decade now, those on the losing side of small wars and increasingly minor crimes had provided the manpower for a gigantic space-settlement boom, applying whatever skills they had—or could rapidly learn—to pay off their crime-debts as quickly as possible. At the same time, the proliferation of space-movement enclaves, each of which incited a horde of beleaguering barbarians or a swarm of furious bureaucrats, had provided an endless pool of new convicts. Quite a large proportion of the prisoners, on completion of their payback time, had seized the abundant employment opportunities the space projects offered.

Mutual Protection was now the armature of a global coalition of defence companies, launch companies, space settlement programmes, political campaigns and a host of minor governments—many of them creatures of these same companies. The space-movement coalition was on the point of assembling enough forces to re-create a stable world government and to bring the former Space Defense battlesats back under UN control. Their objective, long mooted, was to roll back the environmentalist and anti-technological opposition movements, and shift enough labour and capital into Earth orbit to create a self-sustaining space presence that could ride out any of the expected catastrophes below—of which, God knew, there were plenty to choose from.

The coup itself was expected to proceed on two levels. One was a political

move to take over the rump ReUN, by the votes of all the numerous ministates that could be subverted, suborned or convinced. The other was a
military move, thus legitimised, to seize the old US/UN Space Defense
battlesats. That, Myra reckoned, was behind the speed-up in the labour-
camps. No doubt massive subversion was going on among the orbital military personnel, but by the nature of the case there wasn't much she could
know about that.

She stared at the virtual screen for a long time, until the clenchings of her
fists and the twitching grimaces of her face and the blinking-back of tears
confused the 'ware so much that it shut off, and left her staring at the wall.


Sovnarkom—the Council of People's Commissars, or, in more conventional
terminology, the Cabinet—was the appropriately small government of an almost unviably small state (population 99,854, last time anyone had bothered
to count, and dropping by the day). The structures of the ISTWR were an
exercise in socialist camp, modelled on those of the old Soviet republics but
without the leading role of the Party. The result of that strategic omission
had been a democracy as genuine as that of its inspiration had been false. Or
so it had seemed, in the republic's more prosperous days.

Myra arrived early, and took the privilege of the first arrival—the chairman's seat, at the head of the long, bare table of scarred mahogany with a
clunky blast-proof secretarial device in the centre. There were another dozen
seats, six along either side of the table, each with its traditional mineral water
and notepaper in front of it. The room was bare, windowless but lit by full-
spectrum plates in the ceiling. The only decoration on the white walls was a
framed photograph of the long-dead nuclear physicist after whom the city
was named.

Valentina Kozlova came in, her military fatigues elegant as always, her
hair untidy, her hands full of hardcopy. She was in her fifties, a still-young
child of the century, young enough and lucky enough to have got the anti-
ageing treatments before she got old. She smiled tensely and sat down. Then
Andrei Mukhartov, cropped-blond, forty-ish and looking it—probably by
intent—soberly conventional in a three-piece suit of electric-blue raw silk.
Denis Gubanov, younger than the others, ostentatiously casual, needing a
shave, looking as though he'd just come in from sounding out an informer
in some sleazy spaceport bar. Alexander Sherman arrived last, giving his usual
impression of having been pulled away from more urgent business. His fashionable pseudo-plastic jump-suit was doubtless just the job for his post, but
Myra liked it even less than she liked him. He sat down and glanced around
as though expecting the meeting to begin immediately, then pursed his lips
and slid two sheets of paper across to Myra.

'More resignations, I'm afraid,' he said. 'Tatyana and Michael have . . .'

'Taken off for richer pastures,' Myra said. 'I heard.' She looked at the empty spaces around the depleted table, and shrugged. 'Well, according to revolutionary convention there is no such thing as an inquorate meeting, so . . .'

'We really must co-opt some new members!' Sherman said.

'Yes,' said Myra drily. 'We really must.'

Her tone made Alexander snap back, 'It's a disgrace—we have no Commissar for Law, or the Interior, or—'

'Yes, yes,' Myra interrupted. 'And half the fucking members of the Supreme Soviet have fucked off—the wrong half, as it happens. *I* couldn't find a competent commissar for *anything* among the remainder. At the rate we're going, we won't have enough of an *electorate* to make up the numbers! So what do you suggest?'

Alexander Sherman opened his mouth, closed it, and shrugged. His mutinous look convinced Myra that he'd be the next to go—as Commissar for Industry, he had the right connections already.

'OK, comrades,' Myra said, 'let's call the meeting to order.' She took off her eyeband and laid it formally on the table, and those who hadn't already done so followed suit. It was not quite a rule to do so, but it was the custom— a gesture of politeness as well as an assurance that everyone was paying attention—to set aside one's personal for the duration of the meeting. Myra could never make up her mind whether it was mutual trust, or mutual suspicion, that lay behind the custom of not doing the same with one's personal weapons. Nobody'd ever pulled a gun at a Sovnarkom meeting, but there were precedents . . .

'Recorder: on. Regular meeting of the Council, Friday 9 May 2059, Myra Godwin-Davidova presiding, five members present.' She looked around, then looked back at the recorder's steel grille. 'I move that we shelve the agenda and go straight to emergency session. Starting with the death of Citizen Davidov.'

No dissent. Seconds of silence passed.

'Don't all talk at once,' she said.

Valentina Kozlova (Defence) spoke first. 'Look, Myra—Comrade Chair— we've all spoken to you about Georgi's death. We were all very sorry to hear of it.'

Myra nodded. 'Thank you.'

'Having said that—we need to decide on our political response. Now, obviously the police in Almaty are investigating, and so far there seem to be no indications of foul play.' She shrugged. 'That, of course, is hard to prove, these days. However . . . Georgi Yefrimovich had a great deal of responsibility—' she gestured vaguely at Andrei Mukhartov, the International Affairs Commissar '—and in the circumstances, natural causes do seem likely.'

Myra sighed. 'Yes, I appreciate that. And I appreciate what all of you have said to me. Let me say for the record that personally I don't accept that Georgi's death was anything but an assassination.'

She faced down the resulting commotion.

'*However*,' she continued, 'I don't ask or expect any of you to take this as more than a suspicion. At the moment, even the question of who might benefit from it is very unclear—if Georgi was murdered, it might have been by one side or the other. Possibly some elements in the space movement saw him as an obstacle to their . . . diplomacy. Possibly some forces opposed to the space movement thought we'd think exactly that, and had him killed as a provocation. Or maybe, just maybe, his heart gave out. Whatever—it's come at a bad time for us.'

Mukhartov grunted agreement.

After a moment of gloomy silence Valentina spoke again. 'We've all studied your message,' she said. 'What's your own suggested course of action?'

'We try to stop them, of course. Damned if I want the fucking UN back on top of us, let alone one controlled by the goddam space movement and its proxies.'

Valentina leaned forward. 'For my part,' she said, 'I agree with your assessment. We have to be ready for the new situation in which the space movement controls the ReUN, and with it the Earth Defense battlesats. But—' she hesitated a moment, sighed almost imperceptibly, and continued '—I think that the death of Georgi, the understandable suspicions this has aroused, and the, ah, unexpected and unauthorised increase in labour-camp output may have given your response a . . . subjective element.' Kozlova glanced around the table. 'The coming shift in the balance of power can't be stopped by us, or by anybody. The most we've been able to do—thanks to Georgi's diplomacy—has been to help keep Kazakhstan neutral, with a tilt against the take-over. Even they wouldn't take direct action against it, though God knows Georgi tried to persuade them to. They assured us they just didn't have the clout, and I believe them. Now you seem to be suggesting that *we* throw our weight, such as it is, against it. My own view is that we'd accomplish more by staying neutral. It could work to our advantage—*if* we accommodate ourselves to new realities in good time.'

Myra unfroze her face. 'Get in on the winning side, you mean?' she suggested lightly.

'Yes, exactly,' Kozlova said. She seemed encouraged by Myra's response, or lack of response. 'After all,' she ploughed on, 'we ourselves are in a way part of the space movement, we go back a long way with it, and the Sheenisov are as much a threat to us as the barbarians and reactionary governments are to some other enclaves. Frankly, I think we should put out some diplomatic feelers to the other side before the crunch, which as you correctly point out is a matter of days or weeks away. And we're not exactly in a position of strength at the moment. So there is indeed a certain urgency to our decision.'

'Interesting,' Myra murmured. 'Anyone else?'

Denis Gubanov (Internal Security) broke in sharply. 'The Chair spoke in her message of states being suborned and subverted. I don't think we should let ourselves become one of them! Whatever the rhetoric, and the propaganda of inevitability, it's obvious what's going on. Imperialism took a severe blow with the fall of the Yanks, but the blow wasn't fatal, worse luck. Monopoly capital always finds new political instruments, and the space movement, so-called, has proved an admirable vehicle.' He snorted, briefly. 'Literally—a launch vehicle! Through it, the rich desert the Earth. Why should we help them on their way?'

'More to the *point*,' said Sherman (Trade and Industry), making his disdain for Denis's rhetoric emphatically clear, 'there is the question of what we will do for a living when the camps are worked out.'

'We could always—' began Kozlova, as though about to say something in jest, then glanced at Myra and shut up.

'What?'

'Nah. Forget it. The business to hand is what we do now, about the coup.'

Myra let the argument go on. There was a case, she admitted to herself, on both sides. But Valentina had been right—there was a subjective edge to Myra's response. The space movement's central element was Mutual Protection, and Mutual Protection's central element was David Reid. If the space movement got its way he would be the most powerful man in the world.

No way was she going to let that bastard win.

# 3

## THE SHIP O THE YIRD

An hour later, after a run across town that was bloody hard in (and on) my boots, and a hasty wash and change into my work clothes, I stood at the station bus-stop with my steel safety-helmet in one hand and my aluminium lunch-box in the other. Packing my lunch was the only non-basic service that my landlady provided, but for me that was enough to forgive her the absence of breakfast, dinner, laundry and reliable hot water.

The sun's growing heat was burning off the morning mist on the loch and between the hills. I felt as though I might at any moment rise and float away myself. My eyes felt sandy and my brain felt hot, but these discomforts did not diminish the kinder glow of elation somewhere in my chest and gut. In a strange way I could hardly bear to think about Merrial—every time I did so brought on such an explosion of joy that I quivered at the knees, and I almost feared to indulge it to excess. I wanted to keep it, hoard it, dole it out to myself when I really needed it, not gulp it all down at once. (Which is of course a mistaken notion—that particular well, like all too many others, is bottomless.

What I thought about instead was another woman—the Deliverer, under whose memorial I had met Merrial, and under whose remote and ancient protection she and her people lived. (Protected from persecution, at any rate, if not from prejudice.)

Over the past four years, History had been one of the arts I had struggled to master. It hadn't been easy, even in Glaschu, where the place fair drips with it, as they say. The baffled aversion expressed by Merrial was a common enough reaction. In a time of so many opportunities, and a place buzzing with innovative work in so many fields which could be applied to bring about manifest human betterment, it seemed perverse (sometimes even to me) for a vigorous and intelligent young man to turn aside from such arts as Literature, and Music, and Kinematography, or from the sciences: Astronomy, Medicine, the many branches of Natural Theology; from the improving pursuits of Practical Philosophy and Mechanical and Civil Engineering—to turn aside from all these useful works of the intellect, not even for the understandable and, within reason, commendable attractions of business and pleasure, but to fossick about in mouldering documents and crumbling ruins, and to fill his head with bloody images and mind-numbing figures from the megadead past.

It was a distasteful and faintly disreputable fascination, with a whiff of necrophilia, even of necromancy, about it. But, whether we will or no, we're all historians, each with our own outline of history in our heads. This was a point I'd often had to make to sceptical listeners, from parents and siblings through to patronage committees and on to friends and workmates in drink-fuelled debate. We pick up the outline from parents and teachers and preachers, from songs and statues and stories.

In the beginning, God made the Big Bang, and there was light. After the first four minutes, there was matter. After billions of years, there were stars and planets, and the Earth was formed. The water above the sky separated from the water below the sky, which brought forth all manner of creeping things. Over millions of years they were shaped by God's invisible hand, Natural Selection, into great monsters of land and sea. The Earth was filled with violence, and God sent an asteroid, Katy Boundary, to destroy it. The sky was dark at noon for forty days, and almost all the living things were destroyed. Among those who survived were little beasts like mice, and they replenished the Earth, and burrowed into it and became coneys, and climbed trees and became monkeys, and climbed down and became Men—

—ape-men and cave-men, Egyptians and Babylonians, Greeks and Romans, Christians and Americans, Chinese and Russians. The Americans fell but their empire lived on as the Possession, until the Deliverer rose in the east and struck it down. Troubled times followed, and then peace.

*So why disturb it—answer me that, lad!*

Because the truth is more interesting and ultimately more instructive than a farrago of fable? I had acquired the taste not just for truth but for detail; for the peculiar pleasure that comes from seeing the real relationship between events in terms of cause and effect rather than narrative convention. It's a satisfaction which I'll defend as genuinely scientific.

*But what* use *is it, eh?*

To that I had no ready answer, except to define the result as art, in the same way as the method could be defined as science. The argument that those who do not learn from history are doomed to repeat it failed to impress most people, convinced as they were that there was no risk whatsoever of history's more ruinous errors being repeated. So I had to reach for the argument that real history told a better story because it was a truer story; that reality had its own beauty, sterner and higher than that of myth.

The particular story I wanted to tell was of the life of the Deliverer. My proposal for a thesis on her early years as a student and academic in Glasgow, long before she became the figure known to history, was only the beginning of my own world-conquering ambition: to reconstruct, as much as one can across that gulf of time, the mind and personality and circumstance that had shaped the future that was now our past.

It might take decades of research, years of writing. Whatever else I did, this biography would define my own: a life for a Life. Perhaps it was an unconscious balking at that price, or some half-baked, self-justifying attempt to pay my dues to what my more practical-minded contemporaries called 'real work', or something more positive, a dimly felt attraction to the world of material striving and measurable success, a turning towards the future and away from the past, that led me that summer to Carron Town and the Kishorn Yard.

'Thank God it's Thursday,' said a cheerful voice behind me. I turned and grinned at Jondo, who was leaning against the bus-stop sign and eating a black pudding and fried-egg roll. Behind him a score of workers were by now queuing up. Vendors of snacks, hot drinks and newspapers worked along the line.

'It's Friday,' I pointed out.

'That's what I meant,' he said around a mouthful, hand-waving with the remainder of his breakfast. 'Force of habit.' He swallowed. 'Pay-day, at any rate.'

I nodded enthusiastically. Half my pay was telegraphed straight to my account at the Caledonian Mutual Bank; out of the remainder I had to pay for my lodgings, food and drink, and a modicum of carousing at the weekly fair. By Friday mornings I had just enough cash to get through the day. Pay was high, but so was the cost of living—the project had pulled up prices for miles around it.

Jondo was a man about my own age, his beer-gut already as impressive as his muscles. His long red hair, now as usual worn in a pony-tail, and his pale eyes and eyebrows gave him the look of a paradoxically innocent pirate; inherited perhaps from his ancestors who'd gone a-viking, and come to this land to pillage and settled down to farm, and to whom the Christian gospel

had come as good news indeed, a welcome relief from heathendom's implacable codes of honour and vengeance. He spoke with the soft accent of
Inverness, where—rumour had it—there were Christians still.

I tried to imagine Jondo drinking blood at some dark ceremony. The
momentary absurd image must have brought a smirk to my face.

'What's so funny, Clovis?' he growled. Then he smiled, balling up the
waxed paper and chucking it, wiping the grease from his hands on the oily
thighs of his overalls. 'Ach, I know. A good night with your tinker lass, was it?'

'You could say that.'

'Aye, well, each to their own, I suppose,' he said, in the tone of one making
a profound and original observation. 'Here's the bus.'

The bus, already half-full, drew to a halt beside us in a cloud of wood-
alcohol exhaust, its brakes squealing and its flywheel shrieking. I hopped on,
paid my groat to the driver and settled down in a window seat. Jondo heaved
his bulk in beside me, gave me another lewd grin and a wink, released an evidently satisfying fart and went instantly to sleep.

Some passengers busied themselves with newspapers or conversation,
but most dozed like Jondo or stared bleary-eyed like me. The discrepancy
between the time-honoured four-day week and the project's more demand-
ing schedules reduced Friday work to a matter of clearing up problems left
over from the past week and preparing for the next. Not even the inducement of double time could make more than a handful of the labour-force
encroach on the sanctity of Saturday and Sunday, although it could make
most of us work overtime through the week. No amount of patient lectur-
ing from managers with clipboards and redundant hard hats could persuade
us to adopt what they considered a more rational work pacing.

The bus lurched into motion. I lit a cigarette to dispel Jondo's intestinal
methane and laid my temple against the welcome throbbing coolness of the
window. As we crossed the Carron and passed New Kelso I gazed beyond
the suburb's neat bungalows to where morning smoke rose from the tinker
camp. A vivid image of Merrial asleep—the tumble of black hair, the white-
sleeved arm across the pillow—lit up my mind. I wondered what my chances
were of seeing her through the day. I didn't even know which office she
worked in, and a desultory fantasy took shape of finding some fantastic excuse to visit them all: of working my way through the administration blocks
and drawing-offices, spurning the flirtations of giggling girls and pensive
older women with hunky pin-ups above their desks, until I finally walked
into an engineering lab to find Merrial alone and in a day-dream of her
own, about me, into which my real arrival would be a passionately welcomed
incursion . . .

Probably not.

My head swung away from the window as the bus turned left on to the main road along the northern shore. I jolted upright, making sure my head didn't swing back and crack against the pane. Even at this hour in the morning the road was busy with commuter traffic and heavy trucks. The bus chugged slowly along, picking up yet more passengers in Jeantown, another village that the project had expanded, its packed buildings teetering perilously up the hillside. Out on the loch a pod of dolphins sported, their leaps drawing gasps and sighs from the less jaded or dozy of my fellow-passengers.

Then, with a great clashing of gears and screeching of flywheel as the auxiliary electric motors kicked in, the bus turned right, on to the road up into the hills between the two mountains, An Sgurr and Glas Bhein, that dominated the northern skyline of the lochside towns. To me, this afforded an inexhaustibly fascinating view of further ranges of hills and reaches of water. Everybody else on the bus ignored it completely. Someone opened a window to let out the smoke and let in some fresh air; a bee blundered in, causing a ripple of excitement and much brandishing of rolled newspapers before it bumbled out.

Above the last houses, above the meadows, the trees began: twenty-metre-tall beeches, then pine and rowan and birch, all the way up to the crags and the scree. Centuries ago these hills had been bare of all but rough pasture and heather, cropped by the infamous black-faced sheep. But these same bare hills had somehow sustained the sparse guerilla forces of Jacobite and Land Leaguer and Republican. Far below I could see the rocky peninsula known as the Island, a sheltering arm around the harbour, still with a small bunker on its top. During the First World Revolution a thirteen-year-old had written herself into local legend by bringing down a stealth fighter with a nuclear-tipped rocket-propelled grenade. In Jeantown's poky museum you can see an ancient photograph of her: the grubby, grinning cadre of a Celtic Vietcong, posed with the rocket tube slung on her shoulder, beside unrecognisable wreckage on a scarred hillside where to this day nothing will grow.

Over the top of the saddleback and down into the long, dark glen where the Pretender had evaded Cumberland's troops, where the Free Kirk had preached to the dispossessed, and where, later, the Army of the New Republic had cached their computers, the hardware of their software war against the last empire. The grim glen opened to another fertile plain of woods and fields and recently grown town, Courthill. Beyond it, at the edge of the sealoch, lay the great scar of the Kishorn Yard. There was a trick of the eye in interpreting the sight—everything there, the cranes and the platform and the ship, were much bigger than their normal equivalents, like the Pleistocene relatives of familiar mammals.

The bus pulled up at the works gate. The stockade around the yard had been constructed more to protect the careless or reckless from wandering in than to safeguard anything it enclosed. I nudged Jondo awake and we alighted in a dangerous, fast-moving convergence of buses and cars and bikes. We strolled through the gate just as the seven-o'clock klaxon brayed. Hundreds, then thousands, of workers streamed through the gate and swarmed out across the yard. The place looked like a benign battlefield, crater-pocked, vehicle-strewn, littered with the living. I clamped the heavy helmet on my head, and with Jondo puffing along behind me, plunged in; ducking and dodging along walkways, over trenches, under cables; leaping perilous small-gauge railway tracks and over waterlogged trenches and dried-up culverts (drainage here had always been a bit hit-and-miss); past haulage vehicles and earth-movers, air-compressors and power-plants, portable cabins and toilets set down as if at random in the muck, until at length we reached the immense dry-dock that was the focus of the whole glorious affray.

The dry-dock was a giant rounded gouge out of the side of a hill where it sloped down to the sea—hundreds of metres across, tens of metres deep. Its rocky cliffs were old and weathered; it looked like some work of Nature, or of Providence—even of Justice, the smiting of the Earth by a wrathful God; but in fact it was the centuries-old work of Man. (It is their civil engineering that most impresses, of the works of the ancients, but this is perhaps because so much of it endures—greater works than these have gone to the rust and the rot.) Iron sluice-gates, on an appropriately Brobdingnagian scale, held back the sea—though pumps laboured day and night to counter the inevitable seepage and spill.

Within it towered the platform, a—someday soon—floating bastion of concrete and painted steel, and within that towered the ship. The *Sea Eagle* (*Iolair*—pronounced something like 'Yillirrih'—in the Gaelic) looked like a rocket-propelled grenade buried nose-down in the platform. Four fin-like flanges sloped from its central tower to intersect the ovoid surface of its reactor-shell and reaction-mass tank, which was forty metres across at its widest diameter. The part of it concealed by the platform tapered from this equator to the aerospike of the main jet, around which the flared nozzles of attitude jets made a scalloped array.

By now I was tramping along in the middle of my work-gang, Jondo and I having been joined by Machard, Druin, the Lewismen—Murdo One and Murdo Too—Angelo and Trike. We descended a zig-zag iron stairway, down and down again, and walked across the floor of the dock, splashing through puddles of rainwater and seawater (some of which were so long-established that they had their own ecosystems) to the door at the base of the platform's southwest leg. It was like going into a lighthouse: up and up, around and around the winding stair. The air smelt of wet metal, hot oil, damp concrete. Every surface dripped, every sound echoed.

After two minutes' climb we reached the level of the internal scaffolding where we were working. I ducked through a service door in the inner side of the leg and emerged on to a walkway facing one of the platform's turbines across a twenty-metre gap. At our current worksite, a dozen metres along the walkway, ladders, more scaffolding and planks disappeared into—in fact appeared to merge with—the unfinished structure of struts joining the support leg to the platform's engine mount.

Our contract for the month was to finish that structure. There was no flexibility in the contract: there was only a month to go before the platform was floated out. Angus Grizzlyback, the foreman, was sitting at a wooden pallet mounted on crates to form a table, on which were spread some disassembled welding-torches, a small tin of kerosene and a few now very dirty seagull quills. He stood and glowered at us, reflexively lowering his head so as not to bash his pate on the next level up. You could see the white hairs on his chest and forearms which had inspired his nickname (or, for all I know, his surname, local custom being what it was). He was nearly two metres tall and about a hundred and fifty years old.

'Ah, good afternoon, gentlemen,' he said. 'I trust you all enjoyed your long lie? Let's see if we can think of something to occupy our leisure for the rest of the day.'

He drew a sheaf of finger-marked papers from his pocket as we gathered around the pallet. His pale grey eyes, under white brows, fixed me for a second.

'And you can get started right away, colha Gree,' he added.

I nodded brightly, winced at the effect of this sudden violent motion, and went off to make the tea.


The morning meeting—twenty minutes of sitting around, drinking tea and smoking—was the routine start to the day. Work on the project was organised through a sort of ecological pyramid of contractors and sub-contractors, from the great kraken of the International Scientific Society all the way down to frantically scrabbling krill like myself. Angus Grizzlyback combined the functions of entrepreneur and foreman, which partly cut across, and partly complemented, the job of the shop steward (in our case, Jondo) who held the equivalent position in the parallel pyramid of the union.

Conversation at the meeting, in my two months' experience, revolved around rumour, the day's news and sport. At the end of it everybody would drain their mugs, fold their newspapers, stub out their cigarettes, glance at some scrap of paper or doodle of slopped tea, nod to Angus and get cracking on some complex job to which only the most recondite allusion had been made. I would clear up the mess, rinse out the mugs if we were near a tap, and listen to Angus spell out my task for the day in terms suitable for the simple-minded.

Today's agenda was dominated by a motion before the Strathcarron district council, reported in the *West Highland Free Press*, that the locality should delegate its coinage to the regional council at Inverfefforan. This dangerous proposal for centralisation found no favour around the pallet. It was forensically dissected by Angus, vulgarly derided by the Lewismen, angrily dismissed by the Carronich. I myself pointed out a recent lesson of history. A few years earlier, a similar proposal had been passed in Strathclyde. The Glasgow mark had lost all public confidence, and the scheme was abandoned when annual inflation reached a ruinous two per cent. The discussion moved on to the national football league, and my attention wandered.

You can guess where. This time, however, my thoughts were more rational, and troubling, than my previous delighted memories, eager anticipations and fond fantasies. High as my opinion was of myself, I could not shake off my impression that Merrial had expected to find me; that she had known me, or known of me; that her first glance had signified recognition. Love and lust at that sight there had been, on both sides I was sure; but I was equally, though more obscurely, sure that this was not the first sight. I had recognised her too, but had no idea from where; with her it was conscious from the beginning, unconcealed but unexplained.

For a moment—I admit with shame—I considered the notion that we might have *known each other in a previous life*, whatever that may mean. On an instant I dismissed the idea as the foolish, womanish, oriental superstition that it is. Metempsychosis (though undoubtedly within the power of Omnipotence) has no place in the natural and rational religion.

So I lounged, elbows on the rough wood of the crude table, and sipped tea and smoked leaf while my companions argued about finance or football, and tried to apply my infinitesimal portion of Reason to a problem on which my passions were fully, and turbulently, engaged. The rational conclusion was that if we recognised each other we must have met before, not in an imagined previous life, but previously in this.

There were a number of possibilities on my side of the equation. (Merrial's I set aside—there were any number of ways in which she, from her privileged vantage, could have observed me, unobserved herself, and investigated me, undetected.) Was it conceivable that one of the hundreds of faces I saw nearly every day had been hers, unnoticed at the time? It seemed unlikely: hers was the kind of face I couldn't help but notice. I'd have given her a second look, and more, in a crowd of thousands.

Had I seen her, then, in another context, perhaps not even in the flesh? In, for example, some poster or moving picture about the project (all of which, for understandable reasons of recruitment, lied about its complement of pretty girls)? The same objections applied—I'd remember the film, I'd *have* the poster.

By further elimination I quickly returned to the first explanation that had struck me: that we had met, or at least seen each other, in our earlier years; in childhood. Merrial, I now recalled with renewed interest, had not explicitly disavowed the possibility—only discounted it, saying that she wasn't from around here.

Neither, of course, was I. There was no reason why I couldn't have seen her. I couldn't remember any such encounter, but I already knew that our childhood memories are as vagrant as our childhood selves, and as elusive; and as capable of innocent, shameless deceit.

The brute-force approach suggested itself: interrogate my parents, brothers and sisters; ransack family photographs . . . not yet. Already, the conscious thought that I sought the memory would have released the insensible agency in my mind that I privately thought of as the Librarian. That part of me would do the rest, and bring back the record if it were to be found at all—no doubt at some time as unexpected as it would be inopportune, but welcome nonetheless.

'—the torch parts?' said Angus.

I realised I had missed something. Angus sighed.

'You understand how to fit them, test and adjust?'

'Sure,' I said, nodding with more confidence than I felt.

'Fine, fine,' said Angus, standing up and briskly brushing the palms of his hands together. 'Let's get on with it, gentlemen.'

The others were grinning at me.

'Some night that must have been,' said Murdo Too, setting off another round of ribald teasing. I took it in good part but was relieved when they'd all clambered away into the support structure, leaving me to get on with my job without benefit of Angus's unheard instructions. A couple of hours passed quite pleasantly, if dangerously, and at the morning tea-break Angus was happy enough with the results to turn me loose on some sheet metal a dozen metres inward and ten up. I perched in the din-filled open space of the support structure, with nothing visible while I worked but what my own torch's jet illuminated, and with little else on my mind.

About twelve o'clock I decided to knock off for lunch. I throttled down the torch and lifted my mask. As I gathered up the bits of kit to carry back I heard Merrial's voice. I blinked and looked down. There she was, looking up from under a safety-helmet.

'Hi, Clovis!' she shouted, waving a lunch-box.

I waved back and returned to the scaffolding, dropped my tools and grabbed my lunch-box and descended to the dock's floor so quickly that my boots made the stairwell ring. By the time I'd reached the bottom, Merrial had walked over and was waiting for me. She was wearing the standard boiler-suit and boots, an outfit which—with her tied-back hair—gave her a boyish look. Her hug and kiss of greeting were sweet and warm; the rims of our helmets clanged, and we pulled apart, laughing.

'This is a fine surprise,' I said.

She caught my hand. 'Come on,' she said. 'I know a good place.'

We set off across the dock, to the predictable whistles and cat-calls of my mates, high above. Around the vast perimeter of the platform we went, and out into the daylight on the seaward side. Just left of the huge sea-doors Merrial turned towards the cliff, where a series of shelves and foot-holds formed a dangerous-looking natural stairway, which she skipped up on to and nimbly ascended. I followed, not looking down, until she stopped on a wider, grassy, heathery shelf a good thirty metres up.

We sat down. Merrial leaned back against the rockface, and I, unthinking, did the same—then jerked forward as I discovered again the scratches and bruises on my back. With our legs stretched out, our feet were almost at the edge. I felt more uneasy on that solid rock than I ever had at greater heights on the platform. Across the top of the gates, across the sea-loch, the Torridonian battlements of Applecross challenged the sky. The scale of those ancient mountains dwarfed the ship itself to a metal sculpture some eccentric artist had made in his back garden in his spare time.

'My place,' Merrial said.

'Some place,' I acknowledged. 'It's you who should be working on the platform, with a head for heights like this.'

'I'll keep to my cosy lab and my long lies, thanks.'

We opened our boxes and spread out and shared the contents, then got stuck in, both ravenous. For a few minutes we ate, without saying much, then Merrial topped up the mugs, lit herself a cigarette, passed one to me and leaned back against the rock.

'Clovis, I have something to ask you—'

She stopped. She was looking straight ahead, as though she wanted to talk without looking at me.

'What is it?'

'Something you can maybe tell me. Something you might not be supposed to. It's to do with the ship.'

This was getting more serious than love.

'You want to know about welding?' I asked, trying to be flippant.

She laughed. 'No, about history.'

'Oh.' I waved a hand. 'Any time. But there must be plenty better qualified than I, all I know about in any depth is—'

She watched me as the penny dropped.

'The life of the Deliverer?'

'That's the one,' she agreed cheerily.

'You're serious?'

'I'm serious,' she said. She wasn't looking away from me now, she was looking at me with a fixity and intensity of gaze I found alarming.

'All right,' I said, my mind treading water. 'You seriously want to know something about the Deliverer? I can tell you anything you want. But what has that to do with the ship, for God's sake?'

She took a deep breath, gazing away from me again at the tall ship. 'It's a fine ship there, colha Gree, and proud I am to be working on it. But consider this: it'll be the first ship to have lifted from the Yird for many a hundred year. The first since the Deliverance. We don't know much of what happened then, but we do know there were people and machines in space before the Deliverance, and we've heard never a word from them since. There's no doubt they're all dead. Why do you think that is?'

'There was a war,' I said patiently, 'and a revolution. The Second World Revolution, or the Deliverance, as we call it. The folk outside the Yird had followed the path of power, and they fell with the Possession. Starved of supplies, or killed each other, most like.'

'So the story goes,' she said, in the tone of one tired of disputing it. 'But what if it's wrong? What if whatever cleared the near heaven of folk and machines and deils alike is *still there*?'

'Ah,' I said, glancing involuntarily up at the clear blue sky. 'But it stands to Reason, the people in charge of the project will have considered this. Why don't you take it up with them?'

'They've considered it all right,' she said, 'and rejected it. There's no evidence of anything up there that could do the ship any harm. There's no evidence that the loss of the space habitations was anything but what you've said.'

'So why do you think I might know anything about this—' I waved my hand dismissively '—*supposed* danger?'

'Because . . .' At this point, I swear, she looked around and leaned closer, almost whispering in my ear. 'There has long been a tinker tradition, or rumour, or hint—you know how it is with the old folk—that whatever *did* destroy the space settlements and satellites and so on might still be there, and that it was . . . the Deliverer's own doing.'

My mouth must have fallen open. I could feel it go instantly dry, and I felt a moment of giddiness and nausea. My fingers dug into the tough grass as the world spun dangerously. I looked at her, sickened, yet fascinated despite myself. The natural religion has no sin of blasphemy, but this was blasphemy as near as dammit. 'That's deep water, Merrial.'

'You're telling *me*!' she snorted. 'I've had trouble enough for even suggesting it. Everybody thinks the Deliverer was a perfect soldier of God, like

Khomeini or somebody like that! Oh, among my own folk there's a more realistic attitude, they'll admit she had faults, but that's just among ourselves. In public you won't find a tink saying a word against her.'

I smiled wryly. 'Except you.'

'This is not public, colha Gree.' She ran a finger down the side of my face and across my lips.

'You must be very confident of that,' I said. 'To tell me.'

'I'm confident all right,' she said. 'I'm sure of you.'

To distract myself from the turmoil of mixed feelings this assurance induced, I asked her, 'So what is it that I can tell you?'

'What you know,' she said. 'I've always thought the scholars might know more about the Deliverer than they're letting on.'

I laughed. 'There are no secrets among scholars, they're not like the tinkers. All we find out is published. If it doesn't square with what most folk believe, that's their problem; but most folk don't read scholarly works, anyway. And—well, I suppose they are like the tinkers in this—they have a more realistic attitude among themselves. It's true, the Deliverer was no perfect saint. But I've seen nothing to suggest that she ever did anything as dire as . . . as you said.'

She made a grimace of disappointment. 'Oh, well. Maybe it was too much to hope that something like that would be written down on paper.' She plucked a pink clover and began tugging out the scrolled petals one by one and sucking them; passed one to me. I took it between my teeth, releasing the tiny drop of nectar on to my tongue.

'On paper,' I said thoughtfully. 'There could be other information where we can't reach it.'

'In the dark storage?'

'Aye, well, like I said last night—it's there, but we can't reach it.'

'I could reach it,' Merrial said casually.

'Oh, you could, could you?'

'Yes,' she said. 'I can get hold of equipment to take data out of the dark storage and put it in safe storage.'

'Safe storage?' I asked, too astonished to query more deeply at that moment.

'You know,' she said. 'The seer-stones.'

'And how would you know that?'

Again the remote gaze. 'I've seen it done. By . . . engineers taking short cuts.'

'There's a good reason why the left-hand path is avoided,' I said.

' "Necessity is its own law",' she said, as though quoting, but the expression came from no sage I'd ever read. 'Anyway, Clovis, it's not as dangerous as you may think.'

Curiosity drove me like prurience. 'How do they do it safely? Draw pentagrams with salt, or what?'

'No,' she said, quite seriously. 'They make lines with wire—isolated circuits, you know? That's what confines anything that might be waiting to get out. There are other simple precautions, for the visuals—' she made a cutting motion with her hand in response to my baffled look '—but ninety-nine times out of a hundred there's nothing to worry about anyway. Just words and pictures.' She chuckled darkly. 'Sometimes *strange* words and pictures, I'll give you that.'

'And the hundredth time?'

'You meet a demon,' she said, very quietly but emphatically. 'Most times, you can shut it down before it does any damage.'

'And the other times?' I persisted.

'It gets loose and eats your soul.'

I stared at her. 'You mean that's actually *true*?'

She laughed at me. 'Of course not. It makes your equipment burst into flames or explode with a loud bang, though.'

'I can see how that might be a hazard.'

She reached over and touched my lips. 'Shush, man, don't go on like an old woman. Most of the stuff in the dark storage is useless to us, or evil in a different way from what you think. Evil ideas from the old times, they can make you sick, and make you want to share them, so they spread like a disease.'

She leaned back again and closed her eyes, enjoying the sun like a cat. 'I reckon you and I are strong enough and healthy enough in our minds to be safe from that sort of thing.' She opened her eyes again and gave me a challenging look.

The path of power is always a temptation, as Merrial had so lightly said last night. Until now, it had never seriously tempted me; I knew the dangers, and knew no way of getting to the undoubted rewards. Now such a way was being offered; it might reduce by years the time required for researching my thesis, it might even give me a head start on the Life. The lust for the lost knowledge made my head throb.

The question was out before I knew what I was saying. 'Do you want me to help you to do it?'

Her eyes widened and brightened. '*Could* you? That would be just—wonderful!'

She was looking at me with so much admiration and respect that I could not imagine not doing what it would take to deserve it. But even in my besotted eagerness to please her, my genuine concern about the problem she thought she'd uncovered, and my own desire for the knowledge and for the adventure of obtaining it—even with all that, my whole training and my natural caution came rushing back, and I wavered.

'Oh, God,' I said. 'I'll have to think about it.'

'Can you get your thinking about it over by eight tonight?' Merrial asked drily.

'Maybe. And what if I say no?'

She held me in her level gaze. 'I won't think any the less of you. It won't change a thing about that.'

'Sure?' I said, not anxiously but mischievously. I had already decided. She had seduced me into a frame of mind that feared neither God nor men nor devils. 'Then what will you do?'

She shook her head. 'I'll find some other way, or at the worst just register my protest in the record, and go on with my work as I'm told.'

'That sounds like a more sensible course in the first place.'

'It is that,' she said. 'But I'd rather have the satisfaction of knowing the ship is safe, one way or another, than of saying "I told you so" afterwards.'

I couldn't argue with that, and I didn't want to. What she said must have had some deeper effect on me, because when we descended the perilous steps down from the heathery eyrie, each of us one stumble away from the welcoming arms of Darwin, I wasn't afraid at all.


My room was narrow and long, under the slope of the roof. After the heat of the day it was full of the smell of old varnish and warm rust and the sound of creaking wood. The westward-facing skylight let in enough light to see by, and enough air to breathe.

I came in from work and threw off my overalls and shirt, tossed my temporarily heavy purse on the bed, and uncapped a chilled bottle of beer I'd bought at the bus-stop. I opened the skylight to its fullest extent and sat myself under it on the room's one tall chair, and leaned my elbow on the window's frame as though sitting at a bar. Beside my forearm tiny red arachnids moved about on the grey and yellow lichen like dots in front of my eyes.

Merrial and I would meet again in two hours. Plenty of time to wash and shave and dress, to consider and reconsider. I was almost tempted to have a brief sleep, but decided against it, attractive though the barely straightened bedding seemed at this moment. After soaking up the beer I'd get a good jolt of coffee. I lit my fifth cigarette of the day and gazed out over the rooftops towards the loch, my parched body gratefully absorbing the drink, my tired brain riding the rush of the leaf.

Merrial's disturbing but alluring proposition had preoccupied me all afternoon, and although my decision was made I had plenty of doubts and fears. I would not be the first to mine the dark archives in the interests of history, or of engineering for that matter; it was neither a crime nor a sin, but it had always been impressed upon me that it was a dangerous folly. And, to be sure, I could think of no good reason for doing it, other than the ones which motivated myself and Merrial; no doubt everyone who had taken that path had felt the same about *their* reasons. Rationally, it was obvious why the dangers were better publicised than the benefits—those who found only madness and death in the black logic could not but be noticed, whereas those who found knowledge or wealth or pleasure discreetly kept their sinister source to themselves.

What hypocrisies, I wondered, did the tinkers practise, if they themselves would on occasion turn their hand to the leftward path? Until Merrial had mentioned it, I'd suspected no such thing: but then, with the tinkers' virtual monopoly of an understanding of the white logic, it was in their interests to publicly disparage the black. Optical and mechanical computing, and more especially the delicate interface between them—the seerstones set like gems in the shining brass of the calculating machinery—were their speciality and secret skill. What would happen if people outside their guild were to start exploring the left-hand path in earnest, as a public enterprise rather than a private vice, heaven only knew. A new Possession, perhaps; in which case the tinkers might have to engineer a new Deliverance. It was not a reassuring thought.

I stubbed out the cigarette and sent the butt tumbling down the slate roof-tiles to the dry gutter. The sounds of people going home, of engines and hooves and feet, rose from the street below. I turned back into the room and finished the beer, then undressed and went into the sluice-shower and washed myself down. The water ran cold just before I got the last soapsuds off; I gritted my teeth and persisted, then leapt out and dried myself off while the electric kettle boiled. I filled a ewer with a mixture of cold and hot water and shaved carefully, then set some coffee to brew while I got dressed: in the same trousers and waistcoat as I'd worn the previous night, but I thought the occasion deserved a clean shirt.

The bed was close enough to the table for the two items of furniture to form a somewhat unergonomic desk. I sat down with the coffee and looked at the stack of books and papers I'd brought with me to read over the summer. I reached over and hauled a volume from the stack, cursed and got up and found a rag and wiped dust and cobwebs from all the books, washed my hands and sat down again. Sipping the cooling coffee, turning over the pages, I tried to focus my mind on the matters they contained.

When I was awakened for a third time by my forehead hitting the table I gave up and poured another coffee and turned my mind to my real worry, the one I didn't want to think about: what if Merrial were simply using me? That she had sought me out in the first place because she wanted me to do a job for her?

I walked up and down the room's narrow length, turning the question over almost as often as I turned around. After several iterations I decided that I couldn't have been fooled about her feelings, that her passion was real—and that if she'd been intent on manipulating me, she would have done it more subtly—

But then, perhaps that itself was evidence of how subtly she'd done it. At that point I stopped. To suspect manipulation that subtle—an apparently clumsy and obvious approach disguising one devious and elegant—was to undermine the very confidence in my own judgement on which all such discriminations must perforce rely.

So I forgot my suspicions, and looked once more at the books, and at a quarter before eight went out into the evening to meet her, and my fate.

# 4

## PAPER TIGERS

Three flags hung behind the coffin: the Soviet, red with gold hammer and sickle; the Kazakhstani, blue with yellow sun and eagle; and the ISTWR, yellow with black trefoil.

About two hundred people were crammed into the hall of the crematorium. The funeral was the nearest thing to a State occasion the republic had had since the Sputnik centenary. The entire depleted apparat was there, and a good proportion of the workers, peasants and intelligentsia was probably watching on television. The distinguished foreign guests included the Kazakhstani consul, the head of the Western United States Interests Section, and David Reid, who was wedged between a couple of Mutual Protection greps. Myra sat with the rest of Sovnarkom in the front row, dry-eyed, as one of Georgi's old comrades—another Afganets—delivered the eulogy.

'Major Georgi Yefrimovich Davidov was born in Alma-Ata in 1956. At school, in the Pioneers and the Komsomol, he soon distinguished himself as an exemplary individual—studious, civic-minded, with great athletic prowess. After obtaining a degree at the University of Kazakhstan, where he joined the Communist Party of the Soviet Union, he completed his national service and chose a military career. In 1979 he qualified as a helicopter pilot, and later that same year was among the first of the limited contingent of the Soviet armed forces to fulfil their internationalist duty to the peoples of Afghanistan.'

A ripple of dissidence, expressed with indrawn breaths, or sighs, or shifting of feet, went through the room. Myra herself sniffed, compressed her lips, looked down. All those nights he'd woken her by grabbing her, holding her, talking away his nightmares; all those mornings when he'd said not a word, given no indication that he remembered any interruption to his sleep, or to hers.

The speaker raised his voice a little and continued undaunted.

'His service earned him promotion and the honour of Hero of the Soviet Union. In 1985 he applied for transfer to the space programme, and after training at Baikonur he won the proud title of Cosmonaut of the Soviet Union. However, many decades were to pass before he was able to fulfil this part of his destiny.'

By which time it was a fucking milk-run, and there was no fucking Soviet Union, so get on with it—

'During the turbulent years of the late 1980s, Major Davidov took some political stands about which his friends and comrades may honestly differ—'

Nice one, he was a fucking Yeltsinite, get on with it—

'—but which testify to his true Soviet and Kazakh patriotism and the seriousness with which he took his civic duty and the Leninist ideals of the armed forces, which in his view proscribed the use of violence against the people.'

Myra was not the only one who had to choke back a laugh.

'After the Republic of Kazakhstan became independent, Major Davidov's expertise in the areas of nuclear weaponry and questions of nuclear disarmament gave him a new field for his great political skill and personal charm . . .'

Myra bit her lip.


He was in front of her in the taxi queue outside the airport at Alma-Ata. Tall, even taller than she was, very dark; swept-back black hair, eyebrows almost as thick as his black moustache; relaxed in a stiff olive-green uniform; smoking a Marlboro and glancing occasionally at a counterfeit Rolex.

Myra, just arrived, lost and anxious, could not take her eyes off him. But it was the yellow plastic bag at his feet that gave her the nerve to speak. Printed on it in red were a picture of a parrot and the words:

THE PET SHOP
992 Pollockshaws Road
Glasgow G41 2HA

She leaned forward, into his field of vision.

'You've flown in from Glasgow?' she asked, in Russian.

He turned, startled out of some trance, and looked at her with a bemused expression which rapidly became a smile.

'Ah, the bag.' He poked it with his foot, revealing that the carrier was

bulging with cartons of cigarettes and bottles of Johnny Walker Black Label.
'You're a stranger here, then.'

'Oh?'

'These plastic bags have nothing to do with Glasgow. They're used by
every shop from here to China, God knows why.' He laughed, showing
strong teeth stained with nicotine. 'Have you been to Glasgow?'

'Yes,' said Myra. 'I lived there for several years, back in the seventies.'
Something cooled in his look. 'What were you doing?'

'I was writing a thesis,' Myra said, 'on the economy of the Soviet Union.'
He guffawed. 'You got permission to do *that*?'

'It wasn't a problem—' she began, then stopped. She realised that he'd
taken her for a former-Soviet citizen. Former *nomenklatura*, if she'd had
clearance for such dangerous research.

'I'm not a Russian, I'm from the United States!'

He raised his eyebrows.

'Your accent is very good,' he said, in English. His accent was very good.
They talked until they reached the top of the queue, and then went on talking, because they shared a taxi into town, and went on talking . . .


Would she ever have spoken to him, Myra wondered, if it hadn't been for
that yellow bag? And if she hadn't spoken to him, would she ever have seen
him again? Perhaps; but perhaps not, or not at such a moment, when they
were both free, and on the rebound from other lovers, and in that case . . .

She wouldn't be here, for one thing, and Georgi wouldn't be in that coffin, and . . . the consequences went on and on, escalating until she didn't know
whether to laugh or cry. For want of a nail the kingdom was lost—and the
result of that triviality, the fictitious Pollockshaws pet-shop address on the
plastic bag, had gained her a republic, and imposed on others losses she could
not bear to contemplate. Or so it might seem, if anyone ever learned enough
about her to see her hand in history.

But then again, maybe not, maybe old Engels and Plekhanov had been
right after all about the role of the individual in history: maybe it did all
come out in the wash—at the end of the French Revolution *someone*, but, of
course, ha-ha, 'not necessarily that particular Corsican', would have stepped
into the tall boots which circumstances, like a good valet, had laid out for a
man on horseback.

She'd never found that theory particularly convincing, and it gave her
small comfort now to even consider it. No, she was stuck, as were they all,
with her actions and their consequences.

'—in recent years Georgi Yefrimovich played a leading part in the diplomatic service of the ISTWR, in which duty he met his death.' The eulogist

paused for a moment to direct a stabbing glance at the distinguished foreign guests. 'He is survived by his former wife and loyal friend, Myra Godwin-Davidova, their children and grandchildren—'

Too many to read out, and none of them here, get on with it—

Messages were, however, read out from all of the absent offspring, other relatives, old friends. The eulogist laid down his sheaf of papers at last, and raised his hand. The crematorium filled with the oddly quiet and modest sound of Kazakhstan's national anthem. The coffin rolled silently through the unobtrusive hatch. Everyone stood up and sang, or mimed along to, the Internationale. And that was that. Another good materialist gone to ash.

Myra turned and walked out of the crematorium, and row by row, from the front, they fell in and walked out behind her.

Her hands were shaking as she fumbled with her black fur hat and tried to light a cigarette in the driveway. Out on the street, cars were being moved into position to carry the dignitaries off to the post-funeral luncheon function. Somebody steadied her hand, helped her with the cigarette. She lit up and looked up, to see David Reid. Dark brows, dark eyes, white hair down to the upturned collar of his astrakhan coat. He looked less than half his age, with only the white hair—itself an affectation—indicating anything different; none of her give-away flaws. She was pretty sure his joints didn't creak, or his bones ache. They had better fixes in the West. His minders hung about a few steps away, their gaze grepping the surroundings. People were milling around, drifting towards the waiting cars.

'Are you all right?' Reid asked.

'I'm fine, Dave.'

He scuffed a foot on the gravel, scratched the back of his neck.

'We didn't do it, Myra.'

'Yeah, well . . .' She shrugged. 'I read the autopsy. I believe it.'

*You'd be dead if I didn't*, she disdained to add. She believed the autopsy; she had no choice. She believed Reid, too. She still had her doubts about the verdict: natural causes—it might be one of those dark episodes where she could never be sure of the truth, like Stalin's hand in the Kirov affair, or in the death of Robert Harte . . . But Reid took the point she wanted him to take. He seemed to relax slightly, and lit a cigarette himself. His gaze flicked from the burning tip to the crematorium chimney, then to her.

'Ah, shit. It seems such a waste.'

Myra nodded. She knew what he meant. Burning dead people, burying them in *a fucking hole in the ground*—it was already beginning to seem barbaric.

'He didn't even want cryo,' she said. 'Let alone that Californian computer-scan scam.'

'Why not?' Reid asked. 'He could've afforded it.'

'Oh, sure,' Myra said. 'Just didn't believe in it, is all.'

Reid smiled thinly. 'Neither do I.'

'Oh?'

He spread his hands. 'I just sell the policies.'

'Is there *any* pie you don't have a finger in?'

Reid rubbed the side of his nose with his finger. 'Diversification, Myra. Name of the game. Spread the risks. Learned that in insurance, way back when.' He reached out, waiting for her unspoken permission to take her arm. 'We need to talk business.'

'Car,' she said, catching his elbow firmly and turning about on the crunching gravel. They walked side by side to the armoured limousine. Myra, out of the corner of her eye, watched people watching. Good: let it be clear that she no longer suspected Reid. Not publicly, not politically, not even—at a certain level—privately. Just personally, just in her jealous old bones. But there was more to it than making a diplomatic display; there was still a genuine affection between them, attenuated though it was by the years, exasperated though it was by their antagonism. Reid had never been a man to let enmity get in the way of friendship.


Myra glanced at her watch as the car door shut with a well-engineered clunk. They had about five minutes to talk in private as the big black Zhil rolled through Kapitsa's city centre to its only posh hotel, the Sheraton. She settled back in the leather seat and eyed Reid cautiously.

'OK,' she said. 'Get on with it.'

Reid reached for the massive ashtray, stubbed out one cigarette and lit up another. Myra did the same. Their smoky sighs met in a front of mutual disruption. Reid scratched his eyebrow, looked away, looked back.

'Well,' he said. 'I want to make you an offer. We know you still have some of your old—' he hesitated; even here, there were words one did not say '—strategic assets, and we'd like to buy them off you.'

He could be bluffing.

'I have no—' she began. Reid tilted his head back and puffed a tiny jet of smoke that, after a few centimetres, curled back on itself in a miniature mushroom-cloud.

'Don't waste time denying it,' he said.

'All right,' said Myra. She swallowed a rising nausea, steadied herself against a dizzy, chill darkening of her sight. It was like being caught with a guilty secret, but one which she had not known she held. But, she knew too well, if she had not known it was because she had never tried, and never wanted, to find out.

'Suppose we do. We wouldn't sell them to anyone, let alone you. We're against your coup—'

It was Reid's turn to feign ignorance, Myra's to show impatience.

'We wouldn't *use* them,' he said. 'Good God, what do you take us for? We just want them . . . off the board, so to speak. Out of the game. And quite frankly, the only way we can be sure of that is to have control of them ourselves.'

Myra shook her head. 'No way. No deal.'

Reid raised his hand. 'Let me tell you what we have to offer, before you reject it. We can buy you out, free and clear. Give everybody in this state, every one of your citizens, enough money to settle anywhere and live more than comfortably. Think about it. The camps are going to be wound down, and *whoever* wins the next round is going to move against you. Your assets aren't going to be much use when Space Defense gets back in business.'

'That's a threat, I take it?'

'Not at all. Statement of fact. Sell them now or lose them later, it's up to you.'

'Lose them—or use them!'

Reid gave her a 'we are not amused' look.

'I'm not fooling,' Myra told him. 'The best I can see coming out of your coup is more chaos, in which case we'll need all the goddamn *assets* we can get!'

Reid took a deep breath. 'No, Myra. If you do get chaos, it'll be because we haven't won. This coup, as you call it, is the last best chance for stability. If we fail the world will go to hell in its own way. Your personal contribution to that will then be no concern of mine—I'll be dead, or in space—but you *can* help make sure it *doesn't* happen, and benefit yourself and your people in the process.' He was putting all of his undeniable charm into his voice and expression as he concluded, 'Think it over, Myra. That's all I ask.'

'I'll think about it,' she said, granting him at least this victory, for what it was worth. She looked around. 'We've arrived.'


The hotel's ornately furnished function suite was filled with people in dark clothes, standing about in small groups and conversing in low voices. Already they were beginning to relax out of their funereal solemnity, to smile and laugh a little: life goes on. Fine.

Myra and Reid walked together to the long tables on which the buffet was spread, and contrived to lose each other in the random movement of people selecting food and drinks. With a plate of savouries in one hand and a large glass of whisky in the other, Myra looked around. Over in one corner Andrei Mukhartov was deep in conversation with a lady in a black suit and a large hat; she was answering his quiet questions in a loud voice. Myra hoped this representative of the tattered Western fringe of the former

United States wasn't talking about anything confidential. Possibly that was the point. She noticed that Valentina was standing alone, in an olive-green outfit whose black armband was rather shouted down by an astonishing amount of gold braid. Myra made a less than subtle beeline for her.

'Ah, there you are,' she said, as Valentina turned. She nudged her defence minister towards the nearest of the many small tables dotted around the vast floor. They sat.

'New uniform?' Myra asked.

Valentina's rigid epaulettes moved up and down. 'Never had much occasion for it before,' she said.

'Never knew you'd accumulated so many medals, either.'

Valentina had to laugh. 'Yeah, it is a bit . . . Brezhnevian, isn't it?'

'All too appropriate, for us. The period of stagnation.'

Valentina devoured a canapé, not looking away from Myra. 'Indeed. I see you had a little chat with our main inward investor.'

'Yes. He made me an interesting offer.' Myra looked down at her plate, picked up something with legs. 'I do hope this stuff's synthetic; I'd hate to think of the radiation levels if it isn't.'

'I think we have to rely on somebody's business ethics on the radiation question,' Valentina said.

'Ah, right.' Myra peered at the shrimp's shell; it had an ICI trademark. Full of artificial goodness. She hauled the pale pink flesh out with her teeth. 'Anyway, Madame Comrade People's Commissar for Defence, my dear: our inward investor gave me to understand that he knows we've done a little less . . . outward divestment than I'd been led to believe.'

Valentina, rather to her credit, Myra thought, looked embarrassed.

'I inherited the assets from my predecessors . . . and I never mentioned them because I thought you already knew, or you didn't and you needed to have deniability.'

So it was true. The confirmation was less of a shock than Reid's original claim had been. It would take a while for the full enormity of it all to sink in.

Myra nodded, her mouth full. Swallowed, with a shot of whisky. 'The latter, actually. I didn't know. I thought they'd all been seized by the Yanks after the war.'

'Most of them were. There was one exception, though. A large portfolio of assets that made it through the crackdown, that the US/UN just couldn't get their hands on; one contract that was always renewed. Until the Fall Revolution, of course. Then it . . . lapsed, and I was left holding the babies. They were sent back to us in a large consignment of large diplomatic bags, from various locations, all controlled by . . .'

'You can tell me now, I take it?'

Valentina looked around, and shrugged.

'The original ministate, with the original mercenary defence force.'

Myra had to think for a moment before she realised just which state Valentina was talking about.

'Jesus wept!'

'Quite possibly,' said Valentina, 'quite possibly he did.'

There are times when all you can do is be cynical, put up a hard front, don't let it get to you . . . Myra joined in Valentina's dark chuckle.

'So what happened to the assets, and why is our investor concerned about them?'

'Ah,' said Valentina. 'You'll recall the Sputnik centenary a couple of years ago. We rather extravagantly launched one of our obsolete boosters to celebrate it. What I did at the time was take the opportunity to place most of our embarrassing legacy in orbit.'

'In *Earth* orbit?' Myra resisted an irrational impulse to pull her head down between her shoulders.

'Some of them,' said Valentina. 'The ones designed specifically for orbital use, you know? They're in high orbit, quite safe.' She frowned, and against some inner resistance added, 'Well, fairly safe. But the rest we sent to an even safer place: Lagrange.'

Myra had a momentary mental picture, vivid as a virtual display, of Lagrange: L5, one of the points where Earth's gravity and the Moon's combined to create a region of orbital stability, and which had, over half a century, accumulated a cluttered cluster of research stations, military satellites, official and unofficial space habitats, canned utopias, abandoned spacecraft, squatted modules, random junk . . . It was the space movement's promised land, and with the new nanofactured ultralight laser-launched spacecraft its population was rising as fast as Kapitsa's was falling.

'Oh, fucking hell,' said Myra.

'Don't worry,' Valentina assured her. 'They're almost undetectable among all the debris.'

Myra didn't have the heart to tell her how much she was missing the point.

'Why the fuck did you park them *there*?' she demanded. 'Safe, in a way, yeah, that I can understand, but didn't it occur to you that if it ever came out, we might find our intentions . . . misunderstood?'

Valentina looked even more embarrassed. 'It was—well, it was a Party thing, Myra. A request.'

'Oh, right. Jeez. Are you still *in* the fucking Party?'

Valentina chuckled. 'I am the Party. The ISTWR section, at least.'

'Now that Georgi's gone. Shit, I'd forgotten.'

They hadn't even put the fourth flag, the flag of the Fourth, on his coffin. Shit. Not that it mattered now. Not to Georgi, anyway. And not to

those who'd gathered to pay their respects—the only one present who'd
have understood its significance was Reid.

'Don't worry,' said Valentina.

'What does the International want with—oh, fuck. I can think of any
number of things it might want with them.'

Valentina nodded. 'Some of them could be to our advantage.'

'Hah. I'll be the judge of that. You've kept the access codes to yourself?'

'Of course!'

'Well, that's something.'

'So our man's proposing in a buy-out, is he?' Valentina continued. 'Could
be worth considering.'

'Yeah.' Myra stood up, taking her glass. 'I'm going to talk to him some
more. Thanks for the update, Val.'

She refilled her glass, with vodka this time, and set out in a carefully casual
ramble to where Reid stood chatting to an awestruck gaggle of low-level
functionaries. Denis Gubanov and one of Reid's greps circled unobtrusively,
keeping a wary distance from the group and from each other, each at a Lagrange point of his own. She couldn't hear the conversation. On her way, she
was intercepted by Alexander Sherman. The Industry Commissar was wearing the same sharp plastic suit, its colour adjusted to black. He looked shiftier
than usual; a bad sign.

'Ah, Myra. A sad day for us all.' He shook his head slowly. 'A sad day.'

'Yes,' said Myra. The phrase *get on with it* once more came to mind.

Alex took a deep breath and, as if telepathic, announced, 'I have something to tell you. It's not a good time, but . . . Well, I've had an offer from
Mr Reid.'

'To buy out our assets?'

'No, no!' Alex looked surprised at the suggestion. 'An *employment* offer.'

'Oh, right,' said Myra dismissively. She waved a hand as she walked past
him. 'Take it.'


She could see herself in the big gilt-framed mirrors as she walked up; they
faced similar mirrors at the far side of the room, and for a moment she saw
herself multiplied, a potential infinity of different versions of herself: a visual, virtual image of the many worlds interpretation. She had entertained a
childish notion, once, that mirror images might be windows into those
other worlds. Did the photon ever decide, she'd wondered, did it ever turn
aside in its reflection?

What she saw was the endlessly repeated image of a tall, thin woman in
a long black dress, moving towards the still oblivious Reid like some MIRVed
nemesis. She saw the flickered glances exchange their messages, between

her Security Commissar, Reid's security man, Reid, and herself, until Reid's reflected eyes met her actual eyes, and widened.

She encountered a sort of deadness in the air, and realised that the security men were, between them, setting up audio countermeasures, casting a cloak of silence around the group. Then she was through the region of dead air, where the voices were garbled and strange, and suddenly the conversation was audible—for the moment before it died on the lips of those who noticed her arrival.

'Well, hello again,' she said. Her gaze swept the half-dozen of her employees gathered around Reid; they were all making comical efforts to flee, walking backwards as discreetly as possible. 'Headhunting my lower-middle cadres as well as my commissars?'

'Yup,' said Reid, quite unabashed. He made a fractional movement of his fingertips and eyebrows, and his supplicants—or applicants—dispersed like smoke in a draught. The grep and Gubanov continued their watchful mutual circling. A waiter went past with a salver of glasses and a tray of Beluga on rye; Myra and Reid helped themselves from both, then stood facing each other with a slight awkwardness, like tongue-tied teenagers after a dance.

'I could do some head-hunting the other way, you know,' Myra said. 'Perhaps I should buy a spy or two from you. It turns out you're better informed about our investment portfolio than I've been. Particularly its, ah, spread.'

Reid acknowledged this with a small nod.

'Puts us in a difficult position,' he said. 'You have the drop on us, frankly. Earth orbit is the high ground, after all.'

*Oh?* she thought to herself. So he didn't know about Lagrange? Or didn't want her to know he knew.

'However,' Reid went on, 'I'm pretty confident that you won't, um, liquidate. For obvious reasons.'

'So why the offer?'

'Peace of mind . . . nah, seriously. Between us, you and I know everyone who knows of the current level of exposure. But neither of us can guarantee that that'll last. A word in the wrong place and there could be severe market jitters on my side. Which, I hasten to add, would not be to your benefit, either, so we have a mutual—'

'Assured deterrence?'

Reid gave her a *shut the fuck up* look. 'You could say that . . . but I'd rather you didn't.'

Myra grinned evilly. 'OK,' she said. 'It's still no deal, Dave.'

He gazed back at her, expressionless, but he couldn't hide the plea in his voice. 'Will you at least agree not to dump your assets during the takeover bid? Not to make any offers to the competition?'

Oh, Jeez. This was a tricky one. She had no intention of doing any of the things he feared. On the other hand—if he were to fear them (even if only theoretically, and only at the margin, but still . . . ) it might restrain him. It might keep him, and his allies, from crossing that invisible border, that terminator between the daylight and the dark. Let them hate, as long as they fear.

She shook her head, and saw her multiple reflections do the same, in solemn repetition. The act of observation collapses the wave-function, yes: the die cast, the cat dies.

'Sorry, Dave,' she told him. 'I can't make any promises.'

His gaze measured hers for a moment, and then he shrugged.

'You win some, you lose some,' he said lightly. 'See you around, Myra.'

She watched him walk away, as she so often had. His grep followed at a safe distance. Denis raised his eyebrows, rolled his eyes, came over.

'What was all that about?'

'Oh, just some old stuff between us,' Myra said. 'We don't see eye to eye, is all.' She took his arm. 'Let's see how Andrei is getting on with that lady from the Western United States, shall we?'


Not well, as it turned out. This was not the place for secret diplomacy, even if they'd been using the privacy shields, which they weren't. Juniper Bear, the West American unofficial consul, was making her diplomatic position no secret at all. Her broad-brimmed black hat with black wax fruit around its crown seemed chosen to amplify her voice, even though her pose indicated urgent, confidential communication.

'. . . Just in the last month we hit a Green guerilla incursion from SoCal, and at the same time a White Aryan Nations push across the Rockies, and would you believe the First Nations Federation, the goddamn *Indians*, lobbing significant conventional hardware on our northern settlements on the Cannuck side of the old border? Let me tell you, Comrade Mukhartov, we could do with some orbital backup, this time on our side for a change.' She laughed, grinning at Myra and Valentina as they joined the conversation. 'Would you *believe*,' she repeated, 'the goddamn Greens are actually lobbying the old guard to keep the battlesats as asteroid defence? Like we ever really needed that, and now we got everything bigger'n a pea out there mapped and tracked, we might as well worry about a new ice age!'

'Well, that's coming,' said Valentina.

Juniper Bear's hatbrim tilted. 'Sure, the Milankovitch cycle, yeah, but it isn't a worry, now is it?' She laughed. 'Hey, I remember global warming!'

'And *that's* happening,' Myra said. 'But, like you say, it isn't a *worry*, not any more. And the ozone holes, and the background radiation levels, and the synthetic polymers in every organic, and the jumping genes and all that, yeah, we're not *worrying*.' She felt surprised at the sound of her own voice, at how angry she felt about all that, now she was articulating it; it was as though she had a deep Green deep inside her, just waiting to get out. 'But to be honest, Ms Bear, we are worried about something else. About the plan to revitalise the Reunited Nations. Even if they *will* be the enemies of our enemies, in the first instance. We don't want that kind of power turned against anyone on Earth, ever again.' She took off her hat, fingering the smooth hairs and running her thumb over the red star and gold sigil; realised she was standing there, literally cap in hand, begging for help.

Juniper Bear shook her head. She was an old woman, not as old as Myra; she looked about thirty, by pre-rejuvenation reckoning, when her face was in repose, but the weight of her years showed in her every facial expression, if you were old enough to notice these things. You learned to transmit and to receive those non-verbal tics, in parallel processes of increasing wisdom.

'That's what our opposition are saying,' the woman said. '"No more New World Orders!" Well, I'm sorry, but we need a real new world order, one on our side this time. It'll be only temporary—once we get enough forces out there, there's no way anyone can keep central control. Once the emergency is over, it'll just . . .' She made a downward-planing gesture.

'Wither away?'

Juniper's creased eyes registered the irony, her compressed lips her refusal to let it deflect her. 'Speaking of states that wither away,' she said, changing the subject adroitly, 'if any of you find yourselves looking for new opportunities, when all this is over one way or another . . .'

Valentina and Andrei said nothing, at least not in Myra's presence; but Myra herself smiled, and nodded, and said she'd bear it in mind.


'Well!' said Andrei Mukhartov, when the function was over and the guests had departed, the diplomats, the apparatchiks and captains of industry. Andrei, Valentina, Denis and Myra had retired to one of the hotel's smaller and quieter bars. Hardwood and mirrors, leather and glass, plush carpets and quiet music. There were plenty of people in the bar who'd had nothing directly to do with the funeral. This made for a degree of security for the four remaining Commissars, huddled as they were around a vodka bottle on a corner table, like dissidents. 'Thanks for your intervention earlier, comrades. I thought I was getting somewhere until you turned up.'

'You thought wrong,' said Myra. She didn't feel like arguing the point. 'I know Juniper, she'll seem to agree with you and then start talking about the war. Which is where we came in. You didn't lose anything.'

'Huh,' grunted Andrei. He knocked back a thumbnail glass. 'Tell me why you need a Foreign Secretary at all.'

'Because I can't do everything myself,' Myra told him. 'Even if I can do every particular thing better than anyone. Division of labour, don't knock it. It's all in Ricardo.'

Andrei and Valentina were looking at each other with eye-rolling, exaggerated bafflement.

'Megalomania,' said Andrei sadly. 'Comes to all the dictators of the proletariat, just before the end.'

'Think we should overthrow her before it's too late?' Valentina straightened her back and sketched a salute. 'Get Denis in on it and we can form a troika. Blame all the problems on Myra and declare a clean slate.'

'That is not funny,' said Myra. She poured another round, watched the clear spirit splash into the crystal ware, four times. 'That is exactly how it will be. One day all the problems of the world will be blamed on me.' This was not funny, she thought. This was her deepest suspicion, in her darkest moments. She grinned at her confederates. 'To that glorious future!'

They slugged back the vodka shots and slammed down the empty glasses. Myra passed up an offer of a Marley or a Moscow Gold, lit up a Dunhill from her last trip out. The double foil inside the pack, the red and the gold of its exterior—there was still, to her, something wicked and opulent about the brand, which she'd first smoked when duty-free still meant something.

'So, what's the score, Andrei? Apart from today's subtle approaches.'

'Ah.' Andrei exhaled the fragrant smoke through his nostrils. 'Not good, I have to say. Kazakhstan's still keeping out of it—after all, they have Baikonur to think about, and the Sheenisov threat. If it weren't for previous bad blood between them and the space movement, I think they might be tempted to side with it. So their neutrality is something, when all's said and done. As for the rest—I have canvassed every country, I have checked with our delegates in New York, and frankly it looks as if next week's vote will go through.'

'Valentina?'

Myra didn't need to spell anything out. Kozlova had spent days and nights tracking reports from agents in the battlesats and the settlements. She replied by holding out her spread hand and waggling it.

'Nothing much we can do up there,' she said. 'The other side have all the resources to tip the balance their way, whichever way the argument is going.'

'Not *all* the resources,' Myra said.

'Oh, come,' said Valentina, with careful calm. 'We couldn't.' She might have been talking about cheating at cards.

'But they don't know we couldn't,' Myra said. 'We do have a hard reputation, after all. Most of the new countries, not to mention the settlements, probably think we're some kind of ruthless Bolsheviks.'

They shared a cynical laugh.

'I'm sure Reid is disabusing them of that notion right now,' said Andrei. He seemed to have picked up on what they were talking about; and as for

Denis Gubanov, he was leaning back with a smug smile, as if he'd known it for years. Probably had.

'Oh, I don't know,' Myra said. 'He's a devious son of a bitch. He says his side don't know what we've got, and he might still hold out a hope of winning us over—or using us as a threat to keep his own side in order.'

She inhaled again.

'Besides,' she added, 'he doesn't know all we've got. Or so I gathered. He thinks it's all in Earth orbit.'

'It *isn't*?' Denis's smile faded instantly. 'So where is it?'

'Good question,' Myra said. 'See if you can find out.'

Valentina was intently studying the reflection of the chandelier in the bar mirror.

'Is this a joke, or what?' Denis demanded.

Myra shook her head, laid her palm on the back of his hand. 'Easy, man. Don't waste too much time on it—just treat it as an exercise, see what you can find out about what people know or suspect—'

'And I'm not to know myself?'

'Double-blind,' Myra said firmly. 'And double-bluff. I'll let you know after you've brought back some results, but I don't want your investigation dropping any inadvertent hints.'

Denis scowled. 'OK,' he allowed, 'I see the point of that.' He looked at his watch, sighed and stood up. 'Three-fifteen,' he said. 'Time I was back at the office.'

'The unsleeping sword of the Cheka,' Myra said. 'Time we all went back, I guess.'

'No,' said Andrei. 'You and Valentina stay here and get drunk.' He pushed back his chair and raised himself ponderously to his feet. 'We Russian *men* will take care of the rest of the day's business.'

'Sure?'

'Sure.' He put his hand on her shoulder. 'Relax, Davidova. The coup won't come today, or tomorrow.'

'I know that,' she said. 'But we just lost one more commissar today—'

'Alex, huh, son of a bitch. No loss. I cleared his desktop and locked him out the second he mentioned he was leaving us.'

'He was good at his job, and we don't have a replacement.'

'The economy can get along fine without a commissar for a while,' Andrei said. 'The free market, don't knock it. It's all in Ricardo.'

The two men walked to the bar. Andrei gallantly laid a wad of currency on it, indicating Myra and Valentina with a glance, nodded to them and left with Denis.

'So,' said Valentina, looking after them, 'what do you suppose they're up to?'

'Anything but going back to work, I hope,' Myra laughed. 'Hitting the spaceport bars, or plotting our demise. Whatever. What the fuck.' She downed another vodka; stared at the tip of a cigarette that had burnt down, unregarded; lit another.

'You're drunk already,' Valentina accused.

'And bitter and twisted. Yeah, I know.'

'I'll tell you why they left,' Valentina said. 'Apart from the spaceport attractions, that is.'

'Yeah?'

'They're giving us space, my dear. For a caucus.'

'Women's caucus? Bit dated, that.'

Valentina loosened her uniform jacket, removed her tie and rolled it up carefully. 'Not—what was it called?—feminism, Myra. Socialism. A Party caucus.'

'But I'm not even in the Party!'

'Are you so sure about that?' Valentina asked. '*I've* never seen a resignation letter from you. And I would have, you know. I'm sure you're at least a sympathiser, even if—' she giggled '—you've been missing branch meetings lately.'

Myra had to think about it. She supposed there *was* still a direct-debit mandate paying her dues to some anonymous Caribbean data-haven account. She still got the mailings, filed unread. She still wrote for *Analysis*, the International's online theoretical journal. (Its contributors had nicknamed it *Dialysis*, because of its insistent theme that everything was going down the tubes.)

Myra frowned at Valentina. The noise in the bar was louder than it had been. People were drifting in from other functions going on in the hotel: a business conference, an anime con, and at least two weddings.

'What does it matter?' she asked. 'We're nothing, we're probably among the last Internationalists in the whole fucking *world*.'

'Indeed we are,' said Valentina. 'But there's still a couple of things we can do. One is give our comrade a good send-off, by getting absolutely smashed in his memory.'

They knocked glasses, drank.

'And the other thing?'

'Oh, yes. We can see if there's anything the International is planning to do about the coup.'

'You must be fucking joking.'

'I am not. If you want my guess, that's what they wanted the assets for.'

'Whoever thought of that must be out of their tiny fucking minds. Talk about adventurism.'

'I'm not so sure. Remember, there may not be many of us left in the world, but—' Valentina leaned closer '—there isn't only one world.'

'Oh, don't be—' Myra gave it a second thought. 'Oh,' she said. 'Our friends in the sky.'

'Yeah,' said Valentina. 'The space fraction.'

'I don't want to discuss this right now,' Myra said. She looked around, wildly. The place was jumping. One beautiful Kazakh girl whom she'd thought was a bride yelled something in what sounded like Japanese. Her big white dress shrank like shrink-wrap to her body, changing colour and hardening to a costume of pastel-shaded plastic armour. A smart-suit—made from, rather than by, nanotech—was a heinously expensive novelty, offering a limited menu of programmed transformations. Myra wondered how long it would be before its price plummeted, its repertoire exploded; how long it would be before people could as readily transform their bodies. A world of comic-book super-heroes—it didn't bear thinking about. The girl struck a combative pose, to a scatter of applause from the other anime fans.

'Let's get drunk,' Myra said.

# 5

## THE CHURCH OF MAN

Merrial was, as promised, waiting. She sat on the plinth, as I had done, under the Deliverer's equestrian statue. She wore a loose summer dress with a colourful tiered skirt. Something stirred in my memory, then vanished like a dream in the morning. She was in animated conversation with a man sitting beside her. They both looked up as I arrived.

'Hello,' I said warily.

He was a tall, thin man, about thirty, I reckoned; quite brown, with sharp features and dark eyes which had a sort of quirky, questioning look in them; black hair curly on top, short at the back and sides; dressed in leather trousers and jacket and a white cotton T-shirt with a red bandana. A fine chain hung around his throat beneath the bandana, its pendant—if any—below the T-shirt's round collar.

'Hello,' Merrial said warmly. 'Clovis, this is Fergal.'

The man stuck his right hand out and I shook it, noticing as I did so that one of his thumbs pressed the back of my hand and that he held on, as though waiting for some response, for about a second longer than I subconsciously expected, before letting go.

'Pleased to meet you, Clovis,' he said. His voice was low and deep, his accent was hard to place: correct, but by that very correctness of intonation in each syllable, somehow foreign; it reminded me of a Zanu prince I'd once heard speak at the University.

'Let's get some drinks,' he said, rising to his feet. We strolled to the nearest vacant table outside The Carronade. Fergal took our requests and disappeared inside.

'Who is that guy?' I asked.

Merrial favoured me with a slow smile. 'You sound jealous,' she teased.

'Ah, come on. Just curious.'

·'I've known him a long time,' she said. 'Nothing personal. Just . . . one of us.'

'Well, I had kind of figured he was a tinker.'

Merrial's eyes narrowed slightly. 'Yes, that's it,' she said.

Fergal returned in a few moments, taking his seat beside me and opposite Merrial. I offered him a cigarette, which he accepted with an oddly ironic smile.

'Well,' he said, lighting it, 'you know about the . . . concern, for the ship?'

I nodded. 'Yes, but Merrial said nothing about its being shared.'

He grinned. 'Oh, it's quite widely shared, I can tell you that. It's a brave offer you've made, and—' he spread his hands '—all I can say is, thanks.'

I was more puzzled than modest about this reference to the bravery of my offer, so I just shrugged at that.

'Are you on the project too?'

He seemed amused. 'I'm not on site, but I am on the payroll, if that's what you mean,' he said. 'All of—' he glanced at Merrial '—our profession are very much involved in the project as a whole.' He took a long swallow of beer, and a draw on his cigarette, becoming visibly more relaxed and expansive as he did so. 'Its success matters a lot to us. We're very keen to see the sky road taken again.'

'I like that,' I said. ' "The sky road".'

'Yes,' he said. 'Well, it took you people long enough to get back on it.'

'Back?'

'You walked it once.' Another glance at Merrial, then a smile at me. 'Or we did.'

'Our ancestors did,' I said.

'That's what I meant to say,' he said idly. 'But to business. I'll have to get a piece of equipment that you—or rather, Merrial—is going to need. That's going to take some time, but I'll manage it this weekend. You'll have to book some time off and seats on the Monday train.' He smiled wryly. 'Not much point trying to travel on the Saturday or the Sunday, anyway. No trains and damn slow traffic, even if you wanted to drive.'

I nodded. 'And the University would have all its hatches battened anyway.'

'Yeah, that's a point. Still, can't complain—the free weekend is one of the gains of the working class, eh?'

'You could call it that,' I said. 'Mind you, whether what goes on at the University should count as work—'

We went on talking for a bit. Fergal was cagey about himself, and I didn't press him, and after another couple of beers he got up and left. We had the evening, and the weekend, to ourselves.


Merrial slept, leaning against my shoulder, all the way from Carron Town to Inverness. It seemed a shame for her to miss the journey, but I reckoned she must have seen its famously spectacular and varied scenery before, many more times than I had. Besides, I liked watching her sleep, an experience which, in the nature of our past three nights, I had hitherto not had much time to savour.

We had caught the early train, at 5.15 on the Monday morning. Each of us had separately arranged to have the first two days of the week off, by seeking out our different supervisors in the Carron bars on the Friday evening. It was to be hoped that Angus Grizzlyback would remember that I was not coming in this morning; but if he didn't, I was sure my loyal friends would remind him, with predictable and—as it happened—inaccurate speculation as to how I intended to spend the day.

We had, in fact, spent the Saturday and the Sunday in just that way, very enjoyably, in bed or out on the hills. On the Saturday afternoon Merrial had guddled a trout from a dark, deep pool in the Alt na Chuirn glen; leapt up with the thrashing fish clutched in her hands and danced around, sure-footed on the slippery stones. Again, something had moved in my mind, like a glimpsed flick of a tail in the water, which had—as soon as the shadow of my thought fell on it—flashed away.

The sun rose higher, the shadows shortening, apparently in the face of the train's advance. We stopped at all the small, busy towns built around forestry and light industry and—increasingly as we moved east—farming: Achnasheen, Achnashellach, Achanalt, Garve . . . The electric engine's almost silent glide surprised the short-memoried sheep, rabbits and deer beside the track, and set up a continuous standing wave of animals, sauntering or lolloping or springing away. I saw a wolf's grey-shadowed shape at Achanalt; as we rounded the cliff-face at Garve I saw a wild goat on a shelf; and spotted an eagle patrolling the updrafts above the slope of Moruisg.

I didn't wake Merrial for any of them.

I smoked, once, with a coffee brought around on a rattling trolley by a lass in tartan trews. Neither the sound nor the smell nor the smoke stirred Merrial at all, except to a few deeper breaths, long ripples in the spate of her hair across her breast and over my chest. I let her head nestle in the now awkward crook of my left arm, and alternated the cup and the cigarette in my right hand. It was a quiet train, for all that it was busy, with clerks and traders on their weekly commute from their coastal homes to their work in Inverfefforan or Inverness.

On Merrial's lap, with her left arm—crooked like mine—protectively over it, lay a bulky poke of polished leather, fastened with a drawstring thong. It may have bulged a little larger, and weighed a little heavier, than the kind of bags that lasses tend to lug around, but it would have taken a close and sharp observer to notice. Inside it, concealed by a layer of the sort of oddments one would expect to find in such a poke—a cambric kerchief, cosmetics, small-bore ammunition and the like—was the complicated apparatus that Fergal had delivered to her house early on the Sunday evening. It was built around a seer-stone about fifteen centimetres in diameter, nested in neat coils of insulated copper wire. The strangest aspect, to me, of this device was an arrangement of delicate levers, each marked with a letter of the alphabet, queerly ordered:

QWERTYUIOP...

Probably, I thought, a spell.


'Grotty old place,' said Merrial, rubbing her face with her hands and looking around the damp, flagstoned concourse of Inverness station. Her cheeks reddened, her eyes widened under the smooth friction of her palms. Her dress, this time of blue velvet, looked a bit rumpled. We were standing at the coffee-bar, having twenty minutes to wait for the 8.30 to Glasgow.

I looked up at the creosoted roof with its wide skylight panels and suspended electric lamps. 'At least it doesn't have pigeons.'

'Can't say herring-gulls are much of an improvement.' She kicked out with one booted foot, sending a hungry, red-eyed bird squawking away. One end of the station opened to the platforms, the other to the main street. The arrangement seemed peculiarly adapted to set up cold but unrefreshing draughts. Despite its mossy walls and paving, the station was more recent than the buildings outside, most of which pre-dated the Deliverance, if not all three of the world wars.

I finished my bacon roll, smiled at Merrial—who was mumbling, half to herself and around mouthfuls of her own breakfast, some irritated speculation about the degenerative evolution of scavenging sea-birds—and wandered over to the news-stand. There I stocked up on cigarettes and bought a copy of the *Press and Journal*, a newspaper which outdoes even the *West Highland Free Press* in its incorrigible parochialism and venerable antiquity.

Most of its pages consisted of small advertisements, to do with fishing, farming, uranium and petroleum mining and, of course, Births, Marriages and Deaths. The last of these could take up half a tall column of small print: 'Dolleen Starholm, peacefully in her sleep, aged 251 years, beloved great-great-grandmother of . . .' followed by scores of names; and sometimes (as in this case) the discreet indication of cult affiliation: 'RIP' or 'IHS'. More frequent, and more prominent, were proud affirmations of the orthodox hope: 'Returned by the Flame' (or the Sky or the Sun or the Sea) 'to the One'.

I went back to the counter and, while Merrial finished off her breakfast, scanned the sparse snippets of national and international news that had managed to wedge their way in among the earth-shakingly important football and shinty reports, fishing disputes and Council debates.

The Congress of Paris had ceremonially opened its ninety-seventh year of deliberations, and had immediately plunged into bitter controversy about a proposal to empower the Continental Court to adjudicate border problems between cantons and communes; the apparently more difficult matter of disagreements between countries having been resolved by the Congress long ago, its success had apparently gone to its collective head.

I sighed and turned the page. Another American republic had voted a contribution from tariff revenue to the spaceship project, which was gratifying but mysterious—there was even an editorial comment about it, full of sage mutterings about how their ways were not ours, and that we should not disdain such assistance, immoral though it might seem to us. I wasn't too sure; to me, it smelt of stealing money, but the Americans have a much greater reverence for their governments than people have in more civilised lands. If offered some loot by an African king or Asian magnate or South American cacique, I should hope the International Scientific Society would politely decline, and this case seemed little different. But all of this was, at this moment, quite theoretical, as no such offer, and indeed no news at all, from Asia or Africa appeared in today's edition. I rolled it up and decided to leave the national news until later.

Merrial brushed crumbs from her lips and looked at me with amusement. 'You really look as though you're paying attention to all that,' she said, picking up her leather poke. I hitched my canvas satchel on my shoulder and we strolled to the Glasgow train.

'Well, I do follow the news,' I said, somewhat defensively, as we took our seats, this time facing each other across a table. 'What's wrong with that?'

Merrial shrugged. 'It's so . . . ephemeral,' she said. 'And unreliable.'

'Compared with what?'

'Don't misunderstand me,' she said. 'I'm sure this, what is it—' she reached for the paper, and spread it out '—Congress here is real, and really did do what the article says it did. But it is only a tiny part of the truth, and perhaps not the most important part of what is going on there in Paris. Let alone what is going on elsewhere in Paris. So that, and all the other such pieces give you, really, a false picture of the world.'

I could have been offended, but was not. 'I'm a scholar of history, remember?' I said. 'I understand how newspaper reports, even documents aren't everything—'

'Oh, you don't want to hear what I think about *historical documents*!'

'So what else can you do?'

She frowned at me, puzzled. 'You travel around and find things out for yourself.'

'Aye, if only we all had the time.'

She touched the tip of my nose with the tip of her finger. 'It's what tinkers do, and they have all the time in their lives for it.'

The train pulled out, the Moray Firth in sight at first, with its kelp fields and fish-farms, and then nothing to see for a while but the close-packed pines of Drumossie Wood as the train turned and the engines took the strain of the long, slow ascent to Slochd.

A couple of hours later, maybe, after Speyside of the malts and bleak Drumochter, we were in the long and beautiful glens between Blair Atholl and Dunkeld. On one side of the line were streams full of trout and turbines, on the other hillsides buzzing with the saws and drills of workshops. The train stopped for five minutes at Dunkeld. A small, old town of stone, still with its Christian cathedral.

Merrial looked out of the windows, around at the scene, and sat back with a slight shudder.

'A strange place,' she said, 'with the hills around it like an ambush.'

'But that's why it's a great place,' I said, and told her the story of how the Cameronians had held off the Highland host and saved the Revolution to which they owed their freedom. She listened with more interest, even, than my telling of the tale deserved, and leaned back at the end and said, 'Aye well, maybe there's some use to history, after all. I'll never be afraid of these hills again.'


It was two in the afternoon by the time the train reached Glasgow's Queen Street Station, and glad enough we were to get off it. Sometimes two people who can fascinate each other endlessly when alone together, and who can spark off each other in convivial company, find themselves inhibited among strangers who are unignorably in earshot, and find themselves growing shy and silent and stale. So it was with us, towards the end of that journey. I couldn't even find it in my heart to talk about the Battle of Stirling when we passed through the town.

We both brightened, though, on jumping down on the platform. The familiar Glasgow railway-station smell—of currying fish, and curing leaf, and spark-gapped air, and old iron and wood-alcohol and hot oil and burnt vanilla—hit my sinuses like a shot of poteen. Merrial, too, seemed invigorated by it, taking a deep breath of the polluted stench with a look of satisfaction and nostalgia.

'Ah, it's good to be back,' she said.

I glanced sidelong at her as we walked down the platform. 'When were you in Glasgow? And how could I have missed you?'

She smiled and squeezed my hand. 'Oh, I forget. Ages ago. But the smell brings it back.'

'That and the noise.'

'The what?'

'THE—'

But she was laughing at me.

We crossed the station concourse, agreeing that, on balance, pigeons were a worse nuisance than sea-birds (though, as Merrial gravely pointed out, better eating). This comment, and some of the more appetising components of the smell, reminded us that we were ravenous, so we bought sandwiches and bottles of beer from a stall in the station and carried them out to George Square.

We sat down on a bench by a grassy knoll under the statue of the Deliverer.

'Shee that,' Merrial said, pointing upwards as she munched. 'It'sh mean.'

'What?'

She swallowed. 'The statue. The old city fathers must have been a bit stingy.'

I looked up. 'No argument about the city fathers,' I said. 'They're still tight-fisted. But that statue looks fine to me.'

'The horse is black,' Merrial pointed out. She tapped the handle of her knife on a fetlock. 'And cast in bronze. The lady herself is green—just copper. They got out the oxy-acetylene torches and hacked off the original rider, a king or general or whatever, and stuck the Deliverer in his place!'

I stood up and paced around it, peering.

'You're right,' I said. 'You can see the joins. I must have looked at that statue a hundred times, and not noticed anything wrong with it.' I looked up at the lady's head. 'And she has a different face from the one in Carron Town, and they're both different from any pictures I've seen of the Deliverer.'

'Well, there you go, colha Gree,' she said. 'Some things a tinker can teach a scholar, eh?'

'Oh aye,' I said. I sat down again. 'Mind you, it could hardly be just parsimony—it's a fine piece of work after all, and they've done her hair in gold.'

'Yon's gold *paint*,' she said scornfully. 'And as for artistry, the breed and the trappings of the horse are all wrong for the time and the circumstances.'

She was right there, too, when I looked. This was no steppe horse, bareback broken, roughly saddled, such as was shown quite authentically in Carron Square. Instead, it was a hussar's mount, in elaborate caparison. But I thought then, and still think, that the representation of the Deliverer herself was well done. A fine example of the Glasgow style; which, perhaps, makes the equine bodge appropriate, and part of the artist's point.

We binned our litter and headed for the nearest tramway stop, in Buchanan Street. The transport system is one of Glasgow City Council's proudest public works, a more than adequate replacement for the great Underground circle, which was—it's said—one of the wonders of the ancient world. Judging by the remnants of it that here and there have outlasted centuries of flooding and subsidence, it is quite possible to agree that such it must have been.

The tram came along, bell clanging, and we jumped on and paid our groats and clattered like children up the spiral steps to the upper deck. The bell rang again and the tram lurched forward, creaking up Buchanan Street and swaying as it turned the corner into Sauchiehall.

Glasgow's main drag looked clogged with traffic, but everything—steam-engine and motor-car and horse-cart and bicycle alike—made way for the tram's implacable progress. The pedestrians, at this time of the day, were mostly women shopping. But all of them, whether young lasses just out of school or mothers with young children or retired ladies at their leisure, had to pick up their skirts, their pokes or their weans and run for their lives when the tram bore down on a crossing. The shops and offices from recent centuries are built of logs and planks, and rarely go higher than two storeys. The older, pre-Deliverance buildings are of stone; some have as many as five floors. In ancient times there were much higher buildings, but most of them were made of concrete, which doesn't last well, and—agonising though it may be for archaeology—almost all of their structures have long since been plundered for steel and glass. Their foundations give rectangular patterns to the growth of trees in the forests around Glasgow: Pollock Fields, Possil Wood, Partick Thorn.

Farther away, to the west, we could just make out the haze and smoke from the Clydeside shipyards, on which most of Glasgow's prosperity depended. The shipyards were the seedbed of the skills which—along with Kishorn's deep-water dock, almost unique on this side of the Atlantic—had made Scotland the logical site for the launch-platform's construction.

At the top of Sauchiehall there's a new stone bridge, to replace the original concrete one that has crumbled away. It carried us over the Eighth Motor Way and into Woodlands Road, which runs along beside the Kelvin Woods. (They, and the river that runs through them, are named after Lord Kelvin, who invented the thermometer.)

We stepped off the tram at the crest of University Avenue, and stood for a moment looking at the main building, a huge and ancient pile called Gilmorehill. It looks like a piece of religious architecture that has run wild, but it is solely devoted to secular knowledge, a church of Man.

'It's not as old as it looks,' Merrial said, as though determined not to be impressed. 'That's Victorian Gothic.'

I didn't believe her, but I didn't argue. I had felt in its chill stone and warm wood the shades of Scotus and Knox and Kelvin, of Watt and Millar and Ferguson, and no disputed date could shake my conviction that the place was almost as old as the nation whose mind it had done so much to shape.

'Whatever,' I said. 'Anyway, the department we're going to isn't there.'

'Just as well,' Merrial said.

It was actually in one of the small side streets off University Avenue, all of whose buildings date back at least to the twentieth century. The trees that line it are probably as old, gigantic towers of branch and leaf, taller than the buildings. Their bulk darkened the street, the leaves of their first fall formed a slippery litter underfoot.

'So we just walk up and knock on the door?' Merrial asked.

'No,' I said. 'I've got a key.'

She glanced down at her leather bag. 'And you're sure we won't be challenged?'

'Aye, I'm sure,' I said. We'd been over this before. As a prospective student, with my project already accepted even if as yet unfunded, I had every right to be here—in fact, I should have been here more often, through the summer. So no one should question us, or our presence in the old archive. We'd planned how we'd do the job, but its proximity seemed to be making Merrial more nervous than I was.

'All right,' she said.

The key turned smoothly in the oiled lock, and the tongue clicked back. I pushed the heavy door aside and we stepped in. I locked it behind us. The place was silent, and as far as I could tell it was empty. The hallway was dim and cool, its pale yellow paint darkened by generations of nicotine, and it divided after a few metres into a narrower corridor leading deeper into the Institute and a stairway leading to the upper floors. The place had a curious musty odour of old paper and dusty electric light-bulbs, and a faint whiff of pipe-smoke. I checked the piles of unopened mail on the long wooden table at the side. A few notes for me, which a quick check revealed were refusals of various applications for patronage. I stuffed them in my jacket pocket and led the way up two flights of stairs to the library, switching on the fizzing electric lamps as we went.

Merrial wrinkled her nose as I opened the library door and switched on the lights.

'Old paper,' I said.

She smiled. 'Dead flies.'

I made to close the door after we entered the room, but Merrial touched my arm and shook her head.

'I couldn't stand it,' she said.

'You're right, me neither.' The still, dead air made me feel short of breath.

I held her hand, as much for my reassurance as for hers, as we threaded our way through the maze of ceiling-high book-cases. Merrial, to my surprise, once or twice tugged to make me pause, while she scanned the titles and names on cracked and faded spines with a look of recognition and pleasure.

'*The Trial of the Anti-Soviet Bloc of Rights and Trotskyites*!' she breathed. 'Amazing! Do you know anything about that?'

'It was some kind of public exorcism,' I said, hurrying her along. I'd once glanced into that grim *grimoire* myself, and the memory made me slightly nauseous. 'People claimed they had turned into rabid dogs who would go out and wreck machinery. Horrible. What superstitious minds the communists had.'

Merrial chuckled, but shot me an oddly pleased look.

At the far end of the library the ranks of book-cases stopped. Several tables and chairs were lined up there, apparently for study—but no one, to my knowledge, ever studied at them. The most anyone could do was to put down a pile of books or documents there for a quick inspection of their contents under the reading-lights, before rushing out of the library. I recalled Merrial's comment that people today are more claustrophobic than their ancestors.

Beside these tables was another door, of iron, with a handle but no lock. The mere thought of the possibility of that door's having a lock was enough to give me a cold sweat.

'Here we are,' I said, and added, to make light of it, 'the dark archive.'

'What's inside it?'

'I don't know,' I said. 'I've never been in it.'

She frowned. 'Is it off limits, or what?'

'No, no.' I shook my head. 'It's not forbidden or anything. Hardly anybody wants to go in.'

'No point in hesitating,' said Merrial. 'Let's get it over with.'

I turned the handle and pulled the door back. To fit with my feelings, it should have given off an eldritch squeak, but its heavy hinges were well-lubricated. A couple of times I worked the handle from the inside. It appeared to be in good order, but I dragged one of the chairs over and used it to prop the door open, just in case it closed accidentally.

I switched on the overhead light and stepped with an assumed air of boldness across the threshold. The small back room appeared innocent enough. It had a desk, with a couple of chairs in front of it and on its top a cluster of boxy, bulky structures like models of ancient architecture. Aluminium shelves lined the walls on either side. The air held a different, subtler smell, almost like the smell of washed hair or polished horn, with a sharp note of acetones.

Merrial sniffed. 'Like a rotting honeycomb,' she remarked cheerfully. I fought down a heave.

'Would smoking get rid of the miasma?' I suggested.

'Yes, but it might damage the disks.'

While I was still looking around for anything that remotely resembled a disc, Merrial began rummaging along the shelves. The boxes arrayed there were translucent, the colour of sheepskin, with dusty, close-fitting lids. They contained flat black plates about nine centimetres square and two millimetres thick. She picked out a few at random, held them up and shook them slightly. From every one, a sooty black dust drifted down. Oxidation crystals crusted the small metal plates at their edges. She shook her head. 'Hopeless,' she said.

In other, smaller boxes there were smaller, shiny wafers. These, when she picked them out, simply crumbled to the touch.

'So much for them,' she said. 'We'll just have to see if there's anything on the hard drive.' She pulled up a seat in front of the machines. The largest, before which she sat, had a sort of window-pane on the front of it. She opened her poke, rummaged out the clutter on top and carefully extracted her strange devices. She laid them on the table: the seer-stone glowing with random rainbow ripples, a small black box and the frame of lettered levers, all connected by the coils of insulated copper wire.

'Oh, look, that thing there has the same—'

'Don't touch it!'

'All right.'

She glanced up at me. 'Sorry to snap. I'm a bit jumpy.'

'Aye, well, me too.'

'Also I'm in tinker mode.' She smiled. 'Courtesy doesn't come into it. If you want to help, see if you can find a power source for this thing while I set up my system.' She waved a hand vaguely in the darkness under the table.

Suppressing a qualm, I stooped down into that darkness, and after a moment while my eyes adjusted I saw a dusty power-socket, with three holes. A centimetre-thick cable hung from the back of the table and ended in a

three-pronged plug. Deducing how plug and socket fitted together was the
work of a moment, as was inserting the one into the other.

The light around me brightened suddenly. Merrial's boot hit my ribs,
and she simultaneously uttered an odd imprecation.

'What?'

'Christ, don't *do* th'at!'

Another strange prayer. I crawled backwards from under the table. Mer-.
rial gave me a glare.

'I thought that was what you wanted me to do,' I protested.

'Oh.' She thought about it. 'I suppose you could have taken it that way,
yes. I forgive you. Now come here and sit down.' She patted the seat beside
her.

As I got to my feet I noticed what had happened to the machine, and
where the extra light was coming from. The window on the front of the box
was glowing a pearly grey with darker and lighter flecks swirling through
it, like the sky above a port on a snowy day. I took a step backwards. The
temperature in the room seemed to have dropped a few kelvins. Now I understood why she'd been making these invocations. At moments like that
even the most rational person will utter whatever name of the deity springs
to mind.

'It won't bite,' she said.

I sidled forward, keeping a wary eye on the thing, as one might do towards a dog about whom one had received just such an assurance. With the
hand that Merrial couldn't see, I made the sign of the Horns, then realised
that this was shamefully superstitious and began instead mentally to recite a
few Names of the One, and of the Prophets: Allah, Buddha, Christ, Deity,
Jordan, Justice . . .

'Did I do that?' I asked.

Khomeini, Krishna, Mercy, Mary, Odin, Necessity, Nature . . .

'When you switched the power on, yes.'

Paine, Providence, Quine, Reason, Yaweh, Zoroaster. That should do.

She gazed into my eyes with impish amusement, and reached forward and
stroked my face. The rasp of my stubble sounded uncannily loud.

'It's all right, *mo gràidh*,' she said. 'I'm a tinker. I know what I'm doing.
This thing here—' she patted the top of it '—is just a machine that does the
same thing as the seer-stones, only not so well. It's no a deil, ye ken. It's a
computer.'

'Aye, I know that . . .'

'Well, start acting as if you believed it,' she said.

'But is it a *television*?' I shuddered inwardly at naming that dark instrument of the Possession.

She shook her head. 'No. This here is a keyboard, and this here is a screen. The screen, or monitor, works on a similar principle to a television, but it is not a television. And even if it was, it couldn't do you any harm.'

Easy enough for her to say that, I thought, but wisely didn't say.

'Assuming it still works at all,' she added cheerfully. 'The chips got fried in the Deliverance, for the most part.'

(Me neither, but that's what she said.)

She rattled a few keys. The screen's snowstorm responded not at all.

'Control alt delete,' she said to herself, and hit three keys simultaneously. Nothing happened, again.

'Hmm,' she said. She reached forward and prodded a stud on the machine. The screen turned black.

'So much for that one,' she said. She stood up and leaned over the table and started looking more closely at the various boxes.

'Hey!' she said. 'Got it! One of these looks like it's radiation-hardened!' She reached in among the boxes and started fiddling dangerously with live cables, removing a lead from the back of the box we'd used and sticking it in the back of another one. What had seemed to be merely the blank front of that box suddenly lit up, a smoothly shining grey, revealing itself to be a screen.

'Yess!' said Merrial, punching the air.

By this point I was beginning to get a grip on myself, though I must admit I almost lost it completely when Merrial turned around and prodded a letter on the keyboard and the words 'Demon Internet Software' flashed up on the screen.

Allah, Buddha, Christ . . .

'All right,' Merrial said briskly, as the screen with the three sinister names disappeared and was replaced by a picture with lots of tiny pictures spread out on it. 'We've got this bugger up and running, but Christ knows how long it'll stay up.' (She talked this way, I'd come to notice, with its curious combination of obscure sexual and religious references, when she was in what she'd called her 'tinker mode.') 'So what we better do is whip the stuff out of it ay ess ay pee.'

'Out of it what?'

'As. Soon. As. Possible.'

'Oh, right. Toot sweet.'

'What?'

I waved a hand. 'Let's get on with it, as you say.'

'Yip.'

She carefully uncoiled one of the strands of copper wire, and attached a little peg with a copper pin to the end. This she inserted in a round hole (which, she explained, did not fucking have to be round the fucking back, but fucking was) in the pediment of the computer.

'Right,' she said. The tip of her tongue between her lips, she tapped out the words 'Myra Godwin', the name of the Deliverer, on the keyboard. They simultaneously appeared on the screen and on the now black seer-stone.

'Go,' she said, hitting another key.

A few seconds passed (tongue between the teeth again) and the screen and the stone filled with a list of titles which crept slowly upwards, its top moving out of sight, and which kept on going for several minutes.

When the list had stopped its crawl she said, 'OK, copy,' and rattled at the keyboard again. A picture of an hourglass appeared on the screen, and the sand began to run. The seer-stone, meanwhile, showed a tree, branching and budding and growing leaves.

After about a minute and a half the sand had all flowed from the top half of the glass, and the stone was filled with green. Both displays vanished.

'That's it,' Merrial said.

'That's all?'

'Yes,' she grinned. 'That's all the files that mention Myra Godwin transferred, from the dark storage to the stane. No bad going, eh?'

'Brilliant,' I said. She stood up, leaned around behind the computer again, disconnected her wire and wound it quickly around her hand. Then she poked a few more keys on both keyboards. The screen went that shining grey again, and the stone went back to black.

She smiled at me. 'You have my permission to turn the power off.'

We left the small room, and the larger library, exactly as we had found them, and walked quietly down the stairs and out of the Institute. When we were a few metres down the street and away we hugged each other and yelped.

'We did it!' Merrial gloated. 'We actually fucking did it!'

'Yes, I still can hardly believe it,' I said. I caught her hand. 'Now what do we do?'

'We look at what we've got,' she said. 'Somewhere no one will see us, or bother us.'

I knew just the place.


Because it was vacation time there were few students around, so my landlady was happy to rent me my usual small room above the bookshop on Southpark Avenue for one night. She didn't raise an eyebrow as she took my five marks and handed over a bedroom key, even though it was only about half past four in the afternoon. I suppose she assumed we wanted to use the room for sex.

She gave us a quick cup of coffee and shared a smoke, and a couple of months' worth of local gossip, in the back of her kitchen, then waved us upstairs with a wink at me. The room had a fairly generous, though notionally single, bed and a chair and table and power socket. The window had been left open, but its only view was of the back yard. Still, one could look out and see the sky any time one wanted.

'Perfect,' Merrial said.

She unloaded the seer-stone and its peripheral pieces again and set them up on the table, running a small cable from the black box to the wall socket. The little box began to hum faintly, and at the same moment a human face loomed out of the dark of the seer-stone, mouthing distress.

'Ah, fuck that,' Merrial said. She rubbed the stone with a cuff, and the face fell apart into flecks of colour. 'Now,' she said, 'let's get on with sorting and searching. We're looking for stuff from before the Deliverance, but finding it in this lot won't necessarily be easy. Let's hope the files are date-stamped.'

She sat in the chair, motioning to me to perch on the table, and started tapping away at her version of a keyboard. 'Ah, good, we can sort by date.'

The list reappeared in the depths of the glassy stone, this time with a stack of articles at the top with a single date of 28 May 2059. Merrial stroked with her finger gently and slowly along a tiny bar on the keyboard, then tapped another key. 'Let's see what this is.'

We peered together into the glass and began to read.

Bankrupt of any perspective for overcoming the crisis, the ruling elite can only sit and watch as society disintegrates beneath it. Factories fail to fulfil their obligations, corruption is rife, and the real value produced in the economy continues to plummet. Many industrial sectors actually produce negative value: their output is worth less—in market or any other terms—than the raw materials they take in; in essence, they are vast organisations for spoiling resources.

In the absence of any genuine move towards a market, or—from the other side—any initiative from the workers, the system can only continue to disintegrate.

'Sounds like 2059 all right,' Merrial said. 'That was what the Deliverance delivered us *from.*'

I nodded, cautiously. 'Let's just look further down . . .'

What cannot be ruled out is that the Moscow oligarchy could launch some diversionary military adventure, but this too would rapidly develop its own problems, and intensify those of the centre.

'Damn!' I said.

'What?'

'This isn't 2059, it's more like 1999!'

The invasion of Afghanistan must be seen in this context.

'No, it's 1979! Well—' I frowned at the date at the foot of the article '—actually 1980, but it was written about the situation in '79. In the Soviet Union.' I laughed bitterly. 'The reason it's a bit difficult to tell at first what period she's talking about is that it was in the Soviet Union that the collapse started, right there in the 1970s. After the Soviet Union disintegrated it just got worse, and spread.'

This much was a fairly well-accepted historical account, which I'd covered in my undergraduate studies in Ancient History.

'So why's it dated 2059?' Merrial asked. She stroked the bar and rolled the list down again. 'Hah!' she said. 'This file, and a whole lot of others by the look of it, were put *on to* the computer at that date. Which doesn't mean they were created then. I don't know if I can extract the original creation date, either.'

'Wait a minute,' I said. 'Maybe this is where I can help. I should be able to tell the rough date from the titles of the files, or maybe a quick look at their contents.'

'There are thousands of files in there,' she pointed out. 'If dating each of them takes as long as it did to date that one, we'll be here all night.'

I smiled. 'Why should that be a problem?'

It turned out not to be a problem. Although the bulk of the files had the same date in the 'date' column of Merrial's machine, and she gave up looking for a way to find what she called the 'create-date', quite a large number of the files had a date reference of some kind in their titles. These were apparently articles from magazines or newspapers, by Myra Godwin or about her. We quite quickly got into a way of working that let me identify such files, and Merrial deal with them, copying the date from the title to another 'date' column. After ten minutes of this she hit her forehead with the heel of her hand and cried, 'Stop!'

'What is it?'

'We're wasting our time. *I'm* wasting our time, I mean.' She rubbed her hands. 'What we need here is a wee program, to scan the titles for dates, extract them, reformat them and then sort by date . . .'

'I'll take your word for it,' I said, not having understood all of her words. She waved me away, with a look of abstracted concentration on her face.

'This'll be easy,' she said. 'It'll save us hours.'

I sat on the windowsill, smoking a cigarette, while her fingers flickered over the small keyboard, making a pattering noise like rain on a roof. It struck me that there seemed to be no discernible difference between the white logic and the black, but no doubt this only showed my ignorance.

'Yess!' she said. 'No bother.'

She hit a key and sat back. Then she leaned forward again, peering at the stone.

'Oh fffuck!'

I eyed her warily.

'I used fucking two-digit year-dates. Force of habit. Fucking thing falls over on the year 2000.'

The pattering started again.

About half an hour later Merrial had the files partially ordered by date, and we could dig about in them with a little more confidence in their relevance to our concerns.

' "Defence Policy Contract (Expiry), Vatican City, 11 December 2046",' Merrial read out. 'That looks interesting.'

She pressed one of her keys and the file, as she put it, opened: instead of the title glowing a little brighter among the others, we could see the whole document. Parts of it were in impenetrable legal language (parts of it, in fact, were in Latin) but there was enough there for us to form a good idea of what it was about.

Merrial paused before opening another file, one labelled 'Mutual Protection/Space Merchants/2058'.

We looked at each other, both a little pale, each waiting for the other to speak first.

Merrial swallowed hard, and reached for one of my cigarettes.

'You do know,' she said slowly, 'just what the Deliverer had to do to make a living, under the Possession?'

'Well . . .' I could feel my lower lip moving back and forth over the edge of my teeth, and stopped it. 'Yes. It's one of the aspects of history that historians tend not to talk about. In popular works, that is.'

'Ohh!' Merrial let out a held breath in relief. 'You know about the slave camps, then.'

'What?' For a fleeting instant, I literally saw a black shadow before my eyes. I pointed at the seer-stone's script. 'I thought you were talking about the nuclear blackmail!'

Merrial looked puzzled. 'Nuclear blackmail? I know she got some nuclear weapons from the *Papanich*, that's right here. What has that to do with how she made her living?'

'Oh, Reason above!' I clutched my head. 'Let's get this straight. *You* think the dirty secret is that she ran *slave camps*. I think it's that she trafficked in nuclear threats.'

Merrial sighed. 'Yes, that's it.' She unfurled her hand and forearm with parodied politeness. 'You first.'

'All right.' I noticed that my left knee was juddering up and down; I stood up, and paced the floor as I spoke. 'You know about nuclear deterrence?'

'Oh, aye,' she said, with a grimace.

'Well, yes, to us the policy of threatening to burn to death many great cities and their inhabitants seems wicked, but the ancients didn't see it that way. In fact, some of them began to see nuclear deterrence as a good, which like all goods would be better bought and sold by businesses than provided by governments. The trouble was, all nuclear weapons were owned by governments, and were impossible to buy and hard to steal.

'So Myra Godwin and her husband, Georgi Davidov, stole a government. Davidov was a military man, and he carried out a military coup in a part of Kazakhstan, in a region which was very unpleasant and barren but which did happen to have a large stockpile of nuclear weapons. In a way, what happened was that the soldiers who manned the nuclear weapons decided to claim some territory, and nobody dared gainsay them.

'The local people had suffered grievously under the rule of the Communists. Stalin had starved at least a million of them in the 1930s. But things had improved a lot, and after the fall of the Communists they found themselves worse off under the lairds and barons and usurers. The real answer to their problems was not known at the time, or not known widely enough, and they began to hanker for the secure if limited life they had known before.

'This was where Myra and Georgi had their stroke of genius. While Myra was studying here she was a follower of a man called Trotsky, who had been killed by Stalin and who became a banner for a different kind of communism, purged of Stalin's crimes. As if there could be such a thing!'

'What do you mean?' Merrial asked, narrow-eyed.

'Oh, come on, you know, *communism*—' The word made me physically nauseous, as though dirty hands were pawing me. 'Everybody minding each other's business, everybody *owned* by everybody else, and that's just the ideal! What could that be but evil? Let alone the reality, of a small ruling group doing the minding and the owning!'

'How did that help the Deliverer?'

I shrugged. 'She may have believed it when she was young. Nobody's perfect. But when the Davidovs set up their state, they did so in the name of Trotsky, even though they did not really believe in him anymore. They kept enough communism to keep people secure, and enough freedom to let them be happy and rich.'

Merrial's face was set in an interested but carefully neutral expression.

'And the way they got rich,' I went on, 'was this. They started selling options to use the nuclear weapons they held. That way, states that had no nuclear weapons of their own could have nuclear deterrence. They were quite open about it, but they had to stop after the Third World War, when the last empire consolidated its grip.'

I sighed and shrugged. 'It's a blot on her record, I'll give you that. But they never actually used them.'

Merrial looked a bit shaken. 'So the scholars have known that all along? Well, I know what Godwin's people did after they lost their little nuclear threat business.' She smiled, thin-lipped. 'It seems you don't.'

She opened the other file. This one, which I read with growing horror, was about a very different contract. It was a monthly report on work done by prisoners, guarded by a company called Mutual Protection, for another company called Space Merchants.

'Prison labour was another *good*,' Merrial said, 'that our Deliverer thought best to supply on the free market.'

'But that's slavery!'

'Indeed it is,' said Merrial. 'That's why we don't talk about it. I wouldn't be surprised if some of your scholars have covered it up too.' Her eyes narrowed. 'Maybe some of the senior tinkers know about this nuclear business, and all. But they don't talk about it.'

We sat looking at each other, with the sudden passion of people who have lost something that they believed in, and have only each other left. It was all the more bitter because we each had separately thought we had been told the worst about the great woman, had smugly thought we were mature enough to know it and keep it quiet from the gullible populace, and we each had found that we had ourselves been gulled by our own guild; that there was an even darker tale to tell. My mind was racing, and I could feel a headache coming on. At the same time I felt a sense of release, a small deliverance, as the image of the Deliverer toppled in my mind.


With a short break when we wandered out into the warm evening for dinner in a fish restaurant by the Kelvin, we worked through the files. We found plenty about Myra Godwin's strange career—more than enough to write a pretty sensational biography—but nothing about what had happened around the time of the Deliverance itself. It was after nine when Merrial jumped up and hissed, 'Shit! Shit!'

'What's the matter?'

'I've found a catalogue file. No meaningful title, wouldn't you just fucking believe it. And it's got far, far more entries than we've got files here. We just got the low-security stuff! The rest is still in the University's dark storage.'

I rubbed my sore eyes, and reached out for Merrial's hand. 'So what's still there might be *worse*?'

'You said it. It might even contain the stuff we're looking for. We have to go back.'

# 6

## LIGHT WEAPONS

Long ago there had been another country, called the International. It was a country of the mind, a country of hope, and it encompassed the world. Until one day, in August 1914, its citizens went to war with each other, and the world ended. Everything died in that war, God and Country and International and Civilisation; died, and went to hell. Everybody died. The survivors thought they were alive, but they were not. After August 1914 there had been no living people in the world—only dead people on leave, the damned and the demons.

The last morally responsible people in the world had been the Reichstag fraction of the German Social-Democratic Party. They had voted the credits for the Kaiser's war, against every resolution of their past. They had known the right thing to do, and they had chosen the wrong. All subsequent history had been that of the damned, of poor devils struggling in the hell these men had pitched them into; and nobody could be judged for how they behaved in hell.

This thought, with its bleak blend of Christian and Marxist heresies, had originally been expounded to her by David Reid, one night many decades ago, when he was very drunk. It had sustained Myra through many a bad night. At other times—in the days, and the good nights—it seemed a callow undergraduate nihilism, shallow and wicked and absurd. But in the bad nights it struck her as profound and true, and, in its way, life-affirming. If you thought of people as *alive* and *each having a life to live*, you'd get so depressed at what so many had got instead, this past century and a half, that on a bad night you'd be tempted to add your own death to theirs, and thus make an undetectable increment to that already unimaginable, unthinkable number.

A number which Myra, on her bad nights, suspected she had already increased quite considerably. Not directly—if she had sinned at all, it had been a sin of omission—and nobody had ever blamed her for it, but she blamed herself. If she had sold the deterrence policy to the German imperialists when they'd needed it, torn up all her existing contracts and sorted them out later, how many people would now be alive who now were dead? On the bad nights the answer seemed to run into millions. At other times, on more sober reflection, she realised she wasn't in that league; she wasn't up there with the Big Three; there was almost a sort of adolescent self-dramatisation in the pretension; if she belonged in that company at all it was in the second or third rank, below the great revolutionaries but up there with the more destructive of the great imperialists, Churchill and Mountbatten and Johnson and people of that ilk.

Her shoes were kicked off under a chair, the black crêpe and dévoré dress was across the back of the chair, the sable hat was flung in a corner, the black fur coat was on the floor, the whisky bottle was open on the table and Leonard Cohen's black lyrics disturbed the smoky air: Manhattan, then Berlin, indeed.

Myra was having one of her bad nights.

The late-spring night outside the thin, old curtains was cold, and the central-heating radiator didn't do much to hold back the chill. The main room of the flat felt small, almost cramped, like a student bedsit. She had a kitchen, a bathroom, a bedroom; but most of what defined her life was crammed into this living-room. The shelves were lined with books, two or three rows deep, though she had the entire 2045 edition (the last) of the Library of Congress, sharing space with its Sterling search engine on a freebie disk somewhere in the clutter. Her music, her computer software and hardware, her pictures, all were piled up in similarly silted layers of technological generations, with the most recent stuff at the top or on the outside, and everything back to CDs and PCs and even, at some pre-Cambrian level, vinyl, in the strata below. She had, in her eyeband, ready access to any scene on Earth or off it, but she still had posters on the walls.

Once, these posters had consisted mainly of old advertisements for the ISTWR's exports. But in recent years, one by one, the tacked-up shots of lift-offs and payloads, missiles and explosions had been tugged down in moments of shame and fury, to be crumpled and binned, and replaced by scenes of Kazakh nature and tradition. Mountains and meadows, horsemen and peasants, dancers in embroidered costumes—a whole oriental Switzerland of tourist attractions. Kazakhstan was not doing too badly, even today. It had moved away from its disastrous, Soviet-era polluting industries and extractive monocultures, and put its prairies to a more productive and natural use in cattle-raising. The Kazakh horsemen were back in the saddle.

Myra leaned back and stretched. It was nearly midnight. She'd had far too much to drink. Her few hours in the bar with Valentina had been followed by an hour or two of drinking on her own. She was so drunk she was lucid, 'fleeing' as Dave used to call it. Or possibly she was sobering up, smoothly and gradually, and was in the state where repeated applications of the hair of the dog were postponing the inevitable hammer-blow of the hangover. But drunk or sober, with or without Reid's antinomian justification, she had to act. She had to reach the International.

There were two Internationals ('for large values of two' as Reid had once put it, alluding to the numerous splits): the Second and the Fourth. When most people talked about *the International*, they meant the Second—the successor of the one that had torn itself apart in 1914, and had painfully reassembled its severed limbs in the course of three world wars, five world slumps and one successful world revolution. Even today it was massive: the Socialist International's affiliated parties and trade unions and co-operatives and militias had an aggregate membership in the tens of millions, still.

What Myra meant, and Valentina meant, and Georgi had meant by *the International* was a less imposing institution, a remnant of a fragment, most of it embedded in the greater body of the Second, a splinter travelling slowly through its veins. The Fourth International's membership was in the low thousands, scattered around the world—and, as Valentina had reminded her, off the world, thanks to its pioneering efforts at unionising the space rigs back in the 2020s. It was now almost dormant, a tenuous network of old comrades who couldn't quite say goodbye to each other, or to the dreams of their fervent younger days.

The radical sects of the English Revolution, the Muggletonians and Cameronians and Fifth Monarchy Men, had persisted as dwindling, marginal congregations for centuries after their Kingdom had failed to come; so it would be, Myra thought, for the erstwhile partisans of the Fourth. She knew that, but still she had paid her dues.

Now it was time to get something back for her money. For a start, she could find out what her comrades had done with her country's nukes.

Myra flew through virtual space, drunk in charge of a data-drive. New View floated before her, its image filling her eyeband's field. The habitat was a sort of orbital commune—world socialism, in a very small world—which had been put together by the left wing of the space movement, back when such ideas seemed to matter. The graticule showed it was hundreds of metres across, a circular accretion of habitats, salvaged fuel-tanks, cannibalised space-craft. She reached out and turned it about in her datagloved hands, mildly amused at the chill, prickly tactile feedback, and peered at the small print of addresses on the hull until she found the name she sought.

Logan; whether forename or surname, real name or party name she didn't know; she'd never heard the man called anything else. There it was, scribed on a hull panel from an old McDonnell Douglas SSTO heavy-lifter. She tapped it and the view zoomed in, to show a window with the man's face peering out. It was an engagingly apt interface. Myra zapped a hailing code, and the face at the window responded.

'Oh, hi? Myra Godwin? Just a moment, please.' The fetch wavered and Logan's real face, subtly different, seamlessly replaced it, pulling back as the window icon widened to an interior view of an actually windowless room.

The compartment was full-spectrum strip-lit, the glowing tubes like shafts of sunlight among intertwined vines and branches, cables and tubes. Logan floated in the centre of the room. His cropped white hair matched his white stubble. He wore a faded blue singlet and baggy pants. Around his brow was a toolkit headband on which a loupe and a light were mounted; a standard eyeband was shoved higher up on his forehead. He was bent around the open back of a control-panel which he had gripped between his feet and was working on with a hand laser and a set of jeweller's screwdrivers.

He flipped the loupe up from his eye and grinned at her.

'Well, Myra, long time no see.' He still had the London accent, overlaid with a space-settler drawl. His space fraction had picked up a lot of people she and Georgi had known in Kazakhstan, tough trade-union militants blooded in the Nazbarayev years.

'Yeah, I've missed you too, Logan. How's life on New View?'

Logan gestured with one hand, automatically making a compensating movement with the other. 'OK. We've got pretty much up to complement population-wise, near a thousand last time I checked. We're making a good living, though—got a lot of products and skills the white settlers need. And the old Mars project is chugging along.'

'You're still doing *that*?'

Logan turned up his thumb. 'Kitting out the expedition, bit by bit. No intention of hanging around here forever—not with the white settlers staking out the Moon, anyhow. Nobody's even got much scientific interest in Mars any more, 'specially after that contamination thing came out.'

Myra nodded glumly. It had indeed come as a bit of a disappointment that Mars had an entire biosphere of busily evolving micro-organisms, of recent origin; in the 1970s the Soviets had proudly deposited a piece of paper autographed by Leonid Brezhnev on the Red Planet, which was now being very slowly terraformed by the descendants of bacteria from the General Secretary's sweat.

'So we're gonna go for it,' Logan went on. 'Some time in the next couple of years, we're moving it out.'

'You're going to move *New View*?' Myra smiled at Logan, and at herself—each question so far had ended on a high note of astonishment.

'Minus a few hundred tons of stuff we won't need, but basically, yes. Fill her up—well, fill up a few tanks, I mean—with Lunar polar water, buy a fusion engine from the white settlers and push off on a Hohmann orbit. We got enough old spacecraft lashed into this junk-heap to build landers, then habitats on the ground.'

'You've got it all worked out, I see,' said Myra. 'Well, good luck to you with that.' The Mars colony scheme had been pending, Real Soon Now, on Logan's agenda for as long as she'd known him. 'However, I've got something a bit more urgent to ask you. These white settlers of whom you speak, they aren't by any chance the people I once made a lot of money out of sticking on top of Protons and Energias and sending out there?'

'That's the ones,' Logan said. 'And the new lot coming out on the diamond ships, of course.' He laughed. 'The colonial bourgeoisie!'

'Well, whatever you want to call them,' said Myra, 'you know they're planning to take charge, through the ReUN and the battlesats?'

'Oh, sure,' Logan said. 'Everybody knows that.' He shrugged. 'What can you do? And anyways, what difference is it gonna make to us?' He flourished his tiny laser. 'We're safe.'

'No, you're not,' said Myra. She flicked her gaze upwards, checking the firewall 'ware. It was sound. 'I've just learned—from my Defence Minister, no less—that *I* have a clump of city-buster nukes stashed somewhere in the clutter around you.'

'Is that a problem?' Logan asked. 'Best place for them, surely.'

She had to admire his cool.

'Somehow I don't think that was why the International asked for them to be put there.'

'Ah,' said Logan. 'So you know about that.'

'Yeah,' said Myra. 'Thanks a bunch for not telling me.'

Logan mumbled something entirely predictable about need-to-know. Myra cut off his ramble with an angry chop of her hand.

'Give me a fucking break,' she said, exasperated. 'I can figure that out for myself. The nukes are an element of the situation, but they're not my main concern right now. I just thought I should let you know that I know about them, for the same reason that you should've told me: for the sake of politeness, if nothing else. OK?'

'Well, yeah, OK,' Logan allowed, grudgingly. 'So what is your main problem?'

'I was wondering,' said Myra, 'if you'd grabbed them because you intended to do something about the coup. Like, you know, stop it.'

Logan laughed. 'Me personally?'

'No. The International. And don't tell me you *personally* are the only member it's got up there.'

'Oh, no, not at all.' Logan stared at her, obviously puzzled. 'We got plenty of comrades, I mean New View is basically ours, but it's been a long time since the Party had an army, Myra, you know that as well as I do. We do have a military org, like, but it's just a . . . a small cadre.'

'Of course I know that. But I also know what a small military cadre is *for*. It's so that when you do need an army you can recruit your soldiers from *other* armies. You telling me the space fraction's done no Party work on the battlesats? In all those years?'

Logan looked uncomfortable. 'Not exactly, no, I'm not saying that. We have—well, naturally we have sympathisers, we get reports—'

'And so do we,' she said. 'Some of them from the same comrades as you do.' She wasn't entirely certain of this—need-to-know, again—but it would give him something to think about. 'Who actually knows about the nukes?'

'Valentina Kozlova,' said Logan. 'And your ex-husband, Georgi Davidov.' If Logan noticed Myra's involuntary start at this news, he gave no sign. 'And me, obviously. That's it. The only people who know. Unless there's been a leak.'

'Hmm,' said Myra. 'Reid doesn't seem to know about them—he knows we have nukes in space, but he thinks they're all in Earth orbit.' She paused. 'Wait a fucking minute. If you're the only person up here who knows about them, then the request from the Party a couple of years ago was in fact a request from you. You, personally.'

'Well, yeah,' Logan said. He didn't seem bothered at all. 'In my capacity as Party Secretary for the space fraction, that is.'

'You took it upon yourself to do *that*? What the fuck was on your *mind*?' God, she thought, there I go again with the incredulous screech. She added, in a flat, steady voice, 'Besides, what gave you the right to interfere in my section, and in my section's state?'

Logan squirmed, like someone shifting uncomfortably in an invisible chair. 'I had a valid instruction to do it. From the military org.'

'Ah! So there *is* someone else who knows about it!'

'Not as such,' said Logan. 'The military org is . . .' He hesitated.

'Like you said, a small cadre?' Myra prompted.

'In a manner of speaking,' said Logan. He looked as though he was steeling himself for an admission. 'It's an AI.'

Myra felt her back thump against the back of her chair—she was literally thrown by this statement. She took a deep breath.

'Let's scroll this past us again, shall we? Tell me if I've got this right. Two years ago, at the Sputnik centenary, Val gets a message from you, asking for part of our stash of nukes. It's a valid Party request, she decides I don't need to know, and she blithely complies. And the reason this happened is because *you* got a request from a fucking *computer*?'

'An AI military expert system,' Logan said pedantically. 'But yeah, that's about the size of it.'

Myra groped blindly for a cigarette, lit it shakily.

'And just how long has the Fourth International been taking military advice from an AI?'

Logan did some mental arithmetic.

'About forty years,' he said.


It was no big secret, Myra learned. Just one of those things she'd never needed to know. The AI had originated as an economic and logistic planning system devised by a Trotskyist software expert in the British Labour Party. This planning mechanism had been used by the United Republic of Great Britain, and inherited by its self-proclaimed successor, the underground Army of the New Republic, after Britain had been occupied, and its monarchy restored, by the Yanks in the Third World War. It had acquired significant upgrades, not all of them intended, during the twenty-year guerilla war that followed, and had played some disputed role in the British national insurrection during the Fall Revolution in 2045. Its central software routines had been smuggled into space by a refugee from the New Republic's post-victory consolidation. It had been expanding its capacities, and its activities, ever since.

'Most people call it the General,' Logan told her. 'Aces the Turing, no sweat.'

'But what's it doing?' Myra asked. 'If it's such a shit-hot adviser, why aren't we winning?'

'Depends what you mean by "we",' Logan said. 'And what you mean by "winning".'

Myra had, she realised, no answer to that. Perhaps the AI adviser had picked up on the *Analysis* analysis, and agreed that the situation was hopeless.

Logan was looking at her with sympathetic curiosity, a sort of reversed mirror-image of the hostile bafflement she was directing at him. He must have gone native up there; he'd got used to this situation, and to this style of work, over the decades, and had forgotten the common courtesies of even their notional comradeship.

'Anyways,' he was saying, 'you can ask it all that yourself.' He poked, absently, at the control-panel between his feet; looked up; said, 'Putting you through.'

Before Myra could so much as open her mouth, Logan had vanished, and had been replaced by the military AI. She'd had a mental picture of it, ever since Logan had first mentioned it: something like the *Jane's* software, a VR gizmo of lines and lights. At best a piece of simulant automation, like Parvus.

He was a young man in sweat-stained camos, sitting casually on a rock in a clearing in temperate woodland: lichen and birch-bark, sound of water, birdsong, leaf-shadow, a wisp of woodsmoke. It looked like he'd paused here, perhaps was considering setting up a camp. The man looked every inch the commandante—his long, wavy black hair and his black stubble and dark eyes projected something of the glamour of Guevara, the arrogance of Trotsky. He also reminded Myra, disturbingly, of Georgi—enough to make her suspect that the image she saw was keyed to her personality; that it had been precisely tuned to give her this overwhelming impression of presence, of charisma.

'Hello,' he said. 'I've wanted to meet you for a long time, Myra.'

She opened her hands. 'You could have called.'

'No doubt I would have done, quite soon.' The entity smiled. 'I prefer that people come to me. It avoids subsequent misunderstandings. Anyway—I understand you have two concerns: the nukes at Lagrange, and the space-movement coup. Regarding the first—the nukes are still under your control. Your Defence Minister still has the access codes. I requested that the weapons themselves be moved here for security.' He shrugged, and smiled again. 'They're all yours. So are the weapons in Earth orbit—which are, of course, more immediately accessible, and usable. This brings me to your other concern—the coup. It is imminent.'

'How imminent?'

'In the next few days. They'll ram through the vote on reorganisation of the ReUN, and the new Security Council will issue orders to seize the battlesats. They have the forces to do it.'

He paused, looking at her, or through her. 'But we have the forces to stop it. I can assure you, Myra, it's all in hand.'

She shook her head. 'That isn't what our intelligence indicates. I've checked, my Defence and Foreign ministries have checked. We have agents in the battlesats, as you must know—hell, some of them must be in your own military org! *If* such a thing exists.' She wished she had read some of those mailings.

'It most certainly does exist,' the General said firmly. 'And it's been feeding you disinformation.'

'*What?*'

The entity stood up and stepped towards her in its virtual space. It spread its hands and assumed an apologetic expression, but with a sly conspiratorial gleam in its eyes.

'Forgive me, Comrade Davidova. This was not done against you. It was done against our common enemy: Reid's faction of the space movement.'

'How—' she began, but she saw, she saw.

'I'm telling you this now,' the General said, 'because today you lost your last disloyal Commissar. Alexander Sherman has been passing on information to Reid for months. He wasn't the first, but he was the last.'

'Who were the others?'

The General moved his hand in a smoothing gesture. 'I can't tell you that without compromising current operations. That particular information is of no further use to you anyway.'

'I suppose not,' Myra concurred reluctantly. She wished she knew who the traitors were, all the same; hoped Tatanya and Michael hadn't been among them. She'd quite liked those two . . .

'So you used them—and *us*—as a conduit for disinformation?'

The General nodded. 'And for information going the other way—your updates to *Jane's* have been most helpful.'

'Jeez.' Her reactions to this were interestingly complicated, she thought distantly. On the one hand she felt sore at having been used, having been lied to; on the other, she could admire the stagecraft of the deception. Above all she felt relieved that the gloomily negative assessments she'd worried over were all wrong.

Unless the situation was even *worse* than she'd thought—

'The situation is better than you think, by far,' said the General. 'We have our people in place—the battlesats won't be taken without a struggle, which in most cases we expect to win.'

'*Most cases* won't be enough. Even one battlesat—'

'Indeed. Which is where your orbital weaponry comes in. The lasers, the EMP bursters, the smart pebbles, the hunter-killers, the kinetic-energy weapons . . .'

Myra hadn't known her arsenal was so extensive. (God, to think that stockpile had once belonged to the Pope! Well, to the Swiss Guards, anyway—quite possibly His Holiness had been discreetly left out of the loop on that one.) She shivered in her wrap, tugged it around her shoulders, lit another cigarette. She didn't know what to say; she felt her cheeks burning under the General's increasingly quizzical regard.

'What do you want us to do with them?' she asked at last.

'I'm sure you can work that out,' he said. 'I'll be in touch.'

'But—'

He gave her a smile; heartbreaking, satanic.

'I hope I see you again,' he said. He reached out a hand and made some fine adjustment to the air. The link went down.

Myra took off her eyeband and rubbed her eyes. Then she walked unsteadily to the kitchen and made some tea, and sat drinking it and smoking for about ten minutes, staring blankly into the virtual spaces of her mind. She supposed she should do something, or tell someone, but she couldn't think what to do, or whom to tell.

Time enough in the morning, she decided.

Her bedroom was small, a couple of metres' clearance on three sides of the double bed giving barely enough space for a wardrobe and dressing-table. Over the years the room had accumulated a smothering snowfall of soft furnishings, needlework and ornaments; pretty things she'd bought on impulse and never had the heart to throw out. The process was a natural selection for an embarrassingly large collection of grannyish clutter. Now and again—as now—it infuriated her in its discrepancy with the rest of her life, her style, her look. And then, on reflection, she'd figure that the incongruity of the room's appearance was what made it a place where she could forget all care, and sleep.


In the morning it seemed like a dream.

All the more so, Myra realised as she struggled up to consciousness through the layers of sleep and hangover and tangled, sweat-clammy bedding, because she *had* dreamed about the General. She felt vaguely ashamed about that, embarrassed in front of her waking self; not because the dream had been erotic—though it had been—but because it had been besotted, devoted, *servile*; like those dreams the Brits used to have about Royalty. She sat up in the bed and pushed back the pillow, leaned back and tried to think about it rationally.

The entity, the military AI, would have had God only knew how many software generations to evolve an intimate knowledge of humanity. It had had time to become what the Japanese called an *idoru*, a software representation that was better than the real thing, smarter and sexier than any possible human mind or form, like those wide-eyed, faux-innocent anime brats or the simulated stars of pornography and romance. Sex wasn't the half of it—there were other codes, other keys, in the semiotics of charm: the subtle suggestions of wisdom, the casual hints at a capacity for violence, the assumed readiness to command, the mirroring glance of empathy; all the elements that went to make up an image of a man that men would die for and women would fall for.

So, she told herself, she wasn't such a pathetic case, after all. Happens to the best of us. As she reached for her medical kit and clicked out the tablets to fix the hangover, she caught herself smiling at the memory of the General's smile. Annoyed with herself again, she got out of bed and padded to the kitchen in her fluffy slippers and fuzzy nightgown, and gulped cold water while the coffee percolated. She added a MoodLift tab to her ReSolve dose and her daily intake of anti-ageing supplements and knocked them back all at once. She felt better.

The time was 8 o'clock. She put her contacts in and flicked on a television tile and watched it while spooning muesli and yogurt and listening to the murmured morning briefing from Parvus. The news, as usual, was bad, but no worse than usual. No martial music or ballet on all channels—that was enough to count as good news. After a coffee and a cigarette she felt almost human. She supposed she might as well get up and go to work.


The walk to the government building woke her up even more, boosted her mood better than any tab. The air was crisp, the morning sky unexpectedly colourful, reds and oranges and yellows shading to green at the horizon. She noticed people staring up at the sky.

Its colours were changing visibly, flowing—suddenly she realised she was looking at an aurora, thousands of miles south of where aurorae should be seen. As she stopped and looked up, openmouthed, the sky brightened for a few seconds from some great illumination below the horizon.

She ran. She sprinted through the streets, barged through the doors, yelled at Security and bounded up the stairs. As she strode into her office her earpiece pinged, and a babble of tinny voices contended for her attention. She sat heavily on the edge of her desk and flipped down her eyeband, keyed up the news.

The tanks were rolling, all around the world.

Without taking her eyes off the newsfeeds, Myra slid across her desk and lowered herself into her chair. She rattled out commands on the armrest keypads, transforming the office's walls into screens for an emergency command-centre. The first thing she did was secure the building; then she hit the emergency call for Sovnarkom. The thrown fetches of Andrei, Denis and Valentina sprang to attention on the screens—whether their physical bodies were in their offices, on their way in or still in bed didn't matter, as long as their eyebands were online.

Myra glanced around their virtual presences.

'OK, comrades, this is the big one,' she said. 'First, is everything clear with us?'

It was unlikely that the ISTWR's tiny Workers' Militia and tinier People's Army would have joined the coup, but more unlikely things were happening before her eyes every few seconds. (A night-time amphibious landing at South Street Seaport! Tanks in Pennsylvania Avenue! Attack helicopters shelling Westminster Bridge!)

'We're sound,' said Denis. Even his fetch looked drawn and hungover. 'So's Kazakhstan, they're staying out of this. Army's on alert, of course. Baikonur cosmodrome's well under government control. So's the airstrip at Yubileine. Almaty's mobilised, militia on the streets, but they're loyal.'

You hope, Myra thought. The neat thing about a military coup was that mobilisation against it could quite easily become *part* of it, as the lines of command writhed and broke and reconnected.

'Good, great. North-eastern front? Val, you awake?'

'Yeah, I'm with you. No moves from the Sheenisov so far.' Valentina patched in a satellite feed, updated by the second: the steppe was still.

'What about Mutual Protection here?'

'Haven't moved from the camp—and the camp's quiet.'

Myra relaxed a little. 'Looks like our immediate surroundings are secure, then. Any word from orbit, Val?'

Valentina shook her head. 'All comms are very flaky, can't get anything coherent from the settlements, the factories, the battlesats—'

'That's impossible!' She thought about how it might be possible. 'Oh my God, the sky—'

'About ten minutes ago,' Andrei announced, from some glassy trance, 'somebody nuked the Heaviside Layer. Half a dozen bursts—not much EMP, but quite enough of that and of charged particles to scramble radio signals for a good few hours.'

'So how are we getting even the news?' Myra demanded.

'Cable,' said Andrei. 'Fibre-optics aren't affected. And some stuff's getting through by laser, obviously, like Val's spysat downlink. Should increase as people switch, or improvise. But for the moment it's dust in everybody's eyes.'

'Didn't know the space movement had orbital nukes,' Denis said. 'In fact, didn't know anybody but us had *any* serious nukes.'

That was a point. Nuclear disarmament had been the only universally popular, and (almost) universally successful, policy of the US/UN after the Third World War. Even Myra, at the time, had not resented or regretted the confiscation of the ISTWR's complement, along with all the rest. Only by sheer accident had an independent stockpile survived, in the hands of a politically

untouchable institution that counted its supporters in billions, its age in millennia and its policy in centuries. All other strategic nuclear weapons had been
dismantled. There were thousands of battlefield tactical nukes still around, of
course, but nobody'd ever worried much about *them*: the consequences of
their use had never been shown live on television.

(The images went through her mind, again, and the names of cities: Kiev,
Frankfurt, Berlin. She shook her head with a shudder, shutting them out.)

Valentina was giving her a hard stare. 'They weren't *ours*, were they?'

'Not as far as I know,' Myra said. 'Unless you happened to turn over the
access codes to somebody else, eh?'

Valentina shook her head, thin-lipped. 'No. Never.'

'Right, so much for that theory,' Myra said briskly, to assure Val that she
wasn't under any suspicion. 'Andrei, any ideas?'

'Excuse me,' said Andrei. 'I'm still trying to get through the front door.'

'Oh, fuck!' Myra tabbed a code to let him in.

'Thanks . . . OK, I think the nukes were from the *UN* side, against the
coup.'

'And where did they get them?'

'What I think is that the UN hung on to some nukes for itself, the secret
stayed with some inner cadre of bureaucrats who made it through the Revolution and the purges, and they put it at the disposal of the current Secretary General.'

'Makes sense, I suppose,' said Denis. 'What I'd do.'

'What's the politics of this, Andrei?' Myra asked. 'We were so sure they'd
wait for the ReUN vote—' she stopped and laughed. Trotsky himself had
used just such a stratagem. 'Have the coup before the vote—I wonder where
they got that idea. Still, it kind of undermines the appeal to legitimacy.'

She still had one eye on the virtual screens of the cable news. 'Ah, wait,
something coming in—'

They sat in silence as the presenter read out a communiqué from a large
group of small governments calling themselves the Assembly Majority Alliance. The gist of it was that the present Security Council had violated the
Revised Charter of 2046 by planning to use nuclear weapons in space; and a
call for immediate action to depose the conspirators and usurpers. The forces
of the Alliance governments and of Mutual Protection were offered for immediate, co-ordinated action to that end. A swift resolution of the emergency
was anticipated. The population was urged to remain calm and stay away
from work for the day.

'God, that is so cynical,' Val said. 'They must have had dozens of back-
dated statements, prepared for every contingency, so they could claim to be
acting to prevent whatever the Security Council decided to do.'

'Yes, yes,' Myra said. 'All SOP for a coup. And a diversion, anyway. It's in space that the real battles are being fought. Maybe right at this moment! The whole thing will be decided at the speed of light. Come on, let's get into command mode.'

The others nodded, fell silent, turned to the screens and started pulling in all available data and throwing analysis software at it. After a minute or two they'd begun to mesh as a team in their common virtual workspace. Information flashed back and forth between their personal networks, the government network, the *Jane's* system, the newsfeeds, and field reports from their own troops and agents.

The big picture became as clear as the situation it revealed was chaotic. Myra clocked through most of the world's significant capitals: Beijing, Pyongyang, Tokyo, Vladivostok, Seattle, LA, Washington DC, New York, London, Paris, New Berlin, Danzig, Moscow. All of them reported military strikes of one kind or another, but they all had the aspect of *putsches*—short-term grabs of public buildings or urban strongholds, which could be held more by the reluctance of the government forces to reduce them than by the strength of their occupiers. It all had a suspiciously diversionary look about it.

All of the committed technophobe governments, from the Khmer Vertes rulers of Bangkok, through the Islamic Republicans of Arabia to the White Nationalists of Dallas, had their forces on full alert and their media screaming imprecations against the enemies of God, Man or Gaia (depending on local ideological taste); but Myra judged them well aware that they were not, themselves, immediate targets—it was the more liberal governments, those who compromised between the pro-tech and anti-tech forces, which were taking the fire.

The more serious action was taking place in the imbricated global hinterland of enclaves and ministates and company countries; along their fractal borderlines the local defence forces were massed and mobilised, in a posture that was aggressive in the Assembly Majority Alliance statelets, generally defensive in the rest. Meanwhile, in the shadowy lands beyond and behind even these anarchic polities, the forests and plains and badlands and shanty towns bristled as the Green neo-barbarians, the marginals and tribals awoke to the unlooked-for opportunities of this new day.

*Jane's Market Forces* registered unexpected shifts in the balance of power; minor skirmishes could have major effects, putting troops and tactics and weapons to the test in new conditions, or in real rather than simulated combat. Not much blood was being shed, but fortunes were being made and lost, alliances and antagonisms updated; the process had its own gory fascination. Myra felt she could sit and look at it for hours.

But this was Earth, this was not where it was at. The battles here, real or virtual, were fundamentally a diversion, and she was duly being diverted. She turned her attention determinedly skyward.

With Val's well-practised help she spun a neon orrery of near-Earth space, separating out the relevant threads from the skeins of commercial and military orbits. The planet itself appeared as a transparent globe, etched with political and geographical outlines, clouded with weather patterns, cross-hatched with confrontations, pin-pricked with flashpoints. Again its intricate patterns compelled her attention; again, she turned away.

Their own space-borne *matériel*—nuclear and kinetic-energy weapons—were depicted as black rods and cones, deep in the ever-growing ring of space-junk that tracked the main orbital thoroughfares.

'Anything coming through yet from the battlesats?'

'Some,' said Val, sounding distracted. 'I'm pulling in laser comms via various ground stations. Shit, this is tricky—hold it, hold it . . . ah!'

The battlesat locations lit up, one by one; those with which communication had been established blinked invitingly. Myra zoomed in on one of them. A classic von Braun space station, with a rotating tubular ring joined by thinner tubular spokes to an inner ring surrounding the contra-rotating spin-compensated axial tower. The living-quarters and hydroponics were around the ring, in the fake gravity of the spin; the laser-cannon and rocket-racks and particle-beam weapons and military command-centre were in the free-fall hub. The whole enormous mandala had a camp Nazi grandeur, spoiled only by the ungainly arrays of solar panels it had sprouted while its nuclear reactor had run down.

It was one of dozens in various orbits. Space Defense had enforced the Pax Americana of the US/UN Imperium, a twenty-year Reich between the Third World War and the Fall Revolution. In that revolution the battlesats had passed into the hands of their personnel—soldiers' soviets in space—and, ever since, they'd sought a role to replace their lost empire. Everything from power-beam transmission to asteroid defence had been tried, to little profit. The stations survived on a trickle of subsidy—or 'user fees'—from the similarly diminished UN, paid mainly to prevent the battlesats' going rogue out of sheer desperation.

Now the forces of the coup were offering them a new empire, one a lot more justifiable and enforceable than the old.

'So what's the score with this one?' Myra asked.

'Still loyal,' replied Val. 'They just reported in to say they weren't going with the Alliance.'

'Any way of checking that?'

'Don't know, I'm hailing them—ah! they're letting us in.'

'I'll go,' said Myra, 'you stay with the big picture.'

With a clunky, disorienting transition, she found herself standing in a real-time representation of the battlesat's bridge. It was about fifteen metres across, and crowded. The interior matched the exterior's style: banks of flashing lights among chrome and black surfaces; a cluttered overgrowth of retrofitted modern kit among a profusion of plants, like in a civilian space settlement. The layout was optimised for free-fall, with the crew-members strapped into seats and couches at unexpected angles to each other. In this section of the shaft there were actual windows, through which she could see the great wheel turn in the sunlight, and the Earth's swirling clouds below. She blinked, and overprinted the real view with its software image.

The crew were wearing eyebands, and some of them could see Myra's fetch in their own virtual palimpsests of the scene—but they spared her no more than a glance. Another spectral presence had all their attention.

The General sat on a window sill, surveying the bridge with narrowed eyes. He'd been saying something; his words seemed to hang in the air, resonating in the circuits of the display. He interrupted himself and turned to face her.

'Ah, Comrade Davidova—thanks for coming.'

'I wasn't aware I'd been asked,' she said.

'Oh, you were,' the construct said. 'This is, as they say, no accident.'

Myra nodded. No doubt it was indeed no accident that the first battlesat to allow her into its internal systems was the one in which the General was addressing his troops.

He waved a hand. 'Welcome to a quick emergency session of the military org's local cell.' He grinned. 'Which is pretty much the command of this station.' The watching crew-members gave her longer looks now; some of them even smiled.

'We need your help,' the General told her flatly. 'Nice display,' he added. 'May I?'

He reached over, thumb and forefinger pinching into her translucent globe, and with frightening insouciance overrode all her protocols and relocated her virtual view of the Earth and near-Earth space into the centre of the bridge.

She stared at the spinning shapes, fuming. He shouldn't have been able to do that—

'We still hold most of the battlesats.' A quick sharp look. 'That is to say, the anti-coup forces do, whatever their other alignments. But the struggle is still in the balance. We have about a sixth of the battle-sats securely on our side, the enemy likewise, and the others undecided.'

Myra was momentarily stunned. Despite what the General had said to her earlier, she'd had no idea, no expectation that the military org's penetration of Space Defense was so thorough—it must have taken years of work. But the General gave her no time to question or congratulate.

'Here, here and here.' He stabbed a forefinger at three battlesats, whose footprints between them covered most of the planet. 'These are in enemy hands. We can't hit them from the battlesats we hold, because that would risk a spasm of retaliation. But we need to hit them fast, to warn any others who are about to go over to the enemy. Take them out.'

He ran a finger lightly around the republic's orbital caches of smart pebbles, lasers, KE weapons.

'I can't,' Myra said. 'I don't have the skills, I don't have the automation. None of us do.'

The General snapped his fingers. 'The keys, Comrade, the keys. That's all I need. The access codes.'

'Let me consult my Defence Minister,' said Myra, and backed out hastily. It was a relief—even with the sudden, swallowed surge of cyberspace sickness that it brought on—to find herself back in her office, looking at screens.

'Val—' she began.

'I got that,' said Valentina. 'Kept half an eye on you with a partial piggyback. Who *is* that guy?'

Myra looked sidelong at her. 'Good for you,' she said. 'That was the head of the FI military org. An AI. Our very own electric Trotsky.'

'Fuck your mother,' said Val, in Russian.

'Right. We gonna give it the codes?'

'Up to you,' said Val. 'You're the PM.'

'What,' said Myra through clenched teeth, 'would you *advise?*'

Val licked her lips. The others were either pointedly ignoring them or concentrating on their own areas.

'Well, hell. Go with the military adviser, I'd say. Give it the codes.'

'Will that work? Do we really have munitions up there that can down battlesats?'

'Hard to say,' said Valentina. 'Ancient, never combat-tested, poorly maintained—but so are the battlesats! In theory, yes, they can overwhelm a battlesat's defences.'

Myra was trying to think fast. It struck her that the battlesats themselves might be a diversion—old and powerful, but inflexible and vulnerable: an orbiting Maginot Line. Perhaps the General was fighting the last war, and *winning* it, while the real battles raged elsewhere.

She hesitated, then decided.

'Give me the codes for the smart-pebble bombs,' she said. Val zapped them across; Myra tabbed back to the battlesat and passed them to the General. He was waiting for her, with puzzled impatience.

'Thank you,' he said heavily, then disappeared. Myra looked around at the now frantically active crew, gave them an awkward, cheery wave, and dropped back to her own command-centre.

'That was quick.' Valentina pointed at the display. Already, some of their orbital weapons had been activated. Myra devoutly hoped that what she was seeing as a representation wasn't appearing on the enemy's real-time monitors. In three places a cloud of sharp objects had burst out of cover and were moving in the same orbital paths as the three enemy battlesats, but in the opposite direction. They were due to collide with the battlesats in ten, eighteen and twenty-seven minutes.

What happened next was over in less than a second—a twinkle of laser paths in the void. The action replay followed automatically, patiently repeating the results for the slow rods and cones and nerves of the human eye.

Myra watched the battlesats' deep-space radar beams brush the oncoming KE volleys; saw their targeting-radar lock on. Her laser-platform drones responded to that detection with needles of light, stabbing to blind the battlesats—which had, in the momentary meantime, released a cloud of chaff to block that very manoeuvre. Then the battlesats struck back, with a speed still bewildering even in slow motion. Each one projected a thousand laser pulses, flashing like a fencer's swift sword, slicing up the KE weapons and their laser-platform escorts.

'Wow!' she said, admiring despite herself.

'Yeah, that's some defence system,' said Valentina. 'Not standard issue for a battlesat, I'll tell you that.'

Myra zoomed the view. Each attack cloud was still there, as a much larger cloud of much smaller objects. They would bombard the battlesats, sure enough, they'd even do some damage, but it would be more like a sandblasting than a shelling.

The time was 09.25. Forty minutes had passed since the Heaviside nukes. The disruption they'd caused was easing off; radio comms were still haywire, but more and more centres were coming back online via patches and workarounds. The outcome of this first serious exchange was already being analysed. Myra cast a quick glance at *Jane's*. The coup's stock was fluctuating wildly.

'Shit—'

She was about to transfer her workspace to the battlesat again but the General beat her to it. He—or it—suddenly appeared in the command-centre, as a recognisable if not very solid figure. Andrei and Denis, by this time evidently having been brought up to speed by Val, didn't react to the apparition with more than open-mouthed astonishment.

'Too bad,' the General said, staring sadly at the display. 'These defences are portable, not fitted to the station but brought in by the conspirators.'

'Any other battlesats have them?'

A sketch of a shrug. 'We don't. Maybe they're already being deployed among the waverers. Mutual Protection nanofactures, is my guess.'

Better than a guess, Myra reckoned.

'You want another strike?'

'No. Only one thing for it now. Nuke 'em.'

Myra glanced at Valentina. 'Wait. Give us a first-cut sim, Val.'

Valentina ran down the locations of their orbital nuclear weapons and launched a simulation of an immediate strike, in the light of the new information about the battlesats' capabilities. Stopped. Ran it again; and again; all in a few seconds, but a waste of time nonetheless. The answer was obvious. The nukes could get close enough to the battlesats to take them out—but near-Earth space was a lot more crowded than it had been when the doctrine of that deployment had first been developed. There was no way to avoid thousands of innocent casualties and quadrillions of dollars' worth of damage to space habitats and industries.

'It's worse than that,' Valentina pointed out. 'The direct effect of the explosions and the EMP would be just the beginning—there's every possibility that the debris would set off an ablation cascade—each collision producing more debris, until in a matter of days you'd have stripped the sky.'

The ablation cascade was a known nightmare, one of the deadliest threats to space habitation, or even exploration. Myra had seen discussions and calculations to suggest that a full-scale cascade would surround the Earth with rings of debris which could make space travel unfeasibly dangerous for *centuries* . . .

The General had a look which indicated that he was weighing this in the balance. She could just see it now, that calculation—even with a cascade, it was possible that the new diamond ships could dodge and dogfight through the debris—the barrier might not be impenetrable after all, and meanwhile . . .

'Forget it,' Myra said. 'We aren't going to use the nukes.' Her fingers were working away, codes were flashing past her eyes—she was trying to find the channel the General's fetch had ridden in on.

Something in her tone told the General there would be no argument. Instead, he turned to the others and said, quite pleasantly, 'The comrade is not thinking objectively. Are you willing to relieve her of her responsibilities?'

'No,' they told him, in gratifying unison.

'Very well.' He smiled at them, as if to say he was sorry, but it had been worth a try.

'And you can fuck *right* off,' said Myra. She tapped her forefinger, triumphantly, on an input-channel key, and tuned him right out.

# 7

## THE CLAIMANT BAR

Out we went into the summer dusk. Moths sought the sun in streetlamps, baffled. The few quiet roads between the house and the Institute were crowded
now, with local residents taking advantage of the slack season in bars normally
jammed with students. Lads strutting their tight dark trousers, lasses swaying
their big bright skirts. We must have looked a less happy couple, harried and
hurrying.

A few lights burnt in the Institute, one of them the light in the corridor.
As we stepped in and closed the door, the smell of pipe-smoke was stronger
than before, and familiar.

'Someone's around,' Merrial whispered.

'Yes,' I replied, 'it's—'

Right on cue, an office door down the corridor opened and Anders Gantry
stepped out. A small man with strong arms and a beer-barrel of a belly, hair
curling grey like the smoke from his inseparable pipe. His shirt was merely
grubby—his wife managed to impose fresh linen on him every week or so—
but his jacket had not been cleaned in years. It smelled like it had been used to
beat down fires, which it had.

He was the best historical scholar in the University, and quite possibly in
the whole British Isles; and the kindest and most modest man I'd ever met.

'Ah, hello, Clovis,' he boomed. 'How good to see you!' He strode up and
shook hands. 'And who's your friend?'

'Merrial—Dr Anders Gantry,' I said.

He held her hand and inclined his head over her knuckles. 'Charmed.' He looked at her in a vaguely puzzled way for a moment, then turned to me. 'Now, colha Gree, what can I do for you?'

Gantry had agreed to supervise my project; it was a persistent irritant to my conscience that I hadn't seen or written to him all summer.

'Oh, nothing at the moment, Dr Gantry. I've been doing a fair bit of preliminary research up North, and I've about finished the standard references.' I rubbed my ear, uneasily remembering the dust on the books. 'And I thought I'd take the opportunity of a wee visit to Glasgow to drop by the library.'

'That's very commendable,' he said. I was unsure of the exact level of irony in his voice, but it was there. 'We've rather missed you around here.'

'He works very hard,' Merrial put in. 'The space-launch platform project is on a tight schedule.'

'Oh, so that's where you are. Kishorn. Hmm. Good money to be made up there, I hear. And you, miss?'

'I have an office job there,' Merrial said blandly. She shot me a smile. 'That's how I know he works hard. He's saving up money to live on next year.'

'Well, I suppose there are ways and ways of preparing for a project,' said Gantry, in a more indulgent tone. 'No luck with patronage yet, I take it?'

'None so far, no.'

He clapped me around the shoulders. 'Perhaps you should try to extract some research money from the space scientists,' he said. 'Our great Deliverer had much to do with spaceflight herself. There might still be lessons in her life story, eh?'

Merrial's face froze and I felt my knees turning to rubber.

'Now that's a thought,' I said, as calmly as possible.

Gantry guffawed. 'Aye, you might even fool them into thinking that!' he said. 'Good luck if you do. Now that you're getting stuck in, Clovis, I have something to show you.' He grinned, revealing his teeth, yellow as a dog's. 'It's in the library.'

With that he turned away and bounded up the stairs. I followed, mouthing and gesturing helplessness to Merrial. To my relief, she seemed more amused than alarmed.

By the time we arrived at the open door of the library he'd vanished into the shadows.

'What are we going to do?' I whispered to Merrial.

'If he stays around, you keep him busy,' she said. 'I'll get the goods.'

I was about to tell her how unlikely she was to get away with that when Gantry came puffing up, carrying a load of cardboard folders that reached from his clasped hands at his belt to his uppermost chin.

'Here we are,' he said, lowering the tottering stack on to a table. He sneezed. 'Filthy with dust, I'm afraid.' He wiped his nose and hands on an even dirtier handkerchief. 'But it's time you had a look at it: Myra Godwin's personal archive.'

'That really is amazing,' I said. My voice sounded like a twelve-year-old boy seeing a girl naked for the first time. I picked them up and put them down, one by one. Eight altogether: bulging cardboard wallets ordered by decade, from the 1970s to the 2050s.

I hardly dared to breathe on them as I opened the first one and looked at the document on the top of the pile, a shoddily cyclostyled, rusty-stapled bundle of pages with the odd title *Building a revolutionary party in capitalist America. Published as a fraternal courtesy to the cosmic current.*

'Why haven't I seen these before?' I asked.

Gantry shuffled uncomfortably. He glanced at Merrial, rubbed his chin and said, 'Am I right in thinking you're a tinker?'

'You're right, I am that,' Merrial said, without hesitation.

Gantry smiled, looking relieved. 'Um, well. Between ourselves and all that. Scholars and tinkers both know, I'm sure, that we have to be . . . discreet, about the Deliverer's . . . more discreditable deeds and, ah, youthful follies. So, although previous biographers have seen these documents, we don't tend to show them to undergraduates. What I hope, Clovis, is that you'll see a way to go beyond the, um, shall we say hagiographic treatments of the past, without . . .' He paused, sucking at his lower lip. 'Ah, well, no need to spell it out.'

'Of course not,' I said.

I looked at the master scholar with what I'm sure must have been an expression of gratifying respect. 'Shall we have a look through them now?'

Gantry stepped back and threw up his hands in mock horror. 'No, no! Can't have me looking over your shoulder at the raw material, Clovis. Unaided original work, and all that. This is yours, and there's a thesis in there if ever I saw one. No, it's time I was off and left you to it.' He hesitated. 'Ah, I shouldn't need to tell you, colha Gree, but not a word about this, or a single page of it, outside, all right?'

I had a brief, intense tussle with my conscience, which neatly tripped me up and jumped on me. 'Nothing for the vulgar, of course,' I said carefully. 'But in principle I could, well, show it to or discuss it with other scholars?'

'Goes without saying,' Gantry confirmed jovially. He tapped the side of his nose. 'If you can find anyone you'd trust not to claim it as their own.' He winked at Merrial. 'Untrustworthy bunch, these scholars, I think you'll find.' He punched me, playfully as he thought, in the ribs. 'Confidence, man, confidence! I'm sure you have the wit to understand and explicate this lot yourself, and it'll make your name, you mark my words!'

'Thank you,' I said, after a painful intake of breath. 'Well . . . I think I'll make a start right now.'

'Yes, indeed. Splendid idea. Don't stay up too late.' His complicitous grin made it obvious that he thought it unlikely that we'd stay up too late. 'Best be off then,' he said, as though to himself, then backed to the door and turned away.

'Good night to you, sir!' Merrial called out after him.

'Good night,' came faintly back from the stairwell.

Merrial let out a long breath.

'What a strange little man,' she said, in the manner of someone who has just encountered one of the Wee Folk.

'He's not entirely typical of scholars,' I said.

'I should hope not,' Merrial said. 'Wouldn't want you turning into something like that.'

'Heaven forbid,' I said, adding loyally, 'but he's a fine man for all his funny ways.' I looked down at the stack of folders. 'Maybe it would be a good idea,' I said slowly, 'if you were to do your thing with the computer, and I could stay here, just in case he comes back.'

'Oh, and leave me to face the deils all on my own?' Merrial mocked, then laughed, relenting. 'Aye, that is not a bad idea. If he or anyone else comes in, keep them busy. I'll not be long, and I'll be fine.'

'What about this security barrier?'

She waved a hand and made a rude noise. 'Faugh! This wee gadget here has routines that can roast security barriers over a firewall and eat them for breakfast.'

Considering how she'd had to program something a lot simpler than that to sort out the dates, I doubted her, but supposed that was the black logic for you.

She smiled and slipped away; after an anxious minute of listening, I heard the sound of the inner door being opened and the scrape of a chair being dragged across the floor and propped against it. I relaxed a little and turned again to the files—to the paper files, I mentally corrected myself, for the first time making the connection between 'files' in Merrial's and, I presumed, tinkers' usage, and my own.

I was eager to get into the early decades, but I knew that would be somewhat self-indulgent, and that I would have plenty of time for that. It was the later years, closer to the time of the Deliverance, that were hidden from history. I picked up the folder for the final decade, the 2050s, and was about to open it when I heard Merrial scream.

I don't remember getting to the door of the dark archive. I only remember standing there, my forward momentum arrested by a shock of dread that stopped me like a sparrow hitting a window. The file folder, absurdly enough, was still in my hands, and I held up that heavy mass of flimsy paper and fragile cardboard like a weapon—or a shield.

Merrial too was holding a weapon—the chair she'd been sitting on, and had evidently just sprung out of. In front of her, and above the computer, in a lattice of ruby light, stood the figure of a man. He was a tall man, and stout with it, his antique garb of cream-coloured jacket and trousers flapping and his shock of white hair streaming in the same invisible gale that had blown his hat away down some long corridor whose diminishing perspective carried it far beyond the walls of the room. His face was red and wrathful, his fist shaking, his mouth shouting something we couldn't hear.

Holding the chair above her head, her forearm in front of her eyes, chanting some arcane abracadabra, Merrial advanced like one facing into a fire, and seized her seer-stone and machinery from the table. Its wire, yanked from its inconveniently placed socket, lashed back like a snapped fishing-line. The little peg at the end, now bent like a fishhook, flew towards me and rapped against the file-folder. Merrial whirled around at the same moment, and saw me. She gave me a look worth dying for, and then a calm smile.

'Time to go,' she said. She let the chair clatter down, and turned again to face the silently screaming entity she'd aroused. As she backed away from the thing, it vanished. A mechanism somewhere in the computer whirred, then stopped. A light on its face flickered, briefly, then went out.

All the lights went out. From downstairs we faintly heard an indignant yell. I could hear Merrial stuffing her apparatus back in its sack. She bumped into me, still walking backwards.

Holding hands as though on a precipice, we made our way through the library's suffocating dark. I could smell the dry ancient papers, the friable glue and frayed thread and leather of the bindings. From those fibres the ancients could have resurrected lost species of trees and breeds of cattle, I thought madly. Pity they hadn't.

After a long minute our eyes began to adjust to the faint light that filtered in past window-blinds, and from other parts of the building. We walked with more confidence through the maze towards the door. On the ground floor of the building we could hear Gantry blundering and banging about.

Then, behind us, I heard a stealthy step. Merrial heard it too and froze, her hand in mine suddenly damp. Another step, and the sound of something *dragging*. I almost broke into a screeching run.

'It's all right,' Merrial said, her voice startlingly loud. 'It's a sound-projection—just another thing to scare us off.'

Behind us, a low, deep laugh.

'Steady,' said Merrial.

My thigh hit the edge of the table by the door. 'Just a second,' I said. I let go of her hand, grabbed one more file-folder, put it in my other hand and then caught Merrial's hand again.

We reached the library door, slammed it behind us and descended the stairs as fast as we safely could, or faster. Then we lost all caution and simply fled, rushing headlong past Gantry's angry and puzzled face, lurid in the small flame of the pipe-lighter he held above his head, and out into the night.

Night it was—for hundreds of metres around, all the power was off. We stopped running when we reached the first functioning streetlamps, on Great Western Road.

I looked at Merrial's face, shiny with sweat, yellow in the sodium puddle. 'What in the name of Reason was that?'

Merrial shook her head. 'My mouth's dry,' she croaked. 'I need a drink.'

My feet led me unerringly to the nearest bar, the Claimant. It was quiet that evening, and Merrial was able to grab a corner seat while I bought a couple of pints and a brace of whiskies. By the empty fireplace a fiddler played and a woman sang, an aching Gaelic threnody of loss.

Merrial knocked back her whisky in one deft swallow, and summer returned to her face.

'Jesus!' she swore. 'I needed that. Give me a cigarette.'

I complied, gazing at her while lighting it, glancing covertly around while I lit my own. The pub, which I'd patronised throughout my student years, was a friendly and comfortable place, though its wall decorations could chill you a bit if you pondered on them: framed reproductions of ancient posters and notices and regulations about 'actively seeking employment' and 'receiving benefit'. It was something to do with living on public assistance, which is what many quite hale and able folk, known as claimants, had had to resort to in the days of the Possession, when land was owned by lairds and capital by usurers.

The usual two old geezers were recalling their first couple of centuries in voices raised to cope with the slight hearing impairment that comes with age; a gang of lads around a big table were gambling for pennies, and several pairs of other lovers were intent only on each other; and the singer's song floated high notes over them all.

'You were about to say?' I said. My own voice was shakier than Merrial's had been at any point in the whole incident. At the same time I felt giddy with relief at our escape, and a strange exciting mixture of dread and exaltation at the sure knowledge that my life was henceforth unpredictable.

'I wasn't,' Merrial said, 'but I'll tell you anyway. That thing we saw was the deil that guards the files. But,' she added brightly, 'blowing fuses for several blocks around was the worst it could do.'

'Hey, that's comforting.'

'Yes, it is,' she said, in a very definite tone. 'Better that than an electric shock that burns your hands or a fire that brings down the whole building. Or—'

'What?'

'I've heard of worse. Ones that attack your mind through your eyes.'

'And there you were laughing at the very idea, back at the yard.'

'Aye, well,' she said. 'It was just me that had to face them. No sense in getting you worried.'

'Oh, thanks.'

She took my hand. 'No, you were brave in there.'

'Ach, not a bit of it,' I agreed.

'So, after all, we didn't get much,' I said, returning to our table with refilled glasses about two minutes later. Outside, I could hear a growing commotion of militia rattles and whistles and fire-brigade bells. Somewhere across the street, a vehicle with a flashing light trundled slowly past.

Merrial looked up from riffling through the folders.

'Well, you got the 2050s and the 1990s,' she said. 'That's something. What *I* got—' she patted her bag, grinning '—was a whole lot more. Maybe everything, I don't know yet.'

I put the glasses down very carefully.

'The . . . um, barrier . . . didn't work, then?'

'Up to a point. Like I said, my machine, and the logic on it, are stronger than the other one. It just couldn't stop that thing from doing what it kept warning it *would* do. You can steal a bone from a dog if you ignore the barks and don't mind the bites.' In a less smug tone, she added, 'But it all depends on how much I pulled out before I had to . . .'

'Pull out!'

'Yes.'

'So what do we do now?' I looked down at the folders. 'I suppose I'll have to try and square things with Dr Gantry.' Confused thoughts fought in my mind, like those programs Merrial talked about. One sequence of impulses made me think through a scheme of grovelling apology and covering up and smoothing over. Another made me realise that I was almost certainly in very deep trouble with the University authorities, and had quite possibly affronted Gantry in ways that he might find hard to forgive.

'Oh, and how are you going to do that?' Merrial asked. 'I reckon he won't be too pleased about your running off with this lot.'

'That he won't,' I said gloomily. 'But I could always say I grabbed them to save them, or something, and that I'll return them in a few days. After photocopying them, of course. No, it's the other thing that'll have him pissed off. Heaven knows what damage that thing did—I doubt it was just a power cut. More like blown fuses all over the place, maybe worse. That'll be looked into, and not just by the University. And he's going to want to know who you are and what we were up to.'

'Hmm.' Merrial blew out a thin stream of smoke, observing it as though it were a divination. 'Well, seeing as he knows my name, and where I work . . . tell you what, colha Gree. Assume he does make a fuss, or somebody else asks questions. What I do not want getting out is that this has anything to do with the ship, or with . . . my folk. What we can say, and with some truth, is that you were led by excess of zeal to poke around in . . . the dark place. That you inveigled me into helping you. That you're very sorry, you got your fingers burned, and you won't do it again. And that of course the files you took will not be seen by anyone outside the community of scholars. Their *photocopies*, now, they might be seen, but you need say nothing of that.'

I had been thinking of counting Merrial as an honorary scholar in my own version of that bit of casuistry, but hers would do at a pinch. My two conflicting programs meshed: I was in trouble, yes, but I could get out of it, by the aforementioned grovelling and covering up.

The clock above the bar showed the time was a quarter past ten.

'I doubt Gantry's still around,' I said. 'And I don't know where he lives, or his phone number, if he has one. I suppose the best thing to do is see him in the morning, before we leave.' I took my return ticket from my pocket. 'Train leaves at forty minutes before noon. I'll be round to see him at nine, and try and straighten things out.'

Merrial nodded. 'Sound plan,' she said. She cocked an ear. 'Things seem to be quietening down, but I don't think wandering around back there would be a good idea right now.'

'D'you want to go back and check over what we've got?'

'*Dhia*, no! I've looked at enough of that for one day. I want to stay here and drink with you, and maybe dance with you—if a wee bit of siller can make that fiddler change his tune—and then go back to the lodging and test the strength of that bed with you.'

That is not what we should have done, I grant you; but are you surprised at all that it is what we did?


I sat on the steps outside the Institute, in the still, chill morning under the shadows of the great trees, and looked at my watch. Ten to nine. I sighed and lit another cigarette. A couple of hundred metres away a pneumatic drill started hammering. Brightly painted trestles and crossbeams and piles of broken tarmac indicated that some similar work had been done already during the night.

The path of power, indeed. One reason why it's called that is that electronic computation is inextricably and unpredictably linked to electrical power generation, and can disrupt it in expensive and dangerous ways. I had an unpleasant suspicion that the cost of all this was, one way or another, going to meander through some long system of City Council and University Senate accountancy, and arrive at my feet.

'Good morning, Clovis.' I looked up at Gantry. He had his pipe in one hand and a key in the other. 'Come on in.'

His office had a window that occupied most of one wall, giving a soothing view of a weed-choked back yard, and bookcases on the others. Every vertical surface in the room was stained slightly yellow, and every horizontal surface was under a fine layer of tobacco ash. I wiped ineffectually at the wooden chair in front of his desk while he sat down on the leather one behind it.

He regarded me for a moment, blinking; ran his fingers through his short hair; sighed and began refilling his pipe.

'Well, colha Gree,' he said, after a minute of intimidating silence, 'you have no idea how much my respect for you has increased by your coming here. When I saw you a moment ago, stubbing out your cigarette on the pavement, I thought, "Now, there's a man who knows to do the decent thing." Considerable improvement on your blue funk last night; considerable.'

I cleared my throat, vaguely thinking that whatever the doctors may say, there *must* be something harmful in a habit which makes your lungs feel so rough in the morning. 'Aye, well, Dr Gantry, it wasn't yourself I was afraid of.'

'Oh,' he said dryly, 'and what was it then, hmm?'

Without meaning to, I found my gaze drifting upward. 'It was, uh, the demon internet software that I'm afraid I and my friend, um, accidentally invoked.'

Gantry lit his pipe and sent out a cloud of smoke.

'Yes, I had gathered that. And what on earth possessed you—so to speak—to poke around in the dark storage when I'd just given you more than enough material for years of study?'

I met his gaze again. 'It was my idea,' I said. 'Call it—excess of zeal. I got the idea before you gave me the papers, of course, but even after that I thought we might as well go through with it. I'm afraid I was—rather blinded by the lust for knowledge.'

'And by another kind of lust, I shouldn't wonder,' Gantry said. 'This *friend* of yours, she's more than that, am I right?'

There seemed no point in denying it, so I didn't.

'All right,' he said. He jabbed his pipe-stem at me, thumbed the stubble on his chin, and gnawed at his lower lip for a moment. 'All right. First of all, let me say that the University administration has a job to do which is different from the self-administration of the academic community. It has to maintain the physical fabric of the place, and its supplies and services and so forth, and with the best will in the world I can't interfere with any measures of investigation *and discipline* which it may see fit to take in this unfortunate matter. You appreciate that, don't you?'

'Yes, of course.'

'Fine. Well . . . as to any academic repercussions, there I can speak up for you, I can . . . refrain from volunteering information about how the demonic outbreak took place. But I can't lie on your behalf, old chap. I'll do my best for you, because I think it would be a shame to throw away someone with so much promise over what, as you say, was excess of scholarly zeal. Very understandable temptation, and all that. Some of the Senatus might well think to themselves, "Been there, done that—young once myself—fingers burnt—learned his lesson—say no more about it," and all that sort of thing.'

I relaxed a little on the hard chair. I'd been fiddling with a cigarette for a while, unsure if I had permission to smoke; Gantry leaned over with his lighter, absently almost taking my eyebrows off with its kerosene flare.

'Thank you.'

'However,' he went on, leaning back in his own chair, 'there are some wider issues.' He waved his pipe about, vaguely indicating the surrounding shelves of hard-won knowledge. 'We British are beginning to get the hang of this civilisation game. When the Romans left, there wasn't a public library or a flush toilet or a decent road or a postman to be seen for a thousand years. When the American empire fell, I think we can honestly say we did a damn sight better, and indeed better than most. We lost the electronic libraries, of course, and a great deal of knowledge, but the infrastructure of civilisation pulled through the troubled times reasonably intact. In some respects, even improved. A great deal of that we owe to the very fact that the electronic records were lost—and along with them the chains of usury and rent, and the other . . . dark powers which held the world in what they even then had the gall to call "The Net".'

He stood up and ambled along to a corner and leaned his elbow on a shelf. 'What we have instead of the net is the tinkers.' He waved his hands again. 'And telephony and telegraphy and libraries and so forth, of course, but that's beside the point. The tinkers look after our computation, which even with the path of light most of us are . . . unwilling to do, because of what happened in the past, but are grateful there's somebody to do it. This makes them . . . not quite a pariah people, but definitely a slightly stigmatised occupation. And that very stigma, you see, paradoxically ensures—or gives some assurance of—the purity of their product. It keeps the two paths, the light and the dark, separate. You see what I'm driving at?'

'No,' I said. 'I'm afraid I don't.'

'Oh.' He looked a little disappointed at my slowness on the uptake. 'Well, not to put too fine a point on it, it's one thing for scholars to risk their own bodies or souls with the dark storage. Not done, so to speak, but between you and me and the gatepost, it *is* done. It's quite another for a tinker to do it. Could contaminate the seer-stones, y'see. Bad business.'

He stalked over and stared at me. 'The upshot, my friend, is that you had better get your tinker girlfriend back here with whatever she took, and get those file-folders you *borrowed* back here with it, if you want to have this episode overlooked. Clear?'

'Yes, but—'

'No "buts", Clovis. You don't have much time. Get out and get back before anyone else notices, that's the ticket.'

'I'll do what I can,' I said, truthfully enough, and left.

As I hurried back to the lodging I kept trying to think what the hell we could do. I'd been hoping to hang on to the paper files for at least a week, which should give me enough time to see if there was anything of urgent significance in them. There was no way, however, that Merrial could 're-turn' whatever computer files she had managed to retrieve. She could pretend to delete them from her seer-stone's memory, but I doubted if that would fool Gantry. He would want the stone itself, and she was most unlikely to give it to him.

The landlady let me in, because I'd left the outside door key with Merrial. I gave her a forced smile and ran up the stairs, and knocked on the door of the room where I'd left Merrial drowsing. No reply came, so I quietly opened the door.

Merrial wasn't there. Nor was anything that belonged to her. Nor were the two file-folders. I looked around, bewildered for a moment, and then remembered what Merrial had said about photocopying the documents. I felt weak with relief. I gathered up my own gear, checked again that there was nothing of ours left in the room, and went downstairs.

'Aye,' said the landlady, 'the lassie went out a wee while after you did. She left the key wi' me.'

'Did she ask about photocopying shops around here?'

'No. But there's only one, just around the corner. You cannae miss it.'

'Aw, thanks!'

I rushed out again and along the street and around the corner. The shop was there, sure enough, but Merrial wasn't. Nobody answering to her— fairly unmistakable—description had called.

I wandered down Great Western Road in a sort of daze, and stopped at the parapet of the bridge over the Kelvin. The other bridge, which we'd crossed on the tram, was a few hundred metres upstream; the ruins of an Underground station, boarded-off and covered with grim warnings, was on the far bank. The riverside fish restaurant, where we'd eaten last night, sent forth smells of deep-fried batter. The river swirled along, the ash of my anxious cigarette not disturbing the smallest of its ripples.

She could not have just gone off with the goods; I was loyal enough to her to be confident in her loyalty to me, and did not even consider—except momentarily, hypothetically—that she'd simply used me to get at the information she sought. The most drastic remaining possibility was that she had somehow been got at herself, and had left under some urgent summons, or duress. But the landlady would surely have noticed any such thing, so it couldn't have happened in the lodging.

Between there and the copy-shop, then. I formed a wild scheme of pacing the pavement, searching for a clue; of questioning passers-by. It seemed melodramatic.

More likely by far, I told myself, was that she'd simply gone somewhere for some reason of her own. She had her own return ticket. She'd expect me to have the sense to meet her at the station. I could picture us laughing over the misunderstanding, even if some frantic calls would have to be made to Gantry.

Or even, she could have gone to another copy-shop!

A militiaman strolled past, his glance registering me casually. I stayed where I was until he was out of sight, well aware that heading off at once would only look odd; and also aware that staring with a worried expression over a parapet at a twenty-metre drop into a river might make the least suspicious militiaman interested.

By then, naturally, I was wondering if she'd been arrested, for unauthorised access to the University, necromancy, or just on general principles; but then again, if she had been, it was not my worry on anything but a personal level: as a tinker, she'd have access to a good lawyer, just as much as I would, as a scholar.

So the end of my agitated thinking, and a look at my watch, which showed that the time was a quarter past ten, was to decide to go to the station and wait for her.


The train was due to leave at eleven-twenty. At five past eleven I put down my empty coffee-cup, stubbed out my cigarette and strode over to the public telegraph. There I tapped out a message: GANTRY UNIV HIST INST REGRET DELAY IN FILE RETURN STOP WILL CALL FROM CARRON STOP RESPECTS CLOVIS.

I was on the point of hitting the transmit key when I smelled the scent and sweat of Merrial behind me. Then she leaned past my cheek and said, in a warm, amused voice, 'Very loyal of you, to him and to me.'

I turned and grabbed her in my arms. 'Where the hell have you been?'

'Just fire off that message,' she said. 'I'll tell you on the train.' She was grinning at me, and I felt all worries fade as I hugged her properly, then stepped back to hold her shoulder at arm's length as though to make doubly sure she was there. Her poke looked even larger and heavier than before.

'You've got the paper files?'

'Yes,' she said, hefting the bag. 'Come on.'

I transmitted the message, and we dashed hand in hand down the platform. The train wasn't heavily used, and we found a compartment—half a carriage—to ourselves and swung down on to the seats and faced each other across the table, laughing.

'Well,' I said. 'Tell me about it. You had me a wee bit worried, I have to admit.'

She curled her fingers across the back of my hand. 'I'm sorry,' she said. 'But I thought it seemed like a good idea to disappear. That way, if Gantry or anyone else leaned on you to give the files or the, you know, other files back, you could honestly say you couldn't, you really wouldn't know where I was and would look genuinely flummoxed, say if they went so far as to come back to our room with you.'

'Oh, right. I was genuinely flummoxed, I'll give you that. But if anyone was with me they could have made the same guess as I did, and come to the station.'

She shrugged. 'I'd have kept out of sight.' She combed her fingers through a hanging fall of hair, smiling coyly. 'I'm no bad at that.'

'And caught the train at the last second?'

'Or something.' She didn't seem interested in raking over speculative contingencies. 'Anyway, we're here, and we've got the goods. Nothing Gantry can do to get them off us now.'

'Aye. Still, I'll have to wire him from Carron, reassure him they're in safe keeping.'

'Like you said. So it's all square.'

The train began to move. I looked out at the apparently shifting station and platform, gliding into the past in relative motion, then looked back at her.

'No,' I said. 'It isn't as straightforward as that.'

She listened to my account of what Gantry had said about the tinkers and the dark storage. When I'd finished she shook her head slowly.

'You should have just covered up about my being a tinker,' she said.

That was a shock. 'How could I?' I protested. 'He'd figured it already, and it would be easy enough to check. I didn't want to lie to him. Especially not lie and get found out as soon as he picked up a phone.'

Her mouth thinned. 'I suppose not. Fair enough. Your man's trust matters in the long run. And maybe even being evasive would've confirmed his suspicion.' She looked as if a weight had settled on her shoulders at that moment.

'I would have been evasive—Truth help me, I would have *lied* if you'd asked me!'

'I couldn't do that,' she said. 'Ach, this is so complicated!'

'Hey, it's all right,' I said. 'We'll think of something. I'll string Gantry some kind of line, give us time to check out the files, and we'll have them back in a week. Take next Monday off too if I have to.'

Merrial's eyes suddenly brimmed. She blinked hard.

'*Dhia*, I hope it's that easy!' She sighed. 'I wish I could tell you more right now.' She shook her head. 'But I can't.'

'Why not?'

'Oh, *mo chridhe*! I'm a tinker, and tinkers have to mind their tongues. Even if—especially if—their tongues are spending time in other mouths!'

'So you have secrets of your craft,' I said dryly, 'which you have to keep. That's all right with me.'

She looked as if she were about to say something urgent, and then all she said was, 'I shouldn't worry so much. It'll probably all turn out all right.'

'Yes, sure,' I said, pretending to agree with her. 'Oh, well. Shall we have a look at the files, then?'

'OK,' she said, pulling them out. 'Tell you what. You can look through the early one, and I'll look through the late. That'll increase the chances that either of us will find something we can *understand*.'

'Fair enough,' I said.

I opened the folder from the 1990s and flipped impatiently through thoroughly dull and worthy stuff about medical charity, and some fascinatingly improbable economic statistics from Kazakhstan. Towards the end I found something more personal: pages ripped from a spiral-bound notebook, apparently a diary. I pored over the Deliverer's scrawl:

*Thurs Jul 16 98. Trawl of NYC's remaining left bookshops—nostalgia, I guess. Picked up Against the Current in St Mark's—trendy place, left pubns marginalised, seems apt. The old Critique clique still banging on—Suzi W in AtC, etc. At least they're loyal—unlike moi, huh. Then trekked over to Revo Bks—Avakian's lot, madder than ever. They have a dummy electric chair in the shop for their Mumia campaign. Flipped through old debates on SU etc. De-*

*pressing thought 'Marxism is a load of crap' kept coming to mind. Then Unity Books on W 23d. Couldn't bear going to Pathfinder. After my little adventure, not sure I want to face the Fourth International cdes either. Or they me. Agh.*

> *Fri Jul 17 98. Hot humid afternoon, rainstorm later. Met M on Staten Isl ferry. Leaned on the rail and looked at old Liberty thro near fog. M seems to know I'm telling the old gang about his approaches. Thing is he doesn't seem to mind. (Girl with pink hair on the ferry. Swear same girl was in Boston. Am I being followed or getting paranoid?)*

I couldn't make head nor tail of this, and turned over to the last of the entries.

> *Thurs Dec 17 98. Almaty again. Hotel lounge TV tuned permanently to CNN. Green light of city falling in the night. Hospital filling up. Fucking Yanks. Here I am trying to help development, there they are trying to roll it back.*

After that, nothing but a stain and an angry scribble, where the pen had dug into and torn the page. Perhaps she'd reached the end of that notebook, or stopped keeping a diary. I leafed through the rest of the papers, with an oppressive feeling that seeing through their present opacity would take even longer than I'd thought. Then an idly turned page brought me to a stop.

It was a photocopy of an old article she'd written, but it was a small advertisement accidentally included at its margin that caught my eye. It was for a public meeting on 'Fifty Years of the Fourth International' and it had in one corner a symbol which was identical to the monogram on Merrial's pendant. It was all I could do not to knock my forehead or cry out at my own stupidity. What I'd thought were the letters 'G' and 'T' were in fact the hammer and sickle of the communist symbol, and the meaning of the '4' was self-evident. I'd missed the connection just because the symbol faced in the opposite direction to the one on the Soviet flag.

The sinister significance of the hammer and sickle made me feel slightly nauseous; the implication of that same symbol appearing across such a gulf of time induced a certain giddiness.

I closed the file and looked up, and found myself meeting Merrial's equally baffled eyes.

'It's all either not very interesting, or completely fucking incomprehensible,' she said.

'Same here,' I said. 'Let's leave it.'

All that long afternoon, we talked about other things.

Battles, mostly, as I recall.


The train pulled into the station at Carron Town on the dot of six. The sun was still high, the late afternoon still warm. Once again tired and jaded by our journey, Merrial and I left the train with an access of energy and a surge of hunger. Merrial led the way straight to The Carronade, and we settled into a dark corner of the strangely polished-smelling bar with plates of farmed trout and fresh-picked peas and new potatoes, accompanied with a shared jug of beer.

'I can't wait to get back to your place,' I said, 'get a bit of privacy, and get my face right down into . . . the files.'

She laughed. 'Aye, it'll be great to get a good look at them at last, without having to look over our shoulders.'

But as she said it she was looking over my shoulder, as she had done every minute or so all through the meal. She had her back to the wall, I had my back to the bar. The pub was beginning to fill up with people from the project, in for a quick drink on their way home or to their lodgings. As yet I'd heard no voices I recognised.

'You seem a wee bit on edge,' I said.

'Aye, well, like I said on the train . . .'

'Fergal?'

'Yes.'

'You're expecting to meet him here?' I asked, remembering that we were in this bar on her—albeit welcome—suggestion.

She opened her hands. 'Maybe. Depends.'

'On what?' I piled up our empty plates and lit a cigarette.

'Och, on how they want to play it,' she said, sounding unaccustomedly bitter.

'Secrets or no secrets,' I said, trying to keep my tone light, 'you're going to have to let me in on this, sooner or later. I'm getting thoroughly tired of seeing you looking worried.'

'I don't *have* to do anything!' she flared. 'And you don't *have* to see me looking like anything!'

I said nothing, staring at her, shocked and annoyed but already forgiving her; she'd been under a lot of tension, for reasons I knew about and reasons I knew I didn't.

'Ach,' she said, gentle again, 'I didn't mean that, colha Gree. You've not been taught as I have, to be hard.'

At that I had to smile; she seemed more vulnerable than hard, at that moment. Her eyes widened. I heard a footstep behind us, and then Fergal swung uninvited on to the bench beside me.

'Hello,' Merrial said, not warmly. Her glance returned to me.

'Oh, hi,' I said. He looked at our drinks. 'My round, I think.' He reached back over his shoulder and snapped his fingers; most people wouldn't have gotten away with that, but he did. In half a minute the barmaid was laying another full jug on the table.

'So, Merrial,' he said quietly, 'you got it?'

'We did,' said Merrial. 'As far as I can tell. I checked through it all this morning, and it's the whole archive.'

'And where did you do that?' I butted in, a little indignantly.

'Kelvin Wood,' Merrial said, giving me a disarmingly unabashed grin. 'In the bushes.'

'So that's what you were up to.'

Merrial nodded, with a flash of her eyebrows. Fergal looked at her, then at me, as though to remind us that he had more important things on his mind.

'Fine,' I said.

'That's good news,' Fergal said, to Merrial. He laughed briefly. 'To put it mildly, eh?'

'Aye,' she said. 'It is that.'

'Anyway, Clovis,' Fergal said, 'you'll appreciate that the information you've helped to retrieve needs to be looked at with an expert eye. Rather urgently, in fact, considering how long it may take.'

'Of course,' I said. 'Any chance that I could take a look at it first, just glance through it?'

He shook his head. 'Sorry, Clovis. You have no idea—no offence—of how much is there. It's an incredible quantity of not very well organised information. In the time it would take for you to make sense of any of it, we could be searching for information we *know* how to interpret. Every hour might count.'

'Just a minute!' I said, dismayed and indignant. 'Nobody mentioned anything about this. I want to get a look at them too, and not have them disappear into—'

'Some tinker hideaway?' Fergal raised his eyebrows. 'It won't be like that, I assure you. You have my word that we won't keep them long—weeks at the most—and that you'll get to see them and search them at your leisure as soon as we've finished.'

'But,' I said, 'how will I know they haven't been changed—even accidentally? Because I have to be able to rely on it.'

Merrial was looking desperately uncomfortable. She gave Fergal a quick, hot glare and leaned closer to me across the table.

'Think about it, man,' she said quietly. 'This stuff is all illicit anyway—
you could not exactly cite it in footnotes, could you? You can only use it to
find leads to mȧterial you *can* refer to. So you'll just have to trust us—trust
me—that the information won't be tampered with.'

'All right,' I said reluctantly.

'Good man!' He drained his glass and stood up. 'Thanks for your help.'
Fergal reached out a hand across the table. Merrial was already emptying her
personal clutter out of the leather bag. She tightened its thong and passed it
over; Fergal had caught it while I was still gazing, puzzled, at Merrial's actions.

'Wait!' I said. 'The paper files are still in there. You can't take them!'

Fergal raised his eyebrows. 'Why not?'

'These papers belong to the University.'

'I'm afraid they don't,' said Fergal, sounding regretful. 'They belong
to us.'

I looked frantically at Merrial, who only gave a small, sad nod.

'Who the fuck is this "us"?' I demanded, though I already suspected the
answer. 'Come on, I can give you photocopies if you must.'

'Not good enough, old chap.'

'Then give me them back.'

'Sorry,' said Fergal. 'I can't.'

I shifted on my feet, moved my elbow; all by reflex. Fergal's eyes narrowed.

'Don't,' he said very quietly, 'even *think* of messing with me.'

I was actually thinking of yelling out and calling on the others in the bar,
some of whom had their eye on this confrontation. But something in Fergal's
stance and glance suggested that the only outcome of such a brawl would be
his escape after inflicting some severe damage on our side, starting with me.
And whichever side Merrial came in on, or even if she tried to stay out of it,
she was likely to get hurt.

My honour wasn't at stake in preventing Fergal's departure with the
papers—it would be at stake in getting them back—and for now I had no
right to risk life and limb of myself or others over it.

'Take it, tinker,' I said. 'I can bide.'

He smiled, without condescension.

'I hope I see you again,' he said, and was out the door.

I looked over at a few curious, tense faces at the bar, shrugged and
returned to the table, where Merrial was shakily lighting one of my cigarettes.

'Some explanation might be in order,' I said, as casually as I could manage. One of my knees was vibrating.

Merrial took a long breath and a long draw with it.

'Sorry,' she said. 'I can't, really.'

'But look,' I said. 'Why didn't you just tell me to hide the files, or say we'd put them back—'

I was getting exasperated and confused, and then the penny, finally, dropped.

'You agree with him!' I said. 'You actually *agree* that he has some kind of a *right* to those papers, and to see the files first, and that nobody else can so much as look at them without his sufferance. Including me.'

She looked levelly back at me.

'And you're not going to tell me why.'

A small shake of her head.

'And you knew all along this could happen.'

A smaller nod.

'All right,' I said. There were still two half-litres in the jug; I poured for both of us, and lit a cigarette myself, leaning forward into Merrial's smoke, almost into the tent of her hair. 'All right.' The heel of my hand was rubbing beneath my eye; irritated with myself, I stopped doing that and fiddled with the cigarette instead. The sound of the laughter and conversation at the bar was like the noise of a burn over a rock, washing over and hiding our talk. We could say anything.

'I'm really at a loss,' I said. 'I can't believe you just set me up, but unless you tell me what's really going on—'

'I told you,' she said. 'I can't. Can't you trust me on that?'

'Oh, I can trust you on that all right,' I said. 'But if I don't get those files back like I promised, nobody at the University will ever trust me again.'

She looked as tense, as torn, as I felt.

'I'm very sorry about that,' she said. 'But there's nothing I can do about it.'

'Come on,' I said. 'There must be. Hell, if I get the files back, I can give your lot copies of all the files. Isn't that worth more to them than just what they've got?'

'You don't understand,' Merrial said. 'Now that we know about the other files, we're going to have to get them all. Like Fergal said, they're ours.'

'Ours', indeed! I was unwilling, or unready, to challenge her about the society to which that might refer. I spread my hands. 'You can't expect me to accept that without a damn good reason, which you're not giving me.'

'I've told you. I can't. So why don't we just forget about all this?'

'Merrial,' I pleaded, dismayed at the depths of her lack of understanding, 'these files are part of my work, my whole career depends on them. So, please—'

I reached out, touching her hair.

Her eyes glinted.

'Oh, *fuck off*!' she told me, not quite a yell but loud and emphatic enough to turn heads.

'I'll do that,' I replied, and rose and stalked out. I glanced back from the door, and saw only the top of her head, and the forward fall of her hair, and her hands over her face. The door swung shut behind me.

# 8

## WESTERN APPROACHES

'It's over,' Valentina was saying.

'What's over?' Myra asked. She shook her head, looking around her office. Val and Andrei and Denis were all there, perched on desks or window sills. The command-centre screens had vanished like a dream. Parvus hovered on the edge of her vision, looking as though about to speak.

'The *putsch*,' Valentina explained.

'Just like that?'

Myra stared, blinking through options presented by Parvus. The personal had its own analysis, and it was busy agreeing with Valentina. The battlesats seized by the space movement were enough to guard their beleaguered enclaves and launch sites, but not to tilt the balance of world power in their favour. The Security Council nations retained their control over the ReUN, but the battlesats that had resisted the coup had done so in their own name, not that of the ReUN. They remained dangerously autonomous.

At ground level all sorts of local balances had been tilted, almost entirely by the rapid re-evaluations of the real weight on the various sides that the bloody flurries of actual combat had induced. Disputes had been resolved or reopened, entire armies had mobilised or disbanded on the strength of the gigantic shadows thrown on the screens of analysis by the small engagements in the field.

'God,' said Myra disgustedly. 'This is *so* decadent.' It reminded her of the

Renaissance mercenaries that Machiavelli had moaned about in the *Discourses*, working out who would have won if they'd fought and abiding by that decision like gentlemen, while omitting the bloody business of actual battle. 'Nobody wants a real fight, they'd rather follow the sims. Talk about the pornography of violence. Wankers.'

'It's worse than that,' Denis said coarsely. 'We're fucked.' He threw a projection of a time-slice from *Jane's* and laser-pointed the relevant areas. 'Look.'

The ISTWR's military profile and general credibility was no longer something that cautious strategists, estimating from past actions and present rumour, rated highly. It was negligible.

'We've been found out,' said Denis Gubanov. 'In exactly the wrong way. They must have always reckoned with at least the possibility that we had nukes. Mutual Protection—or Reid, anyway—knew we had them. Point is, we didn't use them, so it's assumed we either don't have them or don't have the stomach to use them. We've gone from being Upper Volta with nukes to being Upper Volta without. And the weapons we did use didn't work.'

'They worked—' Valentina began, rather defensively.

'Huh!' Myra snorted. 'They worked just fine, only they didn't destroy the targets. Yeah, I can see that doing our deterrence posture a power of good.'

The hotline phone—a solid, old-fashioned, unambiguous red phone on Myra's desk—began to ring. She looked at it doubtfully for a moment, then shrugged and picked it up.

'Myra Godwin-Davidova.'

Pause.

'Hello, Myra. Dave here.'

She gave him a moment of nonplussed silence.

'Myra? It's *David Reid*.'

'Yes. Hello,' she said. 'What do you want now?'

There was a second's delay in his reply.

'What do you want, is more like it.' Even over the crackly laser-to-landline link, she could hear his fury. 'You had the whole situation in the balance, you know that? You had the fucking *casting vote*, Chairman Davidova! You had the nuclear option, and you threw it away! I'd almost rather you had used your goddamn nukes against us—at least that way the Security Council would have had control, and would've had to take responsibility. There'd be some chance of an end to the chaos, which is all we really wanted. As it is you've turned what should've been the endgame into another fucking stalemate.'

'I don't see how that makes you any worse off.'

She heard a knocking noise and realised after a moment that he was banging something on his head.

'It's made us *all* worse off! It's like entropy, Myra, can't you see that? Everybody's climbed up a few flights, *escalated*, that's the fucking word for it. We're all higher up but relatively we're no better placed, and we've lost energy, wasted work in the process. And you know the only people who'll gain from that? The marginals, the fucking barb, that's who. Including your local godless communists.'

'It's you who should have thought of that. Before you launched your bloody coup.'

Reid took a deep breath, a long sigh down the wire.

'Yeah, you're right. It is my fault. Didn't expect a counter-coup, that's all.'

'What counter-coup?'

Again the odd delay.

'Don't play the innocent. Somebody's taken over most of the battle-sats, and it sure wasn't my lot. Nor the UN's, come to that.'

'You don't know who it was?'

'No. So who was it? You must know.'

Myra thought about this. Ah, hell, he'd find out anyway.

'The Fourth International,' she told him. 'Space fraction, mil org.'

A second ticked past, then she heard Reid's loud laugh. 'Ha-ha-ha! OK, Myra, be like that. I'll find out anyway. Meanwhile, take a look at the north-eastern border, and see if it all still seems so funny. I'm well out of it—I'm on a shuttle for Lagrange. Bye.'

He closed the connection in some manner that sounded like slamming down the receiver on an old-fashioned phone, with an impact that made her wince.

Before she could look at the north-eastern border, Parvus stepped into frame and raised a hand. Myra gestured to the others to wait.

'Yes?'

The stout phantom waved his hands expansively. 'Ah, Myra, I have had to move fast on your investments. I received the hot inside tip—' he laid a yellowed finger to his ruddy nose '—that Mutual Protection are liquidating their assets.'

'What!' Myra had by this time got so used to 'assets' being a euphemism for 'nukes' that she almost ducked under the desk. Her startled gaze raced down the latest news bulletin—nothing.

'Oh, you mean *financially*.'

'Of course financially. When the last war starts I will tell you straight. No, Mutual Protection are selling up, pulling out.'

'Pulling out from where?'

'From here. From Kazakhstan.' He looked at her sadly, almost sympathetically. 'From Earth.'

Over the next few days it became clear that the main gainers from the brief lurch into actual violence were the marginals, who took their own advantage of the distraction—and Mutual Protection's hasty liquidation—to expand their domains in country after country; and the Sheenisov.

They made a push along the pass at Zaysan, to the south-east. Kazakhstani long-range bombers pounded the Sino-Soviet combat drones—devices of unsettling and diverse appearance, combinations of almost Soviet mechanical clunkiness with quasi-organic nanotech sheen. Their wrecks, or corpses, littered the roads and hillsides outside Buran. Any functioning components had a disturbing tendency to reassemble. The Kazakhstani bombing-runs stopped as supplies of bombs began to run out. Sheenisov *spetsnatz* teams—casting hologram feints, radar ghosts, sonic body-doubles—skirmished among the wreckage and dug in at the furthest limit of their advance. Meanwhile, a tank-borne human army, or horde, was outflanking the Altay Mountains at the northern end of the range: rolling south and west from the Katun basin, and down the road and railway from Barnaul, unopposed. By the end of the fourth day after the coup attempt they'd crossed Kazakhstan's northern border, and paused.

The *oblys* council in Semipalatinsk—evidently softened by intimidation or subversion—invited them in, and they cheerfully accepted the invitation. They rode in like liberators, welcomed by cheering crowds, and settled down with every appearance of being there to stay.

The red phone rang again.

'Chingiz Suleimanyov,' the caller identified himself. The current President of Kazakhstan; his nickname of 'Genghis President' was not quite fair. 'I have a proposal for your government, Madame Davidova, and for you personally . . .'

The following morning Myra got up and dressed, and packed. She had most of her luggage sent on to the airport. She loaded stacks of old files, in formats going back all the way through floppy disks to actual paper, into a couple of crates, sealed and diplomatic-bagged and sent off to another destination. Then she began stripping her flat, with a kind of rage at herself. She commandeered some kids from the militia to take the stuff down the stairs—physically, she wasn't up to that, and she knew it.

The bedroom's contents went first, all the cushions and throws, the tatting and trim, the lacework and lacquer and lapis lazuli—out, all of it, into big black plastic sacks that went straight to the nearest craft-market stall for a derisory sum. Let them make their own way again, let them travel the circuits like trade-goods, like cowrie shells and crated Marlboros, back to the Camden Locks and Greenwich Villages of the world. The posters on the walls went next, to another stall, for other collectors. The vinyl records and the compact discs—that was what they were called, she thought with a smile, as she hefted their stacked bulk—to a third.

And then the books. That did hurt, but she went on with it; grimly, grimily hauling them down from their shelves, sorting and stacking. Again and again tempted to sift, to stray; now and again lost in a book, or in the reminiscences it provoked. Blink, knuckle the eye, slam the covers shut, sneeze out the dust, move on. Her eyes reddened, her fingers blackened and her shoulders ached.

Most of the books, too, went to the bazaar. The remainder she had loaded in the back of a small truck. She washed herself and looked around the echoing emptiness of her flat. It was still habitable; it was a place to which she could return; but in it nothing of herself remained.

She shoved her 2045 Library of Congress and her other libraries and concert halls, art galleries and archives into the top of her overnight bag, and distributed her knives and pistols about her belts and pockets. The lads who'd lugged her stuff to the market came back one by one, with sheaves of money. She peeled off more than enough to pay them, one by one.

The truck with the books went ahead of her, well ahead, as she hefted her overnight bag and herself on to the horse, and rode out for the last time to the camp.


'Open up!'

Myra yelled, rattling the iron gate. The truck had parked itself in front, waiting with robotic patience for the obstacle to clear. Any electronic pleas it had made had evidently been ignored.

Myra could see why. There wasn't much left of the camp but the fence, and away to one side—too far away to be useful for her—she could see men taking it apart with wire-cutters and rolling it up in great bales and wheels. Nothing but grass and roadway stretched ahead of her for a few hundred metres. Where the huts had been she could see only clumps of dark material on the steppe, with men and women wandering around and children racing about. The factories were not gone, but they were visibly shrivelling, as though their construction were being run in reverse.

She flipped down her eyeband, upped the gain, gazed at the scene. Nobody'd heard her shouts. Damn. She eased her old New Vietcong knock-off

Glock from its holster, steadied and soothed the horse, and fired not into the air but carefully at a tussock a few tens of metres distant. The mare shied and the bullet ricocheted anyway, but the shot got the result she wanted. A figure detached itself from the milling crowd and marched towards her. Kim Nok-Yung, carrying a rifle.

'Hi, Myra.' He couldn't stop smiling. He tapped a code into the lock's plate. The gate creaked open, and he left it open. Myra led the horse through, and the truck followed, then kept pace beside her. Nok-Yung hopped on the running-board and hung on with one hand, flourishing the rifle triumphantly with the other, as if he was riding a tank into a liberated capital.

'Isn't this great!'

She got caught up in his enthusiasm.

'Yes, it's wonderful. I'm so glad it's over, Nok-Yung.'

They passed one of the factories, vanishing before their eyes, crumbling back from its edges into curiously ordered dust, dust that trickled like columns of ants along paths on the remaining machinery, or on the grass. Some of the dust heaped itself up into blocky stacks that hardened into colour-coded cubes, inert, from which the wind blew not a speck. Other lines of dust coalesced into glassy spheroids, obsidian-black or crystal-clear, that lay in the tall grass like gleaming pebbles and stones and boulders.

'Control components, computers and so on,' Nok-Yung indicated. 'The cubes are construction material.'

'Will anyone collect them, I wonder?'

The Korean laughed. 'We'll take some of the control parts with us—they might be valuable, where we're going.'

'Oh?'

He glanced sidelong at her, almost apologetic. 'Semipalatinsk,' he said. 'To the Sheenisov.'

Myra restrained herself from reining in the horse. 'What? Why, for God's sake?' She waved an arm, wildly, around and behind. 'You can stay with us— you're welcome here, in our republic or anywhere in Kazakhstan. Hey, man, Baikonur will take you on, think of that!'

He shook his head. 'Some of the prisoners will settle here, of course. But I and Se-Ha and the others, we are going to the Sheenisov. Some of us have friends and family with them already. There is no other place for us. Even with Mutual Protection—' he turned aside and spat on the grass '—gone, we still have the debts, and the blacklists. No work to be had back home but debt-bondage. Among the Sheenisov we will be free.' He grinned, no longer apologetic but feral. 'And there is work to be done there—work for us. They are the future.'

'But you don't know anything about what they're really like. Just because they call themselves communists doesn't mean they're *nice*—you should know that!'

Nok-Yung laughed harshly. 'They have no Great Leader or Dear Leader, you can love it or leave it, and we're going to try it.'

By this time they had reached the edge of the crowd. Myra reined in the horse and signalled the truck to stop. Nok-Yung jumped off the running-board. What had seemed from a distance like aimless wandering resolved itself into people moving about purposefully, retrieving and stacking their possessions from the self-disassembling huts. Most of them ignored her arrival. Myra was not surprised or put out. The benefits of her oversight were easy enough to overlook, and the camp committee itself was not a popular body among the prisoners, elected though it was. Like a company union, it had partially represented the interests of the labourers, while often enough relaying the will of the owners.

She noticed Shin Se-Ha, dapper in a sadly dated *sarariman* suit which he'd probably worn for the first and last time at his trial, but which for now signified his new freedom. He carried a small case through the scooting children and trudging adults. By now other vehicles and beasts were trundling or plodding into view, summoned by phones restored to their proper owners.

Myra stood, fondling the mare's neck, quieting it, as the Japanese mathematician picked his way towards her. She tried to search her memory of what he'd been sent down for: misuse of company resources or some such pretext—he'd run refinements of Otoh's neo-Marxian capital-reproduction schemata, primed with empirical data, on the university's computers. The real reason was his results, which he'd indiscreetly spread-sheeted around: the sinister algebra of the Otoh equations added up to complete breakdown in two more business-cycles.

That had been one boom and one slump ago.

'Hello, Myra,' he said. He put the case down. Probably contained all he owned, he was that sort of guy. Frightening, in his way.

'Hi, Se-Ha. Nok-Yung tells me you're going—' she nodded forward '—East.'

'I am. Sorry if you do not approve.'

Very direct! The sun shone in her face like an interrogation-lamp and the wind made a constant white noise. It was a time for telling the truth or facing worse ordeals.

'Whether I approve or not is not the point,' she said. 'You're free, and I have no say in what you do. But I should warn you that the Kazakhstani Republic will resist the Sheenisov, and so will I. We will not be rolled over. I would be sorry to be on the opposite side to you in a battle, but—'

She shrugged.

'I would be sorry too,' said Shin. 'But "so it goes", *ah-so?*'

'*Ah-so* indeed,' she smiled, and suddenly realised how Reid had been able to keep up his no-hard-feelings enmities for so long. 'Meanwhile, I have something for you.' She waved a hand at the truck. 'This, and everything in it.' She tossed him the truck's control-panel, which he deftly caught. 'Go on, have a look.'

Doors clicked open, banged shut. He came back. He caught her hand; he bowed over it, as though about to kiss her knuckles, and stepped back.

'I am in your debt,' he said, stiffly. Then he spread his hands, looking Western and abashed rather than Eastern and indebted. 'What can I say, Myra? You're very kind.'

'Ah, don't be silly, my friend,' she said. 'You and Nok-Yung and the others made my work here a lot more rewarding than it would otherwise have been. I owe you it, if anything.' She shared with him a conspiratorial chuckle. 'And a library of revolutionary theory might just come in handy where you're going, eh?'

'Yes. I don't know if I can take the responsibility.' He shook his head, thinking about it. 'There are books and documents in that van which have *never been scanned in.*'

Myra patted a pocket. 'Not even in the 2045 Library of Congress?'

'Not even that!' He seemed to find the thought awesome, a violation of the order of nature. It gave pause even to Myra's resolution, as half a lifetime's easy assumption that everything was archived, that every jot and tittle lived unchanged in silicon heaven, was suddenly confronted with the reality that some thoughts might only face eternity in the frail ark of woodpulp, and that she was responsible for them. Her commitment rallied.

'Oh, well. I should have read them by now, and if not, it's too late for me.'

The bustle around them was increasing. Vehicles were whining, horses and camels were whinnying and spitting. Some children, even some adults, were in tears at leaving this place, which for all its duress had not imposed any too severe privation, and which was familiar. Some folk were assiduously picking up the glassy stones, whether as talismans or as trade-trinkets Myra couldn't tell. The thousands of former prisoners were dispersing to all the round horizon.

Half a dozen other men were converging on where she stood, gathering around, talking in Korean or Japanese, smiling at her and climbing into the back of the truck. Nok-Yung came up and shook hands.

'We'll keep in touch.'

There was so much to say, so much that could not be said.

'We'll meet again,' Myra said. 'All the best, guys. Good luck with the commies.'

'Hah!' Nok-Yung raised a clenched fist and grinned at her. 'You'll be with us some day, Myra, you'll see. Goodbye, and thanks!'

He threw his bag in the truck and sprang into the driving-seat, then laughed as Shin Se-Ha climbed through the opposite door and flourished the control-panel under his nose. Still shouting and waving, the men drove off, bumping across the steppe, resolutely north-east.

Myra watched them out of sight and then mounted her horse and rode back to the town. Only once did she look behind, and saw that there was nothing left to see.

The airport of the capital of the International Scientific and Technical Workers' Republic had only one terminal building. It was a big, open-plan space, dotted with franchises. They'd never bothered with Customs, or Immigration Control. Between the floor-to-ceiling windows—with their charming views of steppe, runway, apartment-blocks, gantries and more steppe—hung equally gigantic posters of Trotsky, Korolev, Kapitsa, Gagarin and Guevara. The idea, many years ago, had been to make the concourse look Communist: a bit of macho swagger. Right now it had the look of a place about to *fall* to the commies, rather to Myra's disgust. Crowded with people sitting on too much luggage, their expressions flickering between impatience and resignation with every change on the departure screens. For heaven's sake, thought Myra—Semipalatinsk was a hundred miles away, they were over-reacting.

Her own flight's departure-time was not for another hour. She confirmed her booking at the check-in, made sure her luggage was on board, and declined the offer of waiting in the first-class lounge. Instead she made her way to the old Nicafe franchise, and sat down with a coffee and a cigarette, to rest her feet and indulge in a little nostalgia.

In the good old days before the Third World War she'd sipped many a coffee here, with many a man on the other side of the table. Always a different man, and almost never one that she'd liked: ugly, jowly military men for the most part, jet-lagged and stubbled, in creased dress uniforms heavily medallioned; or diplomats or *biznesmen*, sleek and shaven and cologned in silk suits. And always, hanging around a few metres away, outside the glowering ring of bodyguards, would be the photographers and reporters, there to record the closing of the deal. The ISTWR had never gone for secret diplomacy—openness was the whole point of tradable nuclear deterrence.

It had worked fine, until the nuclear war.

The Germans had launched the War of European Integration without a nuke to call their own. This hadn't been an oversight—it had been essential to the element of surprise. Once their first wave of tanks was safely over the

Polish border they'd made Myra a very generous offer for some of her tradable nuclear deterrence. Myra's frantic ringing around her clients had found
no one willing to deal: not for any amount of money, on the entirely rational basis that the Third World War was not a good time to sell. Myra had
considered cutting them out and selling the Germans the option anyway,
but her business loyalty had got the better of her. It had also got the better
of the German occupiers of Kiev, and the German civilians of Frankfurt
and Berlin. She still felt guilty about that.

For want of company, she flipped down her eyeband and summoned
Parvus. For a laugh, she sat his virtual image in the seat across the table from
her. The construct triangulated his apparent position, saw the joke and smiled.

'What can I do for you, Myra?'

'Tell me what you think of the General.' She wasn't bothered by appearing
to talk to empty air; she wasn't the only person in that café area consulting a
familiar or a fetch.

'That is a tricky one,' said Parvus. He ran his fingers through his thatch,
rummaged in his crumpled jacket for cigarettes. Lit up and relaxed; the ad-
dictive personality was part of the package, an aspect of how the thing hung
together. 'There are of course rumours—' dismissive smoketrail '—that the
FI has long had access to a rogue AI. Or the other way round, according to
its opponents.' Parvus showed his teeth. 'It goes back to when AIs of that
sophistication were rare—before the Revolution, or the Singularity.'

'This is the Singularity?' It was Myra's turn to wave a cigarette. 'Not like
you'd notice.'

'It's one of these things you don't notice, when you're in the middle of
it,' agreed Parvus. 'Like the mass extinction event that's going on around us
right now.'

'But that's slow, that's the point. The Singularity's supposed to be fast on
something more than a geological scale.'

'It was.'

'Oh.' She wasn't sure she wanted to take this discussion any further. 'Anyway, back to the General, and what you make of him.'

'Ah, yes. Well. Very dangerous, in my opinion. His use of face and
voice is remarkably effective at getting under the skin of . . . people with
skin. Count yourself lucky he can't use pheromones, at least not over the
net.'

'You're impervious to his charm yourself, I take it.'

'Yes,' Parvus sighed. 'Fortunately for me, I lack self-awareness.'

Myra was still gaping at her familiar's unexpected remark—surely ironic,
though she wasn't sure on what level—when Parvus's place was occupied
by a Kazakh man with smooth clothes and a lined face. He had a distract-

ing small child in tow, and a silently accusing puffy-eyed woman behind him. The woman took another chair, held the squirming toddler in her lap.

Myra blinked Parvus out of her sight, vaguely hoping that the AI wasn't offended, raised her eyeband and smiled at the man and his family. His returning smile was forced.

'Good morning, Madame President. Why are you leaving us?'

Myra looked around. Nobody else seemed to have noticed her. The cult of personality was another strategic omission from their socialist democracy. Just as well—she didn't want to be mobbed on her departure. 'I'm not leaving you,' she said earnestly, leaning forward and speaking as though confidentially. Her mission had not yet been publicly announced, but she had no objection to starting a truthful rumour in advance. Only the details were sensitive, and at that level secrecy was pointless—she was confident that her full itinerary was already circulating the nets, buried among hundreds of spurious versions, all of equally authoritative provenance. 'I'm going to the West, to get help. Economic and military assistance.'

The man looked sceptical. 'Against the Sheenisov? But we haven't a chance, against them. We have no defensible borders.'

'No, but Kazakhstan has—and it's on behalf of Kazakhstan that I'm going.'

'For Chingiz?' The man's face brightened; he glanced at his wife, as though to cheer her up. 'So we are going to drive the Reds out of Semey?'

'We can't bomb Semey,' Myra said, repeating exactly President Suleimanyov's words to her. 'But we can hold the pass east of Lake Zaysan, and we can stop any further advance in the north-east. If we get help soon. The SSU forces are unlikely to try anything for some weeks, because they're stretched. And they don't like frontal fighting. As long as the Kazakhstani Republic stays hostile to them, they won't come in.' She grinned encouragingly. 'And I can be sure our own republic will stay hostile.'

She was not sure at all. There was enough social discontent, understandable enough, in her redundant workers' state for the Sino-Soviets to work on. No doubt the first agitators were already drifting in, among the first refugees from Semipalatinsk. But the man took her words to heart.

'Yes,' he said, adding, 'if Allah wills. But we are leaving, with all we have.'

'I can't blame you,' Myra said. 'I wish you well. I hope you see your way clear to come back, when things are more . . . settled.'

'Perhaps.' The man shrugged, the woman smiled thinly, the child suddenly bawled. They departed, looking up disconsolately at the screens, leaving Myra depressed.

The man had looked like a small trader, one of the large middle class raised by the republic's mixed economy. Despite all the devils it painted on its walls, the ISTWR had always stood more for a permanent NEP than a permanent revolution: only its defence and space industries were state-owned, and apart from the welfare system everything else (which in GNP terms didn't add up to much, she had to admit) was more or less *laissez-faire*. She wondered what the family had to fear from the Sheenisov, who by all accounts would have left their property and piety alone. In a way it was not surprising: the Sheenisov had made their advances by bluff and intimidation, by looking and sounding more radical and communistic than they actually were, and their absence from the comms net left a great blank screen for the most sinister speculations to play on. So perhaps this kind of unwarranted fear was the price of their progress.

Well, she would make them pay a higher price, in a harder currency. She drained her coffee and headed for the departure lounge.


At Almaty she picked up her documents, diplomatic passport and line-of-credit card in a snazzy Samsonite Diplock handed over by a courier, and on the flight to Izmir she sifted through them. The papers were literally for her eyes only, being coated with a polarising film tuned to her eyeband which in turn was tuned to her. Even so, and even sitting in the company class section at the front of the jet, alone apart from the flight-attendant, Myra felt the impulse to hunch over the papers, and wrap her wrist and elbow around their corners like a kid in class trying not to be copycatted.

Suleimanyov had struck a bold deal with the ISTWR, and with her. It was a deal which had been proposed by Georgi Davidov, who'd died before he'd been ready to return with it. Myra's lips tightened whenever she thought of that; her suspicions stirred and were not soothed back to sleep. He'd had the contracts drawn up in the briefcase that was found with his body in the hotel room. The terms were simple, a straightforward offer of economic union and military alliance. Kazakhstan would take over the ISTWR's residual social responsibilities, assimilating all of its inhabitants who wished to become Kazakhstani citizens, subsidising the rest. It would provide for the smaller state's conventional defence, leaving to its People's Army and Workers' Militia the only functions for which they were actually fitted—internal security and border patrols, principally the guarding of the spaceport and airport. In return, Myra's government would integrate its space-borne weapons, including the nukes, into the greater republic's defence forces. They would retain ultimate operational control—there was no way Suleimanyov could expect them to surrender that—but for all public and diplomatic and military purposes, they'd work together under one command. At a stroke Kazakhstan would have a military force commensurate with its land area rather than its population.

This new Great Power could then negotiate assistance from the West. It could stand as a solid bulwark—possibly even an entering wedge—against the Sheenisov, which the inchoate regimes of the Former Union and warlorded China could not. The nuclear weapons would be their bargaining counter. Useless themselves—in any but the shortest term—against the Sheenisov, they could be made available to the US or UN in exchange for the hardware and orbital back-up and even, at the outside, troop deployments that *could* hold back this new Red tide.

Myra, as the oldest available politician, with the longest experience and the widest range of Western knowledge and contacts, would make the initial approaches. In a way she would be going back to her old business of selling nuclear deterrence policies; the only difference being that there was, now, only one logical customer. And because it would be an arduous job, on a tight schedule, they were going to give her a week's break before she started, and a lot of money. She was to use that time and money to get young again.

Rejuvenation was something she should have done long ago. Now, thinking it over, she found it difficult to disentangle her reasons for procrastinating. It wasn't that the process was unaffordable, or even obscenely privileged— many of her own citizens and employees had made a trip to some Western clinic. Dodgy black-market strains of the relevant nanoware circulated wherever health services existed at all, and patches for their shortcomings were a widespread and legitimate trade. But Myra'd never gotten around to it, partly because she had been satisfied with her present condition—attractive enough to pull interesting and interested men, fit enough for her work and her undemanding exercise routines, but in no way good enough to fool anyone that she was actually young, once they saw more of her than her face, or saw her face close up.

Another aspect, she realised, was a certain patriotic stubbornness, of the kind that kept her driving her ancient Skoda Traverser. She didn't want to buy youth from . . . not so much the West as . . . the new breed, the post-nanotech generation. She wanted to muddle along with the fixes that had worked for her so far: the Swiss collagen jabs, the British circulatory-system microbots, the Georgian bacteriophage immune-system back-ups, the Vietnamese phytochemical neural regenerators, the American telomere hack . . . all assembled in a post-Soviet package deal that the health services of the Former Union and the communistans had been doling out for decades.

The Kazakhstani President had taken about thirty seconds to persuade her that it was her personal right and patriotic duty to go for the full works, the one-shot nanotech silver bullet for death. Freed from the burden of responsibility for the ISTWR, given a mission on which even history might some day smile, that legitimacy somehow legitimised her selfish stab at immortality.

But still, *memento mori*, when her mind drifted the words came back. *Death follows me.*


She thought that death had caught her several times over the next few hours. The journey from Izmir's airport, Adnan Menderes, to Olu Deniz on the Aegean coast was terrifying, even in the armoured limo. It wasn't just the hairpin bends, the appalling driving, the precipitous drops and—after nightfall—the way the headlamp beams swung out into empty black space. It was all that, and the dead men.

The car had just laboured up an incline, overtaking a couple of coaches with centimetres to spare between the booming metal of the coaches on one side, and a tyre-width away from the drop on the other, and two seconds to get out of the way of an oncoming truck. In the crook of the bend, a stand of pine a little away from the main forest; three bloodied men hanging from the branches, by the neck, dead. The mind retained from the sight a shocking impression of absences: at the faces, at the ends of limbs, at the crotch. Blink and you'd miss it.

Myra yelped. The driver's gaze met hers in the mirror. The crinkles around his eyes deepened to a smile.

'Greek partisans.'

He started telling her the story, of how Izmir had once been Smyrna before Kemal liberated the nation, and had—only thirty-five years ago—been Smyrna again, and the airport had been named after the Greek fascist Grivas rather than the Turkish democrat Menderes, and how the Greeks had begun to re-colonise, and how the New Turks had risen to again drive out the Hellenic chauvinist pawns of imperialism, and . . . and so on. Myra listened intently to the long, winding tale of nationalist grievance; it distracted her, it kept her mind off all but the worst of the roadside attractions and the most heart-stopping turns in the road. This was a place where the small wars were real, with no simulations played and no quarter given.

Why had Suleimanyov booked her into a clinic here, of all places? She knew the answer had something to do with the complex diplomacy of the rest of her journey—the Turkish Federation was as usual in dispute with the Russians, who were backing the Bulgars and Serbs and Greeks, and most of the US successor regimes were backing Turkey, and Kazakhstan's on-again-off-again relations with the rest of the Former Union were currently in 'off' mode, so . . .

But still.

At last, in the darkness, she saw that they were heading down a long incline, towards the bottom of a valley that opened to the sea. Lights dotted along the roadside and along the sides of the valley increased in frequency to a cluster behind the beach, beyond which were the lights of ships. As the road levelled out the driver turned left, then right through a big iron gate which opened for them. Concrete walls topped with coils of razor wire, a short gravelled drive. She stepped out and looked around. She could see a swimming-pool with a bar, and multilevel apartments. The driver handed her luggage to a couple of lads in jeans and polo-shirts. She tipped the driver, checked in, followed the guys to her room, dumped her gear, tipped the lads and made her way down the stairs and over slippery tiles to the bar, where she ordered a Pils. She sank it in seconds. After the air-conditioned interior of the car the heat was horrendous.

She was on to her third lager and fourth cigarette when a small, dark woman in a white lab-coat strolled over to her.

'Madame Davidova?' She stuck out a hand. 'Dr Selina Masoud.'

'Hi. Pleased to meet you. You're looking after me?'

'Yes.' Dr Masoud clicked a tablet out of a dispensary. 'Swallow this. Wash it down with—'

Myra swallowed. Dr Masoud smiled. She had curly hair and pretty white teeth. 'Something non-alcoholic, I was going to say. But it's all right—it'll just make you sleepy, now, that's all.'

'Fine,' said Myra, covering a yawn. 'I'm tired already. Smoke?'

'Thank you.' The doctor took her cigarette and flipped a gold lighter, slipped it back into her pocket, inhaled gratefully. 'Ah . . . I needed that.' She sat up on the stool beside Myra, ordered a Coke.

'So when do I go for treatment?' Myra asked.

Dr Masoud flashed her brows. 'That *was* your treatment,' she said. 'You stay a week in case there are any complications, any bad reactions. There won't be. Slightly feverish is normal.'

'Oh,' said Myra. It seemed something of an anti-climax. 'So what should I do?'

'Relax. Drink a lot—mainly non-alcoholic, to avoid dehydration. If you want to help the process along, smoke and sunbathe as much as you can. Both are carcinogenic, and they denature collagen too, you know—'

She said it as though relaying a recent and controversial discovery.

'Yes,' said Myra. 'And?'

'They catalyse the telomerase reactions.'

She smiled, downed the Coke, hopped off the tall seat. 'I must go. Enjoy your stay.'

The muezzin's taped cock-crow cry from the minaret's tannoy woke her before eight. She lay for a while enjoying the coolness of the room, and the fast-growing light. The room was, compared with her own, refreshingly uncluttered: painted and furnished in shades of white, the crisp straight lines of the decor and fabrics jiggled here and there with a twiddle of eyelet or a tuft of lace, as though the white ambience wavered between clinical and bridal, undecided whether it signified a hospital or a hotel. Not a bad honeymoon destination, Myra guessed—she'd noticed plenty of young, loud couples at the bar the previous evening, though she couldn't help wondering if the implications of staying together *for ever* might not strike home a little too hard, too soon, in a place like this.

By the pool she sat on a lounger and rubbed suncream on her limbs and torso. Her hands were as claw-like (but supple), her muscles as stringy (but strong), her skin as mottled (but taut) as they had all been for forty years.

On her left, behind the clinic's main buildings, the ground rose as a farmed foothill to a high, barren cliff. Across the kilometre or so of valley bottom, it faced a lower cliff, which sprouted scrub and trees. Overhead, the sky was deep blue. Paragliders, their canopies shaped like brightly coloured nail-parings, drifted by, from a higher range far behind the high cliff, to the beach a mile or so distant. Cicadas whirred like small electrical devices. The rest of the people here seemed to be either young, getting their fix, or old like her, getting their rewind.

For two days it was great. The sun rose above the cliff on the left, set behind the cliff on the right, regular as clockwork. In the evenings the barren cliffs looked red and martian, and the clinic like a Moon colony, a little artificial environment over which the gravity-defying paragliders swooped. Myra spent her days in sunshine and swimming and not dying. It was better than heaven. She rolled over and let the sun bake her back.

Big bare feet stopped in front of her face, in a spreading stain of water on the concrete tiles. Her gaze tracked up hairy brown legs, wet stretched trunks, hairy brown chest, to a face. Beaky nose, bright brown eyes, dark red-brown strandy hair swept back. The man smiled down at her, nodded unconsciously to himself.

'Myra Godwin?'

'Yeah?' Like, what's it to you?

He squatted. Big, white, irregular teeth.

'Jason Nikolaides,' he introduced himself. 'I've been asked to speak to you.'

She felt slightly befuddled.

'You're Greek?'

He laughed. 'Oh no. Not for generations. American.' He bowed slightly. Drops of water fell from his hair. 'CIA. We have a few things to talk about.'

Myra rolled over, swung her legs round, sat upright. Fumbled a cigarette. She looked at him, eyes screwed up against the sunlight and the smoke. She sighed.

'It's been a long time,' she said.

# 9

## THE SICKLE'S SANG

I looked back at the pub door, shook my head, and then walked along the side of the square and turned a corner to the street where I lodged. I went to my lodging, ran upstairs and dumped my bag, then downstairs and out again.

Without taking thought, I turned right, in the opposite direction from the station and the square. I crossed a pedestrian bridge over the railway and walked along the road out of the town, past the floodplain of the Carron River and along the southern shore of the Carron Loch. The railway line was on my right, between the road and the sea. The sun was lowering ahead of me, but not yet shining into my eyes. On my left the wooded hills shouldered up. I walked past the hamlet and glen of Attadale, and on beside and beneath the slope of Carn nan Iomairean.

I'd walked about five kilometres before I stopped, walked over the railway line and sat down on a rock on the shore at Immer. The tide was high and the loch was still; I could hear clear across it the fiddler playing at some revel in the wood at Strome Carronach. The Torridonian hills, their rocks older than life, older than the light from the visible stars, loomed black behind the hills of Strome.

In all that walk I'd met no one, and encountered few vehicles. The whole landscape seemed to shut me out, and to remind me that I was a stranger here, excluded from everything but God's terrible love. A couple of hundred metres away, a man with a scythe was working the long grass of a meadow, as his ancestors had done and his descendants, no doubt, would do. Merrial had, on Saturday up in the hills, recited a bit of tinker doggerel that meant more to her than it did to me:

> *The hammer rang in factory*
> *The sickle sang in field*
> *The farmer proved refractory*
> *The hammer made the sickle yield.*

No hammer, no factory had stopped this man's scythe; its rhythmic swing slashed the grass as though the centuries had never been.

Then the man laid it carefully aside, and jumped to the seat of his tractor, and its methane-engine's fart scared the birds as he lowered the baler and set about raking up the hay.

I laughed at myself, and stood up, and walked back to the town.

She'd left, the barmaid told me, shortly after our quarrel. I thanked the girl, avoided my mates and headed for the tinker estate.

'She isna here.'

I turned from my futile chapping on Merrial's white door. A small boy in shorts and shirt, both too big for him, regarded me solemnly from the path. I stepped over.

'Do you know where she went?'

He was very clean, as far as I could see in the low sunlight, except for a red and evidently sticky stain on his chin, furred with fluff. I resisted the urge to spit on my finger and wipe it.

'I canna say,' he told me, with artless guile.

'Well, can you take me to somebody who can?'

As he shook his head I became aware of the crunching of gravel around me and realised that I need not look far. A dozen tinkers, young and old, male and female, seemed to drift in from nowhere. They gathered in a loose semi-circle around me, none closer than three metres away. Some of their faces I'd seen on my previous visits to the camp; others were altogether strangers to me. All of them were dressed in that mixture of simplicity and artifice which I was beginning to recognise as a peculiarity of tinker garb; it was as though the rest of us wore the cast-off finery of some reduced aristocracy, while the tinkers alone cut their own elegant cloth.

'I'm looking for Merrial,' I said, boldly enough; in the silence my voice sounded as startling and thin as a curlew's in a field.

'Aye, we know that,' said a young man. 'But you'll not find her here.'

'And I know that,' I retorted. 'So where can I find her?'

He shrugged. Somebody tittered. Finally, and as though with sympathy, an older man added, 'That's for her to say. If she disna want you to find her, it's no for us to help you do it. If she does, you'll find her soon enough.'

'So you do know where she is?' I sounded, even to myself, pathetically hopeful. The only response was more shrugs and a giggle.

'There's someone else I want to see,' I said. 'Fergal.'

'Oh,' said the older man, with a pretence at puzzlement, 'there are a lot of men by that name. You wouldn't happen to know his surname, would you?'

'You know damn well who I mean,' I said. 'Let him know I want to see him.'

Everyone took a step closer. The semicircle became a close-packed horseshoe of people who began to move so that the open end was in the direction of the road. I had never thought of the tinkers as intimidating to one of the settled folk—more usually it's the other way round—but I felt intimidated at that moment, possibly because of their greater numbers. I decided to give way with as good a grace as I could, rather than make them make good on the implied—or perhaps imagined—threat. So I kept my distance as they continued to move forward.

'Ah, you'd best be off,' said the young man.

'I reckon so,' I said. 'Good night to you all.'

I turned on my heel and stalked off with as much dignity as I could muster. A stone bounced on the paved road as I reached it, but I didn't look back, or quicken my pace. Inwardly I was boiling with shame at having been, twice in one evening, faced down by tinkers. I was determined, however, that no one among my friends and acquaintances should know about this—not because of the embarrassment to myself, but because they might feel obliged to engage in some collective counter-intimidation of their own.

It was not a busy night on the square, and I didn't feel like meeting people and talking. In fact I felt like doing some solitary drinking. I bought a bottle of whisky in The Carronade, for a mark, and ducked out without greeting anyone with more than a wave.


Back at my room I found an envelope pushed under the door. It contained a telegram, which I unfolded and read in the ruddy sunset light by the window.

'CLOVIS C/O CATHERINE FARFARER MAIN ST CARRON STOP AM V CONCERNED RE MISSING FILES REQUEST RETURN BY SEALED POST TOMORROW TUESDAY OTHERWISE HANDS TIED RE POSS DISCIPLINARY ACTION ALSO INVESTIGATION IMMINENT STOP YOURS AYE GANTRY.'

On my walk along the shore I had concluded that I was a fool to walk out on Merrial, whatever the provocation; and now I felt this even more bitterly. She had warned me at the beginning that loving her would not always make me happy, and she had been right about that. Learning that she could be a member of a secret society made her refusal of confidence more understandable, even as the basis of that society filled me with dismay. My historical erudition had not disabused me of the vulgar view: that the communists had, in their blundering, bloody way, done much to fight the Possession, but that the final victory had not been theirs, and we could thank Providence that there was not a communist left on Earth. I could not bring myself to believe that Merrial really, in her heart, espoused that evil creed.

Any more than the Deliverer had. Perhaps Merrial, and even the other tinkers in the society, used its rituals and phrases for their own purposes, just as the Deliverer had exploited it to found her republic.

On that happier thought I drank a dram or two and fell asleep on the bed.


The following morning Catherine Farfarer, the landlady, handed me two telegrams. One was from the Disciplinary Sub-Committee of the University Senate, suspending me from membership of the University *sine die*, withdrawing all rights and privileges other than representation at a University court, just before the beginning of the academic year. The other was from Gantry, expressing his sympathy and saying that he would APPL THIS OUTRGS DECN.

And it was outrageous—in effect I was being punished before trial, because my chances of sponsorship or patronage were now nonexistent. Even if I were cleared, I would lose at least part of the first year of my project, which as good as meant losing it all. I wired Gantry back, thanking him; but I held little hope that he could do much to help, or that I, with my stubborn closed mouth, deserved it.

Not to my surprise, Merrial was not at work. I got through most of my dangerous day in the arc-lit dark of the platform leg without incident, and was just cleaning my tools (and everyone else's) at a quarter past four when Angus Grizzlyback loomed out of the dim scaffolding and sat down at the crate.

'Clovis,' he said. I looked up. He scratched the back of his head with one hand, and looked away from me and at a piece of paper he held in the other.

'Something wrong?'

Even then, the thought that leapt on me was that he was the unwilling bearer of bad tidings about my parents, or some such family matter.

'Aye, I'm afraid so,' he said. 'I'm going to have to let you go. Pay you off.'

'What for?' I asked, simultaneously relieved and shaken.

'Nothing you've done here,' he assured me. 'It's much against my own inclination, Clovis; for all I've slagged you off you're no bad at what you do, and you're a sound man, but—' He shrugged, and looked down at the paper again. 'It's the Society. They've withdrawn your clearance to work on the project.' He looked up at me sharply, a question in his eyes. 'Some trouble you've got into at the University.'

I put the tools down on the rough table and clasped my oily hands to my head. 'How can they do that?' I asked, but I knew the answer. The University had fingered me to the Society—of which it was, of course, a part—as a risk to the project's security. It all made sense, unjust though it seemed.

'You can appeal, you know,' Angus said. 'I'll back you up.'

I swallowed bile. 'Thanks,' I said. 'I'll bear that in mind. Of course I'll appeal it.'

The only reason I could think of to appeal it was that not doing so would seem like an admission of guilt—and, indeed, I was guilty of plenty, none of which I'd want brought out in a work tribunal. Confident though I was that nothing I'd done could endanger the project, others might not regard being madly in love with a stranger as a sound basis for this conviction.

'Ach, well, I'll set the machinery in motion,' Angus said. 'I'll tell Jondo and he'll take it up with the union.' He forced a grin. 'Have you back in no time.'

'Thanks, Angus,' I said.

'But right now,' he went on, 'I'll have to ask you to leave straight away. It says here I should escort you off the premises, but I'll not do that.'

I was very grateful indeed that he trusted me as far as the gate; but as I turned and looked back on my way out of the yard, I noticed his tiny figure on the outside of the platform, and realised that he'd discreetly watched my every step.


I took an early and almost empty bus back to Carron Town, and went to my room. The whisky bottle, at that moment, felt like my only friend. By morning, it would seem false; we'd have had a severe falling-out, but we'd both know it was only a matter of time before we'd make up. I knew all this perfectly well as I sat under the skylight and tipped myself a generous measure of the malt. Its fortifying fire rushed through my nerves, and I could contemplate my unravelling life with a degree of detachment.

I thought about what I'd lost, and what I hadn't, and determined that what I had left was enough to win me back the rest, if only I could think of a way. So, instead of settling down to some sad solitary drinking, I cleaned up and shaved and changed and went over to The Carronade.

The doors of the pub, heavy with glass and brass, swung shut behind me. After the sunshine the light seemed low. As I walked to the bar my eyes adjusted. At that time, about half past five, it was almost empty. The barmaid was the same girl who'd served us on Monday evening. She was a local girl, tall and thin, with long fair hair bundled up, and strong arms from pulling the pumps. Her name, as I learned in a few minutes of chat as I leaned idly on the bar, sipping at a half-litre of pale ale, was Jeanna Berrymead. She'd grown up on a farm up the glen a bit, at Achnashellach.

Carron Town, before the project had started, was a place where everybody knew everything about everybody else, or at least talked as though they did. Jeanna's knowledge of my meeting with, and parting from, Merrial was elaborate enough to suggest that local gossip was fast catching up with the influx.

'That tinker who was in here—' I said, trying to steer her away from her obvious probing of my side of the story.

'Oh, aye, Fergal.'

'You know him?'

She shrugged and made a mouth. 'To see. He drops in now and again. Bit of an arrogant sod, but he stands his round.'

'Any idea where he works?'

'Aye, in the old power-station up at Lochluichart. It's no' a power-station any more, you understand. But folk still call it that.'

'So what is it now?'

She grimaced. 'Not a place you'd like to go to. It's said the tinkers make their seer-stones there. I've heard tell it feels . . . haunted. A creepy place. Mind you, I've never met anyone who'd been there. Or who'd want to,' she added pointedly.

'Anyone who wasn't a tinker, you mean,' I said. 'Presumably Fergal has mentioned he's been there.'

She shook her head, frowning. 'He's never said a word about it, even when he's drunk. Not that he's drunk often! He can hold his drink, that one.'

'So how do you know that's where he works?'

'Ah, I don't know,' she said, as though impatient to be off the subject. 'It's just—you know—what people say.'

I was about to try to get more than that out of her when another voice joined our conversation.

'Is this you back on the pull, Clovis, so soon after the quarrel with your last lassie?' My workmate Druin sounded amused. I turned and grinned back at him as the barmaid poured him a half-litre. Druin was a local man, married and in his thirties, his weskit showing bare brown arms still oil-stained from his day's work, and scarred from years of work before it too.

'That's not it at all,' I said. 'I thought better of it, as who wouldn't? But she's not to be seen. So I'm trying to find out more about the tinkers.'

He laughed. 'You're a character. The reading makes you funny in the head.' He said this not as an insult but as a charitable explanation. 'Mind you,' he added, 'that's a girl I wouldn't walk out on myself.'

I asked Jeanna for another half-litre and, noticing a temptingly cheap bottle, said, 'Oh, and a couple of shots of the Talisker, please.'

Druin raised his glass. 'Thanks, mate.' He took a sip of the Talisker and asked, 'What's this about you getting the sack?'

'Some trouble with the University,' I said. 'I borrowed some papers, and found I had little choice but to let Fergal take them. The ISS seems to have taken it as a sign I'm not to be trusted. I take that as an insult.'

'As well you might.' He looked at me curiously. 'You don't seem too bothered about it, though.'

I made a twist of my lips, turned my hand over. 'Aye, I'm bothered, but there's no sense letting something like that get to you. I'll appeal it, Jondo's going to take it up. It'll get sorted out. I'm more worried about why Merrial isn't at work.'

'Ah,' he said. 'She isna taking the day off, or suspended or anything like that. She's finished her contract.'

'How d'you know that?'

He tapped the side of his nose. 'Jondo told me, because naturally he asked Admin if she'd been chucked out as well.'

I sighed. 'I suppose that's a relief, in a way. But she said nothing about it to me, even before.'

Druin nodded. 'Aye, they're a close-mouthed lot, the tinkers. So, what is it you wanted to know about them?'

'Well, we sort of take them for granted, right? Some people do one kind of work, and nobody else knows much about it. How did that start? Why can't just anybody follow the path of light? How do people become tinkers in the first place?'

Druin looked at Jeanna, and then at his drinks. He scratched his chin. Jeanna unaccountably blushed a little, and held her hand over a giggle.

'That's a lot of questions,' Druin said. 'To answer your last one first, most people who become tinkers are born into it. They're tinkers because their parents were tinkers.'

'Aye,' I said, 'but look at the tinkers. They're not an inbred people, whatever else they may be. So they must get new recruits, so to speak, but I've never heard of such.'

Jeanna's giggle broke through. She turned away and moved down to the other end of the bar. Druin glanced after her and back at me, smirking.

'Well,' he said carefully, 'it is rumoured that those of the settled people who become tinkers do so through sexual intercourse.' He laughed at the look on my face. 'You might have been well on the way to becoming one yourself, I gather.'

'Oh, come *on*,' I said. 'That's ridiculous.'

Druin shook his head. 'It's no ridiculous,' he said firmly. 'You think about it. A tinker won't settle down without ceasing to be a tinker, and damn few do that. So if you want to be with a tinker, you have to become a tinker yourself. And wander off, and never be seen again, often as not. The tinkers don't stay in the one place more than one or two year, if that.'

'All right,' I said, 'I can see there might be something in that.' My mind was turning over a lot of possible implications, none of which I was in any mood to share with Druin. 'What about the other questions?'

He shrugged. 'As to why they and only they do what they do? I've given that some thought myself, and the only thing I can say is, it goes back to the Deliverance, and it works fine. What more can you say?'

'Oh, plenty,' I said. 'Like whether it's the best way of doing things.'

'Aye, well, like I said. It works.' He leaned closer. 'Here's a bit of tinker cant I picked up: "If it ain't broke, don't fix it." Sound advice, wherever it comes from.'

He drained his mug and knocked back the whisky, then grinned and clapped my shoulder. 'I can see I've given you a lot to think about, but I haven't the time to talk any more. I'm off. Home to the wife and the tea, then out on the hills with the rifle.'

As he slid off the stool and stood up he gave me a canny look and asked, 'You happen to fancy coming along, Clovis?'

'Deer hunting?' Suddenly it felt like something I desperately needed to do to get my head clear. My first inquiries had already given me far too much new information to assimilate.

'Sure,' I said. 'Thanks.'

'Great, well, come along for your tea as well.'

'Oh, I couldn't, your wife's not expecting any—'

'Ach, man, if you saw how much she tries to make me eat, you'd come along out of sheer sympathy. Nah, you'll be welcome.'

'Thanks a lot. See you, Jeanna.'


Druin's wife's name was Arrianne. A calm, solid, dark woman who took my arrival entirely in her stride. We sat around a heavy table in the living-room, under a loud-ticking ancient clock, with the two children: a boy of about fourteen called Hamish, already working at the fish-farm, and a girl of six called Ailey, who unfussily helped her mother to serve the dinner.

The dinner—or 'tea' as they called it—consisted of fresh mackerel, limpets boiled in salt water, new potatoes and carrots and fresh-picked peas. I had to stop at the third helping, but Druin and Hamish went right on through it. This kind of feeding didn't seem to have put an ounce of fat on either of them; Arrianne insisted that I looked undernourished, and she may have been right.

After the woman and the girl had cleared away the plates Druin stood up and reverently lifted two rifles down from a rack on the wall. He pushed one across the table to me.

'You know how to handle this?'

Single-shot, bolt-action, scope. I demonstrated my familiarity and safety to Druin's satisfaction.

'Has a hell of a kick,' he warned, passing me a half-dozen shells. 'Still, you'll no get more than one shot in even if we're lucky.'

He said goodbye, and I said thanks to his family, and then he led me out the back and to the side of the house where his pick-up truck was parked. We racked the rifles on the back and climbed into the cab. The seats were leather, the dashboard hardwood and stainless steel, all lovingly polished.

'Fusion engine,' he said proudly as he turned the key and got an instant low thrum in response. 'Eighty years old, and not a thing wrong with it. Been in the family that long. None of your wood-alcohol or methane stinks for us.'

The vehicle purred into the main street and on to the road past New Kelso. Druin caught me craning my neck to look over at the tinker estate, and laughed.

'Ach, you'll find her,' he said.

He turned right at the junction, up the glen. The evening traffic surge had eased off and we made good progress at about forty kilometres an hour.

'Where are we heading?' I asked, as he slowed for the main street of Achnashellach. A small herd of Highland cattle were being walked through the town, for God knows what reason.

'Ah, you'll see when we get there.' He looked at me sideways. 'You can smoke if you want, just make sure the ash goes out the window, and the butt goes in the ashtray.' He hit the horn. 'Ah, move yer fucking arse,' he advised a hairy beast, which looked back at him as though it had heard, tossed its horns and plodded obliviously in front of us for a further couple of minutes.

Clear of the obstruction he speeded up for the long, slowly rising road to Achnasheen, which we passed through about twenty minutes later. The streets of that town climbed high into the forested hills, and its greenhouses across the floor of the glen.

'In my grandfather's day this was all a fucking bog, the way he tells it,' Druin remarked. 'The station, and the hotel, and fuck all else. Aye, we've got the land back and no mistake, just like the Brahan Seer said.'

'Who?'

'Och, some prophet from the old time, he said the people would come back to the glens. The Nostradamus of the North!' He laughed. 'They say he looked at the future through a hole in a stone, and that very stone is at the bottom of a loch somewhere.'

'A seer-stone?'

Druin guffawed. 'You've got tinkers on the brain, Clovis! The Seer lived and died long before even computers. Which he did not foresee. No, it was an ordinary wee stone with a hole in it that he looked through.'

'Do you believe that?'

'I don't think there was anything special about the stone,' Druin said. 'But there may have been something special to the eye or the brain behind it.'

'The second sight?' I said sceptically.

'I don't know about that,' said Druin. 'The Brahan Seer saw the future in his imagination, and so do we all.' He chuckled. 'He was just better at it than most.'

Druin stopped at a wee place called Dark, and, leaving the truck parked off the road, led me up through the pines on the left.

'No smoking,' he said quietly. 'And no talking either.'

I nodded, concentrating on heaving myself and the increasingly heavy rifle up the slope. The thick needle-carpet made for slow, if silent, progress. I had a bit of difficulty keeping up with Druin, and decided then and there that smoking was indeed unhealthy. At the same time, I was feeling a tension that only a smoke could relieve. Something in Druin's manner, and something about our location, was bothering me, but I couldn't think what. We climbed steadily, away from the road and up the hill.

Druin reached the top of the ridge ahead of me, and there paused, hands on one knee, while I caught up. He pointed down through a gap in the trees to where the other side of the ridge sloped back to the road. Looking down, I could see the road, the railway line and a long, narrow loch.

Loch Luichart. I recognised the place with a sudden jolt at remembering that this was where—as Jeanna had told me—Fergal worked and the tinkers made their strange stone computers. The old power-station, at which Druin was pointing, was a large, dark, block-shaped building at the foot of the slope below us.

'What's this about?' I asked Druin, as quietly as I could.

He grinned at me and began walking slowly up the ridge.

'Thought you might want to hunt more than deer,' he said. 'You're after your man Fergal, and your lassie Merrial. Down there might not a bad place to look.'

I gasped, and not with the exertion of keeping up with him. 'We can't just march in there!'

'Why not?' he grunted. 'But anyway, we won't just "march in".' He stopped, and took a few paces off to the right, into a clump of bushes. 'Ah, here it is.'

He'd arrived at a cylindrical structure of weathered, creeper-covered ceramic, about a metre high and a metre across. As I approached he leapt up on top of it and began scraping away the overgrowth with the side of his boot. In a moment he'd exposed a rusty hatch.

Not so rusty it didn't open, though. I looked in and saw a series of rungs disappearing into the blackness. Druin dropped a pebble in and cocked his ear.

'It's only about twenty metres deep,' he told me.

'Good grief, man, you're not talking about going down there, are you?'

'Aye, I am that,' he said. 'It's safe enough, so long as you hang on.'

'But do you know what's at the bottom?' I looked at him suspiciously. 'And how do you know about this, anyway?'

Druin sighed theatrically. 'What's at the bottom is a tunnel—I don't know if it's part of the original hydro-station or something that got added later. This whole hill has been tunnelled and mined; it was used as an underground base by the British army, and by the Republicans during the civil war before the First World Revolution—changed hands a few times, I think. As to how I know about it—' He laughed. 'There's a map and a diagram of it all in the museum at Jeantown! Mind you, I guess the tinkers will have made yon diagram out of date, one way or the other.'

'Looks pretty dark,' I said.

'Ach, there'll be some kind of lighting down there. And I've got a torch.'

'Was this on your mind all along?'

'Aye,' he admitted. 'But I didn't want to tell you beforehand, in case you got cold feet from worrying about it before we even got here. As it is, I'm just beginning to wonder if I was right in thinking you had a spirit of adventure. You've done nothing but raise objections this past five minutes. Do you want to go after this woman, or no?'

'Of course I do,' I said, stung into action—as he no doubt intended—by his hint at cowardice. I slung the rifle across my back and scrambled up and set my feet on the rungs as I lowered myself in. 'You'll be coming too, will you?'

'I'll be right above you,' Druin said.

For the next couple of minutes I concentrated entirely on descending the laddered steps. The rungs looked rust-free, as did their bolts—in fact, the metal and the ceramic of the shaft were both unknown to me. But I could not be sure that every rung had survived the centuries, so I tested each one before putting my full weight on it. The slung rifle made it even more awkward. One upward glance confirmed that Druin was following. Above him the hatch was visible as a small, bright hole.

After what seemed a long time my foot encountered empty air where a rung should have been. After a moment of fright I lowered the foot further, cautiously, and touched a floor. I grunted with relief and stepped down and away from the ladder, still taking care where I placed my feet. Druin completed his descent a moment later and we stood together in dark and silence.

On the descent my eyes had adapted to the diminishing light and even here, at the bottom of the shaft, it was not entirely dark. I became aware, without quite knowing why, that we were indeed in a tunnel and that it sloped fairly sharply. Looking around, I could see a brighter area lower down. I peered at Druin and gestured in that direction. The pale oval of his face made a bobbing motion which I interpreted as a nod. Together we turned and headed down the slope.

After a few steps I stubbed my toe on something hard. 'Damn,' I muttered, pulling up short. Druin bumped into my back and we both swayed dangerously.

'Fuck this for a game of soldiers,' said Druin. He unclipped the torch from his belt and switched it on. A powerful beam of white light illuminated the tunnel in front of us. It revealed that the floor was indeed littered with obstacles—oddly shaped seer-stones of various sizes. It also revealed that the tunnel was full of people.

Druin yelped a curse and brought his rifle to bear in a surprisingly smooth and swift movement. The torch-beam wavered hardly at all. I was still stiff with shock; the instant I recovered from it I looked over my shoulder and saw more figures crowding behind us, dim in the backwash of the torch's light. One such figure was apparently in the act of reaching out for me—I struck wildly at his arm, and almost fell over because my fist passed right through it. Druin whirled around at the same moment, and the torch-beam cast my shadow grotesquely on the figures before me. They responded neither to the shadow nor the light. Druin let out his breath in a gusty gasp, then laughed.

'They're just hollows, man!'

'Ah.' I stood looking at them in amazement. 'Aye, like the tinkers scare children with at fairs.'

'That's it. God, they had me scared enough.'

'No wonder Jeanna said the place was haunted.'

'She said that, did she now?' Druin pondered. 'I'll have another chat with yon lassie sometime. Anyway. Let's go on. Keep the voice down a bit though.'

Neither of us had spoken loudly at all, but the slightest sound seemed magnified by the tunnel's acoustics. We turned again and walked on, the pool of light from Druin's torch enabling us to avoid the stones on the floor, and almost to ignore the apparitions they cast. Almost—for the still faces of the men and women depicted in this intangible statuary were caught in a moment of anguish and alarm, which, as they repeatedly loomed out of the dark and passed us—or passed through us—was enough to inspire, in me at least, a creeping sensation of disquiet. They looked uncannily like the lost souls, the damned of the Christian and Mohammadan superstitions, and it would have taken a stouter faith in Reason than mine to have walked that dark path unshaken. Irrational as it may be, I drew some comfort from the fact—known to any child old enough not to be frightened by the 'ghost tent' at a fair—that hollows have no existence outside the light, and that, therefore, there was not an unseen crowd of them in the darkness behind us.

Presently we passed beyond their eerie company, and closer to the source of light at the end of the tunnel (an expression whose full force I for the first time appreciated). The air smelt damper, and at the same time fresher. We had reached the foot of the slope; the rocky floor of the tunnel here was flat. Druin switched off his torch and we proceeded very slowly and silently for the remaining few metres. The reason for the light's vagueness turned out to be a sharp bend in the tunnel; we crept around it, keeping close to the outer side of the crook, rifles gripped (though not, I recalled at that very moment, loaded).

I nudged Druin and, taking a shell from my pocket, made to put it in the rifle. He shook his head, firmly, and I desisted, reassuring myself with the reflection that the pistols on our belts were ready for immediate use. We rounded the bend and found ourselves looking out at a brightly lit space of great size—at least twenty metres across, I guessed, and ten high. The lighting came from overhead panels, and seemed like sunlight. The walls curved over to the ceiling, all stone; a cavern then, and not a natural one. Its full length was not obvious from where we stood, at one corner of it.

It contained row upon row of stone troughs, connected with stepped open pipes through which rivulets of water trickled; some arranged to feed the troughs, others to carry away waste—or so I guessed, from the fact that no channel that came out of a trough went into another. I could make out half a dozen people working there, moving from trough to trough, making undetectable adjustments to the flow or sifting some powdery material in. They looked like hydroponic gardeners, and I thought at first glance that they were following this familiar trade, possibly for some recondite component of the tinkers' food-supply. Then I noticed the contents of the troughs farther to my right, and—as I quickly realised—of more mature growth.

They were growing seer-stones—I could distinctly see the larger ones lined up, five to a trough.

'Well, well,' said Druin, as though thinking, as I was: so *that's* how it's done! He slung his rifle on his shoulder, glanced at me and shrugged.

'No point in creeping about now,' he said.

With that he marched boldly out into the light.

# 10

## FORGET BABYLON

They made their way back from the ossuary, ducking under arches and through hammered holes in the walls, into the church. Beneath pocked, defaced Orthodox murals a Turkish woman sold silver and jade and crochet. They ignored her gestured pitch, stepped outside, stalked past more stalls. Across the hollow from the hilltop where the church stood, a hillside of streets of empty, roofless stone houses fought the slow green entropy of birch and bramble. The light was blinding, the heat choking, the silence intense. The cicadas broke it, the birds, the skitter of a lizard.

Jason wandered around to the front of the church, traced a date in coloured pebbles on the paving.

'1912,' he said. 'That's when they finished it. How proud of it they must have been. Ten years later, they left. Voluntary population exchange, hah.'

Myra squatted in the sunlight, swigged Evian, sucked Marlboro. 'Worse things have happened since.' The dry, ancient ribs and femurs in the ossuary hadn't disturbed her as much as the fresh bodies she'd seen the evening she arrived.

'No doubt.' Jason shrugged. 'But you know, this place, it makes me feel like I'm a Greek, for the first time in my life. Even a goddamn *Christian*.' He glanced at the hawkers a few tens of metres away, hunkered down beside her and spoke in a low, earnest voice. 'As in, you know, Western. It's a different culture. They don't like us.'

Myra stared at him, shocked. Karmilassos, or Kaya, or Kayakoi, or what-

ever it was called (the Turks shamelessly called it 'the Greek ghost village')
oppressed her too, but the CIA agent seemed to be drawing entirely the
wrong moral from it.

'This is what nationalism does,' she said. 'And what that kind of thinking
does. No, thank you. I don't buy it.'

Jason looked somewhat hurt. He tilted his hat back and started skinning
up a joint. His age—he claimed, and she believed, though who could now
be sure?—was twenty-four. The last time she'd been seriously hassled by
the CIA had been just over sixty years earlier. There was something awesome
about a man following up a file so much older than he was.


(Last time: the man from the Agency had talked to her over lattes in a Star-
buck's off Harvard Square, in July 1998 when she was touting for medical
aid to Kazakhstan's fall-out victims; the campaign's poster child had a cleft
palate. A surgeon she'd met had set up the contact; someone who'd worked
at the consulate in Almaty, he'd said, but she wasn't fooled. She brought a
tape-recorder, discreet in the pocket of her blouse. She expected someone
who looked like a Mormon, a Man In Black. He was young, dark, bright;
blueberry T-shirt, baggy camos. Called himself Mike.

They chatted about Britain. Mike was interested in Ulster. The Orange-
men were marching at Drumcree. Myra told him nothing he didn't know;
he knew more about her than she did, casually name-dropping demos she'd
been on in the seventies as he idly turned the foreign news pages of the
Boston Globe. They took their coffees outside, sat on a low wall while Myra
had a smoke.

Mike nodded at the clenched black fist of a faded black power mural high
on a wall on the other side of the street, above the map shop on the corner.
'All that's over,' he said. 'No more arguments about the politics, Myra. All of
the line-ups are new, now. We aren't asking you to betray anyone, or anything. Just share information. We have mutual interests. You're going to a
dangerous place, after all.' (Ah, there it was, the threat.) 'You never know when
the right contacts might be crucial.'

'Indeed,' she said. She was staring abstractedly at a teenage girl with pink
hair, sure she'd seen her before. She shook her head. 'I'll bear it in mind,' she
said. 'Here's my mobile number.'

Mike gave her his, and went away. That night Myra phoned her tape of
the whole conversation through to the office of one of the local sections of
the FI, and to a reporter on Mother Jones. The journalist was dubious, the
local cadres—after a quick, panicky consultation—told her to play along.

Two weeks later she was in New York, and met Mike again, leaning on
the rail of the Staten Island ferry. The last round trip of a day which had

been humid, and was now hazy. Commuters dozed on the benches, tourists posed for pictures of themselves with the Statue of Liberty or the towers of Manhattan, the *apparat* of capital, looming in the background. She agreed to liaise with the consulate when she got back; and in the years that followed, she did, now and then, as she and Georgi clawed their way up the structures of post-Soviet Kazakhstan, through revolutions and counter-revolutions. Mainly she reported on people who were as much her enemies as they were the CIA's; smugglers of drugs and people and arms, dealers in corruption and mineral concessions and resource looting. She told the FI about every such encounter, and nothing came of it, and it all faded out. After the Fall Revolution a lot of files were opened. Myra had idly run searches on her own name and code-names in them, and found that most of the individuals and companies she'd shopped to the CIA were working for the CIA.

But they still had her down as an asset, the bastards, after all those years and changes.

And the girl with pink hair had been on the Staten Island ferry, too. She never did figure that out, and in the end put it down to coincidence.)


Jason passed her the joint, and they smoked it together as they ambled down the steep, rocky path through neglected olive-trees to the foot of the hill, where they'd left their hired jeep. The dingy little settlement there had consisted of newly built concrete houses, and a few of the stolen stone houses in the first street of the long-emptied Greek town. All of them had been gutted years ago, the Turkish families living there slaughtered by Greek partisans in the last war. The blue-and-white ceramic eyes—for good luck, against the evil eye—above the doors were cracked, the timbers blackened. Myra ground the roach into charcoal ashes that still lay inches deep. She didn't feel high, just focused, her sight enhanced as if by a VR overlay. She could *see* why this land was worth fighting over.

Jason got into the driver's seat as Myra climbed in the other side. He looked at her sympathetically, as though half-sorry for having brought her here.

'Sometimes God is just,' he said.

'Yeah. In a very Old Testament way.'

Jason started up the engine and swung the jeep around on to the narrow road to Hisaronu. The road climbed, scraping trees, edging precipices. Pine and rock and dry gullies—it was like a hot day in Scotland. Myra remembered a day with David Reid, by a river between Dunkeld and Blair Atholl, that had felt just like this. He had talked about depopulation and forced migration in biblical terms as well, she recalled.

'*Mene, mene, tekel, upharsin,*' she heard herself say.

'What?'

'That thing from the Bible. You know, about the king of Babylon? "Thou art weighed in the balances, and found wanting."'

'I'm aware of the source,' Jason said, keeping his eyes on the road. 'It's the relevance that kind of escapes me.'

'It's the way I feel,' Myra said. She stuck her hand in the air above the windscreen, feeling the cool rush between her fingers.

'That's how you feel about yourself? That's bad.'

'No,' she told him. 'About the fucking *world*.'

'That's worse.'

She laughed, her spirits lifting.

'Anyway,' Jason went on, 'it's just the rejuve talking. People get like that.'

'You would know, huh?'

'Not personally. With me, it's just stabilising, right? With you—' he smirked sidelong at her '—it's got a *lot* of work to do.'

'Thanks.'

'It makes you feel strange. Euphoric and judgemental.'

'Yeah, that's me all right!'

It was the fifth day since she'd swallowed the surgery. The nanomachines had differentiated and proliferated inside her, spreading out through her circulation like an army of sappers, tearing down and rebuilding. She felt their waste heat like a fever, burning her up. Her moods swung from normal to high, she didn't have depressions any more, it was like a biological Keynesianism, except that in the long run she was not going to be dead. She was not immortal, not really—who could tell? The best guess was centuries and in that time something else would come along—but she felt immortal, she felt like people did in their twenties before their cells started running down and their neurons began to die, no wonder she could remember the seventies so vividly, no wonder she was getting so arrogant!

Sex with Jason had been a foregone conclusion, from about the second she saw him. He was an imperialist agent, a strategic enemy even if a tactical ally, and she didn't care, she wanted to seduce him and subvert him herself, turn tricks learned in a lifetime that would curl his toes and grey his dark-copper hair. If he had any inhibitions or revulsion from her still-aged body they had been dissolved in the first evening's first bottle of raki. She'd sucked him rigid, fucked him raw, taught him much and told him little.

The little she told him was about Georgi, and the circumstances of Georgi's death. For reasons which Jason didn't spell out, but which Myra suspected had 'Agency asset—poss future use?' scribbled in their margins, the CIA was conducting its own investigation into that death which had been so deniably convenient for *somebody*.

In the early hours of the mornings, when he thought she was asleep, he would go out to her room's tiny balcony and talk for a long time on the phone. She pretended not to notice and didn't object, instead using these times in murmured pillow-talk on her own, using the eyeband to consult Parvus and to listen to v-mail from her Sovnarkom colleagues about the situation back home. It wasn't good.

Denis Gubanov, in particular, was glum. His summaries of popular attitudes—derived from agents' reports and readers' letters to *Kapitsa Pravda*—indicated what to Myra was a surprising groundswell of opposition to the whole deal with Kazakhstan. All unnoticed, a thick scrub of patriotism had grown up over the years on her tiny republic's thin, infertile soil. Its independence had come to matter to its citizens, far more than it ever had to her. Each night she looked at shots of the growing daily picket outside the government building: red flags, yellow-and-black trefoil flags, pictures of Trotsky. She'd sigh, turn over and pretend to be asleep when Jason came back.


At Hisaronu, a pleasant small town scattered across a hilltop surrounded by higher, distant mountains, they stopped at a pavement café on the main street. They drank Amstel and ate Iskander kebabs, under a striped plastic awning. When they were smoking, and sipping muddy coffee, Myra leaned forward across the table and clasped Jason's hand, letting their fingers intertwine.

'What do you want from me?' she asked.

He clasped back.

'Apart from what I've got?'

'Yeah.'

He disentangled his fingers from hers and pulled from his pocket and unfolded a Mercator projection world-map, furred at the creases. He elbowed aside his drink and a plastic ketchup bottle and spread the map out on the metal table.

She pointed. 'We're here.' She dusted off her hands and made as if to rise. 'Glad to be of help.'

'Sit,' he said, laughing. 'Look.'

She sat down again. 'Who else is looking? If you're about to give me a briefing, wouldn't VR be better?'

Jason waved his hands and looked around. Tourists and soldiers and locals ambled along the noonday street. 'Nobody's looking.' He combed his fingers through his hair. 'And you'll have noticed, I don't have an eyeband.' He shrugged. 'All the networks are compromised anyway, have been for years. That's why I listen to the radio, and read newspapers, and write in a notebook, and carry paper maps.'

'Fair enough,' said Myra, lightly, to hide her cold shock at what he'd just said. Then she realised she couldn't let it pass. 'What do you mean, "compromised"?'

'Insecure, no matter what you do. Codes, hiding the real message in the junk, whatever—there are systems that'll crack every new variant as soon as you set it up. Quantum computation killed cryptography, and there are better methods than that now, implemented on things *nobody* understands. They're out there, Myra. I've seen them.'

She smiled sceptically. 'Things that man was not meant to know?'

Jason nodded vigorously. 'Yes, that's it exactly!' he said, as though he'd never heard the expression before. Perhaps he hadn't. The youth of today. He looked down again at the map, dismissing the subject with a twirl of his hand. Myra let it drop too, but she didn't dismiss it. She was pretty sure he was mistaken, or lying, or had been lied to. And in whose interest might it be for her to distrust her 'ware?

Hah.

Jason jabbed a forefinger on North America, ran it around the Great Lakes and partway down the Eastern seaboard. 'OK, here's my country, was yours. The United States, as we still call ourselves. Not exactly "sea to shining sea" any more. "From St Lawrence to the Keys" never quite caught on, and even that's hard to hold. I mean, we need Maine between us and the Canadian hordes, but, shit. We're holding down major insurgencies everywhere between Baltimore and Jacksonville. And the only reason we hang on to Florida is for Canaveral, frankly, and the only reason they stay with us is they're scared of *El Barbudo*.' He glanced up under his brows, cast her a wry smile. 'You should hear the old boys at Langley kicking themselves about that one. After the Pike Commission put a stop to the exploding cigar capers they just thought fuck it, the bastard's gotta die sometime. Not.'

He opened his fingers like dividers and straddled the continent. 'West Coast . . .' He sighed. 'La-la Land. They got a rival claim in to be the successor state, so diplomatically we don't get on, but between you and me and the *garçon* here—' he absently waved his other hand, snapped fingers, pointed to their glasses '—we're the best of friends.' He brought the heel of his palm down on the middle of America, masking off a large area between the Appalachians and the Rockies. 'Compared with how we get on with the rest. The Mormons, the militias, the fundies, the White Right, the Indians—name it, we lost to it.'

'Yeah, well,' Myra said. 'I had heard.'

'Lucky for us,' he went on, 'they're a bit down on scientists. They got oil and minerals, all right, but with Flood Geology they won't find much more of it. This ain't rocket science. Speaking of which, we and our La-la friends got all the aerospace and comp sci and nuke tech experts. At least, we got the ones who didn't die trying to convince some hick inquisitor with a mains supply and a jump-lead that they really, really didn't know where the alien bodies were buried. Or where the crashed saucers were stashed.'

'You're kidding.'

'I wish. Turned out more people believed in the UFO cover-up than ever believed in the Jewish bankers. When they got their hands on some of yer actual *eevill guvmint scientists* . . . you can imagine the fun they had.' He had a thousand-yard stare, past her, for a moment. 'Some of the scientists confessed. In astonishing detail. Names, dates, places, A-to-Z files.'

The kid serving tables put down another couple of bottles. Myra smiled at him, shoved him a few greasy gigalira notes, waved a cigarette at Jason.

'Any of it true?' She laughed uneasily. 'I've sometimes wondered, like about the diamond ships . . .'

Jason blinked, shook his head. 'Oh, no. Total corroborative hallucination. Like alien abductions, or witches' sabbats. *They'd* heard the stories too, see? Hell, maybe some even believed it themselves, who's to say. The diamond ships, nah, that was just black tech from way back. Your basic Nazi flying saucer. Neat idea in principle, but it never was practical until the right materials came on-stream with the carbon assembler.'

Myra leaned back, refilling her glass, wishing she could consult Parvus. 'You're telling me,' she said, 'that East America has border security problems too? Well, let me put your mind at rest. We're not about to embarrass you by asking for *ground troops*. Or even teletroopers.'

'God, if it was that . . .' Jason had the long gaze again. 'No, it's a bit more complicated. You're going to Ankara next, right?'

'What?'

'You're going to ask the Turks for ground troops.'

'I don't know where you got that idea,' Myra said, carefully not denying it. Ankara wasn't on her itinerary at all, but she was very curious to know why Jason thought it was, and what bothered him about it.

'Sources,' Jason said. 'Anyway, that's what I'm here to tell you would be a very bad idea. If you want to get any help from the US, that is.'

'Hmm,' said Myra. She glanced at a soldier trawling a souvenir rack a few metres away. 'I'm just looking at a US-made GI uniform, US KevlarPlus body armour, a US Robotics head-up with Raytheon AI, a US Colt Carbine-14 . . .'

'Yeah-yeah-yeah,' said Jason impatiently. 'Valued customers. Old friends. Doesn't mean we'd be happy to see their standard-issue US Army boots tramping all over Central Asia.'

'Even to stamp on the Sheenisov?'

Jason leaned his elbows on the table, steepled his hands in front of his face to mask his mouth, and spoke quietly.

'Look, Myra, these ain't communism's glory days. I mean, in *our* glory days we'd have been pounding them with B-52s round the clock, for all the good that would have done. I understand your, ah, fraternal allies have tried that in their own inimitable way, with Antonovs. I've been authorised to let you know—off the record, and deniably—that if you come to New York or DC you'll be welcome, and your requests will be listened to sympathetically. But. Our threat assessment of the Sheenisov—where the *fuck* did that name come from?—is pretty low-key. If a motorised horde of Mongols in plastic yurts want to plan their economy with steam-driven computers, that's their problem, and if it turns out to be popular in your country, that's yours.'

Myra stared at him, rocked back. 'Jeez. That's me told.'

'Hey, nothing personal. It had to be me—or someone like me—who told you this, because at the level you're gonna be dealing with in NY or DC it'd be . . . undiplomatic and impolitic to put it to you so bluntly. I'm not saying you won't get anything. You will, just—maybe not as much as you'd like.'

She narrowed her eyes, leaning forward again. He looked so straightforward, so frank. He couldn't know about the nuclear card up her sleeve.

'OK, OK,' she said, as though not too bothered, which she wasn't. 'So, you're more worried about the Turkish Federation expanding than you are about the SSU?'

'You got it. And, well, there are bigger concerns than that. The coup attempt has—let's say it hasn't made things easier for us.'

'How?'

Jason compressed his lips. 'You'll find out,' he said gloomily.

'All right,' said Myra. She swirled her beer, looked in it, divined no clues. She looked up and smiled at Jason. 'Nothing personal, point taken. So let's get back to personal.'

Jason relaxed suddenly. 'Yeah, OK.'

'And it's from the Gaelic, by the way.'

'What?'

'The name—Sheenisov. I think it was David Reid who coined it.'

'Well, whaddaya know.'

'What I want to know,' said Myra, draining her glass and getting up, 'is what's this about them having steam-driven computers?'

'Ah,' said Jason, as they returned to the jeep, 'I can tell you all about that.'

'Should you be driving?'

'Ah, I guess not.' Jason switched the jeep over to autopilot, and as it

took them back down the long road to Olu Deniz he told her all about the
Sheenisov's strange machines.


It was a strange machine that took her to America.

On her last morning she woke before Jason did, lay for a while, then
reached automatically for her contacts. She was on the point of putting the
disposables in when she noticed that she could see clearly, all around the
room. A quick look out of the window confirmed that she wasn't myopic
any more. She brought her hand within two inches of her face, and it stayed
in focus; she didn't have long sight, either.

In the shower she looked down at her body, but apart from seeing her
toes clearly she couldn't see any difference. Towelling her head afterwards,
she found a loose hair in her hand. She stared at it.

'Jason, lookit that, lookit that!'

'Wha'?' He sat up, looked at her, examined the hair.

'It looks like . . . a hair.'

'No, look at the *end*. No, the *other* end.'

'There's something to see?'

Was he awake? She shook his shoulder again.

'There's a quarter inch of blonde there! Not grey!'

'Oh, Jesus. I'll take your word for it.'

'Hah,' she said. 'Obviously the fix hasn't done anything for *your* eyes. I'd
have them checked, if I were you.'

'They're good enough for the road, anyway.'

He helped her load her luggage on the jeep, disappeared politely—
probably for another surreptitious phone-call—while she sweated through a
final check-up by Dr Masoud, and was waiting at the wheel of the jeep when
she skipped out of the clinic and hopped in beside him.

'All set?'

'Yup. All clear.'

'Welcome to eternity,' he said, gunning the engine and slewing the jeep
out of the driveway in a spatter of gravel.

'Just don't *send* me there first!'

'Ah, I'll be fine,' Jason said, turning right on to the road up into the hills,
towards Fetiye. They climbed and climbed, overtaking taxis and trucks and
dolmushes, being carefully polite to the troop-carriers. The valley farms
and roadside stalls were almost all worked by astonishingly old people, who
looked as though they'd had the basic metabolic rejuvenations but couldn't
afford the cosmetic ones. Instead of being small and stooped they were tall
and straight, but their faces were like Benin masks, dark and corrugated,
with bright eyes glittering out.

So, as Jason remarked, no change there.

They crested a rise and Myra could see again before and below them the impossibly blue, the Windolene-dark sea. A mile or so offshore, visible even from that distance, that height, was the ekranoplan. Smaller craft buzzed around its hundred-metre length. Beyond them all the naval hovercraft and hydrofoils busily patrolled; still further away, across the strait towards Rhodes, Myra could make out their equally assiduous counterparts, the patrol-boats of the Greek Threat.

They followed the long swooping road down to Fetiye, passing the Lycian tombs in the cliffs and turning right before the mosque and down along the edge of the bazaar to the harbour's long mole and esplanade. They pulled up at the embarkation point, beside a star-and-crescent flag and a glowering statue of Kemal.

The engine spun to a halt. Jason looked across at her.

'Well,' he said. 'Will I ever see you again?'

'If we're both going to live forever,' Myra said wryly, 'probably yes.'

'I'll take that as a no.' Jason stuck out his hand. 'Still. It's been a good few days. Keep in touch. And if the investigation turns up anything, *I'll* be in touch.'

She caught his hand, her newly sharpened sight blurring suddenly. 'Oh, don't take it as a no!' she said, dismayed at his casual acceptance of her casual words as a permanent parting. This was like adolescence all over again, this was more than lust, she had a crush on him and she was saying the wrong things. She startled him with a fierce embrace, her lips wet on his, her eye-lashes wet on his neck, and all the while thinking this wasn't like her, this wasn't right, she was supposed to be a diplomat and she was falling for a fuck-ing *CIA agent* who had been sent to do a different kind of job on her; this was Not The Done Thing, at all.

They pulled apart, holding each other's shoulders, staring at each other, oblivious to the chattering crowd of small boys around the vehicle.

'Myra, you're amazing,' Jason said. 'I'll never forget you, I'll keep in touch, I'll try to see you again, but we both . . .'

'Yeah,' Myra said. She made a long sniffly nasal inhalation. 'We're both grown-up people, we have jobs, we might not always be on the same side and—' she giggled '—"we only have fourteen hours to save the Earth".'

'Or something. Yes.'

Jason disengaged, with a smile that to Myra still looked like a regretful adieu. They remained awkwardly formal with each other as Jason dismissed the boys' unwanted offers of porterage, helped her take her luggage to the shuttle boat, and shook hands as she stood at the top of the ladder.

As the small boat chugged out across the harbour to the larger craft,

Myra watched Jason restart the jeep, turn it around and drive it away, vanishing at a turn off the boulevard.

She sighed and turned around to face the ekranoplan. The vast machine looked even more improbably huge as it loomed closer: an aircraft the size of a ship, with stubby wings. A ship that flew. It was on the regular Istanbul to New York run, which stopped off at Izmir and Fetiye before hitting its stride. The boat steered its way through its competitors and hove to under the shadow of the port wing, where a set of steps extended down to a pontoon platform. Officials officiously tagged the luggage for loading into the cargo hold, and the passengers ascended into the ship.

Myra made her way to the forward lounge, bought a gin and tonic at the bar with her remaining handfuls of Turkish gigalira notes, and took the urgent multilingual advice to sit down before the ship took off.

She'd never before travelled in one of these hybrid vehicles—a Kruschevera Soviet invention, she remembered with residual pride—and she was suitably stunned by its speed and above all by the *impression* of speed, as the great machine roared across the Med at a mean height of ten metres and a top speed of three hundred miles per hour. It left Fetiye at noon, chased the day across the Atlantic, and arrived in New York fourteen hours later at 6 p.m. local time.

Myra spent most of those fourteen hours relaxing, sleeping, sightseeing and thinking about how to save the Earth.


From the sea, Manhattan had a weird, unbalanced look, the Two Mile Tower growing from the Lower East Side throwing all the rest out of perspective. South Street Seaport was still battle-damaged from the coup, and smelt more than ever of fish. Myra made her way along the duckboarded temporary quay, indistinguishable in the stream of disembarking passengers until she stepped into the waiting embassy limo with its sun-and-eagle pennant and welcoming chauffeur, who had the door slammed before anyone could so much as gawk.

The long car nosed arrogantly into the traffic flow. The driver, a stockily built Kazakh who looked as though he moonlighted as a bodyguard, caught her glance in the rear-view.

'The embassy, Citizen Davidova?'

Myra leaned back in the upholstery. Outside, through the armoured one-way glass, she could see people sitting around fires. 'No, the UN, thank you.'

'Very well, Citizen.'

The car lurched as its front, then rear, suspension coped with a shallow shell-crater. Or maybe a pot-hole, NYC's municipal finance being what it was.

'But I'd appreciate it if you could track my luggage from the ship to the embassy, thank you.'

'You're welcome.' He began talking rapidly in Russian into a phone.

They pulled in at the UN building about ten minutes later, the heavy gates of the compound rolling back for them, closing quickly behind. Myra checked her make-up in a hand mirror, stepped out of the car and checked her jacket and skirt in the bodywork sheen. Everything looked fine; in fact, she felt rather over-dressed for the grotty old place. Puddles on the plaza, repairs on the windows, rust on the structural steel, and the Two Mile Tower overshadowing the glass-fronted obelisk. On a coppice of flagpoles the two thousand, three hundred and ninety-seven flags of the nations of the Earth and its colonies flapped in the breeze like a flock of birds preparing to migrate from some long winter to come.

She took the driver's mobile number, and told him he'd have at least a couple of hours before she called him on it. He thanked her, grinned and walked off briskly. Myra walked slowly past the old late-Soviet sculpture—St George slaying the Dragon of War, in ploughshared missile metal—careful in her Prada heels, around the puddles and across the crumbling tarmac, to the doorway. An expert system recognised her; a guard saluted her.

In the foyer she stood lost for a moment until she remembered that the whole place had been gutted and refurbished, probably several times, since she'd last been here. This time around, it had been done out in the modish retro futurist style, rather like her own office. The colour-theme was leaves, from shades of green through brown to copper. Soothing, though the people in this calming environment scurried about looking haggard. A huge UN flag, blue ground with stylised globe and olive wreath, hung above the reception desk. Myra registered a momentary shock; it was like seeing a swastika.

Two men approached, their steps light on the heavy carpet. She recognised them both: Mustafa Khamadi, the Kazakhstan UN ambassador, short and dark; and Ivan Ibrayev, the ISTWR's representative, tall and cropped-blond, some recessive Volga-German gene manifesting in his bearing and complexion.

Khamadi shook her hand, his smile showing the gold Soviet teeth he'd kept through two rejuvenations; Ibrayev bowed over her hand, almost kissing it.

'Well hi, comrades,' Myra said, eager to break with formality. 'Good to see you.'

'Well, likewise,' said Khamadi. 'Shall we go to my office?'

Ivan Ibrayev shot her a look.

'Ah, thank you,' Myra said. 'But perhaps for, ah, diplomatic reasons, Citizen Ibrayev's might be . . . ?'

'Very good,' said Khamadi.

As they waited for the lift his tongue flicked his lips. 'Ah, Citizen Davidova—'

'Oh, Myra, please—'

'Myra,' he went on in a rush, 'please accept my belated condolences on your former husband's death.'

'Thank you,' she said.

'I only knew him slightly, of course, but he was widely respected.'

'Indeed he was.'

The doors opened. The two men made way for her as they all stepped in. The doors closed.

'I still think those spacist bastards killed him,' Ibrayev said abruptly. He glared up at the minicam in the corner. 'And I don't care who knows it!'

The whoosh and the rush, the slight increase, then diminution of the g-force. Myra felt her knees wobble as she stepped out of the lift into a long corridor.

'Investigations are continuing.' She shrugged stiffly. 'Personally, I don't think Reid had a hand in it, that's all I can say.' She flashed a smile across at Ivan, down at Mustafa. 'I knew the man . . . intimately.'

Ivan's fair face flushed visibly. Mustafa displayed a gold canine.

'It leads to complications, the long life,' he said. 'It makes us all close, in the end. What is the theory, the six degrees of separation?' He laughed harshly. 'When I was very young, I shook hands with a woman who had been one of Lenin's secretaries. Think of that!'

Myra thought of that. 'Come to think of it,' she chuckled darkly, 'so did I.'

But it still hit her, the pang like a blade in the belly: *all my ships are gone and all my men are dead.*

No, no. Not yet. She still had ships, and she might still have Jason.

Ivan Ibrayev's office was small. They sat with their knees up against his desk. The trefoil flag hung on one wall, rocketry ads on the others. The window overlooked the East River. The door was open. A flunkie appeared with coffee and cups, then vanished discreetly. Ivan closed the door and turned on the audio countermeasures. Myra swallowed, trying to make the strange pressure in her ear-drums go away. It didn't.

She swallowed again, sipped her coffee. The two men leaned forward, glanced at each other. Ibrayev gestured to her to go ahead.

'OK,' she said. 'You know why I'm here, right?'

'To negotiate US military aid,' said Ibrayev.

'Yeah, well. East American, anyway.' They laughed. 'I've already been given to understand that not much will be forthcoming. What the person who told me that didn't know, what you probably don't know, is what we have to offer them.' She paused. Their faces showed nothing. 'The ISTWR still has some functioning nukes.'

'Nuclear *weapons*?' Khamadi asked. Ibrayev smirked, as though he'd always suspected that the little state he served still sheathed this hidden sting.

'Weapons,' Myra nodded. 'City-busters, mostly, but a reasonably comprehensive suite—all the way down to battlefield tactical nukes, which—' she shrugged '—aren't that hard to come by. But still.'

'We knew nothing of this,' said Khamadi. Ibrayev nodded emphatic concurrence.

'Chingiz Suleimanyov didn't tell you?'

'*Nyet.*'

'Good,' Myra said briskly. 'Well, that's what I'm here to tell you. Kazakhstan is now a *de facto* superpower, for what that's worth.'

Ivan Ibrayev steepled his fingers. 'How do we use them, that's the question. They're not much direct use against the Sheenisov—no point in nuking steppe, eh?'

Khamadi's eyes brightened, his mouth shaped a shining snarl. 'We could point out that they need not be aimed Eastward . . .'

'Huh!' Myra snorted. 'Citizens, *comrades* . . . I *am* an American, and I can tell you one thing the Americans—East, West or Middle—won't stand for is nuclear blackmail. This is a people whose nuclear strategy involved megadeath write-offs on *their* side. They may have come down in the world a bit, but they're not too demoralised to take us out before we know what hit us if we even try that. No. What the President wants me to do is almost the opposite: offer them—under our control of course, but a public, unbreakable deal—to the US, or the UN, in exchange for a military alliance that can stop the Sheenisov in their tracks.'

The two men pondered this proposal with poker-faced calm. Ivan opened a pack of Marlboros and offered one to Myra. She lit up gratefully.

'It's worth trying,' said Khamadi. 'I must say, between ourselves, I think we may regret giving up the new power which the nukes would place in our hands.'

'It's not much of a power,' Myra said. 'In a sense we are proposing to blackmail the Americans, not with possible use against them but with possible use against someone else without their permission.'

Khamadi refilled the cups, frowning. 'The UN still has some nukes itself, as we've just seen. I suspect their stock has been significantly depleted by their use. So they might just be keen to replenish it.'

Ivan gestured at his wall posters. 'It has occurred to me,' he said, 'that we could go *all the way* back into the old business: selling deterrence to everyone who wants it!'

Myra laughed. 'Deterrence against whom? The UN? I don't see that working for long.'

Khamadi grimaced, as though the coffee were more bitter than he'd expected. 'Yes, I take your point. Perhaps it is for the best. So what can we do to facilitate this?'

Myra drew hard on her cigarette. 'Apart from verifying my authority?' She smiled at them. 'You can arrange—I hope—somebody to represent the other side. I've given this a lot of thought on the way over, and checked through the US personnel here, and I have a suggestion for the right person to approach.'

'Sadie Rutelli,' Ibrayev said.

'That's it! How did you know?'

Ibrayev tapped his eyeband. 'Great expert systems think alike.'

'Oh, well,' Myra said, feeling a bit deflated. 'I guess she's the obvious choice. What are the chances of meeting her?'

Ibrayev rolled his eyes and blinked a couple of times. 'According to her public diary . . . pretty good. She has a blank space between 10 p.m. and midnight, which is when she intends to go home. Would you like me to set up a paging program to arrange a meeting?'

'I sure would,' Myra said.

'It's late,' Khamadi said. 'She'll be tired.'

'Make it the offer of a dinner date,' Myra suggested. 'She can choose, I'll pay. Just the two of us—I hope you don't mind, guys?'

The diplomats dismissed the very idea that they might even have the slightest thought of such a deeply unworthy emotion. Myra and Ivan matched fetches, and their electronic secretaries got busy trying to reach Rutelli's.

'It may take some time to get through to her,' said Ibrayev. 'She's busy.'

Myra stood up. 'Then I'll get a shower and some sleep at the hotel. If somebody says they want me urgently, call my fetch. If Rutelli comes through, call me straight away, direct. Otherwise—call me in the morning!'


'I hope you're not still enough of an ex-commie to be embarrassed about all this,' said Sadie Rutelli. She passed Myra a flute of chilled champagne from the minibar of the limo that had picked her up at the Waldorf.

'Indeed not.' Myra toasted her ironically. She was leaning back in the leather seat and enjoying every second of it. 'I know all about the expenses of representation. It's all in Marx. We ex-commies are all hardened cynics on these matters.'

'It's great to see you again, Myra. It's been a long time.'

'Yeah, what? Thirty-four years. Jesus. And you look like 2025 is when you were *born*.'

Sadie, sitting in the seat opposite, looked quite stunning with her long black hair, sable bolero and indigo evening-dress. Myra remembered her as having been just as stunning in blue fatigues. She'd been one of the UN Disarmament Commission agents who'd stripped the ISTWR of its nukes after the war. She had done it with tact and determination, and despite the strained circumstances, Myra had warmed to her.

'Oh, you flatter me,' Sadie said. 'I must say you look younger yourself than I remember.'

'Ah, I'm still working on that. Or the little machines are.' Myra stroked the backs of her hands, relishing their now smoother and softer feel, the kind of thing that cosmetic creams promised and nanotech machines delivered.

She felt vigorous, as well—she wasn't experiencing jet-lag (ekranoplan-lag . . . ) and her snatched two hours' sleep had refreshed her more than seemed proportionate.

'Still,' said Sadie, 'you can't beat back-ups, if you really want to be sure of living . . . a long time.'

'Oh, really?' Myra tried not to scoff. 'You believe that thing works?'

'To the extent that I've had a back-up taken, yes.'

'Has anyone ever come *back* from a back-up?'

Sadie frowned. 'Not as such, no. Nobody's ever been cloned and had their backed-up memories imprinted on the clone brain. Though there are rumours, about some tests Reid's men did, way back . . .'

'With apes. Yeah, I know about that. How do you tell if a fucking chimp's personality has survived?'

Sadie smiled. 'Ah, Myra. You're still a goddamn dialectical materialist. I was going to say, there have been cases where people have got the backed-up copy to *run*, in VR environments. It's expensive, mind. Latest nanotech optical computers, those things that look like crystal balls. Takes one *hell* of a lot of processing-power, but there are some people who can afford it: rock-stars, film-stars and such.'

'Don't they worry about the competition?'

'No, no!' Sadie stared at her. 'That's the point. The copies do the performances—the originals just retire!'

'Sounds like a raw deal,' Myra said. 'Imagine waking up and finding you're living in a silicon chip, and you have to work for the benefit of your selfish original. Jesus. I'd go on strike.' She struck a guitar-holding pose, sang nasally, 'Ain't gonna play Sim City . . .'

Sadie laughed. 'Until your management reboots you.'

Myra was laughing too, but it chilled her to think of this new way for the rich to desert the Earth, not to space but to cyberspace, with their bank accounts; to live for ever on television, where their faces had always been. And what a laugh it would be if, in their silicon heaven, they were to meet the General . . .

Ah, shit. Back to business.

'Is this car secure to talk?' she asked, suddenly sure that the restaurant wouldn't be.

Sadie waved a languid hand. 'Doesn't matter,' she said. 'I know what you have to offer—the fact that you asked to see *me* kinda gives it away, yeah?'

'Seeing you put it like that . . . but the devil's in the details.'

'We don't need to worry about the details,' Sadie said. 'Not tonight. Just a little discretion and circumlocution, and we'll be fine.'

Myra smiled thinly. Probably Sadie knew a lot of the details. It was still her job to keep track of nuclear deployments. Her eyeband—Myra guessed the fine sparkly band around Sadie's forehead was an eyeband—would show her every suspected tac nuke on Earth and off it. And she'd have a shrewd idea where Myra's strategic nukes were, too.

Myra glanced out of the window. The car was making reasonable speed up . . . Amsterdam Avenue, getting to the high numbers. The old buildings were blistered, the pavements cluttered with nano-built squatter shacks like spider bubbles, linked by webbed stairways and ladders and swing-ropes. Their dwellers, and the people on the street, were in this part mostly white. Office-workers, mostly black and Hispanic, threaded their way among the crowds, ignoring their importunity.

'Middle-American refugees,' Sadie said. 'Okies.'

The restaurant, when they reached it a few minutes later, was well into the Harlem spillover. Black flight had long since changed the character of the area; Myra and Sadie stepped across the stall-cluttered pavement under the incurious, inscrutable stares of Peruvians and Chileans. It looked like an America where the Indians had won. In fact, these Indians had lost everything they had to the Gonzalistas, a decade or two earlier. The Gonzalistas had been defeated, but their intended victims had no intention of leaving the US. Now the former refugees' petty commerce filled the offices and shopfronts and spilled on to the pavements, just as their huge families filled the old public-housing projects.

But still, Myra thought, getting away from the killing peaks at all was winning. The Gonzalistas had been a nasty bunch, even for commies; the kind who would dismiss Pol Pot as a revisionist.

The restaurant was called Los Malvinas. Inside it was crowded, mainly with young old-money Latinos, preppily dressed, snootily confident of their social and racial superiority over the newer immigrants on the streets but exploiting—in their fashion-statements as in other ways—their cultural connection. The air smelt meaty and smoky, the walls had huge posters of Perón, Eva, Che, Lady Thatcher and Madonna. Sadie was welcomed by name by an attentive head waiter who escorted them to a table out the back, in a small yard enclosed by trees and creeper-covered walls.

'Nice place,' Myra said. She looked down the menu. 'Doesn't look like it'll take a big chunk out of the company card, either.'

'Knew you'd like it,' Sadie said. She shrugged her bolero on to the chair-back, revealing her bare shoulders. 'Jug of sangria?'

'Good idea.' Myra tapped the menu. 'You'll have to advise me on this. Just as well I'm not a vegetarian.'

They put together an order which Sadie assured her would be both good and huge, and sipped sangria and smoked a joint and gnawed garlic-oil-dipped bread while waiting for it.

'OK,' said Myra. She glanced around, reflexively. Half a dozen Venezuelan oil engineers, in shirts and shorts, were talking loudly around the only other occupied table; she shrugged and shook her head. 'OK. Let's talk. Hope you don't mind me saying, but, hell. You got authority to negotiate at the level we're talking about?'

'Sure,' Sadie told her. 'Don't worry about that. Straight line to the top. Not that this is one of the Boss's top priorities, mind you.'

'How about on the UN side?'

Sadie waved a chunk of bread dismissively. 'That's all squared.'

'No change there then, huh?'

'Changes, yeah, but we've rolled to the top again. For what it's worth.'

'Right, I know what you mean. "For what it's worth" seems to come up in conversation a lot these days. Anyway. Here's the deal. We sell you exclusive rights to the package, you back us up against the commie hordes. Shopping-list to follow, but like you say, later for details.'

The waiter arrived with a hot platter and a couple of dishes; a girl followed with bowls of salad and rice. The main dish was like a salad of meat, in which most possible cuts from a cow were represented, along with the tastier internals and a few of the less tasty.

'Enjoy your meal, ladies.'

'Thank you,' said Sadie. She stubbed out the roach. 'Oh, and another sangria, please.'

Myra was ravenous, her appetite honed even keener by the joint, and spent about twenty minutes in atavistic carnivorous ecstasy and exclamation before slacking off enough to take up the conversation properly again.

'So, Sadie.' She put down a rib, wiped her fingers and chin. 'What do you say?'

Sadie took a long swig of sangria, the ice chinking slushily.

'You know, that guy we sent to speak to you? From the Company?'

'Bit hard to forget him.'

'Uh-huh.' Sadie sighed. 'Well, Myra, sorry about this, but.' She scratched her ear. 'It's still the deal, basically. We can give you some kit, sure, but nothing like what you're asking. Definitely no alliance.'

Myra rocked back. She heard the feet of her metal chair scrape the flag-stones.

'That's even *with* what we're offering?'

'Even with.' Sadie picked up something intestinal-looking, dragged it through her teeth. 'Because we can't take it. It's no use to us anyway, frankly.'

'Oh my God. Oh, shit.' Myra reached for her cigarettes. 'Mind if—'

'Go ahead. Yes please.'

'What's the problem with our package?'

'Skill sets and legacy systems, basically.' Sadie looked at the tip of her cigarette, wrinkled her nose and sucked grease from her lips. 'Look above my head. Up. What do you see?'

Myra gazed southward and upward.

'Top of the Two Mile Tower?'

'Right. Know what's in it? Squatters, mostly. Damn thing damn near built itself, like a stone tree. But the builders couldn't find enough businesses to rent work-space in it.'

'That sort of thing's common enough,' Myra said. 'Speculative spectacular buildings are usually finished just before the recession hits, and stay empty until the next boom.'

'If there is another boom . . .' Sadie said gloomily.

Myra remembered Shin Se-Ha's version of the Otoh equations. 'There will be,' she said. One more, anyway, she didn't say. 'What's your point?'

'We're losing people,' Sadie said. 'It's no secret. The coup has succeeded in more ways than it's failed. A hell of a lot of our best scientists and engineers have migrated to the orbital colonies, and they support the faction that Mutual Protection have been running supplies for.'

'The Outwarders.'

'Yeah. Think civilisation on Earth is doomed, and they're getting out. And, more to the point, so is a lot of the big money. Most of the corporations have been headquartered in orbital tax-havens since at least the Fall Revolution. Now they've got the muscle—technical, military—to back that up. And the on-site personnel. They'll finance us, all right, but strictly as user fees, like hiring a defence agency, and only as long as we don't step out of line. You may think of the US as the old imperialist oppressor, but these days we're just another banana republic. The whole Earth is one Third World. Big money and skilled labour are in space, and what's left down below is mostly surplus population.' Sadie smiled wryly. 'And bureaucrats, like you and me.'

'So you're saying the US empire still exists,' Myra said. 'But its capital—in both senses—is now in orbit.'

'Yeah, exactly!'

'Fair enough,' said Myra, 'but how does that affect our offer?'

'Well.' Sadie leaned back, took a short draw, like a sip, on her cigarette. 'Let me draw you an analogy. Suppose, just hypothetically, for the sake of argument, that the US wanted to go back to a strategic nuclear posture.

Leave aside the fact that the Third World War did for nukes what the First did for gas. At least in terms of using them on Earth—the UN got away with the Heaviside Layer blasts, but that was a bit of a fluke. Leave aside the fact that the big money in orbit is becoming virtually Green with paranoia about nukes in space, too.'

Aha, Myra thought. She would not leave that aside, at all. This was the crux, however valid the rest of Sadie's points were.

'Leave aside the fact that there simply aren't that many big nukes left around. Suppose somebody came to us with, I dunno, a stash of old post-Soviet city-busters: laser-fusion jobs, long shelf-life, low maintenance. They still wouldn't be any use to us, because our whole military doctrine has shifted away from reliance on nukes. There's a lot more to maintaining a credible strategic nuclear deterrent than maintaining the actual weapons. You need missile and bomber crews, tactical boys, analysts, constant practice. Hell, I should know, I worked hard enough at dispersing the teams and scrubbing the records, back in my disarmament days. We don't have people with the relevant skills any more, and we don't have the people to train new ones. We need all our available skill pool to keep our stealth fighters flying, and our teletroopers, smart-battle tactics and techniques up to scratch.'

'I think I see your point,' Myra said dryly. 'So, by the same kind of reasoning, our offer of, uh, mining rights in Kazakhstan isn't really of interest.'

'You could say that. That is the analogy, yes.'

Myra doubted that their reversal of analogy and actuality would have fooled any snoop for a second, but there was a protocol to be followed on these things. It was, she recalled, illegal for public officials under UN jurisdiction—after the Fall Revolution as much as before—to even *discuss* nuclear deterrence as a serious policy option.

And of course they hadn't. Not in a way that would stand up in court, which was all that mattered.

'There is of course one advanced country that isn't a banana republic just yet . . .' Myra said. 'Never even rejoined the UN, come to that.'

Sadie shrugged. 'Go to the Brits if you like,' she said; lightly, but she acknowledged the implied threat. 'Not my problem. But it will be somebody else's.'

'Just so long as we know where we stand,' Myra said, likewise taking the hint. 'OK. Forget about the package deal. What about ground troops and air support?'

'The latter, maybe. At a pinch. And hardware. Hardware, we got. Troops, no.'

'Oh, come on. Even mercenaries. We can pay good rates.'

'Mercenaries?' Sadie laughed. 'Mercenaries are the best *we* have. We use them to put some backbone into our crack regiments. And the crack troops are about all that's left. It's become just about impossible to raise ordinary grunts. Conscription? Don't even think about it.'

Myra still looked sceptical. 'I'll show you,' Sadie told her.

They chatted amiably for a while longer, agreeing to dump on Khamadi and Ibrayev the detailed work of negotiating what little aid the US had to give; but basically, the discussion was over. Myra settled the bill, left a generous tip and followed Sadie out. As they recrossed the crowded pavement to the limo, Sadie startled Myra by walking boldly up to a bunch of Andean lads hanging around a headware stall. The boys looked her up and down, lazily curious.

'Hi, guys,' she said. 'How're you doin'?'

'Fine, lady, fine.'

'How 'bout work?'

'This our work.' They grinned at the stall's owner, who smiled resignedly back.

'Ever thought of joining the Army? Good pay, great conditions. Tough guys like you could make a good go of it.'

They had to hold each other up, they were laughing so hard.

'Not gone get killed fighting hicks and geeks,' one of them said. The sweep of his arm took in everything from the Two Mile Tower to the stall's bristling headware whiskers. He spat away, on to the pavement.

'You preferred tech to men,' he said. 'Let tech defend you.'

# 11

## THE ROCK COVENANT

I followed Druin out of the tunnel and into the gallery of the seer-stone growers without any idea of what he intended to do. Like him, I had my rifle slung and my hands empty. He strolled across the floor to a central aisle between the ranks of stone troughs and turned down it, walking in the same overall direction as we had been following in the tunnel—downwards, towards the old power-station.

'Hey!'

One of the growers came hurrying up. He was a stocky, dark man with sharp, darting eyes. His overalls were blue, dusted with white powder that caught the light like ground glass. He stopped a couple of metres in front of us and glared.

'What are you doing here?' he demanded. 'How did you get in?'

'We're—'

Druin motioned to me to be quiet.

'We're just passing through,' he said. He gazed around the chamber with an expression of slack-jawed wonder. The other tinkers had stopped work and stood about watchfully. 'It's a fascinating place you've got here, I must say.'

'How did you get in here?' the tinker repeated, taking a step closer.

Druin jerked his thumb over his shoulder. 'Oh, we were out chasing the deer,' he explained casually. 'We came across a kind of—' he looked at me, as if searching for a word '—a manhole, would you call it? In the woods up there. We went down it for a bit of a lark, like, and made our way down through yon tunnel.'

Druin hitched his thumb under the rifle's strap and added, 'So if you don't mind, we'll just be on our way.'

The tinker showed more real amazement than Druin had feigned.

'You came through the tunnel?'

'Aye,' said Druin. 'It's got some real eerie hollows in it,' he added, with an appreciative wink. He began to walk forward, and I beside him. To my surprise the tinker stepped aside, with a glance and a small shake of the head to his colleagues. I suspected that no outsider had made it past the cavern's spectral guardians for a long time, and that the tinkers here just didn't know what to make of us.

On either hand of us were the stone troughs; the ones we passed first each contained a layer of tiny stones, gravel almost; subsequent ranks had larger and fewer stones, until we reached the very end, where a trough—or rather, by this point, a large circular tub—might contain a single boulder. On the floor below the troughs were oddly shaped stones, apparently discarded; some of these casualties of quality-control had evidently ended up in the tunnel. However, we saw no hollows in that chamber, and I wondered if I'd misunderstood the implied sequence of events, or if the light in there was too bright for such displays.

Within the stones themselves, queerly distorted by the rippling water, strange fleeting scenes played themselves out with a coherence that increased with the size of the stones. I had no leisure to inspect them, but several times I felt that the faces flickering across these smooth surfaces were faces I had seen in the tunnel.

The walls and ceiling of the unnatural cave converged to an entrance-way to another passage, about two and a half metres high and two wide. It continued for about thirty metres ahead of us, beyond which a darker door-way loomed. This corridor was unmistakably artificial, its squared walls and ceiling being made of the same glazed substance as the shaft. Its lighting, too, was subtly different from that of the growing-gallery—though it came from similar glass panels, it had that overtone of yellow which marked it as ordinary electric lighting, if more powerful than usually encountered. Our footsteps rang on the ceramic floor, echoing sharply.

'You carried yourself cool in there,' I said to Druin.

'Ah, it's all bluff,' he said. 'They've got used to folks being scared by *their* bluff. But I reckon we'll soon meet some who're ready for us—our friends back there will have signalled ahead.'

'You're not bothered?'

'Not a bit.'

I was, but I wasn't going to show it. My heart was hammering and my head was buzzing with bewildered images, like the seer-stones themselves, and my hand clutching the rifle's strap was slick with sweat.

The response that Druin had expected—or, possibly, a stronger response—came when we were about two-thirds of the way down the corridor. Fergal and two other men appeared in the exit, barring our way. They carried rifles of an unfamiliar design, not aimed at us but ready for use. We walked forward. He stepped out in front of the others and raised a hand.

'Stop right there!' he ordered.

We stopped.

'What are you here for?' Fergal asked.

I decided it was about time I spoke up for myself.

'I'm here to see you,' I said. 'And Merrial.'

'You're seeing me,' Fergal said. He waved a dismissive hand. 'I'll talk to you later.' He stalked closer, to a few metres away, and stared at Druin. 'I know you,' he said venomously.

Druin shrugged. 'You'll have seen me around.'

Fergal's weapon was instantly aimed square at Druin's gut. My companion made a twitch towards his rifle strap, then raised both hands above his head. The other two tinkers brought their rifles to bear at the same moment.

'I know who you *are*,' Fergal said slowly, 'and what you are. Give me one good reason why I shouldn't kill you now.'

Druin took a deep breath. 'Och, man, if you have to ask that there is no help for you,' he said in a steady voice. I looked at him sideways, frozen except for a severe shaking in my jaw and my knees. 'You see,' Druin went on conversationally, 'if you were to kill me, now, my friend Clovis here would some time soon have to kill you. He would kill you and cut your head from your neck, and carry it to my widow and my weans to prove that you were dead and the matter was at an end.'

He glanced at me. 'You would, aye?'

'I would,' I swore. I had eaten under Druin's roof, and could not well refuse the task, if required. The thought of it made me feel sick, but it didn't shake my resolve. I had no idea why Fergal might want to kill Druin in the first place, and I didn't care. That he was willing to contemplate murder told me all I needed to know about him.

'Well, there you are,' said Druin. 'You could kill Clovis too, I suppose, but that would just double your problem.'

I did not find this last consideration quite as definite and reassuring as Druin made it sound.

Fergal's glance flicked between the two of us, his tongue unconsciously touching his lips. He backed off a little.

'Put down your weapons,' he said, then added, as we lowered our rifles, 'all of them.'

As I unbuckled my belt I looked at Druin. He shook his head, almost imperceptibly. I placed my knife and pistol and multi-tool beside the rifle.

'The *sgean dhu* as well.'

I felt naked when I stood up. Quick hands passed over or patted my body.

'They're clean.'

Fergal picked up my gear, and one of the other tinkers picked up Druin's. Fergal jerked his chin at the exit and moved around behind us.

'This way.'

We walked forward to the end of the corridor. Beyond it was the open interior space of the old power-station; we descended a short flight of steps to a concrete floor and were told to halt. Behind us I could hear some low-voiced consultation. We waited for its decision, hands on our heads, and I looked about. The turbine, of course, was long since gone, as were most of the original fittings; all that remained was a haunting afterlife of odours, of flaked paint and rusted metal and antique brickwork. Above these whiffs rose the newer smells of concrete and solder. The whole big cuboidal building, with its long windows, had been turned into a complex factory full of workshops and walkways, noisy and bright with the screech and sparks of metalwork. From the number of people I glimpsed at their benches or hurrying along, I guessed that about a hundred tinkers were at work in the building.

Strangely I felt on safer ground here, amid those scores of busy people, and hard by the road and rail of civilisation. I knew this comfort was delusory, but clung to it anyway. The thought of calling out for help crossed my mind; then I reflected that Fergal and his comrades would hardly be so bold if their actions were unknown to the rest.

Suddenly the tinkers clattered down the steps behind us and we were each roughly jostled away, in opposite directions. I heard a door slam, from the other side of the stair, just before I was pushed through another.

The room into which I stumbled was a few metres square, with an overhead light, a table and a couple of chairs. Along its sides rough stacks of copper piping, coils of cable, sacks and so forth suggested that the room was one that currently didn't have a definite use, and was used indifferently as a store, a meeting-place and—now—an interrogation cell. There was even, as somehow seemed inevitable, a sink and an electric kettle and some grotty opened bags of coffee, sugar and tea.

Fergal stepped past me, spun a chair into place on the opposite side of the table and gestured to the other.

'Have a seat.'

He put the weapons he'd taken off me on the draining-board, keeping his own rifle trained on me all the while. Then he sat down, not at the table but tilting his chair against the far wall, and cradling the black rifle with its odd, curving ammunition clip.

'OK, man,' he said. 'Looks like I underestimated you, Clovis.' I let this flattery pass. He rocked the chair forward again, gazing at me intently. 'You've got yourself into a bit of a mess,' he continued in a confidential tone, 'and the others are pretty riled with you, but I think I can square it with them. We can sort this out.'

I said nothing.

'Do you know what Druin is?'

After waiting a moment for some response, he went on, 'He's a management spy, that's what. He works for the site security committee of the ISS at Kishorn. He reports on union activists, among other things.'

Fergal said this in such a tone of loathing that I was surprised. The minor hassles between the unions and the contractors and subcontractors seemed to me hardly a matter for such moral outrage, let alone death threats. I folded my arms and cocked my head slightly to one side. Fergal leaned back again.

'He pushed to have you sacked, you know,' he said. 'That's why he was in the bar at The Carronade.'

I admit I felt slightly shaken by this, because it was entirely plausible and because it implied that someone in the bar had been watching us, but I still made no reply.

'He has not come here, with you, to spy on us. He's here to spy on *you*, to find out what your real connections to us are.'

'If that's what he's doing, it sounds reasonable enough to me,' I said, goaded at last. 'I'm sure none of what you're doing is a threat to the project, anyway. That's why I helped Merrial in the first place. So what's the problem with his being here?'

'Oh, it has nothing to do with that. Merrial told you the truth—we think there's a possible threat to the ship, we're investigating it urgently and if we find evidence for it we'll present the evidence to the project's management. No. Druin—and whoever is behind him—are looking for any stick to beat the tinkers with. He's out to discredit us, and arouse hostility to us.'

I shook my head. 'No—he's never shown any hostility to the tinkers, as far as I know.'

'Naturally,' Fergal said derisively.

'Why should he or anyone want to do that, anyway?'

'God, you are so fucking naïve!' Fergal waved a hand to indicate everything outside the room and inside the building. 'We're a somewhat privileged group, by virtue of our monopoly on skills which, frankly, are not hard to learn. Why should you depend on us to build and run your computers?' He laughed. 'You've seen how we make them. It's an ancient technology, called *nanotech*. We don't understand it, but we can apply it. A farmer could do it, just as a farmer can grow crops without understanding how the molecular genetics and replication work. A competent mechanic, with maybe a skilled jeweller or watchmaker for the fiddly bits, could incorporate the seer-stones, as you call them, into machinery.'

'They'd have to know the white logic.'

'That too is not hard to learn. So what's stopping you?'

'Me?'

'Your *people*,' he said impatiently.

'Funnily enough,' I said, 'I asked Druin that very question. He said it was—well, tradition, you would call it. It works, it goes back to the Deliverance, no point questioning it. That's what he said.'

'No doubt. And it wouldn't have been long before he was complimenting you, saying he'd mulled it over and he thought it was a good question.'

'Do you mind if I smoke?' I asked. I wanted to give the impression of weakening; my craving made it credible.

'Sure, go right ahead,' said Fergal.

I took the materials from my pocket and lit up.

'What I don't understand,' I said, 'is why you're so bothered by his turning up here. You even threatened to kill him. Maybe that was a bluff—'

'It wasn't!'

'But why? Even if he's as hostile as you say, he'll have people searching for him if he doesn't return, and it won't take anyone long to think of looking here.'

Fergal flicked his fingers. 'We could make it look like an accident that had nothing to do with us. It's a dangerous sport, deer-hunting.'

'And I would go along with your story, or join him at the bottom of a cliff?'

'Something like that.'

'What,' I asked, trying to keep my voice from betraying my rage and fear, 'is important enough to justify doing *something like that*, now?'

'Ah.' Fergal frowned. 'He—and you—have arrived at a very awkward moment. We've found something in the files that Merrial retrieved—something we've been missing for a very long time, and which we only recently realised might be stored at the University, of all places. We—'

He paused. 'Let's just say we'd lose a lot if anyone started poking around now. There's obviously an investigation going on, and we really aren't in a position to resist any intrusion in force.' He dusted his palms and stood up, laying the rifle carefully aside across the sink, within his reach and out of mine. 'Which is where you come in, Clovis. Obviously we don't want to kill Druin, or yourself.'

'If you can possibly avoid it.'

'Exactly!' he smiled, damning himself with his grin. 'No need for any of that. You're an intelligent bloke, Clovis, and you can help us. All you have to do is persuade Druin that there's nothing here to threaten the project, and that he should leave well alone.'

'That shouldn't be hard,' I said. 'And Druin shouldn't worry you. Even if he is what you say, he's only doing his job. And speaking of jobs, I've just lost mine and I want an explanation. As well as the files you took, and a chance to speak to Merrial.'

Fergal narrowed his eyes. 'Merrial might not want to speak to you.'

'That's for her to say.'

'As for the files—'

He frowned, considering. I got the impression that he was beginning to feel the files were turning out to be more trouble than they were worth.

'Look,' I said, 'I understand why you feel they're yours. But they're not mine to let you have, or yours to take. The Deliverer left them to the University, not to the Fourth International.'

Fergal jumped up as if he'd sat on a wasp.

'Who told you about the Fourth International?'

I shrugged. 'I'm a historian,' I said. 'It's common knowledge among scholars.'

This double lie deflated Fergal somewhat. He sat back down and eyed me warily.

'So what do you know about it?'

'It's a communist secret society that goes back to before the Deliverer's time.'

'Hmm,' he said. He rubbed an eyelid. 'That's about right. Though "communist" doesn't really tell you what it's all about, these days.' He laughed harshly. 'God, I sometimes feel if we could get *capitalism* back—'

'The Possession?' I asked incredulously.

'Well, you would call it that. Let me tell you, it would be better than this dark age you people have got yourselves bogged down in.'

'This is a dark age?' I laughed in his face. 'We're building a spaceship not fifty kilometres from here.'

'Oh, Christ.' Fergal knotted his fists. 'Aye, building it out of boiler plate. You build everything, up to crude atomics and even fucking *laser-fusion engines* with skills handed down from master to apprentice. Compared to the ancients, you people are complete barbarians. Compared to what you could be—'

He sighed and stood up, and began pacing the room like a beast in a cage. 'You could have a world where nobody has to do any work that isn't like play, where almost any sickness or injury could be mended, where nobody has to die, where we live like gods and fill the skies with our children's children. Instead we have *this*.' He smacked his palm with his fist and looked around with an expression of disgust.

'And who would do the work in this paradise?' I asked, perhaps more offensively than I intended.

'Machines, of course. Every bit of work in the world can be done by machines, linked up and co-ordinated.'

'Oh, right,' I said, disappointed. 'The path of power.'

'It doesn't have to be like that, next time—'

'*Next* time?'

Fergal leaned over the table on his fists, in a manner simultaneously intimidating and confidential. 'That's what the International exists for: the next time. The next chance humanity has to break out of this prison. Our time will come, again. And next time, we'll be ready.'

I shook my head. 'I don't understand.'

He looked at me with some regret, then straightened up and moved back to his seat. 'It's no use trying to explain it to you now,' he said. 'There's so much you need to know to make sense of it, and you have no way of getting—'

He was interrupted by a banging on the door.

'Who's there?' he shouted.

'It's me—Merrial! Fergal, you've got to—'

'Wait there!'

His shouted command came too late. The door burst open and Merrial charged in. She rushed past me and placed something on the table and then snatched her hands back from it as though it were a dish too hot to handle. It was a seer-stone apparatus, and the stone in the middle of it was glowing with colour and alive with movement, forming a tiny scene under the domed surface, a bubble of life startling in its virtual reality.

The scene was of a forest glade, in which a man sat elf-like on a rock. He looked out at us, quite calm and uncanny. He spoke, and his voice came from a speaker in the side of the surrounding apparatus. The volume was too low to make out what he was saying—certainly not above Merrial's shouting.

'You never told me there was a deil in it!'

Fergal had jumped up, and was staring down intently at the stone. He raised a hand, without looking up.

'Calm down, Merrial,' he said mildly. 'This is no deil. It's what you were looking for.'

'What in hell is that?' I asked. I too was on my feet, peering entranced at the amazing, beautiful thing.

'It's an artificial intelligence,' the tinker said, his voice thrilled with awe.

He stooped to the seer-stone and placed his ear close to the speaker and listened. Merrial seemed to have noticed me just as I spoke.

'What are you doing here?' she asked. Her eyes were reddened, her cheeks pale with fatigue. She looked scared and puzzled.

'I came here for you,' I said. 'I hoped you might want me to come back.'

'But I thought—'

'You two, please leave now,' Fergal said. He didn't even look up at us. He waved a hand absently to one side. 'Take your weapons and tools, Clovis, take this woman if you want and get the hell out of here with your friend, the company spy.'

Merrial turned and looked down at Fergal.

'You want me to go?' She sounded hurt, but hopeful as well.

'Yes, yes,' Fergal said, impatiently deigning to spare her a glance. 'You've done your job, and very well too. Your skills won't be needed in the . . . next phase. Oh, and Clovis—take the bloody paper files while you're at it. We won't be needing them any more, either.'

Merrial glowered at Fergal for a moment and clutched my hand.

'Clovis, what's going on?'

'I think we'd better do as he says,' I said. I let go of her hand and edged around the table, picking up the rifle I'd carried and the gear from my belt. I buckled them back on, shoved the sheathed dagger back in my boot and took Merrial's hand in my left, keeping the rifle in my right. Together we backed out of the room. Fergal didn't watch us go, or even—as far as I could see—notice. He was talking quietly to the sprite in the stone. I pushed the door shut with my toe.

'Do you want to come with me?'

Merrial blinked. 'Of course I do.'

I hugged her (rather awkwardly with the rifle in one hand, but I wasn't letting go of it again) and then said, 'We better get out before that bastard changes his mind.'

'Or something worse happens. Yes, come on.'

The big work-shop space was still busy, with lights coming on here and there as the evening shadows lengthened—the time, I was startled to realise, was only ten o'clock—and the ambient light reddened. A few people on the overhead walkways glanced down at us curiously, but that was all.

The room in which Druin was being held was only a few quick strides away. I opened the door and walked in, Merrial close behind me. This room had only a chair in the middle, with one very bright light above it. Druin was sitting on that chair with a bored, sullen and stubborn expression on his face, while the two tinkers who'd accompanied Fergal stood, one in front of him and one behind. Their raised voices fell silent as we entered.

Their rifles—and Druin's—were propped against the back wall; mine was pointing straight ahead. It still wasn't loaded, but they weren't to know that.

'Fergal says you're to let him go,' said Merrial.

'What have they been doing to you?' I asked.

Druin stood up and stretched. 'Och, nothing to speak of,' he said. 'They have merely been boring me with an account of my sins. I have not yet found it in my heart to confess.' He deftly retrieved his weapons and kit. 'I'll thank you to escort us out, gentlemen.'

One of the tinkers found his voice. 'I want this confirmed by Fergal.'

'You do that if you like,' Merrial said. 'But I warn you, he's not in a friendly mood.'

The tinker opened his mouth and closed it again. He smiled at Merrial in a surprisingly complicit way, which made me suspect that he and Merrial had some shared experience of Fergal's moods. 'Oh, well, it's your responsibility,' he said.

We stepped outside the room.

'Wait a minute,' said Merrial.

She skipped away up a stair-ladder and ran along a walkway, her feet setting the metal ringing. We waited in uneasy silence until she returned, the two file-folders hugged to her chest.

'That's us,' she said. 'All set.'

The two men walked ahead of us down a long central passage through the machine shop to the building's ancient green copper doors, then turned sharply left and showed us out through a rather less imposing wooden door.

'Goodbye,' said Druin balefully.

The tinkers ignored him.

'Are you leaving?' one of them asked Merrial.

'I'm going home,' she said. 'I hope I see you again.'


Druin's truck was just over a kilometre away. We hastened along the quiet road, the late sun in our eyes. Druin strode briskly in front. Merrial's hand was clasped in mine, fingers intertwined. None of us said very much; we had too much to say all at once.

At last we reached the truck. Druin stopped and looked at the rifles.

'Och, I forgot, we have some deer to kill.'

He laughed at my face, and took the two rifles and racked them again on the back of the truck. We went around to the cab and climbed in. Merrial shared the double passenger-seat with me; it was comfortably crowded. For a minute we all slumped gratefully. I passed Merrial a cigarette and lit for both of us. The Kyle train clattered past.

'You know,' Druin said reflectively, 'I've never before had a gun pointed at me, thank Providence. It isn't an experience I'd want to repeat.'

'I don't think they'd really have killed either of us,' I said. 'It was us who marched in with rifles, after all.'

'Aye,' said Druin indignantly, 'and I've carried a rifle into The Carronade many's the time, and nobody ever took it ill.'

'Different situation—'

'Fergal could have killed you!' Merrial interrupted. 'If he was in the mood. It was only the possible consequences that stopped him. You did something *stupidly* dangerous going there.'

'Well, we went there to get you, and to get yon papers that Clovis makes such a fuss about,' Druin grinned. 'And that's what we've come out with.'

'What a charming way to put it,' said Merrial, unoffended. I leaned past her and frowned at Druin.

'What about you? Fergal said you were working for site security, spying on the unions and on the tinkers. And that you argued for getting me sacked. Is that true?'

'I don't *spy* on anyone,' Druin said. 'That's just the tinkers' way of putting it, at least those three who caught us. There'll be the deil to pay for that, you know!'

'How?' Druin's non-denials hadn't passed me by, but this was more urgent.

Druin turned the engine on and began to steer the truck back on to the road west. 'False imprisonment!' he said. 'And assault with a deadly weapon, which is what threatening someone with a gun is. You and me, Clovis, we could sue the bastards.' He glanced across at me sharply. 'You haven't any idea, by any chance, why they kept us in the first place, and why they let us go when they did? I mean, with me they just kept banging on about what a scab I was. What did Fergal have to say to you? And, come to think of it, what are you two up to anyway? I know you're up to something, and that it concerns the ship. Which means it concerns me.'

I slid my arm around Merrial's shoulders. She smiled at me, then gazed straight ahead.

'Tell him,' she said. 'Tell him it all.'

So I did, as we pulled out of Dark and drove into the sunset.


'Aye, well,' said Druin, 'you've told me all you know, Clovis.' He sipped his whisky and flicked at a midge. 'Quite a tale! But I haven't heard Merrial's side, and I reckon that's more than half the story.'

We were sitting around a roughly made, age-smoothed table in the broad stone-flagged kitchen of Druin's house, ourselves surrounded by the shelves of crockery, the shining electric oven and a sink with a dripping tap. Arrianne and the children had long since gone to bed. The back door stood open to the warm night, and the smells and sound of the sea-loch. A saucer on the table was filling up with our cigarette-butts. Beside it a bottle of whisky and a pot of coffee were emptying fast.

Merrial rubbed her eyebrows, ran her fingers through the wide swathes of her hair and flicked them back behind her shoulders. She had not expanded on any of my account, beyond the occasional corroborative comment or nod.

'Well, all right,' she said. 'From my side there's—well, some of it I'd rather talk about with Clovis—it really is personal, it really is no concern of yours, Druin.'

Druin tilted his hand. 'OK. And the rest?'

'Ah, well, it goes back a wee bit, to when I started worrying about . . . stories I'd heard about what happened at the Deliverance. Basically, it was that the Deliverer, Myra Godwin herself, had set off something that physically destroyed the settlements and satellites, and that in doing so she'd not only killed God knows how many people, she'd created a barrier to anything ever getting safely back into space again. Every orbiting platform that was destroyed would have been broken into fast-moving fragments which in turn would destroy others, and so on until there was nothing left but a belt of debris around the Earth—and anything that goes up now would just end up as more debris! Now, Fergal is a well-respected tinker, apart from his being a . . . leading member of the International.' She shot us a glance. 'Which is not as sinister as you think! But that's by the way. Fergal's in charge of the tinkers who're working on the project, though he doesn't work on the site himself. So after getting nowhere with the project management, I took it to him, and he said we should try to investigate it for ourselves. It was myself who suggested we could look for someone who might have access to anything the Deliverer left at Glasgow, and that, well, there were students working on the project for the summer who might . . .'

'So you came looking for me?'

'Aye,' she grinned. 'But I wasn't to know what I'd find. Could have been somebody who was only interested in scholarship, or who would not have gone along with the idea. Anyway, I kept my ears open, and it was not long before I heard about you.'

Druin laughed, as much at my embarrassment as at her account.

'Clovis was not exactly quiet about his interests! He's been bending our ears about the Deliverer and history all the bloody summer. But back to your Fergal. It sounds like he took your worries seriously.'

'Oh, sure,' Merrial said. 'I got the impression that quite a few tinkers have the same idea, and . . . at least some people in the International had even stronger reasons to think it.'

Druin took a sudden wasteful gulp of his good whisky.

'Why would the tinkers—or this International—want to keep that a secret?'

Merrial stared at him. 'Because the Deliverer's reputation, and her last message to the world, is what protects the tinkers! If the ordinary folk, the outsiders—no offence—got to think she was some mass-murdering monster like Stalin, what would they care about anything she said?'

Druin cupped his chin with his hand and regarded her quizzically.

'Is that what you think, or is that what Fergal told you?'

'Both, but, well, yes. I see what you mean.'

'More than I can say,' I said.

Merrial turned to me. 'What he means is, it's something I've accepted as long as I can remember without thinking about it, but when you say it out and think about it, it just doesn't seem very likely.'

'Exactly!' said Druin. 'It's true up to a point, mind, but fundamentally it doesn't explain why the tinkers and the rest of us rub along fairly well for the most part. The story that they're the Deliverer's children, as it's said, is just a symbol, a signpost or landmark, like the statue itself. We don't get on with the tinkers because we respect the Deliverer—we respect the Deliverer and maintain her statues because we get along with the tinkers. And we do that because we need the tinkers, and they need us.'

I looked at the man, astonished. In all my years of study I had never read or heard a hint of anything like that. I had certainly never had such a reflection on my own. That something so self-evidently true—once stated—yet so unobvious and against the grain of what Gantry would have called 'vulgar cant' should come from this metalworker and not from a scholar was something of a shock to my estimation of scholarship, not to mention of myself.

There was no way I could say all this without sounding condescending, so I only said, 'Druin, that's brilliant. Never thought of that.'

He gave me a thin-lipped, narrow-eyed smile, as if he knew my unspoken thoughts. 'Aye,' he said, 'brilliant or no, I'm pretty sure the thought has occurred to our man Fergal. So his secrecy has other aims than that. If you, Clovis, were to publish your great work on the Deliverer when you're an older and wiser man, which proved beyond a shadow of a doubt that she was the most wicked woman who ever walked the Earth, do you think for a minute that folk would start throwing stones at the tinkers?' He laughed. 'No, they'd be throwing stones at you!'

'Where does that get us?' I asked, somewhat defensively.

'It gets us to this,' Druin said slowly, tapping the table with a blunt finger-nail. 'Like I said, Fergal's desire for secrecy in this matter is not for the reason Merrial and you thought. In fact, from the way you say he behaved when Merrial found the wee man in the stone, I would say that finding yon thing, whatever it is, was his real aim all along. That was what he sent you both to seek in Glaschu. Now that you've found it for him, he doesn't give a damn about any supposed space debris. And don't forget, Merrial, you raised the matter with the project and the only reason you were slapped down hard is that *of course* the designers have thought of that—whether the Deliverer's doing or no, the stuff that was up in orbit in the past must have gone somewhere! In the old records, such as they are, you could see them like moving stars with the naked eye—is that not so, Clovis?'

I nodded.

'Well, they're no there the now, and our best telescopes—which isn't saying much, I admit, compared to the ones with which the ancients saw the Universe born, but still—can't see a speck up there. And there's no more shooting stars now than there was in antiquity—we know that for sure, because these records were on paper and were passed on. So there's likely no cloud of debris around the Earth, although if the Deliverer did as you said, I guess there could be some heavy stuff up there in the high orbits yet. But even that's unlikely. It's said that in the troubled times the sky fell, and the best scientists' guess is that that was our ancestors' way of saying what they saw when the great space cities, long deserted or filled with dead, were eventually brought spinning down by the thin drag of the air up yon and fell to Earth of their own accord.'

By this time I was beyond being surprised by Druin; his words were just further nails in the coffin of my conceit.

'Did you find anything in the computer files about this?' I asked Merrial.

She shook her head. 'No, there's nothing that goes up to the date of the Deliverance itself. It was when I was searching through them that I opened the file that released what Fergal called the "artificial intelligence".' Her eyes widened at the memory. 'At first I thought it was just one of they faces that appear in the stones.'

'What are those, by the way?' Druin asked.

Merrial waved her hand. 'We don't know. We've found references to things called Help programs, and that seems to be what they are—they're aye spelling out "help", anyway! Just some old stuff that got passed down, I think. But this thing wasn't one of them at all. It looked straight at me, and spoke.'

'What did it say?'

'"Hello",' she said, in an unnaturally deep voice.

We all laughed.

She gave an exaggerated shudder. 'My next thought—when I'd got over the shock a bit—was that it was a security demon, like the one you and me ran across in Glasgow. But it wasn't that, either. It wasn't warning me off—it was inviting me in. That's when I ran with it to Fergal.'

'Who seems to have accepted its invitation,' I said. 'He lost interest in all else as soon as he saw it.'

'Hmm,' said Druin. He stood up and stepped over to the doorway, perhaps to get away from our smoke. The sky, an hour after midnight, was still light—or growing lighter again—behind him. 'Which rather suggests to me that that was his objective all along. As why shouldn't it be?' He turned back to us, his eyes shining. 'Who wouldn't want to talk to an artificial intelligence? The ancients had them, and even the tinkers have lost them—am I right, Merrial?'

'Oh, sure,' she said. 'I've never seen or heard of us having anything like that myself, and I . . . I think I would have.'

'You know,' Druin said, 'this is a relief, really. All right, the two of you were used by Fergal, maybe put through a bit of anguish and inconvenience, but no great harm has come of it. And no, Clovis, I don't count your little difficulties as great harm—you'll have worse trouble than that before you're my age!'

'All right,' I said, holding back some irritation, 'I can see how it might not seem important to you. But Fergal has got hold of this thing, and what's worrying me is what he intends to do with it.'

'What he intends to do with it,' said Druin, 'depends on what it is. Any ideas there, Merrial?'

'No,' she said. 'It was in Myra Godwin's files, and we know that some people had these things back then—it could have been some kind of adviser or counsellor. Maybe Fergal knows what it is, but I don't.'

'I hate to think what Fergal might do with an adviser that has access to knowledge from the past,' I said. Druin shook his head.

'So what if Fergal has found a new toy, or a new friend for all I know? It's none of our damn business, and certainly none of mine—it has nothing to do with the security of the ship, now has it?'

'You've got over your annoyance at being held and disarmed pretty damn quick,' I said sourly.

'Ach!' Druin said. 'Hot words. Forget it. Who would sue a tinker, anyway?'

At that Merrial and I both had to laugh. The futility of 'taking a tinker to court' was proverbial.

'That doesn't solve the problem though,' Merrial said.

'What problem?'

'The problem isn't the thing itself. Fergal is the problem.' She frowned, evidently troubled. 'He's no exactly evil—his intentions are good, in a way, and he can be a very . . . charming man in his way, on a personal level; but he's very . . . single-minded, you know? He has a tendency to focus on one thing at a time, and to over-ride anything and everybody else.'

Druin snorted. 'Hah! I don't know Fergal, but I know the type. More by repute than experience, thank Providence.' He chuckled. 'Mind you, if ever I run across a manager like that, he tends to have a short career thereafter. As a manager, anyway.' He stomped over and sat down again. 'But still— that's a problem for your lot, no for mine. I still say we'd best let the matter drop. The project's getting awful close to completion, we're actually ahead of schedule, and there's big bonuses riding on getting the platform out the yard before the end of August—which could make the difference between getting it out before the winter and having to wait till the spring. That's no small thing, and trouble wi the tinkers is the one thing that could blow it at this stage.'

'What worries me about Fergal,' I said, 'is not so much his personality as his beliefs. I know you're not that kind of person, Merrial, but communism is notoriously susceptible to characters who are . . . who can twist it into a reason for doing what they'd like to do anyway, which is living outside the covenant.'

'What do you mean by "the covenant"?' asked Druin.

'Och, what you said—when Fergal seemed to be threatening to kill you. Blood for blood, death for death—that's the covenant, the rock. Or what you said about us and the tinkers, having to live together—same thing, on the side of the living.'

'Fergal sometimes says things like that,' Merrial interjected hastily. 'That so-and-so ought to be shot, or whatever. He doesn't mean it, it's just hot words, as Druin put it.'

Druin made a conciliatory gesture. 'What you're both saying may well be true enough,' he said mildly. 'The covenant is strong in our days, for reasons which—och, we all know the reasons! So a man like Fergal can rant and rave, but he can't do much harm. How many of the tinkers would you say follow his ideas, as opposed to, say, respecting him as a man and an engineer?'

'Not many,' said Merrial cautiously.

Druin leaned back and took a sip of whisky, then topped up our coffees. 'Well, there you are,' he said in a relaxed and expansive tone. 'Like I said, no business of mine.' He leaned forward, becoming more concentrated in his expression, fixing us both with his gaze. 'As to what my business is, Fergal and his two sidekicks were right in one respect—I do have a place on the site security committee. I'm no spy—I was put there by the union, dammit! And I did push for having your clearance revoked, Clovis. What else could I do, with the information I had? But I can equally well push to have it restored, and I will. You'll be back at your job in a day or two, if you want it, whatever your University decides about you.'

'That's—' I shook my head '—that's great, that's what I want. Thanks.'

'But before you return yon files to the University, have another look through them, and try to see if there *is* anything in them about what happened at the Deliverance. Or anything about this artificial intelligence. Tell me what you find, even if it's nothing, just to put my mind at rest. Put that couple of days to good use, you and Merrial.' He grinned slyly. 'I don't need to tell you to do the same with the nights. Speaking of which, I'm off to my bed. And meanwhile, not a word about all this. Keep the peace with the tinkers, and we'll get this show on the road.'

'The sky road,' I said, quoting Fergal.

'Aye. Everybody happy?'


We walked to Merrial's house, and on the way we talked.

'I thought,' she said, 'that you were too committed to your history, your research and your old papers, to be willing to stay with me. That was what I was upset about, not your questions.'

'Ah,' I said. 'And I thought you were too committed to the secrets of your society to trust me.'

'Aach,' we both said at once.

I told her what Druin had said, about the tinkers' methods of recruitment.

She laughed, clinging to my arm and swinging away out on it, looking up at me and looking away, giggling.

'It's true!' she said. 'It wasn't what I'd planned.'

'So you—'

'Fell for you and hoped you'd join us, yes.'

'Ah-ha-ha! Become a tinker!'

'Well, why not?'

She swung around and caught me by both elbows and looked me straight in the eyes.

'Why not?' she repeated.

I thought of what I'd seen and felt—and smelt—in the library when I went there with Merrial, and I thought of what I'd seen in the old power-station. This was history, this was the real thing, not dead but living, a continuity with the past and an earnest of the future, the sky road indeed. But

who's to say it was those considerations that weighed with me, and not the
sight of Merrial under the stars, on her way to a bed I could share for all the
nights of my life?

Not me, for sure.

'Why not,' I said. 'Yes.'

# 12

---

## DARK ISLAND

Coming in from the West on the M8, the taxi hired by the Kazakhstani consulate to take Myra from Glasgow Airport was hit by small-arms fire just as it came off the flyover at Kinning Park.

Myra saw white starry marks pock the smoky armoured glass, *did-did-did*, heard the wheels' *whee* of acceleration; her hand went reflexively to the shoulder holster under her coat and got caught in the strap of the seatbelt. For a moment, as she looked down at her recently, newly smooth and now suddenly white hand, she thought death had found her at last—that she was going to die old and leave a good-looking corpse.

Then they were out of it, smoothly away, swinging around up and on to the Kingston Bridge over the Clyde. Myra twisted about and looked back and to the left, where the standard-practice burning-tyres smokescreen rose somewhere among the office-blocks and high-rises into the pale-blue late-May morning sky. A helicopter roared low and fast above the motorway, making the big car rock again, and flew straight at one of the tall buildings. A diagonal streak of punched square holes was abruptly stitched across the reflective glass of the building's face. The helicopter paused, hovering; the car swooped from the brow of the bridge, and the scene passed out of sight.

'Jesus,' she said, shaken. 'What was all that about?'

The speaker in the partition behind the driver's seat came on.

'Greens,' the man said. 'They sometimes shoot at traffic from the airport.' She saw his reflected eyes frown, his head shake. He wasn't wearing a peaked cap. He was wearing a helmet. The car slowed as the traffic thickened. 'Sorry about that.'

'Can't be helped, I guess,' Myra said. 'But—' she put on her best ignorant-American tone '—I thought you folks had that all under control. In the cities, anyway.'

Not what she'd call a city—there were taller buildings in *Kapitsa*, for fuck's sake! Even with its hills Glasgow looked flat. She could see the University's bone-white tower above the stumpy office-blocks. The place had changed considerably since the 1970s, but not as much as she'd expected, considering all it had been through: the 2015–2025 Republic, the Third World War and the Peace Process; then the Restoration and the guerilla war against the Hanoverian regime, and the Fall Revolution and the New Republic, itself now in its fourteenth year of (what it too, inevitably called) the struggle against terrorism. The blue, white and green tricolour of the United Republic and the saltire of the Scottish State flew from all official or important buildings.

'No, I'm afraid it's not all under control at all,' the driver was saying. 'They're right here in the towns now, and there's bugger all we can do about them. Apart fae bombing the suburbs, and it's no that bad yet.'

'Just bad enough to be strafing tower-blocks?'

'Aye.'

Myra shivered and settled back in the seat. Her not very productive mission to NYC had taken up less time than originally scheduled, leaving her a couple of days before her pencilled-in meeting with someone from the United Republic's Foreign Office. She was beginning to wish that nostalgia—and an itch to personally sort out the disposal of her archive—hadn't made her decide to spend that Saturday and Sunday in Glasgow.

The United Republic, though not her first choice of possible allies, was still the next best thing to the United States. It was politically opposed to the Sheenisov advance, but hadn't done much to stop it because it had a healthy distaste for entanglements in the Former Union. On the other hand, thanks to shared oil interests in the Spratly Islands it was a strong military and trading partner of Vietnam, which was standing up pretty well against the Khmer Vertes, which . . . after that it got complicated, but Parvus had the story down to the details. The upshot was that with an actual state on offer as a stable ally, the UR might well be interested in a deal, nukes or no nukes.

The taxi exited the motorway and took a few sharp turns to arrive at the western end of St Vincent Street, slowing down just across from the New Britain Hotel, where she had a room booked.

'Bit ay a problem . . .' said the driver.

A crowd of a couple of hundred was outside the hotel, almost blocking the pavement, and spilling over on to the street. It consisted of several small and apparently contending demonstrations; three separate loud-hailer harangues were going on from perilous perches on railings and ledges of next-door buildings; lines of Republican Guards segmented the groups. The reverse sides of placards wagged above bobbing heads.

'Ah, no problem,' Myra said. 'Just a lefty demo.'

Probably protesting the presence of a representative of some repressive regime, or possibly an unpopular government minister staying at the New Brit. As the big car described a neat and illegal U-turn and glided to a halt a few yards from the left flank of the demonstration, Myra idly wondered what specimen of political celebrity or infamy she'd be sharing residence with.

The driver stepped out—on the wrong side, as she momentarily thought—went around the rear, pinging the boot open on his way, and opened the door for her. She gave him a good flash of her long legs as she swung them out and emerged, in tall boots, short skirt, sable hat and coat. The rejuvenation was definitely making her legs worth seeing again; she'd have to re-think her wardrobe . . .

The driver lifted her two big suitcases from the boot; she waited for a moment as he clunked it down and closed the nearside door, then she walked towards the hotel entrance, looking curiously at the demo as she hurried past it. There was about three yards of clearance between the shopfronts and the half-dozen or so Republican Guards deployed along the pavement to demarcate the front line of the demo. Behind the Guards the crowd was jumping up and down and yelling and chanting.

She glanced up at a placard being waved above her and saw at the centre of it a blurrily blown-up newsfeed-clip picture of her own face. Suddenly the contending chants became clear, like separate conversations at a party.

'Victory to—the SSU!'

That one was in a battle of the soundwaves with, 'Sheenisov—hands off! Viva—Kazakhstan!'

Above them both, not chanted but being shouted repeatedly through one of the loud-hailers, 'Support the political revolution in the ISTWR!'

A competing loud-hailer was going on in a more liberal, educated and educational tone about the crimes of Myra Godwin's regime—she caught the words 'nuclear mercenaries' and 'shameful exploitation' in passing.

For a moment Myra stopped walking; she just stood there, too shocked to move. Her gaze slid past the reflecting shades of a Guard to make eye-contact with a young girl in a tartan scarf. The girl's chant stopped in mid-shout and Myra couldn't look away from her disbelieving, open-mouthed face. Then the girl reached over the Guard's shoulder and pointed a shaking finger at Myra.

'That's *her*!' she squealed. 'She's here!'

Myra smiled at the girl and looked away and walked steadily towards the steps up to the hotel door, now only about ten yards away. The driver puffed along behind her. The chants continued; it seemed she was getting away with it.

And then a silence spread out, just a little slower than sound, from the girl who had identified her. The chants died down, the loud-hailer speeches ceased. The crowd surged through the wide gaps between the Guards, blocking the pavement. A young man, not as tall as Myra but more heavily built, stood in front of her, yelling incomprehensibly in her face.

Her old understanding of the Glasgow accent restored from memory.

'Ah despise you!' the man was shouting. 'Yi usetae call yirsel a Trotskyist an yir worse than the fuckin Stalinists! Sellin nuclear threats and then sellin slave labour! And noo yir fightin agin the Sheenisov! They're the hope o the world and yir fightin them for the fuckin Yanks! Ya fuckin sell-out, ya fuckin capitalist hoor!'

He leaned in her face ever more threateningly as he spoke. His fists were balling, he was working himself up to take a swing at her. Three yards behind his back somebody holding up a 'Defend the ISTWR!' placard was pushing through the press of bodies. Myra took one step back, bumping into one of her suitcases—the driver was still holding it, still behind her. Good.

She slipped her right hand inside her coat. The yelling man's clamour, and forward momentum, stopped. Another silence expanded around them. Myra reached into a pocket above her thumping heart and pulled out her Kazakhstani diplomatic passport. She thumbed it open and held it high, then waved it in front of the nearest Guard's nose.

'Officer,' she said without turning around, 'please escort my driver into the hotel.'

'Aw right, ma'am.'

'Thanks!'

The driver passed by on her left surrounded by uniforms. Myra took advantage of the accompanying flurry of distraction to dive behind the man who'd yelled at her, and to push herself into the small huddle of pro-ISTWR demonstrators. She glanced quickly around five shocked but friendly faces, noticing lapel badges with a flashed grin of recognition and pride—the old hammer-and-sickle-and-4, a solidarity-campaign button with the ISTWR's signature radiation trefoil, sun-and-eagle stickers . . .

'Comrades,' she said, 'let's go inside.'

The comrades clustered around her and together they stepped back on the pavement. The angry man was being restrained by some of his own comrades, but still denouncing Myra at the top of his voice. Myra's group marched up the steps and through the hotel's big swing doors into the now crowded foyer. White marble floor, black-painted ironwork, fluted mahogany at the reception and stairwell, a lot of flowers and stained glass. The militiamen and the driver were standing off to one side, some hotel-management chap was hurrying up with a politely concerned look and a mobile phone, and—looking back—she saw that everyone was inside and the steps were clear and the door was being secured.

'Jesus H. Christ,' she said. By now she was thoroughly rattled. She reached inside her coat again. Everybody froze.

She stayed her hand, and looked around; smiled grimly.

'Anybody else need a cigarette?'

The iron fire-escape door was spring-loaded and would clang if she let it swing back, so she closed it slowly, letting go of its edge at the last moment.

It clanged.

Myra looked up and down the fire-escape and around the back yard of the hotel. Dripping pipes, rattling ventilation ducts, soggy cartons; moss and lichen and flagstones. She padded down the steps, almost silent in her battered sneakers, old jeans, sweater and padded jacket. At the bottom she pushed her eyeband under the peak of the baseball cap under which she'd piled her still-grey hair, jammed her fists in the deep pockets, feeling the reassurance of the passport and the gun, and strolled across the yard, through another one-way gate, along an alley to Pitt Street then down on to Sauchiehall.

She caught her reflection in a shop-window, and smirked at how like a student she looked. It wasn't a perfect reflection, so it also made her look flatteringly young—like she'd look in a month or two, she hoped. And she already had the bearing, she could see that as she glanced sideways at the reflection of her walk, jaunty and confident. Her joints didn't hurt and her heels didn't jar and she had so much energy she felt like running, or skipping, or jumping about just to burn some of it off. She couldn't remember having felt this good when she really was young.

And things were coming back, memories of an earlier self, earlier personal tactics, like, before her rejuve, if she'd got caught up in a situation like that outside the hotel she'd have turned to the Guards to protect her, as though by reflex, and no doubt sparked a riot right there; not now, it had been a lightning calculation that the demonstrators, however hostile to each other or to the militia, would not attack an innocent minion like the driver and would not attack her while she was shielded by the comrades. No violence in the workers' movement, no enemies on the Left—it didn't work all the time, but by and large the truce was honoured; mutual assured deterrence, perhaps, but then, what wasn't?

Sauchiehall, Glasgow's main shopping street, had been depedestranised since she'd last been here and it thrummed with through traffic, electric mostly but with a few coughing old internal-combustion engines and speeding cyclists and, jeez, yes, cantering horses among them. Myra raced the red light at the end of the street, kept up her jog as she crossed the pedestrian bridge over the howling intersection above the M8 and up into Woodlands Road. There she slowed and strolled again, relishing the old patch, the familiar territory, the nostalgia pricking her eyes. (God, she'd flyposted that very pillar of that overpass for a *Critique* seminar in 1976!)

But the area was posh now, full of Sikh men in suits—bankers and lawyers and doctors—and women in saris accompanied by kids and often as not a Scottish nanny; pavements over-parked with expensive, heavy Malaysian cars. Not like old times, not at all, except for the occasional curry aroma and the feel of the wind and the look of the scudding clouds above.

Talking to the comrades in the New Brit, *that* had been like old times. It had been like fucking *time travel*, and far more like homecoming than any encounter she'd had in New York. After she'd thanked the militia officers, flatly refused to press assault charges, and insisted on giving a huge tip to the driver, she'd retired to the hotel's café for a coffee and a smoke with the five young people who'd escorted her in: Davy and Alison and Mike and Sandra and Rashid, all proud members of the Glasgow branch of the Workers' Power Party, an organisation much fallen-back from its high-water mark in the 2020s under the old Republic but still struggling along, still recruiting and still the British section of the Fourth International.

And they really were young, not rejuvenated old folks like her; she could hardly understand it, because she'd been thinking of the International, for decades now, as a club of ageing veterans. But then she thought of how the most formative and exciting experience of their childhoods had been a revolution—the British section of the Fall Revolution, yes!—and how that might have given them an idea of what the real (that is to say, ideal, never-actually-existing) Revolution might be like.

They'd regarded her, of course, as an old comrade, a veteran revolutionary who'd actually made a revolution, and actually ran a workers' state; but they'd soon lost their reserve, perhaps unconsciously misled (she fancied) by her increasingly believable apparent youth; and told her in more detail than she needed to know of the inevitable rancorous rivalries that had pitted them against, and the rest of the local Left for, her regime's liberal critics and/or Sino-Soviet communist foes.

She was grateful for their support, of course, and told them so; but she thought their ingrained acceptance of far-left factionalism was blinding them to the depth of genuine hatred and moral outrage she'd aroused, and indeed to its justification. There had been nothing in the angry man's diatribe which she hadn't at one time or another said to herself.

*You fucking sell-out, you fucking capitalist whore.* Yes, comrade, you have a point there. There may be something in what you say.

At the same time she found that the comrades were over-solicitous, certain that she'd be in danger if she wandered around on her own in Glasgow. They urged her to contact the consulate, and to travel officially. Myra had demurred, pointing out that that was exactly what had got her into this trouble in the first place. She hadn't told them what she did intend to do, however—*somebody* must have leaked the news of her unheralded and early arrival, and she had no reason to suppose it might not be one of them.

She passed the old church, St Jude's, which still looked much too grand, too *catholic* for the tiny denomination it served, and opposite it the Halt Bar where she'd drunk with David Reid and with Jon Wilde, separately and together, during and after the brief, intense affairs that had nudged all their lives on to their particular paths.

And thus, the lives and deaths of countless others. Jon had virtually started the space movement, and founded Space Merchants. Reid had built up Mutual Protection, and Myra the ISTWR. All from small beginnings, inconsequential at the time, all eventually affecting history on a scale usually attributed to Great Men.

Perhaps if they had not, there would have been some other Corsican . . . but no. Chaos reigned, here as elsewhere.

At the green bridge over the Kelvin she paused, gazing down at the brown spate and white swirl. How trivial were the causes of the courses of any particle, any bubble on that flow. No, it was wilder than that, because the water was at least confined by its banks: it was more like how the whole course of a river could be deflected by a pebble, by a grain of sand, a blade of grass, at its first upwelling; where the great forces of gravity and erosion and all the rest did minute but momentous battle with the surface tension of a particular drop. History was a river where every drop was a potential new source, a fountainhead of future Amazons.

She walked on, past the salient of Kelvingrove Park on the left and up the steepening slope of Gibson Street, and turned to the right along the still tree-shaded avenue to the Institute. She rang the bell, smiling wryly at the polished brass of the nameplate. Once the Institute of Soviet and East European Studies, then of Russian and East European Studies, then . . .

The Institute for the Study of Post-Civilised Societies, was what they called it now.

The woman who opened the door looked very East European, in her size (small) and expression (suspicious). Her dark eyes widened slightly.

'Oh, it's you,' she said. 'Godwin.'

'Yes, hello.' Myra stuck out her hand. The woman shook it, with brief reluctance, tugging Myra inside and closing the door at the same time.

'This place is watched,' she said. She had black bobbed hair; her age was hard to make out. Her clothes were as shabby as Myra's: blue denim smock, black jeans grey at the knees. 'My name is Irina Guzulescu. Pleased to meet you.'

They stood looking at each other in the narrow hallway. Institutional linoleum, grey paint and green trim, black stairway. The place smelt of old paper and cigarette smoke. Posters—shiny repro or faded original— from the Soviet Union and the Former Union: Lenin, Stalin, Gorbachev, Antonov, solemn; Gagarin, smiling. The Yeltsingrad Siege: heroic child partisans aiming their Stingers at the Pamyat Zeppelins. The building was completely silent and there was nobody else around.

'I was kind of expecting more people here,' Myra said. 'I left a message.'

'Like I said.'

'Oh.' Myra felt baffled and miffed.

'Your cases arrived safely,' Irina said, as though to mollify her. She escorted her up the narrow black-bannistered stairs to the library. The stair carpet was frayed to the point of criminal negligence. The library itself was cramped, a maze of bookcases through which one had to go crabwise. Several generations of information technology were carefully racked above the reading-table. Myra's crates were stacked beside it.

'I'll leave you to it,' Irina said.

'Thanks.'

Myra, alone, pulled down her eyeband, upped the gain, looked down at the crates and sighed. They were still bound with metal tape. She clicked her old Leatherman out of its pouch and got to work opening them, coiling the treacherously sharp bands carefully into a waste-paper basket. Then she had to pull the nails, like teeth. Finally she was able to get the files out.

She sorted the paper files into stacks: her personal stuff—diaries and letters and so on—and political, sorted by time and organisation, all the way back from her ISTWR years through to internal factional documents from that New York SWP branch in the 1970s. These last still made her smile: had there really ever been anyone daft enough to choose as his *nomme de guerre* for a debate about the armed struggle 'Dr Ahmed Estraguel'?

She worked her way, similarly, through the formats and conversions from Dissembler through. DoorWays to Linux to Windows to DOS, and through storage media from the optical disks and bubble-magnetic wafers and CD-RWs ('CD-Rubs', they used to be called) to the floppy disks, almost jumping out of her seat at the noise the ancient PC made when it took the first of those. In the quiet building, it sounded like a washing-machine on the spin cycle.

After about an hour and a half, which passed in a kind of trance, all her optical and electronic files were copied to the Institute's electronic archive. She blinked up her eyeband menu, and invoked Parvus.

'Hi,' she said.

'Hello,' he said.

She felt almost awkward. 'Do you mind having a copy taken, and its being downloaded?'

The entity laughed. 'Mind? Of course not! Why should I mind?'

'OK,' Myra said. She uncoiled a fibre-optic cable from the terminal port and socketed it to her eyeband. 'I want your copy to guard this collection of files—' she ran her highlighting finger over it '—and anything you've got with you right now, applying the kind of discretionary access criteria that your existing parameters permit. Give the scaling a half-life of, oh, fifty years. Got that?'

'Yes.' Parvus smiled, doubled, then one of him disappeared dramatically like a cartoon genie swooshing back into a bottle.

'Done,' he said. It had taken longer than she'd expected—she must have had more files on her personal datadeck than she'd realised.

'Thank you,' said Myra. 'Anything to report, by the way?'

Parvus shrugged expansively. 'Nothing that can't wait. Except that Glasgow Airport is closed.'

'What?'

Surely not a coup, not here—

'Fighting on the perimeter. Damage to the runways. Just Green partisans, nothing serious, but there's no chance you'll get your flight on Monday.'

'Oh, shit. Book me a train. For tomorrow, OK? Catch you later.'

She disengaged the cable link and let it roll back. Then she got to work labelling the stacks, dating the paper folders and making notes for the Institute's archivist.

Somebody clattered up the stairs, strode into the library and flicked the light on. Myra turned around sharply and met the surprised gaze of the girl who'd identified her at the demo.

'Oh!' said the girl. She slowly slid her tartan scarf from around her neck and flicked her long, thick black hair out from under her denim jacket's collar. 'What—what are you doing here?'

Myra straightened up, feeling irrationally pleased that she was marginally taller than the younger woman.

'I was about to ask you the same question,' she said.

'I work here! I'm a post-grad student.'

She said it with such confusion of face, such a widening of her big brown eyes, that Myra couldn't help but smile.

'And a political activist, too, I understand.'

The girl nodded firmly. 'Aye.' The comment seemed to have allowed her self-confidence to recover. She stepped over to a chair and sat, stretching her legs out and propping her boots on a book-caddy. Myra observed this elaborately casual behaviour with detached amusement.

'I was an activist myself, when I studied here,' Myra said, half-sitting on the edge of the table.

'I know,' the girl said coldly. 'I've read your thesis. *Detente and Crisis in the Soviet Economy.*'

Myra smiled. 'It still stands up pretty well, I think.'

'Yeah. Can't say the same about your politics, though.' She frowned, swinging her feet back to the floor and leaning forward. 'In a way it's nothing . . . personal, you understand? I mean, when I read what you wrote, I like the person who wrote it. What I can't do is square that with what you've become.'

That was laying it on the line! Myra felt a jolt of pain and guilt.

'I don't know if I can, either,' she said. 'I changed. Real politics is more complicated than—ah, fuck it. Look—uh, what's your name?'

'Merrial MacClafferty.'

'OK—Merrial. The fact is, the Russian Revolution got defeated, and never got repeated—perhaps because the defeat was so devastating that it made any subsequent attempt impossible.' She laughed harshly. 'And like the man said, it's gonna be socialism or barbarism. Socialism's out the window, it was dead before I was born. So barbarism it is. We're fucked.'

Merrial was shaking her head. 'No, nothing's inevitable. We make our own history—the future isn't written down. "The point is to change it." Look at the Sheenisov, they're building a real workers' democracy, they've proven it's still possible—and what do you do? You fight them! On the side of the Yanks and the Kazakhstani capitalists.'

'Like I said,' Myra sighed. 'Real politics is complicated. Real lives, mine and those of the people I've taken responsibility for. The future may not be written but the past bloody well is, and it hasn't left me with many options.'

'You mean, you haven't left *yourself*—'

'Tell you what,' Myra said, suddenly annoyed. She waved at the stack of cardboard and paper around her. 'Here's my life. There's a lot more on the computer.' She jerked a thumb over her shoulder. 'Password's "Luxemburg and Parvus" for the easy stuff. You're welcome to all of it. The hard stuff, the real dirty secrets, I've put a hundred-year embargo on, and even after that it'll be the devil of a job to hack past it. If you're still around in a couple of centuries, give it a look.'

'This is what you're doing?' Merrial asked. 'Turning over your archives to the Institute? Why?'

Myra could feel her lips stretch into a horrible grin. 'Because here it has a very slightly better chance of surviving the next few weeks, let alone the next few centuries. You want my advice, kiddo, you stop worrying about socialism and start getting ready for barbarism, because that's what's coming down the pike, one way or another.'

Merrial stood up and glared down at Myra. 'Maybe you've given up, but I won't!'

'Well, good luck to you,' said Myra. 'I mean that.'

The young woman looked at her with an unreadable expression. 'And to you, I suppose,' she said ungraciously, and turned on her heel and stalked out. Whether automatically or deliberately, she switched off the light as she went. Myra blinked, fiddled with her eyeband and got back to work.


'Everything all right?' Irina Guzulescu was limned in the backlight of the library doorway.

Myra straightened up and dusted off her hands.

'Yeah, I'm doing fine, thanks.' She laughed. 'Sorry about the dark, I was using my eyeband to see with, instead of putting the light on.'

'Probably just as well,' the small woman said. She advanced cautiously into the room, past the opened crates and labelled stacks of Myra's archives. 'Some of the books in here are so fragile, I fear sometimes one photon could . . .' She smiled, and handed Myra a mug of coffee.

'Oh, thanks.' It was cold in the library's still, stale air. She clasped her hands around the china's warmth. 'Is there anywhere I can go for a smoke?' she asked.

'Oh, sure, come on down to the basement.'

The basement seemed hardly changed; the big table that took up most of the room brought back memories—the long discussions and arguments around it, the adventures planned there, the afternoon she'd talked with Jon and Dave, and gone with Jon.

Along the way, Irina had picked up her own mug at the kitchenette cubbyhole. She sat down opposite Myra and shoved an ashtray across the table. In the unforgiving light she looked older; she'd obviously had the treatments, but the weight of her years still pulled at her face; it didn't sag, but it showed the strain.

'Well,' Myra said, lighting up, 'uh, that thing you said? About the place being watched? Why's that?'

Irina moved her hand as though flicking ash. 'Police mentality,' she said. 'Obviously if we study the post-civilised, we're potentially sympathetic to them, and to the enemy within.'

'The what?'

'The Greens.' Irina laughed. 'The FU and the Greens, it's like it used to

be with the SU and the Reds. In the good old days of the Cold War, being interested in the other side at all was suspect, no matter how useful it might be.
And of course the same on the other side.' She smiled. 'I worked at the Institute of American Studies in Bucharest. *Securitate* on my case all the time.'

'Jesus. You must be nearly as old as I am.' Myra thought the remark tact-
less as soon as it was out of her mouth, but Irina preened herself at it.

'Older,' she said proudly. 'I'm a hundred and ten.'

'Wow. Hundred and five, myself. Had the earlier treatments, of course,
but I've just had the nano job.'

'Ah, good for you, you won't regret it.' She smiled distantly. 'You know,
Myra Godwin, you are part of the history. Of this Institute, and of the
societies it was set up to study. I supervised a student a few years ago in a
PhD thesis on the ISTWR.'

'Never thought I'd end up in charge of my very own deformed workers'
state.' A dark chuckle. 'Not that I ever believed that's what it was, or is,'
Myra hastened to add. 'Or that such a thing could exist. Ticktin cured me
of that delusion a *long* time ago.'

'Hmm,' said Irina. 'It was Mises and Hayek for me, actually. Ticktin didn't
rate them very highly. Or me.' She laughed. 'Used to call me "Ceaușescu's last
victim." '

'Well, yes,' Myra said. 'Never found the liberals terribly persuasive myself, to be honest. The question that always used to come to mind was,
"Where are the swift cavalry?" '

Irina shook her head. 'I'm sorry?'

'Oh, it was something Mises said. If Europe ever went socialist, it would
collapse, and the barbarians would be back, sweeping across the steppe on
swift horses. Well, half Europe was—not socialist as I would see it, but as
Mises would see it—and where are the swift cavalry?'

Irina stared at her. As though unaware of what she was doing—the reflexes of a habit she must have thought was conquered coming back—she
reached across the table for Myra's cigarettes and lit one up.

'Oh, Myra Godwin-Davidova, you are so blind. Where are the swift cavalry, indeed.' She paused, narrowing her eyes against the stream of smoke.
'What mode of production would you say exists in the Former Union?'

'The post-civilised mode?'

'A euphemism.' She waved smoke. 'What would your Engels call a society where cities are just markets and camps, where most people eat what
they can grow and hunt for themselves, where almost all industry is at the
village level, where there is no notion of the nation?'

'Well, OK, it's an old-fashioned term,' Myra said, with half a laugh, 'but
I suppose technically you could call it barbarism. Technologically advanced
barbarism, but yes, that's what it is.'

'Precisely,' Irina said. She looked at her cigarette with puzzled distaste and stubbed it out. 'There are your swift cavalry. Look outside our cities, at the Greens. In fact, look inside our cities. There are your swift cavalry!'

Myra really had never thought of it like that.

'The only swift cavalry I'm worried about,' she said bitterly, 'are the goddamn Sheenisov.'

To her astonishment and dismay, Irina began to cry. She pulled a grubby tissue from her pocket and sobbed and sniffled into it for a minute. On a sudden impulse, Myra reached across the table and grasped her hand.

'Oh God,' Irina said at last. 'I'm sorry.' She gave a long sniff and threw the tissue away, accepted Myra's offer of a cigarette.

'No, *I'm* sorry,' Myra said. 'I seem to have said something to upset you.'

Irina blinked several times. 'No, no. It's my own fault. Oh, God, if you just knew. I stayed here to see you, not just to let you in.' The cigarette tip glowed to a cone, she was sucking so hard. 'Nobody else wanted to come in this morning and meet you. They think you are a terrible person, a monster, a criminal. I don't.' She blinked again, brightening. 'I go back, you know. To Romania, and to . . . other "post-civilised" countries. All right, to the Former Union. And you know what? People are happy there, with their farms and workshops and their local armies and petty loyalties. The bureaucrats are gone, and the mafias have no prohibitions to get rich on, and they are gone. The provinces have their small wars and their feuds, but—' she smiled now, sadly '—I sound like a feminist, if you remember them, but the fact is, it's just a testosterone thing. Young men will kill each other, that's the way of it. For a woman, Moscow—hell, any provincial post-Soviet town—is safer than Glasgow.'

Oh, not another, Myra thought. A Green fellow-traveller, a political pilgrim. I have seen the past and it works.

'And when I see something like communism coming *back*,' Irina went on, 'when I see the goddamn Sheenisov riding in their tanks, collectivising again, assimilating all those little new societies, I want to see them stopped.'

She looked straight into Myra's eyes. 'You can do it, you can stop them. You must fight, Myra. You're our only hope.'

Myra felt like crying, herself.


The Brits just didn't *do* trains.

They'd invented them. They had a couple of centuries' experience with them. They had more actual enthusiasts for trains per head of the population than anywhere else. They'd invented *trainspotting*. And they still couldn't seem to figure out how to make trains *run on time*.

So here they were on a bright, cold Sunday morning, somewhere south of Penrith, and under traction from one electric engine that sounded like it came from the sort of gadget you would use for home improvements. Wooded hillsides slid slowly past. At least she had a seat in First Class. The train's guard was just wandering through the adjoining Second Class, where all the screaming kids were, and the refreshments trolley was being trundled along behind him.

Myra lit a cigarette and gazed out. She felt relatively content, even with a long journey, made longer by bloody typical Brit inefficiency, ahead of her. She had plenty of reading to do, right there in her eye-band. Parvus had prepared her a digest of recent British foreign policy, last time she'd done a download. About 100 kilobytes, not counting hyperlinks and appendices. Stacks of v-mail to catch up with.

Not to mention the news. By now there was a regular CNN spot, on the world-affairs specialist newsfeed, dealing with the ISTWR. The demos opposing the policy of federation with Kazakhstan had grown to a daily assembly of two thousand or so, with a couple of hundred people braving the chilly nights in tents in Revolution Square. Some of their banners were what Myra would've expected from her local ultralefts, the sort of folks she'd tangled with outside the New Brit. Others were liberal—pro-UN— or libertarian, with a pro-space, pro-Outwarder undertone.

Nobody on the street—or on the net—seemed to have yet found out about the nukes; a small mercy, but Myra suspected that some at least of those behind the various demonstrators knew about them. Reid, for one, certainly did, and she thought it possible that his hand was reaching for them through the ISTWR's home-grown space-movement militants.

Myra had spent the first hour or so of the journey at her virtual keyboard, writing out reports back and instructions and advice for her commissars, Denis Gubanov in particular. She wanted every chekist he could spare to get busy infiltrating and investigating these demos.

The partition doors hissed and thunked open. The guard came through, a tall, stooping man in a uniform, with a holstered pistol on his hip.

'Tickets from Carlisle, please.' He had a slightly camp voice, gentle and pleasant. He smiled and checked the tickets of the business executive sitting opposite and across from Myra.

"Scuse me,' the steward sang out, behind him. The steward was a small, scrawny youth in a white shirt, tartan bow-tie and trews. Spiky black hair.

The trolley rattled and jangled into the compartment. The guard stepped aside to let it pass. As he did so the train lurched a little, setting the trolley's contents ringing again, and the brakes squealed as the train came to a halt.

There was a crackly announcement, from which Myra could only make out the words 'trees on the line'.

A ripple of derision ran through the carriage. Myra added her hoot to it, and glanced out of the windows. There were trees beside the line, to the right, but they were about a hundred yards away, across a puddled meadow. On the other side, a sharp slope, with trees above the scree.

She heard a gasp from the steward, and a sort of cough from the guard. A large quantity of some red liquid splashed across the table she was sitting at, and some of it poured over the edge and on to the lap of her skirt. Myra recoiled, looking up with a momentary flash of civilised annoyance—her first impression was that somehow the steward had spilled a bottle of red wine over her.

The guard fell sideways across the table with a shocking thud. His throat gaped and flapped like a gill-slit, still pumping. She could see the rim of his severed windpipe, white, like broken plastic. His mouth was open too, the tongue quivering, dripping spittle. His eyes were very wide. He raised his head, and looked as though he were trying to say something to her. Then he stopped trying. His head hit the table with a second thump, *diminuendo*.

The steward was still standing, clutching a short knife in one hand and an automatic pistol, evidently the guard's, in the other. His shirt-cuff had blood on it, as did the front of his shirt. It looked like he'd had a nose-bleed which he'd tried to staunch on his sleeve. It was surprising how thin a liquid blood was, when it was freshly spilled, still splashy, a wine-dark stream.

The steward flicked his tongue across his lips. He waved the pistol in a way that suggested he was not entirely familiar with its use. Then, in a movement like a conjuring trick, he'd swapped the knife and the pistol around and worked the slide. Lock and load; he knew how to use it, all right.

'Don't fucking move,' he said.

Myra didn't fucking move. She'd stuck her small emergency-pistol in the top of her boot when she'd taken off the holster with the Glock, which was now lying under her jacket on the luggage-rack above. There was no way she could reach either weapon in time. Nor could she blink up a comms menu on her eyeband—the phone was in her jacket, too. The other passenger, who was sitting across the aisle and facing the opposite direction, didn't move either. Somebody, not a child, in the Second-Class compartment was screaming. The steward had his back to that compartment, and at least several people in there must have been aware of what had happened. Without moving her head, or even her eyes, Myra could see white faces, round eyes and mouths, through the glass partition.

She was thinking *why doesn't someone just shoot this fucker in the back?* Then, out of the corner of her eye, she saw movement outside, along both sides of the train. Men and women on horseback. Long hair; feathers and hats; leather jerkins and weskits; rifles and crossbows brandished or slung. Like cowboys and Indians. Green partisans. Barbarians.

Far behind her, near the back of train she guessed, there was a brief exchange of fire and a distant, thin screaming. It went on and on like a car alarm.

Every door in the train, internal and external, thunked open. OK, so somebody'd got to the controls. Myra felt a cold draught against the warm and now sticky liquid on her knees. The colour washed out of the world. Myra realised that she was about to go into shock, and breathed hard and deep.

Some of the horsemen, dismounted, leapt aboard the train. At the end of each carriage, a pair of them faced opposite ways, covering the passengers with rifles. The man who landed facing Myra filled the partition doorway. 'Barbarian' was not an epithet, applied to him; he was tall and broad, he had a beard and pony-tail gleaming with grease, and his jacket and chaps bore smooth-edged, irregularly shaped plates of metal attached to the leather with metal rings, a crude and partial armour.

'Hands on heads! Everybody outside! On to the track!'

Myra put her hands on top of her head and stood up and shuffled sideways into the aisle. The steward-punk who'd murdered the guard still had her covered, and was backing out past the big fellow, whom he obviously knew. The businessman, standing up, had a curiously intent look on his face. Myra guessed instantly that he was about to make himself a hero, and in a fortuitous moment of eye contact she shook her head. His shoulders slumped slightly, even with his hands in the air; but he complied with the shouted command and the minutely gestured suggestion, jumping out to the right and landing on the permanent way on his feet and hands, then scrambling up and running across the adjacent track to the low bank with the fence by the flooded meadow.

Myra raised her hands and stepped over the guard's buckled legs, edged past the barbarian and the steward and jumped out. She landed lightly, the impact jolting her pistol uncomfortably but reassuringly deeper down the side of her boot, and walked across the track and up the bank, then turned to face the train.

People were all doing as she had done, or helping kids—silent now— down to the broken stones. The Greens strode or stood or rode up and down, yippeeing, all the time keeping their rifles trained on the passengers. There were at least a score of the attackers on each side of the train, probably more. About a hundred people, passengers and crew, had come off the train. Somebody was still on the train and still screaming.

Myra stood with her hands on her head and shivered. The sight of so many people with their hands up made her feel sick. The barbarians probably intended to loot the train—they must know that some at least of the passengers would be carrying concealed weapons, but they weren't as yet even bothering to search for them. The hope that they would be spared would be enough to stop almost anyone from making an inevitably doomed attempt to fight. It might just stop them until it was too late. If the Greens intended a massacre they would do it, of that she was sure, just when least expected. The Greens would manoeuvre inconspicuously so that they were out of each other's lines of fire, and the fusillade would come. Then a bit of rape and robbery, and a few final finishing shots to the head for the wounded if they were lucky.

One tall man in a fur cloak and leather-strapped cotton leggings was stalking around from one group of passengers to another, peering at and talking to every young or young-looking woman. When he reached Myra he stopped on the slope just below her, rested his hand on his knee and looked up, grinning. He was clean-shaven, with long sun-bleached red hair tied back with a thong around his brow. On another thong, around his neck, hung a whistle. Beneath his fur cloak he wore a faded green T-shirt printed with the old UN Special Forces motto: SORT 'EM OUT—LET GOD KILL 'EM ALL.

'Ah,' he said, '*you* must be Myra Godwin!'

He had a London accent and a general air of enjoying himself hugely. Myra stared at him, shaken at being thus singled out. He recognised her, and she had a disquieting feeling that she'd seen him somewhere before.

'Yes,' she said. 'What's it to you?'

'You got any proof of that?'

'Diplomatic passport, jacket pocket, above the seat I was in.'

'I'll check,' he warned, eyes narrowing.

'Oh, and bring my fucking Glock as well. You are in deep shit, mister.'

'We'll see about that,' he said. He turned around and yelled at the big man who'd emptied her carriage; he was still standing in the doorway, rifle pointed upward.

'Yo! Fix! Get this lady's stuff out. From above her seat.'

He didn't take his eyes off her as the big man passed him the folded jacket and he fingered through it. One quick glance down at the opened passport, and he put the whistle to his lips and blew a loud, trilling note, twice.

'Right, Fix, spread the word,' he said. 'We got her. Tax them and leave. Let's get outta here before the helicopters come.'

The other man jogged off, shouting orders. In a minute, out of the corner of her eye, Myra could see the tax being organised: the people from the train had all been herded into one group, and a man with a shotgun and a woman with a sack were going around, taking money and jewellery and small pieces of kit and personal weapons. People handed their stuff over with a sickeningly eager compliance.

'Want your jacket back?'

Myra nodded. He tossed it, still folded, to her; held on to the holstered automatic, the passport and the uplink phone.

'You'll get these back later,' he said.

She put the jacket on. It was a thin suit jacket and didn't do much to keep out the chill.

'What do you mean, "later"?' she asked.

He laughed at her.

'You're coming with us. We'll let you go soon.'

The wind just got colder.

Myra gestured at her blood-spattered blouse and blood-soaked skirt.

'Excuse me if I don't believe you.'

'War is hell, init?' he agreed brightly. He moved his hand as though tossing something light away. 'The guard was a spy, anyway.'

Myra said nothing.

'OK, youse lot!' some guy on a horse was shouting. 'Get back on the train and stay there. Don't try chasing us, don't anyone try shooting after us. 'Cause if you do, we'll come back an' kill youse all. And don't leave the train after we're gone, neither, or the choppers will pick you off in the fields.'

The group filed into the train through one of the doorways. Myra could see them dispersing along the carriages.

'That's all you're going to do?'

The red-haired man nodded. 'This time.' He jerked his thumb over his shoulder. 'I mean, I feel sorry for these people, but not sorry enough to kill them. And I'm not going to waste time searching the train for valuables. No point in being greedy, otherwise the trains would just stop coming through. Just enough tax to cover the op, you know.'

'What op?'

He stared at her. 'Getting hold of you.'

Oh, shit. She'd thought that was what he'd been driving at. She blinked rapidly, recording his image, and triggering a search protocol on her eyeband, to see if this knowledgeable bandit was known himself.

'You did all this just to get me?' She smiled sourly, over chattering teeth. 'How did you know I was on the train?'

The man looked at her scornfully. 'That wasn't difficult,' he said. He waved a hand expansively but evasively. 'We're everywhere.'

'Seems a bit excessive.'

'Some things you just can't say in a phone call,' he said idly. Then he shifted his feet and straightened up, grinning. 'Besides, raiding is such fun.' He drew in a long breath of fresh air as though inhaling a drug. 'It's a lifestyle thing.'

A slender, dark-skinned woman with curly, wavy blonde hair down to her waist rode up on a big black horse, leading a similar horse and a dun mare. She smiled at the tall man, and turned a colder smile to Myra.

'You know how to ride?'

In a moment everyone was mounted. Myra tugged up her bloody skirt as she settled in the saddle. The tall man waved and whistled three blasts. Suddenly the Greens were dispersing away from the train, diagonally up the scree-slope to the trees or, as those around Myra did, straight across the wet meadow. She found herself on a hell-for-leather gallop behind Fix, with the blonde-haired woman and the red-haired man on either flank. Over a hedge, down a path, into a narrow wooded dell.

Somewhere far away, the sound of a helicopter. Then some short machine-gun bursts, though at whom they were aimed, Myra did not wish to guess.

Myra rode silently like the others, but in the spectral company of Parvus; the AI was murmuring into her bone-conduction earclip and flashing Grolier screens up in front of her eyes. Nothing more current was available without the uplink phone. He'd provisionally identified the man who'd captured her, but it wasn't very enlightening—the latest pictures of him were from about twelve years ago, and he hadn't been a land-pirate then. He had been a net commentator, and—before that—a minor agitator in the Fall Revolution. The television clips of his rants explained why he looked vaguely familiar— she'd watched the British national democratic revolution in the time she'd been able to spare from following the Siberian Popular Front's assault on Vladivostok.

The dell opened to a larger valley, thickly settled. Old stone houses, geo-desic domes, wattle huts, new thatched cottages, a few nanofactured carbon-shell constructions. A lot of cattle and sheep in the fields; kids running everywhere. The path became a gravel road which widened, at the centre of the main street, to a small cobbled square. In the centre, just by a verdigrised copper statue of a Tommy with a fixed bayonet, memorial to the fallen of three world wars, was an outdated but still effective anti-aircraft missile battery. No higher than the statue itself, it held a rack of a dozen metre-long rockets. Myra could read the small print of what they were tipped with: laser-fuser tactical nukes.

People crowded around, welcoming the returning raiders. They called the red-haired man what she thought at first was 'Red', which made sense; then realised it was 'Rev', which made no sense at all. It certainly wasn't the name her search had come up with. The kids were cheering and doing the high-stepping, high-jumping Zulu war-dance called *toyi-toying*.

Fix reined in his horse in front of a large stone building which had a low-ceilinged front room open to the street: a café. Myra followed suit, dismounted and was led through into a back room with a fire, and high leather chairs around a table. The room smelt of woodsmoke and alcohol and unwashed humanity and damp dogs.

'Have a seat.'

Myra sat and the two men and the woman sat down opposite her. They regarded her in silence for a moment. She decided to hazard the Grolier's guess.

'Jordan Brown,' she said. 'And you must be Cat Duvalier.' That name was in the entry's small print as Jordan Brown's wife.

'Well done,' the man said, unperturbed. 'Nifty little machine you've got there.'

Myra flipped the eyeband back. 'Yes. So tell me, Mr Brown, what it is you want.'

'It's *Reverend* Brown,' he said. 'First Minister of the Last Church of the Unknowable God.' He smiled. 'But please, call me Jordan.' He looked over his shoulder and shouted an order. 'Beer and brandy!'

He slung his cloak over a chair; without it, leaning over the table in his T-shirt and wild hair, he looked somewhat more intimidating. Some absence in his gaze reminded Myra of *spetznatz* veterans, or old Afghantsi. The Blue Beret slogan on the T-shirt just might not be ironic, she thought. A boy padded in carrying glasses and bottles.

'All we've got at the moment,' the woman called Cat said. 'What'll you have?'

'I'll have a beer.'

She accepted the drink without thanks, and lit a cigarette without asking permission or offering to share. Damned if she was going to act as though she was enjoying their hospitality.

'You were saying, *Reverend*.'

Jordan Brown spread his hands. 'Just to talk things over.'

'You've gone to a lot of trouble to do that.'

'I sure have,' he said. 'I've risked the lives of my fighters, I've exposed one of my agents, I've had a man slaughtered like a pig—which he was, but that's nothing to you—and had another train guard shot in the belly just for trying to do his job. Quite possibly, some of the passengers have already fallen to friendly fire.' He shrugged. 'And I would have killed more, if I'd had to. The point is, I'll get away with it.' He waved his hand above his head. 'We all will. The helicopter was the worst the British can do against us.'

Myra looked straight at him. 'Like I care. You might not get off so lightly when this gets back to the Kazakhstani Republic.'

Jordan nodded soberly. 'No doubt I'm trampling all over diplomatic niceties. But it's you that came to Britain to get help, not the other way round. So you'll forgive me for not worrying too much.'

'Hah!'

'Anyway,' Jordan went on, 'I've no wish to get into a pissing-contest. I have something more important to say to you. So. Are you willing to have a serious conversation?'

Myra shrugged, looking around theatrically. 'Why not? I don't see any better entertainment.' She poured a brandy chaser, again without false courtesy.

Jordan Brown leaned forward on his bare forearms, took a swig of brandy and began to speak.

'You've come to Britain to get military aid against the Sheenisov. You might even get it. What I want to tell you is two things. One, don't do it. It won't do you any good. You can't fight communism with imperialism. It's just throwing napalm on the fire.'

Myra favoured him with a look that said she'd heard this before. 'If you say so. And what else do you have to tell me? Try and make it something that's news to me, how about that?'

'You're in worse trouble than you think,' Jordan said. 'The entity you call the General is working for the Sheenisov.'

Myra almost choked on her sip of brandy. She coughed fire for a moment. She felt totally disoriented.

'*What?* And how the hell would you know?'

'Strictly speaking,' Jordan Brown said, 'the Sheenisov are working for *it*. As to how I know . . .'

He held out a hand towards Cat. She leaned forward as Jordan leaned back.

'Myra,' she said earnestly, 'I may be a barbarian now, but I used to be like you. I used to be in the International.'

'Oh, Jesus!' Myra exploded. 'Half the fucking world is run by ex-Trots! Tell me something I don't know, like how you heard about the FI mil org— the General.'

'I was coming to that,' Cat said, mildly enough—but Myra could read the younger woman's face like a computer screen, and she could see the momentary spasm of impatient rage. This barbarian lady was someone who'd got dangerously used to not being interrupted. Cat forced a smile. 'I still hear rumours.'

'Rumours? That's what you're relying on?'

'It seems you've just confirmed one,' Jordan said, dryly.

Myra acknowledged that she had. But it seemed a situation where stonewalling would be less productive than admitting that the General existed, and trying to find out where the rumour came from. Parvus hadn't spotted anything like that . . .

'Did you pick this up off the net, or what?'

Jordan looked at Fix and Cat, and all three of them laughed. To Myra, it sounded like a mocking laugh.

'God, you people,' Jordan said. His tone changed as he went on, becoming an invocation, or an imprecation. 'You have a screen between you and the world all the time. We have the human world, and the natural world. We have the whole world that you call marginal, the scattered society of free humanity. We have the whisper in the market, the gesture on the road, the chalked mark on the pavement. The twist of a leaf, the turning of a twig. We have the smell carried on the wind. We have the night sky and the names of all its fixed and moving and falling stars. We have our friends in all your cities and camps and armies. We have the crystal radio that receives and the spark-gap that transmits, in codes you have forgotten, on wavelengths you no longer monitor, in languages that you disdained to learn.'

He tipped his head back and began glossolaliating in Morse code, *da-da-dit-di-da-dididididah* . . . Cat and Fix cocked their heads, listening, and after a minute grinned and guffawed.

Jordan looked a little smug at this demonstration. 'See, I can joke in tongues. We have our own Internet, and our own International. Don't bother looking for a leak from yours.'

'Besides,' said Fix, speaking up for the first time, 'we know this thing from way back. Jordan and Cat fought in the revo, and so did it. It was called the Black Plan, and it was used by—or it used—the Army of the New Republic. We've all encountered it, and we know where it went. To New View, your commie-cult commune in space.'

'And we know how it thinks,' said Cat. 'We can see its hand in what the Sheenisov are doing, in their tactics and in their strategy. It's not exactly malevolent, but it is . . . ambitious.'

'So?' Myra shrugged, trying hard to stay cool, and to reassert her control over the conversation. 'We—that is, my country, Kazakhstan—' there, she had said it, and the words *my country, Kazakhstan* could not be unsaid '—we are not relying on this thing. We take no orders from it, not since—well, it got on the wrong side of me, put it that way. I don't say I believe you about its taking the side of the Sheenisov, but—let's say I wouldn't put that past it. If you're so worried about it, why do you object to my getting help to stop it?'

'Because,' said Jordan, emphasising each word with a chop of the hand, '*it can not be stopped.* Not by fighting it. If it finds itself on the losing side it will change sides, or work for both sides, and it will win. Its only real enemies are rival AIs, such as those of the space movement, and those strange ghosts of genius that some of the spacers are trying to turn into. It will defeat them, or absorb them, and then it will be content in its . . . singular godhood, spreading with humanity to all the worlds to come. It will look after our best interests, whether we like it or not.'

'Hah, come on you can't possibly know that.'

Jordan sat back and looked at her with an ironic expression. 'Oh, yes I can, but call it an educated guess if it makes you feel better. If the British Republic were to come in on your side, I'm sure they'd be delighted to get their old planning-system back. They'd jump at any offers it made them. Or they would accept similar Greek gifts from the space movement's AIs. So whoever wins—the Western powers, the space movement or the Sheenisov—humanity will be living inside some machine or other, for ever.'

'Would that be so bad?'

'No,' said Jordan. 'That's what I'm afraid of.'

He jumped up. 'But what the hell. You do as seems best. If you still want to ally with the British when you get to London, go right ahead. Much good it'll do you.'

He downed his remaining brandy and looked around at the others, then at Myra. 'Come on,' he said. 'I'll take you to the road.'


She rode along beside the red-haired man, troubled but unconvinced by his strange tirades. Wet branches of beech and birch brushed past them, making her duck and blink. The stony path led up the side of the hill above the settlement. Myra looked back down at it before it passed from view.

'How do you people live?' she asked. 'You can't live just on raiding, and some day soon, according to you, there'll be nothing left to raid. Like, who pays for these anti-missile missiles?'

'We all do,' Jordan said. 'We don't have taxes, that'd be a laugh. We—not just this village, all of the free people—have a couple of simple economic principles that have been applied in communities like this for nearly a hundred years now. One is that we don't have rent, but land ain't free—God ain't making any more of it, but we keep right on making more people. So we apply the equivalent of rent to community purposes, like defence. The other is that any individual, or any group, can issue their own currency, backed up at their own risk. No landlords, no usurers, and no officials.'

'Oh, great,' said Myra. 'A peasant's idea of utopia. Single tax and funny money! Now I've heard everything!'

'It does work,' Jordan said. 'We, as you can see, flourish. We're the future.'

'Jordan,' she said, 'you know I found some clips of you on my encyclopaedia? Well, from them I'd never have figured you for going over to the Green Slime. Or for a preacher, come to that.'

Jordan laughed, unoffended. 'The world will fall to the barbarians or to the machines. I chose the barbarians, and I chose to spread some enlightenment among them. Hence the preaching, which was—to begin with—of a kind of rationalism. I can honestly say I have led many of my people away from the dark, heathen worship of Gaia, and from witchcraft and superstition. But I also found, like many another missionary, that I preferred their way of life to the one from which I'd come. And along with loving nature, I came to love nature's God.'

'You were an atheist.'

'So I believed. I later realised that I was an agnostic. A *militant* agnostic, if you like. All theology is idolatry, all scripture is apocrypha. All we can say is that God is One. God encompasses the world, there is nothing outside him, and nothing opposed to him. How could there be? So God approves of all that happens, because all that happens is his will. God loves the world, all of it, from the Hubble to the Planck, from the Bang to the Crunch. God is in the hawk hovering up there and in the mouse that cowers from its claws in yonder field. God is in the sickle and the sheaf, the hammer and the hot iron, the sword and the wound. God is in the fire and in the sun and in the holocaust. God was in the spy I had killed today, and in the man who killed him.'

Antinomianism was, Myra knew, a common enough heresy in periods of revolution or social breakdown. Four hundred years ago, these same words could have been ranted forth on those very hills. There was nothing new in what Jordan said, but Myra felt sure it would not disturb him in the slightest to point this out. He had probably read Winstanley and Christopher Hill for himself.

'You seem to know a lot about this unknowable God of yours.'

'That I do.'

'Is God in the machines, in the AIs that you fear?'

'That too, yes.'

'What's the difference between a God who makes no difference and takes no side and no God at all?'

They had reached the crest of the hill. Jordan reined in his horse. Myra stopped too, and looked down the hill at the grey ribbon of the motorway and the white blocks of a service-station.

So close, all the time.

'You can walk from here,' Jordan said dryly. He took her horse's reins as Myra dismounted. He soberly returned her holstered weapon, her passport and her phone.

'Oh, and to answer your question. There is no difference, in a sense. But to believe that God is in everything, and is on your side whatever you do and whatever happens, gives one a tremendous access of energy.' He grinned down at her. 'Or so I've found.'

And with that, the agnostic fanatic was gone, swift on his horse.

Myra slogged down the hill to the service area, cleaned up, made some phone calls while she ate in the cafeteria, and hired a car to take her to London.

She arrived, through all the obstacles thrown up by the small battles on the way, on the evening of the following day. She had long since missed her appointment with the Foreign Office; she had told them that in advance, and they'd asked her to call back when she arrived, to make another.

But, after all she had seen along the way, and all she had not seen—such as any evidence that people like Jordan's band, and worse, operated with anything other than insolence and impunity, give or take the odd gunship attack—there didn't seem to be a whole hell of a lot of a point.

# 13

---

## THE SEA EAGLE

Rain drummed on the roof of Merrial's house. The view outside was dreich. I'd looked out the window earlier, down the glen and the loch; ranks of cloud were marching in off the sea, and one after another shedding their loads on the hills. Inside, it was warm: we sat huddled together, backs to the piled-up pillows, sipping hot black coffee.

'No work today, thank Providence,' I said.

'Not at the yard anyway,' said Merrial. She waved a hand at the soldering-iron and seer-stones and clutter in the corner of the room. 'You start learning a different work, here.'

'Aye, great,' I said.

'What is this Providence you talk about, anyway?' she asked.

'Um.' I stared at the slow swirl of the coffee. 'It's . . . the helpful side of Nature, you might say. When things work out as we would wish, without an apparent cause.' I looked at her. 'You must know that.'

'But that's just coincidence,' she said. 'All things come by Nature.'

'Some things are more than coincidence, and Nature is more than—' I was going to say 'more than Nature' but stopped and laughed. 'You really don't know any Natural Theology?'

'No,' she said cheerfully. 'I've always just taken for granted that the out-siders have strange beliefs. Never gone into the details.' She put her empty mug down at her side of the bed and snuggled up to me. 'Go on. Tell me the details.'

'Oh, God. All right. Well, the usual place to start is right here.' I tapped her forehead, gently. 'Inside there. From the outside we see grey matter, but from the inside we think and feel. We know there are billions of cells in there, processing information. So thinking and feeling—consciousness—is something that information does. It's what information is, from the inside, its subjective side. Where there's information, there's consciousness.'

'But there's information everywhere,' she said. 'Wherever anything affects anything else, it's information. The rain falling on the ground is information.'

'Exactly!' I slid my arm around her shoulders. 'You've got it.'

'Got what? Oh.' She shifted a little and looked straight at me. 'You mean there's consciousness everywhere?'

'Yes! That's it!'

'But, but—' She looked around. 'You mean to tell me you think that clock, say, has *thoughts*?'

The ticking was loud in the room as I considered this.

'It has at least one,' I said cautiously.

'And what would that be?'

' "It's later . . . it's later . . . it's later . . . " '

She laughed. 'But the whole universe—'

'Is an infinite machine, which implies an infinite mind.' I put my hand behind her head, cradling the container of her finite mind. ' "And this all men call God",' I concluded smugly.

Merrial punched me.

'And the computers, I suppose you would say they are conscious too?'

'Aye, of course,' I said.

'What a horrible thought.'

'They may not be conscious of what we see from the outside,' I said. 'They may be thinking different thoughts entirely.'

Merrial gazed abstractedly out of the window.

'What thought is the rain thinking?'

'Can't you hear it?' I said. 'It's thinking "yesssss".'

'Hmm,' she said. 'Now *there's* a coincidence . . .'


We used the couple of days before my reinstatement in my job at the yard for the beginnings of an education in fine soldering and in programming, the latter subject being simultaneously fascinating and maddening. We also made a painstaking study of the Deliverer's documents, which continued— after we'd returned the originals to Gantry, and I'd returned to work at the yard—with the photocopies, but they yielded no information relevant to the ship's mission. The folder from the 2050s reinforced, in its casual refer- ences and assumptions more than its explicit statements, the staggering extent of the orbital activity of pre-Deliverance humanity. But it contained no hint of the Deliverance itself.

There was one moment when I thought I had won a real historical insight, albeit one tangentially relevant to our immediate concerns.

I looked up from the stack of papers on Merrial's broad table. Every evening after work, I'd slowly sifted through them, as now, in the late sun.

'Merrial?' I said. She turned from the seer-stone apparatus on which she was working, and laid down her soldering-iron.

'You found something?'

'No, just—realised something. These Greens she talks about in some of her articles, the marginal people who lived outside the cities. She makes the point here that they had a lot more practical skills than folk gave them credit for, that they weren't just ignorant barbarians but farmers and smiths and electricians and so on.'

'Yes,' she said, with a mysterious smile. 'That was true.'

'Well! These people, the Greens, they must have been the ancestors of the tinkers!'

'Here,' she said, passing me a cigarette. 'You're going to need this.'

'Why?' I asked, lighting up.

'Because—oh, *Dhia*, how can I break this to you gently? You've got it the wrong way round entirely! Why do you think we call the settled folk "the outsiders"?'

'What?'

'Aye, the Greens, the barbarians, these are not our ancestors, Clovis. They're—I was going to say yours, but I can't say that any more, *mo gràidh*, now you're one of us. They're the ancestors of the outsiders! We are the survivors, the descendants, of the city folk!'

'So how is it that we—I mean the outsiders—live in the cities now?'

She stood up then, walking around the small room like a lecturer, gesturing with her cigarette. 'Oh, but your face is a picture, colha Gree! They live in the cities now because they invaded them, they moved in at the Deliverance when the old civilisation and city life had broken down. And they're still there, bless them, blundering around like the barbarians they are, in the borrowed costumes of the past. All these scholars that you wanted to emulate, they're just rummaging about in the ruins, reading books they misunderstand so badly it isn't funny. You're well out of that, my love, you'll learn more from us in a year than in a lifetime at the University!'

Indeed.


A huge cheer went up, almost drowning the inrushing roar of water, as the sluice-gates opened. The water poured over the edge of the drydock in a

saline Niagara that went on and on, until it seemed that the loch itself would
be lowered before the deep hole was filled. Faster than a tide, the water crept
up the legs and pontoons of the platform.

Merrial's hand gripped mine as we made our way through the crowd,
pushing to the front like children. The entire accessible part of the cliff-edge
around the dock was lined with people. Everybody who'd worked at the
yard, on the platform or the ship, was certainly there, along with casual visitors from the surrounding towns, keen sightseers from all over the Highlands,
and outright enthusiasts from even farther afield. A couple of hundred metres around the cliff and inward, officers of the International Scientific Society, project managers and exemplary workers made speeches from a wooden
stage with a raised dais and an awning. Nobody farther away than fifty metres, at the outside, could make out a word these dignitaries said, particularly
not from the PA speakers strung out like fairy-lights on catenaries of cable all
over the place. Squawks and howls and crackles worthy of a railway station
echoed around the cliff-faces.

I ducked in between a couple of workers at the front who'd incautiously
allowed a quarter of a metre to open up between them. Merrial followed
with, no doubt, a smile at both of them which made them feel they were being done a favour.

And then we were there, a metre or two from the crumbling, tussocked
edge. The platform and the spaceship loomed startlingly close. At that moment another cheer went up, as though to acclaim our arrival, and I realised
that the capsule at the tip of the probe was, minutely but perceptibly, swaying. The platform was afloat.

'Hoo-rrayy!' I shouted, joining enthusiastically in the applause. Merrial
yelled something almost too high to hear beside me; I could hardly hear
myself. Though a less spectacular moment than the flooding of the dock, it
was freighted with greater significance: the beginning of the *Sea Eagle/Iolair*'s
journey, which would end in space.

It was a strange launch vehicle, simultaneously more primitive and more
advanced than anything sent into space in the first age of space exploration.
The ancients could, no doubt, have built a fusion torch-ship, but they didn't.
They went straight from massive liquid-fuelled rockets to the nanotech
diamond ships of the last days. In our time, with chemical fuels relatively
expensive and nanotech (other than the tinker computers) quite beyond our
reach, and the secret of controlled fusion still extant, the fusion torch is a
logical choice.

But, as Fergal had implied, building it out of boiler plate was a trifle in-
elegant. On the other hand, the skills were there, locally available from ship-
building; and the weight—given the immense power of the engine—was not
a significant constraint. And say what you like about red-leaded steel plate,

it is reliably resistant to sea-water. There was, of course, no question of launching such a monster from anywhere on land, which is less forgiving—of intense heat, high-energy particles and unstable isotopes—than the sea.

Its mission, too, was primitive, or at least simple: to launch into orbit an experimental communications and Earth-observation satellite. That payload had required the co-operation of scientists and engineers (tinkers or otherwise), lens-makers and photographers, from all over the civilised world. Its electronic and electrical systems strayed suspiciously close to the path of power—even deploying, if you wanted to be awkward, a system very like television. But after much soul-searching and acrimony, the majority of the most respected practitioners of Natural Theology had, with some reluctance, nodded their long-haired heads. Television, they gravely pointed out, had been destructive only as a mass medium. To object to it as a method of communication from a satellite to a ground station would, they averred, be crass superstition, unworthy of this enlightened age.

Needless to say, a minority of their equally respected, though (it has to be said) usually older, colleagues insisted that this was the first step on a slippery slope at the bottom of which lay a population reduced to a passively rotting mass of mental and physical wrecks. With equal inevitability, given the nature of Natural Theology, a much smaller (and, yes, younger) faction were pointing out that the sort of abject helotry described and decried by their conservative colleagues were in fact the peoples better known as *the ancients*, who had watched television assiduously and had an achievement or two to their credit before they fell. To which, of course . . . but the argument's further iterations would be tedious to elaborate.

Merrial walked forward more boldly than I would have and sat down cheerily on the very lip of the cliff, her legs dangling over and her skirt elegantly spread on the heather to either side of her. I sat beside her and tried not to look down at a drop to the sea, direct and vertical except where it was interestingly varied by jutting rocks. We had found ourselves a viewpoint slightly in front of the platform, between its foremost extension and the open gates of the dock.

The shouting and cheering had stopped now, replaced by the susurrus of conversation, the continuing surge of the rising sea and the deep whine of the platform's turbines as they laboured to move the gigantic structure. Very slowly, the mast-like rocking of the ship's shaft was intersected by a net forward motion. Slow though it was, this set up a noticeable bow-wave at the front, clashing and splashing against the incoming waves. Complex interference patterns formed as the waves rebounded off the sides of the dock and the platform itself, and the sun, already past the zenith and dipping towards the west, made spectra in the spray.

Even at five kilometres per hour, the platform didn't take long to pass us, to the sound of further cheering, and waving to and from the operational crew down on the decks. Another significant moment, duly registered by another round of applause, came when the platform passed through the gates and into the open sea—or at any rate Loch Kishorn. After this there was really nothing to see except the slow departure of the rig, and people began to drift away. The platform had a long voyage ahead of it, out of the loch and into the Inner Sound, from whence it would pass the headlands of Rona and Skye before heading out into the Atlantic. Barring any serious mishap—and the weather forecasts were optimistic—it would proceed for seven more days before it was far enough out in the ocean to hold a position for the launch of the ship itself. The onboard crew would transfer to an escort vessel and stand off on the horizon, triggering the launch by radio control when the scientists and engineers had determined that the conditions were right. Given the robustness of the *Sea Eagle* and the power of its drive, little short of a severe storm could stand in its way. Only the platform was, in theory, vulnerable to the wind and the waves—so the chanciest part of the whole venture, the part which could literally sink it, was the one that had just begun.

Unless Merrial's fears about the orbital debris were borne out. Nothing more had been heard about this from Fergal or any other tinker, according to Druin, and he could be trusted on such a matter, according to Merrial. Although her own contract on the project had come to an end, those of other tinkers working on mission-critical systems (as the cant had it) had not; and she was still well up on the latest tinker gossip—as, increasingly, was I.

In the weeks between our reconciliation and the floating of the platform we had had an interesting time, in which our joy in each other was countered—though not in any way diminished—by the reactions of other people to it. At the yard, I daily endured the merciless mockery which my mates seemed to think entirely compatible with continued friendly relations in other respects. In the softer circumstances of my previous experience—in childhood, schooling and University—some of their insults and abuse would have occasioned life-long, smouldering enmity, if not immediate physical violence. Here they passed as light-hearted badinage, and it was their ignoring rather than avenging that was taken as a token of manly honour.

The stand-offish attitudes of the tinkers at the camp were harder to take, but Merrial insistently reassured me that they were a similar test, of the strength of my commitment to their ways, and to her. As the days and weeks passed their reactions to me had gradually warmed to the point of a frigid, prickly politeness.

Merrial and I were, by tinker custom, bundling—trying out the experience of living together before making a public commitment. I was enjoying the experiment and I was as committed as I could ever imagine being, and so was Merrial, but neither of us was in any hurry to move our relationship on to a more formal basis. A tinker marriage is a serious matter, involving among other horrendous expenses—seamstresses, cooks, musicians—that of keeping hundreds of people drunk for a week.

Merrial looked over at me.

'Time to go?'

'Aye.'

We stood up and made our way back, easier now, through the thinning crowd. For obvious reasons, alcohol was strictly banned from the site, and from this day's event. Everybody was heading back for the towns, starting with the nearest, Courthill. The end of the project, and the final pay-packets and bonuses, would be celebrated by drinking the pubs dry over the course of the afternoon and evening.

We wandered along the path back to the main road, occasionally greeting people we knew. The stage from which the speeches had been made stood empty, and was already being dismantled. The various dignitaries were moving down the path in a compact group, and I hurried a little to overtake them on the grass, eager for a closer glimpse of the famous men and women who had travelled far to honour our achievement. Merrial observed this behaviour with sardonic toleration.

I was pointing out a renowned Russian astronomer and an English spacecraft engineer to Merrial when we both noticed Fergal towards the rear of the procession, walking alone among them all. I was surprised to see him, then realised that I shouldn't be—he had been the project manager on the guidance system, after all. At the same moment, he noticed us. He beckoned us over.

Merrial glanced at me. I shrugged. We went over and joined him, I making sure that I walked between him and Merrial. I felt uneasily that we had no place there, but the rest of the dignitaries politely paid us no attention whatever, to the extent that they noticed us at all, and weren't simply caught up in their own deep conversations.

He looked at us sidelong, without hostility. Our confrontation might as well never have happened, for all that he showed of bearing any grudge. For myself, it was different.

'How have you two been getting on?' he asked. He'd obviously heard of our bundling.

'Oh, fine. Great!'

Merrial caught my hand and swung it. 'This one's no an outsider any more, I'll tell you that.'

'Good.' He smiled, and changed the subject. 'It's a great day for us all.'

'Aye,' I said. 'But I'll not be sure of it until the ship's in orbit.'

'Oh, I wouldn't worry about that,' he said. His gaze flicked to Merrial's eyes. 'The ship is safe.'

'How are *you* getting on?' I asked boldly. 'With your new friend?'

'Who—oh, the AI!'

'What?'

'Art-if-icial In-tell-igence,' Fergal and Merrial articulated at the same moment. I glanced from one to the other and laughed.

'I have to learn that sort of thing sometime!'

'Indeed you do,' said Fergal indulgently. 'Still, you have plenty of centuries ahead to learn it.'

'Well, I suppose two is plenty, at that,' I replied, puzzled at this odd remark.

Fergal stopped, then hastened on as others trod on our heels.

'She hasn't told you?'

Merrial was looking at him and at me with a mute appeal that somehow seemed to mean something different for both of us. Fergal firmly shook his head.

'Well, she bloody should have.'

'I didn't want to—' began Merrial.

'Give him an improper inducement? Or scare him off?' Fergal smiled sourly. 'Like it or not, Merrial MacClafferty, it's a bit late for either now, wouldn't you think?'

'Oh, I'm not sure he's ready—'

'Will you two,' I said, 'please stop talking as if I wasn't there?'

Fergal glanced over his shoulder, looked ahead, then turned his gaze to the ground and spoke in a low voice.

'Do you know why people today live longer than they did until some time before the Deliverance?'

'Aye,' I said. 'I found references to it in the Deliverer's papers. Life-extension treatments. I suppose in some way the effects must have persisted, and become hereditary.'

'Close enough,' he said, evidently resisting an impulse to quibble. 'Well, the people who became the ancestors of the tinkers had a better treatment.'

My heart thudded. 'How much better?'

He looked around again. A couple of metres separated us from the others on that path, before and behind.

'So much better that we don't know how much better it is.'

I looked at Merrial, feeling the blood drain from my face, and then rush back. I squeezed her hand.

'Well, if you'll have me, I don't care if you do outlive me, and stay young while I grow old.' Easy enough to say, when you're twenty-two and don't believe that ageing or death have any personal application in the first place. But to my surprise, Merrial laughed.

'This one isn't genetic, any more than the other,' she said. 'It's—'

'Infectious,' said Fergal. 'Or is it contagious? I can never remember.'

'Whatever,' said Merrial. 'It's, um, sexually transmitted.'

She sounded almost embarrassed.

Fergal, it seemed, was still welcome in The Carronade, and even Druin, when he passed him at the bar, was affable towards him. I guessed, myself, after my third litre and sixth whisky, that the tinker Internationalist was anxious to show us his friendly side. I remained unpersuaded by it, but decided to make the most of it while it lasted. I had still not assimilated the news that I could expect to live longer than I'd ever expected, and it would take me long enough to do it.

'So what,' I asked him, at a corner table in the security of the raucous din around us, 'was that thing Merrial found? The AI?'

'It's . . . a planner,' he said. 'A mind that can co-ordinate an entire economy. Something we're going to need, some day.'

'After your glorious revolution?'

'Yes, and maybe before. It's a revolutionary itself.'

'So what are you going to do with it?' I asked.

Fergal might have been, as Jeanna had said, able to hold his drink. He may well have not done or said anything without calculating its effect on the vectors of his purposes. But I'm sure it was a reckless impulse that made him say what he said next.

'It's on the ship. Well, a copy of it, anyway.'

He was looking at me, not at Merrial, as he spoke. He didn't see what I saw: the momentary flash of triumph and delight on Merrial's face. That glimpse, as much as his words, must have drained the colour from mine. And then—I could see her dissembling—by the time Fergal turned to her, she looked even more shocked than I felt.

'Why the hell did you do that?' she asked.

Fergal leaned in and lowered his voice. 'I learned a few things from the AI,' he said. 'Its memories go right up to a few days before the Deliverance. It knows nothing about what happened but it does know that the Deliverer had control of nuclear and other weapons in space. So the possibility that— you know, what we feared—was true is too strong to ignore. But at this stage—hell, if the mission were aborted, or if the ship were destroyed, God alone knows how long it'd be before we'll see another. There was only one way to do it, and that was to make a copy and let it into the ship's own seer-stone control systems. Out of sheer self-preservation, the copy would be forced to take the kind of fast-reacting control over the ship's drive that would let it dodge through any debris that's still there.'

'Would that work?' I asked Merrial, who was staring at Fergal as though seeing past him.

'Oh, aye,' she said, without looking around, 'we couldn't do that ourselves, but an AI would be in with a chance, I reckon. But what happens once it's up?'

Fergal grinned. 'It just sits in the centre of a new communications web, that's all. A useful thing to have.'

'Bloody dangerous, you mean!' I said.

'Don't worry,' said Fergal, realising he'd gone too far. 'It's not going to interfere with the satellite. It'll just . . . gather information. For the future.'

'Oh God!' Merrial exclaimed. 'You're out of your fucking mind! That thing is a deil! It'll have the world in a new Possession before you know it!'

'It'll be our Possession,' Fergal said.

'Yours, you mean!'

Fergal stretched out his legs.

'And what would be wrong with that?'

He looked at our appalled faces and burst out laughing.

'Don't be stupid,' he said. 'There's no way it can do anything without having people to work with, and there are no such people yet.' He placed a thumb on Merrial's chin for a moment. 'As you fine well know.'

She smacked his hand away, none too gently.

'That was not funny,' she said. She got up with unsteady dignity. 'I'm going for a piss.'

Fergal watched me watching her thread her way through the throng. If he detected the tumult in my thoughts he gave no sign.

'No chance of persuading you, Clovis?'

'Not a chance in hell,' I said, still distracted. His casual banter fooled me for not a second; this was a man who wanted power, Possession indeed, and his current scheme with the AI would not be his last. He was a man I would have to watch, and might one day have to kill.

'Oh, well,' he said. 'Our day will come, and you'll see it.'

I was about to contest this when I felt a hand on my shoulder.

'Oh, hello, Catherine.'

My former landlady smiled down at me; like everyone here, she was already a bit drunk. She nodded at Fergal and looked back at me.

'Hi, Clovis. I hope you like your new accommodation.'

'Oh, aye.'

She reached into a pouch on her hip. 'I've got something for you,' she said. 'A letter that arrived a few days ago, I didn't get round to—'

'That's all right,' I said, taking the bulky envelope. 'Thanks.'

Fergal, perhaps subdued by his rebuff, was moodily studying his drink, or tactfully respecting my privacy, as I opened the package. From the handwriting of the address, I knew it was from Gantry. It contained a letter and a thick booklet. The letter was neatly typed. I glanced down the predictable hand-wringing about my expulsion from the University (the trial had been a farce, not that I cared any more) and about my choice of tinkering as a career; then turned over to the next sheet.

*However, Clovis, and just as a little reminder of the joys of historical research—you may remember I looked a little puzzled when you introduced your girlfriend, Merrial? The reason was that I thought I recognised her from somewhere. Actually, of course, I hadn't—but I'd come across a picture of what may be an ancestor of hers by the same name, in one of the institute's old yearbooks—2058, in fact. You may even have glanced through this once yourself. Have a look at page 35—the resemblance is quite striking.*

*(Needless to say, I expect you to return . . .*

I almost dropped the papers as I fumbled open the booklet and turned to the page. It showed—in much sharper detail and better colour than in modern photographs—some kind of social occasion. People were sitting, smartly dressed, at long tables, clapping their hands as others in their company danced. In the immediate foreground was a girl, caught in mid-twirl, her thick black hair swaying around behind her head, one hand swinging her long, layered skirt out to the side, her bare feet lightly, precisely placed. A fine dancer. Merrial.

She was even named, in the small print of the caption.

It could be an ancestor, I tried to tell myself, as Gantry thought. But I knew it was not so. If anyone could be identified from a photograph, Merrial could. She looked, in the picture, no different from how she looked this day.

I had, from the first moment I'd seen her, thought her younger, fiercer, fresher than myself, and attributed her occasional ironies and unreasonably intelligent remarks to her native wit, which I was quite unenviously happy to regard as greater than my own. It was a shock to realise that they were the wisdom of age. Dear God, how old was she? She had lived since the Deliverer's time! The thought was enough to make me feel dizzy.

Gantry was right about one thing—I had seen this picture before, on an idle trawl through the Institute's public-relations archive. And, as I had anticipated, the memory of seeing it did come back. It had only been a few seconds' pause as I'd turned the pages, a couple of years earlier, my attention momentarily caught by this pretty image from the past.

Fergal's voice broke into my appalled reflections.

'Bad news from home?'

I shook my head, folding the letter around the booklet again, inserting the sheets in the envelope and slipping it into my pocket.

'No, no,' I said, forcing a smile. 'Nothing like that. It's just—I feel faint, I think I've had too much to drink, on an empty stomach, you know?'

I clapped my hand to my mouth.

'Oh God.' I swallowed. The tinker's sardonic, sceptical eyes regarded me. I realised that I had still to decide what to do about another shock, delivered only minutes earlier: that he—apparently with Merrial's expectation—had put the AI on the ship. All it would take to expose him, and blast whatever schemes either or both of them had hatched, would be a word to Druin . . .

'You sure you're all right?'

'Yeah, I'll be fine. I just need some fresh air. I'm going out. Could you tell Merrial to come out too?'

'Sure,' he said, already scanning the crowd for other company. 'Where'll you be?'

'In the square,' I said. 'At the statue.'

# 14

---

## FINAL ANALYSIS

To Almaty then, and apple-blossom on the streets, smoke in the air, and the Tian-Shan mountains beyond; so high, so close they were improbable to the eye, like the moon on the horizon. Myra almost skipped with relief to be back in Kazakhstan.

President Chingiz Suleimanyov's office was a lot grander than Myra's. She felt a tremor of trepidation as she walked past the soldier who held the door open for her. A ten-metre strip of red carpet over polished parquet, at the end of which was a small chair in front of a large desk. The chair was plastic. The desk was mahogany, its green leather top bare except for a gold Mont Blanc pen and a pristine, red-leather-edged blotter. Glass-paned book-cases on either side of the room converged to a wide window with a moun-tain view. The room's central chandelier, unlit at the moment, looked like a landing-craft from an ancient and impressive alien civilisation making its presence known.

The President stood up as she came in, and walked around his intimidat-ing desk. They met with a handshake. Suleimanyov was a short, well-built Kazakh with a face which he'd carefully kept at an avuncular-looking fifty-ish. He was actually in his fifty-eighth year, a child of the century as he oc-casionally mentioned, which meant that he'd grown up after the Glorious Counter-Revolution of 1991 had passed into history. The reunification of Kazakhstan in the Fall Revolution had been his finest hour, and he always called himself a Kazakhstani, not a Kazakh: the national identification, not the ethnic. He didn't have any of Myra's twentieth-century leftist hang-ups. He had never had the slightest pretension to being any kind of social-ist. However, he followed Soviet tradition by wearing the neatest and most conventional business-suit that dollars could buy.

'Good afternoon, Citizen Davidova,' he said, in Russian. She responded similarly, and then he waved her to her seat and resumed his own. The sol-dier closed the door.

'Ah, Myra my friend,' Suleimanyov said, this time in BBC World Service English, 'let's drop the formality. I've read your reports on your mission.' He gestured with his hands as though letting a book fall open. 'What a mess. Though I must say you are looking good.'

'I'm sorry that I was not more successful, President Suleimanyov—'

'Chingiz, please. And no need to apologise.' He pinched the bridge of his nose, closing his eyes for a moment. He looked tired. 'I don't see how anyone else could have done better. Your action in leaving Great Britain was perhaps . . . impetuous, but even with hindsight it will probably turn out to have been for the best. What a long way down they've come, the En-glish. As for the Americans—well, what can I say?' He chuckled, with a cer-tain *schadenfreude*, and gazed upwards at the crystal mother-ship. 'Fifteen years ago they were stamping their will on the whole planet, and now a few nuclear weapons are too hot for them to handle. In my father's time they were willing to contemplate taking multiple nuclear hits themselves.' He looked back from his reminiscence to Myra. 'Sorry,' he said, suddenly abashed, 'no offence intended. I forget sometimes that you were—*are*—an American.'

'No offence taken,' Myra said. 'I entirely agree with your assessment. What a crock of shit the place is! What a pathetic lot they are! The chance of a long life has only made them more afraid of death than ever.'

The President's bushy eyebrows twitched. 'It has not done that for you, then?'

Myra shook her head. 'I can see the rationality of it—people think they have more life to lose if they have a long one to look forward to—but I think it's a false logic. A long life of oppression or shame is worse than a short one, after all.'

She stopped, and looked at him quizzically. He smiled.

'True, we are not here to discuss philosophy,' he said. 'Nevertheless, I'm happy that you think it better to die free than to live as slaves. We may get the chance some day, but let's try to delay our heroic deaths for a bit, eh?'

'Yes indeed.' She wanted very badly to smoke, but the President was no-toriously clean-living.

'Very well,' said Chingiz. 'Something I did not tell you before . . . I arranged for other cadres with similarly relevant experience to make similar approaches to the governments of France, Turkey, Brazil and Guangdong.

They have encountered a similar lack of interest. So we have to face the Sheenisov on our own. I need hardly tell you that we don't stand much of a chance, over anything but the short term.'

'I have a suggestion,' Myra said. 'If the West is unwilling to assist us, then to hell with them. Let's cut a deal with the Sheenisov! All we want is our territorial integrity, their withdrawal from Semipalatinsk and access to the markets, trade routes and resources of the Former Union. What they want, presumably, is a passage across or to the north of Kazakhstan, as they make their way west to the Ukraine, which is the nearest soft target but still one that will take them many years, perhaps decades, to assimilate. I don't think they're ready to take on Muscovy or Turkey just yet. It strikes me that these aims are not incompatible.'

'Yes, yes,' Chingiz said, 'the option of our switching sides has occurred to me, and to my Foreign Secretary. The difficulty is that no one has ever "cut a deal" with the Sheenisov. They have no leader, or even leadership— at least, none that the world knows. They are indeed a horde, without a Great Khan like my namesake. That makes them difficult to deal with—in every sense.'

'Ah, come on,' Myra said, feeling bolder. 'Even the anarchists had their Makhno. I don't believe a leaderless horde could accomplish what they have, even in military terms. It's applying guerilla tactics at the level of strategy and of main-force confrontation—that is novel, but it requires precise co-ordination. There is nothing random going on here.'

Chingiz's lips set in a thin line for a moment. He shook his head. 'A system without a centre can achieve more than we may intuitively expect, Myra. That after all is the lesson of the twentieth century, no? It works in economics, and in nature, and to some extent in military affairs too.'

'Good point,' Myra said. She didn't want to bring the deranged Green rumour about the General into this level of conversation. 'Let's assume they have no leadership. In order to have the co-ordination they display, they must have horizontal communication between the units, and some method of arriving at a common response . . . even if it's only some social equivalent of excitation and inhibition in a neural network. In that case, any offer made to a sufficiently large unit would be spread through the rest, as would a response. It would still be worthwhile contacting them.'

'Hmm,' said Chingiz. He steepled his fingers. 'And what do you propose? Walking towards them until they take notice, then talking to the first person able to understand you?'

'That's about it.'

'It sounds dangerous, apart from anything else.'

'Actually, I propose announcing my intention beforehand, through whatever channels we have, then heading for Semipalatinsk.'

'Come, come,' said Chingiz. 'Things are not that bad, not yet. You can still fly in, direct.'

'And out?'

'Oh, yes. Air-traffic control is still functioning. As are radio and television, on selected channels. It's only computer interfaces that are being blocked—by physical cutting of landlines or by electromagnetic jamming. It's incredibly differentiated stuff—very clever. We couldn't do it.'

She peered at his calm face.

'What reports are we getting?'

'About life under the Sheenisov? Hah. In some respects, life goes on as normal. There are certainly no democidal activities. There are what the Sheenisov call *reforms*. Workplace democracy, and so forth. They are very insistent about that. Many businesses dependent on the net are failing—they either re-orient to the Sheenisov internal communications system, whatever that is, or they pick up sticks and go, or they are expropriated on the grounds of abandonment.' He rubbed his hands. 'Needless to say, this is giving our republic a temporary influx of people, of capital, and of comms gear and computer capacity. Some refugees are destitute, but not many.'

'Any willing to join the fight back?'

'No mass rallying to our armed forces, I must say. The usual *dashnik emigré* diversions—plotting, pleading, mounting sabotage expeditions, low-key terrorism. We don't encourage it.' He rubbed a finger up and down the side of his nose. 'Naturally, we try to prevent it . . . to the best of our ability, but our resources are quite inadequate for such a task.'

'But of course.' Myra smiled. 'Could you raise me some *muj*? Two or three good men, not fanatics, not suicidal, but willing to take a risk and have a go if necessary. I'm still deeply reluctant to fly into Semey. Too much opportunity for an opportune mechanical failure—frankly, I'm getting a little paranoid about anything that's computer controlled, on either side. So, if I may, I'd like to drive, with bodyguards.'

Chingiz raised his eyebrows. 'Drive all the way?'

'No, no. Fly to Karaganda, announce what I'm doing, then drive to Semey, bypassing the ISTWR.'

'Ah, yes.' He teased some of the hairs in one shaggy eyebrow back into place. 'A little local difficulty there.' He sounded reproachful.

'The situation's under control,' Myra said.

'Perhaps. But, on balance, I would suggest that you don't go back there, or even bypass it by truck or jeep through the Polygon. Far more dangerous than flying.' He raised a hand, stilling her incipient protest. 'I know what you mean about the computers, and flight control. I too have thought about this. You will get your bodyguards. You make your announcement, fly to Semey, then wander where you will until someone makes contact—which, as you say, someone surely will. You will pass on the proposals and await developments. Then you will fly from Semey back to Kapitsa, and either declare the conflict settled, or rally your people for their part in the common defence.' He smiled thinly. 'Either way, your internal political problems will be over. Externally, however, it may turn out that the Sheenisov are not our most immediate problem . . .'

'Ah, yes,' said Myra. 'The next move. Presumably at least one of the countries we made our offer to will start to worry about what we're going to do with the nukes, and the option of disarming us will move up the agenda pretty damn quick.'

'Precisely,' said Chingiz. 'The US-spacer nexus is the one we probably have to worry about most—as your friend in New York said, the space industrialists and settlers are understandably edgy on the subject.'

'They're your nukes now,' Myra said. 'We'll go along with anything you say. Presumably you'd want us to stand them down and turn over the operational codes.'

Chingiz slammed his fist on his massive desk, making Myra jump.

'No!' he said. 'We are not going to be pushed around. We are not going to give up our nukes without guarantees of military aid. And we are willing to threaten nuclear retaliation against any attack.'

'So you're ready to go to the wire on this one?'

'Absolutely,' said Chingiz. 'To the wire. But not beyond.'

'All right,' said Myra. 'We'll go with you. We'll see who blinks first.'

'Thank you,' said Chingiz. His face relaxed a little. 'It's a high-risk strategy, I know. But the endgame is upon us, and I for one am not going into it defenceless.'

Myra nodded.

'The best thing you can do,' she said, 'is act as though you're ready to wash your hands of us—of the ISTWR. Denounce and disown us—privately of course, on the hotline—and urge the UN or US or whoever to negotiate directly with us. That should buy us some time.'

'Only if they believe you're mad enough to do it.'

Myra bared her teeth. 'They will.'


Semipalatinsk, or Semey, was a pleasant enough town, whose steppe location had let it spread out so much that even its taller buildings looked low, even its narrower streets wide. There was room in those broad streets for trees whose dusty leaves had been an object of suspicious Geiger-counter monitoring on her first visit, in the late 1980s. The good old days of the Nevada-Semipalatinsk Association against nuclear testing. Of all the betrayals she'd perpetrated against her youth, this one stung the most. Marxism,

Trotskyism and socialism could go hang; it was the implacable naive humanist internationalism of that protest, its irrefutable medical and statistical basis, its sheer bloody outrage rooted in biology rather than ideology, which had been her purest, fiercest flame. She had thought nuclear weapons the vilest work of man, whose very possession contaminated, and whose mere testing was murderous.

Nurup Kerbayev and Mustafa Altynsaryn, her proudly counterrevolutionary bodyguards, strolled a polite step or two behind her, beards and bandoliers bristling, Kalashnikovs slung on their shoulders. Nurup was ethnically Kazakh-Russian; Mustafa looked more Mongoloid, almost Han Chinese. With their AKs and baggy pants and scuffed boots and bulging jackets they both looked just like counter-revolutionary bandits. They also looked like Sheenisov soldiery or the local population, whom the Sheenisov had encouraged to carry arms as a deterrent to counter-revolutionary banditry.

They walked down the streets and across the squares quite unchallenged, though one or two people gave Myra a curious glance, as though recognising her from her television appearance the previous evening. Apart from the parked tanks on the street-corners, around each of which a curious crowd, mainly of children and young people, fraternised with the relaxed-looking crew, the town so far showed little sign of being caught up in a social revolution. It was the weird fighting-machines that were alarming. They stalked and lurched about like Martian invaders; but the locals treated them with casual familiarity, like traffic or street-furniture. Perhaps, Myra thought wryly, it was the absence of searing heat-rays and writhing metal tentacles that did the trick.

As well as those combat drones, big clunky calculating-machines were being installed, indoors in shop-fronts and factories, outdoors in the squares. Gears and teeth and crystal spheres, building to frenetic orreries of some alternate solar system, Copernican with Ptolemaic epicyles. Nanotech dripped and congealed around the brass and steel, like epoxy that never quite set. Around noon Myra and her companions watched one being winched off a flatbed truck and placed carefully in a plaza below a cosmonaut monument.

'Fucking bizarre,' said Myra, half to herself, as a Sheenisov cadre clambered on to the plinth and began an explanatory harangue in Uzbek, not one of her languages.

'With this they will replace the market,' Nurup scoffed, under his breath. 'God help us all.'

A lively market in soft drinks and hot food was already forming around the strange device. Nurup and Mustafa bought her Coke and kebabs, and themselves a hotdog each. Both talked quietly to the stall-keepers. Taking the food, they sat down on a bench and ate.

'There is much discontent,' Mustafa said eagerly.

'Bazaar gossip,' Nurup said. 'Stall-keepers will tell you anything. They will tell the Sheenisov they love them.'

The two men argued obliquely but intensely for a few minutes about the prospects for terrorist action against the Sheenisov.

'We're not here for that,' Myra reminded them. She shared out cigarettes, then together they walked out of the square. Neither of the men raised any questions about her random following of the streets, until they ended up at the bank of the broad Irtysh river. Flats on the opposite bank, a riverside walk on this. A small pleasure steamer chugged downriver, ferrying a calculating-machine on its promenade deck.

Myra leaned against a railing, gazing into the river. The two men leaned against the railing, looking the other way. People passed. After a few minutes of this Mustafa asked what was going on.

'Nothing,' said Myra, not turning around. 'Or maybe something. I'm assuming we've been followed, or watched. I'm quite prepared to wait here for at least an hour. Make yourselves comfortable.'

But they were too edgy and too alert to be comfortable. The most they did was light another of her Dunhills. Myra slipped her eyeband down and was at once struck by a sense of *déja vu*, as the whole scene around her hazed over, sleeted with grey flecks. After a moment she realised the source of that sense of recognition—it reminded her of how she'd first seen towns like this, back in the 90s: through their Soviet pollution haze. She blinked, moved the eyeband up and down, tried to pick up the nets. Nothing but the grey snow. Even Parvus, summoned from memory, looked frazzled by it.

Sheenisov jamming. Shit.

She'd just given up this experiment when she heard her name called. She turned. Shin Se-Ha and Kim Nok-Yung walked side by side up the pathway, waving to her.

'It's all right,' she told her swiftly tense bodyguards. 'I know these guys.'

She shook hands, smiling, with the Korean and the Japanese; introduced them to the Kazakhstanis. Discreet compliments on her rejuvenated appearance were exchanged with her admiration for their now healthier physiques. Even their relatively humane imprisonment had marked them, weighing them down with something which their new freedom—if freedom it was—had enabled them to shrug off. They walked taller. They confronted the Kazakhstani *emigrés* unabashed.

'So, you are *Sheenisov*,' said Mustafa, in a disgusted tone.

'Lay off,' said Myra. 'They're OK. We have to talk.'

'Yes,' said Nok-Yung. 'We have to talk.'

It was a mild day, for the time of year. Not shirt-sleeve weather, but comfortable if you dressed warm, as they all had. Myra indicated a semi-circle of benches in a concreted picnic area along the bank a little. The two ex-prisoners shrugged, then nodded.

Nok-Yung and Se-Ha sat on either side of her, the two bodyguards on separate benches a few metres away. Children, snug-wrapped in quilted satin bomber-jackets and padded trousers, capered about and yelled, oblivious to the adults.

'So how are you getting on, in this brave new world?' Myra asked.

'We're fine,' said Nok-Yung, his comrade nodding emphatically. 'Our families are joining us soon, and in the meantime we have much to do.'

'You both got jobs?' Myra smiled.

'There are no *jobs*,' Se-Ha said primly. 'There is work. We have been . . . co-opted, and we have been sent to talk to you.'

'Well, I had guessed this was hardly a coincidence,' Myra said. 'But I had not expected to see you as Sheenisov cadre already.'

'It's an open system,' Nok-Yung said. 'Interesting contributions are quickly taken up; amplified; discussed.'

'The opposite of the nets, then,' Myra said. They laughed.

'And the opposite of the Leninist system,' Nok-Yung said earnestly. 'Once you are in, you are *in*, there is no . . . apprenticeship? No candidacy, no working your way up. Past experience,' he added rather smugly, '*counts.*'

Myra flashed her eyebrows. No doubt the militant and the Marxist mathematician had found their niches quickly. 'I'm sure that's all fascinating,' she said. 'But I'm here to put a diplomatic proposal to the Sino-Soviet Union as a whole. Can I do that, just by talking to you?'

'Yes.'

'Very well.' She put it to them, straight: the deal, the crossing corridors. Let the revolutionary horde flow around Kazakhstan, like a flood around a rock, and they could swamp the rest of the world, for all she cared. (Could and would run into the sand, she did not say, but that was what she expected.)

They listened politely, now and then asking for clarification, making notes and doodling maps on hand-held slates that—while obviously information-retrieval devices—looked as though they were made of . . . slate. Se-Ha stood up.

'I must consult,' he said, nodded, and walked briskly away. Nok-Yung accepted a cigarette, and leaned back luxuriantly, sprawling out with his elbows on the back of the bench. He regarded Myra through narrow eyes and curling smoke.

'Why do you resist the SSU, Myra?' he asked mildly. 'It is only democracy. It is only socialism. A means—and an end, compatible at last, after all the disasters and crimes done in the name of both.' He spread his hands. 'There are no secrets here, no deceptions. When you were as young as you look—' he smiled '—you would have thought this revolution, this liberation more wonderful than your wildest dreams.'

'Don't let my *mujahedin* friends hear you say that!' she warned, half in jest. She glanced over at Nurup Kerbayev. He smiled back, eyes and teeth flashing like knives.

'But you're right,' she went on. 'Let's just say . . . I may look young again, but I've had a long, long life in the meantime. I've come to believe in myself, and in . . . my country, Kazakhstan. And I will not be assimilated, and nor will we.' She waved a hand around. 'These people, they may seem . . . happy enough to wait and see. But deep down, no—just below the surface—they are seething with suspicion. They are not your Mongolians or Siberians, who God knows had it bad enough under Stalinism but who found everything since was worse. To the Kazakhs socialism means "the tragedy" of the 1930s: the forced settlement, the famine. It means the nuclear tests, the cancers, the birth defects. They don't want to be the subjects of any more experiments. And if you want to point to the ISTWR as a counter-example—that was a special case. A self-selected minuscule minority. Our socialism was always a joke, more black humour than Red. Trotskyism in one country—what a laugh!'

What a laugh she gave. She frightened herself. One of the scampering children playing around them stopped, put his thumb in his mouth and ran away.

'We ran a benign state capitalism, nothing more,' she went on. 'In your case, my friend, it was not even that. God, I feel disgusted with myself that we did it, that we ever allowed ourselves to be compradors for Reid's goddamn private gulags.'

Nok-Yung stared at the sky for a moment. 'I don't know what to say, Myra,' he said at last. 'Your regret over the Mutual Protection camps is . . . well taken. But about the other matters—you must surely know that none of what you have been talking about, the USSR and so on, is socialism as we understand it, and as you understood it. So stop confusing the issue.'

'Oh, I'm well aware that you are different. That you may well be the genuine article: Marx and Engels, Proprietors. And you know what? I don't care. I don't want it, for myself or for anyone.'

'Why not?' Nok-Yung sounded more puzzled than offended.

Myra pointed across the river to the insectile shape of a fighting-machine, patrolling the water's edge with heron-like steps.

'Because of those damn things,' she said. 'And the calculating-machines.'

'What!' Nok-Yung's eyes creased up in amusement. 'Luddism is not your true ideology, Myra. I cannot believe this. These machines are one of the most marvellous achievements of the Sheenisov—a whole alternative nanotechnology, worked out quite independently of the West. You know how the machines scale down, all the way to the molecular scale, and are all mechanical and chemical and optical, with no need for electronic interfaces? That's their—our—secret weapon, an open secret. A computer system that the enemy cannot penetrate, but that everyone can understand and access. I've just begun to use it, and I tell you, it has the most intuitive interface I've ever come across. The capitalists would kill for it. Or rather, they would kill to be able to monopolise it. But it's free, so they can't.'

'I know about your strange machines,' Myra said. 'The CIA told me all about them.' She tapped her temple, smiling ironically. ' "I have detailed files." '

Nok-Yung caught the allusion. 'It is not *The Terminator*, you know! Not—what was it in the films?—Skynet. It is not . . . inimical.'

'Not now, perhaps. But what will it do, when it—or you—have covered the world, like a banyan tree?'

Nok-Yung spat a puff of air and smoke. 'More Luddism! The machines will form a benign human environment, a second nature, within which human nature can flourish, truly, for the first time.' He leaned forward, speaking confidentially. 'Let me tell you what we have done, something that no other system would have dared to do. We have nanofactured a virally distributed, genetically fixable version of the anti-ageing treatment. It spreads before our migrations like a benign plague. You may be already infected, yourself. A gift.'

'God, that is *so* irresponsible!' Myra jolted rigid. 'Viruses *mutate*, dammit, in case you hadn't heard!'

Nok-Yung made a planing motion with his hand. 'Not this one. It has self-repair built in. It has tested stable through a million virtual generations.'

'*Virtual* generations, yes! Man, you did enough design work in the camp to know what *that's* worth in the real world!'

'Different system, different design philosophy,' he said, with infuriating complacency. 'Our testing kits are themselves *part* of the real world. It's like the difference between a working scale model and a simulation. There is simply no comparison. And the computing resources are vast, vaster even than anything the spacers have yet built.'

Myra felt her gaze sinking into the bottomless pool of his self-confidence. It was truly terrifying; it was, she realised, what she most feared for herself—to be so sure. To be absolutely certain that she was right would, as far as she was concerned, be the end of her. Doubt was her only hope, her comfort and companion since childhood, her scepticism her sole security.

Shin Se-Ha returned and sat down, affecting not to notice their frozen moment of mutual incomprehension. He looked at Myra, gravely, and shook his head.

'No deal, I'm afraid.'

Myra could scarcely believe it.

'Why ever not? The alternative is to fight your way through Kazakhstan! All you have to do instead is not fight us! What more can you ask of us?'

Se-Ha shook his head sadly. 'It is not that, Myra,' he said. 'It is not aggression, or animosity. It is simply the imperative of our mode of production. It will be global or it will be nothing, as your Trotsky always said. We have to keep running, or fall over, until we meet ourselves, on the other side of the world.'

He saw this wasn't getting anywhere with her. 'More concretely,' he continued, 'we can't have . . . unassimilated areas within the Union. It would be too much of an opportunity for our enemies. And we can't stop for long, because that would force us to engage in internal class struggle, particularly with the small-property owners, which we do not want.' He smiled. 'To put it mildly! We have so far been able to avoid the whole dictatorship of the proletariat scenario by simply carrying the remaining small and large businesses along with us. The machine-based common-property economy expands, and they expand in its interstices. They can live like nits in our hair, as long as we are running. If we stopped, the itch would be intolerable. We would have to . . . *scratch*.'

'Oh, come on,' said Myra. 'You can run a mixed economy indefinitely. We've been doing it in Kapitsa for years.'

'A mixture of state capitalism and private, yes,' said Nok-Yung, 'as you've just reminded me. A mixture of a real non-commodity economy and a market is much more unstable. Conflicts arise very rapidly—if they're both confined to the same economic space.'

An unstable system, that had to expand at just the right speed to stop itself falling over; not too slow, or too *fast* . . . there were plenty of natural and artificial and social analogies to that. Myra almost giggled at the thought of what would happen to them if Kazakhstan just surrendered, if the Sheenisov suddenly found themselves pushing at an open door and fell flat on their collective faces.

But that wasn't an option. She looked around, checking that her guards were still bored and watchful, then back at the two new recruits to the Sheenisov. The absurdity of the situation struck her—she was doing diplomacy by just talking to two guys on the street. For all she knew they could be as deluded as UFO contactees, and not really ambassadors from an alien intelligence at all. Again she felt the urge to giggle—it was just another silly idea; she was feeling lightheaded, flighty, as though her problem had been solved. She couldn't *see* any solution. She was in deeper trouble than ever, but still she felt relieved.

'There is a certain urgency to it,' Se-Ha was saying, a little apologetically.

'Green factions are experimenting with plague vectors. The spacer groups, the Outwarders, have a radically post-human vision. Between them, they threaten humanity with extinction. Our advance is in essence defensive . . .'

She looked sharply at him. 'Tell me, Se-Ha,' she said, 'just who it was you consulted, back there.'

He looked uncomfortable. 'It was . . . a distributed decision. A consensus.'

'Bull*shit*!' she snapped. 'Don't give me that. I didn't see a vote being taken in the streets around here. Did you? So there must be a leadership somewhere, a council. I want to talk to it.'

'You are talking to it,' he said, 'when you talk to us. To the extent that it exists. The policy parameters have indeed been set democratically, but the implementation, the . . . administrative decisions, are made . . .' He chewed his lower lip. 'It's hard to say,' he finished lamely.

'Let me guess,' said Myra, standing up. 'Expert system. AI.'

Se-Ha looked up at her, eyes dark and blank under his thin black brows. 'That is possible, yes.'

Myra straightened and sighed. She was convinced, paranoically perhaps, that the mad preacher Jordan had been right: the General, the Plan, was at the bottom of all this, that it had implemented itself on the Sheenisov's machine ecology and was in the process of taking over the world. With the best intentions, no doubt.

'God, yes, you're right,' she said. 'It's you or the Outwarders. Both sides are like the fucking Borg. "You will be assimilated"—isn't that what you're telling me?'

Nok-Yung shrugged. 'It's not something sinister. We all live in the world machine. Why not live in a world machine that is on our side?'

Myra had to smile. 'You want me to imagine the future,' she said, 'as socialism with a human face—for ever?'

'Yes!' they both said, pleased that she'd got the point at last.

It really would be hard to end this conversation politely, but she would try.

'I'll take your message back to President Suleimanyov,' she said. 'No doubt you will await our response.'

Se-Ha and Nok-Yung stood up and shook her hand gravely.

'Goodbye,' she said.

'Goodbye,' they both said.

Se-Ha smiled mischievously. 'I hope I see you again.'


They'd rented the plane, an executive jet that had seen better days, in Almaty. Just as well; Myra could not have borne to displace any passengers on the commercial flights out of Semipalatinsk, standing room only and a strict baggage allowance.

As soon as they were beyond Sheenisov airspace—and Sheenisov jamming—Parvus made a priority over-ride and poked his virtual head over the back of the seat in front of her.

'Sorry about this, Myra,' the AI murmured. 'Urgent messages.'

'Patch 'em through,' she said.

The message queue consisted of calls from Suleimanyov, Valentina Kozlova and someone with an anonymous code identifier. She worked through them one by one.

As soon as she blinked on the President's identifier, he was through, live from his office. Various aides and ministers hovered in the periphery of the shot.

'Hello,' he said. 'Results?'

Myra grimaced. 'They're adamant that they won't accept it. I was as surprised as you are. In fact, I was shocked. I have a suspicion that the secret of their military and economic co-ordination is a military AI, and that it is . . . calling the shots.'

Chingiz took this with unexpected aplomb.

'It was worth trying,' he said. He waved his hand, downwards. 'However, the Sheenisov are no longer our most immediate problem.'

'What's happened?'

He smiled wryly. 'As we expected. It's all gone public now—everyone knows about the nukes. Our generous offers to the United States, and to other countries, have been referred up to the UN—and referred back to the Security Council, for immediate action. We are to turn over our nuclear weapons to forces under UN authority within twenty-four hours—twenty-three and a half, now—or face aerial and space attack. Specifically, on Kapitsa, which they have rightly identified as the focus of the problem. After Kapitsa, Almaty.'

Myra thought for a moment that the virtual view had gone monochrome, and that the plane had turned over. Then everything was normal again.

'If they carry through their threat against Kapitsa—well, I would hope for air support.' She smiled wanly. 'But please, Chingiz. Don't let them ruin Almaty.'

'I have no intention of letting them do that,' he said. 'I suggest you return to Kapitsa. You have problems of your own. Evacuate the town, if you can. Let them hit an empty shell. We'll send transport and cavalry.'

'Cavalry?'

'For . . . internal security. The stand-off around the government building is very tense.' He glanced away. 'Your own Defence Minister is trying to

get through to you. She can explain the situation better than I can. Goodbye for now.'

'Goodbye, Chingiz.'

Before taking the next call, Myra turned to Nurup and Mustafa.

'We're diverting to Kapitsa,' she said. 'I may be going into a very volatile
situation. Street violence, at least. And possible bombing, maybe up to nuclear level. This is not what I hired you for. We can drop you off at Karaganda first, if you wish.'

The two *mujahedin* looked deeply offended.

'Our job is to keep you safe until you return to Almaty, or until you tell
us to go,' Nurup said.

'OK,' she said. 'I'm telling you to go.'

She reached for the intercom toggle. Mustafa was out of his seat in an
instant, and placed a hand across the switch. His expression and tone were
apologetic. 'We stay,' he said. 'It's God's will.'

And a matter of honour too, she guessed.

'Kapitsa it is, then,' she said.

The two men beamed at her as though *she* had done *them* a favour. Perhaps she had; they probably believed she'd just issued them two free passes
to heaven. There were times when she envied the devout.

As the plane banked around she took the call from Valentina. This one was
v-mail, recorded in one of the offices in the government building. Behind
Valentina, men with Kalashnikovs lurked at windows. Bureaucrats turned
desks into makeshift barricades. Somebody was operating a byte-shredder,
wiping computer memories, setting up a blizzard of interference.

'Hi, Myra, hope this gets through. Jesus, did you hear that the nuke thing's
all over the media? We've got news collectors—warm bodies as well as
remotes—coming in all the time, and the demonstrators are acting up for
them so they can watch themselves being heroic on CNN. Fucking classic media feedback howl. The nuke thing has really freaked a lot of them out—in all
the factions, the lefty headbangers and the pro-UN types and the fucking
spacists. Not to mention our very own patriots. Our agents in the crowd—
hell, even the reporters—are picking up talk about storming the building. We
want you back as soon as you can; we'll have a militia driver on standby at the
airport.'

The message was time-stamped at 1.35 p.m., and it was now 2.50. Myra
blinked up a split-screen of television news channels while taking the third
call. The seatbelt light came on; the aeroplane was beginning its descent to
Kapitsa. Thank God for ultra-precise radio tuning—Myra could remember when you couldn't even take a call in level flight. The pilot's voice was
raised slightly as he argued with air-traffic control for precedence, throwing

diplomatic weight and Kazakh curses about equally. Myra looked out of the window. More aircraft than usual—hastily hired jets, she guessed—were parked beside the runways. The media circus was in town.

Her anonymous caller flickered into view.

'Jason!'

The CIA agent gave her a tense smile, but warm around the eyes. 'Hello, Myra. Good to see you. Wow, you look amazing. Just in time for your global stardom, huh?'

'Hah!'

'Almost as much excitement as the coup. Anyway . . . I'm here to tell you that we've got somewhere with the investigation.'

Undercarriage down, thump.

'What—oh, Georgi's—'

'Yup. I'm sorry to have to tell you this, Myra, but—shit, we got this out of the black labs, it's bleeding-edge stuff. We did an autopsy on a goddamn *cell sample*—don't ask how we got it.'

A bump, a rocking forward, another bump, and the incline of deceleration.

'The point is, Myra, we found traces of a very specific, very subtle bit of nanotech. It's not exactly a poison, that's the clever thing. It builds up into a little machine, then disintegrates when it's done its job. We found a few gear trains, but that was enough.'

The aircraft came to a halt and the seatbelt light went off. The door banged open and the steps angled down. Myra stood up and shuffled forward, behind Nurup and in front of Mustafa, still talking and listening. She waved absently to the pilot, left him a handful of gold coins as a bonus. She was thinking ahead.

'Enough for what?'

'Enough to identify it. It's a spacer assassination weapon. A heart-stopper.'

A heart-stopper. Yes. It was that.

She blinked away the floating image of Jason to concentrate on her surroundings. No signs of actual incoming fire. She followed Nurup towards the terminal building, about a hundred metres away. Jason's voice in her head continued.

'So there's no doubt any more—it was murder. Now, there's no *proof* the space movement had a hand in it, beyond supplying the weapon, but the circumstantial evidence is kind of strong.'

'You could say that,' Myra agreed, making a conscious effort to unclench her jaw. Having her suspicions confirmed after all this time of indulging then dismissing them was a shock.

*Fucking heart attack . . .*

'They don't exactly throw that sort of kit around,' she mused aloud. 'Too easy to reverse-engineer, for one thing. But why would they do it?'

Through the long corridor, letting Nurup and Mustafa do the lookout. Out of the corner of her eye she could see the adjacent, outbound corridor, packed from end to end with a slow-moving queue.

'Well, the obvious motive would've been to stop him making the offer to the Kazakhstanis.'

'And how do you know about that?'

'Uh, that's classified.'

Myra had to laugh.

'But how would they have known about it, I mean before—?'

'You tell me.'

They'd reached the concourse. It wasn't quite as crowded or frantic as she'd begun to expect; most of those intent on leaving must have already left, or at least be in the exit queue. Much to her relief, no newshounds or reporters had spotted her yet, though she identified one or two by their flak-jackets and communications clutter and vaguely familiar faces. Scanning the crowd, she saw a man in the uniform of the Workers' Militia, who caught her eye, saluted and started pushing towards her.

'It was as much of a surprise to everyone else in the government as it was to me,' she said. 'We figured it was Georgi's own bright idea, which he'd spring on us once he'd got some provisional—oh!'

Mustafa bumped into her back.

Jason waved to her, over heads.

'You never told me you were *here*!'

'Yeah, well . . . thought I'd surprise you.'

It was strange seeing his lips move, and hearing the words, beyond earshot. Like lip-reading, like telepathy.

'Who is that guy?' Nurup asked suspiciously.

'He's OK,' said Myra. She wasn't sure whether introducing Jason as a CIA agent would be a good idea, so she didn't.

And then they met up, and to everyone's surprise she and Jason met in a long embrace.

'Jesus, man!'

She broke loose and turned to the militia driver.

'Thanks for coming. Room for these three guys?'

The driver nodded. 'This way please.'

He led them to a service door which Myra knew she must have passed hundreds of times and never seen. Their progress was less inconspicuous— the two *muj* weren't the only armed passengers, but they were the most noticeable. As the driver fiddled with the push-bar latch Myra noticed heads bob and a little buzzing camcopter swoop from the concourse's rafters.

They hurried along a passageway of corrugated iron and unplaned, splintery joists, and emerged beside a jeep in a small bay of the car park.

'Ah, now that's sensible transport,' Myra said as they all piled in. The Militia jeep had a light machine-gun mounted on its rollbar. Mustafa made that his post. Nurup sat in the front with the driver, rifle propped in the crook of his elbow, pointing up. Myra and Jason sat in the back, with Mustafa's legs and the ammo belt between them. As the jeep careered out of the carpark and swerved on to the main road into town, Jason leaned over and said, loud above the noise and the slipstream, 'You were saying?'

'About Georgi's great plan, yeah. As far as we can tell he never told anyone else, not even Valentina. That was him all over—he was a bit of a Kazakhstani patriot, and he *still* tended to act like this whole place was his personal fief. Which it once was!'

The jeep was making good progress—most of the traffic was in the other direction, towards the airport or—judging by the amounts of luggage and household goods piled on top of cars and trucks—towards Karaganda. Her relief at seeing the evacuation already under way was dampened by flashback images of other roads, other columns of vehicles: the road to Basra, the road out of Warsaw, the perimeter of Atlanta . . .

But no, not here! They had their own air cover—Kazakhstan's elite aerospace defence force would surely shield these refugees. She thought briefly of setting up a conference call with Valentina and Chingiz, but decided against it. This conversation with Jason was the most urgent she could have right now, for reasons that were more than personal.

'OK,' Jason was saying, 'as to the motive, right, did anyone *else* approach you for some kind of similar deal, after Georgi's death but before the coup?'

'Only the fucking space movement!' She swallowed hard. 'David Reid himself, at Georgi's funeral.'

'Jesus H. That kind of fingers them, doesn't it?'

Myra found the question of *who knew about what* bugging her.

'Well, there's a problem with that,' she said. 'Whoever killed Georgi, or had him killed, *must* have known that that would make us suspicious of the spacers. I mean, even before you found the evidence, I had them in the frame. And it's a bit hard to reconstruct now, you know how it is, but when I refused to give Dave any hands-off guarantees, let alone any more . . . active support, well, that suspicion must have been in the scales. Might even have tipped them.'

Mustafa shouted something and brought the machine-gun down and around to the rear. Myra shifted her legs smartly away from the ammo belt and twisted her head around. Five hundred metres behind them was a small, jockeying pack of cars and jeeps, in front of a cloud of dust and beneath a halo of camcopters. She clapped Mustafa's thigh.

'Leave them alone!' she yelled.

He replied with some Uzbek profanity, but desisted, swinging the machine-gun muzzle skyward again.

'So you're saying killing Georgi was counter-productive for the spacers?'

'Damn right!'

'OK.' Jason leaned back in the cramped seat and closed his eyes for a moment. '*Cui bono?* Who benefited?'

'Ah, shit,' said Myra, realising, just as the jeep turned the corner into Revolution Square, and stopped. Myra grabbed the rollbar and pulled herself up. Long practice in estimating the size of demos clicked into place automatically, like eyeband software.

About ten thousand.

'Oh, Jeez,' she said.

It was not a particularly militant or angry crowd, at that moment. Tents and shelters and stalls had been set up, and many of the banners were propped against them or leaning on street furniture, or stuck in the patches of now trampled grass or beds of flowers that chequered the square. People stood or sat about, in small groups, chatting, drinking coffee, reading news off broadsheets or eyebands or handhelds, listening to speeches and songs, arguing with each other or with the scattered ones and twos of the Workers' Militia. Some were dressed casually, others in their best outfits or in national costumes or street-theatre radiation overalls.

'Looks pretty dangerous,' said Jason.

She gave him an appreciative nod. 'Yeah, that's a *mass* demo if ever I saw one. Not to mention a big fraction of the remaining population. Shit.'

The kids back in Glasgow had been right: her small state was having a big political revolution. The two *mujahedin* glowered uncomprehendingly at the mingled banners of Kazakhstan, the ISTWR, the old Soviet Union, the International, the red flags and the black.

She ducked and placed a hand on Nurup's shoulder.

'Stand up,' she ordered. 'Look cheerful. Wave your rifle high above your head. Mustafa, for heaven's sake *smile*, man, wave your arms and keep your hands off the LMG. *No matter what*, you got that?'

To the driver, 'Around the inside edge of the crowd, towards the entrance. Slow and careful.'

She lifted herself up, swung her ass around and perched on the rollbar, feet on the back of Nurup's seat. The driver engaged first gear, then second. The jeep rolled towards the corner of the front of the building. It had about fifty metres to go, then another fifty when it would have to turn right and inch along to the entrance. They went unremarked for about half a minute. Then the people stepping out of their way started calling and pointing. A moment later the pursuing reporters caught up and all chance of discretion was gone.

She could see the news of her arrival spread through the crowd like a gust of wind on a field. The camcopters circled at a safe distance, zooming in on her and on reaction shots of the people looking at her. Their only chance, she'd decided, was to look confident and triumphant. She grinned and waved, meanwhile blinking up a call to Valentina.

'You can see us?'

'Yeah, we've got you covered. We'll open the door for you when you reach it.'

Cheers and jeers echoed off the government office's glass and concrete walls. No organised chanting or coherent mood as yet—people were still unsure what to make of her return. She smiled desperately at every individual face that came into focus, and quite a few smiled back. The hovering camcopters had their directional mikes aimed at her, but she didn't speak to, or for, them.

'It's all right, folks, comrades, we're getting it all sorted out, we've got a strong alliance with Kazakhstan, we're negotiating with the UN and we'll hold off the Sheenisov, I'll be talking to you all soon, once I've had a chance to consult—'

The jeep came to a gentle halt outside the main door. Myra glanced sideways, saw a couple of militiamen holding it, ready to open, their rifles in their other hands.

'Go in, guys, all of you, I'll keep talking.'

They hesitated.

'Go go go!'

One by one they ran up the steps and disappeared inside. Myra stepped from the seat-back to the dash, over the windshield and on to the engine hood, then hopped backwards on to a step, keeping in view all the time. She backed up the steps, smiling and waving, and through the doors.

Jason's arms wrapped around her from behind.

'Well done.'

She leaned against him for a moment, tilting her head back on his shoulder, then straightened up and stepped away, turning to smile.

'That was scary.' She laughed. 'It's weird being the *target* of a demonstration—I feel I should be out there helping to organise it.'

Jason's eyes narrowed. 'That,' he said, 'might become an option.'

'Ah, fuck off, you Machiavellian spook!' She caught his hand, swept an encircling arm at Nurup and Mustafa. 'Come on, guys, let's sort out this mess.'

They held the emergency meeting in Myra's office whose broad window overlooked the square. Denis Gubanov had suggested using the Sovnarkom room, but Myra had dismissed the security man's idea. No way did she want to be in a windowless room.

Everybody was sitting on or lounging against inappropriate furniture—desks and filing cabinets and comms junctions. Myra perched herself on the highest convenient surface, the top of a book-case full of unread yellowing hardcopy. She cradled her Glock in her lap. Somehow sitting in a chair seemed frivolous. Two militia guards stood watchfully at the sides of the windows, using their eyebands to sample camcopter views from the news services. Andrei Mukhartov, Valentina Kozlova and Denis Gubanov all looked sleepless and unkempt: the men unshaven, Val's collar and tie loosened, her uniform rumpled.

Myra introduced the two *mujahedin* and Jason. Denis raised his eyebrows, but made no comment. Myra unobtrusively made sure that her three men were in a position to protect her—she wasn't at all sure who, if any, of those present were leaving the room alive, whether or not the room was stormed by an angry mob. She'd once interviewed an unrepentant old Stalinist who'd been in the Budapest Party offices in October 1956 . . .

'OK, comrades,' she began. 'First things first. You know the Western powers have refused our offers. I've just today been on the shortest diplomatic mission *ever*, and I can tell you the Sheenisov aren't interested in a deal either. So it's only a question of time before they're rolling down the road from Semey. But that's just background. We have some urgent matters to discuss.

'I'm going to start with something that may not seem like the first item on the agenda, but bear with me.' She waved a hand at the window. 'These people can wait. It's about Georgi's death. Jason Nikolaides here has told me the results of a CIA investigation—murder, using a spacer nanotech weapon. Hard to detect traces, but Jason says they've done it, and I believe him. What I don't believe is that the spacist bastards did it. Whoever did it wanted two things—one, that Georgi's offer didn't get through to the Kazakhstanis *before* the coup. Two, that we wouldn't co-operate with the space movement *in* the coup. Now, seeing as nobody except Georgi knew he was planning to make that offer, our range of suspects is a bit narrow. Basically, it has to be someone that Georgi would run the idea past, someone outside the government information loop—maybe in the Sovnarkom, maybe not.'

She looked down, playing with the Glock's slide for a moment, then looked up. She'd been thinking aloud, she hadn't had time yet to go through all the possibilities.

'*Val!*' she shouted. Everybody jumped. 'If I thought it was you, I'd slam you against the wall till your teeth rattled to get the truth out of you. You and Georgi were both in the Party, unlike anyone else here.'

She smiled, pleased to see her colleagues off balance. 'But as it happens, I trust you. Same with Andrei, who's never been into that sort of shit anyway. Denis, now—'

The secret policeman looked up and moistened his lips.

'I swear, Myra—'

'It's all right,' Jason interrupted. 'The Company checked him out. He's clear.' He glanced at Myra, then grinned at Denis Gubanov. 'Bit of a commie son-of-a-bitch, but he's on your side.'

'Good,' said Myra, winging it. 'I'm going through this to *confirm* that nobody here is a suspect. That leaves only one possibility. Georgi must have shared his idea with somebody, and it can only have been the FI Mil Org. The General.'

She let them think about that while she explained to Jason, Nurup and Mustafa about the nukes and the AI.

'It has its own agenda,' she concluded, addressing everyone again. 'And it's working through the Sheenisov. It wants those nukes, very badly. So do the spacers. Whether they used each other—the information on one side, the weapon from the other—knowingly or not, Georgi's murder was a move in that rivalry. Whoever controls these weapons has a gun at the head of everyone and everything in Earth orbit and at Lagrange—which adds up to about ninety-five percent of the human space presence. And I would remind you that, thanks to the coup and counter-coup, the General controls most of the Space Defense battlesats. Now, this has a bearing on what we do about the UN ultimatum. Which is—' she grinned ferally '—the *second* item on the agenda.'

'Excuse me,' said Jason, standing up. 'Just who does control these nukes, at the moment?'

'We do,' said Valentina and Myra, at the same time. Myra gave Val an especially warm smile, hoping that her apparent—and partly paranoically real—earlier suspicion hadn't wounded their friendship beyond repair.

'It's dual key,' Valentina explained. 'Defence Minister and Prime Minister have to go into the command-centre workspace at the same time.'

'And, well, it's not hardcoded in, but right now obviously we have a treaty commitment to give the President of Kazakhstan the final say,' Myra added. 'And his strategy, at the moment, is to stonewall until the last minute, to try and get some military aid concessions out of the Western powers and/or the UN against the Sheenisov.'

'So he intends to turn them over eventually?' Jason asked.

Myra hesitated. 'OK,' she said at last. 'This doesn't go beyond this room, and that goes for everyone here. You guys at the window, too—military discipline, death penalty under the Freedom of Information Law if you breathe a word of it. Everybody clear?'

They all were.

'All right then—yes, he does intend for us to turn them over, eventually. What else can we do?'

'We can use the weapons,' said Denis. 'In space.'

Val's lips set in a thin line. Myra shook her head.

'Massacre,' she said. 'I won't do it, except as a last resort.'

'You're all missing the point,' said Jason. He looked around at all of them, as though unsure whether he had a right to speak.

'Go on,' said Myra.

'OK,' said Jason, 'I'm just speaking for myself here, not for the CIA or East America. I don't know if I'll ever get back to either of them. Anyway . . . the point you're all missing is: *who* are you going to surrender your weapons *to*? Formally, no doubt, it'll be the UN. But physically, somebody's gonna have to dock with them, bring them in, disarm them. Space Defense, and maybe some of the space settlers, have the equipment and expertise to do that. There must be ways of getting past the software of your controls— there always are. Believe me, there are no uncrackable codes any more. Your cooperation would be useful, but it's not essential.'

Myra lit a cigarette. 'OK,' she said. 'So?'

Jason paced over to the window, peered out. 'Still quiet,' he said. He glanced at his watch. 'We've been in here, what? Half an hour? Soon be time to talk to the people, Myra.'

'That's cool,' Denis said. 'We've got agitators out there, they're keeping people more or less up to speed. The line is that the President is negotiating.'

'As I'm sure he is,' said Jason. 'But what does either side have to negotiate? Both sides have hit the bottom of the tank. You have nothing to offer, and the West has nothing to offer you. They will not save you from the Sheenisov. So if I were any of the other players—in particular, the spacers and your FI Mil Org, rogue AI or not—I'd be working very fast right now on two objectives. One is taking you guys and your wonderful dual-key command-centre out physically. The other is lining up rendezvous with the nukes in space. You can bet that while you think you're smart, stringing them along, *they* are stringing *you* along, and they're both going after the same things.'

He looked around again, more confident now. 'This is endgame. Not just for us, but for them. One side or the other—the West-stroke-spacers-stroke-Outwarders, or the East-stroke-the-General-stroke-Sheenisov—is going to grab these weapons and *use* them, sooner rather than later.'

'But—' shouted Val, shocked. 'The ablation cascade!'

'Not a problem for either of them, at the level we're talking about. The Sheenisov's horizons are strictly Earthbound, for the next few centuries. And their computers are invulnerable to EMP hits—they're mechanical, not electronic. As to the spacists and the Mil Org, neither of them is dependent on going back to Earth, or on anything else getting off. And each unit of these forces probably calculates that they can cut and run for a higher orbit, or Lagrange. Of course, they'd rather avoid it, but if they have to they'll take it on the chin.

'So my advice to you all,' he concluded, 'and to those people out there, is get the hell out. And warn everybody that at the first sign of any messing with you, or Kazakhstan, or the nukes—you'll blow them all to hell. Use the nukes against battlesats or detonate in place—either way you'll set off the ablation cascade.'

'Christ,' said Myra, shaken. 'That means the end of satellite guidance, global positioning, comsats, the nets, everything! It'll be like the world going blind!'

'Yeah,' said Jason grimly. 'And every army in the world, too. They're so dependent on space-based comms and sims that they'll be fucked. Except for the marginals, the Greens, the barbarians and the Sheenisov.' He laughed. 'If that doesn't scare them, nothing will.'

The guards at the window were moving from the sides to the centre, gazing out with complete lack of concern for cover. One of them turned around.

'The cavalry has arrived,' he said.

For a moment Myra thought he meant the Sheenisov. Then she realised that Chingiz had come through on his promise, and that the cavalry was their own.


The steppe at nightfall was a moving mass of vehicles and horses. As far as Myra knew, every last person in Kapitsa was moving out. She rode somewhere near the front; she tried to ride at the front, but she kept being overtaken by people in vehicles faster than her black mare. The Sovnarkom rump, and Jason and her *mujahedin*, rode in jeeps beside her. With her eyeband image-intensifiers at full power she could see the Kazakhstani cavalry—horse and motorised—outriding either flank of the evacuation, or migration. The scene was biblical, exodus and apocalypse in one. Banners and flags from the Revolution Square demonstration floated above the crowd, used as rallying points and mobile landmarks. The news remotes and reporters were following the process in a sort of stunned awe, not sure whether the angle was *Road People* (refugees, pathetic) or *Kazakh Rouge* (menaces, fanatic).

Something similar, though not as yet so drastic, was happening in Almaty and other towns across the greater Republic. Chingiz Suleimanyov had pitched the appeal to evacuate as the ultimate protest march, against the West's threats and its refusal of aid against the Sheenisov. If they were to be abandoned to the communists, they had nothing to lose by fleeing in advance to a place that claimed it would be defended. The threat of this avalanching into an unstoppable migration was already spreading panic in Western Europe. Northward, in the Former Union, regional and local chiefs were conferring on their own fragmentary networks, bruiting inflammatory talk of joining in.

'Come in, come in, ya bastard,' Myra muttered. She was riding in a hallucinatory ambience of virtual images, some of them pulled down from CNN and other services, others patched up from the command-centre, whose hardware they'd stripped from the offices and jury-rigged in the back of the Sovnarkom jeep. She could see a satellite image of herself from above—she could wave, and with a second's delay see one of the dots on the ground wave back. (The reassuring thing was that it was the wrong dot, a hologram fetch of herself and her surroundings seamlessly merged with the images from several kilometres distant.) She could see her own face, projected to visual displays around the world by the camcopter hovering a few metres in front of her.

Right now she was trying to raise Logan. A residual loyalty to her former comrades in space impelled her to warn them of the probable imminent disaster. The scanning search of the Lagrange cluster wasn't picking up New View. At length, frustrated, she switched to a broader sweep, and to her surprise connected almost immediately.

'Jesus fuck, Myra,' Logan said, without preliminary pleasantry. 'This is your biggest fuck-up since the Third World War.' He didn't make it sound like an accusation.

'Thanks for the reminder, comrade,' Myra snarled. 'I'm going against my better judgement telling you this, but I've fallen out with your General. That little electric fucker has had the bright idea of making his own bid for world revolution, and I don't intend to wait around to see how it all works out in practice, thank you very much.'

'Yes, I had heard,' Logan said heavily. The delay seemed longer than usual; Myra guessed because she was strung out, running on stretched time.

'You called to say that?' He sounded distracted. A very pretty black girl who looked about ten years old stuck her face past his, grimacing at the camera, filling its field with her microgravity sunburst of frizzy hair. Logan shoved at her.

'Oh, push off, Ellen May,' he said, not unkindly. 'Go and pester your mum, OK? Or Janis. She'll have something for you to do, you bet.'

The girl stuck out her tongue, then flicked away like a fish.

'Kids,' Logan grinned, indulgent despite himself.

'Yeah, they're great,' Myra said, with a pang. 'What I called you for is about that, actually. If that kid's gonna have a future, you guys better get your ass out of Lagrange.'

'We have,' said Logan, five seconds later. 'We raced through our preparations after the coup. We haven't got as much gear as we'd like, but the asteroid miners are going to swing in and join us there. We finished the burn twelve hours ago.' He looked about. 'Made a real mess of stuff I didn't have time to lash down,' he added sadly.

'You're on your way to *Mars*?'

'Yes, at last.' His grin filled the screen. 'Free at last!'

'What does the General think about this?'

'Ah,' said Logan. 'When I found it was bidding to use your orbital nukes in the coup, I figured the same as you did. Not safe to stick around. You remember I said we'd have to leave a few hundred tons behind? Well, it's among them, still in the clutter at Lagrange. We ditched the bugger.' His triumphant smile faded to a bleak inward gaze. 'I hope.'

'Is it still in control of the Mil Org?'

'I guess so. We couldn't do anything to it, beyond discarding the section the hardware was in. Its software is a different matter, it gets everywhere, but, hell—'

'What do you mean "it gets everywhere"? I've got a suspicion it's downloaded to the Sheenisov's weird Babbage engines, but—'

Logan nodded. 'Yeah, and it's probably copied its files to anything of yours that's been in contact with it, like your phone, but it's just the source code, it can't do any harm so long as you don't open the file—'

At that point the connection ended.

Myra took her phone from her pocket and was about to jerk its jack from her eyeband, just in case, when she realised the precaution was irrational. If the bugger was actually running on her phone they were doomed already. She thought about the time the General had appeared right in her own command-centre, and could only hope that Logan was right, and that only its source code, and not its live program, had been secreted there. And in other places . . .

Someday, somebody would open a file stored in the Institute at Glasgow, and find Parvus, and the General behind him. She wished that person luck. Then she remembered Merrial MacClafferty, and realised she'd have to do more.

She had just finished rattling out her urgent message when she heard a dull, distant bang behind her, and turned. Through the eyeband's night vision she saw on the horizon the expanding green glow of the first cruise missile to hit Kapitsa.

It was not the last.

Hours later, in the twenty-below midnight, when most of the migration had camped around fuel-dump fires, Myra was sitting with Jason in front of a portable electric brazier, in the shelter of the dozing horse. She was simultaneously in the command-centre with the others, and with Chingiz. The UN and US had never intended to negotiate, and even the pretence had been dropped.

The Kazakhstani airforce was expending missiles, planes and lives above Almaty now. From space the command-centre was pulling down images of moves from the battlesats. Tiny, manned hunter-gatherer probes were burning off, matching orbits and velocities with the cached nukes. They had hunter-killer escorts, and they were obviously from opposed coalitions—already their exchanges of fire were being replayed on CNN, now that the Kapitsa bombardment had stopped for lack of remaining targets.

'. . . no choice,' Chingiz was saying. 'Our first responsibility is to defend our people, the people we've taken on the duty to protect, even if that means killing more innocent people on the other side than would die on ours if we don't.'

That's talking, thought Myra, that's the way to look at it, that's right. Screw the greatest good of the greatest number. Or maybe not.

'That's the end of the world,' said Valentina.

'It's ending anyway,' Myra said. She looked up from the fire. 'That's my final analysis! We may even save lives in the long run, if we blind and cripple the forces that are getting ready for the last war.' She laughed bitterly. 'In both senses of the phrase.'

An officer leaned into the visual field around Chingiz, and spoke urgently in his ear. Chingiz nodded, once, then raised his hand.

'This is it,' he said. 'Some of the space settlers' diamond ships have just entered the atmosphere. They're heading for—'

Connection lost.

Myra jumped up, and to her utter horror and amazement she saw them, jinking and jittering through the sky towards her. Their infrared radiation signature was arrogantly clear—they didn't need to bother with shielding, unlike the stealth fighters they resembled. One moment they were dots on the horizon, the next they were discs overhead, swooping past at a thousand metres. Their laser lances slashed the vast encampment, and were countered seconds too late by futile fusillades of skyward machine-gun fire. Then they were at the other horizon, and—

—banking around for a second run—

—screams of people and beasts in the night, dying under the laser beams and the humming rain of their own misdirected, falling ordnance—

*Earth versus the flying saucers! Way cool!*

Myra shook off that mad thought and reached for the command-centre controls as though through thick mud. Valentina's eyes shone in the firelight for a moment, and Myra saw in them a reflection of her own resolution. Then she and Valentina stooped together to their task. As Myra rattled through the codes, she waited for the laser's hot tongue on her neck.

The diamond ships were far too fast for human control, or even for their enhanced, superhuman occupants. Their main guidance systems were real-time uplinks to the space stations, which a few good nuclear explosions could disrupt.

The sky went white, and the black discs fell like leaves.


The ablation cascade did not happen all at once. Lagrange went to eternity instantaneously, in one appalling sphere of hell-hot helium fusion, but Earth orbit was a different thing. Hours, perhaps days, would pass before the last product of human ingenuity and industry was scraped from the sky. Even so, the comsats were among the first to fail. Most, indeed, were taken out by the electromagnetic pulses alone. Riding into the first dawn of the new world, Myra knew that the little camcopter dancing a couple of metres in front of her might well be relaying the last television news most of its watchers would ever see.

Behind her, in a slow straggle that ended with the ambulances and litters of the injured and dying, the Kazakh migration spread to the horizon. The sun was rising behind them, silhouetting their scattered, tattered banners. There was only one audience, now, that was worth speaking to: the inheritors.

'Nothing is written,' she said. 'The future is ours to shape. When you take the cities, spare the scientists and engineers. Whatever they may have done in the past you need them for the future. Let's make it a better one.'

The camcopter spun around, soared, darted about wildly and dived into the ground. The horses' hooves, the worn tyres of the vehicles, crushed it in seconds. Myra wasn't worried; she could see her own image, with a few seconds' delay, appearing in the corner of her eye-band where CNN still chattered away. The rest of the field was filled with bizarre hallucinations, the net's near-death experience.

God filled the horizon, bigger than the sunrise.

# 15

## THE HAMMER'S HARVEST

I sat on the plinth of the statue of the Deliverer, and smoked a cigarette to fight my stomach's heaves. Gradually my mind and my body returned to some kind of equilibrium. The din of the launch celebrations, the lights of the houses and pubs, became again something I could regard without disgust and hear without dismay. I stood up, and the ground was steady under my feet. I looked up, and the sky was dark and starry above my head.

I walked a few steps from the statue and turned around. The Deliverer on her horse reared above me. Merrial had told me, a couple of weeks earlier, the reason why the Deliverer's features varied on all the statues I'd ever seen. She was a myth, a multiplicity. Her hordes had never ridden from far Kazakhstan to Lisbon's ancient shore, as the songs and stories say. They had never swept all before them. Instead, each town and city had been invaded by a horde raised closer to home, on its very own hinterland. How many hundred, how many thousand towns had met the new order in the form of a wild woman on a horse, riding in at the head of a ragtag army to proclaim that the net was thrown off, the sky was fallen, and world was free?

It was that final message, the last ever spoken from the net and the screens, that had identified them with that singular woman, the Deliverer. I leaned forward, to read again the words chiselled on this plinth, as it is on them all, from far Kazakhstan to Lisbon's ancient shore:

NOTHING IS WRITTEN. THE FUTURE IS OURS TO SHAPE.
WHEN YOU TAKE THE CITIES, SPARE THE SCIENTISTS
AND ENGINEERS. WHATEVER THEY MAY HAVE DONE
IN THE PAST YOU NEED THEM FOR THE FUTURE. LET'S
MAKE IT A BETTER ONE.

The last words of the old world, and the first of the new.

I thought of Merrial, and took another step back, still drawing on my
cigarette. She was older than I had ever imagined possible. But she was also,
I realised, still as young as she'd seemed when I'd first seen her. Nothing
had changed, nothing could change that lovely, eager, open personality. She
was not old, she had merely . . . stayed young.

As I would.

What did I have to complain about?

I laughed at myself, at my own youthful folly. In the long view of history, in the promise of a long life to come, the difference in our chronolog-
ical age, however great, could only be insignificant.

A step, a swish, a scent. Her warm, dry hand clasped mine.

'Are you all right, Clovis?'

I turned and looked at her, and drew her towards the plinth. We sat
down.

'Merrial,' I said, 'I know who you are.'

'Oh,' she said. 'And who am I?'

I handed her the booklet, open at the page.

She sat for a long moment looking down at it, with a slight smile and a
slowly welling tear.

'Ah, fuck,' she said. 'Everybody else there is long gone, as far as I know.
But maybe I wouldn't know, as they wouldn't know about me.' She sniffed,
and handed the booklet back. 'So now you know. I never wanted to be what
people would expect of me, if they knew.'

'But you are,' I said. 'You knew about the AI, and you expected Fergal to
do what he did. I saw your face when he said it, and it was like you'd just
cracked a piece of white logic.'

'Or black! Aye, I knew. The Deliverer told me about it herself, just before the end. She warned me that it was a dangerous thing, though benign
according to its lights. Like Fergal!'

'But *why* did you give it to him?'

Merrial leaned back and looked up. 'Because the deadly debris is up
there, colha Gree. I *know* what happened at the Deliverance, because I lived
through it. I saw the flashes. I was there when the sky fell. I knew the ship

would never get through without a much better guidance system than the one I was working on—well, I knew by the time I'd finished testing it, which was not that long ago. I needed someone to find the AI under cover of seeking something else, and I needed someone who'd put it on the ship—for good reasons or bad.'

She lowered her gaze and smiled. 'So here we are. And now it's you who has to decide, *mo gràidh*. That ship's success will stimulate others, from other lands as well, from the Oriental and the Austral states. Competition between companies and continents, great revolutions to come, and the sky road before us. If it's not launched, or its new mind is ripped out and it fails, or if indeed the AI is not smart enough to save it, then it'll be a long time before it's tried again. And the next to try might not be as benevolent as the International Scientific Society. It could be an army, or an empire.'

She grabbed my shoulders and gazed at me. 'If you walk in there and tell Druin and his boys, that's what could still happen.'

I closed my eyes. 'I can see that,' I said, 'but I'm more concerned about the power Fergal, or someone like him, might have.'

'Open your eyes,' Merrial said.

She was looking very serious. 'That thing, the AI, the planner, it can only do what people let it tell them to do. Fergal said there are no such people yet. What he should have said is, there are no such people *any more*. Your people, colha Gree, they are not the types to let themselves be ordered about by communists—because they have never been ordered about by anyone!'

'Ah!' I said, suddenly understanding. 'Because of the Deliverance, and the Deliverer!'

Merrial laughed.

' "No saviours from on high deliver",' she said wryly. 'Your people delivered themselves. That's another thing I saw, and I'll tell you about one day. If you're still with me.'

'Oh, yes,' I said. 'I'm still with you.'

'Good,' she said. 'We have a lot to do and a long time to do it in.'

She looked around pointedly. The square was jumping.

'So, colha Gree, are you going to ask me for a dance?'

'Of course,' I said. 'Would you do me the honour?'

For a second before we whirled away I stared at the scene before me, fixing it in my memory. Behind the statue Mars was rising, a blue-green dot in the East. Whatever became of the ship, whether it soared to a safe orbit or was blasted to smithereens, other ships would get out there somehow, on the sky road.

Whatever the truth about the Deliverer, she will remain in my mind as she was shown on that statue, and all the other statues and murals, songs and stories: riding, at the head of her own swift cavalry, with a growing migration behind her and a decadent, vulnerable, defenceless and rich continent ahead; and, floating bravely above her head and above her army, the black flag on which nothing is written.